# WILD.

*A Story Conceɪ ɪung*
*Different Kinds of Love*

by Robert Parry

*to Ruby*

*Also by the same author:*
'Virgin and the Crab' 2009
'The Arrow Chest' 2011

# ~ CONTENTS ~

Cover Illustration
*'Westminster viewed to the West on the evening of 27th April 1749'*
*Artist unknown*

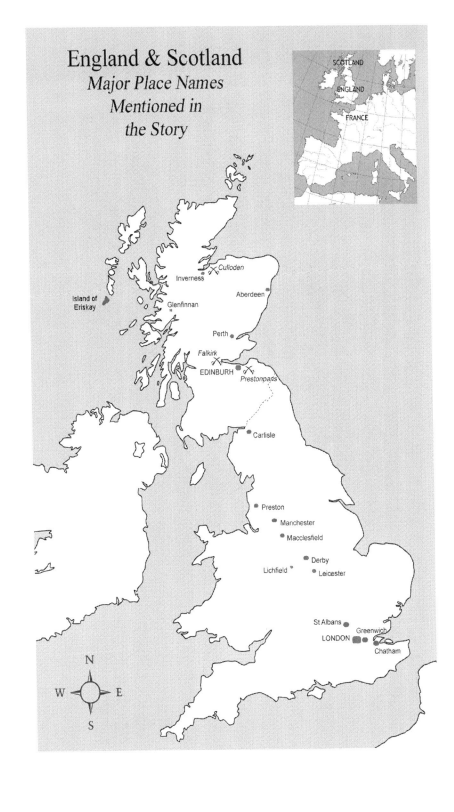

# England & Scotland
## Major Place Names
### Mentioned in
### the Story

SCOTLAND
ENGLAND
FRANCE

Culloden
Inverness
Aberdeen
Island of Eriskay
Glenfinnan
Perth
Falkirk
EDINBURH
Prestonpans
Carlisle
Preston
Manchester
Macclesfield
Derby
Lichfield
Leicester
St Albans
Greenwich
LONDON
Chatham

N
W — E
S

# A Curious Diagram
## Believed to have Belonged to Matthew Wildish

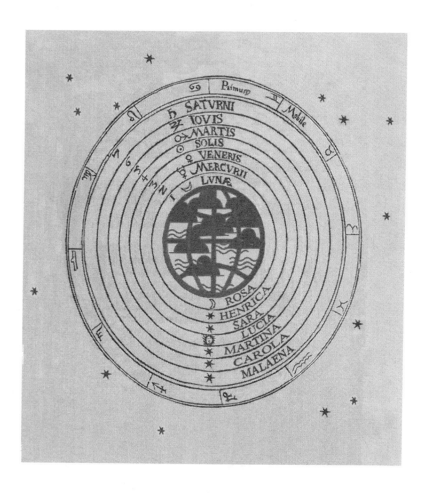

# MATTHEW WILDISH'S LONDON

1 **London Bridge**. Built in medieval times, with numerous houses and shops on top.

2 **Bankside and Southwark**. An area known for its theatres and varied entertainments.

3 **St Pauls Cathedral**. The famous landmark with its dome and baroque style architecture.

4 **The Pig and Whistle** - coaching inn. Matthew Wildish's home and work-place.

5 **Newgate** - one of the old City gates.

6 **The Fleet River** or Fleet Ditch.

7 **Temple Bar**. An elaborate arched gateway. One of the ancient boundaries of the city Demarcation between East-West.

8 **Covent Garden**. Centre for entertainment - opera, theatre etc. Also a market and major shopping area.

9 **Lincoln's Inn Fields**. An open park with theatre. Also famed as a duelling ground.

10 **Seven Dials or the Rookeries**. Infamous area of deprivation, poverty and criminality.

11 **Cockspur Street** leading west from Charing Cross. Joins with The Haymarket.

12 **Charing Cross**. A busy triple junction at the top of Whitehall.

13 **St James Square**. Top residential area favoured by the aristocracy and *Beu Monde*.

14 **St James Palace**. Residence of the King.

15 **Green Park**. Venue for outdoor performances and recreation.

16 **St James Park**. Public space including long avenues for promenading.

17 **Westminster Abbey**, Westminster Palace - and Parliament.

18 **Lambeth Palace**. Residence of the archbishop of Canterbury.

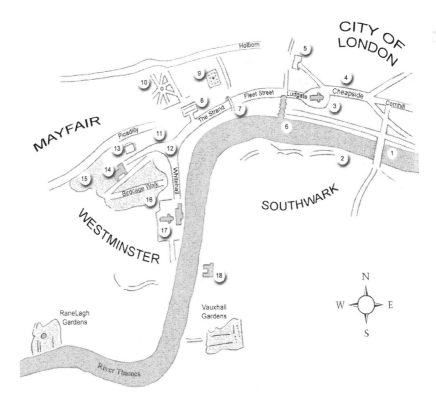

*Created half to rise and half to fall,*
*Great Lord of all things, yet a prey to all,*
*Sole judge of truth, in endless error hurl'd;*
*The glory, jest and riddle of the world.*

Alexander Pope, An Essay on Man

# ~ 1 ~
## THE MAN WHO WOULD FLY

He had thought about it over coffee at The Rainbow and realised it could not be done. It was outrageous, far too risky and ultimately impossible. But that was hours ago. Thinking about it now, out in the open air as he strides through the streets and down towards the river, the whole idea is already starting to look far more plausible. It *can* be done. Of course it can! It just requires a little planning; a certain degree of courage - and probably not inconsiderable funds - but it can be done. He will ask Sam what he thinks. They are due to meet for supper and to exchange intelligence - their usual routine for a Thursday. And Sam is unshockable, anyway. At least, he hopes, he will be unshockable *this time*.

It is a fine summer's evening, the working day ending, and anybody looking for a good time is already out and about in all their finery - the high and the lowly from every stratum of society all mixed together, some walking, some on horseback, some in carriages, others ensconced within the upholstered splendour of gilded sedan chairs. The air is warm; the river swiftly flowing and thereby not too unpleasant upon the nose, and he has money in his pockets and vigour in his loins. Good to be alive! And so many lovely women, too. Ah, yes. How he adores them. People grumble, of course; they say he is 'in love with love,' that his head is turned by every pretty face. But what can possibly be wrong with that! Is love not a worthy emotion? From the most base to the most elevated sentiments, is love not the very essence of existence? Of course. And consequently Matthew Wildish, poet, Master Wig Maker and, more discreetly, occasional spy for the Admiralty, his roving eye full of observation, his inner ear full of joyous music and recollections of various jigs and dances from the recital he has just attended in the city, has already allowed himself to fall in love at least half a dozen times on his brief journey along Thames Street down towards the bridge.

And it is here that he catches sight of his friend - an unmistakable figure, tall and distinguished in his full-length wig and embroidered coat, his sword harnessed at his side. He is standing at their usual place of rendezvous, a rare stretch of open space between the ramshackle buildings, houses and shops that span the river and where this evening an unusually large crowd has congregated, with people jostling and elbowing one another and, in the midst of it all, a most curious sight. Everyone, including Sam, has their attention fixed upon it - a man surely - this fabulous being perched upon a balustrade and who, with outstretched arms, like some exotic bird bedecked in feathers, wings and a tail, is clearly about to jump off *and to fly!*

'Why, Mr Woolveston, a very good evening to you!' Matthew declares, feigning surprise, as soon as he has fought his way through to where his friend is stationed close to the parapet. 'And what, I wonder, would a fine fellow such as yourself be doing here?'

'Searching for an honest man, Sir,' Sam replies in droll fashion, his gaze remaining fixed on the spectacle.

'And have you found one? What's this lunatic up to?'

'No lunatic, Sir!' Sam argues, his bright blue eyes full of laughter now and, with a tug at Matthew's voluminous coat sleeves, pointing with his cane in the direction of the bird-man. 'Look - this brave fellow is about to take wing towards the heavens, or so he assures us.'

'Well, well. Worth waiting for, then - agreed?'

'*Agreed!*' Sam responds with a further enthusiastic smile and an almost imperceptible licking of the lips while at the same time using his considerable bulk and physical presence to jostle one or two fellow spectators aside, the better to observe the imminent take off. This is entertainment - at least it is for Sam - as much as a boxing match, a fine wine or a pinch of snuff. For Matthew, however, it is a nuisance - his own plans that he is so anxious to share with his friend being shouldered out of the way by this unexpected distraction. It would all have to wait now, damn it!

'And may I ask, are you and your good lady well?' Matthew enquires confining himself instead to a more convivial topic of conversation as they continue to observe the careful preparations of the bird-man, balancing now in a curious crouching fashion on the parapet, almost next to them.

'Johanna - oh, yes,' Sam replies brusquely. 'Asking about you, the other day, she was,' he adds with a suspicious sideways glance.

'Oh, really. How very kind,' Matthew says trying not to appear too gratified.

'Yes. *And when are we going to ask good Mr Wildish for supper again,*' Sam continues with increasing petulance, mimicking his wife's voice as best he can. 'I mean, what is it with married women and their constant interest in the welfare of bachelors? As if the very existence of anyone brazen enough to escape their clutches becomes a never-ending source of fascination.'

To which Matthew has no opportunity to respond other than to laugh heartily, because the crowd begins to become very animated. Something is definitely about to happen - made all the more dramatic by the setting sun that has cast a brilliant glow over the whole scene - all the red-brick houses on the southern bank of the river, set within their forest of church spires, and even the old rusting pikes at the bridge end, once adorned in times gone by with the heads of traitors - all bathed in a glorious, piercing radiance, as if bestowing a blessing upon the spectacular plumed creature himself as he spreads his wings in readiness. All is silent, a most untypical silence into which only the rushing waters of the river far below can be detected. And then, at last it speaks:

'Man hereby joins as one with the angels!' comes the cry from the bird-man as he rises from his squatting position and puffs out his chest. 'Open forth the windows of the sky, ye Gods! Mark this occasion all who are gathered here and recount it with pride to your grandchildren in times to come. God save the King!'

To which the brave fellow leaps off - his wings flapping with a curious squeaking sound while everyone holds their breath.

Instantly, he begins to descend - possibly even faster than would normally be the case for a man jumping off a bridge - to plunge feet-first into the swirling waters below. The weight of his wings carries him under the flood at first, which is very swift at the piers of the great stone structure, but he emerges shortly afterwards, down-stream on the other side, minus his feathers and tail, and not to cries of adulation from the crowd, sadly, but to howls of cruel derision.

'Never thought it would work, did you?' says Sam - master of the understatement as always as he turns and hastens away, losing all interest in the poor wretch fighting for his life in the waters below.

Matthew, not willing to quit the scene quite so soon, tarries until satisfied that the man has at least managed to thrash his way towards the shore - by which time Sam is already through the southern end of the bridge and away, down into the crowded lanes of Southwark, so that Matthew has to run to catch him up. It is noisy here, full of the sounds of carts and wagons, the roar of bears and barking dogs from the pits and the cries of hawkers and street traders on every corner, and none too clean underfoot, either with cattle being driven through to market.

'Our feathered friend will survive, you will be relieved to learn,' Matthew announces with irony, overtaking his friend - a portly, robust figure of agitation and nervous energy now, his long, affluent wig of meticulously coiffured curls that Matthew once made for him bouncing and flapping as he goes.

'Oh, good,' Sam responds crisply, oblivious of Matthew's displeasure. Distracted for a moment by the alluring aspect of a young woman on the corner, selling oranges, he is only saved from a collision with a number of cattle by a timely nudge in the ribs from Matthew himself - fortunately a little more alert.

'The devil take these creatures!' Sam exclaims, scowling at the enormous presence of a bull as it passes, all frothing at the mouth and with a big brass ring through its nose, its well stocked neither regions swinging beneath it as it ambles away. 'We have far too many of these beasts being driven through the streets these days - and at all hours. One even entered the courtyard of the Royal Exchange recently. Can you imagine the pandemonium! Oh, by the way, that reminds me: did I tell you I made over twenty guineas the other day at Garraways. Bought on a dip - East India stock at twelve - and then, in no more time than it took to enjoy a dish of coffee, the jobbers were selling it at almost thirteen. Not bad for an hour's work, eh!'

And with an extravagant swing of the arm, he dashes the tip of his cane against a stone upon the ground, sending it flying across the cobbles with a spark. Sam could be so boastful at times - so unbecoming of a gentleman. No doubt a similar level of enthusiasm would have attended South Sea stock some years ago, Matthew thinks - until the bubble burst and everyone lost their savings, their property and in some cases their lives in the process. But the stock market, like Sam, has a short memory.

'Actually, there was someone in Italy who believed in flying,' Matthew volunteers, still with half his thoughts on the bird-man, 'only this was with the aid of a mechanical device upon which a man might be seated, as we would normally ride a horse. Ingenious. And, you must admit, if anyone could succeed in such an endeavour it would be worthy of more than a little consideration among your business friends in Exchange Alley.'

'Nonsense!' Sam replies, chortling in his typical gruff, sanctimonious fashion. 'Only a fool would invest in such insanity. Typical of Italy, though, with all their Popery and ridiculous fantasies. If God had meant us to fly, Sir, he would have given us wings. But no. Instead, he has given us our mental faculties - our reason. And I for one, am grateful for the distinction.'

Sam is jealous, of course. He has never been overseas, never visited Italy, never so much as considered doing the *Grand Tour* as any self-respecting gentleman should have done by his age.

A further minute of brisk walking brings them to their destination, the entrance to one of their regular meeting places, a garden tavern - not exactly one of the haunts of the nobility, but adequate enough for their needs, and ideal for listening to the common talk, to gauge the mood of the populace. Mounting the steps into the outdoor area with its modest entertainments of skittles and occasional music, they collect their ale and then, amid the profusion of pergolas and hanging lanterns, benches and wooden pedestals, locate a seat in a relatively secluded area and settle down. This is business they are to discuss now, serious ministerial business. And therefore Matthew realises he is to be frustrated yet again, unable to explain his unique idea to his friend who has, in fact, already produced a small note-book from his pocket in readiness.

'So, tell me,' Sam begins again, his voice now reduced to an untypical whisper after fetching a lamp and setting it down on a nearby barrel, the better to peruse his notes, 'any interesting commissions lately from Jacobites, ripe for our attentions perhaps?'

Matthew is aware of others in the garden observing them with a blend of curiosity and suspicion - and it always makes him feel nervous, exchanging gossip in a place like this. If only Sam would make the occasional concession to his surroundings in matters of dress. But no. Whereas Matthew would usually choose a simple unembroidered coat and waistcoat for such places, Sam always has to look as if he were going to a banquet at the Guild Hall, with great brass buttons everywhere, all flounces and lace cuffs.

'Actually, I believe I may have something for you this time,' Matthew answers quietly. 'A certain Mr McNiel of Derby, a country gentleman with interests in silk weaving. He approached me at my apartments at The Pig And Whistle some days ago with a commission for a wig, and upon learning that I also excelled in the writing of verse brought forth a miniature of his lady wife, that I might compose some lines of dedication to mark their imminent wedding anniversary.'

'Really!' Sam responds with interest. 'McNiel, you say? How did the conversation go?'

'Oh, I began in the usual way - the odd remark about the unfortunate state of our kingdom, then by degrees revealing my own sentiments as a disgruntled Tory and Jacobite - adding that in order to practice any profession in London, not to mention being able to vote, hold office or serve on juries, I have had to renounce the faith of my Irish forebears. He warmed to me then, and soon we were discussing the plight of the Stuarts in exile and their possible restoration. I have yet to sound him on whether he reinforces his sentiments in any practical sense, but he was so delighted with my poem concerning his wife, a charming lady, by the way, whom I also had the pleasure of meeting briefly, that he even suggested I might be entrusted with executing a tribute to one of his race horses at some future time.'

'Praise indeed!' Sam observes. 'Keep this one warm for me, Matt, and we shall see what comes of it. He will visit you again?'

'Yes: the final time next week to pay monies owing on the wig.'

'Excellent. I'll put a watch on this Mr McNiel of yours - that we might observe exactly how he spends his time in the capital.'

'Um, *safely* I trust?' Matthew inquires, fixing Sam with a questioning gaze - not altogether certain whether this additional occupation as part-time informant for His Majesty's Government is at all to his liking any longer. 'They are a decent enough couple, with young children.'

'I say, you haven't gone all soft on us, Matt, have you?' Sam counters, not entirely in jest. 'Remember, we threw all that nonsense out years ago - the Stuarts - the divine right of kings, and all that. We have a nice, obedient kind of monarchy in this country now, imported from Germany - and I for one will do my utmost to keep it that way. A secret vocation, to be sure - but a worthy one.'

'Yes. Only just lately I suspect yours has become rather a sinister one, as well,' Matthew remarks.

'Not at all!' Sam protests, with again eyes only for the pages of his little book, checking various annotations in the margins. 'If a prominent family decides to throw in its lot with the Jacobites, then our good King George has every right to seize their assets - especially if His Majesty is to undertake useful and important projects like furnishing his palaces and making wars on the French. I advise our friends in Whitehall on the most likely fruits for picking, that's all. Anyway, how's your love life lately Matt? Still with that special lady of yours - the one I saw you with last time. What was her name ..?'

'No,' Matthew answers curtly. 'No, we parted. Good claret is my mistress now.'

'Parted - what after so long! Why you must have been together with this one for all of three weeks.'

'Very funny.'

'Being a romantic fool is all very well for a man in his youth,' Sam continues pointing an accusing finger, 'but it is far less becoming with the approach of maturity. It is high time, Sir - high time you settled down and embraced the blessed state of matrimony, as I have done,' he concludes and, as always, never ceasing to remind the world of what a fine match he has made in his own lovely wife Johanna, the daughter of a baronet – thus uniting his fortunes with someone not only of beauty and intelligence but of considerable wealth, also.

But Matthew resists the temptation to indulge his friend any further - for inevitably his thoughts have turned once again to his newest obsession: an idea so exhilarating that he really must share it with someone, and soon - or else he will simply burst.

'Listen, Sam, I want to tell you how I think a man might fly - and no I'm not referring to mechanical devices, or wings of vellum, or anything you could remotely invest in at Garraways. This is much more interesting. I am speaking of none other than the realm of the mind.'

'The mind ... um, yes,' Sam mutters by way of courtesy, inviting Matthew to continue with a flourish of the hand. He has a tendency, when feigning interest to speak in a slow, drawling fashion - the word *'yes'* emerging from his lips as a long, protracted *'yerrz'* sound, accompanied with the typical vacant stare of a man who is rarely inspired by anything that occurs above the level of the waist.

'Actually, Sam, you have already uttered something quite intelligent this evening,' Matthew continues undaunted, 'namely the Good Lord providing us with the faculty of reason instead of wings, remember?'

'Yerrz,' Sam mumbles and lowers his eyes to his notes once again.

'Well, I agree. But we are also endowed with something every bit the equal. We also have our aspirations, our passions. And it is through these that we might explore realms and dimensions of the intellect far beyond ourselves.'

'Yerrz ...'

'And that one should employ for this purpose the very act of love.'

*'The act of love!'* Sam echoes and suddenly appears for the first time to be gaining interest.

'Yes, Sam, exactly. Imagine you are in the arms of a beautiful woman. Tell me: have you not experienced occasion when, at moments of the most passionate and intense embrace, you have, as it were, become lost to yourself, transported to a condition of mind in which neither envy or fear nor worry or greed can ever reach you? Have you not felt liberated from yourself and your cares at such times?'

'Well ... yes, I suppose so, now you come to mention it,' Sam replies grudgingly. 'Brief as such moments are, alas.'

'Precisely - and brief, always, because we lose all self-control in the throws of our delights, and then - well, the weapon is discharged, we collapse in a heap and all those wonderful sentiments vanish. Well, consider this as an alternative: that one might engage in that embrace in such a way as to rather prolong the ecstasy, and to do so with far more than just one woman.'

'What, you mean like two-in-a-bed? A night at Fanny Cockburn's in Covent Garden?'

'No, no - I am not speaking of a mere fleeting moment of sordid entertainment, Sam - a couple of women of easy virtue.'

'No?'

'Nor even three.'

'Really?'

'No - nor even four or five.'

'Good God! What *do* you mean, Sir?'

'A harem.'

*'A harem!'*

'Yes, Sam, that's right. Oh, I am tired of all these petty romances. I want something different. I want to be inspired and swept up in something grand, something magnificent. A substantial variety of beautiful women, for instance - that should do - and all to be enjoyed within the span of a single day and night, because thereby, by such an uncommon intensity of experience, a man would surely be transported to the heavens themselves!'

Sam takes a long deliberate draft of his ale and wipes his lips on the back of his hand before signalling to a server to replenish their drinks, placing the empty jug down upon the barrel with a slow, deliberate and emphatic thud.

'I see,' he says.

'You understand, then?'

'Oh yes, perfectly,' Sam replies. 'Though you do appreciate, of course, that you are utterly and completely barking mad?'

'Mad - what do you mean?' Matthew protests.

'May I remind you, Sir, this is England we are living in: not some exotic Eastern seraglio. And anyway, presuming you could ever locate so many women and persuade them to oblige you all at once (unlikely enough, if I may say so), you would simply not be able to rise to the occasion with sufficient frequency. I mean could any man! You would be exhausted after the first hour.'

'No, Sam. My intention is that the whole thing be conducted without once surrendering to that fault that is so common in men of our age and disposition of losing one's seed. You know - *popping the cork?'*

'What!' Sam exclaims with a look of utter astonishment. 'Why, this is sounding more and more preposterous by the minute.'

'No listen Sam, believe me, there is a precedent for this. I have heard of it upon my travels. Consider, for example, the exotic East, the Emperor and his concubines; the Sultan and his harem. They say that the arts of love cultivated in such places far outstrip anything any of us can ever aspire to here in the seedy underworld of vice we are so familiar with in the West. Why, they even say there is a science to the coupling, too, which the Sultan controls to such a pitch of perfection that he and his concubines are removed to realms of delight that for us are not only stranger than we imagine, but possibly stranger than we are *able* to imagine.'

'It certainly is stranger than *I* can imagine!' Sam remarks, taking up his ale again.

'So you won't help me?'

'Help you!' Sam exclaims, now utterly exasperated. 'Why in the name of Beelzebub should I help you! If you intend to make a complete arse of yourself, Sir, that is entirely your business. And anyway, where do you expect all this might take place - this orgy of yours? Consider the practicalities. They would all be arguing and giggling among themselves. The noise would be intolerable. And unless, heaven forbid, you are considering having recourse to street girls, which I strongly advise against if you wish to preserve your health, you would simply not find enough eligible women to choose from - none that are not already married, affianced or spoken for in some way. What you are suggesting, Sir, is little more than some ridiculous, juvenile fantasy. Why, a man jumping off a bridge with wings strapped to his back is beginning to look quite sober in comparison to some of your ideas.'

Matthew turns away in frustration. How very disappointing. Of course, he could argue further with his friend, explain that the intention was never to enjoy all the women together in the same place; that they would be separate experiences, ranged over a span of several hours, an entire day even. But it is of no use. Apart from his skills as a musician, which are considerable, Sam is as unimaginative and earth-bound as his boots. In silence, therefore, both men sup at their ale once more - until Matthew notices, standing in conversation beneath a nearby pergola, none other than a former sweetheart of his, Rose. Yes - the delectable, buxom, fair-haired Rose Tidey - a fine young woman who could definitely be considered as a candidate for his amorous project. What's more, the fates have clearly conspired to aid him this evening, because in her company is another young lady - in many ways even more lovely - and both, moreover, are glancing his way, as if speaking about him. The call to action.

'Will you excuse me Sam,' he announces. 'I have resolved forthwith to demonstrate your woeful underestimation of my capabilities in this matter. Observe!'

'Observe what?' Sam demands - but Matthew has already got to his feet.

'Good evening, dearest!' Matthew declares as he approaches Rose - though her eyes, as she raises them to meet his, do indicate a certain disdainfulness, he feels. 'Do you remember me?' he adds with a smile.

'Do I remember you?' she repeats wistfully, glancing as if towards the heavens for inspiration. 'Oh, perhaps, were I to search the catalogue and history of my many romances - of which there have been so many magnificent encounters, so many brave and lustful lovers, perhaps I might indeed be able to locate you somewhere - a faint recollection among the multitude. At the moment, though, the name does escape me ...' At which she glances with unguarded amusement at her more youthful companion, whose wide grin, accompanied by a giggle and twitch of the shoulders urges her on to greater things. 'Let me see, could the name be *Mr Fumble, can't get the laces undone?* or is it perhaps *Mr Softy had too much to drink that night?* If you could enlighten me further ..?'

'It's Matthew,' he replies, patiently ignoring the jibes. 'You know - good old Matt!'

'Oh, yes. Quite right! Matthew Wildish, the wig maker,' Rose finally admits, though still rather uncharitably, he thinks, as she produces a fan, opens it and waves it most languidly beneath her chin.

'*Master* wig maker,' he corrects her with a further smile.

He has heard that Rose is a successful young lady these days, as her fine apparel proclaims: the pearls and tiny glints of precious sparkle dancing upon her breast and throat as she speaks, worldly-wise and comfortable in her expensive silks and brocades. From a humble family of brewers, she has excelled by starting up her own business in the transportation of ale, regulating and organising whole gangs of strong and burly porters to deliver far and wide the products of several breweries in the east of the city - a clever lass and not to be trifled with. So he laughs at her jesting until finally she warms to him, even allowing him to embrace her and to fetch some drinks. Her fair younger companion is, it transpires, none other than her sister, Margaret, visiting from the country. And although Rose is clearly not interested in rekindling any of their former romance, at least not straight away, Margaret, as she takes delivery of a large jug of cider, appears far more amenable. Dressed more humbly than her sister in a neat riding jacket, and returning his glances, with a bashful modesty, she is, indeed, a pretty young lady. Her skin is unpowdered and without blemish, and her eyes, which are probably blue, though he cannot tell for certain in the darkness of the garden, are wide and moist with vitality, reflective of every light that illuminates her tender face. He likes Margaret. And, realising that to win her affections would also be to keep some hope alive with Rose, it is definitely time, he thinks, to turn on the charm.

'Margaret,' he begins, coming a little closer to speak into her ear - and the texture of her fine, silvery hair as it sweeps against his cheek is divine. 'Are you enjoying yourself this evening?'

'I am,' she replies - briefly, cheerfully and with a nod.

'And have you been in London long?' he inquires further.

'I have,' she says with similar brevity and a further nod.

'And do you like it?'

'I do.'

'Good. And - er - what do you think of all us fine, cultured fellows here in the capital, eh?' he asks, leaning back for a moment, so she might behold just such a specimen in all its glory. Margaret, however, in response to this more challenging line of enquiry, can only stare back in confusion this time, before turning to her elder sister as if for guidance - though not much more than a scowl and a rueful shaking of the head appears to be forthcoming from that quarter. 'I mean do you like the men of London?' Matthew adds by way of clarification, accompanied by a coy, wide-eyed smile. He knows his teeth are brilliant white when he does that. Never fails.

'Ooooh, yes, I do!' Margaret replies with a squeal of delight and nods again with the rapidity of a marionette on strings.

He feels he might be getting somewhere, and so is permitted to fetch another round of drinks for both girls, and one for Sam, too - who does, however, continue to sit apart with obstinate disinterest, preferring still the perusal of his notebook.

'Margaret, I have, among my various talents, the cutting of small profiles in relief - you know, those little shadow-likenesses of people you see in picture-frames or brooches? I use them to display to my clients how their wigs might appear when worn, and I cannot help but observe what a fine delicate profile you have. So very pretty. May I enquire, have you ever had yourself rendered in relief?'

'In relief? Oh, no I do not think so,' Margaret answers, this time with a look of appropriate sadness. 'What would I have to do?'

'To have your profile fashioned? Why it's simple,' Matthew answers as, positioning himself to one side, the better to observe the prospect, he continues to explain, indicating with a flurry of his fingers exactly how one would snip away at the card with fine scissors.

'Oh, yes, I understand now,' she responds - though noticing her sister's eyes observing her with something not unlike hilarity at just that moment, her face quickly reverts to being anxious.

'Oh, he would render you most faithfully. Quite right!' Rose declares, joining the conversation at last, and not without a certain irony. 'Usually in a horizontal fashion, as I recall - his preference for the business of *rendering*.' And then turning to Matthew himself and pointing her closed fan menacingly in his direction, she adds, 'I shall of course accompany my little sister, should any of this require a visit, as I rather suspect it might, to your workshop or apartments.'

'Of course - most welcome, Rose, most welcome! I reside these days at the Pig and Whistle, the coaching inn off Cheapside,' Matthew replies, handing her his card - and hardly able to conceal his pleasure, for at a stroke it seems that the voluptuous Rose, and the fair Margaret might soon both be at his door and within the range of his embrace. He could not have hoped for a better start to his endeavours, and so he secures an appointment for Wednesday afternoon next week and then hastens back to Sam to recount his triumph.

'I tell you, Sam, that dear young lady is single and without a sweetheart of any kind here in London,' Matthew insists in a fervent whisper, responding to his friend's renewed and unfailing cynicism. 'And her sister is an old acquaintance of mine who will surely also oblige again. This is going to work, Sam - mark my words. A whole bevy of lovely women, one after the other, all in one delirious, exciting twenty-four hour period. I shall become the toast of the town, the envy of the nation. I am going to rediscover all those secrets of the Orient and recreate the exotic seraglio of the Sultan himself at my very own apartments at the Pig and Whistle.'

But before Sam can argue or protest any further, a huge

commotion is heard and a whole gang of street porters, bare-sleeved with bulging muscles and clearly all very thirsty, come charging along the street and into the gardens, making straight for the tavern door itself where they call inside for their ale. Not surprisingly, the landlord serves them straight away, at which they all turn their attentions to several of the young ladies nearby - and especially to Rose - for yes, of course! These, Matthew suddenly realises, are *her* men: her own team of porters and carters, men of such legendary strength that they are regularly expected to shoulder loads of three hundredweight and carry them around on their backs from street to street. One of these gentlemen, who possesses a breadth almost equal to his height, even seems to be on good terms with young Margaret, so familiar, in fact, as to venture to pick her up by the waist and then, with one sweeping movement of the arm, to swing her playfully over his shoulder as if she were a rag doll. Astonishing. Matthew can hear Margaret's little shrieks of joy as she is further rotated acrobatically around the man's great thick neck onto his other shoulder from where he is able to plant a very intimate kiss upon her lips before allowing her to descend once again carefully onto the grass at his side - there to be informed by her friends, amid much merriment and gesturing, of the presence of a tiny smudge of soot from one of the beams of a pergola that has impressed itself upon the tip of her nose and which Rose, smiling, cleans off lovingly with a lace handkerchief.

'Doesn't have a sweetheart, you say?' mutters Sam with some irony though avoiding raising his eyes to study the spectacle too closely himself.

The girls, meanwhile, and some of the porters, have begun an animated conversation, in which Margaret is clearly remarking on the exciting prospect of having her profile rendered in paper because she is busy making little snipping gestures with her fingers and pointing in Matthew's direction. Her boyfriend, though, does not appear to be sharing in Margaret's enthusiasm, and in fact looks most displeased as he turns to survey the darkness of the gardens and its many occupants, eventually to settle on the face of Matthew and to fix him with a steely gaze.

On his feet instantly, Matthew holds out two imploring palms towards the man as he advances.

'Now, now, my friend, it's not at all as you think, if indeed you *are thinking* at this moment,' he begins verbosely - but this only serves to exacerbate matters, so that before Matthew can say another word he finds himself being lifted into the air by his lapels and hurled against a wooden pillar with a loud thud that robs the very breath from his lungs. Unwilling, as any gentleman would be, to draw his sword on an unarmed man, Matthew can only wait in horror as his assailant advances once more with a view to further violence, but by this time Sam is on his feet also and has managed to stand between them, a most ridiculous look of defiance on his face, one hand resting on the hilt of his sword, though he too will not draw, but instead ventures to prod the man in the stomach with the knob of his cane.

'Desist Sir, at once!' he cries. 'We are men of quality, can you not see that?'

'Oh yeah! Let's see what stuffing you're made of then,' the man growls, just before Sam himself is collared from behind by another one of the porters. Others intervene, and suddenly a full scale brawl is in place, with Matthew trying to ward off the jealous boyfriend with a stool as would a lion-tamer at the circus - and Sam, his cane fallen, now carried aloft at a distance of several feet from the ground as he aims several futile punches into the air and - indignities of all indignities - even loses his wig in the process, revealing the shaven pate beneath. By this stage, the proprietor of the tavern has had enough. Emerging from the building brandishing a cudgel he wades into the fray, endeavouring to grab anyone implicated in the disorder and, with the aid of some colleagues, to eject them. Dozens of jeering spectators have already gathered around, some even peering over the hedges from outside to observe the spectacle as several of the leading pugilists are hurled from the rear of the garden, including, most unjustly, Matthew and Sam - everyone tumbling, or else propelled forcefully down the short flight of steps outside and into the mud of the road. And here, in the relative darkness and confusion, they are able to disengage themselves from the fracas and the bundle of flailing limbs.

'Come on Sam, run for it!' Matthew cries. And indeed they are just about to do so when Matthew slips on something in the gutter and is down again, his face coming to rest in something of an unpleasantly wet and disconcertingly inert furriness.

'Oh my God, I've landed on a dead cat, I swear.'

'Out of the way!' Sam declares, pushing his friend aside rather than assisting him to his feet. 'That, Sir, I'll have you know, is my wig!' he adds, stooping to retrieve the sorry, mud-spattered object that has been flung from the garden and, brushing it vigorously with the back of his hand. 'Damn it! Look at it - filthy.'

From out of nowhere, suddenly, a further assailant appears, roaring like a lion as he advances. But Sam, now far better prepared and clearly furious by this time, lands a blistering upper cut beneath the man's chin - which knocks him down.

'Until Wednesday afternoon, then?' comes a merry voice and a face appearing from behind one of the hedges. It is Rose. Not quite knowing what to say, Matthew smiles briefly in her direction as, together with Sam, his wig restored rather crookedly to his head, they set off at speed down the lane, their fine heels clattering on the cobbled surface like a team of stampeding horses as they go.

## ~ 2 ~
## THE LIGHT OF STARS AND
## WHISPERED INTIMATIONS

It is a fine evening though a little humid after rain as the carriage and four horses that Sam has sent for him with its plush upholstery, its family crest upon the doors and a statuesque groom in a powdered wig stationed upon the platform to the rear, climbs by torturously slow degrees and much slipping and sliding of wheels out of London and up to Greenwich, a burgeoning residential area becoming increasingly popular with the gentry and whose proximity to the naval dockyards and Royal Observatory has made it an ideal site for the building of many splendid new villas and terraces - tall, elegant homes, behind whose impressive, perfectly proportioned facades, the new well-to-do families such as Sam's now live and flourish. The heathland here above the park, broad and flat with seas of grass waving in the breeze and dotted with sheep, still with their lambs grazing, all makes for a pleasantly pastoral scene; a welcome relief from the noises and bustle of the city just a few short miles distant to the West.

The carriage is drawn up beneath the shade of a lime tree, and here, with a curious blend of joy and trepidation, and brandishing a neat offering of cut flowers, Matthew alights and approaches along a short, arrow-straight path to the front door - for it is here, behind this portal of oak and shining brass with its fashionable fan-light window, that the lovely Mrs Woolveston, Sam's wife, Johanna, resides. Apart from the music of Handel, there is scarcely anything in this world more worthy of esteem in Matthew's estimation than the person of Johanna - a woman so well-read, of such intelligence and discernment, as comfortable when speaking of the newest scientific discoveries of the Royal Society as when gossiping over the latest tulip to arrive from the Netherlands, that he can only hope he will not make a fool of himself, as he has certainly done in the past, by being unaccountably tongue-tied in her presence. The bell

is rung and he has only a moment to wait until the door swings
open to reveal the genial aspect of the butler, and also a tiny dog,
the resident pug named Boris, yapping and leaping about with
excitement. Two small children, John and Samantha, aged four and
five years, run to greet him, as does an attractive and nimble-footed
house maid who takes his tricorn and sword belt and curtsies
graciously - the whole place, as always, alive with the buzz and
excitement of a busy family home. And it is here, a moment later,
in the spacious dining room, with its painted pilasters, its oval
mahogany table and stylish chintz-covered chairs that denote a
habitation of both wealth and fashionable taste, that a tasty supper
of jugged meats and cheese is served and conversation commences.

'I suppose you'll be visiting astrologers and soothsayers for
guidance next, eh, Matt?' Sam enquires, looking very suave this
evening in the drapery of his long silk banyan, and with typically
forthright humour as they sit together with Johanna.

'Astrologers and soothsayers?' Johanna echoes with surprise,
her brows concentrating themselves with polite interest into a tiny
nest of furrows just above the bridge of her nose.

Matthew stares back at her across the table, captivated, and
quite lost once more in the serenity of her hazel-green eyes - so full
of observation and intelligence and which this evening, he thinks,
resemble nothing so much as sparkling emeralds there in the
candle-light - while her lips, so artfully shaped into a cupid's bow,
he knows not whether by nature's gift or the skilful application of
colour, purse themselves into the faintest of smiles. She has asked
him a question he realises. About astrologers and soothsayers …
yes, that's it, and he will have to respond. But the words will not
come. Why is she the only woman in the world who has such an
effect upon him? Equally puzzled, though no doubt for a very
different reason, Johanna's smile becomes wider, more inquisitive.
And as she tilts her head askance, enquiring and anticipating still
his reply, one pendulous diamond studded earring extricates itself
from a stray ringlet of fair hair and sparkles its little message of
refinement above the pale, unblemished skin of her shoulder.

'Oh yes, that's right,' Sam continues, filling the silence on his
friend's behalf. 'Our good fellow Mr Wildish here, does nothing by
halves, y'know. He's hoping to become rather an expert in the - er -
traditions of the Orient, isn't that so, Matt?'

Matthew glances swiftly and not without irritation towards his friend. What is he aiming at with that last remark? Is he trying to embarrass him in front of Johanna? She would surely see through any artifice, any subterfuge that he could ever hope to sustain.

'The Orient, you say? Goodness!' she exclaims with interest, taking a sip of wine and regarding his continued silence with those typically large and attentive eyes of hers that often appear slightly startled.

'Oh, yes,' Sam continues, 'the exotic traditions of the Ottomans are what's taken his fancy of late, isn't that so, Matt?'

'Exotic indeed, yes,' Johanna agrees before Matthew can reply, 'their ceramics; their literature and noble architecture. I can understand how these would provide inspiration for your various artistic pursuits, Matthew.'

'Just a bit unfortunate, therefore, that they continue to be oppressed by so much superstition,' Sam contends, 'especially when we compare their scientific ignorance with our own modern achievements. We live in enlightened times. I'm glad to say.'

At which he carves some bread, fixes his fork upon a tasty morsel of hare and, waxing poetical all of sudden, declares with gusto:

*'Nature's laws lay hid in night.*
*God said Let Newton be! and all was light.'*

'Well, yes - yes, I do concur,' Matthew responds at last, able to converse more coherently now that he has Sam in his sights. 'We have, it is true, made no small strides in our understanding of physics and the mechanical nature of the world. But I would also suggest that the East still has much to teach us - in medicine, for example, and in their standards of sanitation and personal hygiene. In these things, I would maintain, we still have a degree of catching up to do - as witnessed in the popularity of the Turkish baths here in our own country of late.'

'Fascinating,' Johanna responds and softly sighs, resting her chin upon the backs of her hands, her elbows upon the table for a second in a pose of rapt attention. But wait. This is all contrived: she is teasing him - of course she is - her finely tapered eyebrows arched in little half-moon shapes of merriment. And inevitably, therefore, he catches himself wondering what exactly she might already be privy to. Has Sam told her already what they spoke of the other night in the tavern? No, surely not! He wouldn't do that, would he? A swift glance in Sam's direction, however, and the smile of wicked amusement on his face are sufficient for Matthew to fear the worst.

'Actually, yes Sam has confided in me already something of your purpose,' Johanna remarks as if reading his thoughts, and in a suddenly far less melodious voice - at which his heart sinks almost through the floor. 'That you intend to draw upon a number of women as inspiration for a sequence of sonnets describing the Muses of classical antiquity? Something of that nature, yes?'

The relief is almost too much for Matthew. 'Oh, yes - that's it!' he cries - blurting out his words a little too vigorously, he suspects. 'My latest poetic endeavours - sonnets, yes. And each one of these shall be modelled on a real person - anywhere where beauty and elegance might be found among those that I know. Women - yes, only distinguished women. I - er - have determined they must be women and distinguished, yes.'

Further glances of bemused suspicion from Johanna upon his by-now quite hysterical elaboration, do eventually compel him to cease his prattling. But Sam is not ready to let him go, not just yet - his face full of mirth now that he has his friend dangling on a hook, and revelling in it. 'Yes,' he chimes in again, 'and even more amazing is that Matthew intends to produce them all at once - in a creative frenzy of activity, as he put it to me just the other evening. Isn't that so, Matt? Rather a tall order, I should say.'

At which, Johanna can only smile and shake her head in further bewilderment before rejoining the conversation with: 'Well, whatever modus operandi you choose, Matthew, do always keep us in mind, won't you, if it is at all possible that we might be of assistance. You know how much we admire your fine verse. Why, perhaps even *I* shall have the honour of becoming immortalised as one of your lovely Muses?'

To which Sam splutters loudly and almost falls off his chair in an all-too-obvious attempt to control himself and rein in his laughter. 'By Jove, not while there is breath in my body!' he finally gasps and coughs loudly several times.

Johanna, meanwhile, imperturbable as ever and with a look of complete resignation by this time over her failure to penetrate whatever private joke is taking place between the two men, merely shrugs her shoulders - and at just that moment, anyway, their two children, John and Samantha, are brought in by their Nanny to say goodnight - a ritual accompanied by numerous demonstrable hugs and kisses, including those that must also be bestowed upon Boris the pug - even though the little rascal is, Matthew reflects, still perhaps at an age when he would prefer to set his canine teeth into things, instead.

It really is a most engaging domestic scene, and Matthew cannot help feeling just a tiny bit envious, like someone looking in from the outside, pressing his nose against the window pane upon such a charming family idyll. How very lucky Sam is to have such a companion as Johanna - so elegant in her plain silk gown, open a little at the neck and shoulders as befits the warm evening, her hair braided and pinned neatly around the crown: an effortless simplicity. Yes, it *is* a desirable state – marriage; the society of a loving wife; the stability of house and home; all those accomplishments that invariably throw the plight of single men like himself into sharp relief: the tedious routine of lonely nights, unwashed linen, dirty dishes and an unfortunate over-reliance on the provisions of taverns and chop houses for sustenance.

Eventually, the children depart to their prayers, while the ever capable mistress of the house attends once more to the table and a further contribution to the meal - a late arrival in the shape of a fruit pudding, wheeled in with good-humoured ceremony by further members of Sam's household staff, including the comely young maid who opened the door to him earlier and whose name, he quickly discovers is Mary. Typical of Sam, of course, to populate his home with a pretty face whenever possible. Though not tall, she has a slender figure, her movements nimble and curiously decorative, and as her eyes meet his for one moment, he feels a stirring at the presence of her youthful vitality. She seems to sense this, and for just the briefest of moments, and unseen to the others, acknowledges his interest by returning his smile. Brandy is served shortly after, while at both men's insistence Johanna remains at table to enjoy not only the excellent liquor but also an aromatic sample from Sam's snuffbox - offered from the hidden compartment, in this instance, and thus exposing the better and more expensive variety of snuff therein, the variety reserved usually for himself.

'Five guineas an ounce, Matt,' Sam remarks as he takes forth a pinch of the fine powder between finger and thumb and holds it deftly to his left nostril. 'As enjoyed by His Majesty King George, no less.'

Matthew is impressed, or at least makes a reasonable demonstration of being so by raising his eyebrows in admiration. Yes, his friend is undoubtedly doing well these days - in fact possibly too well for a junior procurement officer in the Admiralty. Is this astonishing opulence a result of those investments he is always pursuing in the coffee houses around the Royal Exchange? Or is the rumoured fortune of Johanna's family even greater than everyone has been led to believe?

So much remains enigmatic about Sam's wife. Matthew is aware that her father is wealthy and well connected, that the family live somewhere in Kent, but that is about all. She always seems most at ease when in the domestic arena, the home in which she is the capable and unchallenged mistress. There is a tranquil, gentle way about her at such times, always softly spoken - though whenever he has encountered her outside, he often detects a certain unease and vulnerability, as well. Having a garrulous and outspoken husband like Sam probably contributes to this reticence - but he cannot be sure to what extent. How might it be, Matthew ponders, if one were to have the pleasure of conversing with her alone?

As usual, after supper, they hurry off for an hour of music making in the drawing room, with Sam singing in his surprisingly fine baritone voice, a plausible rendition of Handel's heroic 'Honour and Arms,' followed by Johanna playing a delightful fragment of Bach on her cello. In Matthew's case, the occasional modest accompaniment to a vocalist from the harpsichord is all he can usually aspire to - though with suitable encouragement this evening, and an additional glass of claret, he does manage to extend his performance with a few minutes of awkward improvisation before taking delivery of some sheet music in order to join in a trio with the others.

To experience the joy of music is for Matthew a necessity every bit as persuasive and insistent as that of food and drink - a most powerful urge that has become a constant presence in his life. In fact the prospect of a day passing without at least once being exposed to music of some kind, whether attending a recital or simply making it oneself leaves him with a sense of panic. Until someone invents a mechanical device that might bottle it up, he knows they must continue to make it themselves at every available opportunity. Not only that, but it is enormous fun. For no one here is professionally trained or aspires to anything beyond the simple pleasure of mutual entertainment. And when Sam takes up his violin and they all play together, the sound is simply a delight - Sam being by far the most skilful musician among them, and always the inspiration to any performance, no matter how modest. While others must point their noses almost constantly at the sheets of music before them, Sam - his eyes alive and sparkling with fun, his own movements as open and vigorous as if he were partaking of a dance - is to be found instead glancing up at the faces of everyone else as he plays, infectious in his smile and thereby encouraging everyone else to lift their heads, to celebrate the composition more bravely and joyfully. They love their music.

At length, it being such a fine evening, and with the sheer fatigue of hand and mind having compelled them at last to cease and to put their instruments down, they elect to go up onto the wide leads of the roof that weave a path between chimney and parapet, and where Sam's telescope is invariably placed in readiness for stargazing - that most fashionable of hobbies in these parts due to the proximity of the Royal Observatory with its famous astronomical telescope - encouraging many local residents to follow suit and, in their own humble fashion, to become amateur observers as well. Sam is in possession of an excellent refracting telescope with a three-inch lens, well mounted on a sturdy tripod - no match for anything within the great observatory but an instrument, nevertheless, of sufficient magnification and quality to reveal the moons of Jupiter; the majestic rings of Saturn; and even, on a clear July evening such as this, those peculiar misty presences in the night sky called *nebulae*.

Availing themselves of the narrow staircase from the servant's quarters, they emerge through a trap door and settle down together, safely ensconced behind the parapet, reclining on cushions already brought up, and their wine carried with them, too.

'Do you remember the comet?' Johanna asks softly, almost thinking aloud as she locates the widest segment of the lead plating, quite close to Matthew, and arranges the expanse of her petticoats into a comfortable array of folds about her.

Naturally, everyone remembers - how could they ever forget!

'Ah, yes,' Matthew replies, recollecting with much fondness those crisp chilly nights in the early months of last year when they had sat together, sometimes just the three of them, or else in the company of various guests - all huddled together, their backs against the warmth of the chimney stacks, sipping at their wine and gazing across to the horizon in awe at the great comet - a miraculous object with no fewer than six enormous tails emanating from its nucleus, and which blazed forth each night for weeks on end, making its slow and stately progress through the heavens, outshining everything else in the evening sky, including the Moon. Some people even reported seeing it by daylight, so bright was it. The flat area around the rooftop here afforded a particularly spectacular viewing platform, and Sam's telescope revealed all of the comet's details in intricate glory - the filaments within the tails, changing always, night upon night, in subtle variations of colour and texture.

'Huh!' Sam exclaims with a chuckle. 'And do you remember all those kill-joys who assured us it must be some terrible omen; the fall of kings and so on? Always the same, isn't it - upon the occurrence of every comet, every eclipse or conjunction of planets, it is always some calamity, some portent of doom the fortune-tellers anticipate for us; never anything pleasant. Sometimes I think it is because they know so little of themselves, these people, that they seek to be so wise for all the rest of us.'

'Well, correct me if I am wrong, husband, but it *was* almost a calamity, was it not?' Johanna argues with calm confidence. 'Wasn't the Jacobite, Charles Stuart himself in Paris with the French King at the very time, planning an invasion?'

'Why, yes, that's true, my dear, yes,' Sam concedes albeit with reluctance, busy removing the lens cap from his instrument and wiping the glass with a muslin cloth. 'It did all seem a remarkable coincidence, I must say.'

'Perhaps *coincidence* is when the fates just chooses to remain anonymous,' Johanna suggests.

'Um, *Yerrz* ...' Sam mumbles, not very comfortable it would seem, still preoccupied, or pretending to be so. He rarely approves of his wife's little flights of fancy.

'Well, all I can say is I shall never forget it,' Matthew states, wanting to disarm the situation, and still with the recollection of the wondrous object in his mind's eye. He doesn't want it to be a source of disputation. The memory of it lives on, its potency undiminished, and he feels enthralled by the notion that they might be living through extraordinary times as a consequence. 'At the very least, I suppose the Jacobites would have seized upon its appearance as a pretext for invasion. What happened in the end, Sam? It was all kept rather quiet, as I recall.'

'What happened!' Sam exclaims, evidently less than pleased with Matthew's woeful lack of knowledge in such matters. 'A substantial flotilla of fighting men, escorted by over twenty of their finest warships was launched against us, that's what happened. It was only by some timely winds and a spot of clever seamanship that we managed to avert a catastrophe, and most people here knew nothing about it. Unfortunately, though, there is every indication they will try again, possibly from Scotland - with the French navy as always ready to lend support - and we cannot blockade the entire Scottish coastline. Oh, and by the way, none of this to be repeated, if you please. The populace must not be unduly alarmed.'

Matthew nods his concordance. Sam, perhaps as a consequence of his connections with the Admiralty, seems particularly disturbed this evening by the prospect of rebellion. And if he is right, then this continued bid to restore the Stuarts through violent means cannot be kept a secret forever.

It is almost completely dark now, and with every passing moment more and more stars become visible. Atop the hill in Greenwich Park, can be seen the Royal Observatory itself, the familiar shape of Flamsteed House, with its distinctive towers and cupolas, and above this, as the eye lifts towards the zenith, that intriguing, luminous smudge of star-dust, the Milky Way. It is beautiful. But as for any sign of a comet with six tails ... well no, that had been an event of the utmost rarity, a once-in-a-lifetime experience, and everyone knows that in its absence the sky would never be quite as exciting henceforth, never quite as intoxicating in its deep, imponderable mystery as it was then.

'Superstition amongst the common people remains our greatest enemy,' Sam continues, his eye now to the telescope. 'And this is why we must be circumspect. We need to educate people far better. It is science that must be the standard by which we judge things. Can you demonstrate it? Can you verify its significance? These are the questions we must always ask concerning matters of omens, of superstition - and perhaps even of religious dogma, too.'

'Really?' Johanna inquires, a little cynical perhaps, referring still to her earlier variance with Sam's assertions. 'Religion, as well? Goodness me!'

'Well, yes. The same application of reason must be applied in this area, as well, my dear,' he adds, turning to her. 'Can you demonstrate it? Can you prove it?'

'I see,' Johanna responds. 'But tell me, husband: what of God, then? Can you demonstrate that he does not exist? Can you prove it?'

Sam, unable or unwilling to fashion a suitable reply, returns his attentions to his telescope once more, applying adjustments to the calibration with the aid of two small brass knobs as he seeks to track the object of his choice across the sky - though his findings do not appear to be entirely to his satisfaction, even now. 'Confound it all,' he grumbles to himself as he peers through the lens again in some frustration. 'Having the instrument located here on the roof is far from ideal. The heat rising from the house creates a distracting turbulence in the air. I really should have a small building erected in the garden: an observatory.'

'An observatory!' Johanna exclaims, though with laughter in her voice this time, availing herself of a shawl now against the chill 'Goodness, husband, then I should never see you at all! The coffee houses of Exchange Alley by day and your observatory in the garden by night.'

To which Sam, leaving off for a moment to help her wrap the shawl around her shoulders, smiles and chuckles once again by way of demonstrating his agreement - and his understanding, too. Because she is right. And to his credit, Sam is well aware of his own tendency to become just a little fanatical about things at times.

'Perhaps Matthew could join us at the opera next week?' Johanna inquires of her husband, as if keen to put aside their differences and change the subject - but to which Sam voices his compliance only grudgingly.

'Why, yes, of course,' he says, directing his reply as much to Matthew as to his wife. 'At your service, Sir - if you are so disposed.'

'It would please me greatly,' Johanna adds with a special smile of kindness in Matthew's direction - though it is not easy to see her face now. 'A rare summer gala, and an opportunity, moreover, for you to meet our eminent friends, Lord and Lady Snatchal,' she adds with continued enthusiasm, laying a gentle, ungloved hand upon his wrist as she leans ever closer to him. 'We have hired our own box for a while, as Sam might have told you - and I am certain we can accommodate you as well, my Wonder.'

'Thank you,' Matthew says, while Sam coughs and clears his throat, a gruff sort of tone that implies he might not be entirely approving of his wife's sudden gesture of intimacy with their guest, nor of the nickname she has awarded him of late - *my Wonder.*

Matthew tries not to feel too wounded by his ambivalence. To attain *the blessed state of matrimony,* as he described it the other evening, almost always signals a cooling of relations with former friends. Not caring to look back too often to one's bachelor past or to those who still inhabit it seems to be the usual pattern of behaviour, and Sam's attitude this evening is no exception.

'Lord and Lady Snatchal?' Matthew repeats, thinking that the name might be vaguely familiar. 'Do I know them?'

'Possibly,' Sam asserts, taking a moment to pour some wine for everyone and also, having suspended his efforts at observing for the time being, to light a couple of small candle-lamps which he hangs nearby. 'The Earl is becoming a prominent voice in the Privy Council, these days, and in the Admiralty. They have a substantial town house in St James's Square and also - although we have not yet seen it - apparently one of the finest examples of Palladian architecture in the kingdom at Snatchalcombe House in Surrey. With connections of that sort it would certainly be possible for you to secure some major commissions for your work, Matt. Why, the Earl himself was only just the other day remarking on the excellence of my peruke - all crafted in your studios, as I told him. He was impressed. And he has the ear of the King - directly.'

'A worthy outlet for your talents,' Johanna remarks.

'Aye, and lucrative, too. As much as forty, maybe even fifty guineas a commission would be acceptable within those circles,' Sam adds - a propensity to convert everything to a monetary value being always his forte, and to which Johanna withdraws at last her tender hand from Matthew's arm, leaving him with a distinctly bereft feeling and the urgent desire, unlikely as its fulfilment might be, that it be restored at once. His gloomy meditations are broken abruptly, however – because Sam has become all at once unusually agitated, shifting uneasily on his feet and dabbing his lips with a handkerchief in rapid, nervous movements as if suddenly forced to consider something not at all to his liking.

'As it transpires, I must confess to a - er - certain tardiness in respect to the delivery of invitations to this event,' he announces, glancing across sheepishly at his wife.

'Goodness me, husband! Please do not tell me you have forgotten to ask the Snatchals?' Johanna groans, painfully aware of Sam's frequent ineptitude when it comes to social affairs. 'Oh heavens! Well, there will certainly be enough room for us all in the box *now*,' she adds with a sigh and an irritable shaking of the head in her husband's direction.

'I will go at once to seek him out,' Sam declares with an heroic note. 'Yes - immediately. Forgive me, Matthew, that the evening must draw to a premature close. I will arrange the coach if you will allow me a few minutes and then you can, of course, accompany me back to the City. Lord Snatchal will surely be at a certain - er - establishment that is well known to me and where he and a number of his companions can be found on this particular evening of the month. Do not fret, Johanna, my dear. I am confident I shall be able to deliver our invitation by hand, personally, within an hour of setting forth, I promise.'

At which Sam, availing himself of a lamp and the trap-door exit, leaves the rooftop and descends into the house to order up his carriage, which would have been waiting in readiness for Matthew's homeward journey, anyway.

'This series of sonnets that you mentioned - do tell me again, my Wonder, what is to be their nature precisely?' Johanna inquires after a moment, and in a voice of particular softness - though it is not a welcome question for Matthew since he has not yet had an opportunity to fabricate a sufficiently plausible tale.

'Oh, I - er - haven't quite decided yet,' he replies as he sidles up closer, as near as decorum will permit, seeking out her presence in the darkness.

A degree of light is available from the newly risen moon to make up for Sam's taking of one of the lamps, but this is behind her, so that her profile becomes etched in tiny filaments of silver upon the line of her forehead, defining her lips and chin, and thus rendering her appearance almost statuesque: a head that should not be out of place were it carved in antique marble. This and the pale blondness of her hair is almost all he can discern until he reaches over to bring the remaining lantern closer.

'I suspect they might be something a touch more primitive in style to the usual fare,' he continues, setting the lantern down, happy now that he can see more of her face - and also realising, to his own surprise, that the whole idea might not be such a bad one, after all. 'The muses, yes, but also perhaps the Gods of Olympus - something special. I could even accompany each one by the making up of a carnival mask, a hobby of mine, as you know. It would be a fine exhibit, a curio for a drawing room or library, or merely for my own satisfaction. We shall see.'

'The classicism of Olympus would be most fashionable, yes,' she concurs sharing in his enthusiasm, 'or even perchance a commentary on the planets once associated with them? The heavenly bodies.'

'The heavenly bodies?' Matthew echoes.

'Oh, yes. I hope I shall not shock you, my Wonder. But being of the opinion that a woman should have more to do in this life than embroider shirts or play at cards in the afternoon, I have made it my pleasure to study the stars - their ancient mysteries, in addition to their science. And it just occurred to me that the planetary spheres of old might prove a worthy subject for you. Oh, I'm sorry, because then you would also have to become very mystical, and I am being silly suggesting such a thing.'

'No, not at all,' he murmurs. 'Tell me, please. I am not averse to becoming mystical. Not at the present moment, at least.'

How good it is to be with her, he thinks, alone like this as he had secretly wished earlier - and her voice, so hushed and intimate, reminding him of someone revealing a secret. He is acutely aware of her proximity, the rustling of her skirts, the subtle movements in the darkness as she responds to his nearness.

'I have read that at the court of the Medici in Florence, during the flowering of the Renaissance, there was a famed Humanist scholar by the name of Marsilio Ficino,' she continues in careful measured tones. 'To this day, schools of philosophy in France and Italy continue to commemorate his ideas - which, in turn, were derived from the ancient wisdom of the classical world, the re-discovery of the writings of Plato and Pythagoras - oh yes, and with a sprinkling of poetry from Dante thrown in for good measure. A most fertile combination.'

She pauses, to listen for his response, whether she has piqued his interest.

'Please continue,' he murmurs.

'Ficino, in his capacity as astrologer to the court of the Medici at whose summer retreat these secret exercises were practised, maintained that, arranged about each of us in a subtle dimension that we cannot readily perceive with our accustomed senses, are the spheres of the heavenly bodies, seven in number. Oh, and it is here, Matthew, that I must confide in you a further interest which I have long entertained, and that is in astrology - not at a superstitious level, not in the manner of horoscopes and such nonsense sold on street corners for a penny, but rather that which is played as a kind of music upon the human soul. In Ficino's teachings, the aspirant contemplates the occult associations of each planet or luminary in the precise order set out by the ancients, one after the other as upon a stairway to the heavens.'

'Ah, so beginning with the lunar sphere,' Matthew suggests. 'Am I correct?'

'You are,' she answers, her voice still hushed, 'the emotional and sensuous Moon - that body which is closest and thus appears to move the most swiftly in the skies. Then there is the intellectual sphere of Mercury, followed by beauteous Venus, the resplendent Sun, courageous Mars and benevolent Jupiter in turn, until finally the profound and melancholic sphere of Saturn is penetrated, signifying the wisdom and maturity of the enlightened soul. It was by this means, the philosophers maintained, that an individual might loosen his or her mind from the confines of the body, to liberate the spirit and to soar above the material world - a journey that would take the aspirant closer to the source of all wisdom and harmony: the sphere of the infinite starry sky, the *Primum Mobile.*'

'How very interesting,' he remarks, feeling disturbed and yet inevitably drawn to what she is telling him - because it seems to be resonating already, albeit at a somewhat more elevated level, with his own extravagant plans for enjoying a variety of beautiful women in close succession. And her next words leave him in little doubt of the intriguing similarities.

'It was through the use of the senses that they approached their quest - through music, through the contemplation of certain colours or sounds; sometimes certain fragrances, herbs or flowering plants, or even precious stones - all in various combinations of seven - since all things are related, we are told, to one or more of the heavenly spheres. They are united in a magical sense, as part of a great invisible chain of being from the inanimate upwards to the angelic. In this sense, all things are worthy of contemplation - for there is nothing in the whole living world so ugly or base that a sense of spirit does not in some way attend upon it. It is these spiritual forces latent within ourselves which, thus awakened, provide the keys to unlock the mysteries and set the seeker upon the pathway to the heavens.'

'*The pathway to the heavens.* How marvellous that sounds,' he murmurs, almost as if to himself. 'But *seven*, you say?'

'Always. It is the number of perfection. In matters of harmony and proportion, it is the seven colours of the rainbow, the seven notes of the musical scale. The spiritual practices of the East also have the seven heavens. Why even in our Bible, we have seven archangels, do we not! There are seven days of creation; seven lamps that burn before the throne of God. Whether any of this might be accommodated into your project, my Wonder, I can only surmise - yet I know that with your lyrical skills and rich talent you will surely apply what modest inspiration I can provide in order to perfect your work. Have I been helpful?'

'Thank you - thank you so much,' he sighs after a moment's contemplation. 'I should say you have been more helpful than I can possible explain at the moment.'

And suddenly he realises that they have drifted so close to one another that their sides are touching, and he feels her breath on his cheek, so warm in the coolness of the night air. And her eyes seem to be all aglow with moonlight as she lifts her face to look into his.

'*Matt! Matt! Where the Devil are you?*' the fulsome voice of Sam booms out abruptly as if from some infernal region of the building below and which causes them both to start and instinctively draw apart. 'Our horses are harnessed and at your service, Sir, should you ever care to come down and renew your acquaintance with me.'

And so with a wry smile, drawing himself away from the inspiring lesson and the equally enchanting company of Johanna, Matthew gets to his feet - and then, having seen her down safely before him, he bows graciously and, with the utmost reluctance, take his leave of her. Sam, meanwhile, attired more formally in readiness for their departure, is to be found in the hallway examining with pride his latest acquisition, a splendid long-cased marine barometer upon the wall. And as Matthew approaches, his friend opens the glass dome atop with a key and gives the tube within a tap with the finger to check the atmospheric pressure, and thus the weather that might be imminent - be it 'Dry,' 'Set Fair,' 'Change,' 'Rain' or 'Stormy' - as indicated upon its silvered and intricately engraved register plate.

'We bought a number of these for the Admiralty,' he announces, 'and this is one of the very best. At least it is supposed to be. Huh! I regret to say I shall have to take it back to the manufacturers for some adjustments. But a wonderful instrument, nonetheless, would you not agree?'

'Very impressive,' Matthew replies, though without much conviction. The wood in which the long column of mercury is encased is of fashionable mahogany, and the whole thing would have cost a small fortune, he reflects as he harnesses his sword and dons his tricorn ahead of the journey. Sam's home is full of scientific instruments like this - barometers, thermometers, microscopes and telescopes of every latest style and invention and which are always in constant need of adjustments or repair. Matthew, anyway, is hardly listening any longer to what his friend has to say - because everything is different now, his hitherto purely carnal ambitious having suddenly become transformed and ennobled by the words of Johanna, by the alchemy of the mind and the very romance of the stars themselves. And it is to this end, the magical stairway to heaven and none other, that he knows he must now set his course.

# ~ 3 ~
## WINDOWS OF THE SKY

It is, as Matthew well knows, a journey not without its dangers, especially at this time of the evening, when highwaymen would sometimes lie in wait along the more leafy and deserted stretches of the Kent Road. And Sam's new coach and four with its lanterns and gleaming accoutrements would be more-than conspicuous. Quite an allure.

'Do not concern yourself,' says Sam, once they are under way, their carriage slipping and sliding downhill quickly towards the City. 'Our coachman is armed with a blunderbuss and cutlass; our groom, with a pair of pistols - and both have instructions to shoot at anyone approaching with malice aforethought. Anyway what do you think of it - my new coach?' he adds with a particularly aloof, down-the-nose glance at his friend. 'Does up to 25 miles per hour on a suitable road surface, they say. Not that we have any suitable road surfaces anywhere - but no matter. It would if it could, eh!'

Matthew, his eyes trying to penetrate the darkness beyond the windows, does not deign to respond to such nonsense.

'You seem uncommonly pensive, Sir,' Sam observes, breaking the silence again, and also interrupting once more the process of thought that has been instigated by the conversation with Johanna earlier, his plans now imbued with an intriguingly mystical significance - one that until thirty minutes ago he had hardly dreamt of as existing. How exciting!

'Sam ..?' Matthew begins at length.

'Yerrz ..?'

'I must know: how much have you revealed to your good wife about my designs - I mean regarding our discussion the other night?'

'I take it you are referring to the harem you intend establishing at your quarters at The Pig and Whistle?' Sam inquires. 'All I can say is that which passes in discourse between man and wife is a private matter, Sir, and for no other to know.'

'So you won't tell me?'

'Correct - an entertaining diversion for me in which I shall enjoy seeing you squirm for the next several weeks until your preposterous scheme comes crashing to the ground, as it surely must. Furthermore, seeing as you are such a gallant with the ladies,' he adds, turning to him and becoming morose, *'even to the brazen extent of taking my wife's hand this evening up on the leads,* such a torment and punishment shall be all the more to my delectation.'

'Sam!' Matthew protests, 'I did not take your good lady's hand. She rested hers upon my arm, that's all. I can assure you my sentiments towards your dear wife are purely noble.'

'Oh, really. Well, now you are just sounding pompous,' Sam retorts.

'All I can say, then, is I must be learning from the master,' Matthew states, turning his head away, glancing once more through the window on his side and wondering at his own unease, that he should feel so anxious about Johanna learning of his somewhat excessive carnal ambitions. At least their coach is out of danger now - with various domestic dwellings, inns and taverns either side of the road and, just ahead to their right, the broad, winding river coming into view - a forest of tall masts and rigging clustered in and around the dockyards east of the city, and all the busy traffic of passenger boats and wherries - their swarms of tiny lanterns all reflected on the water: a whole universe of stars below.

'Anyway, enough!' Sam declares. 'I have resolved to be nice to you for once, because this evening I am going to introduce you to some men of quality. Lord Snatchal to whom I must deliver our invitation is the head of a most noble society of gentlemen who ...'

'What, you mean Masons?' Matthew interrupts in dismissive tone, assuming what his friend is referring to would be any one of the various gatherings of fraternities, clubs or lodges favoured by the aristocracy, renowned for their extravagant dinners and riotous behaviour - and invariably accompanied by much drinking and debauchery. Matthew has never been invited to a single one, which has always annoyed him intensely, though he refuses to let such disappointments show.

'No, not necessarily Masons,' Sam replies, 'though of course you might encounter one or two among them.'

'Well, probably not anything that would interest me, then,' Matthew concludes. 'Not that I would know, anyway, since no one has ever troubled themselves to extend an invitation to me,' he adds, referring to Sam's reticence over the years in broaching the subject of membership.

'Well, nobody is likely to, either!' Sam counters, 'Not all the time you keep arsing about like you do,' he adds, taking a pinch of snuff for himself before handing the finely worked silver box across to Matthew, who does indulge this time - though not without a sneeze in the taking of the fine powder, thereby revealing his inexperience with the craft.

'What do you mean, *arsing about?*'

'I mean, Sir, your preoccupation with trifles - poetry, for example, and pretending you can make a living out of it. Or constructing carnival masks at a shilling a time. As long as you insist on remaining unmarried, moreover, you will never be taken seriously. You'll never be regarded as a fully fledged member of the male species. At the very least, if you wish to become numbered among people of merit, you must find yourself a proper job, a profession.'

'Stop being so mischievous, Sam! You know full well I have a profession - I am a Master Wig Maker, trained in Paris among the finest in Europe.'

'I know, but listen: nobody wants to have anything to do with the French any more, Matt. Not at the present juncture. I should keep quiet about your Parisian connections, if I were you.'

Even when trying to be kind, Sam always manages to sound so disparaging. It irritates Matthew, such arrogance - and to which he snaps back straight away: 'At least I continue to work in the field I was trained in - unlike yourself: a Barber Surgeon who elected to become a pen-pusher in the Admiralty the day after completing his apprenticeship.'

'It was more lucrative,' Sam asserts, puffing out his chest defiantly. 'Besides I couldn't face the prospect of a lifetime of lancing boils and shaving heads. They say hard work never killed anyone - but why risk it? That's my philosophy.'

'Well, then you would understand that I do not wish to spend the rest of my life just making wigs, either. There are more important things to be doing. And, anyway, the occupation of poet, may I remind you, is a noble one, and an important one too, for any society. We think differently. The world to us is a different place, full of the finer things - the arts and civilised values.'

'Oh yes, well we shall see how civilised we all become if the Admiralty turns its back and the French march up the Dover road into London. The massacre of St Bartholomew's Day in your beloved Paris, though it was long ago, has not been forgotten, y'know. Men women and children, babes put to the sword. It could happen again.'

'I disagree. That's nonsense. And by the way, where has that proper bespoke wig of yours gone to - the one I made?' Matthew inquires of his friend, noticing the poor quality of the one Sam has on. 'I would have thought you would have wanted to wear your best this evening.'

'Can't,' Sam answers. 'A confounded bird has nested in it. I told the valet he should not leave it in a box so near to an open window. The children discovered it, and now of course Johanna won't let me touch the damn thing until the ruddy eggs have hatched and the chicks fledged. That could be weeks - and then it will need to go to the cleaners, you can rely on that! What with one thing and another, what with the one we picked out the gutter the other night languishing in your studios for repair - *and still not ready yet, may I remind you* - I am left with this old moth-eaten specimen.'

'I will have the damaged one ready for you by the weekend, my friend. Do not fret. Perhaps you could send your new housemaid over to collect it,' Matthew suggests, with a fond recollection of his exchange of glances earlier this evening. 'I must say, I rather like the look of her. Mary, was it not?'

'Desist, Sir! The young woman you speak of is a member of my most valued household retinue.'

'Ah - keeping her all to yourself, then, eh?' Matthew jests.

'Now now, Matt - I don't know what you are implying, but that which takes place between myself and certain members of my household staff, particularly in the laundry room downstairs, for instance, on a Friday evening, is entirely a matter of the utmost confidentiality.'

'Sam - surely not!'

It pains him, the thought that Sam could even contemplate fumbling with the maid when he is married to one such as Johanna. And Sam seems to sense this, as well.

'It was difficult to resist, Matt ...' he explains with untypical bashfulness, 'it being darkish at the time.'

'*Darkish!* What has that got to do with it? Are deeds committed in the absence of light any the worse for those that are visible? How could you!'

What a peculiar business marriage must be, Matthew thinks, if this is all it leads to. And he wonders what might be the extent of Sam's possible infidelities, real or imagined, and how far afield he might already have cast his net. Their coach is passing through the suburbs south of the bridge at that moment, the worst areas of Southwark where the streets at this time of the evening are populated with numerous touts, pimps and whores. To be sure, temptation and opportunity enough are always to be found in the city for any man who might be dissatisfied at home. As if to confirm his worst fears, Sam suddenly becomes most lively as he gazes outside with a mixture of feigned disapproval and admiration.

'Huh!' he exclaims. 'Look at those wenches out there plying their trade. Hot blooded women, eh!'

'You think so?' Matthew responds. 'I venture to suggest it might be the ever-present prospect of starvation that is more likely responsible for any fulsomeness of the blood. That or the allure of fine apparel for which the wages of any honest trade would not suffice.'

'Oh, don't you be so sanctimonious, my friend,' Sam retorts. 'If you are ever to bring to fruition such an extravagant and ambitious scheme as you spoke of the other evening you may well need to draw upon the services of females of precisely this persuasion. And then heaven help you!'

'Sam - really - have you learned nothing of my intentions? It is not some orgiastic melee, or idle lechery to which I have set my purpose. Why, the more I contemplate things lately, the more I begin to appreciate that it's a far more subtle experience that I am seeking. Yes, that's it - even more refined than what we spoke of the other day: a quest for the *philosopher's stone*, no less.'

'God help us!' Sam exclaims as they turn up onto the bridge and begin to negotiate its crossing, a slow process amid the usual congestion of wagons, hackney chairs and ambling pedestrians. 'Now you're beginning to sound like some cranky old alchemist. What on earth is all this about?'

'It is about flying, Sam - remember?' Matthew replies, and with laughter in his voice now as they approach the very spot above the river where, he recalls, the incident of the bird-man took place. 'You see, contrary to the authority of your Mr Newton, many among us philosophical folk still maintain that we are each at the centre of our own universe, at the focus of a precise sequence of heavenly emanations, seven in number, and not normally perceived by the senses. In order to fly, therefore - not in a physical sense, you understand, but via our mental faculties - one must avail oneself of - er - certain subtle experiences.'

'Yerrz ...'

'Yes, certain experiences, Sam. Life is infinite in the variety of pleasures that can be combined to liberate the spirit by this means: seven notes of the musical scale; seven colours; even seven glasses of wine, if you like. I intend to avail myself of seven beautiful women, each reflecting the physical characteristics of the planets of occult tradition - the Chaldean order, beginning with the Moon, therefore, and ending with Saturn. Yes, I can see it now, the way it will work. I shall begin with a lady of pale and delicate complexion, rounded and voluptuous to represent the fair Moon. That is the first step upon the ladder, so to speak. Then a good feisty maid for Mercury comes next; succeeded by a well-proportioned beauty for Venus ...'

'Followed by a blond, I presume, to represent the solar sphere?' Sam interjects with an encouraging turn now the subject matter has become more to his liking. 'And then a fiery redhead for Mars?'

'Why, yes - yes, that's right,' Matthew answers, rejoicing in his friends growing understanding. 'A nice chubby bunny for Jupiter comes next - and finally a rather more - er - *mature* lady, dark and melancholic who would represent Saturn at the end of the journey. All this would need to be accomplished within a short time, and without any distractions or interruptions - and, as I believe I have indicated to you already, the magic must not be broken by any moment of reckless abandon. Rather, each of these seven intoxicating stages must be prolonged and savoured, with devotion and attention to every sound, every mysterious secret touch and fragrance along the way. Ah, can you imagine the intensity of such an experience, Sam! Who knows where this journey might take whoever is bold enough to set his prayers to such a purpose - the discoveries that might ensue as each window of the sky is opened and passed through, its mysteries unveiled.'

They have reached the other end of the bridge now, and Sam, gazing out at the busy streets of the city to gauge their progress remains silent for a while, and then when he does finally respond it is in a surprisingly calm and thoughtful tone. 'Well, Matthew, my friend, according to my calculations at the present stage of our journey, we are not too distantly located from the lunatic asylum at Bedlam. Would you like me to instruct the driver to direct us to the door so I might drop you off?'

'Sam, for Heaven's sake!'

'Where on earth do you get all these ridiculous ideas, anyway?'

'Oh ... as a matter of fact this was from Johanna,' Matthew answers, trying to sound casual.

'What! You mean you've been in conversation with my wife concerning your outrageous proclivities!' Sam bellows, his face a brightening scarlet, an effulgence detectable even in the semi-gloom of the carriage. 'You, Sir ... *you* are utterly beyond redemption!'

'In your absence for a short time this evening, our discourse merely revolved around those very ideas that you yourself had alluded to earlier,' Matthew protests with dignified calm, 'the Muses, remember? One thing led to another and we finished up with the planets, that's all.'

But Sam, still furious, brushes the matter aside with an irritable wave of the hand. Their coach has turned into Cornhill now, a high-walled thoroughfare where, even at this late hour, so many of its shop windows, its silversmiths and drapers, mercers and haberdashers are all lit up - and their destination also, a substantial and brightly illuminated coaching inn, coming into view. 'I shall have to speak to you about this another time,' he grumbles. 'For the time being, whatever you do, I strongly advise you not to discuss anything of this preposterous nature among the gentlemen you will be meeting here this evening. I also recommend that you refrain from shaking anybody's hand or revealing yourself in any sense as belonging to the - er - *the uninitiated*. If anyone asks, just say you are my valet. Understand?'

'Certainly not!' Matthew replies angrily. 'Do I look like a valet, damn it!'

'Well no, not exactly - but you don't have a wig.'

'You know perfectly well I rarely wear a wig,' Matthew argues.

'I am fortunate in not needing to. And my apparel is the equal of any man. Introduce me as your friend and colleague or not at all.'

And, reluctantly, Sam agrees.

The night is still young, and, once they have stationed their coach safely in the courtyard, they enter by the front doors and climb the wide stairway together to the first floor where, by the sounds of it, a rowdy gathering is well under way. And it is with a blend of keen anticipation but also considerable trepidation on Matthew's part that they approach the doorman waiting at the top and are admitted to a busy and candlelit interior of a large dining room. Sam, peering into the smoke and gloom, searches for any sign of the man he has come to see amid the crowds of smartly attired gentlemen - some clearly well-inebriated, some leaning on the shoulders of their companions or, in one instance, apparently engaged in a game of leap frog - while elsewhere another is intent on relieving himself into a chamber pot, an item that appears to be in constant circulation among those attending. Lord Snatchal, it transpires, is located over the other side of the room, reclining on a couch in conversation with two equally opulent and distinguished looking colleagues, all in monstrous sized periwigs - their clothing all braid and buckles and their stockings fastened above their knees in the old fashioned style. Snatchal also appears to be in command of a small baboon on a chain, dressed in perfectly tailored coat and breeches, who cavorts nearby among the disorderly chairs and benches, his big round eyes going from face to face with a lively and curious intelligence so acute that it puts the rest of the occupants of the room to shame - for they all seem more than a little befuddled and worse for drink - the preferred preoccupation here being the pledging of various loyalties or devotions every few minutes in copious quantities of brandy and claret.

'My noble lords and gentlemen, I give you the delectable charms of Mrs Lucy Armstrong of Cockspur Street!'

To which everyone raises his glass and responds with an almost devotional repetition of the name 'Mrs Lucy Armstrong!' they all cry in unison.

'To the Mistresses of all good noblemen, wherever they may be!' cries another a few moments later.

'To the Mistresses of all good noblemen,' follows the chorus as they all drain their glasses with enthusiasm.

'And may a Thousand Frivolous Favours of Fantasy attend upon your every endeavour!' cries another - this last foray into the realms of alliteration proving too great a challenge for most and tending to trail off incoherently, the gentleman responsible hoisting up his glass almost to the ceiling and thereby losing most of its contents in the process.

'Don't you think this is all rather childish?' Matthew inquires of Sam, realising that his worst misgivings of such gatherings are being confirmed. He always feels irritable when solely in the company of men

'No not at all,' Sam replies, indignant over the suggestion. 'These are men of the world, Sir. And if a man of the world is to be taken seriously he must celebrate the society of a mistress or two as well as that of a valet or a pastry cook. Here, it is not only the arts and sciences that are venerated, but the charms of womanhood - and fulsomely!'

'All the more puzzling, then that no women are in attendance,' Matthew remarks icily.

But Sam shakes his head in despair. 'You wait,' he says, leading Matthew farther into the room with a guiding hand upon his shoulder. Here, they request a jug of wine and take their seats at the end of a long dining table which, by its scattered and spilled remains indicates that a considerable feast has earlier taken place upon its ravaged surface. It is entirely vacated of diners now, apart from one gentleman asleep, his head upon the table itself, the lower portion of his wig resting within a dish of partly consumed oysters, the curly tresses darkening as they soak up the various oils and juices therein. Upon the wall to their side hangs a large, elaborately framed mirror, and Matthew when catching his refection therein and observing his demeanour alongside those of the other guests, realises that he is by far the youngest person in the room and that he must surely be conspicuous because of it. It is as if a lesson in mortality, the very march of time itself were being presented to him in the glass. For whereas many in attendance are grey-haired, weak and curved in the spine, their skin without lustre, as though covered in a coating of ash, his spine is erect, his hair all shiny and dark about the temples and with a sharply delineated hairline etched against the lustrous skin. His eyes are sparkling, his lips full and moist. The vitality of the living shines from him - so that regardless of any comparison in height, for there are many of a height similar to him, he appears as a giant among them, a paragon of strength and vigour. What would they all be thinking of him - an interloper? He has heard terrible stories about secret societies and of offenders being punished, having their tongues cut out or being hanged for their indiscretions.

Meanwhile, the gentleman with his wig in the oysters has been roused at last with a friendly prod from the cane of one of his colleagues, a man who next climbs up onto the table - a position from which he wobbles precariously and in a full, resonant voice addresses the assembly thus: 'My Lords, Knights and Companions! Gentlemen! Silence and due reverence if you please. Our most venerable and ancient ceremony is about to commence.'

'What's this?' Matthew inquires of his friend in whispered confusion.

Sam appears agitated. 'Oh, that means it's time for the navel ceremony,' he replies. 'That is, n.a.v.e.l.'

But Matthew has no opportunity to demand further clarification - for at just that moment a ship's bell is rung and the hitherto all-male assembly is joined by a woman, her hair all loose, clad merely in a long silk dressing gown and carnival mask and who has just been ushered in through another door at the far end of the room. She promptly removes the gown and, to much sighing and a salacious, almost audible smacking of the lips among the gentlemen present, reveals her complete nakedness. She is not young, but with her finely proportioned and slender form, she would, Matthew reflects, be the envy of many a woman who is. Escorted to the table by two gallants, she promptly rolls herself over onto its surface, a space hastily cleared and prepared in readiness with a fresh table covering, and upon which she lies, perfectly supine and still.

It is Lord Snatchal, no less, who gets to his feet next from the far end of the room and, with an adroit and delicate touch clearly born of much practice and repeated experience, approaches and pours a small quantity of red wine into the inviting hollow of the woman's navel. He mumbles some kind of incantation in Latin and then, one by one, the assembled men file past the supine lady herself, taking each in turn a sip of red wine - with Lord Snatchal in the role of some outlandish priest, renewing the wine each time. With studied authenticity, he even traces a blessing in the air with his fingers as each man passes. Even Matthew, inured to the brazen hostility of the English towards the religious faith of the enemy, can only look on with revulsion at what is in essence an outrageous blasphemy, a gross parody of the Mass.

'No more than harmless entertainment,' Sam whispers into Matthew's ear, his voice one of embarrassment. 'Do not, Sir, I pray you, be offended,' he adds, before stepping up to take the bizarre sacrament himself. Matthew has to follow suit, naturally, to avoid any suspicion - for he is still acutely aware of all those mistrustful eyes upon him. But Lord Snatchal gives him a wink and nudge of encouragement as he steps forth, and within a second or two the deed is done. It is quite decent wine, he thinks to himself, afterwards, even if a little salty. The woman's scent is of the highest quality, too, and her eyes, well-visible, through the apertures of her mask, engage him as he steps away and seem to burn with a special intensity. Whether this is from her approval of him alone or a sentiment fuelled by her overall state of excitement he cannot determine - though she continues to regard him with study, even as the next gentleman steps up to receive his benefaction.

'And you have the cheek to imply that *I* have some peculiar ideas! Matthew remarks as he and Sam take their seats again at the far end of the table. 'This is most unchivalrous, if you ask me - to be disrespecting the ways and customs of others, and that so blatantly.'

'Well, yes, the Earl can appear, how shall we say, a trifle idiosyncratic in the mental department, I'll grant you that,' Sam agrees grudgingly. 'But a formidable opponent in parliament, they say. I even heard he's tipped to become the next Chancellor of the Exchequer.'

'Oh, really. How very reassuring,' Matthew responds.

Meanwhile, the serious business of the ceremony of the navel being concluded, Lord Snatchal returns to his former position reclining adjacent to his pet baboon on the couch. Having acknowledged the familiar face of Sam at last, he beckons him and Matthew over; and they, after bowing and making a suitable leg to the noble Lord, each draw up a chair in front of him. Sam's invitation to the opera is duly delivered, and Matthew is introduced as: 'Mr Wildish, a most excellent poet and one of the finest wig makers in London, destined for the highest of patronage.'

'Really!' the noble Lord exclaims, stowing the invitation away into his pocket before taking a candle-lamp and holding it up to examine Matthew's hair in more detail. 'Why, that is a most excellent piece you're wearing at present, Wildish, if I may say so,' he adds. 'Don't think I've ever seen a more natural looking specimen.'

He is not an old man, but his voice is lacking in resonance, like somebody already old before his time - and with a scrawny, ribald kind of face, disconcertingly goat-like and upon which two scarlet painted lips appear forever in a position of being extravagantly pursed as if surveying some eternally recurring scene of voluptuousness before his inner eye. 'Anyway, Wildish,' he continues, 'welcome to our humble little gathering, a place where you will certainly find men of elevated sensibilities like yourself - those who celebrate the cult of Priapus and who appreciate the fine arts and the excellence of the female form in equal measure, since these are indisputably the salvation and glory of mankind, would you not agree?'

To which, Sam, a look of admiration upon his face, squeezes his palms together and nods earnestly his complete concordance - while Matthew, still more than a little stunned and repulsed by it all, finds his attentions being drawn more and more to the baboon at the other end of the chain and also to the incongruous presence of a riding crop at the noble Lord's side. What on earth is that for?

'Do not take our peculiar devotions too much to heart, Wildish,' the noble lord continues with a friendly wink, perhaps sensing the newcomer's unease. 'The origin of the little parody that you have just witnessed is born out of genuine veneration, I can assure you - the veneration of rationality and enlightenment over superstition and blind faith - the Popish faith of our enemies, which we do just tend to mock rather savagely, I will admit.'

Matthew's continued lack of enthusiasm, however, does not appear to entirely meet with the noble Lord's approval. 'I take it our young friend here is loyal?' he suddenly enquires of Sam, though making sure Matthew himself can well hear and, oddly, as he does so, his mouth appears to drop open in a curious fashion, and stays that way.

'Indeed, Sir - and a person moreover who has frequently aided me in my endeavours on behalf of His Majesty's deputies at St James's and Whitehall.'

To which Snatchal nods his approval and with a discreet little movement puts his fingers beneath his chin and pushes his mouth closed. This curious manual adjustment to his jaw being accomplished, he then draws his face ever-closer to his listeners, his red lips pursed into a somewhat cankered rose-bud, his narrow eyes turning towards Matthew and squinting in examination of his very soul. 'Well and good - because you should know, Wildish,' he begins again, 'that even as we speak, our kingdom is in the gravest danger. The Stuarts and the Papists have united their fortunes in France once more, and since the French know full well that unless we are distracted elsewhere they have no chance of a direct assault across the Channel, they are just about to do their damndest to ferment rebellion among the Scottish Highlanders and to incite civil war here at home. We will be powerless to stop any of it unless we know who is prepared to aid them, especially among those buggers up North where, given half a chance, many of the families would like to see the monks and priests back in charge. The Highlanders meanwhile are a bloodthirsty race, as I well-know from the last time they tried it on, the 1715 rebellion. We must maintain vigilance, therefore. And with fellows like my good colleague Sam here on top of things, I know we can rest happy in our beds at night - as the actress said to the bishop, what!'

And thus, concluding with that singularly lewd jest, the noble Lord taps the side of his nose twice with his forefinger in a gesture of complicity followed by a further extravagant wink.

'Your ever-faithful servant,' Sam responds fervently, hand on heart, his fleshy chin wobbling with demonstrable veneration.

All seems well, until just then Matthew catches sight, out of the corner of his eye, of the baboon; the creature itself listening to the noble Lord's words with an expression of utmost concentration on his tiny, wrinkled face - so that Matthew discovers that it is becoming increasingly difficult not to laugh. A fit of the giggles is coming on, he knows. The very idea that the salvation of the kingdom might be in Sam's hands is preposterous enough, but that his superior here in all such endeavours transpires to be a man who enjoys the company of a pet baboon on his evenings out is simply beyond the maintenance of sanity.

Fortunately, an opportunity arises for them to escape, because Lord Snatchal appears to be in need of the chamber pot at just that instant, and Sam, perceiving Matthew's imminent loss of self control, his shoulders beginning to tremble with little convulsions of hilarity, nudges him none too kindly in the ribs as he shepherds him away to a more discreet position away from prying eyes.

'Why does the old fellow never smile?' Matthew asks in a whisper as they retake their seats. 'And that mouth of his that keeps opening - it looks most odd.'

'A matter of false teeth,' Sam replies, 'combined with an unfortunate injury during his days in the Household Cavalry. His lower dentures are a good fit, and easy to keep in place - they can do wonders these days with hippopotamus ivory, apparently - but the upper ones must be retained by the aid of springs. A certain challenge is experienced, therefore, in closing the mouth once open. It doesn't happen often, fortunately; but if he smiles too broadly, the whole thing can malfunction.'

'I see,' says Matthew, assuming that nothing more this evening could possibly surprise him. But he is wrong. The serious business of discussing the preservation of the kingdom now being over, and it still being early (a glance at the mantel clock indicates that it is only a little after midnight, after all) there is apparently yet further ceremony and entertainment to be enacted - for abruptly, the entire company, to a man, begin to clap and then to chant, a repetitive refrain of: 'blind man's buff! blind man's buff …' until one among them finally steps forward and appears to volunteer his services - which are indeed, quite singular and unlike any other game of blind man's buff Matthew can ever recall having witnessed because the gentleman in question - in addition to being blindfolded and spun around three times - has to have his breeches pulled down around his ankles before the game can commence. The object of his quest, as he stumbles about the room, is to locate, among the many males, the one female still present - she of the earlier navel ceremony, clothed in a chemise now but also drenched in her distinctive perfume that Matthew remembers from earlier to aid the process of detection. She is pursued to a mighty uproar of laughter and ribald shouting - the poor fellow in the blindfold searching for her with outstretched arms and twitchy hands, being eventually allowed the reward of a pleasant fumble upon catching her. This being accomplished, he removes his blindfold and hands it over so that another volunteer, who in readiness has already dropped his breeches, might take up the challenge. Chairs are overturned, tables bumped into and general pandemonium ensues for a good fifteen minutes as each takes his turn, with Lord Snatchal himself applying strokes of his riding crop upon the backside of whoever is 'it' for the moment, or in fact bringing it down soundly on any available buttock, clothed or otherwise - all the while leaping about in a frenzy of mischievous delight and shrieking: 'Woo, ha! Woo, ha, ha!' as he prances from one bum to the next, pausing only to close his mouth now and then with a timely slap of the hand beneath the chin.

'Surely we are not expected to join in?' Matthew asks with exasperation, getting to his feet - also thinking of Johanna again for some reason and of all the tranquillity, beauty and charm that awaits Sam at home. What on earth are they doing here!

'Now don't go all puritanical on me, Matt,' Sam continues to harangue his friend, 'not after all you've been prattling on about the past few days. This is one of the Club's traditions, the way things work here - and not to be trifled with.'

'What, groping about with some common whore!' Matthew exclaims.

But Sam is unrepentant and shakes his head as if in amazement at his friend's naivety as, rising also, he hauls Matthew to one side again by the arm. 'I'll have you know, Sir, that the woman you see here is no common whore, but belongs to that illustrious genre of females termed the *Demirep* - women of quality for whom the normal constraints and obligations of married life are thrown aside at moments, but only, of course, if their security can be assured. I'll wager she would have been selected from any number of amenable wives or mistresses of those present - hence the mask she wears, and the darkened room the better to preserve her anonymity. Desist, Sir, therefore, in using that derogative term here. Oh, and by the way, I think we might be arousing suspicion by our reluctance to take part.'

But Matthew has already had quite enough. 'We are leaving, Sam,' he insists, ready to drag his friend away if need be. 'We are leaving at once!'

But just as Sam is about to protest, the room falls unusually silent. A newcomer has entered - by his simple apparel, a messenger or page of some kind, and clearly in possession of important news for Lord Snatchal himself. Approaching him, he whispers into his ear, looking stern and grave-faced as he does so. This accomplished, and with a brief bow of acknowledgement towards one or two of the other gentlemen nearby, he then departs as swiftly as he had arrived - leaving Snatchal, meanwhile, in a condition of some introspection for a period before eventually turning to speak to some of his colleagues nearby who, in turn, begin to speak with others close to them. A buzz of muted conversation spreads around the room - the hitherto boisterous and rowdy gathering becoming transformed into one of sober and serious contemplation as it becomes abundantly clear that all their high jinks has come to a very swift and, for them, unwelcome conclusion.

Sam, pushing his way forward to join them, has his ear whispered into as well - only to return straight away to Matthew's side, where he also seems lost in thought for a moment before turning to his friend, and with a mixture of concern and growing passion on his slightly flushed features declares: 'Well Sir, now there's a thing. While you have been mincing around London, chasing the ladies these past few days, your head full of trifles and absurd fancies, Charles Stuart, the Young Pretender, has set sail from France in a frigate laden with artillery and gunpowder, and escorted, furthermore, by a sixty-four-gun French warship. What do you think of that! The ship has been engaged by our navy and damaged well enough that it has limped back to its home port, but the other has sailed on - its direction north-westerly. Destination, it is surmised, the Western Isles of Scotland.'

Matthew looks back at his friend with some indifference and confusion. 'Is that -er - anything to worry about?' he inquires in all innocence, not being much of a military man himself and feeling that the occupation of *mincing around London chasing the ladies* sounds infinitely preferable, in any case.

'What?' Sam explodes, but lowers his voice straight away by necessity as heads turn. 'As a would be-spy for the Crown, Sir, you really ought to be doing better in these matters. The Stuarts, you might recall, are convinced they are still the rightful heirs to the English throne. Once on Scottish soil, the Prince's intention will be to draw as many Highland clans and Papists to his standard as he can in preparation for a full-scale invasion from the North. Just as Snatchal mooted earlier. It is war, Sir - war, and God knows where it will end; how many good men and women will perish before it is over.'

'Well, he still has to get to Scotland, doesn't he?' Matthew argues, 'this Young Pretender or whatever they call him. He still has to gather support. It might come to nothing. Don't worry so much.'

But even as he glances around the room, now so utterly transformed by the presence of the news from sea, Matthew knows that most of those present are, indeed, most worried. Even the demirep has lost her sparkle and allowed a dressing gown to be placed upon her shoulders before retiring despondently into another room, while the men themselves, who a moment earlier had their breeches down around their ankles, begin by slow degrees to compose themselves, to fasten their buckles and secure their belts, to replace their swords and to comb and straighten their wigs, all in readiness for their departure. In demure, hushed tones, footmen and pages are called; carriages and chairs are ordered. It is all over - and so very quickly - reminding Matthew of the conclusion of a play when all the actors wipe away their make-up and return to the real world: the evening at an end.

Once outside, and as soon as he has seen a by-now somewhat inebriated Sam safely into his carriage where he will be taken the short distance to his sister's home in The Strand - there is now for Matthew merely the prospect of a short walk back to Cheapside and his own apartments at the Pig and Whistle. Being late, and with most of the shops and households having long since extinguished their lights, or let them burn down, it is very dark. Having taken an unfamiliar alley, moreover, which he had wrongly assumed would bring him back into Cornhill, Matthew realises, to his surprise, that he is lost. His overwhelming emotion is not one of anxiety, however, since he is confident in his swordsmanship and knows he can see off any would-be assailant, but rather one of annoyance - that, for someone who professes to know the city like the back of his hand, he could become so quickly disoriented. Fool!

Just then, out of the gloom he sees a light coming towards him and the small figure of a link-boy - one of the many children who scratch a meagre existence on the streets guiding sedan chairs or pedestrians about in the dark and who, with his torch of pitch held aloft, will, for a few pennies, usually deliver you safely to your destination.

'Light home, Sir?' the little fellow asks - and even with the meagre illumination thus supplied as the boy approaches, it is sufficient for Matthew to become aware of his location.

'Oh, no thank you, I know where I am now,' Matthew replies. 'I have but a short distance to go.'

'Oh, that's all right Sir, I'll light your way for you. It is very late - and not a light showing anywhere.'

Heavens! Matthew thinks as he looks down at the shiny face with its curly head of hair surmounted by an undersized and threadbare cap, these children are getting younger and smaller by the day. Probably on the border-line of starvation, and clothed in not much more than a collection of old rags, the poor little wastrel would be in need of the money, that's for sure. So he does acquiesce

'A wretched business for you, being out so late,' Matthew observes as they hasten along, the link-light carried aloft a couple of paces in front as the boy marches off ahead - so frail and emaciated, his tiny frame, that one might fear that a breath of wind could carry him away. Compared to the affluence of those in whose company Matthew has just spent the evening, it seems a most disturbing contrast.

'It's a living Sir,' the child replies.

'Ah but it'll be a tough one, I'll warrant,' Matthew argues - though the boy appears unconcerned.

'Keeps me off the streets,' he declares, throwing a cheeky, sideways glance back over his shoulder - a well-worn jest no doubt, but it makes Matthew smile nonetheless.

In distinction to most boys of his class and calling, he is unmarked by any of the usual scars of smallpox. He has been lucky. And as they go, Matthew cannot help reflect that, given different circumstances, given opportunity and a half-decent education, this fine little man might have just as easily be destined for an apprenticeship somewhere: for a city guild, a voice in a cathedral choir or even a clerk at the Inns of Court. Anything would be possible. But no … here he is just a street urchin, and surely without a home of any kind, for no one would permit their child to be out at such an hour. And were he to perish, as Matthew knows so many do, and were he not to wake tomorrow from beneath some heap of filthy blankets in an alley or stable yard, no one would mark his passing with so much as a shrug of the shoulders.

Within minutes they are in Cheapside and, at Broad Lane, the entrance to the inn and the arch beneath which coaches and horses pass into an expansive, galleried courtyard - the very place where Matthew lives and works in apartments on the first floor. *'Matthew Wildish esquire,'* as his calling card proudly displays, *'for the provision of bespoke wigs and carnival masks, to be found at the sign of the Pig and Whistle, Broad Lane, off Cheapside.'* And the very board that depicts those two unlikely companions, a handsome wild boar and an over-sized penny whistle, hangs over the entrance, and swings in the wind with various assorted creaks and groans for the best part of nearly every night, as anyone who might attempt to get a full night's sleep here will readily testify.

Their destination thus attained, the boy, availing himself of the conical receptacle on the wall, extinguishes his light, and all is suddenly terribly dark again as Matthew searches for his purse. But when he looks around again, to pay his dues, the boy is gone.

'Hello?' Matthew calls softly in the darkness, realising to his consternation as he does so that in the process of guiding him home, the little fellow had not once asked him for directions or for an address. How had he known where to go? 'Hello ..?' Matthew calls again. But no reply can be heard, only his own voice echoing from the walls of the arch. How odd!

Weary suddenly almost beyond endurance, and relieved to be safely back, Matthew strolls through the yard to his door, climbs the stairs to the gallery above, and within moments is inside and upon his bed. He is exhausted, yet in what remains of the night, his sleep is fragmented and shallow, his dreams and thoughts combining in fitful visions of warfare - of London under siege, surrounded by fierce rebel warriors from the far-away Highlands of Scotland, and of the lovely Johanna, too, and all the beautiful and fragrant people who inhabit the capital he loves so dearly, at the mercy of hoards of bloodthirsty savages in tartan skirts.

'What is to become of us all?' he wonders. How very inconvenient it all seems.

# ~ 4 ~
## RANDOM APPEARANCES
## OF COLOUR

With a roll of the shoulders, he allows his valet, Francis, to help him into his best embroidered waistcoat and then to make some final adjustments to his cravat. Matthew is feeling pleased with himself this morning because he has received a letter from Greenwich which would most likely be from Sam or Johanna, and he is looking forward to an opportunity to open it and to peruse its contents as soon as the business of choosing his clothing for today has been finalised.

'Good man!' he says, throwing a brief look towards the solicitous face of the valet at his side, and then back again to the adjustable dress-mirror in its frame where he glances again with approval at his own aspect. Yes, Francis is a good fellow, Matthew has to admit, and he definitely knows how to iron and prepare his clothes for him. Sometimes, though, he does appear to be rather tall - yes, too tall - which normally for a valet would not be a disadvantage, but here especially where the rooms do have such low ceilings, the man seems to fill the entire space at times: taller even than Matthew's own six foot, and consequently rather out of proportion in an aesthetic sense. For all that, Francis is an excellent and discreet companion, serving as his personal secretary, butler and valet combined, for almost two years now. Invaluable. The truth is, it would be difficult to replace him.

'Ah, Francis, it is a foolish thing to be too well-dressed,' Matthew observes, fussing with the elaborate ruffles of his neck stock, 'and yet a man who would make his way in the world is a fool if he fails to dress well. Would you not agree?'

To which Francis, with his long serious face and drooping eyelids, bows very slightly his concordance. 'Oh yes, Sir,' he answers in his usual smug, slightly condescending voice. 'That's fashion for you, Sir. Each social group wishes to emulate those above it, while at the same time distancing itself from those below. And fashion is the way, Sir. The more elaborate and impractical the better. It gives a man something to strive for.'

'Um, quite the philosopher we are this morning, Francis,' Matthew responds. 'Where do you learn this sort of thing from, anyway?'

But the valet merely sighs to himself with forbearance as he continues to go about his labours, taking a clothes brush briefly to Matthew's shoulders. 'And may I ask, do have a busy day in prospect today, Sir?' he inquires, preferring to respond with a question of his own, and without any qualms over being forthright, because part of his job, after all, is to keep track of appointments and to ensure the smooth flow of visitors and clients. This is important, because here, in the light and airy rooms situated along one side of the gallery that runs around the perimeter of the coach yard of the Pig and Whistle Inn, are not only Matthew's private lodgings and bedchamber but also his workshop, a long, substantial room with a row of large windows; a place where clients are received and where some of the finest wigs in the kingdom are manufactured by his own hand, a bespoke service.

It is a curious choice of profession, Matthew often reflects, for one who is so enamoured of female society, because only very occasionally would a female grace his studios with a visit, and usually some elderly dame in search of a modest postiche that might be attached to cover an area of baldness. He would match the colour and texture with his customary skill, and was widely regarded as one of the best in the field. But as for his daily work, the regular clientele providing income ... well, that is composed solely of those who adorn themselves with wigs: gentlemen only, and therefore all very dull. To mitigate this unfortunate state of affairs, Matthew has in recent times expanded his business into the making of carnival masks - and many fine examples of these line the walls of his rooms - all of which, in addition to the freakish collection of wigs and disembodied mannequin heads, contributes to a most unusual ambiance, to say the least.

'Yes, Francis, I do have one or two jobs to be finishing off today,' Matthew responds at length. 'But first there is the matter of a certain Mr McNiel, I believe, yes?'

'At two o'clock this afternoon, Sir,' Francis confirms with a glance at his pocket book in which he always makes a note of his master's business appointments - for his employer has, to put it mildly, a poor memory - his mind often distracted, his head forever up in the clouds contemplating some poem or another. Without constant reminders he would miss the half of all his appointments. At least that is how Francis would perceive it. Quite exaggerated, of course.

Matthew has been here in residence for over a year now, and there are many reasons why it suits him well. The inn, with its frequent coach services to and from the north of England, is an ideal place to gather gossip and intelligence - though fortunately it is not necessary to enter the inn itself or to run the gauntlet of the rowdy guests below in order to gain entry to his apartments, since these have a doorway and stairs all to themselves accessed from the courtyard below which bring visitors up to the gallery outside, a smart, roofed promenade around the central courtyard - and thus Matthew has always been at liberty to receive his clients and informants discreetly. By the same token, it is an ideal location in which any self-confessed libertine such as himself might flourish and entertain the ladies, with just sufficient activity about the building and stables outside so that visitors can slip in and out relatively unobserved, and unchaperoned too if need be, while any extraneous noises resulting from his amorous encounters become likewise lost in the general hubbub of activity that inevitably attends the place, all hours of the day and night.

'Ah, yes, thank you Francis,' Matthew declares, taking his watch and examining the time before returning it to his waistcoat pocket. 'Mr McNiel it is! I have not forgotten, you know. A final fitting, and payment for his wig, as I recollect. Yes. Do remind me, though, won't you, that I must fetch those wax figurines and icons from their boxes before he arrives. I would like them to be on display for the gentleman. He is a Tory, and rather fond of devotional items - religious bits and pieces, you understand.'

Francis responds with his usual slow, imperious nod that signals that everything is, indeed, understood perfectly, that the requirements of being in a business such as wig making often engender peculiar practices; that here in the employment of Mr Wildish they are likely to be more peculiar than most; and that, despite all these tribulations, the two watchwords of discretion and loyalty remain forever his constant companions. In truth, however, and as Matthew well knows, Francis is not a political animal. It is all he can ever do to remember that the country is divided into two factions that extend not only across political divides but also religious ones as well; there being, on the one hand, the Whigs, the rational, sensible reformed party who favour classical architecture and protestant ideals and to which, coincidentally, Matthew himself adheres; and then on the other, the Tories, the disgruntled, old fashioned, often suspiciously Catholic party, who have too much interest in all things French and who are, therefore, irredeemably *outré*.

'And will you be requiring the crucifix upon the wall again this time, Sir?' Francis asks.

'Ah, yes, that too, thank you,' Matthew replies. 'You are becoming quite an expert in how to please some of my visitors, Francis,' he adds with an approving nod, making one final re-alignment to his extravagant lace cuffs, and then allowing just one final adjustment to the silver buckles on the knees of his breeches. 'Stockings in good order, Francis?' he inquires, to which Francis places himself at a distance behind his master and surveys the calves with a professional eye to ensure the white stockings are without blemish and aligned neatly.

'Absolutely, Sir,' he answers.

'Excellent. Good man! Oh, and Francis, by the way, I don't suppose you know the whereabouts of a good astrologer do you?'

'An astrologer, Sir? A *good* one?'

'Yes, I rather would like to learn a bit more about the subject for - er - a certain project I have in mind.'

'There is Doctor Alcock, the most fashionable and sought after at present. Whether he is good or not, Sir, I cannot say. He is an apothecary, also, and renowned, I have heard, for predicting the time of one's death with remarkable accuracy - oh, and also for determining times of financial hardship or penury among his clients and which he usually manages to ensure through the application of his own fees.'

'Ah, sounds like a lively sort of fellow. Leave me his details sometime will you, Francis? Good man!'

Francis once again signals his understanding and, before retiring to his own quarters outside and farther along the gallery, makes a precise note of this very task in his trusty ledger.

Electing to spend what remains of the morning attending to his letters and perchance working on a poem, Matthew brews a jug of coffee and takes it over to his couch, his celebrated couch, the place of many a line of inspired verse. Being also a place of many an amorous conquest or hour of pleasure, it should come as no surprise that it is set discreetly within an alcove out of sight of the large windows. And it is here, seated upon this very item of most comfortable *and comforting* furniture, that Matthew is at last able to open that letter from Greenwich.

To his surprise it is from Johanna only:

Woolveston Cottage, Greenwich, Kent

Salutations, my Wonder,

I trust this finds you well. Apropos your sonnet sequence and our discourse the other evening, I have discovered some quotes among my library papers and wondered if you might find them of value?

1 'Divine emanations are conveyed through the spheres of the planets via a hierarchy of subtle energies, from spirit downwards into base matter.'

2 'All creation stems from one source, and every physical aspect of creation has its counterpart in the world of the spirit.'

3 'The planets and stars are, almost in their entirety, inside of us, where the light of life and the origin of heaven dwell.'

As you can see, my Wonder, your creative journey is therefore as much an inner quest as an outward one.

Sam sends his kindest regards, and we both look forward to the pleasure of your company at the theatre next week, as arranged.

Affectionately yours,
Johanna Woolveston

How wonderful - this message from a quite different world of gentility and refinement. He had no idea she was so keenly anticipating the fruits of his labours. And as he reads through it once more, intrigued by the ideas it contains and feeling hugely flattered that Johanna should take the trouble to share her thoughts with him at all, he quickly becomes lost in a wealth of poetic fancies, sketching in his mind, at long last, some proper, serviceable ideas for his sonnets - a sequence of seven which, in a most satisfying way, he is now persuaded, have every possibility of resonating with his own amorous intentions - the seven very special women that he intends to enjoy. The world of the spirit, yes - but one that he intends to make most palpably real in the world of the flesh.

And thus, as so often happens on mornings such as this, reclining, and taking up his special graphite stylus, that very latest acquisition of his bought from a little shop in Golden Square and which enables him to write with complete spontaneity wherever he might be, Matthew endeavours to compose some verse, to daydream and, eventually, even to doze off a little, too - his waking visions populated, each time as he closes his eyes, with the face of Johanna: so fair, so inquisitive, so full of the most alert intelligence and kindness. The desire for her society is as powerful as ever - a deep, aching space in his heart that can only be filled by her presence, an all-to-rare event for him, of course. Would he or any mortal ever write a poem to her loveliness? That really would prove a challenge too far, surely.

It is a good while before the appointed hour of two o'clock when, still reclining upon his couch, Matthew is roused from the most pleasant of slumbers by the distinctive sounds of his own yard door, swinging open at the bottom of the stairs, followed by the equally distinctive and familiar clatter of footsteps, dainty footsteps in this instance that denote a female visitor ascending to the gallery. What could this mean? With Francis still away in his own chambers, Matthew hurries to the door - and there, to his surprise and delight outside on the walkway and just about to put her hand to the disused bell-cord is none other than Rose Tidey, his former sweetheart, the very one he so recently became re-acquainted with that evening in the garden in Southwark when Sam had almost lost his wig in that unfortunate brawl.

'Rose!' he exclaims as a gasp of surprise escapes his lips. 'Please, do come in. The door bell refuses to function, alas, but I heard your footsteps.'

'Oh, were you not expecting me?' she inquires, slightly reproachful, he senses.

Of course! He remembers now. Today is the day on which she and her sister Margaret were due to visit, though he had rather dismissed the possibility from his mind after the brawl that evening and then forgot about it entirely. What a pleasant surprise.

'My pretty little sister Margaret is indisposed, you will be sad to learn,' she announces, as if anticipating his question and regarding him with heavy-lidded eyes for a moment as she saunters in and glances, not entirely with approval along the length of the chamber. 'I had some moments free this afternoon, so I thought I might take a chair to come to you anyway. I can see, at any rate, that your new rooms are every bit as disorderly as the old ones,' she adds, running her gloved finger along a shelf, as if to confirm the presence of dust.

How strange, to see her standing there, so elegantly turned out in a delightful combination of jacket and skirts, the celebrated *pet-en-l'air* and the very epitome of fashion, therefore, amid all the coarse working paraphernalia of his studio - the youthful sheen of her fair hair, so resplendent against the cream-satin. He does not mind her show of disapproval and knows she is only teasing him - though the smells of the glue he uses for his work do not seem entirely to her liking, he notices, genuinely so, and he is just about to apologise when outside - though the noise is so loud that it might just as well be *inside* - a coach-and-four comes thundering into the yard below, preceded by a shrill blast on a bugle and then joined by the almost equally loud and frantic ministrations of the stableboys and grooms as they race towards it and begin their changing of the horses in double-quick time.

'Matthew!' she declares, raising her voice to be heard. 'With so much going on - and surely all hours of the day and night - how do you ever manage to work, let alone sleep?'

And they laugh together as he leans over to draw the casements to, explaining that one simply gets used to the racket - being assailed by the constant noise and commotion of the place, all the regular services that come and go - the 'Daily Rocket' from Colchester, the 'Tally-Ho' from Norwich, and a dozen others. At least, he tells her, he may now come and go now as he pleases, with no longer the inconvenience, as so often in the past, of being locked out by irate landladies and having therefore to spend his nights with the constable in the Watch House.

'And still making those enormous towering wigs for the men, I see,' she observes as mercifully the noise outside abates, inspecting with amusement the long wefts of hair hanging in rows, and the various blocks and mannequin heads upon his bench. 'You will need to adapt to the changing times, Matthew, as young men are becoming tired of them. These great long perukes will only be used for formal occasions soon, and unless you can interest the women in adopting them, you will be out of business.'

'Well, maybe we will be able to do just that one day,' Matthew responds with a smile. 'Perhaps women will begin to wear them.'

'Not a chance!' she argues merrily and chuckles again. 'We are far too clever and modest to become entangled in such vanities.'

'Won't you take a seat, Rose,' he says, unconcerned by her efforts to torment him, and knowing her predictions to be inaccurate anyway, because already in France the fashions are changing.

He guides her over to his couch, about the only place free to sit for a woman in a wide gown. 'Please, do make yourself comfortable, my dear friend,' he continues. 'And may I offer you some refreshment, some tea, perhaps, or a glass of sherry?'

'Um, sherry will do nicely, as long as it's genuine Spanish, and dry,' she states, evincing her impressive working knowledge in such matters as she takes her seat, descending gracefully.

'I have the very thing for us,' he announces and, reaching into the furthermost recesses of a cupboard, emerges with a bottle of the very best *Fino* from the hills above Cadiz - just the kind of rare offering always kept in readiness, of course, since it is what his customers expect.

Fetching a glass for her and one for himself, he settles down at her side. What a fine young lady she is, he thinks. Her profile shows a well proportioned face, yet delightfully fleshy, as well, with rounded cheeks that she has blushed with pink rouge today - and with just the suggestion of plumpness beneath her chin, a pleasing curvaceousness that he does not recall from earlier days and which he finds most attractive, at least for the moment as the mood takes him. And what eyes! So unusually large and blue, and with long, curved eyelashes - so expressive and always most lovely with that soft, dreamy aspect to them that he recalls so fondly.

'This is a rarity,' she says in her usual forthright manner, placing the glass to her nose for a second or two prior to sipping with her usual expert judgement. 'It's well-nigh impossible to acquire sherry of this quality these days - what with all the wars going on over there. Most of us have to make do with port.'

'I have a good friend in the Admiralty,' he replies, pleased to have impressed. 'They always manage to smuggle their requirements through, don't worry. Anyway, my dear Rose, I trust we are to have each other to ourselves today and not to be joined by any jealous boyfriends?'

'Quite right!' she answers with demonstrable relief and a giggle of delight. She seems calmer now, and in a voice far milder than earlier, adds: 'To tell you the truth, Matt, I no longer wish to be associated with those men you saw me with the other evening - not unless it is in a professional capacity, that is, since I cannot abandon the family business and those who work for us. But no - I have resolved to keep some distance forthwith. My little sister Margaret, sadly, is not so discerning, and is engaged now to that very brute who assaulted you and your friend in the tavern garden.'

'Engaged? So soon?'

'Yes. I am upset, because I know it will all end in tears. He won't value her. Men like that never value anything other than their own bestial appetites. I do not wish to have that variety of man in my life any more, Matt, that's all I'm saying. I want to be thought of as a woman of cultivated standards. Yes, quite right! I want to be clever and respected.'

'Why, that is a noble sentiment, Rose.'

'I want to be a lady. A clever lady.'

'Indeed. I am certain you are more than qualified in intelligence and wit for such a vocation.'

'Do you think that? Do you really? Oh, Matt, you were always so good with me, so patient. I didn't mean it when I jested and played so unkindly upon your feelings the other evening. The truth is I was disappointed when we ended our friendship. It was not of my doing. It was just that we were both so busy, were we not? I had inherited the family business and was so entangled in it all. And we were young. Yes, we were so very young then.'

'It was only last year,' he reminds her, sliding along a little closer, so he is able to place an arm behind her on the couch. It is, he knows, like a hawk closing in on its prey, relentless, inevitable. He simply cannot prevent himself, nor does he wish to; and within a minute, he knows she will have allowed him to kiss her.

'Yes but a year is a long time when a girl is but twenty-one,' she concludes and assisting him in his endeavours to place himself closer by gathering in her voluminous petticoats. 'It was an age ago. I am grown up now.'

'Indeed, you are, Rose, and most fair and beautifully grown, if I may say so. And now we are alone together once again, we must not question our hearts a moment longer. You know I am ever your most willing admirer, and more if you would allow me to enter into your confidence.'

'Oh, you would *enter*, Matt, I do not doubt it,' she declares, accompanied by a most engaging peal of laughter.

'I would - and to be plain with you, I have considered little else for the past several minutes,' he tells her, watching closely for her reaction, for he knows he is being bold. 'And I have wondered, too, how fine it might be for us to revisit that occupation that afforded us so much pleasure in former times.'

'Have you now?' she responds, and with a sudden turn of immense seriousness – which does not, however, linger long upon her face. For with Rose the moods are always changing. It is like observing the clouds above the mirror of the ocean, where every wave is followed by another that might be of an entirely different sentiment. And although his understanding of the various characteristics and spheres of the planets is still limited, he is beginning to suspect that here at his side might well be the very epitome of fair Luna, the Moon herself. The first of his seven has been located - a cup from which he has already drunk, of course, yet not fully appreciated at the time amid all the fire of youthful desire. Now once again, this treasure of delight is within his reach, and surely the better to be savoured and appreciated this time around.

'Oh, Matthew, how funny you are!' she chuckles, proffering her empty glass to him that it might be filled once more. 'You must know, I am sure, that at such a moment, a woman's heart is full of so many questions. To enter indeed. Quite right! For anyone who succeeds in bringing his flirtation so closely to her door and persuading her to open it must become the most curious of beings. What will it be like, she asks herself, the visit that he makes? Will he enter courteously and be a welcome guest, or will it be a swift call? Will he be rude and indifferent as he departs, or thankful and pleasant. Above all she wonders if he will entertain her and leave her feeling satisfied. As I recollect, you were ever the most courteous guest, Matt. You always arrived at my door bearing gifts; you always pleased me and never outstayed your welcome.'

'Dear Rose,' he whispers, 'you need not fear to open your door to me. Be assured of my devotion.'

At which she turns her face to his once more and gazes into his eyes, a slightly helpless look that he remembers so well and which he knows very few others will have ever been privy to. Her hand strays absently to the ribbons and ties upon her bodice: a nervous movement; and he notices also, at just that moment, an almost imperceptible shudder in her shoulders and breast, a tremble of emotion and desire. All the distractions of the busy world outside fall away now as, admiring the fine silver filigree of her necklace, he instinctively reaches out to her. 'Why, what a lovely piece,' he whispers, and with a confident and direct touch of tenderness examines with finger and thumb the sparkling item with its exquisite inlay of shell, taking care that in so doing his hand is lightly, so very lightly in touch with that special place of delicacy upon the side of her neck to which she responds by bringing that very part of herself just a little closer to his touch. And now he knows she is his.

'Ah Rose, how fine a moment is this - just the two of us together once more.'

'Yes ...'

He kisses her hand and then a moment later their lips have touched.

'Clever, clever Rose,' he whispers, caressing the side of her head, her neck and shoulder once more. 'And clever is she who knows best when to nourish her desires with the food of pleasure. Is that not so, my fair and lovely?'

'Yes - but pray tell, what is that noise, my darling,' she asks, distracted for a moment, 'like a thump, thump?'

'It is surely our hearts beating as one ...'

'No, actually, I think you have someone ...'

'Someone?' he echoes with only vague comprehension.

'Yes. Outside, with a big knob, banging on your door with it.'

'What!'

'The knob of his cane, I mean.'

And to be sure, as Matthew regains the use of his faculties, he is aware of the most loud banging on his front door. A quick glance over his shoulder through his windows to the courtyard below, moreover, reveals a vacant sedan chair - its bearers standing idly close by. Of course! Matthew has clean forgotten. It is two o'clock, and this can only be his client, McNiel who, in the absence of any response, has surely already ascended the stairway and is upon the gallery outside. And then the banging comes again.

'Quick, quick, I must prepare the room!' Matthew cries, leaping to his feet and, to Rose's obvious bewilderment, begins to race about the chamber, frantically removing from boxes and drawers vast numbers of statues and icons of various saints or religious icons and arranging these hastily in lots of different places - upon cupboard and chimneypiece, in alcove and table - in fact upon any available surface not already cluttered with the paraphernalia of his profession. A wooden crucifix is even located and within seconds attached to a hook upon the wall.

'You *were* expecting me, I trust, Mr Wildish,' McNiel inquires as Matthew shows him in - a dapper man, self-confident, though his face startled in this instance by the discovery of Rose standing so fine and lovely with flushed cheeks in the very centre of the chamber endeavouring to regain her composure amid all the untidy and grubby detritus of the workshop.

Hastily, Matthew introduces the two of them; and then, by way of encouraging Rose's departure, presents her with a peculiar handshake as one would do to a client. 'Yes, well, thank you Mrs Tidey,' he says, showing her the door. 'Shall we say the same time again next week, when we can renew our discussion on how exactly we might satisfy your requirements. In the meantime, Good day to you, and please do commend me to your dear mother.'

And with Rose thus dispatched, accompanied by a very private kiss on her cheek unseen in the passageway outside, Matthew, calmer now, returns to deal with his client.

McNiel accepts the offer of a stool which he draws up to the bench, and here, getting straight to business, Matthew asks him to remove his periwig. He then places with great aplomb his own creation which he had measured for him some weeks ago proudly onto the shaven pate. A quick adjustment of the vertical positioning, a moment of re-arranging the curls with a comb, and the customer is quite done within minutes and ready for the looking-glass.

What a pity he has not brought his elegant wife with him this time, Matthew reflects - far more the accomplished person of style and conversation than her husband would ever be. He is turned-out well enough, of course, the man from the north. His clothes are not cheap - but still, and as Matthew recalls from their last meeting, his appearance is still rather lacking in the refinement of a fashionable city gentleman - his attire being so very 'last season' his mannerisms all a little too obviously awkward and rustic.

'Um, very fine, very fine,' McNiel responds with genuine admiration as he examines his own reflection, which would, Matthew well knows, reveal to him a visage of a man many years younger, far more gallant and dashing than anything he would have experienced to date - for of one thing Matthew is confident, and that is the first rate quality of his work, and that wigs of such pre-eminence flatter and roll back the years for a man as powerfully as any spirited young mistress could ever do. McNiel, being clearly not the type for a spirited young mistress, would regard his wig as the perfect treat, therefore, and a bargain at twenty-five guineas.

'I trust you and your lady wife are finding your stay in the capital a pleasant one, Mr McNiel?' Matthew inquires, making a few final adjustments with a comb.

'Oh, well, to be perfectly frank, no not entirely. Such a disparity between wealth and poverty is surely not to be found in any other part of the kingdom. I mean, such opulence in certain quarters where one is assailed constantly by liveried chairs and gilded carriages upon the streets, and then, turning a corner, one almost falls upon some poor wretch begging a penny that he might bring relief to his starving family. I must say I am shocked at the overall degree of filth and squalor, and the buildings blackened from the smoke of so many coal-fires - even more so than upon my last visit some years ago.'

'Really?' Matthew inquires with polite interest, hoping to draw him out.

'Yes, belike it is the fastidiousness that comes with advancing years - but really, such a profusion of crudities - the bating of animals, the cockpits and rings on every corner in some quarters - and the dreadful howling and baying of the spectators as much as that of the poor unfortunate beasts who are everywhere sacrificed merely for entertainment. I must own that I find it all quite demeaning. And then the overall state of the poorer quarters - the rills of stinking mire running down the centre of many of the streets, the remains of butchered animals in the gutters, left for the dogs, not to mention the endless danger of falling debris from the slums in Blackfriars - why, even the hazard of chamber pots being emptied from above onto the pavements! There must be many a fine peruke such as this spoiled by an unwholesome downpour of that kind. And as to the extent of prostitution, and so openly flaunted in public places ... well, what can a gentleman say about such gross offences! Bawdy houses kept in such an open manner almost everywhere, the whole town it seems at times one monstrous stew. Why, it is almost impossible to walk down Fleet Street even in broad daylight without being accosted and taken by the arm by some harlot, and offered the most disgusting liberties of her person for no more than a pint of gin. I have encountered children abandoned to the streets, drunken mothers and violent fathers - poverty, degradation and suffering everywhere. And against all this, one sees the fine folk, of course, all those Hanoverians dressed to such extravagance of taste, tucked up within the safety of their sedan chairs and lifted above the filth so they might not soil their fine shoes as they flit from one *soiree* to the next. And then, if all this were not already bad enough, one hears reports of the resurgence of the dreadful violence of those gangs of young aristocrats that go about by night - what do they call themselves, the Mohocks, or the *New* Mohocks - slitting the noses of young maids or thrusting their swords into the sides of sedan chairs. Why, if this is the civilisation of city life, then all I can say is I long to return to the homespun simplicity of my native Derbyshire.'

Matthew is stunned. It is as if his simple question has ignited a spark within the other man, setting off an explosion of indignation.

'What you say is true enough, Sir,' Matthew agrees, though he has, and much to the other man's disapproval, he suspects, been smiling just a little irreverently throughout. 'To be sure, none of us who live here in the metropolis could ever be unaware of its faults or deficiencies. It might surprise you to learn, however, that the very disorder that you mention does not entirely displease me.'

'Really?'

'No. Maybe because I arrived here from Ireland when still a child,' Matthew continues, feeding his guest more information about his background which he hopes he will find to his liking. 'I have known little else other than London you describe for much of my life - apart from a brief period of travels overseas, that is, and where I spent some time in Paris learning my craft. But even then I longed only for the day when I might return to this fair city.'

'Belike it is the differences in our age, then - a matter of tolerance,' McNiel suggests with some restoration of his good humour.

'Um, perhaps,' Matthew concurs as he pours his guest a generous glass of that very same sherry that he had a while earlier enjoyed in the company of Rose. 'Perhaps indeed it is a matter of tolerance. But let me put a simple question to you, Mr McNiel. Are you a gardener?'

'Why yes, I am fond of growing things,' he replies, accepting his drink with approval. 'I have a glasshouse at my home in Derby, and several exotic specimens.'

'Good, then you might well understand my reasoning, Sir,' Matthew continues, re-taking his seat. 'Let me explain. There are some people who in a quest for quality and perfection in their gardens endeavour to order everything in the best regimental fashion, with neat hedges and parterres in which every prize bloom is nurtured and cosseted by expert hands, its season and time of ripening anticipated and calculated to perfection - so consequently the gardens themselves become as dreary and as predictable as a lesson in Latin. On the other hand, there are other kinds of gardens, are there not - rough-hewn from the land, places of informality and where a sufferance for disorder produces all manner of surprises - where random appearances of colour can spring up and combine unexpectedly from season to season in endless patterns of spontaneous delight. London is just such a garden to my eyes, Sir - a city where fragrance and beauty might well be nurtured from the produce of the dung heap, but where the most rank and unwholesome of places can give rise to instances of astonishing splendour and beauty - so many new varieties of human ingenuity, fashion, music and artistic excellence - so very many, in fact, that it makes all the smoke and grime, all the immorality, all the violence and deformity of manners that it feeds upon, pale into insignificance. I love the ungoverned surprises of London, in other words, Mr McNiel, and I would not exchange a single one for a thousand well-ordered rows of box hedges and parterres in which we might, to our folly, endeavour to cultivate the genus of humanity.'

'Well ... indeed, it may be that I understand then, after all,' McNiel responds with an amused nod of the head. 'The eloquence of a poet, and I will not presume to gainsay it,' he adds, as he drains his glass and prepares to conclude his business, counting out his money, as Matthew in turn writes him his receipt. 'Oh, and you have, I take it, heard the news - on the political front?' he inquires, almost as an afterthought.

'About the arrival of the Young Pretender? Oh yes,' Matthew replies, gratified, for here is his opportunity to probe. 'The winds of change are blowing north of the border, Mr McNiel, are they not?'

'They are indeed,' he concurs, getting to his feet and, to Matthew's satisfaction, wandering over to take a closer look at the crucifix and one or two of the wax icons placed in readiness for him upon the shelving. 'By the way, before I take my leave of you, Mr Wildish, I have been meaning to ask you, for I cannot help but see you are a man of the true Faith. Do you not ever feel anxious that the display of imagery of this kind might be ... well, misconstrued by certain individuals?'

'No not at all. If I am expecting anyone close to the government or the Crown, I will sequester all such items in good time. Naturally, I do not relish such subterfuge, yet it is essential if one is to flourish in any kind of commercial capacity. Besides, the figures are, you will notice, carved in wax and can therefore be disposed of swiftly in any open grate - simply melted away, if need be, in an emergency.'

'Um ... ingenious. It is just that one cannot, in my experience, be too careful. I say this, because I rather suspect I am being followed - spied upon here in the capital - perhaps due to my family's long association with the Jacobites, with the Stuarts and their sympathisers. Do you think that is possible?'

'Well, Mr McNiel, I would say yes it is a distinct possibility,' Matthew responds with candour, deadly serious now, 'and my advice, therefore, would be for you to exercise constraint. And as we are unlikely to meet again in the near future, I would also like to be plain with you and state that I would be gratified if you would consider my services at your disposal - and anyone else who might wish to aid the rightful Prince in his aspirations, should he and his people ever find themselves hereabouts in the capital.'

'You do understand, I take it, that any such presence could only be achieved through force?' McNiel says. 'I regret to say it can be no other way, as the present incumbent on the throne, which to many of us will always be known as merely the Elector of Hanover, is no more than a puppet of the Protestant mercantile classes, governed by the Masons. And they will not relinquish their hold on this corner of Europe lightly.'

'Indeed,' Matthew agrees. 'It would seem, alas, that a violent struggle is inevitable if George is to be toppled. But, still I would like to re-iterate that I am willing, as I say, to help *in any way.*'

'I shall not forget your generosity,' McNiel states, now properly at ease. 'For I can tell you - and I have this on very good authority - that just as soon as he receives sufficient assurances of support from the Highlanders and from those of us in the north of England, Prince Charles will order the deployment of thousands of French troops who are already pledged and waiting in readiness to cross the Channel to aid the cause. The small presence of a few seamen and comrades in arms that have recently landed on the remote Western Isle of Eriskay could, therefore, and I trust *shall*, very quickly proliferate into thousands of well-equipped fighting men. The forces of retribution will fall upon the capital from two directions, from the North and from across the Channel in France. We live in hope.'

'We do - we do indeed live in hope. And that which you have confided in me, Mr McNiel, gives me much solace and encouragement.'

And thus, his intelligence gathered, his understanding of McNiel's true colours now unambiguous, the afternoon's business is concluded. Matthew looks down with satisfaction from one of his windows as his client crosses the yard, his new wig in its bespoke leather bag with Matthew's business name embossed upon it carried proudly underarm as he disappears through the archway into the lane, there to hail himself a chair.

Yes, so many treacherous men are to be found now, Matthew reflects; men who have their lands in the northern counties, places where the refinement and wealth of the far-flung capital continues to feed their jealousies and resentments. Their willingness to lend support to an invasion has not been exaggerated by the Admiralty, and the information Matthew has gleaned today will surely prove a valuable addition to their knowledge. But then, just as he is about to congratulate himself with a further glass of sherry, Matthew's attention is arrested by a most disturbing sight: a man in the yard below emerging from behind an unharnessed coach, as if from hiding. A rough-looking, muscular fellow, yet also of considerable height, he looks quite sinister, Matthew thinks, like some prizefighter in fancy clothes. He has clearly been waiting for McNiel to emerge, moreover, because no sooner has that gentleman walked from the yard, than the man himself has begun to follow, with merely a passing glance of observation upwards towards Matthew's windows as he goes. For one terrible instant their eyes meet and Matthew quickly withdraws.

Is this one of Sam's colleagues - someone sent to keep a watch on McNiel as was intimated the other evening? Perhaps. And suddenly, Matthew feels terribly ill at ease, even with a twinge of remorse. All these spying games he has become embroiled in are not at all to his liking any longer. Oh yes, it had all seemed jolly good fun at the start, sounding out the occasional scoundrel who might be disloyal to the King. It had got him noticed among the higher echelons of society, to be rewarded on merit with any number of prestigious commissions. But he had never really been interested in the politics of the game; never really wanted to keep up with developments any more than was necessary. And now, with the raising of the stakes everywhere and with the prospect of all-out war, it seems his own sordid little discoveries might well be used towards violent ends. McNiel could be in gravest danger. They might arrest him, torture him. And a traitors death was still a dreadful one even in this day and age.

And thus, Matthew catches himself wondering in all earnestness how he might extricate himself from these increasingly unpalatable duties - knowing, also, in one moment of chilling comprehension, that any attempt to do so in the present climate might only serve to cast suspicion on himself - he whose name is there for all to see, moreover, upon the leather bag that McNiel is sporting all over the streets of London at this very moment. Damn it! He is trapped - caught in a snare of his own making - and with no way out that could ever leave him entirely free of it. He can only sincerely hope and pray that he himself might not be under suspicion, and that the brute he had just seen outside would be aware of just whose side he was on. The implications, should it be otherwise, would be just too dreadful to contemplate.

# ~ 5 ~
## A HOTBED OF RAKES
## AND WHORES

It is late, the sun already low in the sky and the shadows lengthening along the pavements and avenues as a swift chaise brings Matthew eastwards between the newly built classical facades of Piccadilly towards the Opera House in Covent Garden where he is to join Sam and Johanna in their box for an evening of music. How exciting!

With time on his hands, he has spent the latter part of the afternoon at Ranelagh Gardens, one of his favourite haunts - his visit this time flavoured with an additional and altogether more intriguing sense of purpose. For not only are the leafy pleasure gardens at Ranelagh the most fashionable location for outdoor entertainment at this time of the year, but they also remain the foremost venue for romantic intrigue, secret assignations and courtships among the *Beau Monde* - and infinitely preferable, in his estimation, to the much larger and disconcertingly inexpensive Vauxhall Pleasure Gardens south of the river. Ranelagh also has the advantage of its famous Rotunda, the rococo splendour of its great circular pavilion, equalling in size, they say, the very Coliseum in Rome - a place to see and to be seen, and to promenade around the famous central tower, its ornate structure concealing a mighty fireplace that serves to extend the season of evening entertainments far into the autumn months - while high above, and seated within the privacy of a circle of tiered boxes as if at a theatre, people gaze down in idle observation and gossip, speculating upon the appearance of this or that masked celebrity or noble visitor in disguise. The Rotunda is also an excellent venue in which to dine - being rightly famed for its fine wines and cuisine and where, in colonnaded alcoves, people sit at well-appointed tables of red baize, pampered and served by whole regiments of waiters and pages. His expectations, therefore, are of a relatively safe and wholesome experience should he chance to encounter any eligible women - those who, by their appearance, mannerisms or predilections might resonate with one of the seven planetary spheres to which he has set his purpose.

He knows it will not be easy, such a series of multiple seductions, yet he is determined to bring his plans to fruition - ideally within a matter of weeks – and a beginning of sorts has already been made, of course, with Rose during her recent visit when she had signalled her availability as the very embodiment of the fair Moon. But all the rest are still lacking. Where is his vivacious Mercury, his sensuous Venus or lusty Mars? Where is his bright solar radiance or dark saturnine beauty? If he is to have any chance of succeeding in his extravagant sexual adventure, he knows he will firstly need to locate and establish an intimate friendship and regular routine with each one, and they must, moreover, be unbeknownst to one another - quite a challenge.

But for now it is time to let go of such lofty aspirations, and gladly, too, for the outlook this evening is every bit as enticing. Through the window, he can detect that his chaise has already crossed the Piazza of Covent Garden and within moments has drawn up around the corner outside the familiar portico of the theatre and where Sam and Johanna, he discovers, are already arrived and waiting in the upper lobby to greet him, looking exceptionally smart and elegant - Johanna, in particular, so very stunning, he thinks: her clothes in various shades of pastel blue trimmed with grey; her skin with that fine, almost transparent paleness and radiance that he adores so well, all contriving to portray a most engaging aspect of ethereal mystery and charm.

'Are you looking forward to the music, my Wonder?' she inquires. 'I understand there is to be a good amount of Handel - a mixed selection of operatic arias.'

The answer, of course, is yes - Matthew adores the theatre, and when combined with fine music and singers to create the marvel that is opera, it is little short of divine. He loves the commotion, the ornamentation, the extravagant clothes, the jewels, makeup and elaborate wigs - and that is only the men! Here, beneath all the sparkling chandeliers of crystal and light, amid elaborate stucco walls studded with mirrors and murals of putti and angels, one does not encounter a single person who does not do their very best to excel - the women being in his eyes irresistibly fascinating, each one trying to outdo the other in their fabulous apparel, to vie in excellence of taste, fashion and display. Heavenly.

Suddenly, though, his heart sinks because he is reminded of the less-than-savoury prospect this evening of having to endure the company of the appalling Lord Snatchal - and the Countess his lady wife, moreover, whom he has yet to meet - so that he finds himself wondering just how he is going to negotiate the process without speaking out of turn and disgracing himself.

As if reading his thoughts, Johanna reaches up to whisper into his ear. 'And don't forget to be nice to Lord and Lady Snatchal, Matthew. They are our friends, and they are extremely well connected - so much so, that through them you could obtain patronage of the highest order, especially for your poetry. The Snatchals are anxious to promote themselves as champions of the arts, you see, and this most vigorously at present in order to attract the attention of the King and his newest mistress.'

'Really!' Matthew declares, adjusting the prominence of the diamond pin in his cravat and feeling that the Snatchals might not be such a bad lot after all. 'So what might be the extent of the King's present involvement in the literary world?'

'Nil!' Sam replies crisply. 'As with all of the arts, the court at St James's is rightly regarded, even among those who visit from Germany, as the ultimate residence of dullness. The Prince of Wales, though, the sworn rival of the King about the capital these days, has always had a penchant for it, and so everyone is looking to emulate him. Play your cards right, Matt, and there could be an annual stipend in it for you. I trust, therefore, that you will conduct yourself accordingly?'

Matthew nods his acquiescence. 'I promise to behave,' he says, hand on heart.

In truth he disapproves of all this social climbing, and especially when observing Johanna's willing participation in it. Though from a good family herself, and an extremely wealthy one, at that, the temptations of rubbing shoulders with the upper echelons remains just too strong for her. Worse, she would often subordinate her intelligence and integrity, it seems to him, just in order to fraternise with people who have little to commend themselves apart from their wealth and their obvious propensity for snobbery. What a waste.

From the upstairs lobby it is only a brief stroll round to the entrance to their box - an altogether more intimate and cosy space with a valance and a half-dozen closely packed chairs and a bench within. It is here he encounters his fellow invited guests for the evening.

'Room for one more?' Sam inquires playful as he guides Matthew in before him and makes all the necessary introductions. The Earl, on his feet at that moment, seems to recognise him and gives him a friendly nod - while Lady Snatchal, and upon turning on her seat to inspect the newcomer, becomes suddenly most animated indeed.

'Oh, how do you do, Mr Wildish!' she replies to his greeting and, brushing from her face her extravagantly curled black hair of tight, almost wiry ringlets, and continuing to glance over her shoulder as he shuffles along behind her chair, she murmurs as an aside only audible to him: 'I'm sure we can always squeeze that little bottom of yours in somewhere.'

'Thank you Madam, you are most kind,' Matthew responds, slightly alarmed and determined to remain civil.

'*Always,*' she assures him, with special emphasis, holding his attention still.

Everyone makes themselves comfortable, the men drawing up chairs behind the ladies, and it is only now upon being able to survey Lady Snatchal at close quarters for the first time that Matthew is able to perceive the variance in her age compared to her distinguished husband. Although not by any means young herself - her black hair being, to his trained eye, all too obviously dyed - she is a woman possessed of considerable vitality and self-assurance; and also clearly quite a character. Everything about her is dark and dramatic: her black gown, with its tightly seamed waist, trimmed only with purple and maroon, her eyes dark and sparkling. Even her eyebrows are long and dark, her skin swarthy - all in all, such a contrast to Johanna, who at her side remains as demure, pale and inscrutable as ever and, in his estimation at least, a thousand times more dignified and elegant than her noble companion.

Leaning forward in his seat, the better to survey the scene below, he realises that only rarely has he observed the auditorium from such an interesting vantage point - with such a comprehensive view of the stage and, perhaps of equal importance, the rowdy parterre below - a large open space in which the audience sit, recline or sprawl upon benches covered in well-worn green cloth or else parade up and down the wide aisles in search of conversation. Everywhere, the fragrances of oranges and tobacco rise and blend with that of perfume and candle smoke in a heady aroma that pervades the entire space, and the noise is astonishing - for there is nothing sedate or sombre about a visit to the theatre or opera these days, nothing that might resonate with the dreadful puritanical tyranny of the London stage of bygone years, nothing either that refers to the sordid streets outside where - as Mr McNiel himself might have so eloquently expressed it the other day - life is short, disease and suffering constant companions, and every gross enormity and vice is prevalent. Here, at least, people can forget, can be merry and may gather to indulge their pleasures for an hour, to celebrate not only the diverse joys of music and dance, but also all the gossip, jealousies and intrigue of society. Everywhere, even at this early hour, they have begun: talking loudly, laughing and flirting outrageously - typical raucous behaviour even during a performance. Then, suddenly, with a fanfare of trumpets and drums, the curtain rises, and from a brilliant stage, lit by a firmament of chandeliers and flickering foot-lights the programme commences. It is an assortment of pieces, and fortunately, therefore, includes plenty of breaks and changes of scenery during which the audience can give vent to their enthusiasm.

'Oh, by the way, my Wonder,' Johanna says, turning to him during one such pause in proceedings and, once assured that Lady Snatchal's attention is also engaged, removing from her bag a small book. 'I brought this for you from our library: a description of the planets and stars. I thought it might provide additional inspiration for your latest literary project.'

'Thank you!' he says, reaching forward to receive the little volume and leafing through its pages briefly. It appears to be an old, dog-eared book of astrological lore, describing the heavenly bodies, their symbolism and various associations with objects, animate and inanimate - including colours, gemstones and, most significantly, the physical characteristics of men and women appropriate to each one. Johanna, he notices, appears anxious that he might find her gift an embarrassment, but then when satisfied by his reaction that he does not, she smiles with a blend of satisfaction and excitement, and her eyes light up with enthusiasm. 'Most interesting,' he declares. 'The stars and planets.'

'Ah yes, always got a bit of a twinkle in his eye, our Mr

Wildish,' Sam observes loudly from behind so all might hear, still taking any opportunity to resume the pitiless baiting of his friend. And once again, Johanna, a cloud of bewilderment drifting across her face, can only stare back at him in confusion. Sam, of course, declines to elaborate, and in fact, being seated next to Lord Snatchal, remains deep in whispered conversation for much of the subsequent performances. Like it or not, Matthew cannot help catch snippets of their exchanges - which return again and again to the prospect of a new Scottish Jacobite rebellion, an unwelcome reminder of the failed uprising of thirty years previous. And thus all the activity upon the bright stage below, the graceful and acrobatic steps of the dancers, the rousing choruses of the singers and the accomplished playing of the orchestra hardly appear to register for either of them. Only occasionally, when a particularly well-known piece is performed, does the hubbub of noise throughout all of the theatre ever subside. This occurs at the start of a rendition of the opening aria to Handel's Serse, and the much-loved *Umbra Mai Fu* - the only piece from that particular opera of some years ago to have survived in the repertoire.

Matthew adores it, and always secretly imagines that the composer, knowing how splendid it was himself and not wishing his audience to miss a thing, deliberately made the very first note so long and lingering that by the time it was complete (and there is a famous castrato in London who is able to make it last an eternity) the audience would have had ample time to cease their prattling and to pay heed. It is evidently a stratagem that continues to work. Silence descends - and consequently Matthew can relish the aria with its beautiful, languid string accompaniment to the full, a few precious moments in which he becomes perfectly entranced:

*Tender and beautiful fronds*
*Of my beloved plane tree,*
*Let fate smile upon you.*
*May thunder, lightning and storms*
*Never trouble your dear peace,*
*Nor may you by the winds ever be profaned.*
*A shade there never was,*
*Of any plant,*
*Dearer or more lovely*
*Or more sweet.*

... until suddenly, quite by chance, he lifts his head just as Johanna turns to glance absently over her shoulder, and their eyes become engaged in one curious moment of mutual observation. It lasts no more than a second but it is astonishing to him, because at just that moment, his heart swelling with this most glorious of music, he realises that he loves Johanna - this eloquent and beautiful woman seated here almost within reach of his embrace, her bare shoulders rising and falling as if struggling to catch her breath, her eyes with that slightly startled look as they meet his - it is an inexplicable joy and a pleasure just to be near to her. Surely, then, this must be the very feeling everyone talks about, a feeling that he does not ever recall having experienced before and yet which he understands now in all its startling simplicity: the sensation of being in love. Yes - so very simple, and yet the realisation of it is overwhelming. He is in love with Johanna.

The aria reaches its conclusion and it is time for the interval, a juncture marked with a re-doubling of conversational volume below combined with an onslaught of similar noise from all the balconies and boxes - a thunderous stampede of people getting to their feet all at once on the wooden floorboards, all stumbling and racing out into the foyer for refreshments so swiftly that one might conclude, if one did not know better, that the very auditorium itself might be ablaze behind them.

'Gawd, I need a drink!' states Lady Snatchal, herself, brandishing a conspicuously empty champagne glass which she casts to one side into the hands of an entering page as she rises. Her husband steps forward to place a shawl around her shoulders, and everyone exits to the passageway outside where sparkling wine and claret are being served by a multitude of footmen ready and waiting with bottles and trays carried aloft.

'Delightful, most delightful!' Matthew declares to the ladies, still clutching his book of astrological lore to his breast. 'The Handel in particular.'

'It was right proper inspirational, I would say,' Lady Snatchal agrees, with a special nod of appreciation also to Johanna at her side, just prior to taking delivery of a fresh glass of champagne which she consumes in its entirety straight away.

With Sam and Snatchal engaged once more in serious talk nearby, Matthew finds himself placed in a triangle with the ladies and, being tall, has to look down upon them both while they, in turn, gaze up at him, with Lady Snatchal in particular seeming to feast her eyes on the entire length of his frame as she does so, from shoes to hair, taking in every detail of dress, all the tiny accessories of buckles, buttons and studs in-between. Although not tall, she has a figure that is slender and well-proportioned, with a long elegant neck and narrow waist which does not appear to be excessively laced in. There is a physical, athletic way about her movements - that of an accomplished horsewoman, perhaps.

'And do you come here *offen*, Mr Wildish?' the noble lady inquires, her eyes still wandering up and down.

'I do, My Lady, though usually below, alas, in the hubbub of the pit where there are so many unfortunate distractions.'

'Oh, yes. A hotbed of rakes and whores it is down there. You are surely much safer up here with us, Mr Wildish. What say you, Johanna, my dear - we'll look after him, won't we?'

Johanna, however, appears embarrassed by this all too obvious flirtation on the part of her esteemed companion. 'Sam and I found it so very stimulating, Mr Wildish - your most recent visit to us at Greenwich,' she remarks, raising her chin and addressing Matthew with a deliberate note of pride. 'I have been thinking further of your sonnet sequence, also, and anticipating its completion with such excitement.'

'How very kind,' he responds.

'Mr Wildish is a most talented poet, Dorothea,' Johanna adds, turning to her noble companion by way of explanation, and placing a hand on her sleeve to arrest her attention, which is at present diverted to the rear aspect of a handsome guardsman nearby. 'We are engaged in a project with Matthew in which he intends to pen a number of sonnets to the seven heavens.'

'The seven heavens. Gawd! That sounds a bit of all right!' Lady Snatchal exclaims, returning to the conversation just as soon as she has replenished her glass with yet more champagne. 'And so jolly romantic, too, of course.'

Odd, the way she converses. It is almost a kind of self-parody - nervous, almost frantic, her head and shoulders sometimes going in all directions as if tossed by the wind; and then, in contrast and without warning, certain moments would arise in which she would become entirely motionless, glancing shrewdly to one side or the other, her eyes, narrowed in observation, but in every other respect statuesque, reminding Matthew of an irritable child wanting to stamp its feet over being made to stand still for too long. All just a bit disconcerting. Responding to a call from her husband, she excuses herself for a moment, and Matthew is not sorry to see her go.

'Well, my Wonder,' Johanna remarks, 'I certainly think you may have made an impression on our Lady Snatchal.'

'Oh, I am glad,' he answers with an attempt at levity, but feeling in fact quite indifferent - his eyes full only of Johanna's extraordinary beauty, while she, as if reading his thoughts and perhaps slightly disturbed thereby, looks away, untypically bashful. 'And thank you again for the loan of the little book,' he continues, endeavouring to mitigate her embarrassment. 'I shall look forward to reading it - and, in fact, I have already given the subject serious thought and have resolved to visit a certain Doctor Alcock for some expert guidance.'

'Alcock?' Johanna echoes, thoughtful as she sips at her champagne, her gaze turned inward.

'Yes - he is an apothecary and, I am assured, also an expert in the field of astrology.'

'Goodness! Well, that could certainly be interesting,' she says, although dubious it would appear by the puckering of her lips as she meets his eyes again. 'There are different levels of astrology, Matthew - the elevated, mystical approach of the classical past, for example, or the rather more banal and commonplace casting of horoscopes that is so popular today. I rather suspect that your Doctor Alcock could fall into the latter category, though I might be wrong.'

'How can I determine which?'

'Well, you could try sounding him out with some of the ancient maxims. *As Above, so Below,* for example. Is that familiar to you?'

'As Above, so Below?' Matthew repeats with curiosity. 'No, not exactly ...'

'Silly me - I should have included it in my letter. It is the relationship between heaven and earth, my Wonder - that at birth the soul descends through the spheres of the planets, absorbing the nature of each one as it passes - as if each of us were a universe in miniature. *As above, so below.* Ask your Doctor Alcock if he is familiar with any of this, and then you will know whether he might be of service.'

'Thank you, I shall,' Matthew responds, as always slightly bedazzled by it all whenever she provides him with such a plenitude of information - and with still so many additional questions he might ask, if only there were opportunity - and for which, sadly, there is none, because at just that moment they are reunited with Lady Snatchal. No doubt having reached the conclusion that conversation among the men is likely to remain insufferably *political* for the near future, she takes Johanna by the arm and then, much to Matthew's disconsolation, wanders away with her, probably, he reflects, as he watches them vanish around the curved passageway of the lobby, returning to the comfort and privacy of the box.

The departure of the ladies, at least provides Matthew with the opportunity to turn his attention to their husbands for once. Speaking softly under his breath, as befits the gravity of the matter, he imparts to them the intelligence gathered from his recent meeting with his Derbyshire client, Mr McNiel. The information is well received, with Lord Snatchal, in particular, his head draped in the most elaborate of powdered wigs with an old-fashioned centre parting, seeming to be most impressed.

'Excellent work, Wildish!' he declares, though without any trace of a smile in his approbation, presumably due to his dentures. At least he is not in the company of his pet baboon this evening, Matthew thinks, which is already a considerable improvement. 'You must come and join us, by the way, one and all, for a weekend at Snatchalcombe House,' he adds, 'our little place in the country and where you might just find a rather interesting commission awaiting you, Wildish - in your professional capacity, that is: a certain item of ceremonial regalia that is due for restoration and which I trust would not inconvenience you too greatly if you care to take it up. I shall elaborate on the precise nature of the project nearer to the time, since it does entail a certain amount of discretion on your part - though I am sure you are more than capable of satisfying us in that respect - as the actress said to the bishop, what!'

'Of course, Sir, at your service,' Matthew replies as he and Sam both quickly bow and confirm their readiness to accept such a profusion of honours and invitations.

'Not sure whether you overhead what Sam and I were discussing a moment ago?' Snatchal continues, fixing Matthew with a penetrating eye, as if ready to allow him even further into their confidence.

'Well, whatever it was, it definitely sounded serious,' Matthew replies, raising his chin in a gesture of inquiry.

'Indeed it was. I was just informing Sam of the latest news from Scotland. And yes, it is serious - *very* serious. The usurper, Charles Stuart has reached the mainland safely and has already taken the irrecoverable step of raising his standard at a place called Glenfinnan in the Highlands. Issued a manifesto, he has - requiring that his father's subjects rally to his cause - that means us, by the way, the English as well as the Scots. Bloody cheek! This would have occurred already some days ago, of course, but news has only just reached us. Thus, we have a fresh generation of rebels up there, already distinguishing the new Pretender, Charles, from the old one, his father James who led them before. Young Charles is a man of far greater military competence, however - and an individual of such charm and wit, that they've already begun to call him the Bonny Prince - or Bonny Prince Charlie. He has, they say, already won the support of several of the most powerful and influential of the Highland clans. And now they intend to march towards Perth.'

'Outrageous! Scandalous!' Sam avows, his various chins wobbling in a suitable demonstration of indignation even though he would have heard the news already, only a few minutes ago, and from the same source.

'Perth?' Matthew responds, sipping at his glass of fine claret and trying to sound interested, his mind still befuddled with thoughts of Johanna. 'Is that - er - a significant development?' he asks, trying as best he can to picture the geographical location of the town itself, somewhere vaguely north of the Scottish border and farther north probably even than Edinburgh, which itself has always seemed to Matthew to be somewhere not too distant from the ends of the Earth.

'Extremely significant, Wildish,' Snatchal responds crisply, as if rebuking him over his nonchalance. 'I and several others will be discussing the whole thing with his Majesty's Private Secretary tomorrow morning. We must mobilise our forces. War is now inevitable - the whole damn show probably coming to a head in just a matter of months - and interfering with Christmas, of course. Bloody nuisance!'

'Do you - er - enjoy opera, Sir?' Matthew inquires of Snatchal, suddenly feeling desperate to change the subject, since the prospect of war interfering with Christmas has clearly thrown the noble lord and much of the Privy Council into the very slough of despond.

'I do!' he replies, and in an immensely serious tone of voice - as though the realisation has only just occurred to him, his jaw dropping and, failing to return to its original position, needing to be corrected with the by-now familiar tap under the chin with the back of his hand. 'In fact, I'll have you know, gentlemen, I am a confirmed admirer of fine music - in all its forms. Why, it even affects me in a physical way. Oh yes. I know this with absolute certainty, moreover, because - and listen, this is really interesting - that following any expedition to the theatre or to a recital of music of quality such as this, I have always experienced a most singular exhilaration of the body - such an excitement and quickening of the blood, such a profound heat and palpitation of the heart, that it can, at moments, be almost overwhelming.'

'Really?' Matthew murmurs, trying not to appear alarmed.

'Oh yes,' Snatchal continues. 'And, like I say, the physical evidence is there for all to see - because whenever I return home from such a venture, and as I climb the stairs and reach the privacy of my boudoir and disrobe, I discover, as I finally remove my waistcoat and britches and look down ...'

'Yes?' says Sam.

'I discover ...'

'Yes?'

'... that I have actually lost weight.'

Sam, nodding dutifully, stares in silence for a moment before pronouncing the entire revelation to be utterly fascinating, while Matthew, anxious to be away already, excuses himself and elects instead to take a stroll - for surely there must be more interesting sights and sounds to explore. And he is right - because even with the imminent conclusion of the interval, the pleasures of gossip and entertainment, wine and champagne are clearly uppermost in the minds of most people here. Any prospect of war seems remote - which suits him just fine. And how many fine women there are, too. Not only that, but as even the most cursory glance through the pages of Johanna's astrological book will confirm, each and every one must now be perceived through the lens of an entirely new faculty of observation. No longer merely a broad spectrum of desirability, the female gender is now divisible in terms of the planetary hierarchy - every face, every elegant gown, every towering hairstyle or artifice of beauty-spot adorning cheek or breast presenting him with a new and refreshing variety of understanding. A vigorous redhead, strong and forthright in manner could now only be perceived as an embodiment of Mars. The more-distinguished woman of age and maturity, especially if slender and lithesome of limb could now only inform him of the dark, impenetrable mysteries of Saturn. Already the alchemy and magic of his new-found understanding has begun to alter his very process of perception. An entire planetary system is circulating around him, with everywhere a heavenly body waiting for his exploration and conquest.

And then what of Johanna? What is he to make of her extraordinary intensity? As so often of late, whenever in her presence, he finds his thoughts are racing - his mind filled not only with his deep regard for her, but also with visions of planetary spheres and starry skies, of mysterious quests and heroic deeds that he must perform in the way of some ancient knight valorised and setting forth at the behest of his beloved. In truth, he does not feel at all confident that his efforts can tally with so many lofty expectations. He will write his sonnets, of course - he has already commenced upon them - but in their interpretation he feels he would rather leave the spiritual side of things to her. His seven heavens will instead be dedicated to his personal odyssey of sensuality - a far more attractive and accessible proposition.

In time, he finds himself having returned to the entrance to Sam and Johanna's box. Suspecting that the two ladies are alone inside with their champagne, and not wishing to intrude, he tarries a while at the entrance - though at the same time unable to resist the temptation to eavesdrop on their conversation.

'Oh, I don't know,' Lady Snatchal's robust and distinctly plummy accent can be heard from within, a little harsh in tone, as though complaining. 'I really do think I could do with something.'

*'Something?'* he hears Johanna echo by way of inquiry, her voice, by contrast lively and full of fun.

'Yes, I don't quite know what it is at the moment, but I could definitely do with something. Your young Mr Wildish, for example. I think I could do with him, as a matter of fact.'

'Dorothea, really!' he hears Johanna exclaim with laughter, admonishing the woman who has clearly become such a close acquaintance of late.

'Well, he is rather dashing, isn't he,' Lady Snatchal continues. 'Furthermore, it is not necessary, I'm sure, for me to reiterate that there has been a certain falling off of vitality lately in respect of my dear Cornelius - something that has also been a particular vexation to me ever since my unfortunate riding accident, the fall that I had. My physician says it's quite likely the only explanation for my unusually vigorous appetites. You do understand, my dear?'

'I do, Dottie,' he hears Johanna respond in a firm but still gently indulgent voice. 'But the gentlemen you are referring to is a dear friend of ours and ...'

'Married?'

'No. Mr Wildish chooses for the present to remain single and fancy free - in fact rather too fancy free in our estimation, so that Samuel and I have become rather protective towards him as a consequence. But, there again, he is young. Our only concern is that he might overstay his position in this state of immaturity, and remain young for a little too long.'

How odd - most peculiar it is, hearing himself being spoken of in this way, and by Johanna, of all people. The revelation that she might disapprove of him, even if only slightly, is most distressing, almost painful.

'Can one ever remain young for *too long*?' Lady Snatchal remarks with a wistful sigh, as if thinking aloud. 'Surely not! Does he have money? Is he rich?'

'Goodness, no!' Johanna replies, the sound of merriment in her voice once again. 'A most kind and worthy gentleman: a fine poet and craftsman; he excels at dancing, and also fencing, I am told; but he has no fortune - a state surely most undeserving. We remain convinced that he is worthy of the highest patronage.'

'Oh, we can soon arrange some of that!' Lady Snatchal responds straight away. 'I reckon I could do your Mr Wildish a favour or two at court very easily. And, as they say, one good turn deserves another, wouldn't you agree?'

'I do not think I entirely approve of this line of reasoning, Dorothea,' Johanna says, and her voice is one of censure now, so much so that Matthew almost fancies he can hear the occasional vexatious flutter of fans beneath chins.

'Don't be ridiculous!' Lady Snatchal retorts. 'What are you insinuating?

'I am not insinuating anything,' Johanna responds, more conciliatory in tone. 'It is just that I would be most saddened to see Mr Wildish compromised by ... by any sort of inappropriate liaison.'

'Oh, you've likely got your eye on him, yourself then?'

'Goodness!' Johanna gasps. 'You are a naughty lady, Dottie. Do you know what, if I were a man, and if you were a man - why I think I would throw down the gauntlet at this very instant and challenge you to a duel.'

And the pair of them laugh - with Dorothea, Lady Snatchal, in particular, having a most audible and singular way about her when amused, and which Matthew has already heard on at least one occasion this evening: a loud, raucous 'honk, honk' kind of noise, like the sound emitted by an over-excitable goose, and usually punctuated with any number of loud snorting noises in-between honks.

'Pistols at dawn, then, my dear,' she concludes once the honking has subsided. And there is, he thinks, just a hint of earnestness in their banter. How terrifying! And suddenly, as the bell is heard somewhere along the passageway heralding the second half of the performance, the prospect for Matthew of a weekend all together at the Snatchal's country estate is one that engenders decidedly mixed feelings.

Following the performance, and with a call at his apartments easy to incorporate into their journey to Sam's sister's house in The Strand, Matthew is offered a ride home in the Woolveston's coach. But not straight away. Hearing word that a display of fireworks is due across the river in Vauxhall Gardens, Sam has ordered that his carriage proceed not westward but instead down to the embankment near Whitehall stairs where they intend to avail themselves of a good vantage point from which to view the rockets.

And so it is that Matthew finds himself carried once more in style inside Sam's prestigious coach-and-four, glancing out from time to time to the dark streets, interspersed with the dying embers of lamps or the occasional passing torch of a footman or link-boy lighting the way for chairs - meagre illumination and all Matthew has by which to survey the faces of his companions seated, side-by-side, opposite. It would, he surmises have been more convenient for Johanna to occupy the width of the coach herself in her wide, panniered robe, but Sam appears intent on nestling in close, not exclusively for the purpose of laying claim to her in Matthew's presence but also out of a very clear and genuine admiration he has for her - his eyes so attentive and full of her presence. It is all rather touching to behold, Matthew thinks - while also secretly wishing it was himself placed so intimately at Johanna's side.

What an enigma she is. He had assumed, when first introduced to her - it must be all of two years ago now - that she was a sorrowful, melancholic young woman, labouring under some deep sadness - or if there was any joy or fun in her life at that time it was never displayed frivolously. Now, however, he understands that what he had observed was in fact an innate decorum, a natural composure and tranquillity of spirit, as rare in someone of her tender years as it was admirable. And in the darkness of the carriage, where her eyes appear to shine with an inner radiance all their own, he likes to imagine that whenever they chance to look his way, as now, that she would be regarding him with some affection. She seems deep in thought for a while, but then, as if having reconciled something within herself, she leans forward in his direction to speak.

'A date for your diary, then, my Wonder,' she announces in a clipped, almost officious tone, handing him a card from her purse. 'Courtesy of Lady Snatchal: your invitation duly delivered, to join us for a weekend at Snatchalcombe House, the Snatchal's country estate.'

'Oh good. Thank you!' he replies reaching out for the card with care inside the rocking and unsteady interior of the coach, just negotiating a sharp corner in the road as it turns into Whitehall. 'I suppose I should bring someone with me, should I not?'

'Well, actually no,' Johanna answers, adjusting the lateral placement of her hat against the drafts of the window and securing it again with its pin. 'Lady Snatchal did ask me to tell you that she would rather prefer you to come unaccompanied - unless you wish to bring your valet, of course. I suspect she has some sort of matchmaking in mind, and will pair you up with someone. Goodness! I do hope that is the reason, anyway, and nothing else.'

Noticing a look of some introspection on her face at this point and a curious glance from Sam at her side, he inquires what she might mean exactly.

'Oh, just that you should ... how shall I put it: be circumspect in your dealings with the Countess,' she replies, responding to his curiosity. 'She is known to be partial to younger men, and her husband is insanely jealous. Oh, I know Cornelius, Lord Snatchal, does not give that impression. He is perfectly charming, and seems to tolerate almost everything. But he has, in the past, been known to be quite brutal, especially if he suspects anything untoward.'

'I see,' says Matthew, though perhaps not entirely convinced.

'Fought a man in a duel, once,' Sam remarks, and deadly serious

'Really!' Matthew responds, a little more persuaded.

'Oh yes. Nasty business.'

'There is one notable exception, though,' Johanna continues. 'The King himself is by all accounts quite smitten with her, and even though Cornelius seems to regard this as an honour, the Countess does not share in his enthusiasm and has so far managed to resist His Majesty's blandishments. As I say, it is more the younger buck that interests her. So do take care, my Wonder, won't you?'

'Be assured, I shall,' Matthew answers just as the coach arrives at their intended vantage point and draws to a halt in one of the many open yards off Parliament Street, and not a moment too soon, for the display of fireworks from the gardens across the river has already commenced.

Without stepping down from the carriage, they are able to see everything perfectly through the window, which Sam has rolled down for the purpose - being himself possessed of an almost childlike excitement all of a sudden, agitated and bustling in his seat. At this distance, the detonations of the fireworks themselves are almost inaudible, but their brilliance is undiminished, reflected on the water as each one rises gracefully into an almost cloudless sky. In silence, they watch the bright trails, often three or four ascending together and then suddenly bursting into life - a globe of tiny embers each one, resplendent for a moment and then fading as it falls away, only to be replaced by others. Quite a good show - the science of pyrotechnics advancing almost on a daily basis here in London to produce such brilliant displays; and the lucky promenaders in Vauxhall would be enjoying this one for sure, Matthew thinks, picturing himself there - since he knows the gardens well.

'How delightful!' Johanna remarks, though wrapping herself in her woollen shawl against the chill breeze as it wafts in from the river.

The moon is up. And, by leaning forward, Matthew can just make out, to the east, the bridge, all bright with its permanent glow of habitation - and the great dome of St Paul's, too, set against the pearly sky. Across the river, the distinctive Tudor crenellations and walls of Lambeth Palace stand equally dark, with hardly a light showing, while out on the water itself, many of the boats and wherries, their lanterns bobbing up and down, have drifted almost to a standstill, their passengers becoming avid spectators, too, emerging from beneath the awnings and balancing on unsteady feet the better to see. And then, all of a sudden, the entire interior of the carriage is lit by a particularly striking burst of yellow light, accompanied this time by an audible rapport which reaches them a second later and echoes off the walls of the tall buildings to their side - and at which all three, and even Sam's coachman and groom outside, cannot help but voice their admiration in a collective roar of approval.

'I love fireworks,' Sam observes, needlessly, for everyone knows how much he does. 'Look - is it not like a ballet?'

'A ballet?' Matthew echoes, puzzled over his friend's singular observation.

'Yes, look!' Sam repeats, almost grudgingly, as if it were not patently obvious to the whole world what he meant. 'Somebody should ask your Mr Handel to put this sort of thing to music - these dancers. I mean, each of those rockets as it climbs, does it not remind you of a life, a person born - blazing forth in all its glory, full of vitality and strength, just for a brief time before it dies away - only to be replaced by another, and then another. Sometimes they go up in twos or threes - look! And all so graceful - launching themselves with such bravery, and such a merry dance, as well, like a little community of souls all sparkling together for a while until they vanish into the night. Good heavens! I trust you will forgive this untypical outburst of philosophising, my friends. I do believe I am beginning to sound like you, Matthew. Daft as a brush!'

Matthew laughs. But Johanna at his side, looking up into her husband's face with an unusual and silent deference, regards his statement without merriment. And then, unseen by him, for he is still gazing out of the coach window, her shoulders tremble and her aspect alters, as if she were in the throws of some sudden and chilling premonition. It lasts only a second. But as the final trail and dying ember from the last of the rockets fades, and as Sam signals with a rap of his cane upon the roof of the carriage to the coachman that they should set off again, Matthew is almost certain, though it is far too dark to know for sure, that there is the presence of a tear in her eye.

# ~ 6 ~
## OBSERVATIONS OF THE
## HEAVENLY BODIES - JUPITER

*Of the planet Jupiter, its general and particular significations:*
*She who bringeth joy. Upright and straight in body. The face being*
*of an oval visage, full and fleshy. The hair a light brown or flaxen.*
*A high forehead, large eyes, strongly proportioned thighs and legs.*
*A lover of sweet and affable conversation. Aspiring in high matters*
*and given to the pursuit of extravagance and all that is special. In*
*apparel flamboyant and preferring of purple and green. The*
*emerald for her gemstone.*

Thus are described the special qualities of those marked at birth by the signature of Jupiter as set out in Matthew's book of astrological lore lent him by Johanna and by which one might detect, according to the very heavens themselves, those examples of male or female excellence best suited to each of the planets. Perhaps, he is thinking, he will encounter a woman of such outstanding character and style here this evening at Ranelagh Gardens, that most convenient of places for courtship and intrigue and where he has ventured once more to sample the delights of music, good company and fine wine. Perhaps, having composed his sonnet to Jupiter this very day, it will make things happen? He has elected for the occasion to wear a short wig, white-powdered and neatly triple-curled upon the temples, because here, in the darkness, his own natural hair colour can, he knows, sometimes set him at a disadvantage to other men. And that would never do.

Though becoming late in the season, with the height of summer having long since passed and autumn approaching, it remains still pleasantly warm, one of those evenings in which it almost feels as though the dusk has brought with it its own particular warmth, and without a breeze at all. The air, therefore, in its stillness, is fragrant with the scent of late-flowering honeysuckle - coloured by golds of calendula and purple heather, all lit by a profusion of lamps and beacons along the walkways: presenting to the visitor, therefore, a most pleasant aspect of enchantment and adventure - the very essence of any pleasure garden after dark. The best of Ranelagh, however, on this night as much as any other, is that there are always so many lovely women - and these often unaccompanied by little more than a maid or a page. And so it is that, although he has not ventured out this evening with the express intention of locating an exemplar of Jupiter in all her glories, it so transpires that he discovers her - in fact he almost collides with her as, quite by chance he enters a fragrant rose walk to sample the final blush of summer flowers - and there she is! - leaning slightly to imbibe the fragrance herself, a fine figured woman, not young, but possessed of such grace and stately bearing that he knows immediately that he has located the very essence of what he desires. She wears a wide brimmed hat lavishly appointed with flowers, and her gown is of a turquoise silk, trimmed with touches of braid and ribbons, all of a most fashionable quality and of such elegance and taste that the sight of her leaves him almost breathless with admiration. And then, a moment later, as she lifts her face, which is elaborately masked, and her eyes meet his, he resolves without hesitation, whether she be alone, in company of a beau, or even under the guard of an entire army of footman or pages, that he must not let this moment pass, and that he must be bold and speak:

'Such fine specimens!' he declares.

'What?' she responds in a voice that indicates she is not entirely pleased with his intrusion.

'The flowers - they have flourished all summer yet still they bloom for our delight,' he continues, pressing his nose closer to the remnants of the roses themselves and hoping his words might ring true.

'Yes. A fading beauty - but one that may still excite the senses,' she concedes, more wistful in tone, as if alluding to her own self perhaps - for the line of her jaw, which has a certain softening, would, he surmises, place her somewhere not too distant from her fortieth year. 'And you are ..?' she enquires, availing herself of the liberty, as many do, of shedding the normal rules of social conduct - a liberty not only allowed in places such as this, but also positively encouraged.

'Matthew Wildish, Ma'am, is my name,' he answers. 'And I have been thinking ...'

'Thinking, Sir? About what, precisely have you been thinking?' she inquires a little impatiently, seizing upon the slightest hesitation in his voice and turning from him as if she would walk away.

'Why, that music and wine are surely waiting for us yonder inside the pavilion,' he answers, 'and that I can thereby promise you something quite special if you would give me leave.'

'Something quite special?' she echoes in a voice of indifference. 'You are confident, young man. Do you not think I have had *special* enough in my lifetime that I should be so impressed by your promises of yet more?'

'Madam, forgive me. For special is as special deserves, and I wish only to offer you whatever entertainment I can - if only you will honour me with five minutes in which I might continue to flirt with you in my own foolish way.'

'Really - *only five minutes!*' she remarks, burying her face in the flowers once more, no doubt to conceal a smile. 'That would, indeed, be a most swift flirtation.'

She has a pleasant voice, full and resonant. Turning to him, she opens her fan, waving it slowly - and thus invitingly beneath her chin before closing it once again and placing it softly to her lips.

'Impetuosity, Madam, I admit, is a fault of mine,' he says with a modest bow as befits the occasion. 'But truly, I believe a concert is about to begin. Let us put aside all misgivings, therefore, and instead raise a glass in celebration of beauty that fades only slowly, and of evenings that may last forever?'

And to which, quite spontaneously, and with outrageous audacity, noticing that she is accompanied only by a solitary maid, a young girl plainly dressed and who has been following from some distance away, he dares to proffer her his arm.

'You are a smooth talker, Sir,' she says, her voice still edged with reticence and disapproval, yet taking his arm, for all that.

'It is an occupational hazard, Ma'am,' he states as they begin to walk together.

'Really. And would your *occupational hazard* be that of playwright or an actor perhaps?' she asks, ambling slowly at his side, and smiling now despite herself. 'You certainly seem capable of putting on a good performance when necessary.'

'I am a poet, Madam,' he replies. 'I also make carnival masks.'

'Oh, then perhaps you have a willing admirer, after all,' she declares, 'for, as you can see, I am a devotee of the mask. I collect them. I have dozens. It is a fascinating exercise in human nature, is it not - for when one dons a mask one immediately undergoes a loss of inhibition. Thus, a skilled maker of masks must strive to interpret not merely who a person is, but what they would be. And that is often very different. They deal in the deeper mysteries.'

'Then consider me at your service, Madam,' he replies, 'for I would gladly learn what you would be - and of your deepest mysteries, also.'

At which she laughs for the first time, as jovial as a peal of bells as they continue to meander their way through the crowds and beneath the arched entrance to the Rotunda where already the faintest strains of a string ensemble, its musicians tuning their instruments, can be detected from within. Matthew, discovering that an hour is free in one of the supper boxes, hands his intriguing companion into a chair. And thus seated together at table, in their own neatly appointed alcove, their glasses filled with Rhenish wine, they are able to listen at leisure to the performance - which this evening is to include the singing of a most-capable and celebrated Italian castrato, the distinguished gentleman himself having just stepped onto the bandstand to join the orchestra.

'Oh, how I adore the castrati!' she states, almost in abandon, her breath rising and falling with the tide of the music, giving herself entirely to it as a lover would to an embrace. 'And not only for the beauty of their voices,' she adds, as if sharing in a secret passion with a friend - and thereby signalling to him, with all the courtesies of formal conversation being now discharged, her complete willingness to be familiar. 'Women do *so!* And men so seldom understand why.'

'Perhaps,' he remarks, 'we are puzzled - that they who are so ill-provided for the satisfying of your desires should be so instrumental in their generation.'

'Oh, fear not, Sir. I can assure you that such creatures are perfectly well equipped for the provision of all manner of enjoyment: their soft skin and delicate complexions, their voices so melodious in discourse, and yet as abundant in the possession of sap and vigour as any man, if not more so. With them, in the absence of all risk and danger, one can safely avail oneself of the best a man might have to offer without incurring the penalties that attend upon being a woman - the perfect aphrodisiac for one who would not wish to grow a belly in return for her pleasure.'

To which, raising her fan once more, she regards him for some time in silence, not only to continue her appreciation of the music, but also to gauge how shocked he might be by her worldly declaration. And thus, at such close quarters, and with the assistance of the soft candlelight of their table he is able to study her and to admire her beauty at last - for yes, despite the bejewelled mask of black velvet that covers a considerable portion of her face, she *is* beautiful. He is certain of that. Her lips, he notices, are most artfully painted, prominent against her fair skin and with a fullness that promises much joy in the taking of a kiss - while her eyes appear to sparkle with the most extraordinary vitality. But who might she be? And why is she here, seeking what? These are the questions that inevitably race through his mind, and yet he knows that to surrender to any misjudged curiosity at this stage would be as futile as it would be unwise. In the event, he need not have worried, for she allows him further into her confidence almost immediately with her next words:

'Be assured,' she begins again, prefaced by a long and self-indulgent sigh, 'that even though I am unable to shock you, I can perceive I have at least aroused your curiosity.'

'Madam, I am amazed,' he responds with calm, 'that you can read so well my thoughts as well as bewitch me with your eyes? Are you a sorceress?'

'No - nor do I need to be. For yours is the curiosity of youth, Mr Wildish, and as with all the wonders of youth it betrays itself most readily to those who no longer possess it.'

'Madam there is much that I would ask, it is true,' he finally admits, 'but I suspect you have not ventured here this evening to answer questions, but rather to *ask* them, and these more than anything of yourself - as surely you will have done many times, for you seem no stranger here.'

'Correct. But do not despair, Sir. I remain willing to satisfy you - your curiosity, that is. My name, you do not need to know, of course. And because I am masked, and because you are a gentleman, you will not ask it of me. Suffice to say, I am indeed a frequent visitor to these gardens - these enchanted gardens - and far more frequent, no doubt, than I dare admit even to myself. As a woman, one can never really enjoy the same degree of liberty anywhere else, while the anonymity of the mask allows me to shed the restrictions of my social position. Ah, but wait! You have the advantage over me already, curious youth, do you not? For now that I have confessed to you so many of my vices, do you not think you should disclose at least one of yours in return? An uncommon attraction towards women of a greater age than yourself, perhaps, which would explain why one so very young should direct his seductive charms to one who, by comparison, must appear so very old?'

'Madam, I must tell you that all women are of interest to me, of whatever vintage.'

'Idle knave - would you compare me to a wine?'

'I would - if for no other reason than your enchanting complexity, Madam, and because you bring intoxication and pleasure to my senses. Young or old, I love everything about women - their sound, their fragrance, their conversation, their range of sentiment and the full spectrum of their desires that seem so more profound than those expressed among us male ruffians. And when beauty is combined with intelligence and wit as I see before me now, the combination is irresistible.'

'Irresistible indeed!' she chuckles, with sportive humour convivial still despite his efforts to match her in boldness of speech. 'But why so intense, Sir? Were you so deprived of the company of spirited women in your formative years? Did you have no older sisters to tease you?'

'None, Madam, and I regret to say I knew my mother only in passing, and she, moreover, was lost to me at an early age.'

'Why, there you have it! For that which is deficient in our youth often informs us of our needs in later years when we crave what was denied to us in even stronger measure. I am as culpable in that respect as any - for I too have my foolish fantasies, born of neglect and frustration. That is why I venture here, you see. It is my theatre, my stage. Beneath the cloak and the mask, I exist here in the concealment of the night as one who travels through a dream - *my* dream - which is why, I confess, you might not recognise me or see me the same from one evening to the next. A different guise, a different outfit and style on each occasion, always as the fancy takes me. For, as you will have perceived by my apparel, Sir, I enjoy the advantages of a certain good fortune and affluence, and can thereby indulge even my most extravagant of whims whenever

I choose - for I believe there is nowhere within this entire city that has such charm, nowhere more accommodating to all the wide and varied temptations of the imagination than here, where all our basest instincts can be enhanced by a thousand alternative delights.'

In the brief silence that ensues they gaze steadfastly into each other's eyes and all his senses are alive - for behind the mask it is the creature of need, at last, that he sees.

'And all the more enthralling perhaps for the lengthy denial of what we most desire,' he concurs and pours a little more wine for them both. 'It is the thrill of the chase, Madam. Though in the proximity of so many probing eyes, of course, one must be discreet. Here the naked and primitive expression of the act is prohibited to all but the most daring and vulgar among us.'

'Indeed yes,' she observes - and by the rising of her breath he senses her desire. 'And of little interest, anyway - since those who *are* most daring and vulgar invariably leave us feeling so very disappointed upon the conclusion of their labours, do they not?'

'Correct, Madam. We long, instead, for a more agreeable alternative.'

'Oh ... then I must tell you, Sir, I am the most accomplished mistress of *the alternative*.'

'Really, Madam. Tell me more.'

'I shall. Because here in these gardens, for an entire evening I will often have for my sport that a man might pursue the predilection, be he so inclined, of experiencing little more than the softness of my glove upon his brow, or to wonder at the symmetry of my ankle or the heel of my shoe. He may thrill, and so may I, at the brush of hair upon a cheek or the scent of desire that elsewhere would make us blush for shame. Above all, I am intrigued that here one may make love to the sound of beautiful music - and where else can that be achieved! I am acquainted with a loving couple who regularly hire a blind fiddler to furnish them with just such an ambiance - but then the good gentleman would surely know what is taking place. The joy of being here is that one can make love to music and nobody knows. Here, therefore, I may go, safely masked and incognito, to an adventure with the beau of my dreams, whom I may have met quite by chance a moment earlier beneath an arbour of roses. And here, too, or somewhere near in the darkness, hidden from observation by a woven trellis or myrtle hedge, I might, if I am so disposed, sit upon a seat or grassy bank and have him whisper sweet and tender obscenities to my willing embrace until by a practised and artful accommodation of my limbs to his I am brought to my perfection. Life is precious, is it not, Sir? And every moment a joy to be treasured - for time and its passing are more swift and more cruel than one of your years can ever imagine. And so, there you have it. There you have my story and perhaps my immediate aspirations also. Take it all for what you will, though my name I shall not divulge to you, not for all the silver in Arabia.'

'Madam, your story has intrigued me far more than I can say,' he declares, resting his hand upon hers.

'Then I shall rejoice in that,' she replies, joining her other hand to his in turn. 'Your presence has made me quite the orator, and more so this evening than I am at all used to - or even thought possible.'

'Then I have given wings to your thoughts, Madam,' he murmurs, closely now. 'But tell me: what would you have for deeds?'

'What would I? Why, I would relish this sweet wine in my glass a moment more. And then I would remove my glove, thus, and have my fingers touch you here upon your cheek, where a certain roughness has settled since the attentions of your razor this morning - just here, where it is a little dark, as would be your hair, I'll wager, were it visible to me. And then, in a location more discreet, I would feel the abrasiveness of it upon my breast. My requirements are modest, are they not?'

'Nay, Madam, I beg to differ. I think rather they are as vast as the mighty dome of this pavilion and the firmament above it, and that what you speak of is but a prelude to something far greater.'

'Then I am obliged to you, Sir. You have recognised my plight: a misfortune of the greatest inconvenience. For you see, by the continual satisfying of one's needs, and so regularly as has been my personal vocation for some time now, one adventure must inevitably feed off another, becoming bolder and more extravagant each time until it is scarce possible to trump any that has gone before. You have much to surmount, therefore, if you would entertain me with your deeds. How then shall *that* be? What, then, are your credentials in the art of love?'

'I have none, Madam – or few that could compete with yours. I shall not pretend otherwise, being as poor a dissembler in your presence as I am an ardent admirer of your beauty. Instead, I would flatter you in lines of verse.'

'What, you have a poem for me as well as your youthful eyes?'

Not answering her, but with a view instead to leaving the Rotunda for the more secret and nocturnal delights of the gardens, he rises from his seat and offers her his arm that they might walk once more - since he knows from frequent experience that a well-spoken line of verse often proves the ultimate means of dispelling doubt in affairs of the heart, and that poetry itself never sounds finer than when whispered outdoors by moonlight - while she, untypically frolicsome all of a sudden and with much enthusiasm, rises also in her readiness to accompany him.

'A sonnet dedicated to those we meet in a moment of delight, that the memory of it might never fade,' he breathes softly as, within only a short time, once outside they have located a secluded bower, a bench beneath honeysuckle in almost total darkness some distance from the paths and here, seated closely, more intimately than ever, without recourse to any written page, he speaks his lines to her in a voice that gains in tenderness as he leans his face towards hers and takes her hands once more in his:

*Boast not to me of life's extravagance,*
*Flaunt not thy velvets, silks or goldsmith's name!*
*Do not fake the rainbow, or feign romance*
*With tailors, cooks or milliners of fame.*

*I also crave the fashion of the hour,*
*My style abides in art and music's skill,*
*And celebrates, as thee, my fragrant flower,*
*Whatever passing fad might strive to thrill.*

*Yet we, in our embrace, seek stronger ties,*
*Where none but our two hearts should ever be,*
*Where sweet delight in all abundance sighs,*
*And touch to touch shall surfeit never be.*

*Rue not if this tired world despair of love,*
*Come cling to me, my special turtle dove.*

And she does, indeed, cling to him then, leaning towards him so that their foreheads touch. 'On hearing your fine poem, Sir,' she whispers, 'I must tell you that your words have a most agreeable effect upon certain parts of my ... more intimate physiology.'

'Why, what mean you, here perhaps? Or here, my darling?' he murmurs resting a hand, unseen by anyone, gently upon the place of her heart, the lovely bodice of lace and tied ribbon that restrains her breast, animated so strongly by the passion of her breath.

'Indeed, yes, my poet. Here - indeed most everywhere,' she sighs - and yet also smiles to herself, most beautifully he notices, at the quickening of her own desire.

He feels quite lost in her now, and she ever more intimate in her presence also, as they launch themselves into a profusion of touches and caresses - and he, exultant, is just about to press his lips to hers when to their utter astonishment they are made aware of the distinctive sounds of a marching band, most incongruous and most unwelcome, and all so very close, moreover, to where they are hidden - music of sorts, yes, but of a variety that does not please either of them, or inspire any further warmth, alas. And suddenly he senses that the moment is no longer ripe for the taking of this succulent fruit; and she, also, appears most unsettled by it all.

'I cannot say I recollect music of this kind here before, not of an evening,' she states, getting to her feet and looking around to identify the source of it, clearly most displeased by the shrill of the pipes and the coarse, insistent drumming, coming ever closer - with the intention, for all they know, of doing an entire circuit of the garden - and a good many assorted cheers and *huzzahs* rising up from those spectators already caught up in the excitement. 'Surely not already in celebration of some foolish sentiment towards war!' she continues, though in a voice of exasperation now.

'Indeed, it would seem so,' he says, recalling news that the King has curtailed his Summer Progress overseas and, with considerable reluctance, no doubt, has already returned to England to address the crisis. 'Come to me tomorrow at my chambers in the city,' he says, quite spontaneously, risking all. 'I can assure you my home is most comfortably appointed - a place of the utmost privacy and where I would fulfil all that special promise that must, it seems, be postponed – though for a short time only, I trust.'

'You are bold, Sir - bold verging on the impertinent,' she responds, more waspish now in her ways, and preparing with all haste as if to leave. 'Your chambers? And where might this be, pray, this fragrant bower of dalliance and perfumed delight?'

'At the sign of the Pig and Whistle, just off Cheapside,' he answers.

'What! A vulgar coaching inn!' she cries, disengaging herself angrily now from any attempt to seize her hands once more. 'How dare you dally with me, Sir! Do you take me for a common strumpet?'

'By your leave, Madam, I wish only to take you for what you most desire, strumpet or wanton as you will,' he urges her in ever more hurried speech, 'for I know you are made for far more than mere modesty or temperance. Why, Madam, should the vulgarity of my invitation not even add a little spice to your appetite?'

At which she alters - and this most dramatically, embracing him with a violent intensity as she sighs: 'Far more. Far more than I dare admit. You have primed me and set me afire, Sir. I shall indeed come to you, and take full measure of your *special*.'

'Tomorrow?' he appeals to her again, taking again her hands in his, successfully this time. 'For there I promise with no idle boastfulness that I shall honour you and, indeed, shall trump all others, as you put it - or else die in the attempt.'

And even with the sounds of the wretched marching band thundering in their ears, he thrills at the warmth of her touch as she presses herself to him once more with a passion.

'Tomorrow, yes. Shortly after noon,' she answers and, accepting his card, reading over the address quickly, adding: 'I shall arrive by chair, and you will know me not by any announcement, but as you see me now … behold.'

To which, disengaging herself and removing her hat, she slowly raises her mask to reveal her face - which even by the modest light provided appears indeed most lovely: a well-favoured complexion topped by what he can now perceive to be a most lustrous head of flaxen hair - her forehead broad, her eyebrows fair and elegantly arched, rendering her appearance even more open and wanting of joy - while even those lines that nature and the passage of time have bestowed upon her face have, it seems to him, been fashioned only from laughter and the experience of frequent and repeated episodes of pleasure. She is, he feels with all his heart and soul, the most adorable of women.

'And so you will, I trust, remember me,' she says, replacing her mask.

'I shall, Madam, do not doubt it.'

The marching band, meanwhile, is almost upon them. He can see it plainly now, being led by a link-boy carrying a gigantic flame twice his own height - and all the soldiers following behind, young men who in the ostentation of scarlet coats and braided tunics seem to be the toast of the town at present and can do no wrong.

'I trust I shall learn tomorrow what new mask you might fashion for me, Mr Wildish,' the lovely Jupiter remarks, calmly now as she re-arranges various aspects of her clothing and once again pins her hat. And although she has managed to restore some laughter to her voice, as if jesting, she is earnest enough, he senses, for she fixes him steadily with her eyes. 'Let me see if you can indeed fathom my mysteries, my *mascarero* - for I am very demanding. You should know that, and you shall not say that you have not been warned.'

And with that, and a final moment's embrace, he escorts the nameless beauty back towards the pavilion - its bright windows ranged high above the tree-tops like a gigantic lantern in the night and where, at the entrance, her girl is waiting amid the crowds. Handing them both into a parked carriage, which is most likely that of the lady herself, he suspects, he bids his lovely Jupiter adieu before commencing upon his own homeward journey. He goes via the river, relishing from his seat at the stern of the wherry the fine starlit evening, his thoughts full of passionate longing and a stirring in his loins that he has rarely if ever experienced before. Tomorrow. Tomorrow for my demanding special one, he murmurs to himself, and smiles. He cannot wait to deliver up his promise.

It is close to noon and everything is set for the anticipated visit today from the fair epitome of Jupiter. Will she come? Will she really come to him as promised? At one moment, as he gazes down to the busy yard below, he thinks she will, then a moment later he doubts it completely - all surely just a foolish fantasy - for here now in the brightness of a glorious sunny day, the events of the previous evening in Ranelagh Gardens seem little more than a dream. At least the prospect of her visit has urged him towards some domestic maintenance for once - and with the aid of Francis, his trusty valet, he has already made significant headway against the notorious untidiness of the place - a condition largely of his own making but one to which he has applied himself this morning with no small measure of transforming zeal, converting his normally chaotic and grubby living quarters (and in particular his bed-chamber) into something far more acceptable. He has thrown out the old rags that once served as curtains, and invested in new drapes from the haberdashers in Cheapside - and these are up already, thanks to Francis, who has installed fresh rush-matting on the floorboards of the workshop, and an expensive rug at the door of the bed-chamber, too. A vase of roses adorns a dark corner, and fragrant pomanders of sweet herbs are placed liberally about the bedroom and studio in order to at least disguise - if not to entirely banish - any unpleasant odours emanating from the yard outside or the dreadful smells from the glue and wet hair that his wig-making trade produces - so that now the place is as fragrant as a duchess's boudoir, and positively gleaming with cleanliness and order.

'Well, this is impressive,' he says to himself with an approving glance around his studio - surprised at the results and wondering why he does not strive to do it just a bit more often.

The hour for his assignation is almost upon him by this time, and so, ever hopeful that something might indeed yet come of it, he commences the process of sprucing himself up, every bit as adroitly as he has applied himself to the interior of his home. Thus, following an uncommonly lengthy flirtation with flannel, soap and water, he sits down at the wash table and shaves carefully in front of the looking glass. Francis is called once more and assists him into his very finest shirt and floral embroidered waistcoat, his silk breeches, white stockings, and shoes of Spanish leather. His lustrous long hair he brushes and is tied with a purple velvet ribbon at the back, and a white silk cravat secured with a silver pin is added as a final embellishment of quality. These essential tasks being completed to his entire satisfaction it is simply a matter of dismissing his man for the afternoon and then waiting - he sincerely hopes for not too much longer for whatever may come to pass.

Anxious not to miss her, lest she fail to locate the sign above his doorway below, he positions himself on the bench that serves as a window-seat overlooking the yard and gazes down to the numerous comings and goings of the busy inn. A small coach arrives and its weary and sore-bottomed passengers fall out and wander into the tavern, but none among them is the lady he is expecting, who did say, in any case, that she would arrive by chair. Horses are unharnessed from the coach, and in the lugubrious heat of the

September afternoon, grooms and stable boys attend to their duties and then retire. For a time, all is uncommonly quiet and peaceful, the sun shining upon the warm brickwork of the walls, and upon the various plants and weeds growing out of the less-trodden areas of paving around the perimeter. Why, it is all so lovely that he even feels a poem might be coming on.

But then suddenly he is shaken from his reverie by a loud cry and commotion from below and when he glances down again it is to see - and he can hardly believe it - an enormous ginger-coloured highland bull, the kind that are regularly driven along Bishopsgate towards market, but which has obviously escaped and bolted from its handler, charging into the yard below, preceded by a terrified gentleman pedestrian - one hand clutching his hat, the other waving his cane - and running as if for his very life. He saves himself only by leaping up onto a bale of hay, leaving the bull itself to charge around aimlessly, snorting, bellowing very loudly and seeming unable to find its way out again, while above, all around the galleries and at every window, people gather and stare in astonishment at the spectacle.

'Well, I'm not about to go down to resolve your problem, whoever is responsible - not in my finery,' Matthew mutters to himself, entertained, he has to admit, as the beast continues to race around. But then, to his horror, the stupid animal comes charging headlong towards his own porch - to the doorway of his stairs below which would, moreover, normally be wide open at this time of the day.

'Oh no, surely not!' Matthew cries as he hears the thud and splintering sound of wood as the animal - which he can no longer see - has come crashing into the passageway and, by the sounds of it, has already got a good part of itself lodged inside. This is, Matthew suspects, rapidly becoming a disaster.

Quickly, he hurries out onto the gallery and along to the top of his stairway and, sure enough, there below, staring up at him, a brass ring in his nose, all foaming at the mouth, and rolling his big brown eyes, is the head of the bull itself. In the narrow, enclosed space, the enormous beast has squeezed itself into a position from which he appears utterly incapable of extricating himself, his forelegs resting on the steps themselves, his hooves caught between the risers.

Meanwhile, various onlookers, mostly a number of elderly

customers from the inn, have begun to gather below in some consternation, and the only way Matthew can deal with any of it - for deal with it now he must - is to locate a different set of steps from the gallery - which he quickly does from the opposite side - racing down and around until within a few frantic seconds he is at his entrance door. Although damaged, the porch, he is astonished to discover, is still intact, with the door having swung itself shut behind the bull and enclosed him entirely.

'I wouldn't go in there, Sir, if I were you,' a passing coachman says.

'By your leave, Sir, I shall,' Matthew says, 'as I live here.'

But the man merely laughs. 'You mean you *did* live here, once. Looks like there's a new tenant in residence now, eh, ha, ha!'

Ignoring the fool, Matthew advances on the door and opens it carefully to behold the vast backside of the animal itself, lodged immovably at the foot of his stairs, his rear legs scuffing and scraping the floorboards and large pieces of splintered wood from the porch itself caught up upon the pinnacles of his horns as his thick, steaming neck thrashes furiously from side to side in frustration. And so noisy! For when he bellows it is as a great acoustic resonance in the enclosed wooden space that causes Matthew to instinctively step back and to quickly shut the door again.

'The creature cannot turn, nor can it back out,' Matthew explains to the onlookers, most of whom respond without sympathy - and in fact, with nothing much new to see by way of proceedings, most of them are already beginning to disperse anyway, including the gentleman pedestrian, down off his bale of hay and by this time clearly enjoying something of a celebrity status among a group of ladies from the inn. No one among them now it seems is in the least bit concerned over Matthew's predicament until, at last, someone competent in the business of dealing with animals arrives on the scene, namely one of the stableboys, a tall lanky youth whom Matthew knows quite well and who, upon opening and closing the door swiftly to appraise the situation for himself, responds merely with a scratch of the chin and dubious shake of the head.

'He thinks he's back home in his barn, I reckon,' the youth says with a wry smile, 'He feels safe in there, see. And he's probably making all that noise cause he's hungry.'

'Hungry!' Matthew cries with exasperation. 'Listen, you must help me. I have to get him out.'

'Oh, I don't reckon that would be a good idea, Sir,' the youth continues patiently. 'He wouldn't be happy being moved, not now. Not happy at all.'

'I don't care if he's happy or not!' Matthew cries, feeling that he might be losing patience with the whole affair - and with just everybody else in the world at present. But then, lowering his voice, more mildly, adds: 'Listen, I haven't got my purse on me at the moment, but I promise you there's a half-crown in this for you if you can remove the animal, only quickly if you please.'

'Take him some hay!' another young fellow, a groom from the coach house suggests as he passes by, though clearly far too busy to stop. 'If you can gain his trust, then you can coax him out.'

'Coax him?'

'Yes - gently, *you know.*'

Grudgingly, with a despairing shake of the head, Matthew breaks out some handfuls of hay from the bale that a moment ago had served the gentleman pedestrian so well. But there is no way that the beast can be proffered so much as a morsel in its current position.

'My God!' Matthew reflects with dismay, his eyes full only of the rear end of the beast, its great arse still very much *in situ and* with all its mighty appendages dangling on prominent display beneath. 'If the lovely Jupiter from Ranelagh Gardens arrives now she will discover something *special,* that's for sure.'

The only remedy, he decides, as he shuts the door on the beast once again, is to retrace his steps back up to the gallery once more and around yet again to the top of the stairs. And this he does. Still determined to put the groom's suggestion into practice, and leaning cautiously forward now from a position above, he is able to hand some hay down to the front end of the animal - that part, after all, where it is most likely to be of use.

'Come on, come on - take it!' Matthew grumbles impatiently, throwing the hay onto the steps above the creature's head. But the animal remains obdurate and simply bellows again most ungraciously his discontent. Glancing down for assistance, Matthew discovers that both the groom and stable boy, meanwhile, have disappeared - and Francis, the valet remains unavailable as well, of course, having been dismissed for the afternoon - which upon reflection seems to have been rather a mistake.

Furious with himself, Matthew is just about to run to the inn to try to find him, when a gilded sedan chair comes racing into the yard, its bearers in perfectly powdered wigs and fine brocaded livery, and clearly in a hurry at the behest of their passenger inside - so that within moments of setting the box down, the handles are slid away, the door is opened and out steps the lady from Ranelagh in a most gorgeous plumed hat, unfurling the vast width of her sumptuous silk and taffeta dress in all its glory and standing there looking like a goddess amid all the filth and muck of the yard. Glancing around and then up to the gallery, she spots Matthew almost immediately and smiles - only moderately puzzled perhaps by his waving of both hands towards her in what he suspects would seem a curiously hysterical fashion. Undaunted, she simply waves back, brandishing his card in her hand.

'Oh, Mr Wildish!' she declares, her manner business-like in the proximity of the chairmen, 'I hope you don't object if I just pop in and see if you have anything special for me today?' At which, without waiting a second longer, she glides towards the door of the stairway.

Feeling as if the world is about to come to an end, Matthew, his face in his palms, can only wait and listen - listen to the swinging open of the door, listen to the blood-curdling scream - so very loud - followed by a further terrible shriek of horror and panic.

'Madam - I can explain!' Matthew calls down.

'How dare you!' she cries, emerging into view once more and clearly not to be pacified. 'You jest with me at your peril, Sir!' she adds, pointing an accusing finger up at him before turning back to her chair and climbing inside.

'Madam, please ...'

But it is no good. And Matthew can only watch helplessly as the chairmen, who have hardly had a second to pause for breath, must do a smart about-face and, lifting up the chair again, hurry their passenger away, their fine shoes clattering on the cobbles as they go, leaving an eerie kind of silence in their wake - a silence broken only by a soft, somewhat melancholic bellowing sound from the poor creature itself, still trapped on the stairs.

Miserable and utterly exhausted by it all, Matthew ambles down into the yard again, realizing now that the only solution available to him is to encourage the beast by slow degrees to demolish the entire, fragile wooden structure in which he is entrapped. And thus, aided by a combination of various kicks, butts and attempted turns, most of it comes crashing down and the animal can at last extricate himself, easing his enormous body out backwards through what remains of the doorway. And then, most fortuitously, at just that very moment, a small boy, scruffy like a street urchin and appearing out of nowhere it seems, steps forward and with the utmost calm and self-possession simply reaches up and attaches a chain to the ring in the bull's nose, and within seconds has secured the other end to a nearby tethering post. Relieved at the timely intervention, Matthew fetches more hay, and this time the animal, more at ease and genuinely in need of sustenance, begins to eat. And thus, at last, some sense of order is restored.

Wiping the sweat from his brow, Matthew looks down at the boy who has helped him. He does not appear to be one of the regular lads, and yet his face seems familiar.

'Who are you?' he asks.

'That's it! Everything's all right now, Sir,' he says cheerfully, not really responding to the question at all as he ambles away. How odd - but then suddenly Matthew knows - of course, this is surely the link-boy who had guided him home in the darkness the other evening after his attendance at the Cornhill Club, the very same little fellow with his curly mop of hair and threadbare cap. Yes - but there is no opportunity to run after him or thank him again, for abruptly the peace is shattered once more by the arrival of a whole group of men, farmers or drovers by the look of them in their country dress of wool and hemp, and who all at once have come storming into the yard. There are half-a-dozen of them, and they are all very agitated and distressed.

'Oi! What are you doing with my bull?' one of them demands, striding up to Matthew, all sweaty and flustered, his sleeves rolled up upon his big, brown muscular arms.

'Sir!' Matthew responds indignantly, 'I rather think the more pertinent question might be *what has your bull been doing with me?* It has demolished the entire stairway to my apartments here, look! - the reconstruction of which will cost me a pretty penny. The whole thing, furthermore, has ruined my chances of having a good ... I mean, of receiving a very important client who was due to visit me in my rooms this afternoon.'

'What - you mean you've had him here all this time, my bull?'

'*Well hardly from choice!*' Matthew replies, loosing all patience now.

'Here, don't you go raising your voice at me!' the farmer says, pointing a menacing finger. 'We've been looking all over the city, we have.'

'Listen ... I am sorry,' Matthew apologises, relenting somewhat, while the farmer also calms himself and seems repentant. It is a very hot afternoon.

'It's just that I thought ... well, that you might have stolen him, that's all,' he grumbles.

'No, Sir, I have not stolen him. Do I look like someone who would wish to steal a bull!'

'No - well, why would you be a feeding him, then?' he asks, still suspicious, his eyes narrow.

'Because he's hungry, of course, damn it!'

'Hungry - *we're* the ones who's hungry!' the man declares, hands on hips looking outraged and exasperated. 'We're the ones who's been chasing around all day searching for the runaway, haven't we boys!'

The other men, by this time having sized up Matthew by his apparel as a gentleman and one of relative opulence, have begun to utter various plaintive noises by this stage, and even the rubbing of one or two rustic bellies can be observed by way of demonstration that they are, indeed, hungry as well - to which Matthew, wanting to keep the peace and be done with the whole affair, decides that the best way to placate everyone would be to offer them a meal in the tavern of the inn - a proposition which, once voiced, is met with universal and vociferous approval. He ushers them across to the tradesmen's entrance in the corner of the yard, therefore, sets them down at a table inside, and then orders from Mrs Block, the landlady, oblivious to everything it would seem, a slap-up dinner for everyone concerned. Ale is also provided in generous measure to help smooth over any grievances, and the entire party become very jolly indeed - with everyone concluding, to a man, that their host is really not a cattle thief at all but a 'right good gent,' instead.

Matthew does not linger to soak up the praise, however. After a swift glass of brandy, he returns outside to the yard and the waiting bull - while also looking around once more for any sign of the small boy who had come to his aid with the chain earlier but who, alas, is nowhere to be seen. The whole place is very quiet and deserted, in fact. It is just him now, Matthew, and the beast itself, still tethered to its post, its thick ginger coat so resplendent in the sunshine. Matthew looks into the creature's eyes, and the creature looks back at him, doleful and without remorse. He is not impressed by the opulence of Matthew's floral embroidered waistcoat or his by his silken breeches. He is not bedazzled by the diamond pin in his cravat or the once shiny silver buckles of his shoes now tarnished by filth. He is not even concerned that he has destroyed Matthew's prospects of establishing an alliance with the beautiful Jupiter from Ranelagh Gardens - now fled in terror. He is merely hungry and in want of hay - and remarkably docile as well - the mask that was once its bovine face somehow transparent for one peculiar moment in which Matthew even fancies he sees some distant origin of life common to his own. It is a peculiar sensation. They have become the best of companions, he realises. And so he takes a little more hay from the bail; measures out the coarse golden stems between his fingers and then, with a peculiar kind of satisfaction at the unfamiliar task, leans forward and feeds him some more.

# ~ 7 ~
## THE WIG

'Do come in, gentlemen, and take a seat, won't you,' Lord Snatchal declares as, nervously, Matthew and Sam, having enjoyed a hearty breakfast with the ladies in the somewhat over-sized morning room downstairs, are now invited to enter the more personal, exclusively male preserve of the Earl's closet. This is high up in a remote wing of the building - situated along a narrow passage, almost beyond the powers of location for anyone not already familiar with the complex layout of passageways, galleries and stairways of the gigantic edifice. They are here amid the extravagant neo-classical grandeur of the Snatchal's principal country seat of Snatchalcombe House in the rolling countryside of Surrey. A coach journey in the early October sunshine brought them to it yesterday - Matthew, Sam and Johanna, together - to spend the weekend with the Snatchals. They had expected upon arrival to discover something reasonably grand, but even Sam appeared surprised by the sheer size of the place - a long-fronted citadel of colonnaded and Palladian stone and marble set amid acres of landscaped parks and rolling countryside; a building of endless corridors, vast atriums and staterooms, of Doric pilasters, painted ceilings and gilt entablatures, not to mention the occasional towering library or echoing ballroom - all far too extensive, of course, so very cold, so very intimidating in scale for the habitation of mere mortals - which must, Matthew concludes, serve in some part to explain why those who dwell in such places must withdraw whenever possible to small cosy rooms such as this, to the personal dressing rooms or closets of their owners, in which they might conduct their day-to-day affairs in some measure of comfort. Consequently, this morning, they find themselves ensconced in the noble Lord's most private domain, a small room no bigger than a modest bedchamber of a town house - and where

Matthew is to take possession of a very important commission, perhaps the very reason for his being asked here in the first place. And he is just a bit terrified by it all. 'What a neat little room!' Sam declares, obsequious as ever.

'Interesting, isn't it,' Snatchal agrees with pride, indicating with a sweep of the hand all the various prints and drawings upon the walls, scenes of ancient Rome or of modern farming activities mostly, interspersed by the occasional trophy or piece of hunting paraphernalia. He is seated in front of an open bureau - upon which, Matthew is intrigued to see, there is a rather crude mannequin head, a wooden block, over which an ancient dilapidated wig has been placed. 'I retreat here for contemplation, y'know,' the Earl continues, 'to write letters or to read. You might just say it is my holy of holies. I can leave behind all the servants, the estate workers and visitors this way, and all the endless demands upon my time - and also, if I'm an honest man, Lady Snatchal, as well. Oh, pleasant company as my dear wife undoubtedly is, a man needs at least a few moments of silence once in a while, would you not say so, Sam? Naturally, I won't ask you for an opinion on the matter, young Wildish, since you do not, I understand, enjoy the society of a loving spouse?'

'Indeed, no,' Matthew replies. 'I have been unfortunate, or perhaps *fortunate*, it that respect, to have remained single.'

To which Sam, having settled down upon a chaise longue, his head covered this morning merely by an informal though expensive silk night-cap, and clearly still relishing the honour of a private audience with such a noble personage, lets forth a cynical, 'Huh!' which, Matthew concludes, could mean anything or nothing, and which he is not at all certain is entirely to his liking, either way.

'Oh, your time will come, m'boy, fear not!' Snatchal remarks wistfully. 'You know, I can still bring to mind those heady days of youth myself, even now.'

'Really?' Sam inquires, continuing to sound genuinely intrigued - a consummate actor.

'Oh yes,' Snatchal confirms. 'And I'll tell you something that is really interesting - a bit of a confession for you, this: I did actually discover my innate fondness for female society at a remarkably early age. Even as a small boy I was most precocious and just couldn't resist showing off in front of the ladies. There's a game I used to play with the village girls that springs to mind even now.

Yes - whenever my father took himself off to the County Fair or on business, he would leave me to my own devices in the village. Well, you can imagine, just a small boy, on the loose - and when I wasn't climbing trees or fishing for tiddlers in the local stream, I would just take off my britches and chase the local girls up and down the road. I'd whirl the britches round and round in the air as I went. Oh, how I loved it when they screamed and ran off. And then I'd chase, them, by Jove! How I'd run after them! Ah ... the County Fair.'

Matthew senses himself becoming distinctly hot under the collar. Even Sam appears to be somewhat embarrassed, before brushing the matter aside and saying, 'Oh, well, I'm sure we all do silly things at that age that we come to regret.'

But Snatchal merely regards him with some puzzlement. 'Oh, no ... no, I'm still doing it,' he says. 'Though of course one has to be more discreet these days and I have to pay for the privilege - an arrangement I have with some ladies at a certain establishment in town, you understand. All part of my avowed mission to grow old disgracefully, gentlemen. Not going to let up on that!'

At which he takes out his watch to examine the time and appears suddenly disturbed. 'My word, it is getting late - and Lady Snatchal has organised a stroll in the park for us this afternoon. We'd better get down to business, gentlemen. The wig - the wig, Wildish - behold!'

It is now, at last, that Snatchal brings forward closer to Matthew's attention the mannequin head with its peruke. And even without leaving his seat, Matthew can see that it is a most singular and odd-looking piece, the hair itself being extremely sparse, unpowdered and hanging untidily in a bewildering variety of different shades and textures. Dreadful craftsmanship, he thinks, though an instinct tells him to keep his own counsel - an instinct which proves well founded.

'The question,' Lord Snatchal continues, 'is can you fix it, Wildish? It does require a spot of maintenance, as you can see, and also, if you please, just one modest addition.'

'An addition?'

'Yes, let me explain. The illustrious gathering of gentleman that you were taken to the other evening was, as Sam has probably informed you by now, the monthly congress of the Cornhill Club or, to give it its full title, the Cornhill *Wig* Club - the origin of that name stemming from a long and venerable tradition reaching back, oh, it must be all of seventy years now, that requires each new member to contribute a quantity of the privy-hairs taken from the person of his mistress, or - er - wife, as the case may be.'

To which Matthew's jaw drops - also in sympathy with that of the noble Lord who has attempted to smile too broadly at the conclusion of his explanation and must therefore, after a moment's awkward silence, staring blankly into Matthew's eyes, lift his fingers to his chin to snap it shut again.

'I see,' Matthew responds at length, endeavouring to keep his composure. 'I assume this would explain the rather irregular colouring of the material itself in places?'

'Precisely, Wildish, precisely,' Lord Snatchal replies. 'In fact, the venerable object that you see before you is comprised, I'll have you know, of at least seventy or eighty different donors. Obviously the esteemed article itself, though possessed of no intrinsic value, is nonetheless of inestimable worth to those of us who sit at the core of the fraternity, the Knights of the Wig as we call ourselves, and which is why, as a rule, it is kept under lock and key in my personal curio cabinet just to the rear of the room here - or the reliquary as I rather wickedly call it - and only brought out on special ceremonial occasions, anniversaries and so on. Our former wig-maker sadly passed away last year, and so we are casting about for someone such as yourself who would not only have the requisite skills to continue to maintain the piece, but could also be relied upon to exercise discretion and secrecy. It would automatically confer upon you the privilege of becoming a probationary member of the club, by the way - or Companion of the Wig, as you would be called at the start. A great opportunity for furtherment, of course, especially for one so young.'

Matthew glances to Sam to gauge his reaction, only to be met with an encouraging nod as if to say: *'See - I told you so! Very important commission!'*

'Thank you, Sir,' Matthew replies. 'Although it is most unlikely that one should ever be so ungracious as to decline such an honour - may I inquire, though, just out of interest: what would be the implications if one did?'

For a moment, the two other men both stare at him in stunned silence, not just surprised but downright shocked it would appear. They glance at each other with confusion before directing their attention back towards Matthew once again.

'Well, young Wildish,' Lord Snatchal replies at length, sounding embarrassed, 'in the event of such a refusal, and what with us having already divulged the nature of the club and its emblem to you, an object venerated by so many distinguished and noble gentlemen from among the very highest echelons of His Majesty's government and Privy Council, we would just have to - er - well, ask a certain gentleman by the name of Webster to attend upon you.'

'Webster?'

'Bone Crusher Webster, to give him his full appellation,' Sam clarifies.

'Yes, that's right,' Lord Snatchal continues. 'You see, whenever we need any embarrassing inconveniences sorted ... well, Bone Crusher Webster is the man we call upon. He usually manages to discourage any indiscretions or anyone who would divulge our business or dishonour any of the ladies who have contributed to the wig. But failing such a warning being heeded ... well, Mr Webster also has a good few associates among the resurrection men.'

'The resurrection men?' Matthew echoes again, puzzled.

'Body snatchers,' Sam elucidates. 'As you know, the surgeons these days are increasingly desperate to get hold of bodies for dissection or anatomical study. It's still not legal to do so, of course, due to the conflict of science with religion - and this is where the resurrection men come in. A number of them operate out of the St Giles area of London. And when they're not skulking around church yards late at night with their shovels and crow bars, they are always willing to do business with people like our Mr Webster.'

'Yes, that's right,' Snatchal confirms. 'In other words, if all else fails, the person in question would just finish up as a skeletal specimen in a lecture room somewhere - all purely in the interests of medical science, naturally.'

'You might already have noticed the presence of Mr Webster,' Sam remarks, clearly enjoying the increasingly disturbing revelations that Matthew is being exposed to. 'He would have been keeping an eye on your informant, Mr McNiel, the other day.'

To which Matthew nods to the affirmative, recalling the disconcerting sight of the man in the courtyard that afternoon as McNiel departed, the one he had thought looked nothing so much as some deranged prizefighter. It could only have been him.

'Is Mr Webster also a member of the Cornhill Club?' Matthew inquires.

'Oh heavens, no!' Snatchal exclaims. 'Good man but - er - not the right sort, you understand. He just does a job for us once in a while, that's all.'

Returning his attentions to the wig, which he is now finally allowed to touch, Matthew draws up his chair towards the bureau and examines the piece more closely. The foundation is badly damaged, he concludes, in fact almost absent in places. The whole thing would probably need re-styling, and with a completely new base to save it from simply falling apart.

Lord Snatchal, meanwhile, and with an additional anxious glance at his fob watch, seems keen that the business be concluded as soon as possible. 'Well, Wildish, what's it to be: yes or no? Can we rely on your services?'

'Why yes, of course, Sir,' Matthew replies, looking up. 'It is an unusual commission, I'll grant you that; and the material somewhat unfamiliar to me - but I am sure I can adapt my working practices to accommodate your requirements, yes.'

'Excellent!' Snatchal declares. 'Oh, and by the way, the piece also has a special container that you may borrow,' he adds, going off to the rear of the room once again and returning with a smart rosewood box with elaborate brass filigree and a cushioned interior and which he places upon Matthew's lap. He then takes the precious wig itself from its mannequin head and lowers it with both hands into the container with a slow and gradual movement no less focused and full of reverence than if he were handling the Holy Grail itself.

'Much obliged, Sir,' Matthew says, looking down at the inert furry bundle, trying desperately to keep a straight face and aware of Sam's watchful eyes upon him all the while. Delivered of an irresistible curiosity all of a sudden, and thinking of Johanna for obvious reasons, he turns to Sam and asks: 'And I suppose in your time you would have contributed a little something to the piece, as well, Sam, eh?'

'Oh yes,' Sam replies. 'Though at a juncture *prior* to my marriage, in case you were wondering, Matt, and therefore the offering in question does not belong to my good wife. I'm sure you will be relieved to discover that.'

'Indeed.'

'Oh, that reminds me - before I forget,' Snatchal interrupts, still on his feet, 'here is that additional material I just mentioned a moment ago.'

At which a secret draw is released from the side of the bureau to reveal a small package wrapped in tissue paper. This is handed across to Matthew with the same veneration and care as afforded to the wig a moment earlier - the reason being not difficult to discern, for upon examination, it reveals itself to be a further substantial wad of red crinkly hair, coarse in texture as befits its hallowed anatomical origin. And this, too, once re-wrapped in its paper, is placed by Snatchal most carefully into the box ready for transit.

'Well, gentlemen - time to go seek out the ladies downstairs once again. Lunch is due to be served, I'll warrant. And afterwards, a little recreational activity. You're up for a good blow with Lady Snatchal, Matthew, I take it?'

'I beg your pardon, Sir?' Matthew gasps, hardly able to contain himself by this time.

'A good walk - *a good blow*, as we say in these parts. The Countess is particularly fond of a good blow in the afternoon - as am I.'

And with that tantalising assertion, and with the noble Lord himself leading the way along the labyrinth of passageways, they begin the long journey back down to the morning room, a substantial distance that takes all of ten minutes to traverse, with Matthew, his lips pressed tightly shut, his shoulders wobbling in repressed hilarity, carrying the box containing the precious cargo in both hands all the way.

It is shortly after lunch, when the afternoon 'blow' commences, much to Matthew's initial consternation, since he has not come equipped for a march through the countryside, especially this time of the year at the onset of autumn when the ground can be so muddy. In the event, he need not have worried, because it proves to be a pleasant enough diversion, at least at the start as they set off across the astonishing and beautiful park in which Lord Snatchal's mansion is situated, a pastoral landscape with clusters of oak and ash trees interspersed with broad expanses of rolling grassland populated with grazing sheep and, at every turn, a magnificent vista, including a wide, meandering lake with islands of willow trees. It even includes a maze located on a hill, an artificial mound surrounded by concentric circles of yew hedging and crowned with a mock castle turret with a swing inside - and where, apparently, one may even take tea. There is, Matthew feels, something quite wonderful about being placed amid such a piece of countryside, contrived and artificial as it might be, for it seems to him to be the ideal scenery for the conduct of civilised life - the fashions, the cut of the clothing of his companions at one moment seeming to resonate with those very shapes evident in the landscape itself - the tilt of a hat with the outcrop of woodland on a hillside; the triangular form of a woman's gown with the shape of a tree; the proportions of a gentleman's coat with that of a column or pediment of a building or temple. It is surely a wonderful time to be alive. And he wonders, despite all their foibles, faults and occasional pomposities, whether humans will ever be quite as close to their perfection as now.

It is also a rare treat to be in the company of Johanna, who today looks most elegant in her riding jacket and flared petticoats, so feminine and graceful in her deportment, and negotiating the rough terrain of the park and its roadways with the utmost ease. Her hair almost golden in the sunshine, is just visible from beneath the brim of her hat - this having but a narrow circumference and trimmed with a few early autumnal flowers and sprigs of heather, so eminently appropriate for the occasion and yet so very distinguished at the same time. Oh, he has tried to hide his feelings for her this weekend, and even to deny them from himself if possible, but to no avail. Every time he sees her, his heart races and he feels an unaccountable longing which he cannot explain - while all the while trying to reconcile such feelings with the loyalties and sense of fellowship he holds for Sam. There seems no remedy for this dizzy, discordant combination of emotions; and as he draws closer to her at one stage and as she turns and smiles in his direction, here beneath the bright and vigorous canopy of the autumn sky, it is an absolute joy to him.

And thus fired up with all the ardour of romantic desire, Matthew, growing more and more in confidence, becomes quite the orator, entertaining everyone as they go with some of his anecdotes and experiences with wigs - always a source of fascination and amusement, he feels. The famous story, for example, of the man who discovered a mouse in his wig after falling asleep at the theatre, or the one about the gentleman having his wig stolen in the street by a small boy hidden in a covered bread-trays usually carried aloft by bakers - or even the dramatic story of a wig being snatched from a man riding in a hackney carriage when the villain on horseback cut an opening in the back of the vehicle and grabbed the wig from behind. It all goes down a treat, and appears to entertain Lady Snatchal in particular who seems willing to burst into raucous laughter (that of the honking goose variety he had the pleasure of encountering at the opera) upon almost any anecdote or witty aside that Matthew is prepared to broadcast. As time goes on, even the slightest glance in her direction seems sufficient to make her grin wickedly and snortle, and even a disparaging glare from Johanna or a somewhat admonishing poke in the ribs from the knob of Sam's cane at one stage are not sufficient to discourage him. What fun!

Among this company of admiring companions, however, it is Lord Snatchal more than any other who remains steadfast in his determination to upstage him, constantly holding forth about the grandeur and magnificence of his estate which, he never ceases to remind everyone, is a proper working farm as well as a mansion, a genuine business concern - which makes it all sound as if he were perfectly familiar with the task of rolling up his sleeves each morning, herding the cattle, milking the cows and collecting every last one of the hen's eggs himself - an inference which annoys Matthew - annoys him almost as much as the fact that the old rake seems intent on monopolising the company of Johanna, with whom he is obviously quite smitten - so that there is a jauntiness in his step this afternoon, a demonstrative swinging of his cane as he goes, like the perfect gallant. Matthew is not impressed, for it seems that the man, upon some account or other, has never acquired the habit of caring for the interests of his listener or their propensity to become bored. A most unfortunate oversight, since none of what Lord Snatchal has to say is anywhere near as interesting as his own anecdotes on wigs. And even if Johanna wishes to be regaled with endless descriptions of sheep dipping or worming for parasitic infestations, the Countess, Lady Snatchal, is evidently equally as bored by the conversation as Matthew himself - and that won't do at all, he decides. And as he catches her eye once more, quite by chance, and without having to even utter a word this time, it elicits an immediate honk of merriment in response.

'Now look, this is really interesting,' Snatchal declares, commanding everyone's attention by pointing with his cane, 'down there one can just make out the village of Little Snatchalcombe on the left - that's not to be confused with Greater Snatchalcombe, by the way, which is not visible from here at all. That had to be moved - ruddy eyesore it was - but rather just there, in front of the church, see our herd of highland cattle there, in the field to the right, see! Magnificent beasts. I know every one by name. Because this is a proper working farm, you know - has been ever since the Reformation when all of this - er - changed hands, so to speak. The only difficulty about a place like this, of course, is pest control - the moles, the otters, the foxes, the badgers, the kites and the buzzards. Naturally, we shoot the lot of them whenever we can. Insects and ants, though, constitute a rather different kind of problem. We are at times quite plagued by the little devils, especially indoors. And of course, we cannot shoot them. For one thing, it would make a terrible mess of the carpets. I don't suppose anyone has any ideas about ants, by the way? What about you Wildish. You seem to know a lot about everything. What's good for ants?'

'Well, my Lord,' Matthew replies straight away, 'I do believe they are rather partial to a drop of treacle.'

To which Lady Snatchal roars, and almost falls over, laughing so hard and raucously that one might think an entire flock of deranged geese had flown overhead. 'Oh, Mr Wildish!' she splutters. 'A drop of treacle. How very funny!'

Her husband, however, appears unamused. Still determined not to be outdone, he embarks upon an elaborate description of the history and construction of the lake, and of how his great grandfather, the 4th Earl, had hewn it from the unforgiving soil himself - albeit with assistance from five hundred Irishmen with picks and shovels - at the time of the Glorious Revolution of 1688.

'Fascinating!' Sam declares, obsequious as ever, and to which Lord Snatchal puffs out his chest - a proud, self-satisfied smirk upon his face as he leads everybody away upon yet another stage of the walk - which Matthew can only hope is a circular route of some kind, because there seems to be no end to it - and even after having been on the go for over an hour they have, to his knowledge, not even turned around yet to retrace their steps.

In time they descend through yet more tracts of rolling

grassland until they find themselves on a lower path with wooded land up ahead and, to their side, a field of pigs, their dilapidated wooden shelters surrounded by the inevitable quagmire of mud and effluent. Consequently, the smell is not particularly edifying and the ladies hold handkerchiefs to their noses while Sam's attention turns to the occupation of fending off flies from the manifold recesses of his powdered wig.

'Ah look - there's some of my boys!' Snatchal declares in his usual haughty way. 'My apologies for the unfortunate smell, but it is a working farm, you know. And these are an excellent breed, the Berkshires. A bit on the feisty side, I'll grant you that, but meaty and with damn good loins. And they do, of course, make excellent sausages.'

'Really?' replies Matthew straight away. 'How on earth do you teach them to do that?'

To which Lady Snatchal breaks down completely, overcome by an outburst of such uncontrollable hilarity and of a honking of such alarming intensity that the others must rush to her aid, for she has collapsed into a heap - totally immobilised with her skirts all about her ears - and has to be raised and set upon her feet again before any kind of order can be restored. 'Gawd!' she declares, a terrible snotty sound at the back of her throat which requires a hearty slap or two from Johanna, none too delicately as it happens. 'I nearly went and had an embarrassing accident then. Oh Mr Wildish, how unlikely. Really! Teaching a pig to make sausages! Ha, ha!'

This latest piece of silliness, meanwhile, seems quite enough for Lord Snatchal and for Johanna, who both begin to stride away together, full of righteous indignation, leaving everyone else to bring up the rear, especially Lady Snatchal herself, who appears in time to be gaining interest in the various fruits and berries of the hedges along the margin of the path, stopping from time to time to pick these for herself and place them with care into the small wicker trug she carries under arm. How curious, Matthew thinks, as he looks back over his shoulder: there she is, a Countess of the realm, a woman so exorbitantly rich that even outdoors in the rough countryside she clothes herself in panniers and silk taffeta and who, if she so wished, could send out for an entire cartload of berries and blackcurrants - and yet for whom today the allure of gathering the gifts of nature for herself is just too great to resist: a basic instinct of acquisition that no amount of money can ever vitiate.

'Control yourself, Sir,' Sam admonishes him, his voice a furious sibilance, even though they are some distance from being overhead by any of the others. 'Remember what we told you the other day - Lord Snatchal can be a jealous man when crossed. And his dear wife back there has an unfortunate tendency to become overawed by fripperies.'

Sam seems very much on edge, Matthew feels - and the reason is not difficult to discern. For as they turn a bend in the path, it is to see once again the Earl himself in his extravagant embroidered coat, the curls of his periwig bouncing upon his shoulders as he continues upon his merry perambulations with Johanna - a sight which, perhaps recollecting the story of the old boy's antics at the County Fair, appears to unsettle Sam constantly. 'Don't go ruining all that you've gained this morning,' he adds struggling to restrain himself, 'the unique honour bestowed upon you.'

'Honour! What honour?' Matthew demands equally as petulant as he kicks through the carpet of early-fallen leaves, especially thick at this place on the pathway so close to the woods.

'Your visit this morning to Lord Snatchal's inner sanctum. The commission for the wig, Sir,' Sam reminds him.

'The wig! Well, the whole thing is most distasteful, if you want my opinion. The last thing I was expecting from your campaign of *social advancement* was to be working on a load of seventy-year old muff clippings.'

'The item you are referring to, may I remind you,' Sam argues, looking down his nose in his most sententious manner, 'is a highly revered emblem, representative of the symbolic bonding among men of quality that holds society together - the Brotherhood, the Club, the process of government and patronage. You should be proud, honoured by the invitation to become associated with it.'

'Oh, no doubt I would,' Matthew protests, 'if only I did not feel as if I were selling my soul to the Devil in the process. And anyway, I hardly had much choice, did I - not with the prospect of a visit from your Bone Crusher Webster as an alternative. Which reminds me, I have been meaning to ask you: these people, I take it they do know whose side I am on?'

'Sorry – I don't understand?'

'Webster - I assume he is aware that I am working for the government, not just some covert Jacobite?'

'Well ...' Sam begins, not altogether convincingly, 'I expect so.'

'*You expect so!* What the hell does that mean? Tell him, Sam, if you please. If it is within your power, make sure my position is clear.'

'Well, I'll do my best. You're right enough to be concerned, though. You wouldn't want to get on the wrong side of that brute. Huh! All your fancy swordsmanship, all your cunning and guile would be useless in the face of such a powerful beast.'

'Thank you,' Matthew responds, hardly pacified. 'That is very reassuring, I must say.'

'Oh, don't go worrying so much!' Sam exclaims. 'You are to become a Companion of the Wig now, remember? It bestows immense protection. Just tow the line, Matt. Play the game and you'll be all right. And anyway, think of where it could all lead.'

'I do - that's what worries me.'

In time, as is normal when any party go for a walk of such duration, the order of procession changes; conversations come and go, and pairings are dissolved and re-established with others, and so it comes to pass that this afternoon, upon their continued hike through the parklands of Snatchalcombe House, Matthew next finds himself walking in the company of Lady Snatchal - with Sam now having joined the others up ahead, his hand resting on the hilt of his sword as he goes, the perfect squire glancing this way and that, as if the very Jacobite army itself might have already traversed the hundreds of miles from Scotland and be lurking in the undergrowth.

'A pleasant afternoon, Lady Snatchal,' Matthew observes, filling a moment of awkward silence in which he is aware of her gazing up intently to his face as she walks at his side.

'It has been a right amusing and entertaining one, as well, Mister Wildish, thanks to you,' she observes. 'I trust that you are settling in nicely, by the way, and that everything is to your satisfaction?' she adds, her voice slightly agitated, he feels, perhaps due to the exertion. She often has a curious way about her of preceding her words with a sharp, audible intake of breath, like a sigh in reverse; and this is most evident at the present time.

'Oh yes, thank you,' he replies. 'I believe your home to be one of the finest Palladian mansions I have seen in all of Europe. The architect should be congratulated.'

'Mr Vanbrugh, yes, with modifications lately by Mr Kent. The

Snatchals have always employed the very best. The only difficulty is there sometimes seems rather a lot of it to get around - a lot of rooms. We do have three hundred, or thereabouts.'

'Or *thereabouts?*' he echoes with polite curiosity as they continue walking at a more leisurely pace.

'Nobody can ever agree on how many. The architect's original plans are of no use, because everything's been altered so much over the years. We did have a proper go at counting all the rooms once - just for a bit of fun when all the family were together one weekend. But we all reached different conclusions. It takes an entire day to do the tour of all the building. And no one can remain sober enough for that length of time to complete the count. Even for those of us who have been coming here, on and off, for years, it is all one can do to prevent oneself becoming lost inside without a map of some kind. How it must be perceived by guests I can only shudder to think - which is why, as you know, we had a trail of coloured sand laid on the floor all the way to your chamber yesterday evening so that you could accomplish your return journey to us in the dinning room in good time.'

'Yes indeed,' he confirms, remembering the sight of the butler going before him yesterday with a small sackful of sparkling, almost scarlet sand which he had sprinkled on the floorboards all the way up to his room.

'It's jolly handy, isn't it!' she declares with a vivacious smile. 'Your trail won't be swept away until after your departure, so don't worry. We have lots of different coloured sands. They come all the way from the Isle of Wight. And of course it enables me to locate the rooms of our guests myself, should I need to speak with anyone - for example, in the night.'

'In the night?'

'Oh, yes. It's quite likely, if I am unable to sleep, that I will leave my bedchamber and wander. It has been that way especially since my unfortunate riding accident, the fall I had.'

'I see.'

'Do you enjoy a satisfying night, as a rule, Matthew - I may call you Matthew, mightn't I? - or are you inclined to lie awake, like I do ... fiddling about?'

'I usually have no difficulty sleeping.'

'No, neither does Cornelius,' she remarks a little disconsolately, Matthew thinks, and still breathless, her voice.

Perhaps, he thinks, it is due to her clothing. Making no concessions to the great outdoors, the edges of her silk gown are laced tightly together above the most elaborate of stomachers, a tapered bodice embroidered with traces of silver. Remarkable. And surely very heavy for her.

All seems well for a time, as the trio ahead vanish around a bend in the path, and at which Lady Snatchal places her hand upon his arm and takes a step towards the wooded area to her side. 'Matthew, I wonder if you might give me a helping hand. I'd like to pick some of them there mushrooms - look, over here.'

And before he can do much to prevent it, for she does not let go of his sleeve, he finds himself assisting her up into the woods. She is determined to go, even though the bulk of her gown is not at all easy for her to negotiate upon the terrain of twigs and brambles, and he becomes anxious that she might stumble. Numerous varieties of mushroom are to be found here, however, and she seems intent on examining them.

'I love the shape of some of these,' she declares, stooping to pick what looks to be a particularly large example of a Panther Cap.

'I believe you would be ill-advised to sample that one, Madam,' Matthew states with a note of urgency, guiding her away to a more leafy area, 'since it is known to be deadly poisonous.'

'Is that a fact?' she responds, though with an untypical softness to her voice, not relinquishing the mushroom but rather caressing the stem and then the distinctly phallic head of it with finger and thumb and then actually raising it to her lips as if daring him as she gazes up into his eyes. 'It isn't half-pretty, though, don't you think - the shape? One rather wants to … well, to pop it into one's mouth. What a shame it's not allowed.'

'Indeed, it would probably mean death within the space of a few agonising minutes,' Matthew insists. 'Do not touch it even with your lips, Madam, I beg you.'

'Dorothea - you must call me Dorothea, please,' she insists, crouching and, still clutching at his sleeve, leaning over to reach more mushrooms. 'Or even *Dottie,* if you wish. My closest friends call me Dottie, because that's exactly what I am sometimes - totally dotty! I'm sure I shall finish my days locked away in some frightful attic. Matthew, I must tell you, how unimaginably difficult it has been walking behind you all afternoon watching that heavenly little bottom of yours in your buckskin breeches. The tails of your coat separate and fall away as you walk - did you know that? - and reveal glimpses of your cheeks constantly. How on earth do you manage to get yourself into something so tight?'

'Madam, I do not think you should be speaking ...'

'I shall!' she interrupts, raising her eyes to look directly at him once more. 'We are alone, Matthew, and no one can hear us or see us. What I have just described has been the most exquisite torment to me this afternoon, so much so that I must own that I am not inclined to leave here or to abandon this place without being brought to completion, if you would so honour me.'

'No I couldn't possibly,' he says.

'Why not?'

'Oh, it's ... it's to do with the wig,' he answers, the very image of Bone Crusher Webster springing most unpleasantly to mind.

'The wig! What bloody wig?' she demands, suddenly far less affectionate.

'Oh, you would not be familiar with the matter, your Ladyship. But there are certain things, certain traditions among men of principle that should not be transgressed and ...'

'Attend me, Sir,' she interrupts, deadly serious, one hand grasping his, the other with the fatal mushroom raised to her mouth. And he suddenly realises they are no longer standing or even crouching but have somehow slipped down into a seated position opposite each other among the softest bed of dried leaves. 'Lend me your hand for but a few moments, Matthew,' she insists, already pulling him towards her - while somehow at the same time clasping the folds of her petticoats and raising them. 'My needs, I assure you, are at such a point of fever pitch that they will be swiftly extinguished. Comfort me now, Matthew, comfort me now in my distress, and without delay.'

'Distress, my Lady?'

'Indeed, the distress of my craving and unrequited passion - here, touch me where I weep not from grief or sadness but rather from longing and desire. Do it Matthew - do it now, or I shall swallow this mushroom. I shall gobble it up and die before your eyes.'

And with no time for him to protest any further, the dreaded object is already between her lips, her eyes staring defiantly at him, and burning so brightly with passion that he finds himself rising to the occasion despite all his own misgivings, ready in fact to oblige to a measure even greater than her modest request. But then suddenly there comes a loud snapping sound - a twig breaking on the forest floor perhaps, yet so very pronounced in the silence of the afternoon that it is almost like a musket shot, and upon which Matthew is on his feet instantly - startled, as is she, staring up through the undergrowth to the ridge of trees above.

'Look what's that up there on the bank? Is that a boy or something?' she cries, pointing towards a shaft of light, all golden and radiant, breaking at just that moment between the trees.

'A boy!' Matthew exclaims, shielding his eyes. 'I can't see anything.'

But Lady Snatchal, with astonishing speed and dexterity, has already scrambled back down onto the path by this time - restoring the jumble of her dress to a more dignified shape and appearing most indignant over the possibility that someone might have been spying on them.

'Come Matthew, we should join the others, quickly,' she says, still picking out a few twigs and leaves from the flounces of her hem. Her voice sounds agitated, even frightened.

'No, no - wait, Madam,' he calls back to her, already some way up the hill, troubled by the fact that it had been such a particularly loud and unusual noise. 'If you will excuse me for just a moment, Madam, I should like to investigate. I shall return within seconds, I assure you.'

'Well, I'm not waiting, anymore. I'm off,' she announces, and begins walking. He sees glimpses of her between the trees, hoisting up her petticoats and hurrying along the path below, her trugful of berries and mushrooms long since abandoned or lost in the confusion. 'Pray, do not tarry long,' he hears her call, as if displeased with him. And then, all at once, he finds himself alone. For a moment, it is most quiet, eerily so - until a breeze springs up and the leaves begin to swirl about him as he climbs higher, upwards through a thicket of holly bushes and oak trees to a ridge where much taller beeches are situated. And then suddenly, looking up once too many times, he loses his footing and tumbles forwards head over heels, plunging down into a broad, deep hollow, sliding the last couple of feet on his backside and where, for good measure, he also bumps his head on an overhanging branch. Breathless for a moment he simply lies there looking up through the canopy of trees, listening to the wind, watching the clouds - until all of a sudden he realises that something has changed, that everything is so very different and that the winds are possessed of a unique and special sound, autumnal winds, in fact - for with the leaves turning brittle, drying upon their branches, the sound is of a rough, abrasive variety, almost a roar: so very different, for example, to the soft breezes on fresh, verdant foliage that would occur in spring. Every autumn he has ever known in his twenty-seven years returns to him abruptly with that sound, a sound never acknowledged until now, and the comprehension of it is exhilarating. And then the sound is joined by others, louder - distant, slightly menacing sounds, like the drums of a marching army - though he sensibly concludes that it is more likely only thunder. But then in a strange kind of way it also reminds him of orchestral percussion, joined to the most sonorous, foreboding chords - a song of the season's dying - of summer yielding to autumn, the season of change and revolution, sweeping all the old order away. And then silence ...

A small boy, a familiar face, since it is the link-boy from London, is standing by his side and holding a looking glass, a round one with a brass handle like his valet has back home. 'Here you are Sir,' he says, cheerful as ever. 'No bones broken. Just a bit untidy.'

'What are *you* doing here?' Matthew demands, sitting up and examining his own by-now dishevelled appearance in the glass, the black ribbon at the back of his hair having almost come undone, and his face besmirched with mud. 'I thought you lived in London?' he continues, sitting up and beginning the task of re-tying his hair, picking out the odd stray leaf or twig as he does so.

'London's a filthy place, Sir,' the boy states in his usual mystifying way.

'Why,' Matthew asks himself with irritation, 'does this child never reply to a question properly, but instead always responds with something totally unconnected, hardly ever an answer at all.'

'You must tell me why you have not yet allowed me to reimburse you for all your trouble?' Matthew asks, and pray do me the honour this time of answering my question. Why always run off before I can open my purse? Do you have some kind of eccentric millionaire for a father or what?'

'My father? Oh, that's a good one, Sir. Ha, ha! Very funny,' he replies.

But then, and it is most disturbing, as Matthew continues to attend to his appearance in the glass, he becomes aware that there are other people behind him, he can see them reflected in the glass, reclining on the banks of the hollow, and when he turns his head he beholds a whole group of young soldiers - all in magnificent scarlet and braided uniforms, all laid out on the ground, motionless, and all in the most peculiar positions, some with their arms flung out, others with their faces set in stony expressions, their eyes staring out into space - their fabulous tunics with their shiny brass buttons all undone and disordered, their black tricorn hats all at odd positions on their heads, or else upon the ground nearby - and all such fair and beautiful young men. So very young! And then as he looks more closely he discovers to his horror that they are all damaged, all casualties of some dreadful battle that has taken place. Impossible surely - not here in the peaceful county of Surrey adjacent to a great country house. Yet here they are, so stark and resplendent, their bright liveries set amid all the gold and bronze of the leaves and bracken. He sees their muskets, some with bayonets fixed, sees the powder flasks on their belts. And then he notices that one has a leg missing, another an arm. And many have blood, dried brown blood upon their hands and faces too, some with terrible, disfiguring wounds.

'That's war, Sir,' the boy's voice comes, softly now, from behind him. 'That's what war looks like.'

To which Matthew, still stunned, the tears welling up in his eyes turns to speak to him, but no one is there. The boy has gone, and then he discovers to his confusion that he is flat on his back again and staring up yet again into that majestic canopy of treetops and clouds above - vast towering clouds racing along in the company of a flock of noisy jackdaws and crows, so black against the sky. Quickly, with a sudden sense of agitation, he leaps to his feet, looks around - but still there is no one; no soldiers, no boy, nothing but the trees and the dappled sunshine and the beautiful golden autumn leaves at his feet.

'*Matthew! What ho! Matthew!*' He hears his companions calling, voices borne upon the breeze from some directionless place, and very far away.

He should answer them, he knows. But, not wishing to give the impression of being lost, he resists the temptation to shout back and respond right away. Instead, he brushes himself down and begins to climb, trying to scramble out of the hollow. 'It'll be easy enough to track them down now,' he tells himself, hearing the cries yet again. 'The last time I saw them they had all just gone around a bend in the path - yes, that's it - a bend to the right hand side. I just need to wander down here, and I will be upon them. I have no need to call out and make myself sound foolish.'

Yet when he does reach the bottom of the bank, there is no path, only an impenetrable thicket of bushes. Worse, the early sunset of autumn is already approaching, the light fading all the while. He resolves, therefore to retrace his steps, to climb right back and then down again to the original place where he had been propositioned by Lady Snatchal. This being accomplished, and having regained the pathway again after another fifteen minutes, he realises to his despair that it is in fact an entirely different path he has landed upon - a more formal, road-like structure made for wagons or carriages. The sky is darkening and becoming tempestuous, with a crescent moon peeping through at moments towards the West - a sight which at least provides him with some sense of direction. Following the road, therefore, with renewed confidence, he eventually comes to the Gate Lodge and the long, long drive leading to the house itself, which can be seen now in the distance, many of its windows already lit from within. Clearly everyone would be home inside by this time and wondering where on earth he had gotten to - perhaps talking about him in various tones of anxiety or disapproval. The greatest discourtesy, on his part, though, even worse than abandoning the party on their walk, is that he might now be too late to dress for dinner. Feeling an utter fool, he can only hope and pray they will not be too angry.

# SWEET AIRS AND BREATH
# OF NIGHT

'I shouldn't say anything if I were you, Matt,' Sam tells him. 'Don't breathe a word.' And even when spoken as a whisper, his voice echoes back loudly from the marble floor of the hall as he motions Matthew towards the dining room.

'Is Johanna upset?' Matthew asks, disappointed that he will not be permitted to speak in palliation of his offence, and noticing, too, as they approach the tall double doors, that the others are already at table.

'Upset! She is furious,' Sam answers, looking impressive this evening in his best embroidered waistcoat and making Matthew, who has hardly had time to wash the mud from his hands, let-alone dress for dinner, feel all the more dowdy. 'She's already emotional anyway because she's missing the children and her little pug, as well, back home. But you, Sir ... you have topped it all and insulted everyone today by running off like that.'

'No, that's not what happened, Sam,' Matthew insists, tarrying with his friend at the doorway and tugging at his sleeve. 'Listen, I need to explain ...'

'Don't explain. We haven't time. Johanna does not, she says, wish to converse with you at all. So, take it from me, your best course of action would be to keep your own counsel this evening. With a bit of luck, then, the whole thing might blow over. Lady Snatchal has told us everything, anyway.'

'She has?'

'Yes, that you suddenly took it upon yourself to go off on your own and said you wanted to explore the woods. What on earth was that all about! Why, Sir, were you so bored in our company that you had to engineer your escape from us? We thought you were never going to return. Johanna feels you have insulted our hosts and embarrassed us into the bargain. Not only that, but there has

been a lot of bad news coming in during the course of the day
pertaining to the conflict in Scotland, and Lord Snatchal is most
annoyed. A disastrous battle at a place called Prestonpans.'

'Prestonpans?'

'Yes,' says Sam, responding to Matthew's vacant stare, 'I
know, I haven't heard of it either, but apparently it's somewhere up
there on the east coast of Scotland. Our army under General Wade
has been badly mauled; the rebels victorious and continuing their
advance south, their sights set on Edinburgh and the north of
England. Therefore, do not, I implore you, jest any further with our
hosts this evening - or with anybody, for that matter. Try to
maintain a sense of decorum, and refrain from any bad language.
Remember these are people of quality here, people of taste and
refinement. Understand?'

Grudgingly, feeling like a mischievous schoolboy being told off
by the prefect, Matthew nods his acquiescence, saddened that he
should have earned the wroth of Sam, one of the few male friends
within his social sphere, and all the more precious because of that -
and now so alienated and angered that he even attributes faults to
Matthew's character that do not even belong to it - for he rarely if
ever resorts to bad language or swearing. How unfair! The worst of
it is he still feels utterly devastated that he has offended Johanna.
How can he ever explain to her the truth - *how,* if she has no
intention of speaking to him? It seems that whatever he attempts to
say this evening by way of trying to redeem himself is going to fall
on deaf ears. And he feels the torment of it tearing him apart,
almost tearfully so, as he takes his seat at the enormous dining
table, her face, opposite him, like those of everyone else,
unresponsive, ignoring him completely, not even deigning to
glance his way through the forest of candle sticks, dishes, salts and
tureens that stand between them, their myriad reflections dancing in
the candlelight - and creating thereby, in the turbulent moisture of
his eyesight, a most chaotic picture.

'What a room is this!' he thinks as he forces some measure of
self-control and begins to look around. So vast - from the marble
floor with its occasional Turkish carpet of vast dimensions, to the
towering chimneypiece, all colonnaded and veneered, and with a
distinguished coat of arms with motifs of grapes and cornucopia
carved into it - while high above, upon the lavishly plastered and
stucco ceiling, flecked with gold leaf, multitudes of painted angels

and putti hover in attendance - keeping watchful eye on the diners and their feasting. Breath-taking. Why, even amid the grandeur of St James's Palace, the King himself would not be living as handsomely, Matthew reflects.

Just one additional guest is included among the party this evening, and to whom Matthew is cordially introduced: a young lady by the name of Miss Wilcox. She has, he gathers, the distinction of being the niece of Lord Snatchal - no doubt brought in for his benefit and to make up the numbers. But they needn't have troubled themselves. He is in no mood to become the subject of any match-making this evening, not least with this poor specimen, who being not only plain of face - though he could forgive anyone that - is also one of such a weak and unspirited constitution as to be almost without any breath of life. Clad in an unbecoming sacque gown, the poor unfortunate young lady seems to be entirely without shoulders, and has instead a neck which finishes at the top of two long, spindly arms that appear to have never engaged in anything more rigorous than the fluttering of a fan - and thereby presenting about as much allure, in Matthew's estimation at any rate, as a garden obelisk. Much of her conversation revolves around the subject of babies. Had they scoured the entire kingdom from top to bottom in search of a more unsuitable companion, they could hardly have surpassed Miss Wilcox. Thank heavens she has been placed away from him at table, she being seated next to her uncle on the one hand and Johanna on the other - which at least affords him some protection. The overall conversation, however, is far from uplifting - in fact downright gloomy with all the talk of the rebel invasion taking centre stage.

'I don't understand,' Miss Wilcox grizzles plaintively after finishing her turtle soup, 'what is it that they want from us, all these horrid people in Scotland?'

'The Jacobites, you mean, my dear?' Lord Snatchal responds. 'Why, a change of government, a different king,' he explains.

The Countess, meanwhile, at the head of the table, signals towards the butler that he might come forth to reveal the main course - which appears to be the remains of something reared not long ago on the working farm and which has already arrived on its lengthy journey from the kitchens in an array of gleaming tureens, all very steamy and savoury looking.

'But what's wrong with the one we already have, with King George?' Miss Wilcox inquires, still mystified, raising a napkin to her lips as she observes the carving of the meat and all its rivulets of bloody juices with some obvious consternation. 'And why do they call themselves Jacobites, anyway, uncle Cornelius? What does that mean?'

'From *Jacobus*, the Latin for James, my dear,' Lord Snatchal continues to explain, and most patiently, 'that being the name of the last English king of the Stuart line before we booted the lot of them out in the last century for going all Popish on us. Among the Catholic countries overseas, though, they are still considered to hold the legitimate succession to the British throne, and thus our present incumbent, King George, is considered a usurper. It is James's grandson - Charles, the Bonny Prince as they call him - who is at this very moment leading the Jacobites south, setting our own people against us and gaining support all the while. Most disconcerting. We don't want to be ruled by the Church of Rome in this country, my dear. We prefer business instead, trade and commerce.'

'Oh, yes, that does sound so much more sensible,' Miss Wilcox agrees as Lord Snatchal, responding to his inveterate weakness rises and disappears for a moment behind a tall, embroidered commode screen, strategically positioned towards a far corner of the room.

The sound of someone availing himself of a chamber pot is heard, tinkling merrily in the background as everyone clears their throats in modest embarrassment, for the vast echoing expanse of the dining room does indeed seem exceptionally quiet at just that moment, apart from the tinkling.

'*Right and Might* will surely prevail,' Sam observes, endeavouring to fill the silence.

'They say that the King's son, the Duke of Cumberland, will be recalled from duties in Flanders,' Lady Snatchal adds - attired this evening in the most opulent of blue damask trimmed with black - her stomacher and stays so tightly laced as to have thrust her bosom upwards to a place almost beneath her chin - a most distracting cleavage presenting itself, therefore - while she, fully aware of the effect herself, invariably manages to catch Matthew's eye whenever his gaze drifts inadvertently towards it. 'He will take over from old Wade,' she adds, looking down her nose at him with disdain. 'The Duke is an excellent general. A man who knows when to act decisively. A man who knows when to take his chances.'

'He does indeed,' her husband concurs, emerging from behind his screen of finest *Chinoiserie* as would the emperor of China himself, before returning to table. 'And even though he has never actually won a battle, I do understand that he has already proved his metal against the French in Flanders simply by ... by having a presence. Yes, *a presence*. Trouble is, even if we do get him back, he can't do miracles, y'know. And if the numbers against us are significant, which they could well be with the addition of French reinforcements, then it will be a damn close run thing. In any dispute, those who have the least justice on their side are invariably the ones who are the most belligerent at first, the most passionate, if only to compensate for their absence of reason. This is what we are facing at present. There could be terrible carnage, therefore - towns and villages the length and breadth of the country overwhelmed, the land devastated by marching armies; ruined harvests; disease; pestilence and even starvation on a massive scale among the common people - why it just doesn't bear thinking about.'

'Oh, how horrid!' Miss Wilcox declares, 'It seems so unfair. And my friend in Cheltenham is going to have a baby!'

A lingering silence ensues, followed by a further ripple of embarrassed coughing.

'Yes, quite, quite, my dear,' the Earl concurs at length, dabbing his mouth with a napkin, the better to readjust his dropped jaw. 'A most challenging time to be having babies for anyone in Cheltenham, yes.'

Everyone drinks up, and glasses are re-filled almost immediately as they all endeavour to put a brave face on things, until suddenly Matthew discovers that the others are staring at him, most likely, he suspects, because there are tears in his eyes, or at least the start of them. It is Sam who is compelled to speak first: 'I say, Matthew, old chap - what on earth's the matter?' he asks, a hand upon his sleeve.

'I am well enough, Sam, do not fret,' he responds, trying his best not to start blubbering. But the prospect of war, especially after his peculiar experiences in the woods this afternoon, is most dreadful to contemplate. 'A foolish moment of emotion. I am sorry.

War is a terrible thing.'

Johanna looks at him, also, though still with an all too obvious disapproval - perhaps even more so now that he seems intent on compounding his earlier faults by making a complete spectacle of himself at the dinner table. A moment later, however, and albeit grudgingly, her eyes do become a little kinder, a little less censorial. How very lovely she looks, he cannot help thinking as he dares to meet her eyes properly for the first time this evening, so elegant in her pale satin dress, her blond hair so neatly braided and coiled, and with a garland of autumnal flowers secured upon her shoulder, as well. Will she find it in her heart to forgive him? He can only hope so.

'I say, don't take it so hard, Matt!' Sam pipes up again, trying to lift his friend's spirits, as he allows him to take his handkerchief, an item of finest silk and lace, and to blow his nose several times loudly into it.

'Yes, do cheer up, Mr Wildish!' Lady Snatchal declares, speaking directly to him and expressing her disapproval in no uncertain terms. 'The worst of our misgivings are so often without foundation, would you not agree?'

Lord Snatchal also endeavours to make light of it: 'Well, at any rate, ladies and gentleman, I do hope you are enjoying our modest repast this evening,' he says with good cheer, his normally long, goatish face lifting at last as he signals that a nearby selection of puddings and cakes should be unveiled.

'The roast beef was particularly delicious, Sir,' Sam concludes with an appreciative dab of the napkin to his lips, while declining with an irritable wave of the hand to take back the wet rag that Matthew proffers him after blowing his nose yet again.'

'Yes - that was old Angus,' Snatchal remarks.

'Angus?'

'Yes, you know, one of my Highland cattle. Don't know whether he was a Jacobite or not - but he was jolly tasty, all the same, what! You see, ladies and gentlemen, we do endeavour here at Snatchalcombe to vie with the royal table for quality, even if not always for quantity, if you catch my drift. Fond of his grub, eh, the King.'

'He does have a prodigious appetite, or so I hear,' Sam remarks with laughter.

'And a girth to match, I understand,' Johanna ventures to

suggest, a little wickedly, too.

'And with his return this summer, rumour has it, a new cargo of German ladies of the largest size, shipped over with him from Herrenhausen,' Lord Snatchal adds, happy for the conversation to become even more irreverent. 'Why, I should think the resources of half the nation will be required to feed them all soon, God bless them.'

'Oh, don't talk to me about the King!' Lady Snatchal exclaims with a glance up to heaven as if in exasperation as she drains the last drop of claret from her glass. 'Really, I mean he is such a hopeless flirt. He tries it on with everybody - and always in that ridiculous German accent of his which he has never quite got rid of. I mean, just the other evening at the Palace I was sat by him at the table after supper, and he goes leaning over to one side and whispers to me: "Dottie, how vood you like to pop outside and sample a piece of zer German sausage?" Well, really! Can you imagine! So uncouth.'

'Goodness! What did you say to him?' Johanna demands, clearly horrified. 'I hope you impressed upon him that you were a lady.'

'I did, Johanna - don't you worry! "Oh no, Your Majesty," I said, "not fucking likely. You should look to have better control over your baser inclinations," I said. Well, he soon turned his roving eye elsewhere after that. But really - what can one say to such coarse behaviour? Heaven only knows what would become of the nation if it were not for men like my dear Cornelius here to advise on things and maintain standards.'

'I suppose his heart is in the right place, though,' observes Sam, amused.

'And, more important, his politics,' Snatchal adds, clearly pleased with his wife's approbation and also, perhaps more covertly, with the King's abiding interest in her, as well.

'Is it true, uncle,' Miss Wilcox suddenly inquires with a complete departure from the present tone of the conversation, 'is there really going to be a nasty war?'

Embarrassed silence descends once more.

'That's right, my dear,' Snatchal replies at length and still with monumental fortitude. 'Hostilities have already commenced, my dear, if you care to recall our discussion of a moment ago?'

'Oh, yes, that's right. I'd forgotten already. Silly me!'

Endeavouring to demonstrate some sympathy, Johanna turns to the young woman at her side in a bid to draw her out. 'Do you enjoy reading, Miss Wilcox?' she asks.

'Reading?' the young woman echoes awkwardly. 'What do you mean, *books?*'

'Yes.'

'Oh, I don't think so ... no,' she replies, shaking her head after careful consideration, her nose crinkling up somewhat as if exposed to an unpleasant stench.

'What, not at all?'

'No. Not really,' she confirms with a further crinkle, thereby drawing a line under that particular topic of conversation.

'Well young lady, not to worry! Lord Snatchal declares, filling the embarrassing silence with a kindly chuckle as he finishes his pudding. 'We have a most entertaining and educational after-dinner treat awaiting you this evening - something that will require no books or reading of any kind.'

'Oh, music - wonderful!' Johanna exclaims.

'No, not music, either,' Snatchal asserts, enjoying the suspense, 'or even cards. No, no, I have arranged for your delectation this evening a practical scientific demonstration - by way of the very latest fashionable apparatus as seen within the hallowed walls of the Royal Society, no less, and which will be performed for us presently in our very own drawing room. The fellow we've hired has already arrived, I believe.'

It is an announcement which, amid a buzz of excitement and loud rustle of taffeta petticoats, provides the women with a good excuse to be up and away, led by Lady Snatchal, eager to 'reconnoitre the man's apparatus in advance,' as she says, and thus leaving the gentlemen alone to savour a welcome glass of brandy. Lord Snatchal, meanwhile, taking up a pipe, and filling it with tobacco, is soon puffing away like a chimney. Leaning back in his great, straight-backed chair, more like a throne, he stares into space for a minute or two before speaking.

'Actually, gentlemen, I regret to inform you that the very latest news from the North is far more grave than I was letting-on earlier,' he says.

'Really?' says Sam, paying heed, and with an obvious sincerity this time, as the remote noises of giggling and joyous conversation waft in from time to time from the ladies in the adjoining room -

leaving Matthew under no misapprehension as to where he would rather be.

'Yes. The truth is, Scotland and the borders are completely lost to us already. Availing themselves of the excellent road networks which we built some years ago for the movement of our own troops, the rebels have been able to garrison just about every major town and city north of the border - including already the capital Edinburgh, along with Perth and Aberdeen. All have fallen, and all at break-neck speed. It's our own fault, gentlemen. General Wade, after the first uprising, insisted on building these roads, and now they have been used by our enemies. They are dancing in the streets of Edinburgh, they say. And as the troops march with ease from place to place, everywhere the refrain is the same: *"If you'd seen these roads before they were made, you'd lift up your hands and praise general Wade!"* What is especially irksome is there is every chance now, encouraged by their victory at Prestonpans, that the French are about to join, supplying heavy ordnance and men at arms. Oh, we are doing our best to blockade the east coast to prevent any shipments. But it is a formidable area to cover. The odds have to be high that the French ships will get through eventually. And if they take it into their heads to launch a full-scale invasion from across The Channel, as they attempted last year, then I'm afraid our forces, fighting on two fronts, will prove woefully inadequate - with not much we can do to stop a complete rout.'

'I suppose we should sell any stock that we have?' Sam ponders aloud.

'Yes, sell. Sell now. Particularly anything connected with property or overseas trade. Once the news is out that London is in their sights, the royal court will probably be off, anyway - into exile. What concerns me most, though, is what will happen once the common herd get hold of the truth. There will be pandemonium. The City will panic and there could be a run on the banks which will collapse the economy. Damn it! You see, that's what happens in a society where information can be got by anyone who can read a newspaper - or have one read to them. Bad show, if you ask me. News is a highly inflammatory commodity, gentlemen. News makes the multitude far too familiar with the actions of their betters, and then they start taking it into their heads that they can act on it and change things. Most unseemly. Oh, what fools they are making of us! I'm not worried over a few French soldiers. We have always managed to deal with them in combat. But these Highland clans, these men who survive the coldest winters up there in the mountains wearing nothing but woollen skirts, these men have got balls, gentlemen - balls of fire. They are strong and muscular, with big hairy faces and sharp teeth. There are thousands of them, maybe tens of thousands already gathered to the Bonnie Prince's standard. They train themselves not as we do with marching and parade ground discipline, but by lifting huge tree trunks and tossing them around at one another - and all these feats of prowess are achieved, moreover, solely on a diet of porridge oats. What they would be like should they ever have access to proper nutrition one can only shudder to think. In the field, meanwhile, they employ hardly any formal dispositions or tactics of any kind - but instead rely on a terrifying charge when they go into battle, straight into enemy lines, followed by fierce and merciless hand-to-hand fighting. Why, they say that the blood-curdling cry they emit as they close on their enemy is enough to put the fear of God up even the most disciplined of soldiers - men who so-often just break ranks and run for their lives upon the hearing of it. Muskets, cannon, bayonets are as nothing to them. They know no fear, and when they strike it is with a huge broadsword, the claymore, that can cleave a man in twain from top to toe - and then they roar like lions and skewer their victims heads on their own pikes. Why even the dagger that they carry, the dirk, as they call it, and which they keep attached to their sleeves, is of a length to vie with some of our swords. And what have we to offer in return? Why the muddled and misplaced heroism of poor old General Wade - even older than me, gentlemen, and I fear that he and his men are simply not likely to be measuring up, in any sense, to the vigour of these tartan savages.'

'Good heavens! Is there really nothing we can do?' Matthew asks, speaking really for the first time this evening and hoping that by now the liberal quantities of wine that he and the others have already consumed will have smoothed the way to at least some manner of reconciliation.

'No, nothing at all,' Lord Snatchal replies shaking his head disconsolately - not unless we can come up with a few more men like Bone Crusher Webster, that is. Ha! No, our only realistic hope lies with the Duke of Cumberland. So come, fill your glasses gentlemen! Let us pray for his speedy return.'

'Amen to that,' says Sam, puffing out his cheeks at the prospect of conflict on a scale no one had really wished to acknowledge or contemplate until now, while the prowess of Bone Crusher Webster, a man who could stand up to a hoard of ravening Highlanders thus described, continues to scale towards ever more dizzying and terrifying heights in Matthew's vivid imagination should, heaven forbid, he ever incur his wrath.

'I do wonder, though,' Matthew ventures to suggest after a moment's hesitation, emboldened by his moderate reception a moment ago, 'whether it really might just be better at the end of the day to negotiate - I mean, to make an accommodation with the enemy? As you know, I have encountered a number of sympathisers from the North over these past several months, and they do all seem to be decent and reasonable enough men. I mean, Catholic, Protestant, whatever - are we really all so very different beneath the surface?'

But this is met only by silence.

'Don't be so bloody naïve, Matt!' Sam finally blusters, and clearly offended. 'Oh yes, they make a show of decency now - when they're the underdogs. But look at how they behave when they have the whip hand. Overseas, the Church and State rule the roost by instilling fear in their citizens - fear of torture in this world or else eternal damnation and hell fire in the next - while in private they engage in vices of such depravity that would make the most profligate of our bagnios here look like a genteel garden fete in comparison. Hypocrites, Sir! Hypocrites of the first rank. They will see us hung, given half a chance. Our lands will be taken from us - our families, our wives and children placed in chains, and the progress of science turned back on itself for a hundred years if we were to do as you suggest.'

'Really, Sam, that is not at all accurate,' Matthew argues. The iniquities you speak of may be the case in rare instances, yes - but believe me I have travelled overseas, in France, in Italy and have seen things for myself, the way people live and the high regard in which they hold their Church. What you are saying is exaggerated.'

But Sam, not at all happy over having his paucity of overseas experience alluded to, merely takes a pinch of snuff, scowling at his friend in a most disparaging way - while Snatchal, who has likewise been listening closely to Matthew's mitigation of the enemy's faults and imperfections, seems equally grave, leaning

forward in narrow-eyed observation. 'Well, come now gentlemen,'
he says getting to his feet. 'Enough of trying to put the world to
rights. It is time to join the ladies. Do not forget, Wildish: you are a
probationary member of the Wig Club now. You will not fail to
remember your loyalties, I trust?'

And Matthew, his heart pounding, nods his complete
compliance and understanding, realising that he might, once again,
already have said too much.

A butler fetches a lamp which is placed nearby to provide
additional light in the dark, cavernous drawing room, hitherto lit
merely by a number of candles. It is time for the demonstration.
And to this end, a dove of white plumage has been placed into a
spherical glass container at the high top of the apparatus, and its lid
secured with a turn of a special key. Just sufficient room is
available within the bowl for the creature to flutter its wings and to
hop about in confusion, while below there is a pedestal attached to
an array of various tubes and handles - the entire edifice itself
having been assembled upon a table in the centre of the drawing
room, the better for everyone to see, and around which they all sit,
waiting patiently for the experiment to begin. Mr Cheetham, Lord's
Snatchal's special guest for the evening, is formally introduced -
this gentleman being one of the growing band of professional
entertainers who tour the country these days demonstrating a few of
the more noteworthy developments that are taking place in the field
of scientific experimentation or, as the pamphlet which Matthew
takes from the table proclaims:

*Benedict Cheetham Esq. Itinerant Lecturer in Natural Philosophy,*
*will undertake touring shows of scientific curiosities. Town Halls,*
*Coffee Houses and Private Residences of Quality where for a*
*modest consideration he will lift the veil from the miracles of*
*science. The fantastical experiment of the pneumatic engine with*
*bird confined to a vacuum as centrepiece of proceedings. Plus the*
*famous demonstration of electricity, its diverse actions upon the*
*dissected legs of a frog, and others that will astonish and amaze.*
*Cash payment preferred.*
*(Frog legs and birds supplied at no extra charge).*

In addition to the apparatus, a large specimen jar is placed upon the table containing what appears to be a pair of shrunken lungs floating in their murky liquid of preservation. Miss Wilcox in particular appears to be repulsed by the sight, her head turned away though with eyes that must return to it again and again, always accompanied by a marked crinkling of the nose.

The experiment is ready to proceed - to which purpose, once assured of everyone's attention, and that the dove is securely sealed in its glass bowl, Mr Cheetham begins to turn a handle. An uncomfortable, rhythmical sucking kind of noise begins to be heard - a sound over which Lady Snatchal in particular appears to be somewhat perturbed, glancing around with eyes as big as saucers trying to locate its origin and which, upon inspection, is found to be emanating from a small cylinder at the base of the apparatus itself.

'Normally, the bird that you sees here sustains life through the uses of her vital organs, specifically the lungs, which all creatures possesses in some ways or another,' the man announces in his own singular rendition of the King's English and which, Matthew thinks, does make him sound like a circus ringmaster. To add strength to his contention he raises the jar containing the lungs at this point in proceedings and wobbles it about, much to Miss Wilcox's consternation who places a hand of obvious distress to her tummy. 'But, ladies and gentlemen,' Mr Cheetham continues, 'let it be known forthwith that the lungs is only of use when operating within what is termed the *Atmo-sphere* - or the air, as the vulgar tongue might describe it. Contrary to popular superstition, this *Atmosphere* possesses no properties of spirit of any kind but is in fact no more than a substance like any other that can be weighed and measured - and which, though invisible, can be removed through the use of suction as is taking place at this very juncture as I continues to turn this here handle - like a sort of bellows in reverse, see.'

'Remarkable!' the Earl declares, pleased with the achievement of bringing such a singular novelty to his home.

'*Yerrz*, very good,' Sam mumbles, endeavouring to demonstrate suitable enthusiasm. Johanna does likewise, though both she and Miss Wilcox do appear to be sharing a certain concern for the bird's welfare, their eyes directed anxiously upwards to the bowl - for the dove, gradually deprived of the breath of life, has already ceased fluttering its wings and, to Miss Wilcox's dismay (for she lets out a plaintive cry at the sight of it) begins to throw itself around most oddly, tumbling this way and that in irregular convulsions, its sharp little beak and claws to be heard chaffing upon the inside of the glass as it goes.

'As you can see,' Mr Cheetham continues, 'by this means, the experimenter has power of life or death over the creature thus contained, which has now already begun to lose control of its faculties - a bit like we might observe, say, in poultry when their heads are wrung off but their bodies keeps dancing around afterwards.'

At which a dull thud is heard and an empty space materialises at that part of the table where Miss Wilcox has hitherto been seated. She has, everyone quickly apprehends, fainted and is now flat on the floor - a discovery that causes instant consternation as the men immediately leave their chairs and rush to her aid.

'Here ... take my smelling salts,' Lady Snatchal cries as she also hastens to the scene, wobbling on unsteady feet, rather the worse for drink, but with a small bottle of ammonia already in her hand which is duly applied to the unfortunate Miss Wilcox's nostrils. Soon the young woman is revived and lifted back on her chair, and thankfully no worse for the experience. The unfortunate dove, meanwhile, has not fared so well. Having been neglected by Mr Cheetham at the critical moment, and still deprived of air, it appears now to have expired completely. This was not how the experiment was meant to conclude, of course - it having been always the intention to revive the bird at the last moment with a turn of the key at the top of the bowl which would allow the vital air to re-enter the vessel - something that is attempted now, and with all haste by an agitated Mr Cheetham himself, but all to no avail. The bird has expired, lying with her breast upwards, her head drooped and her neck all awry, as if broken.

'Too late. Too late,' Mr Cheetham announces as the dove is taken out through the top aperture and then, accompanied by a rueful shaking of the head, thrown down unceremoniously onto the table, dead, much to the dismay of the ladies in particular. This gesture of peevishness being over, the man launches into his final summing up, ignoring the occasional sobbing sounds from Miss Wilcox as he stands in theatrical fashion, his chest puffed out and his thumbs notched into the lapels of his waistcoat as he speaks. 'In summary, my lords, ladies and - er - what have you, although in this instance there has been a bit of an unforeseen conclusion to proceedings, you can all nonetheless observe, I take it, that what hitherto has been considered to be the miraculous gift of life is in fact dependent on nothing more than a physical substance, sustained only by that which mankind can measure and regulate. There is no ineffable mystery present here, and this is as true for the bird as it is for the fearsome tiger, for the whale or for the mighty oliphant, or even for you and me, ladies and gentlemen - even for you and me. All right, the bird costs me a few bob and I'm as upset about it as anybody else. But only by such means can the advancement of science take place, leading us towards a state of enlightenment and into a more comfortable and comprehensible future. And so I suppose it's all worth it in the end. Thank you, thank you kindly!'

At which he bows and a brief ripple of polite applause trickles around the table.

'You will of course be compensated for any additional cost incurred by the unfortunate accident,' Lord Snatchal says.

'Much obliged, thank you, Sir,' Mr Cheetham responds with a gratified nod.

'*Wine?*' Lady Snatchal cries with droll confidence, anticipating unanimous agreement from those present that this would indeed be a suitable conclusion to proceedings.

Matthew, meanwhile, not wishing to rise, simply takes the dove and examines it himself. It is not yet cold. Contemplating with sadness upon the fragility of life, he continues to hold the creature, stroking its breastbone a tiny pink ridge protruding at the sternum where the feathers are so thin as to be virtually absent, wondering whether any sign of a heartbeat can be detected. To his surprise, there is something, though immensely faint.

'Have you been doing this sort of thing long?' Sam asks of Mr Cheetham, as he and Johanna return with their glasses to sit again at the table, curious to watch the dismantling of the complex apparatus as they sip their wine.

'No, not all that long, to be honest,' Mr Cheetham replies as he accepts a glass from Sam and imbibes the ruby red liquid with large extravagant gulps, as if drinking ale. 'Cor, that's a nice drop of stuff!' he says, picking up the dusty bottle for himself and examining the label at arms length for a moment while he pauses in his labours. 'What's that, Chateau Lafite? Oh yes, I likes a drop or two of Chateau Lafite. Exquisite. Now, where was I? Oh, yes, anyway, I always was in the entertainment business, as a matter of fact - used to travel all over the country with performing animals. I had a good collection of animals in them days: dogs and ferrets, and a bear, as well. Used to do all the taverns and theatres, all over the place. Mind you, I sometimes had a bit of trouble getting lodgings for the bear - which was a pity really, 'cause bears is usually well behaved enough, as long as they ain't aggravated.'

'Yes, quite!' agrees Sam, trying to ignore the position of Lord Snatchal's jaw, which is however promptly closed by a swift tap under the chin from the fan of a passing Lady Snatchal, brandished with all the dexterity and accuracy of familiar usage.

'So anyway,' Mr Cheetham continues, proffering his glass for a top up, 'I thought to myself, and the Missus said to me one day, as well, she said, "You ain't getting any younger Mr Cheetham. This ain't the sort of thing you can keep doing forever." And she was right. So, I gave it all up - just like that! Sold all the animals and got myself some of these here gadgets. See, that's where the future lies, I reckon, in gadgets. And now I tours around all the best houses like this, all the gentlemen's clubs in town. Honestly, it ain't a bad sort of living. Know what I mean?'

The dove, meanwhile, warmed and still cradled in Matthew's hands, suddenly opens its eyes and begins to scratch against his palms, with at first one leg, then both - until within just a few minutes, it has become alive again, full of energy, straining to be liberated - a process which Matthew duly resolves to set in motion. Getting to his feet, the bird still cradled in both hands, he whispers to a page nearby to raise one of the tall sash windows and then, with the sudden rush of cool air and silver moonlight flooding into the room, holds the bird itself up to the open sky.

'No, no, Sir! Mr Cheetham ... shouts, 'I can use her again if she's all right, don't ...'

But it's too late, the bird has gone. Fluttering awkwardly and with confusion at first in the darkness, a place in which it would not normally be active, of course, it quickly locates some trees and becomes lost in the tangle of branches. It is a beautiful night, a breeze compelling the clouds rapidly across from west to east, veiling the Moon intermittently, and which is itself almost full and very high. The air feels so fresh and clean after the stuffiness and candle smoke of the drawing room, the sweet airs and breath of night - so that it is almost with regret that Matthew turns and allows the window to be closed once more behind him. The great heavy velvet curtains are drawn again, and the mystery of the night into which the fortunate dove has fled, is now all but vanished from his senses.

'The poor creature, has surely earned its liberty,' Matthew announces, filling the silence in the room as he surveys the assorted faces among the guests - some, like Mr Cheetham, with reproof, others like those of Johanna and Miss Wilcox gazing up at him with a kind of wonderment, that he has somehow brought the dove back to life, almost as if through supernatural means. Lady Snatchal, however, he notices has no expression on her face at all, since she has apparently passed out in her chair by this time, her head dropped down to one side - in an odd kind of way similar to the dove itself a moment earlier, the empty wine glass in her lap.

'Well now, anyway, ladies and gentlemen?' the Earl declares at length as if keen to embark on a summing up. 'Before we allow Mr Cheetham to leave us, shall we just have your verdicts on our little diversion this evening? What did you all think of it?'

'Extraordinary!' Sam declares.

'Goodness, yes - something to power the imagination, certainly,' Johanna agrees with tact, her eyebrows arched in a not entirely convincing expression of amazement. 'And that which we have hitherto considered to be the invisible breath of God should now be regarded as a substance that can be measured and weighed like any other.'

'Yes indeed. Well put, Mrs Woolveston,' Lord Snatchal concurs, employing due formality of address in the proximity of Cheetham who, still listening carefully, has returned once more to the job of dismantling the air pump. 'And Amelia, my dear?' the Earl inquires further, turning next to his niece. 'What about you?'

'Oh, I don't know,' Miss Wilcox replies with an especially savage crinkling of the nose. 'It's horrid. I don't care.'

'I find it tendentious and misleading,' Matthew asserts, ignoring the narrow-eyed look of suspicion that flares up in Mr Cheetham's shrewd and observant eye as he glances covertly in the other man's direction. 'How does providing a new name for air, or merely observing it's effects like this prove that a holy spirit does not attend the lives of those who breathe it?'

To which Mr Cheetham, still occupied with his task, responds: 'It does not disprove the Holy Spirit, Sir. It's just that it makes him unnecessary.' And then turning to Matthew more directly: 'We must not become the enemies of reason.'

'I can assure you I am not at any risk of becoming the enemy of reason,' Matthew argues patiently, though most adamant and assertive all of a sudden. 'On the contrary. I believe all aspects of humanity should be celebrated - the rational and the sacred, the scientific and the spiritual. Anyone who pursues the one at the exclusion of the other is not only a fool, Mr Cheetham, but a dangerous one.'

'That might well be so, Sir,' the man replies, clearly smarting from the criticism. 'But at the end of the day, it doesn't matter if we are dangerous or not, because people are impressed by what we do, and they'll pay handsomely for it. In time, all of society, from the top to the bottom, will be enthralled by machines such as this.'

'And enslaved by them, too, no doubt?' Matthew suggests.

'You said it, Sir. And I shall not argue with my betters. Let's just say, that folks will have a hunger for the fruits of knowledge far bigger than all them things you have now, bigger than all your fancy music and poetry, all your fine clothes and swanky manners - because it will give them power. In other words, through machines and gadgets, people like me are going to rule the world one day, Sir. So you might as well get used to it.'

But this last remark appears to be too much for the sensibilities of Lord Snatchal, a man who can detect, with the vision of a hawk at a thousand feet, any sign of revolutionary zeal among the undeserving poor - and he is not at all pleased with it. 'Our gratitude to you, Mr Cheetham,' he remarks urbanely. 'That will be all for this evening. You will of course be expecting to stay with us overnight, I take it?'

'Ah, yes, thank you Sir. For it is - er - late.'

'Yes, indeed,' Snatchal observes. 'Unfortunately, we are a little short on room at the moment, Mr Cheetham. Would the stables be adequate? One of my men will show you there.'

And with a look of disappointment followed by a shrug of the shoulders, the unfortunate man, his equipment now packed into two large cases, is escorted by a footman from the drawing room, guided on the first stage of a journey that will take him across the floor of the huge, domed atrium, then down the steps of the portico, across the forecourt and far around the sides of the vast building with its hundreds of empty bedrooms to finish in the stable yard behind the west wing and where, in the darkness, he will spend the night on a bed of straw with the animals.

Thereafter the remainder of the evening passes, for Matthew, in a haze of vaguely perceived experiences and fragments of disjointed conversation. More wine is brought in. The utterly inconsequential Miss Wilcox somehow melts away, or has been taken away - he cannot rightly remember the manner of her going. The Countess, Lady Snatchal, having awoken and soon after passed out yet again in her chair, is roused, and with an arm each upon the shoulders of two sturdy maid servants, is taken to her bed chamber. Lord Snatchal, meanwhile, and who continues to drink heartily, is eventually removed upon a field stretcher to his, and Sam and Johanna stagger away merrily, arm in arm, their noses down over the sandy trail which will eventually take them, like a pair of inebriated bloodhounds on the scent, up to their quarters in some distant wing of the enormous building - leaving Matthew quite alone with his thoughts, therefore, and an opportunity in the now peaceful drawing room where almost every candle has burned down, to stroll over to the windows as he had done earlier, to draw back the curtains and to raise one of the frames himself this time to behold the moon again, much lower in the sky by now and farther over towards the West where a tiny ribbon of the lake can be detected gleaming in the distance. He wonders if there are men on the moon, as some astronomers speculate. Maybe there are, and even towns and cities up there, too, with people in them. But if so, they have surely set aside the earth as their Bedlam, with all the fools and madmen down here below.

Everywhere is so silent, the deep and impenetrable silence of the countryside at night - which makes the sudden and piercing cry from a predatory owl flying out over the woods, all the more unnerving - and upon which he slides shut the window, locates a comfortable couch and gradually drifts towards a deep and grateful slumber.

Would the dove be out there still, he wonders, safe in the branches of the tree into which it had flown? He hopes so – somewhere out there in the darkness, waiting for the first light of dawn, and upon which, if such a creature possesses any cognisance or powers of recollection at all, it would regard the evening that has passed as little more than a confused and distant dream of life, a sorrow and a torment from which it has finally been set free.

# ~ 9 ~
## OBSERVATIONS OF THE HEAVENLY BODIES - VENUS

*Of the planet Venus, its general and particular significations: She who bringeth beauty harmony and proportion. A body exceeding well shaped and inclining to tallness. Large eyes, tending to dark. Hair, smooth and plentiful. One who delights in baths, perfumes and all merry meetings, masques, music and plays. Cheerful, full of amorous enticements, often entangled in love matters or prone to venery. Neat in apparel, preferring of blue, pink and pastel shades. The sapphire for her gemstone.*

'May I enquire, Sir, are we expecting any further visitors today?' Francis asks, standing tall in his black frock coat and seeming to fill the entire height of the workshop, from floor to ceiling as he does so.

'Only the laundry collection, this afternoon,' Matthew explains. 'Oh, and my good friend Sam is due - Mr Woolveston, that is. He is coming to pick up the wig I repaired for him. I can show him in myself, Francis, don't worry. You may go, if you wish. The rest of the day is yours.'

With a well-rehearsed bow, followed by a sequence of rhythmic ducking movements as he traverses the length of the room with its low beams, the valet departs, leaving Matthew alone at his workbench.

He is feeling particularly pleased with himself this morning, with his private entrance reconstructed and fully restored after the debacle of last week. Even better, he has just received an invitation to a spectacular Masquerade at a residence in The Strand, and is reading through the letter again with satisfaction, anticipating all the many beautiful women who will be in attendance and all the enticing possibilities this might deliver up. Excellent.

In the meantime, there is always plenty to be getting on with here on the work front. Buoyed up by the almost legendary status of having trained in Paris, the world's capital of extravagant hair pieces, and being tipped as a likely candidate to one day become wig maker by royal appointment, his work is more and more sought after and rightly celebrated for its quality and skill. Fresh commissions are coming in all the while, as any casual glance at his order book or diary will confirm: - a formal periwig for an Alderman, here; a short bob wig for a stockbroker from Garraways, there. Existing pieces are always in need of expert restoration, as well, like Sam's. And then, if all this were not enough, the peculiar hairpiece belonging to the Cornhill Wig Club also has to be dealt with, a task for which, Matthew has to admit, he has scant enthusiasm. He has it displayed in readiness on a mannequin head upon one of his benches, and has studied it carefully, mapped the various components and made notes so it might be re-fashioned again; but that is about as far as he has got with it. The existing workmanship itself is of a low order; and whereas a proper, high-status wig of the kind he specialises in usually has individually woven hairs, especially at the front, all inserted into a fine fabric foundation, measured and shaped to the very contours of the client's scalp, this one just has thick wefts of hair tied together and inserted into a coarse foundation with no attempt at styling whatsoever. He is debating, therefore, just what level of finesse one should bestow upon such an unpleasant object. Certainly, the foundation itself is badly decayed and in need of total replacement.

Should he begin? The light is really not at all that good today, he concludes, casting about for an excuse to set the work aside as he shifts his stool around to the end of his bench and thus closer to the long row of windows, the better to gaze out to the busy coaching yard below; the better, also, to dream up a line or two of verse, as is his wont. He is endeavouring to put the finishing touches to his sonnet to Venus, drawing once again on the lines in the little book of astrological lore lent to him by Johanna. Not only that, but there is always something interesting to see down in the yard; always something to amuse or to inspire - and the wide open vista above the rooftops is forever a source of fascination, as well - the sky today smudged over with a mixture of clouds racing across on a stiff October breeze which occasionally sheds a shower of hail or sleety rain against the glass: already so evocative of autumn.

It reminds him, with regret, that the outdoor season at Vauxhall and Ranelagh Gardens is now well and truly over for the year. There shall be no more moonlit nights beneath fragrant bowers; no more promenades beneath a canopy of stars to the song of the nightingale, arm in arm with one lovely woman or another; no more listening to the glorious music of his beloved Handel at bandstands or pavilions. Autumn has arrived, and cold Winter is an approaching spectre - as is war, of course - and any number of similarly melancholic prospects engendered by the world at large, and which like an unwelcome visitor he allows to steal into his thoughts and remain there for far too long - until, suddenly, with the sound of a bugle heralding its approach and the clangour of ironshod wheels and hooves upon the cobble stones, one of the great northern coaches, hauled by six horses and a postilion mounted up front, thunders into the yard at break-neck speed - literally break neck for any unfortunate passenger riding atop of it who might neglect to lower his or her head upon coming in under the arch. Today it seems to have been a particularly narrow squeeze, with a mountain of cases and boxes piled on top. And then, following another loud blast on a bugle to confirm his arrival to anyone who might be left in any doubt of it, the coachman, a man so heavily attired against the elements that he appears at least twice the girth of any mere mortal, jumps down and is promptly surrounded by an admiring bevy of hostlers, stable boys, grooms, chamber maids and waiters from the inn all eager for the latest news and gossip from 'up North.'

People really are becoming anxious, Matthew reflects - even quite ordinary people to whom one would not normally attribute any interest in politics or current affairs. A humble shoeblack and a paper boy are numbered among them today, their faces gazing up at this giant of a man in genuine anticipation - and Matthew, being no exception to the curiosity of the hour, opens the casement an inch or two wider, the better to listen to what the fellow has to say.

Very few individuals there are of greater consequence, more sought after, celebrated or feted than the coachman assigned to one of the main staging routes from the North. The romance and excitement of his vocation is a draw to everyone, to the men and the ladies alike. This afternoon, moreover, what with the prospect of a rebel invasion from Scotland becoming a very real one, the allure is simply irresistible. And this fellow really knows it, too,

Matthew thinks to himself - standing tall in the centre of the yard, his hands thrust into his pockets of his greatcoat, with a look of unabashed self-importance emblazoned upon his scarlet, weather-beaten face. It is as if he were about to read a proclamation.

'War, ladies and gents!' the coachman bellows, as if it is, indeed, a proclamation - and in this case one of obvious doom. 'The Scottish clans are assembling; the French will join 'em - and you can kiss goodbye to all your comfy, soft-southern ways down here. Rebellion, my city friends, rebellion and bloody insurrection! And there's nothing any of you can do to stop it.'

Everyone sighs, and a low moan of despair circulates around the yard, while those poor, travel-weary passengers on the coach - unimpressed by anything their man has to say, since they have no-doubt heard more than enough of it already these past few days at every stop along the way - gradually begin to emerge from the dark interior of the vehicle, scrambling down unaided as best they can on numb legs and then threading their path through the crowds towards the doorway of the inn - the imminence of any Jacobite uprising being of negligible significance, it seems, when set against the pressing needs for refreshment or the easement offered by the nearest privy.

'So what's it they're after, all these Scots?' one of the stableboys demands, thrusting his chin forwards, his shoulders all tense about his ears as if ready to take up arms straight away.

'Blood!' the coachman declares almost merrily, and removing his heavy leather gauntlet and raising his hand to the level of his neck, provides a vivid demonstration of slitting the throat with one finger. 'Blood and guts - *your* blood and guts, all of you, because they be Papists, see! They who burn and torture the likes of good Christian men and women. You're all done for. All done for in London - the lot of you! Ha, ha, ha!'

Matthew, having heard quite enough, slams the window shut, which engenders a raising of the eyebrows from the coachman himself before he turns from his audience and waddles his way across the yard, following his passengers inside for liquid refreshment - which will, Matthew surmises, be readily provided for him by any number of eager listeners. What a performance. And surely grossly exaggerated.

Determined still not to let any of this nonsense spoil his day, Matthew returns to his bench, and as he takes up some routine tasks, running some newly acquired strands of hair through his hackling iron, he allows his thoughts to settle once more upon far more enticing matters, namely his treasured project and ongoing ambition of enjoying the pleasures of seven beautiful women within the span of a single day and night. Ah yes! In this respect, he has every reason to feel optimistic, because, with a combination of determination and sheer good luck, he has already managed to locate again his lovely and exuberant *Jupiter* from Ranelagh Gardens, she whose name, he has learned, is Miss Caroline Bolter. She resides at an address in Hanover Square and would, he suspects, be a mistress of a person of some eminence. Accepting of his apologies for the unfortunate incident with the bull, she has come to him again, and already they have consummated their amour with an hour of the most passionate and vigorous engagement. As anticipated, she had proved a sturdy and demanding lover, uncompromising in her insistence on being fully pleasured. Restoring it fondly to his remembrance again today, the strength of her embrace, the extravagance of her creature needs, he knows that even in that brief time together, they had enjoyed each other well - he being patient and lingering in the approach, and yet strong and powerful in the final delivery, exactly as he had instinctively recognised would be her requirements. A success! He is due to visit her next time, for an overnight stay in which he intends to press home his advantage, for they will have opportunity this time to play and to explore more fully. He simply cannot wait.

Thus, already, he is sure of at least two among the magical seven, for there is also the clever Rose Tidey, the epitome of fair Luna; and he remains confident that when the time comes for putting his fantastical scheme into operation, that she too will be ready to respond. Two beautiful and fascinating women - and the very thought and recollection of the intimacy he has already shared with them, rouses him again even as he endeavours to concentrate on his work.

It is not too late in the day, when steps, are heard approaching along the gallery outside, followed by a soft rap on the outer door and the melodious salutation of 'Oooh hoo!' that signifies the arrival of his laundry collection - the same day every week. 'Come through, please - the doors are open,' he calls over his shoulder expecting, as he turns, to see someone like the redoubtable Mrs

Biggs, the woman who usually comes to do for him. But it is not Mrs Biggs. Instead, standing in the lobby at the threshold to his workshop, is a lovely young woman. Surely in age no more than eighteen or twenty years, she is dressed humbly in a simple dark-blue gown, unhooped, and with wavy brunette hair which, though not great in length, is brushed free about her shoulders.

'Good morning. You're new,' he says, cheerful and endeavouring to make her welcome. 'I really must get that door bell fixed,' he laughs. 'Have you come for the laundry?'

'I have. Mr Wildish, isn't it? My name is Sarah. I work for Mrs Biggs. Will you show me what to do?'

'I shall indeed, Sarah,' Matthew asserts with enthusiasm, rising from his stool the better to assist in the process of instruction.

Hoping that she will have detected the look of kindness and reassurance in his eyes, he bows in greeting, and to this gesture she reacts by casting her own gaze downwards, out of modesty rather than any fault of shyness, he suspects - for she is a bonny girl, one that men would admire, and she would surely be well aware of it.

'My towels are stacked up by the kitchen door,' he explains, guiding her in, 'but the bed linen unfortunately is still *in situ*. I have been busy and ...'

'Oh, that's all right,' she interrupts cheerfully, 'I can soon strip those.'

'Thank you. It's just through here - look, I will show you.'

Having indicated to her the location of all those items she would be expecting to take with her to the wash house, he returns to his bench, making himself busy once more. But he cannot concentrate. Occasionally, as he lifts his head he catches glimpses of her moving about the apartments, and it is a most pleasantly distracting sight - her youthful aspect being one of very slight awkwardness and diffidence combined with a most upright vigour - most shapely and with a glorious bloom of health to her complexion. He is intrigued by her large brown eyes and long, elegantly formed face and neck - while her generous, moist lips are often to be seen parted as she works, suggesting a certain brooding curiosity of the senses, unencumbered by any unnatural reserve or reticence - and thus promising any man perceptive enough to notice such things much delight. And he suspects, therefore, even now so soon, that providence has gifted him this day with the very image and essence of Venus in all her enchanting simplicity. He has no way of knowing whether her visit this afternoon is a singular event or one that might be repeated. He knows only that he must not allow such a precious opportunity to slip away, and thus as she emerges from the bed-chamber for the final time, one of the sheets tied up and slung over her shoulder as a bag in which all the other pieces are contained, he turns from his workbench and remarks on a number of trivialities to engage her attention - the inclement weather, and so on. She does not reply, but rather seems most disturbed all of a sudden, her eyes with their outstanding dark lashes casting about the room with a distracted, frightened aspect.

'Are you well, Sarah?' he asks.

'Oh, I don't know. It's not normal here, is it - all those masks on the wall, and those heads with their wigs! And, glory be, they've got eyes, some of them, as well. They've been following me around the room, I swear - those eyes!'

'I sometimes have a bit of fun and stick beads on the mannequin's faces,' he tells her, smiling and letting her into his confidence, 'so, yes, they do look like eyes. And I paint the lips, too, if the mood takes me, and even paste on a beauty spot for good measure.'

And, dropping her linen sack down, she wanders over to a number of the heads and inspects them more closely, the faintest of smiles forming at the corners of her lovely mouth, as if thrilling at her own anxiety. She seems fascinated by the luxury and beauty of the wigs, the sensuality of the hair which she clearly longs to reach out and touch.

'Oh, well,' she continues, 'I can see they are not real eyes. But, for all that, I wouldn't want to be here on my own - not for all the tea in China.'

'Well, do not worry, Sarah. Should you visit again, I would be happy to watch over you as you go about your business, for I think there would be much in that occupation that would be agreeable to me. By the way, I was just about to make some tea. I am hard at work, too, Sarah, and we could surely both do with refreshment at this time of the afternoon. Would you care to join me?'

She seems doubtful, even mistrustful at first. But a further reassuring smile puts her at ease. 'Oh, righty-ho, then!' she declares in a pleasingly self-satisfied way, he thinks, as she goes to take up one of the stools.

'Oh, Sarah, do take a more comfortable seat over here on the couch,' he urges her with gentle persuasion.

Still a little diffident, she allows him to guide her over to his comfy nook, that very special place set in the alcove and just about the only part of the workshop not exposed to the windows - the same as Rose had sat upon just the other day, and many others before her, of course, and which, he knows by long and familiar usage, often proves a pleasant size for two, and most accommodating for a little flirtation.

Soon he has made the tea, and this he brings into the studio on a tray which he sets down on the end of his bench nearby. She seems quite overwhelmed by the sight of a gentleman waiting on her, even in such a modest way as this, and from those threads of casual conversation that pass between them next, he gathers that she, like many a girl in her position, must reside in the same place as she works, in communal accommodation with Mrs Biggs herself, in quarters she shares with several lodgers, a dog, a cat and another laundry girl like herself. What a waste. Such a beautiful young woman employed in base labours, and also at the behest of a hard and unrelenting mistress, as she would surely have in Mrs Biggs.

'That's a rum-looking one,' she observes, pointing at the Cornhill Club specimen on the bench nearby.

'Ah, yes, it is in terrible need of repair - the foundation has deteriorated so very badly. I do have a far better piece to show you, though.'

And reaching over he removes from its wooden block one of his finished masterpieces, a sumptuous full-length periwig, dark and lush in texture.

'This would be a far better example of the wig maker's craft, Sarah - look!' he urges her as, holding the wig aloft, he allows the full extent of it to unfurl in all its splendour. 'Naturally there are plenty of wig-makers at large out there, especially in a big city such as this - the common peruke makers, as we call them - those hacks of the trade employed in barbers shops or tiny backstreets along Holborn. But *Master Wig Makers* such as myself that can produce work of this calibre ... ah, we are a breed apart, Sarah, a rarity - wizards in the mysterious arts of weaving, knotting and ventilating - in other words, sewing the hair so finely, shaping the foundation in just such a way, with the aid of the finest positional springs and wires, that the results are every bit the equal, if not better, than most heads of natural hair. And of course I always use the highest quality material. Never for one moment would a Master Wig Maker consider recourse to animal hair or the vile combings gathered from the floor of a barber shop. The very best dark hair, for example must come from Spain or Northern Italy; brown or auburn hair is obtained from France or Ireland. The best blond hair of all from the German states. I know my sources, and they are impeccable, as is every finished item that leaves these rooms.'

'It is very beautiful,' she says, her eyes wide as she reaches out to touch the rich tumbling curls. 'So soft and ... and so clean!'

'Here, let me take your cup from you,' he says, suddenly delivered of a moment's inspiration, 'and you can try it on.'

'Try it on, Sir! What the wig of a gentleman?'

'Yes, let me see what a fine fellow you would make - though I venture to suggest it would be nowhere near as fine a young woman as you are now. But no matter. Let us have some fun, Sarah.'

And after piling up her own hair quickly and helping her into the piece, and following a few adjustments with a comb to the resplendent shroud of curls, he fetches a looking glass to show her how she appears, which makes her quite merry as her generous lips purse themselves ever so slightly in admiration of her own startling transformation.

'Why, what a handsome fellow!' he declares, responding to her laughter. 'Why, you could go to the best of masquerades thus and turn the heads of many a lady, and man as well, with such a fair visage, for they would not know how to fathom your mysteries, Sarah, or which variety of delights they should seek of you.'

'Oh - you are a wag, Mr Wildish,' she admonishes him, somehow far more self-confident seeing herself in her new guise, even to the extent of nudging him in the ribs with her elbow. 'What should a poor girl like me make of such saucy talk!'

Smiling gallantly, and with a gentle lifting movement, he helps her out of the wig - thereby touching her a little more intimately and managing to nestle in closer, too, and to her continued astonishment even takes up his comb again to run it very gently a few times through her own hair to compose it for her once more. 'Sarah, you should make nothing of my foolish prattle,' he announces softly, looking into her eyes, 'nothing at all that does not accord with the receipt of kindness and care, for those are my only sentiments. Listen, will you tell me something?'

'Yes. What is it you would ask?'

'Tell me what would you be, what would you have if you could become anybody or anything in the whole wide world. Tell me and I will wave my magic wand and see what happens?'

'Oh, I don't know. Chances are I would fancy myself as a Duchess. Yes, that's what I'd like. What would you be, then, Mr Wildish?'

'You cheeky minx! What would I be? Why, Sarah, I would be all your pleasure.'

'All my pleasure,' she echoes, a shadow of doubt furrowing her brows. 'Really?'

'All of it. If you will allow me to make my case to you. From the top to the bottom of the range of your innermost wishes and desires.'

'Oh ... so not just having me take your dirty linen from you each week?' she chuckles, at ease now as she permits him to nestle close, so their sides must touch, and shoulders also.

'No, I would rather that you become a maker of it,' he whispers, 'and that you would anoint those very sheets with the issue of your joy, and mine.'

Will she run away, he wonders? Stunned, she gazes back at him with eyes that have become, if anything, even larger, darker and of greater intensity and yet also, surprisingly, a certain sadness - so that when she does finally respond to his bold seduction, it is prefaced with a lengthy sigh. 'Where I live, I have a bed I must share in a garret with an old spinster,' she whispers. 'That's all I've ever known, without a moment of solitude. So I do not suppose I've ever had that much joy that I've ever *anointed a sheet,* as you say - not right proper like you would be expecting.'

'Would you like to?'

'Oh dear! I knew I should not have looked into your eyes,' she murmurs suddenly by way of reply, 'for it is true what they say, that one careless glance gives more advantage than a hundred words. And I have heard a girl can get herself in the family way soon enough with them sort of tricks.'

'Sarah,' he murmurs, taking her hand most gently, 'I can promise you there are many ways two friends might please each other without the burden of such anxieties. I will gladly show you all that I am practised in if you will give me leave, and with all due tenderness and safety of your person.'

'Really ..?'

'Listen, my Pretty: locked in my memory is a poem that I have already made for you. It is in praise of a Goddess who once lived on the shores of a distant sea, a place bathed in sunshine and warmth. And it is she, Venus, who shall be your mistress now, not some shrew who commands your labours for a penny a day.'

'A distant sea, bathed in sunshine and warmth,' she repeats, her lovely lips parted at the conclusion of it, lost in all the sensations of the moment. 'Glory be! I think I like the sound of my new mistress,' she adds, looking so deep into his eyes now. And as their hands and foreheads touch in ever closer intimacy, and as their cheeks brush each other's faces in that typical dalliance of would-be lovers about to kiss, he whispers to her his words:

*Of foaming brine and wavelets were't thou born,*
*Fair daughter of the sea and sun-kissed shore.*
*Come, pleasure all my fancies that are torn,*
*And long for measured sighs of love once more.*

*Humbled in thy mask do thou so oft appear,*
*In places strange and foreign you abide.*
*Unveil! Come forth in all thy splendour, dear!*
*Cast free thy chains, no more thy beauty hide.*

*These hands so fair, for which such praise was sung,*
*Are not for drudge and tyranny of rules.*
*These feet beneath which tender flowers once sprung,*
*Not made for climbing stairs or serving fools.*

*For music, joy and perfumed bowers made art thou.*
*So, come to me, my lovely. Kiss me now.*

She seems quite lost for a moment in the music of the sonnet, in the sound of metre, the like of which, he realises, she might never have heard until now.

'I shall,' she murmurs as if responding to some questioning voice within: 'I shall. It's just that ...'

'What, my darling?'

'I always thought this sort of thing was for the rich, like new clothes all the time or ... or chocolate?'

'No, my Pretty. It is nature's kindness, a gift to us all. You are wanting only of the leisure and opportunity to experience it for yourself. Allow me the honour of becoming your guide and instructor ... in all of your pleasure.'

'All my pleasure. Really? All of it? All mine?'

But he answers her only with kisses now and her lips are as hungry for the experience and as alive with desire as he has ever known in any woman, young or old. It is heaven ... bliss, until gradually he becomes aware, as she does, too, of a sudden noise outside in the yard, a chair arriving. Nothing remarkable in that, he thinks - but then recalling that Sam is due, he glances over his shoulder to check the time - to discover that it is, indeed, the very hour. Quickly, getting to his feet, he glances down - but it is not Sam who exits from the chair but, to Matthew's mixed astonishment and delight, what appears, even beneath the expanse of a wide brimmed hat, to be none other than Johanna! Dressed in a smart jacket and skirt resembling a riding outfit, and with her little pug Boris clutched to her breast, she glances briefly around the yard. Detecting his sign and the open door beneath it, she enters and climbs the stairs straight away, reaching the outside gallery before he can even run to meet her.

'Mrs Woolveston - Johanna! What a pleasant surprise,' he says, opening the door. 'Apologies - I must get that bell fixed. Do come in.'

'Good afternoon, my Wonder!' she says, smiling in her usual composed and gentle way as she brushes by, entering without invitation - and the kindly look in her eyes as she does so tells him that she has, indeed, forgiven him for all the misunderstandings of the weekend at Snatchalcombe House. What a relief! 'Sam has been called away to Deptford,' she announces. 'It was an opportunity for taking his barometer back for repairs once more, as well. So, since little Boris and I were shopping in town, anyway, we thought that we might take it upon ourselves to collect his wig for him and ...'

But at that, she notices - and not without a certain disappointment - that they are not alone, and that at the other, comparatively more gloomy end of the long chamber, a laundry girl is attending to her bag of linen.

'Oh, yes, just some domestic business,' he announces by way of explanation. And, noticing with relief that Sarah is in no hurry to depart, he goes to her briefly and encourages her to continue with her work in another room.

'What work?' she whispers as he guides her through to the bedchamber.

'A labour that you should come to relish, full well, I promise you, my pretty, if you would but stay one quarter of an hour until I have seen to this good lady and her business,' he whispers back to her, taking both her hands, unseen, and planting a kiss on each. She understands.

Meanwhile, Johanna has made herself comfortable, taking a seat in the one-and-only armchair near the fire, the tiny pug still in her lap and where, having discovered the tea, she has even set up a cup and saucer for herself in readiness for his hospitality. He joins her, drawing up a stool from his bench. And as he pours tea and watches her, seated here in his home and workshop, the very picture of loveliness and yet so informal in her actions as she takes the tiny china cup delicately between her fingers, he realises that he is the happiest man in the world that she should be here.

'I will pack the wig for you,' he says after a little conversation, taking Sam's restored piece from its block and laying it with utmost care into a stout leather bag, 'Did you come with anyone - to help you carry?'

'Yes, with a footman. I have dismissed him, though - which I regret because it's not very nice outside. Lots of sailors are wandering about in Cheapside. I am not sure what it all means, but I heard someone say they will be marching on Whitehall later to petition the Palace for a substantial sum of prize money - booty from captured French ships that has yet to be released to them. Some of the shops and taverns have already closed to avoid trouble. So, I will most likely take a chaise straight back to Greenwich now. They should have what is due to them, though, don't you think?'

'Oh, they're always complaining about something, aren't they, those wastrels,' Matthew answers, displeased that she should be bothered by such unpleasantness. 'Why, given the present crisis, one might even conclude it is all just a trifle unpatriotic.'

'Well, yes. At any rate, everybody seems quite distressed,' she remarks, though not, he detects, entirely with approval over his disparaging remarks. 'Anyway, do tell, me, my Wonder,' she continues, changing the subject with a cheerful turn and still making a terrible fuss over the utterly spoiled pug clutched in her lap, 'how are you getting on with your sonnet sequence? That's what little Boris and I would really like to know, isn't it Boris! The planetary spheres?'

He gets to his feet and is just about to fetch some of what he has written so far to show her, when he catches sight of the girl Sarah once more, who is standing at the bed-chamber door, clearly at a loss for anything more to occupy herself with, and suddenly conveying to Johanna's alert and keen intelligence the purpose of it - that she and he are waiting for her to be gone. And as Johanna's face turns to him again, the look of pain and comprehension in her eyes is almost too much to bear. He feels so wretched, because the pain is one that can only be born of love. And he knows now that she cares for him, perhaps every bit as much as he does for her.

'Would you prefer me to go now?' she inquires, her voice broken and faint, as if a profound sadness for all her foolishness - and his - has suddenly overcome her.

'No, no ... not at all,' he says, feeling torn between all the conflicting emotions.

'Grrrr!' comes the sound from the pug, still in Johanna's lap - a snarl, as if voicing on behalf of its mistress all the feelings that she will not express. But there is more - for now suddenly alert and craning its neck, the diminutive animal appears to be turning its attentions towards, of all things, the wig nearby on the bench, the very one belonging to the Cornhill Club.

'Boris - naughty boy, what's this all about?' Johanna rebukes him in a kindly way, and then turning to Matthew explains: 'He has been having trouble with his teeth lately, poor darling, and it makes him rather morose. I do believe he has taken a disliking to your mannequin heads. Be quiet Boris!'

But Boris seems unrepentant and, crouching on his haunches now, his nostrils flaring as he sniffs the air, lets forth a further menacing, 'Grrrr!' in the direction of the wig. And then, before anyone can do anything to prevent it, he leaps from Johanna's grasp straight onto the bench, drags Lord Snatchal's irreplaceable wig from its mannequin head, and then jumps down with it onto the floor.

Matthew and Johanna are on their feet instantly, overturning the trayful of teacups and jugs as they do so - but it is too late. The pug, its quarry firmly clutched between its jaws races the length of the workshop, then back again, with Matthew, Johanna and the laundry girl, stooping all the while as they race after the creature, trying to apprehend it. Despite their best efforts even in the confined space, they can do nothing to intercept it or retrieve the wig from his jaws - and in a moment the miscreant has sped off into the passage, straight out the door, down the stairs and away with it into the yard.

'Stop, Stop!' Matthew cries, almost tumbling down the stairs in pursuit of the creature, only to see it race ahead through the puddles, under the arch and out to the lane beyond, all the while the wig dangling from its teeth. Seeing Matthew giving chase, only serves to increase the animal's determination to make good his escape, which he does at full speed farther out towards the busy, congested market of Cheapside, weaving in and out of the market stalls, along the length of the broad thoroughfare with its expensive shops and taverns - with Matthew, dressed in all his finery and ridiculously impractical shoes, running in desperate pursuit, drawing much unwelcome attention from the large numbers of rough seamen congregated in places, and feeling that the breath is being squeezed from him with the exertion. He has never run so fast - and still there seems no end to it. *'Stop it - stop that dog!'* he screams occasionally at startled bystanders, but no one is alert enough or dexterous enough to be able to stoop so low as to intercept the little fellow. Soon the chase has led down and around to the north wall of St Paul's and the church yard, a less-congested area but, unfortunately, also a place where the pug attracts the attention of two additional stray dogs who decide to give chase as well, all to the accompaniment of much barking and yapping. Faster and faster, around the perimeter of the churchyard they go, with Matthew barely able to keep pace with them now at all.

'Boris! Boris!' Matthew cries again, but to no avail - though as the creature and his pursuers turn into Ludgate Street, which is downhill all the way, he does manage to close the distance once more, with only the occasional stumble as he goes. Soon, Matthew is upon him, therefore, and eventually manages to corner him at the bottom of the hill where the narrow Fleet river runs towards the Thames. The steep hump of the bridge here proves sufficient deterrent to any further progress - though with the two stray mongrels also bearing down on him, Boris himself now seems more intent on survival than anything else.

'Come here, Boris, come here, boy,' Matthew murmurs as he reaches down towards the wig still held in its jaws, placing himself between Boris and the other animals and speaking as persuasively and as nicely as possible, and which under the circumstances is not really very nice at all. *'Come here you ruddy cur!'* he adds in a moment of weakened self-control as the dog swerves away and denies him yet again.

But worse is to come - he cannot prevent it - and a full scale dog fight ensues next - the precious object held between Boris's jaws now having become the bone of contention between the three canines, each competing for a piece of it - until within seconds the now badly shredded, muddy and virtually unrecognisable hair-piece, or what scraps of it remain, is hurled into the air and then down into the watery, flowing midden of the Fleet - no more than an odious, stinking ditch of turbid water at this place - and where, swirling a few times amid the offal and sewage therein is carried rapidly downstream, past the dark walls of Bridewell prison and where, sinking all the while, it vanishes into the depths of the mighty river Thames.

Gone.

Picking Boris up in his arms and defending himself with a few well placed kicks at the mongrels who would assail him still - and who do not abandon the field before biting some farewell chunks out of his once-pristine stockings - Matthew staggers back up Ludgate Hill with the tiny animal under his arm, his own tattered appearance being the target of many a curious and disapproving glance from the good citizens of London - as around the Church Yard he goes and eventually, by slow degrees, for he is exhausted now, returning into the familiar surroundings of Cheapside, Broad Lane and the Pig and Whistle - where he finds Johanna, stationed outside the trunk-makers shop by the entrance to the yard, a sedan chair at the ready, waiting in a state of nervous agitation. With manifest relief at the sight of Matthew's return, and a look of gratitude verging on awe for the obvious heroics he has undertaken on her behalf, she takes Boris from him and clutches the creature to her breast. Matthew has, she declares, surely saved its life and brought the little scallywag safely back to his Mummy, who can only cover its hairy little face in the most affectionate of kisses. But Johanna he notices, is also trembling inordinately, distressed far beyond what one would expect under the circumstances, and the reason for it is not difficult to ascertain as, without a word, she points over her shoulder into the yard to where every available inch of space is taken up by a crowd of noisy sailors; a veritable ocean of tricorns, woollen caps, rough leather jerkins and neckerchiefs all swaying as one; singing, shouting, chanting, and none too sweetly either - for he can hear it clearly now - the threatening and implacable refrain of: *'Drink, drink - we want drink!'* repeated over and over again - the whole place in uproar.

'The inn and the tavern downstairs are all closed up, and they are not at all happy about it,' Johanna states approaching tentatively from behind, as if employing his body as a shield as he steps through, farther under the arch to investigate. 'I am so sorry, my Wonder. I fear you might find it difficult to get back in now. Was that an important wig?'

'Oh ... yes, rather,' he says, realising he had just uttered the ultimate understatement. 'Anyway, Boris is restored to you in one piece, and I am greatly relieved to see you are safe. But, in the light of what is happening here, Madam, I think you had best be getting along now, don't you. You can pick up the post chaise to Greenwich just down the road. Come - I will hand you into your chair.'

'Matthew, no! Look at you: you are wounded - there is blood on your sleeve. My hero! How can I leave you with all these angry people outside your home. I am frightened for you if I go.'

'Then consider how much more concerned I should be for *your* safety, Madam, if you were to stay,' he answers her, and then, after explaining that the graze on his arm is merely the outcome of having fallen in the road, he adds, 'Please, I beg, you, Ma'am. You must go. This could all turn very ugly.'

And with a signal from him to the chairmen that they should open the door for her, he ushers the reluctant Mrs Woolveston into her seat. With Boris nestled in her lap, she gazes out at him forlornly through the open window, her face full of concern. 'Do be careful, my Wonder,' she appeals to him, with Boris, too, looking up with his big doleful eyes, seeming to concur.

'Convey the lady to the nearest coach stop for Greenwich,' he orders the men, and off they go, carrying her down into Cheapside and to safety.

Pushing his way with determination into the yard once again, he can see that all access to his apartments is indeed denied - though fortunately someone has had the presence of mind to have closed the stairwell door; so no harm done, at least not yet. In desperation, he looks about for anyone familiar - discovering at just that moment the landlady of the Pig and Whistle herself, Mrs Block, a stout, bustling woman who comes rushing through the crowd to meet him.

'Oh, Mr. Wildish! Thank the Lord you are here!' she cries, wringing her hands. 'My husband is indisposed - as are all the stable boys, too.'

'Indisposed?'

'Well ... yes. They've run off, in fact. The seamen say they've been marching since morning from Deptford, and are in no mood to drink ditch water here in the City for their pains. I fear that even if we open up and serve some ale, our building will be reduced to ruins. They needs pacifying, Sir.'

'I am flattered, Madam, that you believe I could pacify a mob of renegade sailors?' he states, casting about at the same time for a way by which he might get back up to his apartments - but all the stairs to the gallery appear to be shut. 'What on earth do you imagine I could do, anyway?'

'That you might address them and prevail upon them as a gentleman, Sir. Ask them to proceed in an orderly fashion. Oh, anything - but please do help!'

But just then, a common roar is heard, a bawdy cry, and when Matthew looks up, he beholds, leaning over the gallery outside his apartments, none other than the lovely Sarah, the laundry girl - smiling, her elbows on the balustrade, head in hands, and her ample cleavage without a lace tucker of any kind pressed up under her chin for the edification of all concerned. She appears to be enjoying it all immensely.

'Cor, come on darling!' they roar again. 'Show us your charms!'

'Yeah, or else let us come up and get some of them!' another shouts.

This is getting worse and worse.

'Oh, you cheeky boys!' she calls down to them. 'I have locked the door below and you shall not come in.'

'Why, then I shall soon climb up to you!' one of the young lads declares as, with all the determination of one about to ascend a mast in the teeth of a gale, he wraps his arms around one of the supporting pillars in readiness to climb – and with the intention, no doubt of enjoying all those very pleasures that Matthew himself had so narrowly been deprived of earlier.

'*Oh no you don't!*' Matthew shouts, spontaneously, pointing an accusing finger towards the youth.

Abruptly, a menacing silence descends upon the yard. A hundred hitherto angry or ribald voices hushed to a mere sibilance as they all turn, to a man to stare in his direction - so quiet, in fact, it is even possible to hear the traffic and market chatter of Cheapside - and at which Matthew, by now a sorry spectacle of torn clothes and ripped stockings but realising that he is probably the only one who can avert a full-scale riot, climbs onto an old tree stump in the corner of the yard and, raising himself up to his full height and swallowing a very large lump that has materialised in his throat, addresses the crowd thus: 'Gentlemen, I appreciate that you are thirsty. Do not, however, be anxious.'

Silence.

'We're not the ones who are anxious, mate,' one of the more burly of the men finally responds, pushing his way through closer to Matthew, the better to get the cut of his jib. '*You're* the one who ought to be anxious,' he adds, pointing a finger, 'because if we don't get something to slake our thirsts soon, we'll be breaking this place into smithereens with our bare hands.'

'Gentlemen, hear me out!' Matthew cries and, taking inspiration from the somewhat overblown rhetoric of a typical politician out on the hustings, endeavours to take command of the situation. 'My friends, I can assure you all, that within a few short minutes, I myself with the assistance of the proprietress here, Mrs Block, shall open the tavern door in the corner of the yard here and you shall be given drink. I ask only that you conduct yourself with the dignity deserving of your profession. For you have many friends and supporters here in the capital who will surely sympathise with your contention and I ... yes, *I* am proud to be numbered among them! If you are due prize money for your labours, then I believe you should have it. If you have suffered injustice at the hands of the government, I believe it should be righted. I support your cause, gentlemen. Wholeheartedly, I applaud your boldness. I admire your balls - metaphorically speaking, you understand. I am with you all the way - and, in short, I have an unbelievable belief in you (if that makes sense). Give me, pray, but a few moments and I trust we shall reach an accommodation of all your needs.'

A general hum of approval and acquiescence circulates around the yard, followed suddenly by a loud cheer as Mrs Block scurries through the crowd brandishing above her head a large iron key to open the entrance - and then another cheer almost equally as loud as Matthew finds himself hoisted up and carried in the same direction, aloft upon the broad shoulders and tattooed arms of several enthusiastic seamen, only narrowly avoiding a collision of his head with the lintel of the doorway as they pass inside. Here he leaps down and hurries to the bar. There is but one solitary cask tapped for use, and so, while Mrs Block does her best to fill jugs and tankards, he hastens downstairs to fetch another which he winches up before hurrying back upstairs again. He then takes a mallet and, as he has observed as a customer many times, inserts the tap over the keystone in the barrel and bangs it home, thereafter joining in with the general business of distribution as the ale begins to flow. By the time he serves the final man, however, the first one to have imbibed is already waiting for a top-up, and so once again he must descend to the cellar and do the business of loading another cask onto the hoist. And so it goes, with barrel number two and then three until, half an hour later, worn out in mind and body, he slumps down upon a bench in the corner of the tavern for a moment, wondering just how many barrels a hundred-odd thirsty sailors can consume before they are satisfied - and then, most extraordinary, a small boy, the link-boy it is, once again, appears in the doorway - his little cap upon his curly head, his clothes a bundle of rags, as ever. Surely not coming to Matthew's aid once more? But yes, because a second later, and even more astonishing, raising his fingers to his lips, he lets forth a whistle and with a wave of the arm, the familiar and most welcome face of Rose Tidey appears in the doorway - his clever Rose, the brewer's daughter - and with a couple of her burly porters in attendance, moreover, each with a gigantic barrel of ale upon their backs. *Reinforcements* - and at just the right moment.

'Poor Matthew!' she laughs, advancing on him across the room, hands on hips. 'Word is out all over the city that the Pig and Whistle is under siege. The boy told me that I should bring you enough ale to sustain an army - which I didn't think we could quite manage, but probably there'll be enough to satisfy this lot. We can settle up with the landlord later. What on earth has happened to you? Your clothes are in shreds.'

'Oh, I've been chasing a dog,' he explains, getting to his feet to greet her by placing a rather weary but nonetheless grateful kiss upon her cheek.

'It must have been some chase!' she observes, laughing still.

'It was,' he replies, nodding and with a sense of tremendous relief now that it really does look like there is going to be enough ale to go around.

Much hearty drinking continues, as Matthew returns to his duties at the bar, though this time aided by Rose herself and in which, weary as he is, the process becomes a mechanical one, drawing the ale, serving it, giving each jug or tankard a perfunctory rinse, serving again. In an odd sort of way he even derives a certain satisfaction from the process. Even his lovely laundress is among the crowds, he notices, clearly still enjoying herself while putting up a spirited resistance - endeavouring to 'repel all boarders' and invariably, to her credit, succeeding in doing so. Eventually, with a merry smile and hoisting her bag of sheets over her shoulder once more, she departs - safely he is pleased to observe. And then, all of a sudden, without warning, the men also start to leave. It happens so abruptly. With all the instinct and spontaneous mystery of a gigantic flock of roosting birds, they assemble as one teaming mass in the yard once again before vanishing into the afternoon almost as quickly as they had arrived, destination Whitehall. It is all over and, to Matthew's surprise, so very quickly, too. He is exhausted.

Rose assists him up to his chambers where, upon his bed, the last thing he is aware of is a delicate kiss on his forehead and nothing much else until he wakes in darkness much, much later.

By slow degrees, still hardly able to credit what has happened to him, he rouses himself and gets to his feet. Upon going to the window, and even before lighting a candle, he realises it must be very late - probably around 11 o'clock, as most of the rooms around the perimeter galleries are in darkness. The events of the day appear as little more than some fantastical nightmare now, leaving him with feelings of utter devastation and not inconsiderable bruising and aching bones from the damages inflicted during the chase. How calm and peaceful it all seems, he thinks. Not a soul to be seen anywhere. The sailors are gone. The lovely young laundress, Sarah, is gone, Johanna is gone, the priceless wig entrusted to his care by Lord Snatchal is in a thousand pieces at the bottom of the Thames. Everything is gone.

Eventually, a light appears, approaching from under the

archway and a moment later its bearer comes fully into view, a flare carried aloft revealing the tiny figure of the link-boy, his cap and curly hair all bright in the surrounding darkness. He stops, standing alone for a moment, in the centre of the yard, his distinctive chubby face now illuminated clearly. What *is* he doing, Matthew wonders? Here yet again. Has he been guiding a guest towards the inn? Does he perhaps sleep somewhere nearby? Does he in fact ever sleep at all? These and other idle questions float through Matthew's mind as he gazes down, wondering if the boy can see him as well. He can - for he lifts his head just then and glances up to Matthew's windows, and their eyes meet in recognition. And then, very slowly, the boy raises his arm and he waves, just the once. And Matthew has just enough time to acknowledge him and to wave back, just as slowly, before the little fellow turns and walks away, his hob-nailed boots clattering on the cobble stones as he goes, leaving only darkness and silence behind.

# ~ 10 ~
## ROOKERIES

His chair is carried swiftly to the appointed location in the leafy precinct of Lincoln's Inn Fields, a place where many a duel is fought, and where, beneath the canopy of autumnal trees, it meets with another arriving from the opposite direction and set down at the very same time - a hastily arranged rendezvous in the fading light of a November afternoon, Sam marching towards him, and he towards Sam, each brandishing his cane as some kind of symbolic staff or weapon. Both are very upset.

'Bloody fool!' Sam declares, his first words. 'Johanna has told me all I need to know. The rest I have deduced myself.'

'Well, it is your ruddy dog that's to blame. It would be as well if you could train the cur to have some measure of self-control.'

'Boris, under normal circumstances, is a highly disciplined creature, Sir,' Sam counters straight away. 'But those were hardly normal circumstances - an animal with an acute sense of smell being exposed to such temptation. The wig should have been under lock and key, guarded with your life.'

'Well I'm sorry, but I refuse to go treating a bunch of old muff hair with that level of veneration. It was an unfortunate accident, that's all.'

'Huh!' exclaims Sam, followed for good measure by an additional 'Huh!' - at which, side by side for the first time, they begin to walk, kicking through the deep, crunchy layer of fallen leaves - the setting sun casting a radiance upon their faces as they go. It is very windy, too, which only serves to heighten the intensity of their feelings.

'Even to dishonour just one - *just one* - of the contributions represented in that wig would have been sufficient to evoke a death sentence,' Sam remarks, irrepressible still. 'But you - *you*, Sir, have somehow managed to completely destroy the entire thing! Seventy years of veneration and noble tradition. You do, I take it, understand the implications?'

'Yes thank you, Sam,' Matthew responds, turning up his coat collar against the chill. 'I have gathered that much from my recent conversations with Lord Snatchal - and that the most likely outcome will be my transformation into an anatomical specimen for the edification of medical students. Your concern is most touching, nonetheless.'

'Oh, I'm not bothered about you. It's me I'm worried about! It was I who recommended you. We're both done for.'

At which Matthew cannot help recollect the spectre of Bone Crusher Webster once more, skulking around the yard of the inn that day of McNiel's visit. Worse, Matthew is almost certain he has seen him again recently, this morning being the latest sighting.

'Sam, listen: is it possible that Webster fellow would still be creeping around where I live?'

'I don't know - is he?'

'Yes, I'm sure I saw him again this morning. Surely it cannot be connected to the loss of the wig. How would he have discovered a thing like that so soon?'

But Sam does not answer straight away. 'Other reasons could be at play,' he suggests at length, calmer now.

'Such as?'

'Lord Snatchal. If he suspects, for example, that your dealings with the Countess that weekend at Snatchalcombe House were anything other than proper ... well, as we have already told you, he can be a dangerous man. All in all, Matthew, there could be numerous reasons why you might be enjoying the honour of Bone Crusher Webster's attentions.'

'How very flattering!' Matthew says.

'A flattery that will be as nothing, believe me, should news of your most recent calamity ever become common knowledge.'

'But what can we do? The job has to be completed sometime and the wig handed back. How can we possibly get out of this mess?'

'Well, Matt, my clever friend, the answer to that question is remarkably straight forward, even though I suspect it might prove far from easy to put into practice. You must somehow make a new one.'

'A new one? But where on earth could we obtain such a variety of suitable material, and at such short notice - not unless we could pop along to a bordello or something. Like Mistress Mountfast's. Ask the girls there to volunteer some samples?'

'Don't be ridiculous!' Sam grumbles in response. 'News of that would be all around town within hours, and would certainly come to the attention of members of the club, who are regular denizens of such places. At the moment, we at least have secrecy on our side. And time, I presume? When did you promise the work would be finished?'

'Before Christmas.'

'Less than two months away. Fair enough. How many individual specimens would you say were included in the wig itself? I don't suppose you had time to count them?'

'As a matter of fact, I did - and I also recorded their positions, since it became pretty obvious that a new foundation would be required. There were seventy-eight individual contributions. Um ... that does seem like rather a lot to get hold of, doesn't it?'

'Well there's yours and mine - that's a start,' Sam says. 'No one will be any the wiser as to the gender of the stuff, for heaven's sake - except Boris, perhaps. Little devil. That leaves seventy-six. I suppose normal head hair is out of the question? The wrong shape and texture?'

'Correct,' Matthew answers emphatically.

'But what about animal hair?'

'No, not that, either,' Matthew replies with a despondent shake of the head. 'The texture would in most cases be far too bristly - or else far too soft, like the mouse-skin on a merkin. Moreover, one must assume that those who venerate this material to such an extent would also possess a certain observational expertise in the subject. Oh, bloody hell! It is hopeless, isn't it. You're right, Sam. We *are* done for.'

For a while, they continue on in silence, heads down, each deep in thought, occasionally raising their eyes in idle observation or admiration of the elegant town houses, built by Inigo Jones and others which form the perimeter to the fields themselves, including a well-known theatre where people are already assembling outside. Some lights are showing in the houses, too, and lamps are being lit above the more affluent porticoes and doorways.

*'Beards!'* Sam cries, so loud that Matthew jumps at the sound. He is becoming nervous; edgy.

'Beards?' he echoes. 'What, you mean substituting pubic hair with facial hair?' And for a while, Matthew contemplates the appearance of a typical bushy beard, comparing it mentally with the other variety that it might be called upon to imitate. It is just plausible. And conveniently, at just that moment, they notice, seated nearby on one of the smart wooden benches, a gentleman with just such an appendage - possibly a vagrant, pushing his luck if he thinks the authorities will allow him to stay here, settling himself down into a reclining posture with a jug of gin. Approaching with an audacity that could only be born of extreme need, they join him on the bench, one each side, and ask him if they might examine his beard. Too startled to offer any resistance the unfortunate man, now sitting bolt upright, can only stare ahead wide-eyed as they begin to examine the object, taking hold of chunks of it between finger and thumb, as would tailors appraising the quality of cloth.

'Um, it is reassuringly crinkly,' Matthew remarks, pleasantly surprised.

'And of a workable length, moreover, in this instance,' Sam concurs, teasing out the full extent of it.

'Just a minute, what's all this about?' the man demands at last.

'Hush, Sir!' Sam says. 'Tell me, how many men among your compatriots or friends would you say maintain this unfashionable preference for facial hair? Because we would like to meet them.'

'I beg your pardon!' the gentleman exclaims, none too pleased and feigning a certain refinement, which does however, soon desert him. 'Ere... you're not a couple them Mohocks, are you - them rich kids who go about terrorising folks at night, cutting off ears or slitting the noses of watchmen for their sport?'

'My good Sir,' Sam begins again, 'the so-called Mohocks that you refer to have not been reported in the capital for some twenty odd years. They no longer exist outside of the realm of foolish rumour and hearsay, a figment of the imagination - unless, that is, you mean the fearsome tribe of native American Indians after whom they were once named. And they are nowhere near at hand, Sir, believe me - being on the opposite shores of the Atlantic Ocean. No, my colleague and I are both peace-loving and honest gentlemen of the guild of Barber Surgeons - Mr Smith here and myself, Mr Green. We have a charitable mission to go among the poor in our spare time - not, you will be relieved to hear, to preach or to fulminate against the evils of drink, but in pursuit of a far more noble mission: to attend upon the coiffure of gentlemen in need.'

'Well, I've never heard the like!' the man declares.

'No matter, Sir. We are passionate in our mission,' Sam continues effusively. 'And for no charge, Sir. For no charge whatsoever, do we undertake this philanthropic service. Therefore, if you could perhaps direct us to a few more gentlemen similar to yourself in need of attention we would be gratified, most gratified.'

'All right. But what's in it for me, then?'

'We shall bring plenty of gin. Gin in exchange for the honour of making the Unkempt tidy again, the better to glory the work of the Lord,' Sam replies, becoming ever more grandiloquent (if such were possible).

It is the gin that seems to clinch the deal. And so, with only a brief detour to the shops along Holborn to purchase a sharp pair of scissors, a leather bag and as many bottles of 'Mother Geneva' as their coat pockets will contain, they accompany the gentleman to the north of the city, to St Giles and to those infamous streets and houses around the area of *Seven Dials* which, he assures them, is his home.

By the time Matthew and Sam, still in the company of their new companion, have reached their destination, the temperature has dropped and it is entirely dark - a darkness accompanied by a swirling, pungent fog, aggravated by a thousand autumnal fires and domestic stoves and which has already spread its foul and pestilent murk everywhere. Most unpleasant.

'This way, gents!' the man, whose name, they learn is Tobias, calls from over his shoulder, as if sensing their reticence as the streets become ever more narrow, ever more filthy and eventually no more than a warren of tight, gut-squeezing alleyways running between hovels - these overhung with casements and gables that lean and jut out so far towards their opposite numbers on the other side as to almost meet in places and consequently presenting the appearance, should one dare to look up, of a ceiling belonging to a collection of sinister tunnels. How anyone might find their way along these unmarked ditches is a miracle in itself, and Matthew can only catch himself wondering how on earth he and Sam might ever find a way back out again.

'You know where this is, don't you,' Sam whispers from behind as they go, single file from necessity. 'This is the St Giles Rookeries - the most despicable, dangerous, villainous dive in all of London. No one goes here - not unless they are desperate or mad.'

'Then we are surely both,' Matthew whispers back over his shoulder, knowing the bitter truth of it already, his hand upon the hilt of his sword and feeling they might have made a terrible mistake in coming here at all, for gradually as his eyes become more accustomed to the gloom, he also becomes aware of other people, so many people, all in close proximity, some seated outdoors, upon the ground, their backs against the walls, others somehow behind the walls, yet so close that their presence can be felt as well as heard, like a stirring of vermin behind panels, just inches from him, all the people, talking, arguing, mumbling, weeping, groaning from either side. Occasionally, where a meagre light from a piece of tallow is burning from a window or open door, he can catch glimpses of them, fleeting sights of overcrowded, abject misery - faces, bodies wrapped in blankets, standing or lying where there is hardly space enough for a bed, others trying to cook a meal at an open fire, surrounded by children endeavouring to keep warm by the same means. He had not thought it possible that so many could live together and share such tiny spaces, so very cramped and stifling that many have simply spilled out into the streets for air - and thus, as he goes, unseen hands tug in wonder at his coat tails, his rich apparel here in such a place surely as conspicuous and as resplendent to them as the wings of an angel. The stench is appalling, a stench beyond anything he has ever known from the outside - while beneath his feet as they tread, the ground heaves with glutinous layers of unmentionable filth.

'Here we are gents,' their guide announces as he kicks open a stiff, broken door half hanging off its hinges. They duck to avoid the low lintel and enter down steps through a small hallway into a basement room surprisingly well lit in this instance and which also contains a substantial number of people, mostly men of the anticipated villainous and unkempt variety, clothed in rags, and mostly of a status scarcely above that of beggar or vagabond - all seated around the fireside upon various chairs, mattresses or simply bare floor. Among them are a number of young boys, who might be link-boys but, more likely, pickpockets, as they appear to be locked in negotiations with some of their elders, discussing the merits of an array of watches, purses and even a wig, laid out on the floor at their feet. They all stare up in astonishment at the splendour of the new arrivals.

'Blimey!' one of the men exclaims, getting to his feet. 'I'd better fetch the boss,' he adds, and vanishes through an entrance to another room, curtained off by an exotic and most incongruous length of green chintz.

'Sam,' Matthew whispers closely into his friend's ear, 'I am rapidly coming to the conclusion that the best course of action at this juncture would be for us to take to our heels now, and run as fast as possible, agreed?'

'I think if you care to glance over your shoulder, Sir, you will discover our exit is already barred,' Sam replies with studied nonchalance.

It is true enough, the door has been pushed shut and a stout wooden bar placed across it. They are stuck, everyone continuing to stare at them in silence, feasting their eyes upon their fine apparel, their immaculate coiffure and, perhaps worse, their expensive swords harnessed at their sides. At least plenty of beards are on display, Matthew reflects - *and what beards!* These are beards which, when coming round a corner would precede their owner by a good distance before the face on which it was attached might become visible. Ideal, in fact, for Matthew's purpose, should he and Sam ever manage to escape with their lives, that is - because this, without question, Matthew realises, is a den of the worst possible thieves and procurers of every kind of vice into which they have been brought, a place that might even include those wretches who rob graves and provide cadavers to the anatomists and surgeons for dissection and who are possibly eyeing up their freshest candidates at this very juncture.

The chintz curtain, meanwhile, with an abrupt and theatrical swish, is drawn back and a man emerges, tall of stature and far better dressed than the others in a pair of buff-coloured breeches, a clean white shirt and a bob-wig. He surveys the newcomers for a few seconds, at which Sam and Matthew make each a respectful dip of the head in recognition of one who is clearly the leader, but a leader of what or of whom they dare not contemplate.

'You'll be willing to relinquish your weapons, gentlemen?' he asks in a firm, though melodious voice, possibly of an Irish accent.

Grudgingly they obey, unfastening their sword belts and

handing the articles over to one of the men, who, to their dismay takes them, with their canes, off to some dark recess at the far end of the room - while another, responding to a signal from the boss, gets to his feet to attend to the fire, such as it is, burning from a grate in the chimney breast. 'I'd better get some more fuel,' he mutters - upon which, to Matthew's astonishment, he goes to the staircase and snaps off a couple of banisters from the dilapidated structure and throws them onto the fire. Clearly, having fallen foul of squatters, the property would, Matthew surmises, be one of the many speculative builds of recent times, thrown up quickly for short term gain and which would have a life-expectancy of not much greater than the span of its leasehold. The whole area here is subject to this kind of blight and therefore also to its inexorable decline.

'These gentlemen are men of charity,' their guide, Tobias, explains though not without a certain irony to his voice, Matthew thinks. 'They like to do good.'

'Oh, to do good - is that a fact! Well, that's very kind, I must say, very kind indeed,' the boss responds, speaking now in a fruity, affected manner, as if in imitation of how he would imagine fine folk might talk, and to which a ripple of amusement circulates among the occupants of the room. 'Sure, we do sometimes have gents in here who like to do good, though usually good to themselves, I should say. So maybe you could just get to the point, my friends, and tell us exactly what you would be wanting, eh? And what you'd be prepared to pay for it.'

'Sir, we are in want of nothing,' Sam avers, his chins wobbling as he shakes his head in vigorous denial. 'We are desirous only of undertaking our charitable work, to bring style and comfort to the afflicted.'

A roar of laughter rises up now at this latest remark, which even to Matthew's ears does sound most improbable in such surroundings.

*'What do you want, I say?'* the boss insists, clearly losing patience and still not willing to countenance any alternative explanation of their presence other than that born of his own limited experience and iniquity. 'If it's a job you'll be wanting of us, speak up! You shall not shock anyone here by your request. If it's a skeleton you're needing for your anatomy learning, we've got a fine selection of those upstairs - I can show you. Or do you want

to tidy up some debts? Claim on insurance? To get rid of someone?'

'No Sir, none of these,' Sam asserts.

'Ah, so you want women, eh? Well, we can arrange that.'

'No Sir,'

'Some boys, then? We can get you some molly boys, and no questions asked.'

'Certainly not, Sir!' Sam replies again with barely concealed horror.

'*Sheez!* Not women, not boys. Well, what *do* you want, you pervert!'

'We wish for nothing, Sir, as I say, other than to advance our mission. We will cut your hair, Sir, and give you a trim around the chin while we are at it. And we bring generous quantities of refreshment, moreover. Behold!'

At which Sam empties his coat pockets of four bottles of highest quality gin, and Matthew does likewise.

The boss's protestations are now entirely swept aside as, amid sounds of great enthusiasm and approval, the bottles are opened and within minutes everyone has availed themselves of cups, chipped glasses or any other container available by which to receive the benefaction - for it is gin of a proof and a quality that they would rarely have encountered before.

'Yes, well, I suppose some of us could do with a bit of tidying up here and there,' the boss concedes, smoothing his own long, unkempt beard and evidently quite excited by the prospect now. 'Do me first, will you?'

Sam bows a gesture of gratitude, as a chair is quickly brought forth and placed in the middle of the room - at which, brandishing his sparkling new scissors, Matthew gets to work straight away, combing and cutting the bedraggled hair of the man, ensuring that a generous length of ginger-grey beard is recovered at the same time - and resulting in a transformation so dramatic, that the man himself, with neatly clipped and perfectly pointed beard, comes to resemble nothing so much as a swanky Elizabethan grandee - so very fine, in fact, that it leaves everyone breathless with admiration. Thus transformed, the boss, holding a fragment of mirror that has been found for him, prances up and down the room, admiring himself with all the pride of a tart on parade in the Piazza of Covent Garden.

'Cor, don't I look pretty!' he exclaims. 'Look at me - don't I just!'

'Beautiful, boss!' one of the men declares.

'Yeah, very handsome,' volunteers another. 'A cup of gin and trim round the chin. Ain't we lucky!'

Thus within a very short space of time they are all queuing up for the privilege of being similarly shorn, with Matthew working non-stop for the next thirty minutes, and with increasingly aching fingers as he struggles to meet demand. Sam, meanwhile, has been at work, too - retrieving the beards from the floor and placing them into the leather bag, endeavouring as he does so to keep each sample separate from the others, a pre-occupation that eventually attracts some unwelcome curiosity from others in the room.

'Ah, yes, just doing a spot of - er - cleaning up,' Sam remarks with an attempt at nonchalance. 'Wouldn't wish to leave the place untidy, after all.'

Laying all suspicions aside, Sam's detractors resume their places in the queue once more - essential, since there seems to be no end now to the number of candidates for the sheering, and Matthew is certain that word must have got out around the locality because different men are appearing all the time, coming in from outside to take advantage. He has done twenty already, and more are still waiting – and thus, needing to allow his hands and fingers to recover, he accepts a cup of gin, and takes a few moments repose, accepting a seat next to one of his more successful transformations, Tobias himself, in fact, their original guide and who is hardly recognisable now in his improved state.

'Are you sure we can't interest you in any feminine company?' Tobias inquires. 'We've got plenty to spare, y'know.'

'Well I can't see too many ladies around here,' Matthew remarks, emboldened by the strong gin to be blunt. 'I thought it was some kind of lonely bachelors society when I first came in, to be honest.'

'No, no, they're a-bed, most of them, keeping it warm for us.'

'In bed? What at this early hour?'

'Well there's hardly much else to do, is there!' Tobias exclaims, irascible. 'We can't go wasting money on fancy candles and things. No, we offer beds for hire. That's how we makes our money, some of us, anyway. Thruppence a night for a single bed; tuppence to share a double. Get the drift? So the ladies, if they're down on their luck, with nowhere to shelter for the night, they just slip in with one of us - so it's a lot cheaper than on their own in a cold bed. Oh yeah, we've got it all worked out, mate, don't worry. And now we're all looking so handsome, the lot of us, I reckon we'll be well away tonight.'

'Glad to hear it,' Matthew responds, unable to even begin to imagine the appearance or state of hygiene of any woman willing to share a bed with these wretches. And then he takes up his scissors again.

A further half an hour passes until he feels he has probably cut the hair and beards of half the men in London. Another cup of gin is imbibed and then Matthew requests from the boss, who is by this time reclining like an emperor at the far end of the room on what looks to be some kind of dais, whether their swords and canes might be restored to them so that they might depart - and to which the man himself sits up and then laughs heartily before replying: 'Oh, come now, gents, I don't think we need trouble you with any additional baggage for your homeward journey. Sure, you will not be needing them expensive weapons of yours, since I can guarantee you safe passage at least to the bottom of the lane here.'

'But what then?' Sam inquires.

'Then you are on your own, of course, ha, ha! Oh, and if you don't mind we will also relieve you of your wig, Sir, before you depart. And very nice it is, too.'

To which, one of his minions steps up, and with one swift and adroit movement plucks Sam's costly wig from his head. Very quickly, and with an artful twirl of the fingers, he secrets it within the seams of his waistcoat. Sam is furious, and it is only by a timely hand on his shoulder that Matthew is able to pacify him and thus preserve their safety.

'Sam we should leave now, at once, while we at least still have our britches remaining to us.'

Sam can only agree. And within moments they have been released, out in the cold night air, minus swords and cane, and Sam minus his wig, a bald pate illuminated by whatever faint moonlight is able to penetrate the alleyway in which they find themselves - and which, by all that they can discern, is not even the one by which they had entered earlier. At least they have secured their booty, the bagful of beards. Mission accomplished. They are fortunate, too, in that no one troubles them as they go - for they are still clearly within the territory of their former hosts. But as they reach the end of the lane, they are forced to concede that this might well be the boundary of it and that consequently, as a matter of survival, they must now endeavour to extricate themselves from this warren of dangerous and lawless hovels as quickly as possible.

It is late, and those same streets once so crowded are now eerily quiet and empty.

'Confound these endless unmarked alleys!' Sam curses, as they try to locate the most direct route out of the Rookeries. 'It is imperative that roads should be signed in my opinion - all roads. And it is to this city's shame that the authorities have not yet managed to do so. We are completely lost, I swear.'

'No, no, look, Sam - if that is indeed moonlight up there, which I am almost certain it is, then we must turn and go this way, which will be southward, the better to reach some familiar streets, perhaps even the Piazza itself, if my calculations are correct.'

'I feel naked,' Sam declares irritably.

'What, you mean without your sword? Yes, I know.'

'No, Sir, without my wig. It's ruddy freezing out here without anything on the head!'

'And I have lost my purse and my watch, too' Matthew asserts, feeling with his palms those vacant places where every object of value or worth has been picked from him by those thieves.

'Likewise,' Sam grumbles. 'My treasured watch, my finest silver Le Roy taken from me. Damn their eyes! Those scoundrels.'

In time, they locate a somewhat more open lane leading upwards - everything beginning to look more commercial with the shuttered windows of second-hand clothes shops and the occasional pawnbroker. Surely this would be leading them towards Drury Lane or some such street, Matthew reflects as they hurry along. But just as they reach a narrowing between the buildings and a flight of long, sloping steps up ahead, two men appear - gentlemen from what they can discern by their apparel, though it is impossible to see their faces.

'Good evening, gentlemen,' Sam greets them. 'If you could provide us with directions to the Piazza we would be much obliged.'

'Oh, no, Sir, why, pray, should we do that?' one replies, and Matthew can see now and by their stance they are clearly in no mind to yield or let them pass and that they are both masked and in possession of swords.

'What do you mean?' Sam demands. 'By your leave, Sir, why so unfriendly?'

Both men are young, and probably not a little inebriated. And then, to his horror, Matthew hears a sound to his rear and turns - to discover two more, also masked, coming up behind. It is an ambush. The streets here are terribly quiet at this hour, with every sound, every click of a heel, every word echoing against the walls of the alleyway and the stone steps on which they are all standing. And when one of the pair above, probably the leader, draws forth his sword, the sound of it leaving the scabbard it utterly dreadful.

'I say! Now what do we have here?' he inquires as with his sword tip he deftly lifts the leather bag from Sam's grasp, hoisting it up for inspection before tossing it over Matthew's shoulder to one of the men behind.

Turning once more, Matthew watches as the man catches the bag and opens it to examine its contents.

'Nothing in it!' he declares, picking out the odd tuft of hair. 'Just a load of old packing material.' And then, losing interest, he simply casts the bag to one side.

'We have no money, if that's what you're looking for,' Sam declares. 'We have already been relieved of our purses elsewhere this evening.'

'Oh, I say, George, did you hear that?' The principal among them declares addressing his companion. 'How frightfully unfortunate! Relieved of their purses.'

'Oh, most unfortunate, David, yes!' the other at his side replies with a tut-tut as he, too, draws forth his sword.

'The poor fellows appear to have no means of protection, either,' comes the voice of one of the men behind - though neither Matthew or Sam dare turn to look again, or avert their eyes from the proximity of the blades pointing in their direction from above.

'This is a public highway!' Sam blurts out. 'Who do you think you are, anyway, to inhibit its use?'

'Who do we think we are?' the leader echoes, laughter in his voice. 'Why, we are the Mohocks, Sir. Yes - that's right. And we much prefer the smell of blood to the glint of money, and thus you need have no worry over your possessions. We are in search of amusement, that's all - and have already slit the throats of enough stray dogs and cats this evening to be wanting a change of itinerary. And *you,* we have decided, are it.'

'Um - what was that you said earlier, Sam?' Matthew murmurs, 'just a figment of the imagination, those Mohocks?'

'Yes, well, I might need to - er - revise my opinion on that matter,' Sam remarks with bravado, though Matthew can detect the fear in his voice now, which is tremulous and tight. It is clear they are in deep trouble, and they can only exchange glances of despair.

'Enough! Let us pass, gentlemen!' Sam demands, stepping up once again with amazing bravery, though he must surely comprehend now that it is futile. 'Do you have no fear of the law?' he adds, almost pleading now.

'The law!' George laughs.

'There's not a justice in the land would dare touch *us,*' one of the men behind confirms. 'Friends in high places, don't you know. My father is a Viscount, actually.'

'And mine an Earl,' the other trumps his friend as he begins to amuse himself by pinking Matthew with his sword point. He can sense tiny shreds of his coat being cut, penetrated by the sharp steel. Knowing that they face certain injury or worse, Matthew is left with no alternative, therefore. He takes out his scissors.

This is accompanied merely by further bouts of hilarity, all high-pitched giggling at the sight of a man armed with scissors against four short-swords, which despite the term given to them are at least seven times greater in length than anything a barber might avail himself of in an emergency. It is a chilling sound, the laughter of cruelty and foolish intoxication - the only other sound, oddly enough, being that of somebody in the distance running, a clattering of heels on cobblestones - but too far away to be of any use, even if they were to call out for help.

'Let's cut them now!' one of the men behind urges his companions, losing patience. 'Let's take off their ears.'

'Forbear, Sir!' Matthew declares brandishing his scissors. But a thrust from the man's weapon narrowly misses his hand and rips through his cuffs. He feels the heat of his own blood on his forearm as he leaps back, narrowly avoiding more serious injury.

In the meantime, the footfalls in the distance have become louder, now obviously turning into the lane itself and coming their way - something which the four Mohocks seem to become aware of now for the first time, because David and George turn their heads in that direction, glancing uneasily over their shoulders at the intrusion.

And then the source of it becomes apparent. At first it is scarcely more than a light, a flame that becomes visible, carried aloft by a small boy running down the steps towards them. Onward he comes, steadfast, his stride unbroken, his hobnailed boots clattering so very loudly upon the cobblestones until, to the surprise and consternation of the men above, he runs straight between them, his torch if anything even brighter now for the speed of it, so they must snatch their coat tails away to avoid being singed as the little curly-headed fellow pushes through. But that's not all - for clutched in the boy's other hand, and Matthew can scarcely believe what he is seeing, are two swords, sheathed. Brandishing them proudly and with a twirling movement on his heels, and hardly breaking stride, he throws one to Matthew and the other to Sam, and within seconds both the weapons are drawn and restored to their rightful owners - for Matthew can tell instantly by the precise heft and reassuring feel that it is, indeed, his own sword - yes, his very own weapon at his command once again!

Seizing on the moment of distraction, Matthew hurls the scissors into the face of one of the men behind, a blow which, accompanied by a terrible cry, embeds itself with horrible accuracy even through the thickness of his mask - and then, a split second later, he has leapt into range of the men above.

'Well now - en garde, gentlemen!' Matthew declares, assuming an extravagant, foppish pose, left hand on hip, his sword-hand pronated and held high as he circles the point in front of their noses - calculated to enrage them both.

Sam, meanwhile, has turned his attentions on the remaining man behind - the other one being on the ground by now, groaning and clutching at his face. No further threat.

'Your father may be an Earl, Sir,' Sam declares with studied nonchalance, 'but your mother is surely a whore!'

This deliberate aggravation also does the trick, and Sam's parry and riposte in response to the man's first angry lunge strikes home instantly, accompanied by a horrible scream - a deep penetration to the shoulder - to which he falls back in confusion, only to receive an additional slash to the thigh from the same weapon which draws forth considerable blood, gushing as he collapses.

The two men above, meanwhile, confused for a moment but

now with determination and fury, have already descended upon
Matthew, and it is all he can do to deflect their weapons with a
series of rapid ripostes, especially difficult as they are both on
higher ground. But his swordsmanship is far superior, and the men
are unsteady on their feet, the worse for drink as they slip and slide
in the muddy margins of the lane. It is at that moment, when the
one by the name of George, with little more than a twitch of the
nose at first, notices the appearance of smoke coming from
between his legs and then a second later that his clothing is, indeed,
on fire - a smouldering of his coat tails that has suddenly flared up
into a bright girdle of flame.

'My God, my privies are ablaze!' he cries hurrying away down
the steps in search of the nearest conduit or puddle, going like a
fiery rocket, slapping at his backside as he goes, and stumbling
eventually, too, as Sam follows at a calmer walking pace, leaving
just the one, David, the leader to be dealt with.

'Even odds between us at last, I believe, Sir!' Matthew declares
as, leaping up to the vacant space at the side of his assailant, he
quickly turns him and then, stepping in closely in response to his
initial thrust, has his sword enclosed and then taken from him in
one swift, devastating movement that places the man's weapon
across his own throat. Matthew gives him a knee to the groin and
then, quickly disengaging, thrusts the same sword straight down
into the man's standing foot - penetrating the tiny bones and sinews
as the blade goes right through to the sole - and deeper, twisting
itself into the ground where it remains - followed by a terrible
protracted scream from the man as Matthew steps away.
Whimpering, the tears streaming down his face, the scoundrel
doesn't even have the guts to pull his own sword from his foot, and
so - clutching the hilt in trembling hands, can only sink down on
one knee, still impaled on the spot.

All the commotion, meanwhile, especially the continued cries
from the man with the blazing rear end, does finally begin to attract
some attention - spectators from windows and doorways, residents
and shopkeepers emerging along the length of the lane, so that the
fellow is at least able to have his agony extinguished by the
application of the contents of a chamber pot. But he looks to be
badly injured. The forth man, meanwhile, the wretch still self-
indulgently occupied with the scissors wound to his face, and the
very same who a moment earlier was hoping to relieve two

unarmed men of their ears, remains slumped against the wall, and he can only hold forth an imploring hand, begging mercy as they return to him. A substantial build-up of blood has evidently taken place behind his mask, for as he removes it, a great splash falls forth upon his shirt front - a souvenir of a wound, Sam remarks to him as he stoops to retrieve the leather bag nearby, that no amount of *friends in high places* will be able to remedy - and then off they go, hastening after the boy who has hardly broken stride throughout, continuing to light their way until they reach some familiar streets - and, soon, they are out upon the bright lights and congested pavements of the Piazza and in search of a carriage. The boy will not join them, though - for he is still walking briskly and, despite Matthew's protestations and calling out to him, keeps on walking, so that the last they see of him is his tiny figure, his link-light still carried aloft, disappearing around a corner into Bedford Street. It is over - the whole extraordinary incident since his most dramatic arrival on the scene having lasted no more than a few minutes.

'Cheapside!' Matthew calls to the coachman as they clamber up into the cab and then begin to roll away, safe at last and thanking the good Lord and all their lucky stars for their deliverance.

'I'll trouble you for a little Brandy if you have any,' Matthew calls to the coachman through the window - and a moment later a hip-flask is handed down and into the carriage - the contents of which are quickly applied to his wound, a long flesh wound, as he had suspected, the length of his forearm. The application of the liquor is very painful for a second or two, but the remedy must be carried through, he knows, to avoid any possibility of gangrenous infection.

'That was a ruddy miracle!' Sam declares loudly as he leans back into the seat opposite, for the first time able to let go of the horror of it all as he emits a deep sigh, verging almost on an animalistic growl, because the smell of blood is still in their nostrils.

'Yes. I assume it was your sword, too, that was restored to you, was it not?' Matthew inquires once he has regained his breath and composure after the application of the liquor. 'It was definitely mine - look, my very own restored to me by the boy.'

'Yes. Yes, that's right. But how on earth did the little rascal manage to get hold of them?'

'And how did he manage to find us in time?' Matthew adds. 'I can only think he must have been in that hovel all the while, part of that den of thieves. Well, whatever - I sincerely hope I shall have a chance to express my gratitude when next we meet.'

'What - you know him then, the boy?'

'No, not really. Only that I seem to have encountered him quite often of late. He is almost like an old retainer now - as if somebody has hired him to look after my interests. Most odd.'

'Well, for my part, I would be obliged if you could convey my appreciation, also, Matt, and to recompense him generously with coin. He has saved us both from a terrible fate.'

'I agree,' Matthew confirms as he decides to takes a peep inside the bag and looks with approval upon the mass of crinkly hair therein, and all of a most pleasing variety of shades and textures, too. It should, he reflects, as Sam leans forward to join him in sampling the booty, prove more than adequate for the purposes of remodelling the Cornhill Wig Club's pride and joy.

'To your satisfaction, I trust?' Sam inquires, scratching himself vigorously on the back of the head for some reason.

'It is - even though none too pleasant on the nose at this stage,' Matthew states as he draws the string at the top tightly closed, while also surrendering to the urge to scratch himself in various places. He cannot help himself. 'A bit itchy, it makes one feel, does it not?' he adds, and wonders just what else they might have brought away with them from the Rookeries.

'An unfortunate case of *Roger the Lodger*, I believe,' Sam observes, with a further scratch. And they laugh together, quite hysterically for some time as the brandy flask exchanges hands, back and forth - not overly concerned by the presence of the odd coot or two, but simply relieved to be in one piece, rejoicing in their own miraculous preservation.

# ~ 11 ~
## THE RAINBOW

It is official: the destruction of London by hoards of rabid and bloodthirsty Highland warriors is imminent. The newspapers, and especially those of the Whig press, are full of lurid detail:

*'Relentless Advance. Jacobite Hoards Cross Border into England.'*
*'Rebels Marching on Carlisle.'*
*'Atrocities Inflicted on the Innocent - from our Correspondent in the North.'*

Matthew closes the broadsheet he has been reading and, getting to his feet, replaces it on the rack before returning to his seat in the window and from where, looking back into the room, he surveys once more the comfortable interior of this his favourite coffee house, The Rainbow in Fleet Street - just the right distance from his apartments off Cheapside to warrant a tidy walk, but not too far removed as to require special arrangements of transport. The coffee and chocolate are good, too; there is always a welcoming fire on days that are chilly; and even in these troubled times it remains orderly and the conversation civil. Yes, he likes the Rainbow.

The coffee houses of London come in all shapes and sizes, and in his time Matthew has probably visited every one - each having its own unique and distinct character consistent with the nature of its clientele - some being for academics and scholars, others for lawyers and politicians; some for the musicians and writers, others for jobbers and stockbrokers. Political affiliations are catered for, as well. The Tories have their favourite haunts, the Whig party theirs. What all have in common, however, is the propensity for gathering and broadcasting news, and this with an inexhaustible hunger. It is as if all of cultured society has a voice here - or, as the popular ditty has it:

*There's nothing done in all the world,*
*From monarch to the mouse*
*But every day or night 'tis hurled*
*Into the coffee house.*

Your typical coffee house is not only a place where a gentleman might come for news, however. It is also a retreat. Here a man might fill his pipe and sit alone with his meditations or else enjoy a meal in company with friends or discuss the latest intrigues at Court. It is where he can, if he's of a mind to, browse at leisure through the announcements of shipping, or to peruse the lost-property lists upon the walls. Here he can buy shares in trading companies, or take out an insurance policy on just about anything (or anyone). He can pin an advertisement to a notice board, or leave a letter to be picked up by the post. Occasionally in recent times, women can be found among the society of the coffee houses, too, particularly in those of a more liberal persuasion, catering to those of education and wit. Above all, for Matthew, it is a place to do business, since every profession is represented here, and consequently every variety of wig - because just like the coffee houses themselves, the wigs of gentlemen also come in all shapes and sizes: from the formal, full-bottomed periwigs of the gentry that could use up to ten ordinary heads of hair in the making, to the short and eminently practical bob wigs of the merchants and stockbrokers; or even the 'bag wigs' - the type he is wearing himself this morning, with the hair at the nape neatly enclosed in a silk pocket to protect the collar or waistcoat. And such a range of qualities, and standards of workmanship on display - from the work of the cheap, barber-shop peruke maker, heavily powdered, coarsely woven - he can spot them a mile off - to those modelled at the hands of his own fraternity, the esteemed craftsmanship of the gentleman Master Wig-maker: luxurious and lustrous items, expensive and individually fitted; the envy of many, the possession of so very few.

But all this diversity counts for naught this morning, for the common preoccupation of everyone present - and it would be the same at every other establishment in the capital - is that of rebellion. The Rainbow is as raucous as he can ever remember it. Complete strangers compete for space among the usual crowd of garrulous regulars that he knows and recognises - all crowded together at tables, smoking their long-stemmed clay pipes and engaged in the most lively discussion concerning the latest news from the front line - for that is what it has become now, and must be recognised as such, *the front line* - with divisions of the Jacobite army, having already established themselves across the border in the northern counties and progressing ever farther southwards with the town of Carlisle already in their sights. The Bonny Prince is now at large upon the very roads and highways of England, not just those of some remote Highland Glen, and consequently the mood among the customers of The Rainbow even at this early hour of the day is one of palpable anxiety - the first time Matthew has really noticed such a universal change in sentiment among so many.

'The situation is dire, gentlemen - and, what's more, bad for business,' one of the guests within Matthew's earshot is heard to utter - a smart fellow, sombre of dress, probably to do with banking or the stock market.

'The Young Pretender - he is obviously no fool, either,' states another, a somewhat more elderly man, with the dismal look of one who might even now still be able to recall the previous attempt to restore the Stuarts, thirty years ago and which, thankfully, failed spectacularly on that occasion. 'He's made it clear he intends to preserve all the liberties and freedom of worship, and that he will be in no hurry to disband the union between Scotland and England, either. And why so magnanimous? Because, he views the populace of both countries as his rightful subjects, and he expects them to rally to his standard. His is not a divisive campaign, gentlemen - nor is it a Catholic uprising against our own Protestant King, as some would have it. Why, there are even Catholics up there who oppose it, they say, especially in the Lowlands of Scotland.'

'Precisely,' chimes in the stockbroker once again. 'This is a war of civilised values, not religion. The Lowland Scots are remarkably like us. They are merchants and traders, enlightened and educated men who powder their wigs and bathe once a week. The truth is, they don't want Bonny Prince Charlie and his grubby Highland savages in Edinburgh anymore than we do down here in London.'

'Don't you be so sure!' A third gentleman from a neighbouring table buts in, holding the bowl of his pipe and pointing the stem accusingly in the other's direction. 'It says here, in the paper I am reading, that Charles and his men have been feted and welcomed all over Scotland, his triumphs celebrated with poems, portraits and medallions. The ladies of Edinburgh, in particular, seem inordinately partial to him - and they say he holds court there in Holyroodhouse as would an emperor. Not only that but these so-called savages you talk of have kept good discipline among themselves - at least so far. They have been urged to treat the citizens with the utmost courtesy and to pay for everything they make use of - orders from the very top, from the Jacobite leader in the field, Lord Murray - a brilliant soldier and entirely in favour of this Popish Pretender and his ambitions. And thus they have managed to take possession of the city of Edinburgh - and consequently the hearts and minds of forty thousand people - without spilling a single drop of blood.'

'How, then, do you reconcile that with these reports I am reading in this paper, here, Sir?' yet another, a rotund gentleman in a tight waistcoat and even tighter cravat, joins in - red of face and most animated all of a sudden, loudly tapping the broadsheet with his fingers. 'It states, and I quote: women have been exposed, yes, exposed, Sir - stripped naked at the market in Edinburgh and then butchered by the rebels. Pamphlets have been pouring onto the streets of English towns in the North detailing this and every other atrocity, including, it says here, the devouring of infants - cannibalism, Sir! The *not-so-Bonny* Prince, what! Fine words and deeds on the outside, yes - but in truth a man in league with the Anti-Christ and, worse, the king of France! Our clergymen, therefore, are quite right to denounce this monstrous youth and all his barbarous intentions towards the people of these isles, as the Devil incarnate that he surely is. Our wives and daughters are not safe, Sir, and as it stands are likely to be ravaged by these tartan beasts - coming down here brandishing their gigantic claymores.'

'Claymores? What's a claymore, anyway?' someone asks.

'A broadsword, no less than three feet in length that can slice a man in two with one mighty stroke.'

'Yes - they cut their foes to pieces with their weapons, and eat human flesh, it states here. We are undone, I'm afraid.'

'Nonsense, Sir! The Scots are no match for our plucky redcoats.'

And so it continues, as Matthew, reclining back into his seat, gradually ceases to pay much attention to any of it - this unseemly frenzy of speculation and panic. And that such futile discourse should be taking place here in The Rainbow, moreover, this once so peaceful oasis of etiquette and dignity, is most disappointing. Turning away from them for a while, he glances out the window instead, to all the busy commerce of the roadway and the pavements outside and where, even amid the very hub of the publishing industry of Fleet Street, all seems so much more reasonable and calm - and where he is also pleasantly distracted by the sight of a well-dressed young couple, arm in arm, walking past, clearly in love, their eyes filled only with regard for each other - he being most-dashing in the finest of silks, and she in a riot of pink and blue flounces and ribbons. What does the war mean to them? Would the constant cries of the paperboys proclaiming their dour warnings on every street corner even register with them as they skip past, talking of all their plans and laughing together in their happiness? Would they care? Unlikely.

'Ah yes,' he thinks to himself, 'life must go on.' And for him, too, thus, fortified by the typical warm glow of self-indulgence that an hour here at The Rainbow invariably brings, he turns his thoughts once again to his own very personal campaign of conquest, to his seven heavenly bodies, that magical seven - which, he has to admit, still has a substantial number of vacant positions yet to be filled. So far, he has only three that he can be confident of - the passionate Caroline Bolter from Ranelagh Gardens for the role of Jupiter; the luscious young laundry girl Sarah May for Venus; and of course the lovely Rose Tidey, still his favoured candidate for the Moon, even though he has yet to re-establish in any practical sense their intimacy of earlier times. But even then, he is still in want of at least four more, the Sun, Mars, Mercury and Saturn. Perhaps this evening will present new possibilities. For this coming night, at last, is that of the Grand Masquerade that he has been invited to, organised by private subscription at a mansion in The Strand - a venue in opulent surroundings and yet, like most masquerades, open to a wide spectrum of society, a place where, for those concealed beneath the anonymity of a mask and costume, anything might happen (and usually does) and all manner of intriguing encounters might take place (and usually do). What's more, and this is the greatest jest and audacity of all, he has invited Sarah herself to accompany him - and in disguise! With all the skill at his command, he has decided to pass her off as a young beau, replete with one of his finest wigs. What fun that will be. He simply cannot wait.

Ah, dear Sarah! How remarkable, that on that very day he had set his thoughts to composing his sonnet to Venus, she had appeared and entered his life - as though the very act of writing it had acted as some kind of magical evocation. And already, with far more leisure at their disposal than upon her first visit, they have enjoyed each other in fullest measure - those sweet, secret hours locked in their embrace while he would kiss her lovely lips all swollen with desire, or else would whisper gentle encouragement to her eager ear, so keen of study. Of course, she is young, much younger than he, and her fondness for him is driven, he suspects at least in part, by all those delights that leisure and liberty bring to the discovery of love's rich and varied repertoire. But no matter. Having reached an age at which he might with some measure of authenticity take on the role of seasoned rake and libertine, he has accordingly become the wicked seducer and teacher to her innocence. And he knows, by her sighs, that he has pleased her well and that he will be able to persuade her to come to him whenever the tryst shall need to be repeated. This most ripe, fecund and succulent fruit of Venus is his now - and there has, indeed, been much pleasure in the tasting of it.

And so one must conclude, if such joys await a man so very palpably in the here and now, why should he be concerned over phantoms of war or the strife that exist merely upon the pages of a newspaper! Why, in a universe of so many beautiful women should he allow any of these cantankerous old fools jabbering away around him amid the fetid stench of tobacco smoke and stale coffee dregs to tarnish even for one minute the treasures awaiting him outside - there at every turn of every corner in this fabulous city? He shall not let them spoil his fun. And as he anticipates instead the coming evening with Sarah and thinks fondly upon every kiss and fragrant embrace that awaits him amid all the wine and laughter of the masquerade, it brings a stirring sensation to his very core and a quickening of his pulse in anticipation.

Suddenly, though, Matthew is shaken out of his daydreams because a serious altercation is taking place in the room. Two men are on their feet - and one, wagging an accusing finger at the other in most ungentlemanly fashion, is fulminating against the almost universal contention being voiced against the Jacobite cause: a brave fellow, to be sure - being very much at variance with everyone else.

'It is a disgrace, Sir - an utter disgrace,' he protests, 'that you should be so hell-bent on ignoring so many of your fellow countrymen who are courageous enough to demonstrate their loyalty to the true king in exile - the true king of England, Sir, and his son the Bonnie Prince - the very pattern of all manly virtues and one calculated to render the nation happy should it ever have the good fortune to see his blood-line restored. How much longer should we be governed by the Elector of Hanover - a boorish German who barely speaks English!'

'How dare you, Sir!' the other man, the stock-broker shouts, on his feet now and clearly furious that anyone should venture to make such a seditious remark in public. 'If you are referring to our good King George, Sir, I suggest you hush your mouth!'

'I shall not, Sir!' the man protests, his right hand already across to his waist, covering the pommel of his sword. 'I shall not be silent a moment longer and listen to such drivel, such calumny! This is the biased nonsense of the Whig press - full of innuendo and propaganda, with no foundation of truth whatsoever. God bless him, I say - Charles Edward Stewart! And his father, too, the rightful king of England for whom his son is come amongst us as a lamb. God bless him, and beseech the Lord in Heaven to have mercy, to take him unto Himself and lend him a crown of glory here upon the earth as well!'

'Scandalous, Sir!' the stockbroker bellows, incensed by the obvious religious connotations of the man's speech. Pulling off his glove, he is just about to throw down his challenge when his companions hasten to surround him and prevent him from doing so because it would almost certainly result in a duel taking place to satisfy honour. 'Nay, then let me draw here and now,' he protests, struggling to place his hand upon his sword next, knowing all the while that he would be conveniently prevented from doing so. 'Let me draw, let me draw, I say!' he demands again, though not very convincingly.

Matthew, meanwhile, and instinctively favouring the underdog, finds himself on his feet, too, and at the side of the Jacobite sympathiser, about to remove his glove also. Placing his hand upon his arm, Matthew urges him to desist. 'Be content, Sir, I beg you,' he whispers fervently into the man's ear, who seems not to hear him at first, so full of passion is he, genuinely so in his case, leaning forwards like a bristling boar about to charge, his shoulders heaving with indignation. But eventually, his path blocked by Matthew and several others, he does calm down, and both antagonists are gradually made to see reason. The Jacobite who praised the Pretender in almost messianic terms a minute earlier allows himself to be escorted from the coffee house, while the stockbroker who had responded with such hollow indignation is persuaded by slow degrees to be seated and to imbibe yet more of the same very strong beverage that has possibly been the fuel behind so much of the tumult anyway. Taking out his comb and attending to his wig, he endeavours to make light of it all: 'Beseech the winds to favour my delicate frizz,' he jests, while one or two others take out their combs and emulate him. Order is restored amid a positive orgy of collective preening.

Matthew, meanwhile, though once again returning to his window seat, soon feels it is time for him to depart also, to leave them all to their newspapers and rumour-mongering - lest he come to be regarded with equal suspicion as the poor fellow he has just aided.

It is a fine, though cool afternoon, and shortly after commencing his walk homeward, with still plenty of time to spare before Sarah's arrival at his apartments, Matthew elects to turn down towards the bridge for a look at the river, a favourite diversion for him. The great thoroughfare of the bridge is as crowded and congested as ever - the usual free-for-all of carriages, chairs, horses, cattle and poultry, all competing for their passage from one end to the other, walled-in either side and, in many places, being directed through the narrow spaces that tunnel beneath the very buildings themselves - reminding him of the rumour circulating among the citizens lately that many, if not all, of the ancient buildings will soon have to be pulled down. The modern city simply cannot tolerate the inconvenience of it any longer, this sprawling edifice of shops and businesses left over from medieval times. Other bridges will be built of course - the Westminster bridge is already underway to the West - but that will be years until completion. And so, for now, things remain much as they have been for centuries: chaos prevails.

As is his custom, he locates one of the rare stretches of open balustrade and here, leaning back against some brickwork, sets himself to soaking up a burst of rare autumn sunshine. Is it possible to be in love with a city, he wonders as he gazes westward along the busy river bordered by its forests of church spires and elegant walls? If the answer is yes, then there is surely no better candidate for a man's affections than London - the buildings of Hawksmoor and Wren; the pleasure gardens of Vauxhall and Ranelagh; the theatres and fairs of Bankside and Covent Garden. Never silent, the very air itself is alive with all the varied and dissonant voices of its citizens - a cacophony of hawkers and traders, of street ballads and organ grinders, all vying with the endless clatter of ironshod wheels on cobbled stones and the intermittent pealing of a hundred church bells filling the skies. And then, by contrast, eastwards, down by the docks, the sounds are entirely different - an evocation of the not-too-distant sea, all the creaks and groans that attend the mechanics of ships and their commerce; the cries of gulls circling above the jetties and wharves - all mingling with shanties sung on decks or the taut flapping of canvas upon the yards of the anchored ships. How wonderful a combination of sounds! By day, a chorus of celebration; by night, a whisper and a sigh of pleasure - and whenever he must journey away from it for any length of time it would be as if his very heart were weeping for its absence and urging him to return.

He thinks for a moment of the bird man who had jumped from here some while ago, and whose memory still lingers as a symbol of his own ambition to fly - though in his case not with artificial wings as some hopeless mimic of a bird, but rather through the faculty of thought, through sensual experience - a refinement of passion by which a man might rise above the multifarious distractions of this world and fly *without* wings. It is, he knows, becoming something of an obsession, but a most pleasant one, for all that, and one which he is not inclined to relinquish or even to moderate one bit. And then, as if to emphasise his resolution, at just that moment, during a rare lull in the noise of the traffic, he catches the unexpected sound of music being played, horns and a trumpet emanating from an open window - the melodious fragment carried across the water and echoing from the walls of the buildings on the other side. Musicians practising, no doubt - but what a superb and evocative sound. Music, even here. So typical of this glorious city. And he resolves, henceforth, that it shall be an overture to the rest of his life.

*Art thou troubled? Music will calm thee*
*Art thou weary? Rest shall be thine*

Thus, so engrossed in all these poetic fancies does he become that he hardly notices the chair that has hurried past him, its bearers carrying it rapidly northwards towards the city but which stops just a few yards farther on, and from which an elegant young woman in a tricorn hat trimmed with a long, extravagant plume of ostrich feathers steps forth. It is Johanna.

'Why, Mr Wildish!' she chuckles coming to greet him, her face and hair, or that which is visible to him, all-aglow from the sunshine. 'I thought it could only be my poet, gazing out at the river at this time of the day.'

'Mrs Woolveston - how lovely to see you!' he declares, accepting her hand and addressing her in formal fashion as befits the situation. 'And what, may I ask, brings you into the city this afternoon?'

'Oh, I often come this way on a Friday,' she says, turning up the wide collar of her jacket, which is cut away like a riding coat at the waist - her favoured attire for being out and about. 'I enjoy tea with Sam's sister - and always try to take a chair across the bridge. We then undertake our shopping together in town before I take a coach back home. And look - I do not have little Boris with me today, either, so you are quite safe. Do you like it here, my Wonder? What are you thinking about?'

'Oh, I was thinking whether it is true what I was once told, that in ancient Rome, he who was charged with the job of building and looking after the bridges shared the same title as that of priest - *Pontifex,* being the same word for both professions. So yes, I do like it here. I feel connected to things. I like to look up-river to all the fine buildings. I journey to them in my thoughts and imagine all the people at work and play within. Or I take myself to the opposite wall over yonder and look instead at all the tall ships in the dockyards, and all the glorious billowing clouds driven by the very wind that will take them eastwards and out to sea. I imagine them sailing out to Deptford and past your home in Greenwich. And because that is where London is connected to the sea, I fancy the very air itself over that side is briny with salt and that there is the fragrance of tar and barnacles upon the hulls of every vessel.'

'A poet's eye,' she says, endeavouring to share in his obvious passion for the place. 'Goodness me! Do you know, my Wonder, I was feeling quite heavy with cares this afternoon, until now. I am so glad I hopped out to join you, to share in your fancies for a while.'

'I would be honoured to accompany you, if I may,' he says, realising that it would be difficult for her to locate a vacant chair here in the middle of the bridge. 'I was just about to stroll back, anyway.'

Without reply she smiles her consent and they begin to walk side by side, though sauntering rather, as neither has any urgent desire to complete the crossing or terminate their moment of togetherness too soon. 'Actually, this afternoon is a little different to my usual routine,' she says, 'because Sam and I will be staying overnight.'

'Ah! The Masquerade, then - am I correct?'

'Um, perhaps,' she answers, assuming an air of nonchalance, not very forthcoming. No one really ever admits to their intention of attending a masquerade, no more than they would divulge what style of dress or disguise they might appear in. It is all part of the established tradition, the mystery and intrigue surrounding such events, and Johanna would rightly perceive his line of inquiry as slightly impertinent.

'Goodness - what have you done to yourself?' she asks, disturbed by the discovery of the bandage upon his wrist, a remnant of the sword fight inflicted by one of his assailants a few days ago and which even his most extravagant of lace cuffs cannot quite conceal.

'Oh, that!' he answers, feigning indifference. 'From my fencing lessons. An unfortunate accident.'

'How dedicated you are - that you continue still with your studies. A noble art.'

'A useful one, as well. A gentleman is rarely inconvenienced when he goes forth with sword harnessed. Sometimes one must train in earnest, unprotected, without a *bouton*. It is only a surface wound, a mere scratch.'

'It is. Yet I should not wish to see the like upon your face, Matthew. Do exercise caution, my Wonder, when you practise.'

He agrees - assures her that he shall - and cannot help feeling thrilled, too, that she should care.

As always upon the bridge, numerous uncouth and ill-mannered people are to be found, jostling, pushing their way through. It can sometimes prove intimidating for anyone in their finery, let-alone a beautiful woman, he reflects, a suspicion reinforced a moment later as an unruly gang of young apprentices comes barging its way through the crowds, making Johanna flinch slightly as the young men pass; and in a quite natural and spontaneous way he proffers her his arm because of it.

'Sir, I cannot,' she states by way of response, bashful but with good humour as she declines his offer.

'Why, if I were your cousin or brother, you would consent and feel none the worse for it,' he argues gently.

'You are right, of course,' she chuckles and links her arm beneath his after all. 'Thank you *cousin* Matthew,' she adds with a further smile that, to his delight, has just the tiniest trace of recklessness about it as well.

It occurs to him then that never has he been so near to her, not physically - at least not since that evening up on the leads of her home in Greenwich when, alone for a few precious minutes, they had nestled ever closer, side by side, and talked about the stars. He can feel her arm pressing against his side now, though her hips, unfortunately, remain cushioned from him somewhat by the width of her skirts. Not much to get excited about - and yet in a slightly disgraceful way he finds himself thrilled by the notion of sharing, even if only a little, in some of those pleasures normally reserved for Sam. He wonders if she might feel something similar, for whenever their heads turn to each other as they walk, and their eyes meet, as happens often, she smiles to herself, and so does he. Neither can prevent it - as if taking a special delight in being so reckless, and doing so, moreover, in such a very public place.

A beggar, an elderly seaman by the looks of his clothing, can be seen seated against the pillar of an arch as they approach and pass beneath. An old tobacco box is placed in the darkness upon the ground with a few meagre coins; his wooden crutch and peg-leg genuine enough by way of demonstrating the most likely origin of his hardship: the impact from a cannon ball, no doubt. A sorry sight - but to Matthew's surprise, Johanna insists on stopping in front of the man and then, rummaging through her purse, produces a guinea, taking care to enclose the piece in his palm so that his trembling arm might not let it fall. 'Good man,' she whispers, looking into his eyes, 'your sacrifice does not go unmarked by those of us who have felt it also.'

'How extraordinarily generous of you!' Matthew exclaims as they walk on and she takes his arm once again - while, glancing back over his shoulder, he catches sight of the beggar, still staring at the coin in his palm, as if frozen in disbelief.

Matthew cannot help wondering, also, what she had meant by her remarks. So he enquires.

'Oh, it always makes me behave recklessly, anything of that nature,' she says, dismissing it lightly. 'Any poor man who has served in the navy.'

'I see,' he responds, though still he does not understand - and she, perceptive as ever, senses this.

'Matthew, you speculated a moment ago on the presence of a surrogate cousin or brother upon whose arm I might entrust my safety - but you should know that I did in fact lose my own dear brother at sea. Really. It was some years ago. Edward was an officer. His ship went down in action with the French in the West Indies. Our whole family was devastated. I was so troubled by it that I almost lost my sight and could hardly see for weeks after. It had such an overwhelming effect on me.'

'I am so sorry,' he says. 'I had no idea.'

'He was the most handsome and delightful of young men,' she continues, her head raised unnaturally as if fighting back her tears. 'Our loss compelled us, my parents and I, to meet several people of similar misfortunes, even a number of quite humble families, and ever since then we have always supported those brave men who serve in His Majesty's ships. Never underestimate the might of the Royal Navy, my Wonder. The economy of our nation would be as nothing without it. Over forty thousand men in service as we speak, hard working men who all need supplies of food and clothing, beef, pork, wheat and rum. The navy is the single largest consumer of agricultural produce, especially if you take into account the merchant fleet, as well.'

'I never thought of it that way,' he says, observing her with a mixture of bewilderment and admiration, astonished by her intimate knowledge - though considering her family connections and Sam's position in the Admiralty, it would make sense.

'And don't forget all the coal and ore that has to be mined,' she continues fulsomely, still with her arm linked beneath his as they go, 'all the foundries and blacksmiths that supply the iron for the ships - three tons of iron for a single cannon, and every ship has dozens of them. There are thousands of nails in every vessel to hold it all together. Anchors, chains, rope for rigging, canvas for sail - the list goes on and on, and it all has to be mined, grown or made up somewhere by someone. The navy, Matthew, is the most important institution there has ever been in our nation's history. That is why I am so proud of those who are part of it.'

'Ah, and of course, that is how you met Sam, was it not - to do with the Admiralty?' he asks, feeling how very splendid it is, having the opportunity to converse with her like this, about her family, about what has been and what still remains of such importance to her.

'Yes, that's right,' she replies, 'that is how Sam and I met. Thus, as one fine young man went out of my life, another entered almost straight away. Though of course, Sam was never at sea - not properly. I still live in dread that he might, in the course of his work, which as you know often takes him aboard vessels in dock, ever be required to undertake voyages, no matter how small. Perish the thought! I do not want such a thing. I want my husband to remain always the most hopeless *landlubber* if possible.'

'Fear not, I am sure Sam will give you no cause for concern in that respect,' he jests, knowing how very reluctant his friend would always be to venture too far from home or from all the attendant comforts of slippers and feather-down. 'He would no more allow himself to go to sea than be seen without a wig.'

And she laughs - knowing well enough the truth of that, while at the same time taking a handkerchief from her sleeve and attending to a little moisture at the corner of her eye.

'That reminds me - were you ever told the story of Sam's father?' she asks, and when Matthew replies no, she explains: 'Well, Sampson Woolveston, was a merchant, trading all corners of the globe and tipped for a knighthood, but due to a terrible accident one day when his wig blew off amid a public function when the King was visiting the dockyard, he fell from grace and never really recovered his former status. Rather apt, don't you think - Sampson's fall after losing his head of hair. And so, even though he was not old enough to have witnessed the unfortunate incident himself, my husband has never gone forth without a wig firmly set upon his head. I suppose there is always a reason, a story of some kind hiding behind our worst eccentricities. I cannot suffer the thought of a man I care for going to sea, and Sam cannot suffer to be without his wig.'

And he smiles despite the poignancy of the subject, and again cannot help marvel at what a luxury it is - to have her all to himself like this. He is so very happy.

'Do you know what, my Wonder,' she continues in pensive mood, her voice more gentle once more, 'I never really viewed the two events, the loss of my brother and my marriage to Sam following so hard upon it, as in any way connected, not in any significant sense. How little we understand concerning our deepest motivations - until the leisure of reflection or some other discourse with a friend, such as this, gives us leave to do so. And what about you, my Wonder? What lies behind the creation of Matthew Wildish? What makes you the poet and dreamer that you are?'

'Ah, that's easy. I just always wanted people to be listening to me. I am an inveterate *show off!*'

'Did they listen to you at home in Ireland, when you were young?'

'No - not really. Nothing much happened to me of note until I came to England to study as Barber-Surgeon. Though I did not stick with that, as Sam will tell you - not for very long.'

'Ah yes - and of course that is how *you* met Sam, am I right? Surprising, really - that neither of you has ever used his medical training or put all that learning to any purpose.'

'Well, at least Sam served out his time. Though now I suppose we would both be redundant anyway. You see, the surgeons, they are going their own way, with their own guild, and the barbers their way with theirs - by order the King and parliament. The cleverest, the academics, are being separated from the artisans, who will continue to shave us and cut our hair. But if we want our boils to be lanced or a leech applied to our backsides, we must now seek out the surgeon or the physician - and at what a price!'

'Matthew, you are too funny!' she laughs. 'And what about all those good men who make wigs? What shall become of them?'

'Good question - for there are no guilds of wig-makers to protect them, not in this country. Probably there never will be, not now.'

'Well, fiddlesticks!' she says. 'You need none of it, anyway. With poetry, that is where your future lies - and with patronage shortly, I trust, of a far higher order than at present. Which reminds me: how is your latest project progressing? Do you have a title yet for your sequence of sonnets?'

'Oh - er - yes, I do,' he answers, thinking quickly. 'I'm calling them *Observations of the Heavenly Bodies*.'

She repeats the title with approval. 'Observations of the Heavenly Bodies... Goodness, that's rather good, isn't it! I am sure you will do great things with those. And do you have anything for me to look at yet, anything I might read sometime?'

'Oh, yes,' he replies, wondering which of his recent poems might prove the least provocative. 'I can give you some lines now. Your verdict would be most welcome, naturally.'

'Now?'

'Why, yes. Tell me what you think.'

And thus, reaching a more open stretch of roadway towards the head of the bridge, out into the welcome daylight once more and speaking in time with the rhythm of their steps, he recites some of his lines: a few from the sonnet to Venus, a few more from Jupiter - fragments only in order to convey the mood and character of the work. But when he glances to his side to gauge her reaction, it is only to discover her looking downward, deep in thought.

'They are - er - rather earthy,' she murmurs, 'and with more than a hint of the element of fire thrown in,' she adds, her eyes with their mildly startled look darting to his for an instant but not quite wishing to engage him fully this time - so that he can only conclude, with regret, that he might have embarrassed her.

'I accept that it does make the matter of patronage somewhat delicate,' he admits with haste. 'Perhaps it would be prudent not to mention your involvement in the work any longer - should it ever come to print, that is. I had thought of dedicating the poems to you and Sam, you see, in gratitude, but I am now inclined to think that might be rather improper ...'

'No, no,' she interrupts. 'I would not wish you to consider withdrawing your dedication simply because of their sensuality, and neither would Sam, I am sure. No, no. One must acknowledge these sentiments, as did so many other distinguished poets of the past. Your lines will surely open many doors for those who have leisure to think upon them.'

'Do you think so?'

'Matthew, I do not only think so. *I know so*,' she asserts.

It seems an odd kind of statement. So he speaks up, seeking

clarification. 'To be sure, many a young maid or spinster would be thus enlightened - but not someone such as yourself, I trust?'

He knows his question is very risqué. Will she feel affronted?

'Your trust in such a deduction might be somewhat misplaced,' she argues. 'Many a young maid, yes - but also many a woman embedded within the state of matrimony and for whom such sentiments may, at the very least, be unfamiliar.'

He resists the temptation to make any comment, but instead allows his silence to encourage her. 'What I am trying to say,' she continues in a voice charged with emotion, untypical for her, 'is that what is perceived as worldly experience in some, might in fact be a falsehood, a pretence only and not based upon any genuine breadth of experience or satiety of the senses. For many, I am sure, there is instead merely a notion of longing - a longing for something more - a life that is half-suspected, half-doubted, something wondrous waiting over the horizon and yet always receding the more one strives for it. Your lines remind one of that.'

He has never heard her speaking so earnestly, so wanting for him to understand - and all happening in such an odd location, under such mundane circumstances. He wants to talk more, to pursue the topic. But just then their attentions are arrested by an abrupt burst of sunshine through what is by now a somewhat moist sky, and a spectacular rainbow appears over the ancient ramparts of the Tower to their left hand side, so bright that they must stop, as many do, to admire it - a miracle in seven colours shining out against the slate-grey clouds. Even a trace of a 'double,' a second rainbow, can be seen forming beneath it - the indigo in particular, he thinks, being most clearly delineated. So rare.

'Our very own Mr Newton demonstrated that it is the outcome of light being split into its component colours,' Matthew declares with a turn of rationality that, he cannot help thinking, Sam would approve of, were he here. 'The moist air acts as a prism-lens upon the sunlight,' he continues with authority, 'its seven colours being really different aspects of one pure, undivided light.'

'Goodness, Matthew!' she exclaims. 'You are beginning to sound like quite the man of science. Do you not see, as I do, Joseph's coat of many colours shimmering in the air? Do you not see the rainbow bridge of those old Norse folk, a pathway uniting the world of humans to the realm of the Gods in Valhalla?'

'Why, Madam, I am shocked!' he laughs, feigning indignation

as they continue their walking, 'that you would compare the stories of the bible to those of the pagan Gods?'

'All are pathways to the same destination, Matthew,' she answers. 'When someone points towards the heavens, we would do well to look at the stars, not just to the finger that points.'

'I shall henceforth, I promise, think only of the stars,' he avows with humour, hand on heart - hiding his feelings for her behind a foppish display of nonchalance. In truth he feels very moved. It is an amazement to him, that such a normally routine occupation as walking over London's Bridge could be transformed into such a magical journey. She has given voice to his thoughts at the very moment he had tried to deny them to himself and bury them beneath the weight of rationality. How he longs to continue this most agreeable of pastimes. But it cannot be - because soon, having descended already onto the pavements by St Dunstan's, they find themselves at the end of the bridge. And here, to his regret, as the rainbow vanishes and the rain begins to fall, she disengages her arm. Noticing a vacant chair being set down in the rank at the edge of the highway, she hastens towards it and within moments is inside, regarding him through the open window as she gathers the folds of her dress about her.

Noticing the chairmen making ready, and eager to be up and away, Matthew provides them with directions on her behalf and then returns to bid her goodbye.

'I look forward to your completed poems, Mr Wildish,' she states with a decorous adjustment of her gloves and sleeves, her voice business-like in the proximity of the men. 'What you speak of is the vitality that sustains us all. The fault is not with the author, if some appear uncomfortable when reminded of it.'

'I am indebted to you, Ma'am,' he says with a modest bow of courtesy, every bit as trite.

'Not at all. And so good afternoon to you, Mr Wildish. Until we meet again.'

At which the door is closed and she is carried away. When will it be, he wonders, that *meeting again?* For him, it cannot come too soon, to be once again united with she who is his undivided light.

# ~ 12 ~
## OBSERVATIONS OF THE
## HEAVENLY BODIES - THE SUN

*Of the Sun, its general and particular significations: She who bringeth warmth and vigour. A strong body and the limbs, well composed. A noble forehead. The hair golden or flaxen. Oft-times of a high or ruddy complexion. The eyes large, expressive, and lips full. A great heart - proud yet affable. Bountiful and sincere with a desire to rule. Of excellent apparel and quality of dress, preferring of yellow, scarlet or gay pastel shades. The topaz for her gemstone and all things made of gold.*

With this tantalising description of the Sun firing his imagination, and wondering just where he might possibly locate a woman of such heroic credentials, Matthew, seated at his bench, closes the cover of his book of astrological lore lent to him by Johanna, and endeavours to return to work, but it is already late, and by the sounds of the dainty and rapid footfalls on the stairs outside and the tuneful and by-now familiar call of 'Oooh hoo!' from outside, it would seem that the beautiful Venus, Miss Sarah May, his ardent partner for this evening's masquerade, is on her way to him already.

'Oh, Mr Wildish, I know I'm early - so can't we just go to your chamber?' she asks, tugging at his sleeve, with scarcely a minute having elapsed since her arrival, and they, unable to keep each other at arm's length for more than a few moments. 'I am terrible, I know - but I do so *want it, want it, want it!*'

'No, my pretty,' he states, gazing with determination into her lovely dark eyes, that seem always so inordinately large. 'We must resist ... for now.'

'Resist! Oh, but can't we at least cuddle and make *magic fingers* once more together. Can't we?'

'No!' he repeats, more firmly, all his manly instincts assailed by that most seductive of fragrances that she has brought into the room already - unmistakable - so that it is all he can do to prevent himself from enjoying her here and now. 'Today is different, Sarah,' he continues. 'Let us drink some wine, instead, and begin our preparations - and I promise you we will both share in the fullest measure of satisfaction later, when we return.'

'Oh, yes - the masquerade,' she says, nervously now. 'What will you make of me, then? And how shall we both be attired?' she asks, her excitement turning from one subject to the next with amazing rapidity. 'I have not been able to stop thinking about it all day - my mask, and my costume.'

'Well, Sarah,' he explains, pouring a generous helping of wine into their glasses, 'firstly, you should know that one never attends a masquerade as oneself, but rather as a fantasy of some kind, disguised in the clothes of, say, a shepherdess or a sorcerer; as some exotic fairy creature of some kind, or a king or queen from history - and even of the opposite gender, if one so chooses. This evening I intend to appear in the clothing of a noble Turk, a Sultan no less, while you my lovely will cross over and honour me with your company as a handsome beau from overseas, in clothes lent to you by me, and with the crowning glory of a wig of such lavish, aristocratic quality that people will be breathless at the sight of it - all in keeping with the spirit of the occasion, in which all manner of jests are played out. I predict, Sarah my sweet, that you will become the very magnet to any number of amorous women, and there will be such fun in the deception!'

'Um. I think rather you will clothe me thus so I shall not be approached by any other man,' she surmises with an audacious turn that pleases him, 'and that I shall keep all my desire to be spent on you alone.'

'Correct. That is how we shall entertain ourselves, Miss May. I want to see your cheeks coloured and your face alive with eagerness all evening long. Rein in your appetites for these few intoxicating hours, and I promise you that your sense of anticipation will reach a higher pitch than you can possibly imagine, and that your release from its delicious torment, once we are finally alone and on our homeward journey in the privacy of our carriage, will be all the more gratifying as a consequence.'

'Oh, yes, but how long a wait is that!' she protests with a squeal of anguish. 'I shall explode before it is over.'

But her predicament cannot be discussed any longer. A perfunctory knock upon the door, has Francis the valet already upon the threshold, a newly pressed shirt and breeches of Matthew's own in readiness, though not on this occasion for Matthew but adapted and cut for a very different purpose. And it is with a look of some confusion that Francis bows and takes his leave as the laundry girl is gradually attired in the clothing of what is to become a handsome young aristocrat. Matthew also lightens her complexion with the thinnest dusting of powder, and applies a touch of cochineal to her lips before pinning and concealing her hair beneath a resplendent masculine full-bottomed periwig. The final touch is a crescent-shaped beauty spot, applied just beneath her mouth - a precise signal which, in keeping with the symbolic code associated with such items, signifies the preference of the wearer towards 'silence.' Amid much excitement, he also introduces his lovely companion to the special mask he has made for her, all blue and silver with drifts of small sapphire-like stones and turquoise beads. Fabulous.

'You will require just one final piece of masculine adornment,' he states, taking one of his swords from his closet and harnessing it to her waist. 'Try not to go touching it too often, but rather keep it tucked away behind your coat, and be ready to relinquish it at the door when we arrive. You are not going into battle, remember.'

A few final adjustments are made, including a lesson on how she might stand and walk like a man - until within just a very short time, Sarah with her long body and slender waist has metamorphosed into the most handsome of males, strutting up and down the length of his studio, one hand on her hip, and then, to his astonishment and laughter, thrusting out her pelvis like the very buck, as she stands with pride before the full-length looking glass.

'Oh, Glory be, how good is this!' she exclaims rejoicing in her new altogether sharper appearance. 'Not to be held down by skirts, but to have tight britches and hips that might be shown to the world - and a bottom. Look! Oh what it is to be a man!'

He gazes at her in admiration. The disguise, especially with the addition of the mask, is a tolerably good one, and she really does present the illusion of some exotic young Duke from a foreign land - that, or else a lady of similar status crossed-dressed - her wig being of such an outstanding quality and length that it could only ever be owned by one of considerable wealth and standing. There is not much that can be done to hide her bosom, however, despite the presence of her neck-stock and the stays that she has retained beneath her shirt; and so they determine that those delightful charms should not be repressed unnecessarily. 'Leave the buttons of your waistcoat here undone, my beauty,' he suggests, releasing her a little and feeling the wonderful form of her for himself. 'You will then drive the men wild as well as the women, I swear. You will be the finest young hermaphrodite in London, and no one, man nor woman, will know what to make of you or how to seduce you.'

'What, do women have desires for other women, then?' she inquires with a touching naivety.

'Oh yes,' he answers. 'A masquerade is an occasion upon which you will encounter any number of intriguing deviations from the simple fare that you and I have enjoyed together these past few weeks. And at any venue worth the ticket, you will be propositioned by all variety of individuals. Among all the satyrs and nymphs, priests and nuns, or those who wantonly play the role of tart or cavalier, you will discover every possible guise or fondness of manners in-between. There are, for example, young people who enjoy the caresses of older and more experienced hands while, conversely, you can rest assured, there are a liberal number of older ones who prefer their quarry to be young and fresh. There are ladies who prefer to be entertained by a dwarf or by the unique society of a castrato from the opera house; and there are men who in order to invigorate their failing vitality seek solely those who can wield a whip upon their backsides. Not that such enormities are enacted in any public place as we are to attend this evening. That would never do. Be comforted, therefore, Sarah my lovely. I shall protect you from the any of the more outlandish of these excesses and no one shall harm you.'

And at this she smiles, for the first time with immense tranquillity and composure, drawing herself up to her full height, puffing out her chest, and becoming, in a strange unexpected way in all her new-found self-confidence, every bit the equal of himself.

The broad thoroughfare of the Strand with its tall stately buildings and rows of expensive shop-fronts is as lively and as congested with traffic as ever upon their arrival at eight o'clock, and it is a relief when their carriage is allowed through the open gates of the great house to which they have been invited, and thus into the relative calm of the brightly lit courtyard - the distant faces of spectators gazing through the railings, hoping to glimpse the arrival of a celebrity or two, being of no concern to them, for here it is but a short walk to the steps leading through stone columns to a generous marble-floored atrium, almost full to overflowing with guests, many hurrying in and out of the cloakrooms for those vital last-minute adjustments to their attire. Illumination, meanwhile, is provided by a vast array of candle-lit lamps and chandeliers, their radiance all magnified by the presence of mirrors and crystal. And thus abiding in this most-pleasant confusion to the eyes, bedazzled from all sides by all the multitude of elaborate masks and beautiful shimmering costumes of silk and brocade, he and Sarah relinquish their cloaks and swords and enter the ballroom, arm in arm; and as he looks to her at his side in her lavish wig of resplendent curls, her breast rising and falling with excitement, he cannot help but smile with pride as he beholds and shares with her the spectacle in all its intoxicating glory.

'I take it you have informed your employer Mrs Biggs and also the poor spinster who shares your bed not to wait up, this evening?' he asks with humour.

'Fear not. I have,' she answers, having returned the salutations of a dozen curious glances of admiration already - the slightest bow of her head as she passes, just as he has taught her - while all the time counterfeiting the manner of a seasoned veteran of such places, not humbled or overwhelmed by any of it at all.

'Don't forget, if anyone asks you the origin of your wig, you must give them my particulars,' Matthew reminds her in a moment of calm as, with a glass each of sparkling wine, they seek out a place where they can stand relatively unmolested by staring eyes and yet still continue to survey the exotic traffic of costumes passing by.

'I shall - and my good offices on your behalf will be rewarded I trust when it comes to our re-union later this evening,' she remarks in a haughty way, continuing to learn the manners of society speech with amazing rapidity.

'I shall no doubt be much obliged to you by then, Miss May,' he says.

'And I to you, Sir. Glory be, how exciting is all this! I don't like to stare, but it is impossible not to.'

'Here you need not be anxious about staring,' he assures her, making a brief adjustment to his own mask with the aid of the mirrored wall. 'Amid such a profusion of amazing sights, everyone stares, and everyone expects to be stared at, in turn. And remember, you do not need to hang upon my arm constantly, my pretty, but may instead mingle. Approach anyone you wish and, if you are so inclined, examine at your leisure every detail of any costume or mask that takes your fancy. It will be perceived as a compliment - though the longer you do stare the more you are naturally obliged by the etiquette of the masquerade to speak and engage the person of your curiosity. Ask firstly whether you know them, or they you. That is always a good start. Then, once a conversation has commenced you may venture observations that are more intimate. Be courteous at all times, but entertain no fear of impropriety. You may even touch those you engage with, and explore - because here, all the rules and strictures of normal behaviour are in abeyance, which is why the masquerade is sometimes referred to as *The World Upside Down*. Here a king might become a peasant, and a peasant a king.'

'And a laundress a young prince!' she laughs.

And as she continues to press close, it occurs to him that, were she clothed as a woman, and he consequently kept at a distance by the girth of her gown, the sensations would be so very different to what they are now. For here, clad merely in her breeches and waistcoat, the wonderful rotund softness of her breast and the presence of her hips can be felt against his side. It thrills him, the novelty of it, this pressing so close with the rhythm of her breathing, her nostrils flaring a little now, too, he notices, as if sniffing the very air. He understands, of course - for here one is exposed to a most extravagant combination of fragrances, not only the ubiquitous snuff that, together with the powder of wigs, sometimes fills the air as a fine dust, not only the rose and lavender scents of the ladies that linger about every costume, stocking or glove, but rather that which, in the proximity of so many men and women living out their innermost fancies, is born of the inevitable fragrances of excitement, of that which emanates as much from beneath the clothing as from that which is placed as perfume upon it. The result is an aroma that is unrivalled in its animal vitality and rawness - of such a heady, intoxicating potency that not even the most consummate perfumer of Paris could ever hope to replicate it.

Immersed thus in this ocean of sensation, sights and sounds, one can only be swept along - as surely as they are now, as if taken by a stimulant or drug that threatens to rob them of all rationality and decorum.

Now, whether it has anything to do with such an effect, or whether it might be connected to the book of astrological lore he had been reading earlier with its most florid description of the Sun therein, he cannot rightly tell, but as he and Sarah continue to stroll, Matthew becomes aware of a most outstanding individual - brightly attired and in a mask of scarlet and gold, a wealth of braided blond hair spilling forward from beneath the hood of her cloak, which itself is of a beautiful rich cloth of gold. Tall of stature, stately of bearing, she does not tarry amid the company of any one group, but appears to mix with different segments of the crowd, as if known to many despite her disguise. How very intriguing! And so, while remaining ever mindful of Sarah at his side, he stays alert for any explanation of who she might be - and as fortune would have it, this is provided for him after not too long.

'That's Lucy Armstrong,' he overhears one woman talking with another, in tones that are not entirely approving.

*Lucy Armstrong.* He will remember that. But then to his disappointment, after managing to discover the name of this epitome of solar magnificence, he loses sight of her - she having made her way towards the cloakroom - surely not intent on departure at such an early hour! He sincerely hopes not. But no matter. The lady's name is engraved upon his memory. And thus, deep in thought and wondering how he might make her acquaintance, his attentions are restored to the here and now by a timely nudge in the ribs from the vivacious young woman at his side, reminding him that the joys of the present are considerable, after all - and in any case at just that moment, and as if his dizzy senses were not already surfeit of such blessings, he catches sight across the room of a most elegantly attired Elizabethan lady with a grand lace ruff about her throat, a silver mask of an intricate pearl motif, covering much of her face and who, he realises straight away, is almost certainly Johanna. Standing amid a small group of lively individuals, none among them being Sam, she has recognised him straight away and is staring back, distracted from her conversation, and with considerable curiosity, moreover, being directed to his lovely companion, Sarah. Would she be trying to place her, wondering whether it was the same person she encountered that afternoon at his apartments and whose presence, he recalls, had pained her so much at the time?

As if drawn towards each other by some magnetic force, they are quickly within speaking distance.

'Do we know each another, Madam?' he asks, as, without any care for propriety, they take each other's hands.

'Goodness, no!' Johanna replies. 'I am The Virgin Queen, and from an entirely different century. However, it was my father who founded the guild of Barber Surgeons in 1540, and thus I am allowed all manner of liberties with anyone I suspect as belonging to that noble fraternity.'

Upon which, they find themselves quite spontaneously embracing, as would loving friends - so that all of him becomes filled suddenly with a new and compelling delight. Drawing away for a second, he regards her more fully. This visage of theatrical extravagance - so very like to her, yet somehow so very distinct from anything he has ever noticed previously in the normally so demure and distantly aloof Mrs Woolveston. And as he looks into her eyes, so tightly margined by the mask, for one heart-leaping moment he is not even sure if it is Johanna at all - for these are eyes that are ablaze with such an unfamiliar and irresistible intensity and mischief.

'I am the Sultan of Sultana,' he announces as, belatedly, he acknowledges that it is incumbent upon him to introduce himself - stepping back for a second from this most esteemed object of his affection so that he might bow and display his fine apparel, his wide silk trousers, his abundance of vulgar jewellery and ornamentation.

'And most distinguished, Sir - and with such muscular bare arms!' she remarks, allowing him to take her hands in his once again. And they remain thus for some time, smiling like misbehaving children - for indeed they are misbehaving terribly - before he finally succeeds in tearing himself away and returning to the company of Sarah, and where he is suddenly delivered of an excellent idea. Realising, that this might be the ideal opportunity to unite the two of them and consequently for him to slip away in pursuit of the delectable Lucy Armstrong, he resolves to throw all caution to the wind and to introduce the handsome beau to Johanna forthwith.

'Come, this way, dearest,' he urges her in an encouraging whisper as she once again links her arm beneath his. 'I shall, with your consent, hand you for a short time to a very dear friend of mine.'

At which he introduces her to the Virgin Queen with much aplomb, presenting Sarah herself as a certain *Count Cosimo* of the distant principality of Naples and Capri - and knowing by the customs and traditions that govern such a gathering that it is all perfectly acceptable to speak such utter nonsense.

'Charmed, I am sure, to make your acquaintance,' the Queen declares. 'I am so pleased you are a man, Count Cosimo - otherwise I should suspect you of being merely one of the Sultan's many wanton young female companions.'

Sarah, meanwhile, staying true to the preference for silence as indicated by the placement of her beauty spot, says not a word in response, but merely bows, quite moderately, before raising her eyebrows in mock innocence and gently tapping the tiny black velvet crescent itself with the tip of her index finger. Had she attended a thousand masquerades, she could not have conducted herself with greater tact. What a rare and gifted young woman she is, he thinks.

Once assured of her safety and of Johanna's acceptance, and with the ostensible mission, he tells her, of seeking out a certain gentleman by the name of Sam, he sets himself free and, seizing the opportunity to explore, immerses himself in the crowds of the ballroom once again. Alas no sign of the gorgeous Lucy Armstrong amid this ocean of theatricality, but no matter - for here, among the profusion of common moretta masks or the more ordinary disguises such as his own, he finds himself enchanted by the number of far more sophisticated displays, costumes of such admirable skill and invention that he feels quite overcome at times - and masks, too, that with their elaborate designs, their floral motifs, their jewels or glittering traceries of gold and silver, can only be viewed as creations of art in their own right. Even the plainest and most humble of aspects can become transformed by such an accessory. Thus, rather than the counterfeit of the face beneath, it is the mask itself, shaped by the bearer's own dreams and fantasies, that becomes the true essence, the real self made visible - something which makes the visage he next encounters all the more disturbing. For although its wearer has, even in the short space of time he has been at liberty to observe her, established herself as one of the most noteworthy of this evening's attendees, she is also the one that most others avoid. And the reason is not difficult to ascertain. Her face is veiled as well as masked, a shroud of thin, glittering gauze draped entirely over her head and shoulders, while her vast dress, a court mantua of black silk and cloth of silver is panniered, by a miracle of engineering and whale-bone, to a width almost equal to her height, so that the crowds within the ballroom must part like a biblical sea as she goes among them. But that is not all, because beneath the transparency of the shroud there sits a most grotesque and ingenious wig of writhing serpents which, Matthew sincerely hopes, are animated by springs or some other artificial means and not real. Many people are disturbed by the sight - and most, no doubt fully aware of the mythological significance, do not dare to look directly at her - for this is surely the very head of the Medusa itself they are being shown.

Unconcerned by all the fuss, or perhaps secretly amused by it all, and with a brace of young pages walking behind, she glides majestically into one of the smaller side rooms, away from the music and where, amid a quantity of heavily attended card tables, their occupants, heads down and self-absorbed at their gaming of Faro or Ombre, she is able to locate a place apart and take her repose. Carefully descending onto a long upholstered bench, she arranges her skirts and sips at a glass of dark wine that has been served to her by what is probably her own footman. And yet still none dare approach - none, that is, but Matthew - for how can he resist! Delivered of a moment's inspiration, he locates the most highly polished silver platter available from one of the tables and, buffing its surface with a napkin into that worthy of a fine looking-glass, comes to sit by her side, his back turned from her sufficiently so as not to be exposed to her deadly Medusa's eyes. She, piqued by such a bold gesture, lifts her veil while he, in turn, raises the mirrored surface of the plate until he beholds her dread-pale mask and fearsome aspect in reflection - all margined by her mass of writhing serpents, through which she stares back indignantly at the image of his face.

'Will you not look at me directly, Sir?' she inquires, in a strident voice which would, he surmises, belong to one of advanced years and - even more surprising - seems vaguely familiar.

'No, Madam, for I would then be turned to stone.'

'Not so if you were to be my Perseus,' she argues fanning herself now most vigorously. 'For then you would likely cut off my head and vanquish me.'

'I have no weapon, Madam. You are safe from my blows. But how safe is my heart?'

'Of your heart I know nothing, Sir, for I speak of a weapon of a far different metal - one with which, I cannot help but observe, you are most well-equipped withal, and with which you might prick my pretensions soon enough. You do not recognise me, then?'

'No, Madam. I should remember one such as you.'

'You say no, and yet did you not once drink wine from my navel? And did you not once stay my hand one afternoon in the woods as I was about to pop a pretty mushroom into my mouth?'

Abruptly the revelation falls upon him with a weight so heavy he feels momentarily crushed by its immensity. Of course - and why had he not recognised the voice! This is Lady Snatchal - Dorothea. She had been masked on that first occasion also, he recollects, that warm summer's evening when he had first been introduced by Sam to the appalling antics of the Cornhill Wig Club. Now here she is again, and in an entirely new guise, speaking to him from a dimension far beyond any level of common vice or pettiness he might have previously attributed to her.

'You seem surprised, my hero. But you should not be. I enjoy exhibiting myself - of being the object of many attentions. It has been that way ever since my unfortunate riding accident, the fall I had. I have told you about that, have I not?'

'Yes, Madam, you have. But over the years, your misfortune, I would venture to suggest, would have been the comfort of many a man of quality and discernment.'

'The comfort perhaps but, I must assure you, never to the entire satisfaction of most. I reserve my full favours only for the chosen few. And once I have determined upon my choice, I am not gladly spurned - something you in particular would do right well to remember, young man. For I know ... I know, my darling, all about that there wig.'

'The wig - what do you mean?' Matthew replies, trying not to sound alarmed, his heart pounding.

'I learnt of it yesterday - at Greenwich as a matter of fact, over tea with Johanna. I learned that her naughty little pug, Boris, made off with the item and destroyed it. How unfortunate! The incident must have put paid to her plans with you that afternoon, calling at your quarters unescorted, and it has certainly put paid to your future health and security should news of your negligence ever become common knowledge.'

'Ah, but you are mistaken, Madam,' he responds with an affected nonchalance and gaiety, still dissembling though his pulse is racing as he continues to gaze back to the mask and the persistent creature-eyes full of such lasciviousness. 'Firstly, may I remind you that, Mrs Woolveston has every right to visit my quarters, as it is also a workshop where clients may call. As for the wig, it was indeed one of my projects - and naturally I gave chase when it was taken - and thereby have given rise to many an amusing tale, no doubt, among those who observed me. But the special item belonging to the gentleman's club you are alluding to - and which I appreciate you would have seen on occasion - why, to be sure, that is quite safe. It continues to be undergoing renovations at my studios.'

'I do not believe that statement to be accurate, Sir,' Lady Snatchal countermands him with confidence. 'Johanna, sweet little innocent that she is, and who cannot stop talking about you from one minute to the next, made much of how odd it all looked, the worst example of a wig imaginable, she told me - of so many different shades and textures. Naturally she knows nothing of its true significance, and she found it right amusing to tell me her tale. We laughed together. I, however, found it to be most educational. Do not fear, my noble Turk, your misdemeanours shall not be disclosed by those who are your friends. And we *are* friends, are we not?'

'Indeed, Madam,' Matthew answers, realising that he is becoming ensnared by this cunning and determined woman.

And then, all of a sudden and without warning, she has risen from her place and is there before him - a vast mountain of fabric in motion - and squatting somewhat the body set within it, so that he is compelled to gaze directly into her face now, and with the full horror of her masked aspect.

'All of our life is a masquerade, Mr Wildish, and you would do well to remember that,' she says, as her fan is lowered to reveal her smile of triumph - her eyes, full of a most ribald self-satisfaction and glow of victory. 'We will speak again upon this issue, because now that you have gazed upon the head of the Medusa, my dear, either you must give me the satisfaction of that there weapon of yours, or else be prepared to meet thy doom.'

Furious all of a sudden, more at his own vulnerability and foolishness than anything else, he gets to his feet, bows and then walks from her, feeling overcome by the revelation that he has been found out. Oh what a fool you are Matthew Wildish, he curses himself - to have become embroiled in all of this nonsense, and now to be targeted by this predatory creature! Of course, she is not an unattractive woman, and there would be nothing in a bout or two with her that would cause him any discomfiture. But the danger in which such an illicit act would place him is almost too awful to contemplate. Yes, he could construct the wretched wig again, pass it off as the real thing - and, with any luck, he intends to do just that - but could this adulterous bargain, the securing of this woman's silence in the way she expects, ever go undetected or unpunished by a husband who moves within such powerful circles? The answer has to be a chilling and inescapable 'no.'

Negotiating his path through the crowds of the ballroom, he catches sight of Sarah and Johanna once more, this time not only surrounded by a bevy of young lovelies, male and female, but also receiving the attentions of none other than Lord Snatchal, disguised not very convincingly as a scrawny goatherd, complete with sandals and a tunic - his mask a thin Venetian-style oval, barely covering the inveterate lewdness of his face. The old reprobate.

In his present state of agitation, Matthew cannot bear to approach or speak with any of them; and thus, in need of some light relief, he wonders again if he might be able to locate the allusive Sam? Surely he must be here somewhere. And so he sets himself again upon the mission of seeking him out, walking from room to room, from ballroom to tearoom, to cloakroom to balcony. But still no sign of him - until Matthew is suddenly aware of a Domino approaching, a person, heavily cloaked and hooded in black, so typical of the masquerade and whom he has already observed earlier discreetly handing out calling cards to some of the more obviously wealthy or lonely gentlemen guests. Promoting some dubious service or the other, no doubt, there is always a number of these rascals at venues such as this. Coming closer, and with Matthew clearly in his sites now, the Domino draws forth a card from the folds of his vast black cloak and, without a word, presents it to him before hurrying away into the anonymity of the crowd. It is an advertisement, of course, but when Matthew a moment later reads it he is excited almost beyond measure.

*Gentlemen of refinement and adventure!*
*Come and have fun and games this evening at the private residence*
*of the lovely golden-haired Mrs Lucy Armstrong, a lady of the most*
*robust and sunny disposition who will warm your cockles at the*
*sign of the Sun and Coconuts in Cockspur Street.*

Here, surely at last, is his intuition vindicated! Here this evening amid all his travails, he really has encountered his Sun after all - she who can be found just around the corner from here, moreover, in Cockspur Street - so that the temptation to just pop along quickly and reconnoitre the place and, even better, to survey the charms of Mrs Armstrong herself, is just too much for Matthew in his present state of excitement to resist. Why, he could be there and back within fifteen minutes! The lovely Sarah would scarcely notice his absence. And then, at just that moment, as providence would have it, he discovers Sam - at last! He is reclining amid a group of women, one of whom is probably his sister, and has endeavoured to disguise himself as a Roman Senator, complete with toga and a short hair-piece, copied no doubt from some classical statue. The women, replete with long-handled fans that they wave at times in the air above his head, are also busy feeding him grapes - the whole company intent on rendering him quite the decadent. Matthew, however, approaching within earshot, is resolved instead on begging an important favour.

'Sam, Sam! It's me, Matthew!' he calls.

'Good day my subject,' Sam responds, looking down his nose with complete indifference. 'I am the Emperor Augustus, and if you require an audience, you should send a request in triplicate, care of the Admiralty, Whitehall, where I currently reside.'

'Forbear, Sir, and honour me with your attention please!' Matthew calls loudly and with a beckoning wave - upon which, with some reluctance, Sam abandons his retinue of admirers and saunters over to Matthew, hand on hip, the toga over one shoulder, the other bare. It is very noisy all of a sudden as some buffoon nearby, his stomacher fashioned as a face and with a gigantic, top-heavy hat encasing his entire head and shoulders, makes a spectacle of himself by toppling over.

'Sam, listen, I am popping out for a while,' Matthew states, trying to raise his voice above the din. 'If for any reason I fail to return within half an hour, come and seek me at the sign of the Sun and Coconuts just around the corner in Cockspur Street. Understand? No more than half an hour. I hope to be returned long before that.'

'Where's that, you say? The Fun and Go-go Huts?' Sam repeats inaccurately above the din.

'No - The Sun and Coconuts?'

'Understood, yes,' Sam responds, not very convincingly, nodding in a vague kind of comprehension amid all the noise and chaos, and with people running between them also. But it will have to do. Eager to be away, Matthew knows he must seize the opportunity without further ado - for why should he not avail himself of the services of at least one professional in order to build the cast of his magical seven! The peerless charms of Mrs Lucy Armstrong, clearly a most accomplished and celebrated courtesan, awaits.

Availing himself of his cloak, and reunited with his sword once again, Matthew emerges into the cold night air and quickly locates the corner of Cockspur Street ahead with its large coaching inn, The Golden Cross, all brightly lit and as busy as ever. The sign of the Sun and Coconuts, however, is not to be found on the main thoroughfare, but is instead tucked away just behind the entrance to a small court running off towards the royal mews. It is uncommonly silent and just a tiny bit unsettling, and a pull of the doorbell elicits no response. The door, though, he discovers, is unlocked - and so he steps through into a lobby with another door opposite, this having a notice attached that reads: 'Enter Here for Fun and Games' - which seems under the circumstances a reasonable enough offer. So in he goes, closing the door softly behind him - to find himself inside a well-appointed though somewhat dark lounge, with a good fire in the grate, and containing just one other man, totally naked, sitting warming himself at the hearth, and who upon Matthew's entrance springs to his feet immediately.

'Good evening, Sir!' the man declares urbanely and unabashed in his nakedness. 'Would you care to take off your clothes, please, and wait here? House rules.'

'Certainly not!' Matthew replies indignantly. 'Kindly tell me where I can speak with Mrs Armstrong.'

But the man merely shakes his head. 'I know nothing of Mrs Armstrong, Sir. Rather, I am in desperate need to be away from here. I cannot, of course, because unfortunately I am somewhat exposed.'

'You are, indeed, exposed, Sir! I can well perceive *that!*' Matthew concurs with indignation, still casting about for any sign of where one might have *fun and games* and finding little.

The man, who is not young and of a genteel and educated manner, continues to follow Matthew about the room, however - and when he next speaks it is in a most conciliatory and sincere tone. 'I beg you, Sir, let me explain, please,' he continues. 'I came here approximately an hour ago, responding to a notice I was given at the Masquerade. I confess I was in search of a little alternative entertainment. But then, when I entered this very room, a gentleman, a stranger, appeared through the other door there. Stark naked he was, and asked me if I would care to take off my clothes and wait. I said, "what, my clothes, all of them?" "Oh yes he replied, all of them - house rules." Well, fool that I am, I agreed. That was the last I saw of him, and of my clothes. I have been robbed, Sir. No one else is in the building, I swear - and the door over there through which the rogue disappeared simply leads out into a passage that exits onto the street again. I have no money left to me, no clothes. How am I to return to my home - a place where my arrival, I suspect, is already long overdue? I am a gentleman, Sir - the head of a respectable household, a family of high regard and reputation. My dear wife is involved in much charitable work. I have children, a dear golden-haired little daughter just beginning to take music lessons, and a fine son, an upstanding young gentleman up at Oxford studying law. Can you imagine the shame, the indignity they would be forced to endure should the scandal of their father being found walking the streets naked ever be broadcast among the common kind! I implore you, Sir, please, for I can see you are also a gentleman of refinement, lend me your clothes, that I might return forthwith to the bosom of my family and repent of my foolishness.'

Matthew compelled by the poignancy of this story suffers the inconvenient sensation of sympathy - an unfamiliar enough experience for him at the best of times. He tries to resist but, knowing that Sam would be coming to his rescue, anyway, in a short time, it occurs to him that perhaps he is destined this evening to aid his fellow man rather than to indulge in any dissipation with what, by now, appears to be the entirely mythical delights of Mrs Lucy Armstrong. And so he agrees.

Removing his cloak, his baggy Turkish trousers and shirt, his under-garments coming away at the same time, Matthew is shocked at how quickly the gentleman seizes them and dons them before Matthew can protest - with a speed surely engendered by desperation and probably also a certain anxiety that Matthew might change his mind. In seconds the man is fully clothed, therefore, and Matthew fully naked, apart from his purse and sword which he clutches to his side, lest they be commandeered also.

'Thank you, Sir. My only regret is that I shall be unable to return these items immediately as it would only arouse suspicion at home ... '

'Please, Sir, spare yourself such concerns,' Matthew interrupts. 'A certain person of my acquaintance from the masquerade will be seeking me out here presently. You may keep what you have. I am glad to have been of service, Sir.'

'Thank you. Thank you from the bottom of my heart!' the gentleman repeats, and a second later the newly made-up Turk has gone, slamming the door to the court outside loudly behind him in his haste to be away.

Glancing at the clock on the chimneypiece, Matthew discovers, to his disappointment that it is some time yet before Sam would be likely to appear. And so, with nothing for it but to wait, he sits himself down on the very seat by the hearth where the unfortunate gentleman had been warming his extremities earlier, and endeavours to do likewise. At least an ample supply of logs is available to throw upon the fire. It is precisely 10.30 - the room silent but for the steady ticking of the clock and the occasional spit and crackle of the flames as he waits ... and waits, until, after twenty long, dull and arduous minutes have surely elapsed, he ventures to glance up at the clock again, only to discover that it is still only 10.35. Time passes inordinately slowly, and it seems like an age until 11 p.m. is reached. But even then there is no sign of Sam. And when 11.15 comes and goes, Matthew begins to panic. Damn it! What on earth has happened to him? Surely by now Sarah would be assuming he has abandoned her - his lovely Venus, back there still amid all the excitement and frivolity of the masquerade, exposed to so much temptation and saucy offers. Everyone will be unmasking soon, anyway, revealing their true identities and thus he is forced to conclude it would be nothing short of a miracle if she were still to be waiting for him and not to have gone off with someone. Damn, Damn, Damn!

Endeavouring to keep warm, he gets to his feet and, pacing back and forth, gazes at the magnificent full length portrait above the chimneypiece, the inscription of which indicates that he is indeed in the company, if only in oils upon canvas, of the redoubtable Mrs Armstrong. His earlier expectation that in her might be found the epitome of Solar radiance, is certainly not dispelled by the sight - a tall, shapely woman, gloriously and brightly attired, a complexion that is fair and brilliant, and with the most resplendent golden blond hair which, for the benefit of the portrait, is displayed in a plait coiled neatly about her head but which, he surmises once released from its combs and pins would be of a considerable length and glory. A distinguished portrait, to be sure - and Matthew's imagination has more than sufficient opportunity in his enforced idleness to wonder at how she would appear in the flesh, becoming as he does so enthralled by the prospect of ever encountering her, and already contemplating the composition of a sonnet that might celebrate her distinctive charms.

But just then, a sound can be heard at the front door, someone upon the threshold entering, and then in walks a man. Matthew recognises him from the Masquerade, an unpleasant, bumptious fellow dressed as a friar, complete with rough cassock and an artificial tonsure hairpiece with its bald pate in the centre. Realising that the man has clearly ventured here for the *fun and games* himself, there is for Matthew only a fleeting moment's hesitation before he approaches him and, looking the man directly in the eye, and with the utmost calm and composure, declares, 'Good evening, Sir! Would you care to take off your clothes and wait here?'

'My clothes, Sir? What, all of them?'

'Oh yes, all of them - house rules.'

Matthew, now dressed in the coarse dark cassock of a friar, is almost passed by Sam unseen in the foggy gloom as he encounters him outside in Cockspur Street - his friend, cloaked now against the chilly evening, swaggering up and down the other side of the roadway, searching, as he explains, once Matthew has collared him, for any sign of 'The Bun and Hazelnuts.'

'*The Sun and Coconuts,* I told you, damn it!' Matthew exclaims as they begin a hasty march back towards the Strand. 'Good God, Sam, are you going completely deaf?'

'Well, it was noisy at the time, as you recall!' Sam protests, his face now unmasked and flushed with his typical high colour even out here in the cold. 'By the way, you look different. Why are you dressed like ..?'

'Don't ask,' Matthew grumbles.

'Well, whatever you've been up to, you have missed an absolute treat, Sir,' Sam continues effusively, ignoring his companion's bad humour. 'I cannot ever recollect such a fabulous masquerade. Johanna is equally thrilled - a huge success - though I'm afraid your young *beau* has been taken. Lady Snatchal, unmasked by that time, came over and befriended her - Sarah, wasn't it? Anyway, the last thing the young lady said prior to leaving was to pass on a message to you that Lady Snatchal had invited her back to her house in St James's Square for a *game of flats* - which she, poor dear, was under the impression was something to do with cards. Before I could enlighten her to the contrary, unfortunately, she was gone.'

'A game of flats? *Oh no!* This is not how I wanted my lovely Sarah to expend her pent up urges this evening. I had no idea the Countess was so inclined. Can it be true?'

'Oh yes. The rites of Sapho, you mean? Common knowledge - at least among the *Beau Monde.* Ever since ...'

'Don't tell me! Ever since her unfortunate riding accident, the fall that she had?'

'Yes. That's right. I say, how did you ..?'

'Never mind. I'm going home, Sam. I shall walk back, or at least pick up some transport farther down the street.'

'Well, I trust you will keep yourself safe,' Sam says, and with a genuine concern this time. 'You do not, after all, look all that inconspicuous.'

Matthew watches as his friend, with a farewell wave, returns through the gates to the bright lights of the masquerade, before setting off himself on his homeward journey - this most unlikely Friar, walking along London's Strand at midnight and making his way through the tall arches of Temple Bar and into Fleet Street. A few snowflakes are falling now, and he thinks about picking up a chair. But the streets are peaceful and he discovers that the walk is having the salutary effect of dissipating his bad mood. With the cold air, moreover, there is hardly a street girl to be seen, and he remains untroubled. Shortly after passing through the archway of Temple Bar, however, he is joined by an unexpected companion: the link-boy - trotting up alongside him, his torch already lit. He seems to recognise Matthew straight away, despite his odd attire.

'This way, then, Sir?'

'Ah, yes, thank you,' Matthew responds, feeling as though it were perfectly natural to speak to him again, even though the likelihood of any such chance encounter in the vastness of the city would be remote, to say the least. 'My tiny waif - I wonder what name I should give you?'

'Waif? That sounds like *Ralph.* That'll do. Call me Ralph, Sir. I think one name's as good as another, don't you?' the boy responds merrily as he quickens his pace, walking just ahead of his charge in his usual jaunty step.

It is all very quiet, and their heels echo from the walls of the buildings as, with his chest puffed out and his shoulders thrown back, the boy sings a little tune to himself as they go, making up rhymes.

> *'Ralph the Waif,*
> *By my faith!*
> *That's a good one, I am sure.*
> *I've been called much worse, and more.'*

'What do you want to do with your life, Ralph?' Matthew asks a moment later as they pass the elegant doorway and windows of the Rainbow on their right, all dark and silent at such a late hour. 'You are a hero already in the estimation of my friend Sam, you know - I mean after coming to our rescue the other evening.'

'I reckon a fellow should be doing at least one heroic deed in his lifetime, wouldn't you say so, Sir?' the boy responds cheerfully, turning to glance back over his shoulder. 'A proper moment of destiny. If the honour comes his way, that is.'

'Yes ... I suppose that's true,' Matthew murmurs. '*One heroic deed.* Why, you are quite the little philosopher, this evening, my friend,' he adds, laughing and wondering at his turn of phrase. He certainly doesn't sound like your typical link-boy - but then does he ever! 'So all this dalliance with trifles, all our masquerades, all the music and culture that us fancy folks celebrate, none of it's worth a candle, eh, when set against heroism?'

'Oh, no, Sir - I didn't say that. Only, what you're talking about - it doesn't protect or preserve us, does it! It doesn't put food on our tables or clothes on our backs. And none of it has ever prevented war, which is a-coming now, they say.'

'True enough, Ralph. True enough,' he agrees with a grim smile, for even he has become resigned to it now.

Eventually they reach Cheapside and the familiar lane leading off to the Pig and Whistle.

'Now, my young friend, this time I really must insist on reimbursing you for your trouble,' Matthew says, gazing down at the mop of curly hair beneath its old moth-eaten cap.

'Oh, that won't be necessary, Sir,' the boy replies, looking up - his pale, shiny face suddenly so very serious and all glowing in the dancing light of the flame - though a moment later he does seem to sense Matthew's frustrations. 'Fair enough, then, Sir,' he adds, relenting. 'You may give me some payment on Tuesday, if you wish,' and upon which he turns to walk away.

'Tuesday? Why on earth *Tuesday?*' Matthew calls after him. 'Oh, all right: Tuesday it is. Where might I find you on *Tuesday*, then?'

'Oh, don't worry, Sir. I'll find you,' the boy calls back. 'And if not ... well, days of the week, they're like names, aren't they: one's as good as another. Good night, Sir!'

And with that, whistling a fragment of some popular tune as he goes, the boy vanishes around a corner, being as much a part of the night as an owl or fox or some other vagrant creature at large - and every bit as elusive and strange.

# ~ 13 ~
## ELIXIR MAGNUM
## AND THOUGHTS FROM A CHAIR

During idle moments he sometimes wonders what would happen if, through some perversity of fate by which every pictorial reference, painting, engraving or sketch should somehow be expunged from the pages of history, how one might explain to future generations the nature and appearance of a sedan chair, this infernal yet essential instrument of conveyance about the city streets? Perhaps one would begin by describing a small wooden box, normally painted black with a hinged side and roof, into which humans of various shapes and sizes, even those equipped with swords or wide panniered petticoats, would, with heroic optimism, endeavour to accommodate themselves into a seated position upon a hard bench - and which, once the doors and ceiling were subsequently shut, would afford about as much room to breath and move about in as a coffin. One would also need to explain that the smells within the box itself would be pungent, to say the least, if not down right unpleasant, depending on the cleanliness or otherwise of its former occupants and their state of digestion at the time. One would then describe in turn a number of additional features of this unique mode of transport: that the box would be lifted from the ground, for example, with the aid of two lengthy wooden poles slotted along the sides and then carried in the grip of two sturdy men in blue kersey coats, one in front, one behind; that once underway these same men would brook no obstruction - the cry of 'by your leave, Sir,' often shouted at the last moment to avoid a collision with pedestrians, and this not always successfully; that the speed at which the chair might be carried, especially by those with calf muscles the size of footballs and operating on a fixed rate per mile, could outstrip anyone endeavouring to walk or, in some cases, even *to run* alongside; that the chairmen themselves would, at an early hour in their shift be

tolerably steady and reliable bearers but by the end of it would
stagger and wobble so much as to virtually tip the poor passenger
out through the flimsy door onto the road; that a small panel or
window would usually be available in the side or front door of the
box, through which, once opened, one might shout instructions or
curses according to one's mood to the bearer up front, and which,
in turn, would sometimes be relayed with additional comments, not
always complimentary, to the bearer behind; that during most of
the journey, for anyone caring to glance out through the sides, there
would appear to rush by a bewildering sequence of disparate
images - glimpses of tricorn hats on turning heads, of half-seen
enticements from shop windows, or of endless doorways to
buildings of indeterminate height never encompassed by the eye;
and finally, it would have to be noted that without sedan chairs it
would be impossible, given the state of current civic amenities, for
a gentleman's clothing or shoes to remain clean for more than a
few minutes exposed to certain quarters of the London streets and
pavements - or, in other words, that sedan chairs were, for all their
disadvantages and horrors, an essential component of civilised life.
And because only the wealthy and well connected could afford to
ride within them, it so followed that civilised life in the city
remained out of reach to all but the most wealthy of its inhabitants.

Matthew Wildish, however, whether by dint of hard work or
sheer luck, knows that he is numbered among those fortunate few,
and has no qualms about availing himself of a chair this morning -
for it does at least ensure a cleanly presented arrival at one's
destination - and on this occasion it is essential to do so because he
has an appointment with a certain Doctor Alcock, the astrologer
and apothecary he has been meaning to investigate ever since
Francis his valet had recommended him some weeks ago. At first,
upon being supplied with the doctor's details, Matthew had
concluded with scepticism that it really would not be necessary to
make the gentleman's acquaintance. Johanna, after all, had tactfully
warned him against it. Yet as he continued to work on his sonnets
he came to fear that his own ignorance in the field of the occult was
possibly inhibiting him and rendering his work slightly shallow - or
at least it might be perceived as such by those who were already
conversant with such arcane knowledge. Doctor Alcock, therefore,
might be just the man for some esoteric inspiration at this juncture -
at least that is what Matthew sincerely hopes, as his chair is set

down in the narrow cul-de-sac of Crane Court, home to many prominent organisations, including the Royal Society no less, and where he alights, pays his fare, and - after taking a deep and grateful draft of fresh air into his lungs - ascends the narrow flight of steps to the Doctor's front door, marked by a painted sign depicting a star and a surgeon's lancet in close proximity. Finding no bell upon which to pull, Matthew raps loudly upon the knocker instead - this being eventually sufficient to rouse the attentions of a maid who shows him upstairs to a small chamber lit by a solitary candle. The room also contains a quantity of various bottles and jars, a brass armillary sphere and, suspended from the ceiling, the traditional spectre of the apothecary's stuffed alligator - an object with which Matthew's head inadvertently collides.

'Doctor Alcock?' Matthew calls - the man himself seated with his back towards him at a desk by the window, quill in hand, his shoulders hunched, and with long, somewhat thinning grey hair that extends down from beneath a felt smoking-cap atop his head.

'Ah yes, good day!' he says without turning - and only after some time does he set down his pen and, rising only partly from his chair, at last shakes his visitor's hand in greeting. 'Ah, I see we have a gentleman today,' he declares, as if surprised, squinting somewhat mole-like in the darkness. 'How do you do?'

'Thank you I am well. And you?'

At which Doctor Alcock stares at his visitor with a look of some surprise and bafflement before inviting Matthew to share with him a swift glance at the pendulum clock on his chimneypiece and replying somewhat cryptically, 'Twelve thirty-seven.'

'*Twelve thirty-seven?*' Matthew echoes, puzzled.

'Oh yes - opposition of the Moon to Mars in Aries. Thus portending conflict, tensions and difficult domestic arrangements. At least for the next hour and a half.'

'Would you like me to leave?'

'No, no, that won't be at all necessary. Just don't expect me to offer you any coffee or tea or anything like that. It would be ghastly. And if my maid were to make it, it would probably poison us both. Anyway, how may I help you Sir. I see you haven't brought any piss for me to examine. Would you care to do a sample for me now?'

At which he reaches under his desk for a suitable vessel, a round-bottomed glass flask in which, as part of the time-honoured diagnostic procedure of the medical profession, one would normally present one's urine for inspection.

'I have not come on medical grounds,' Matthew states.

'Really! Well, well - that, if you'll forgive me, is rather unusual for a young man. But never mind. You had better take a seat. Oh, wait a minute, not there. Here take this one. Oak stool, you see. Elm for the ladies, oak for the gentlemen, otherwise we would be pushing our luck a bit. So, what can I do for you, Sir? Romance? Business? A journey commencing? A lost article to be retrieved? Talismans, amulets, a stolen artefact, its whereabouts and condition? Don't ask me for any of those whatever you do - not with Mars and the Moon like it is. It would not come out well for either of us.'

'I - er - am interested in none of those, either, Doctor Alcock,' Matthew asserts. 'I was rather hoping you could provide me with some knowledge of the heavenly bodies, the planets and their more esoteric, occult significance. I am a poet, you see and ...'

'Esoteric significance?' Doctor Alcock repeats, as if dazed.

'Yes - *as above, so below,* and things of that nature,' says Matthew, recalling the maxim that Johanna had once conveyed to him.

'Um, how odd! You seem to have reminded me of something important there,' Doctor Alcock responds. 'Yes. Even though I can't quite remember what it is, it is definitely important. How fascinating! Anyway, tell me, what is the date of your birth, Sir, that I might construct a chart of nativity for you, forthwith?'

'My date of birth, why the seventh day of August.'

To which the doctor picks up a stick of chalk and writes this information upon a slate before turning to look inside a large book of tables - presumably an ephemeris of planetary positions, while also availing himself of an abacus to aid him in his calculations.

'And the year of birth?' he asks bluntly, almost in the way of an interrogation.

'1718,' Matthew replies.

'Location?'

'Dublin.'

'Time?'

'Don't know,'

'Huh! *Always the way, isn't it!* Oh, all right, I'll set the chart for noon instead.'

A few minutes pass without further word as the apothecary works away, writing with speed and yet meticulous neatness upon a large square of paper - eventually producing an intricately crafted chart, a kind of map of the sky, as it is explained to Matthew, with the signs of the zodiac arranged around the outside and which also includes the co-ordinates of the stars and planets at the time and place of his birth.

All seems well, as the doctor fetches an extra candle by which he might scrutinise the work. But then suddenly, clutching his hands to his temples and in a voice of chilling despair, he shouts, *'Oh no!'*

'What is it? What's the matter?' Matthew demands, terrified.

'Nothing. Nothing at all,' Doctor Alcock replies, regaining his composure with remarkable rapidity. 'Just that you have as many as four major bodies in Leo, Sir. Look! All in the closest conjunction. Why, this is an enviable vitality, I must say. How do you cope with it? The arts, I suppose, could just about be your salvation, though I must say this configuration is far from an easy one to live with - it will either be to the eternal glory of your creative genius, Sir, or else it will lead you a merry dance of utter licentiousness and lechery. In other words, young man, you are either going to be truly great or ... you will be a nuisance.'

'I sincerely hope the former,' Matthew replies, trying to make light of it. 'To be sure, I would not wish to be a nuisance.'

But this does not entirely meet with the approval of Doctor Alcock either. 'Does any man!' he declares rhetorically, raising his eyebrows to the heavens. 'And yet so often we become so, do we not. At birth, we are a nuisance, placing our mothers in mortal danger. Later we become a nuisance, placing our father's in penury to pay for our schooling - a place where we subsequently become a nuisance to our teachers. Later, as apprentices, we become a nuisance to our masters, and as workers we vex our employers or argue with the tax collector. As parents ourselves, we browbeat our children.; and as husbands we importune our wives continually to satisfy our fancies - and all the while, in-between, endlessly eating, drinking, consuming precious resources and spoiling the very air with the smoke from our fires to keep ourselves warm. Always a nuisance. And when we do finally depart this life and our bodies perish, we even become a nuisance to our relatives who must dispose of our carcasses. It is a rare man, one in a million, Sir, who succeeds in passing through this vale of tears without becoming a nuisance to somebody or other.'

'Ah, yes ... well, this brings me to my question,' Matthew responds trying desperately to get back to the purpose of his visit.

'Your question, Sir? I'm sorry ...?'

'Yes. When a man does quit this mortal coil, as it were, where does he go? Is there a soul that survives us? That is what I need to know.'

'Why of course. You don't think all this disgusting, puking and fornicating span of three score year and ten is the sole purpose of our existence, do you. Good God! It would hardly be worth having a universe, if that was all there was to it. No Sir, the part that you consider to be yourself is but a small fragment, or so I have been told. We are all like that - small fragments of much greater beings, reaching to the very stars themselves.'

'How can I become aware of that, though?' Matthew asks. 'I want to experience the natures of the planets in a philosophical way, you see. I want to discover whether it is possible for a man to escape the slavery of his baser instincts and to reverse the descent into matter that we all of us experience at birth and to journey back towards the realm of the spirit. How does one approach such a task?'

'Well, don't ask me!'

'You mean you don't know?'

'Haven't got a clue. Oh, all that mysticism stuff is all right, I suppose. But it doesn't pay the bills, does it. I'm more involved in the modern medical line, myself, you see, pills and potions.'

'But if someone like you doesn't know, then how can anyone else, someone like me for example, ever expect to find enlightenment?'

'Enlightenment? Oh, that's a different matter,' Doctor Alcock mutters with a vigorous shake of the head. 'You have to know someone for that.'

'What ... you mean like the Masons?'

'No, no, no - ruddy nonsense. No - you have to commune with the angels. Oh, it's something to do with each of the planets having its own intelligence, I think. Some call it angelic; others demonic. Depends on what mood you are in at the time, I suppose. Anyway, when you find it, whatever it is, you must pop back and tell me about it, won't you. Until then, I hope that has been helpful, young man. That will be thirty shillings.'

'I see, yes. Thank you,' Matthew says, taking out his purse and counting out the money with some reluctance and wondering what exactly he has got in exchange.

'Oh, and an additional half-crown for the chart itself, if you please,' Doctor Alcock adds, rolling up the parchment and securing it with a bright scarlet ribbon. 'You would not wish to leave empty handed, I am sure? And I can supply you with a full list of important dates into the future also - by post tomorrow, if you wish - including your date of death, naturally.'

'Why, yes, thank you, Matthew responds, handing over his business card with the money. That would certainly be most helpful, I should think.'

'Good, and that of course, will be just a tiny bit extra on top of what you have already paid. A further ten shillings, if you please,' Doctor Alcock responds as Matthew gets to his feet and, having already buttoned up his coat in readiness for a quick escape, counts out another quantity of coins.

'Oh, by the way, I don't suppose I can interest you in any of my very own special Elixir Magnum, can I?' the indefatigable Doctor Alcock inquires indicating a row of bottles upon a shelf. 'My own unique physic, Sir - a medicine against all manner of distempers, maladies and peculiar inconveniences. I have high hopes for it. So much so that for this week only I am offering two bottles for the price of one: a bargain at just ...'

'Oh, no, no, thank you. I am fortunate in that I normally enjoy a fairly robust constitution,' Matthew responds, wondering if he is going to escape today with anything remaining in his purse at all.

'Ah, yes,' the doctor admits with a despondent shrug of the shoulders. 'Youth! I remember it well. Always more interested in romance and what the stars foretell than in the serious business of illnesses. To be frank with you, Sir, I would prefer to drop all this astrology stuff and just stick to medicines - if we could only convince people that being unwell was *normal* and that they needed our attentions every day of their lives - then we could really begin to make some proper money. The Promised Land, Mr Wildish - the Promised Land. Until then, though, I suppose we'll just have to keep taking the piss.'

'Good afternoon,' Matthew ventures yet again by way of departure.

'Bye bye,' Doctor Alcock says, and with one final glance at the calculations by which he has drawn up Matthew's horoscope, adds, 'Oh, and by the way, young man: beware of dogs, won't you. You don't do well with dogs. I can see that clearly. Watch out for the little rascals.'

'Thank you. You may be assured of *that*,' Matthew replies, thinking of Boris the pug and realising that perhaps he should have come to see Doctor Alcock some time ago, after all.

Outside, taking a chair westwards from the corner of Fetter Lane, and aware now more than ever that his discussions with Johanna were always of far greater value than anything the illustrious Doctor Alcock might be able to offer, Matthew resolves to dismiss the whole foolishness from his mind forthwith. But it is not that easy. How can something so ancient and venerable as astrology, a subject that Johanna clearly finds worthy of study be represented by men such as this? He longs now only to be able to speak to her - to listen to her guidance and wisdom. Yes, *if only*.

The chairmen are making good progress this time, and the rhythm of their stride is uncommonly steady and even quite beguiling - while the view outside the windows reveals a city in good heart, flattered by the presence of a little sunshine that makes the brick-work glow with gentle colours or else plays upon all the elegant cornices and pediments of stone that make up the noble lines of the city's new streets and squares - London, *his London* as he sometimes dares to think of it, laying claim to his adopted home as have so many poets of the past - a city getting bigger by the day and forever contributing in no small way to that immense ongoing work of art that is *England;* the England of grand homes, classical architecture, parks and gardens; the England of extravagant fashions, urbane and civilised conversation, wonderful music, poetry and theatre - and, of course, in the midst of it all, so many breathtakingly beautiful women.

The best of London, though, the envy of all of Europe, is undoubtedly the shops - not just a few shops, but an entire two and a half mile stretch of them - all the way from Cornhill in the East, to Charing Cross in the West, taking in Cheapside, Fleet Street and the Strand en route - one great pulsating artery of lavish emporiums and arcades running through the heart of the City. Even the approach of darkness does not diminish their abundance. Candle

makers and lamp-shops, mercers and haberdashers, confectioners
and fruiterers - their illuminated windows all dazzling with
enticements, and everywhere the crowds of elegant women of
every age and class floating in and out of the doorways in shoals,
all most smartly attired, attended upon by handsome footmen in
gold-laced jackets as they seek out the milliners and drapers who
will supply them with materials for their homes in the new-built
squares of Mayfair, or else for the clothing and fashions that inspire
their eternal quest for beauty and romantic intrigue. And within the
shops themselves, meanwhile, so many stylish assistants at work,
flitting here and there - gallery upon gallery of lovelies sporting
every latest fashion and coiffure, fragrant with every newest scent.
It is a paradise to Matthew; the greatest pleasure simply to mingle
and enjoy the intoxication of the very air one must breathe in such
places. Yes - here is *his* Elixir Magnum, all the inspiration for a
thousand poems if need be. It is all that any man of romance could
possible wish for, and a walk from one end of it to the other, and
which should normally take no more than an hour, invariably
consumes the better part of an afternoon and evening of pleasant
distraction before he ever completes its course.

He is fortunate, he knows. His position in society enables him to
move upon this fabulous stage as a player of some distinction; with
wealth enough to respond to fashion; with leisure enough to travel;
and, above all, to be in possession of all the education and
cultivated taste sufficient to converse as the equal of any man. Life
is good. And, this afternoon, as he allows his mind to wander
towards various recollections of poetry and music, as is so often the
case when travelling alone, it occurs to him that even the very
music of the age, the melodies of his beloved Handel, are likewise
born out of rhythm and movement - from the sedate and plodding
measure of one who marches to the call of duty, to the impatient
steps of a gallant who hastens to a lover's tryst; from the
perambulations of a well balanced chair, to the canter of a horse,
from the revolution of the wheels of a coach to the very planets
orbiting in the sky above. Rhythm is present everywhere - and
never more so than in the mystery and metre of poetry, the passage
from the first word to the last. And if there is any kind of meaning
or purpose to it all, to all this wild and chaotic business of simply
*being alive*, then the journey itself and the meeting of it with some
measure of humility and grace must surely be the greater part of

happiness. He understands that now - and so Doctor Alcock be damned!

'Where're we supposed to be going, then - anybody know?' comes a loud complaint from one of the chairmen outside, ostensibly directed to his companion to the rear, but as much intended to be overheard by Matthew himself, of course, inside.

Glancing out of the window once more he remembers that he has not supplied the men with any detailed directions yet - other than the vague injunction to carry him westwards. But of course he *does* have an objective, if only half acknowledged at the back of his mind. And as they approach the broad, triangular expanse of the junction at Charing Cross with its equestrian statue and sinister pillory, he is aware of it coming into view already. Rolling down the side window of the chair, he orders the men to cross over into Cockspur Street, therefore, and to stop near the entrance to the narrow court where he had gone on such a fruitless quest not too long ago, on the evening of the masquerade.

'Tell me, gentlemen,' he inquires of the chairmen, once they have placed him down, still speaking through the window - and not, to their puzzlement, in any hurry to alight, 'just a matter of idle curiosity on my part, but do either of you happen to know anything concerning the establishment along there under the sign of the Sun and Coconuts?'

The men outside exchange furtive glances and seem reticent to speak for a moment. 'Oh, yes, Sir,' the one up front responds at length, shuffling uneasily on his feet. 'We - er - carry quite a number of distinguished gentlemen to that door.'

'And one or two we have carried out, as well, in our time, and not always in the best of condition,' the rear chairman ventures to add.

The curiosity on Matthew's face, the raising of a polite eyebrow is insufficient at first to warrant clarification. But eventually, with encouragement in the form of a handsome tip promised them, the men set aside their misgivings. 'It's a place of wickedness, Sir. Of perverse goings on,' the front man declares, though still awkwardly.

'Heavens!' Matthew remarks. 'How terrible! I don't suppose you could - er - possibly enlighten me further?'

'It's a bagnio, Sir - but one of *special services,* if you take my meaning.'

'No - I don't take your meaning!' Matthew grumbles, beginning to lose patience. 'Out with it, man!'

'Well, let's put it this way then, Sir. The royal mews up yonder is a place, as you probably know, where many a fine gentleman can be seen mounting and riding out in pomp and splendour. But what is not so well known, is that many of those very same officers and many a gent from other parts of town as well come to the bagnio yonder to be mounted and ridden themselves - in this case by a sturdy lady going by the name of Lucy Armstrong, and who for their pleasure harnesses them up and applies the whip to their backsides.'

'I see,' Matthew responds, leaning back into his seat and feeling suddenly in the light of such revelations that he might be of a mind to forego the society of the lovely Mrs Armstrong after all. Clearly she is a mistress of flagellation - and though Matthew counts himself as very much a man of the world, he has never felt the urge to wander too deeply into that particular avenue of so-called pleasure. How unfortunate.

Try as he might, though, the recollection of that brief glimpse of Mrs Armstrong at the masquerade, and of her splendid portrait above the chimneypiece in the room that evening still haunts him, so that inevitably he must asks himself: should he really dismiss her from his ambitions so readily, merely because of her chosen profession? Surely not! What would that say about his own limitations and prejudices? It is, he concludes, something that requires just a little more thought and consideration.

'Pall Mall!' he orders the men, for he has resolved to take a stroll in the gardens below St James's to clear his head amid the fresh air and pleasant greenery of London's favourite promenade. The chair is lifted again, therefore, and off they go. The rhythm returns, his mind is steadied, and the great quest to which he has set himself, be it mystical or physical, sacred or profane, or even a peculiar combination of all of these, continues apace.

# ~ 14 ~
## THE SATED LOVER

He has been the night-long with Caroline Bolter, his very special *Jupiter* from Ranelagh Gardens, the kept mistress of a nobleman who at the present time is two hundred miles away in Lancashire commanding a regiment of soldiers endeavouring, not very successfully it would seem by the latest headlines, to repel the Jacobites from the gates of Manchester. They had contrived to meet at Ranelagh again, the final night of the season in the Rotunda, for a meal and for an hour of unbridled flirtation in masks - he having fashioned a fabulous piece for her before-hand, replete with sequins and tiny green beads, all surrounded by a filigree of lilac and gold brocade. Here again she had played the part of the wanton in search of adventure, and boldly too, with a largess worthy of Juno herself - before, together, they had repaired to Hanover Square and her spacious and well-appointed apartments where there had been much teasing of each other, and much rushing from room to room and chasing, rolling and tumbling until the considerable fires of her passion could even begin to be extinguished - as extravagant and demanding as ever. And most loudly did she proclaim her satisfaction, not once, not twice, but, it seemed to him, almost interminably once they had finally settled into their embrace.

Returning now by chair along the uneven and crowded roadways down towards Charing Cross, he suspects the very skin upon his honourable member has been almost flayed from him in the process, for he is aware of a distinct rawness down below. Not only that, but his back feels sore when he reclines into the seat, so that he suspects she has scratched him again, and belike even drawn blood in the throes of her release. Would he be marked, all scarred from her clawing nails? He hardly dared think about it. Oh yes, nothing by halves, a night spent with the indomitable Caroline, and consequently a certain weariness if not exhaustion now accompanies him upon his homeward journey, a dusting of dark stubble upon his cheeks and his clothing more than a little untidy and worse for wear.

He had intended to take breakfast at The Rainbow, but due to the congestion on the roads, with thirty minutes having already elapsed since starting out, he is inclined now to abandon the chair and seek out a carriage instead that might take him directly home via a different route, back to where he has, after all, still a number of urgent jobs to attend to - not least of which would be the commencement in earnest upon the restoration of Lord Snatchal's wig, a task he has repeatedly postponed. At least the raw material itself, gathered at such hazard to life and limb recently in the Rookeries of Seven Dials, has been washed, de-loused and passed through his hackling irons in readiness. But several long days of work still lie ahead to recreate the piece itself, even if he were to emulate the coarse workmanship of the original.

Yes, lots to do - but really, the journey thus far is taking an eternity. Heavens above, he thinks, it would have been quicker to have walked! A wipe of the misty window and a glance out to the side reveals the reason for the delay. The Haymarket with its busy stalls and shop-fronts is packed with people. Worse, many of these appear to be troops - conscripts and volunteers, all milling about on the roads and pavements, some in makeshift liveries, but others in full regalia, their scarlet uniforms all pressed and dapper, their buttons and buckles polished and gleaming in the sunshine. Frustrated by his lack of progress, Matthew rolls down the window and calls to the man up front: 'Sir, the cause of our delay, if you please? This is outrageous!'

'Can't be helped, Sir.' The man calls back over his shoulder above the rising din. 'You can see what's going on. It's the muster.'

'The muster! What muster?'

With a jolt and a thud, the chair is dropped to the ground, though no further explanation is forthcoming. Instead, both the men come round the side to talk - and here, hands on hips, their faces despondent, they appear to arrive at the conclusion that there is not much point proceeding, since the crowds are, if anything, becoming even thicker. The sound of a military band with rousing pipes, bugles and drums can also be heard now, joined by various ecstatic cheers and even some ripples of applause.

'Apologies, Sir,' the other chairmen announces, his long pendulous nose almost entering the compartment through the window. 'It's the muster, you see.'

'I know - I know it's the muster!' Matthew cries. 'Your colleague just told me that. Why are they mustering at all, that's what I want to know? And how much longer is it going to go on for?'

'The Duke of Cumberland, it is - returned from the continent and the fighting of the French,' the first chairman explains with greater lucidity, 'and he's brought his men - whole regiments of foot and horse, and some Dutch as well. The Jacobites are at Manchester, see. There's no stopping them otherwise.'

Despairing of any further progress, Matthew alights from his chair, pays his fare and begins to walk, but not before shouting back angrily to his bearers: '*Manchester* - it's bloody miles away. And I haven't had my breakfast yet!'

But they seem unimpressed by his predicament, and merely shrug their shoulders as they turn their attention instead to a street vendor selling pies - which do, in fact, look damn good, especially to a man hungry after a night's exertions. But Matthew resists. There are too many rumours as to what unscrupulous vendors put into pies these days for him to be tempted, so he keeps walking - squinting somewhat through tired eyes in the way of some nocturnal creature exposed to the daylight.

To be sure, it is an unusual situation, Matthew has to admit, as he pushes his way through as best he can, jostled on all sides, his gentleman's clothing and affluent appearance commanding scant respect - in fact just the reverse amid this rabble. How very unpleasant. With many, if not all, of the fine linen and mercer shops of the district boarded up, there are boisterous and vulgar men everywhere now - converging together from out of the taverns and the cheaper bordellos, some upon the arms of their temporary sweethearts, others brawling or relieving themselves in alleyways or even, like dogs, against any convenient tree - while elsewhere volunteers and citizens with an eye to the glory of combat are enlisting alongside them in droves and being told where they must go to assemble and be supplied with uniforms. Plenty of cheap gin is on hand even at this early hour to moisten the wheels of patriotism, and everyone is very jolly. It fills him only with horror. All these young men rushing off to fight - cannon fodder to be placed in a line and marched helpless into a hail of musket fire and cannon, to be mutilated or cut to pieces by sabres or bayonets - and for what! A kind of hysteria has taken over the city; everyone rushing either to slaughter their fellow man or else to their own doom, as if it were the very greatest of achievements to do so. The fools.

Threading his way through the crowd, it becomes obvious, moreover, that the muster is not the only unusual activity taking place. Hackney chairs and coaches seem to be in particularly high demand, with queues forming everywhere - while any vehicle that does venture along is already filled to overflowing, even to the extent of some passengers hanging on to the pillion or platforms to hitch a ride. There is also an inordinate number of wagons laden with household goods and furniture, some being hauled by horses, but most simply by man-power alone - there being a sudden shortage of horses and mules, now, of course, what with so many animals being requisitioned for the front line. Evidently, the citizens - and not just a few of them - are packing their belongings and leaving. *Leaving London!* It can only be due, Matthew surmises, to the perceived dangers of occupation, since that is clearly what everyone is now expecting. Is it likely? Even possible?

'Sir, a word - may I just inquire where you might be going?' he asks one man waiting for an opportunity to move forward with his goods, all stacked high upon a hand-cart drawn behind him, a burden that looks almost too heavy for any one person to budge at all let-alone travel with any distance.

'Anywhere but here, Sir,' he replies. 'I am hoping to pull these bits and pieces to my cousin's house in Holborn, and from there we will be going in wagons to Kent, or farther afield as needs take us.'

'But surely you don't expect the city of London to fall to those blaggards?'

'What's to stop them!' the man replies, mopping his brow. 'Preston has been taken. And they're outside Manchester now - with all the weapons and food thereabouts seized by them already, they say; in every house, the furniture broken up for firewood, and troops billeted all over the place, drinking and making free with the ladies. There's no laws to prevail against them, no decency in an invading army.'

And with that, and the appearance of an opportune space in the traffic, the man heaves upon the bars of his cart once more and pulls away, slipping and sliding in the mud of the roadway as he goes, now all churned up and most intractable. And there are many like him - men, women, children, and even their livestock, all on the move. The scene is one of panic - the sparkling playground that was once his city and theatre of pleasure, has now all but vanished, governed solely by a morbid preoccupation with some distant, fantastical threat that will surely never come to pass. He wants to shout out to them, to everyone, to come to their senses, to calm down, to return to a more measured state. But it is of no use. Everyone seems preoccupied with their cares. Even as Matthew manages to make his way down into Cockspur Street, he notices that the windows of its fashionable shops, coffee houses and milliners have been boarded up for safety - even here. How unremittingly depressing it all is - though when passing by the narrow court and the sign of the Sun and Coconuts farther up where he had so nearly come to grief the other evening, he cannot help but smile despite it all. Certainly one of his less-successful forays of recent times into the realms of romance and seduction.

But just then, abruptly, his train of thought is broken by a loud cry - and when turning to glance up the lane itself he is just in time to observe a man in the process of tumbling down some steps. Standing at a doorway above him, moreover, is a tall woman in a resplendent robe of candy-stripe silk brocade, all pastel colours, lemon and pink. With elbows folded about her ample bosom, she is glaring down at the unfortunate man, a conscript by the look of him, and clearly the worse for drink even at this early hour.

'Away with you, wretched boy!' she declares, her voice strident and firm, though not without a trace of laughter to it as well. 'This is not an establishment for the likes of you.'

'Mrs Armstrong!' Matthew exclaims, almost involuntarily as he advances up the alleyway - recognising instantly the lady herself from her portrait and also from that fleeting glimpse he had enjoyed of her at the masquerade. Placing himself adroitly between the soldier and the steps, he flourishes his hat, makes a leg and bows, feeling most gratified to discover that she really does exist.

Hearing his exclamation, and sizing up the quality of his apparel with a look of some approval, she acknowledges his intervention with a gracious smile - upon which, Matthew discovers for the very first time that she has the most extraordinary dimples in her cheeks and that her hair is the colour of sunshine.

The importunate conscript, meanwhile, is not so impressed with Matthew's arrival. 'I'm as good a man as any!' he asserts, thrusting out his chest and wiping his mouth with the back of his hand, which hardly makes him any more becoming.

'Now, now, good Sir,' Matthew admonishes him with humour turning to place a kindly hand upon his shoulder. 'Hark, can you not hear the drums yonder?' he adds, pointing a finger at the sky. 'Your service to your country should be all of your calling now.'

The man appears flattered, as though being given his marching orders. But still reluctant to depart, he takes Matthew to one side and, in a meek tone of voice, protests, 'It might be my last day on earth, Sir. I don't want to fight and die without ... you know, having just one more pop at it!'

But Matthew is firm, reminding the fellow that it could be days or even weeks until he might be called upon to fight, and that the establishment here that he has mistakenly alighted upon would require a half-year of his wages before he might enjoy even the most basic of its privileges. On the other hand, lots of willing lasses are to be found up in the Haymarket making merry with the soldiers at this very instant for no more than a pint of gin. He would miss his opportunity for recreation there if he were to tarry any longer. What's more, there are hot pies to be had for sixpence - which finally appears to clinch it, and the man is soon staggering forth into the busy street to confirm for himself the attractions on offer.

'Well, well! I am much obliged to you, Sir,' Mrs Armstrong says, unfolding her arms, her voice now far more soft and genteel.

What a fine looking woman she is, he thinks. Buxom, strong of limb - a person full of vitality and fun. It is as if the clouds have parted, and all the walls of the shady little court illuminated by her presence.

'Glad to be of service, Ma'am,' he responds with a further bow. 'My name is Matthew Wildish, and ...'

'Matthew Wildish - the poet?'

'You have heard of me, Madam? I am surprised ...'

'*Surprised,* Mr Wildish?' she responds, smiling still, though also rather intimidating all of a sudden as she descends the steps to approach him.

'I mean, that you should be familiar with my work,' Matthew answers, discovering as he looks into her eyes, which are large, golden brown in colour and most beautiful, that her height is every bit the equal of his own.

'Why, Mr Wildish, do you not think that your surprise, that a creature of my species should appreciate poetry, might just be a trifle discourteous? Do you not think it might be as irritating to me as the expectations of the soldier you just sent away?'

'I must apologise Madam,' he responds, knowing she is perfectly correct. 'It is my enthusiasm that has robbed me of my courtesy, since I have for some time desired to make your acquaintance - though for various reasons seem to have been unsuccessful.'

But at this she merely laughs once more, perhaps aware of being still a little over-wrought herself. 'Really!' she declares with returning warmth. 'Well, well, Mr Wildish, now that you have succeeded in doing so, may I suggest you return at a later date more convenient to us both, so that I might offer you some hospitality.'

'Madam, be assured of it.'

He should, he knows, be off then, but he does not; and neither does she. Instead, they stand for a moment looking into each other's eyes with growing amusement, both reluctant to conclude their conversation - and with a strange kind of mutual understanding between them, too. For here is someone who, like him, would surely live much of her life in the realm of delicious fantasy. Even now amid the harsh sounds of the troops assembling and the citizens taking flight, even now with the world falling to pieces all around them, here is someone who would doubtless sip champagne and make love in the afternoon: a kindred spirit - and one, moreover, who seems to have sensed the same in him. With neither willing to terminate this delightful and spontaneous liaison, therefore, it is she who breaks the silence.

'I must say you do have the look about you, Mr Wildish, of one who has yet to return home after a night of distraction.'

'Madam, I confess it is true.'

'Then perhaps you would care, even at this early hour, for a little refreshment before you continue upon your way - and pray do not be concerned if you are unprepared in matters of funding. Rather, I wish that you should enter as my guest.'

It is agreed. And with a further bow and exchange of pleasantries, he is admitted to the very interior he had searched for in vain some days ago - this time entering not via the small doorway he had to his folly taken previously, but now from the top of the steps. A far grander entrance, in fact, and from where he is shown through to a spacious atrium - the interior with its mock Near-Eastern decoration and profusion of tiles and mirrors typical of what one would expect of an expensive bagnio, a place moreover which, though modest in size, is clearly designed to cater to an exclusive clientele. He notes the presence of a steam room with the sign of 'Caldarium' above it, and a number of doorways to smaller chambers, each labelled with some pseudo-Roman or mythological association or the other - Elysium, or Parnassus, or such like. Upstairs they go, to settle inside a comfortable parlour on the first floor, wainscoted and painted blue and where a lavishly curtained window with swags of luxurious velvets and silks looks out over the rowdy street below. Taking seats at opposite sides of a coffee table, he upon a chair, she reclining upon a couch, they listen with amusement to all the hurly-burly of the muster for a moment still taking place outside - until, as if by magic, since he cannot remember anyone having been summoned, a maid enters bringing with her a bottle of champagne and the equally welcome sight of a hearty breakfast - a rack of toast, a selection of delicious preserves and some salt ham. It is all very nice, indeed, he thinks, being exposed to such hospitality, though it is also slightly nerve-wracking, because Mrs Armstrong, who rarely takes her eyes from him for a second, is clearly the kind of woman used to being in charge of her men - as one might, with good reason, expect considering her profession. That she might be open to pleasures of a more conventional mode, as her demeanour to him has already intimated, is encouraging, however, and more than worthy of exploration.

Resisting the food for the time being, and upon the maid's departure, he gets to his feet to pour some of the sparkling wine. She continues to watch him - an expression of benevolence and approval upon her face as he, drawn for a moment to the contents of a nearby bookcase, discovers there a volume of his own poetry, a modest anthology made some years ago and no longer in print, but sufficient to assure him that her assertions of a moment ago of being acquainted with his work were well founded. In addition to this, can be seen numerous volumes by other poets, by Milton and Donne, by literary giants of the present such as the redoubtable Mr Pope, and even some by philosophers and men of science. Amazing

- though this time he refrains from saying so, for this most singular and rare individual is, he suspects, one who will brook no foolishness or worldly posturing in any man, and who would see through even the most sophisticated of flirtations.

'Well now Mr Wildish!' she laughs, catching the look of admiration once more upon his face as he returns to his seat. 'You see how I am full of surprises, and that you should congratulate yourself if you were to learn the half of them in the space of a year of study.'

'Indeed, I am beginning to think so, Madam,' he concurs, determined to maintain his composure as he notices that what he had hitherto assumed to be her petticoat is in fact another open robe that has gradually slid itself apart to reveal glimpses of flesh and a leg of heroic proportions, a thread of gold sparkling from around her ankle. 'What else, I wonder might there be to learn about you?' he adds with nonchalance, pretending to be unmoved by the sight.

'Why, firstly, you should learn that I am no simple harlot, Sir,' she replies instantly, her voice as merry as ever, her eyes radiating fun. 'We should best have that out in the open before you seize upon the idea of placing anything else there - since I know full-well the priorities of young men of your society.'

'Ah, but Madam, now it is *I* who should feel affronted,' he states, 'that you presume to know my mind and to attribute such narrowness to its purpose. I am, I assure you, most humble in my desire first and foremost to cultivate your friendship.'

'Oooh, is that a fact!' she chuckles. 'Well, your protestations of humility are not very convincing, Mr Wildish. Especially in one so well furnished with nature's gifts to be practised in the very antithesis.'

To which, found-out yet again, and feeling rather defeated as a consequence, he can only fall silent.

'You know who I am, I take it - and what I do?' she inquires - sipping at her champagne freely now and watching with approval as he does finally avail himself of something to eat - for he is hungry now almost beyond endurance.

'Madam, I believe I have some knowledge, yes - imperfect as that must be,' he answers, looking up and feeling very much at ease all of a sudden in her presence, and - every bit as pleasing - sensing that she feels likewise in his.

'Well and good,' she observes, 'though I'll wager the greater part of your knowledge is inaccurate. 'Despite my calling and profession, Mr Wildish, I am nowhere near as wicked as you may have heard, and I have not committed a thousandth part of the offences that the frivolous, jealous women of this town accuse me of - all those faithless wives or craven demireps who indulge their own vices constantly with man or beast and who seem to think that decrying the sins of others might excuse their own iniquity. I am better than they are - oh yes - many times more powerful, and they know it - and I am no more wanton or free with my favours than any other female of discernment or taste. In fact, my tastes are very simple, Mr Wildish: I insist on the best. That is all. The best in all things. And that, alas, comes but rarely to any of us.'

He continues to look into her eyes, aware of his growing fondness for her, and that if his initial impressions upon their meeting a few minutes ago had been favourable, by now they have become governed by an attraction of almost overwhelming intensity. To add to her qualities still more, he notices that her hair, touched by a little stray sunlight that steals in through the window from time to time, is not only pure golden, but also textured in places with the finest of braiding - whether by a gift of nature or contrived by artifice he cannot say, nor does he much care, for he finds himself longing to reach out and explore the texture of it between his fingers. Her mouth is large and sensuous, and of a curious swollen aspect around the lips - while it is the pleasing dimples that form in her cheeks as she smiles that, perhaps more than anything, continue to charm and fascinate him.

'Madam, I agree,' he remarks in words that bear no relation to his turbulent thoughts. 'We must live in hope that those who venerate excellence might still be among us in this world.'

'Yes ... yes, we must live in hope, Mr Wildish. You are correct. And we are each in our own way fortunate, are we not - for, as you can see, I am also blessed with certain advantages - and these, like yourself, most obviously in my appearance.'

'Indeed, Madam, it has not escaped my attention.'

'I was apprised of this understanding at a remarkably early age,' she continues, altogether far more inclined to indulge him now and allowing him to top up her glass once more with champagne.

'Really?'

'Oh yes. It was when treading the boards in the theatres of this city for a period during my formative years, in fact, that I came to the attention of a certain noble gentleman who taking rather a shine to me, elevated me for a short time prior to his demise to the status of his mistress. Since then, I have been known as *Mrs* Armstrong, though I was never wed.'

'And do you continue to have connections to the stage, Madam, may I ask?' Matthew responds, helping himself to ham and buttering several slices of toast rapidly as if his life depended on it.

'None at all,' she replies swiftly. 'For I can assure you, Mr Wildish there is quite enough *theatre* that takes place on these premises already, more than enough to satisfy any feelings of nostalgia I might have for my former profession. It was, however, during those days that it was revealed to me by the testimony of my paramour (and subsequent experience has done nothing to dissuade me of the validity of his statement) that my leg and foot are of a particularly pleasing and well-proportioned aspect, and have the powers to excite in a way equal to that of the face and voice of others more commonly regarded as merely beautiful. The elegance of heels and silk stockings, of fine lace anklets and gartered thighs add to my appeal - as do, on occasion, and as the wishes of my clients dictate, a nice tall pair of riding boots. Consequently, I was resolved, once I had lost my means of support, and yet endowed as I also was with a handsome settlement in the aforesaid gentleman's estate, to turn such a boon to my advantage, and thus to establish a business in which I could put to good use these my very best assets - a business which thrived to such an extent that I was quickly able to purchase this very building in which you find yourself and where I have made it my occupation to provide specialist services to gentlemen of distinction.

'Here, at my bagnio, therefore, you will discover firstly the ideal location in which to warm, cleanse and refresh your person with the aid of steam, hot water and - beginning at two-thirty in the afternoon each day - the ministrations of an excellent masseur, Mr Mustafa, who is, he tells me, from the distant and exotic empire of the Ottomans. And although I rather suspect by his accent that he is more from the Paddington area than anywhere else, he does know how to invigorate tired limbs, to ease the pains of rheumatism or to snap your joints back into place if they are recalcitrant. Alternatively, you may also hire one or more of my bedchambers for a day or night, and bring with you any *amour* you wish to spend your time with here. Absolute privacy and discretion are assured when undertaking any of these activities, and if you so wish you may also hire the conventional services of our chamber maid or cook. If a gentleman wishes to make an appointment with me, however, he may expect no more than the privilege of removing his clothes and having me restrain him with ropes or chains and to then administer the instruments of flagellation. It is, I should tell you, a speciality of the house, and is the only service I personally provide. My fees are high, *very* high, so that I should inform you here and now, Mr Wildish, that under normal circumstances none may approach me unless, like Jove himself, he does so amid a shower of gold.

'Meanwhile, in the administration of corrective discipline, I have a worthy selection of items to choose from. I apply birch twigs, whips, riding crop and straps, and will, upon request, also take a gentleman over my knee with a slipper. It is a service generally called upon by feeble or elderly men to rouse their blood and to regain, albeit briefly, some recollection of the thrill and rapture that once attended them during their youth - and to this purpose we also provide, upon request, a second female with particularly soft hands who can provide manual assistance while the process is being undertaken. It is a most stimulating combination they assure me - though for most of my worn out old gentlemen, reaching the moment of discharge is, for all that, a somewhat protracted and arduous exercise. Five, ten, twenty minutes of my ministrations are as nothing to them. But they will not have me forbear, not for one second - for even the faintest recollection or remnant of pleasure deep in the recesses of the memory, for a man as he ages, is so alluring that he will seek to summon it forth no matter what pain or indignities he must endure. Generals, admirals, colonels and captains, bishops, judges, barristers, lords and physicians - they all come to me, striving to re-kindle some spark of excitement long after the powers of enjoying the more conventional delights of the opposite sex have deserted them. This very afternoon, for instance, I am appointed to deal with a particularly ancient and venerable peer of the realm with whom I have in the past had so much labour to rouse the blood in his veins, that I would as well be whipping the most obstinate of mules over the frontiers of the Alps. But I keep at it - and he pays me handsomely for my labours. Stamina and endurance are my watch-words, Mr Wildish, and I am not of the name *Armstrong* without good reason.'

Matthew, who has been eating heartily throughout, expresses with a gracious bow of the head his gratitude for such a thorough and entertaining exposition over breakfast. 'I am beholden to you, Madam,' he states, raising the napkin to his lips, and wishing he could move across to join her on her sofa, though this he dares not yet attempt. 'I would say that a man who could win your affections would be a rare creature, to be sure - should there be one of such good fortune at the present time, I wonder?'

'You will not be entirely surprised to learn, Mr Wildish, for your words reveal your aspirations in that respect, that there is none. I am single, in want of nothing ... nothing perhaps other than the full experience of romantic pleasure with a man who might have the courage to bask in the fullness of my light from time to time and reflect it back to me. And do not, pray, ask me to explain such an oddity of speech. Demonstrate to me rather that you do understand and you shall become, I promise you, all that you wish to be in my company. And so, Mr Wildish, for a guest that I have known but half an hour, I should think I have told you quite enough, both for mine own good, and yours.'

'Madam, be assured, I am your most willing listener, and that I remain at your service entirely.'

'Indeed, Sir!' she chuckles. 'Though I do tend to hear that refrain quite frequently between these walls. Never mind, I know your meaning is different to what I am accustomed to. I willingly accept your generosity, Mr Wildish - though in flying so close to the Sun, rash youth, beware that I do not melt your wings.'

'Nay, Madam, for I would gladly be destroyed in pursuit of it.'

'And I with you, Sir. I with you,' she sighs, and most warm-heartedly, he thinks. 'Though for now, sadly, I must frustrate your purpose, and mine - for I must shortly prepare for my afternoon's labours, while a prospect such as this is not one to be quenched with undue haste, as I am sure you would agree. I suspect that you will do well, Mr Wildish, if given half the chance. It is a woman's intuition - though possibly adulterated already with the foolishness and the hopes we all of us entertain of finding happiness, if only for an hour. And so I would be obliged if you could at least demonstrate the validity of my intuition - just a little, if you would care to do so before you depart?'

'*Now*, Madam?'

'Yes - now, though sadly I can permit you no more than five minutes.'

'Five minutes!' he gasps. 'Why, what could I possible do in ...?'

'Why, I wish you to read me a poem, Sir,' she interrupts merrily as ever. 'Heavens above! What did you think I meant? And I trust that it shall not be any longer than five minutes. I do not like lengthy poems, Mr Wildish. A poem is like a man's member. A lively and sensitive presentation of the matter usually proves far more satisfying then excessive length.'

At which, emboldened at last by her delicious humour, he rises and steps around the table, that he might sit beside her on her couch, a manoeuvre from which, he is pleased to observe, she does not withdraw apart from gathering in her wide skirts to make room for him. 'Madam, poetry of the kind I have for you is best whispered softly, and so I will join you here, if I may,' he says.

'You have, Sir, already done so. It would be churlish of me to ask you to rise once more and return to your chair.'

'Then hear me, fairest dear,' he whispers, more earnestly now, taking her hand, 'for your society this morning has been to me the most agreeable of experiences; and these lines of heartfelt verse, inspired already by a glimpse I had one evening of your portrait, are for you, and you alone.'

*When, after winter's bleak and dismal reign,*
*I raise my pallid visage to the skies,*
*And vain ambition doth urge me on again,*
*To honour the acclaim of cheers and sighs.*

*Now would I take thy hand and see thee shine,*
*That we entwine our wings of waxen pride.*
*Our hands, our lips, our tangled limbs combine,*
*Fair ripe and gold, our passions soaring glide.*

*Then are we as to eager youth that fly,*
*Upwards, up, and deep-caress'd, my fairest toy,*
*That rising forth unto the radiant eye,*
*Dissolv'd be in sighs of molten joy.*

*What care then I, if falling, cease to be,*
*If thou should'st only perish there with me.*

With a lengthy breath that seems to come from a place deep within her magnificent frame, she allows him now to take both her hands, as their lips meet in the lightest yet most delectable and lingering of kisses.

'Oh, how fine it is,' she murmurs, 'to be so intimate with one whose company is yet so very strange and new. You have brought moments of magic into this room today, and I am thrilled at it. Come to me again, won't you, my brave Icarus?'

'Madam, I shall. Be sure.'

Yet still they cannot quite bring themselves to part. And steadfast still, they look into each other eyes, her open lips, inviting, confirming still her pleasure at the arrangement. 'I am here at my works most days,' she states at length, taking up her fan and endeavouring to become business-like. 'If you care to call before noon, though, you will find the baths available to you, Mr Wildish, and myself also free for conversation.'

'Then I shall call, Madam, and will look forward to making free with you also.'

'You are blunt, Sir.'

'Nay, Madam, you will find my edge is keen.'

'Oh, I do not doubt it, Sir,' she replies - her ways altogether milder and far more yielding he senses than at any time hitherto, as they kiss briefly once more - one further thrilling, magical embrace that promises so very much delight.

But for now, sadly, he knows he really must leave. The noise outside the window is becoming intolerable, in any case - for it seems that wherever he sports his amorous intentions these days he is destined to be pursued by the sounds of vulgar cheering; of marching men, drums and fife. It is, however, with a far more agreeable outlook that he exits once more into the streets and continues on his homeward journey - along and into The Strand, where at last there comes some welcome respite from the din, and where the traffic, carriages and chairs appear to be moving freely at a more customary pace. He feels better now - restored to life, thanks to his hour with such a fascinating and intriguing woman. And he rather suspects that whatever awaits him in the great and indeterminate 'tomorrow' with all its uncertainties, that the bright and spirited charms of Mrs Lucy Armstrong will be very much a part of any pleasure it contains.

As usual at this hour of the day, the boys in Fleet Street are out selling their papers, and already, every news-stand or bill-board is proclaiming the news, scrawled in thick black letters or else called out in equally thick London accents by the vendors: *'Read all abou'dit! Jacobites march on Manchesta!'* followed a few yards farther on by: *'Rebels capture guns and 'eavy ordnance - cannon and explosiffs. Read all abou'dit!'*

And as Matthew pauses to buy a copy at one of the news-stands, the boy remarks: 'Looks like we'll be 'avin a mighty bang or two coming our way, Sir, eh!'

But Matthew, barely breaking stride and tucking the paper under his arm, merely laughs in response. 'Oh, you may depend on that,' he declares, much to the boy's confusion.

# ~ 15 ~
## A MESSAGE OF DISTINCTION

What on earth is wrong with our army? Matthew asks himself, as he pauses on his homeward journey, sheltering in a doorway to peruse the front page of his newspaper. They seem incapable of winning a single battle. Rather than showing any signs of being halted, the rebel advance seems, if anything, to be gathering apace, which can only serve to give encouragement to the French. And consequently, he finds himself thinking of Sam and Johanna at their home in Greenwich. Surely they would be feeling vulnerable, living so close to all the strategic dockyards east of the capital. Would Johanna be anxious for the children, and Sam for his home and possessions? Would they be contemplating leaving for somewhere safer? The answers must be 'yes' on all counts - so that whereas until now Matthew has felt not the slightest pang of disquiet for his own welfare, suddenly he begins to feel concerned for theirs. The thought of never seeing Johanna again is almost too much to bear. And then, just as he is debating whether to pop into The Rainbow and write letters of enquiry, or even to arrange a visit to them, he notices, striding up the hill amid the crowds towards him the tall figure of Francis, his valet.

'Francis! Francis! Are you looking for me?' Matthew calls with a wave of the arm.

'Good day, Sir,' he says, appearing to be not at all properly attired for the outdoors, but rather still in his waistcoat and dress shoes, his stockings all bespattered with mud, his face flushed from the exertion of walking uncommonly fast. 'I took it upon myself to come to where I thought I might find you, Sir. A calling card was received this morning - one which I believe you might wish to respond to with some urgency.'

'Thank you Francis,' Matthew says, taking the card.

Well now, he thinks, here's a surprise! For the card belongs to none other than Lord Cornelius Snatchal. Printed on stiff vellum of the highest quality, his coat of arms embossed across the top, it also has a brief hand-written note on the back explaining that he would consider it a pleasure if he might call this afternoon. Matthew knows not whether to feel honoured or horrified - though quickly his vanity gets the better of the argument, and he finds himself feeling most gratified. He wonders what mode of transport the noble lord will choose for his arrival. Will it be a smart carriage with gleaming accoutrements that will thunder into the yard and up to his door, or a privately owned chair - a train of footmen in attendance? In any event, the Pig and Whistle would rarely have been so favoured; and the appearance of such a noble personage would definitely cause a stir among all the other tenants and staff. A message of distinction, to be sure.

But his day-dream is suddenly shattered as he turns the card over once again to check the time at which the noble lord intends to be calling: one o'clock - approximately just twenty minutes from now!

'I have, Sir, laid out the wax figurines already,' Francis declares with an aloof smile that indicates how very pleased he is with himself for having anticipated his master's wishes, 'all the devotional ones, is that correct, Sir?'

'Good God no, man!' Matthew cries and immediately quickens his step. 'Those are only to be displayed for the benefit of Tory recusants. Not for a member of His Majesty's Privy Council. Hurry Francis. I shall be hanged at Tyburn if the noble Lord finds those *in situ.*'

But for all the vigour and urgency of their pace, their progress is not easy. It seems that just about everyone Matthew knows is out and about, and every regular fellow from The Rainbow must stop him, grab a hold of his sleeve and interrogate him as to whether he has heard the news - and always the same news, of course. *Rebels at Preston, marching on Manchester.*

'Yes, yes, I have heard, but forgive me, Sir, I cannot stop,' is his repeated refrain - until the next encounter - and the next.

Eventually, after running almost like a pair of athletes around St Paul's yard and along East Cheap, they arrive back at the Pig and Whistle - a glance at the clock tower on the way informing them that if Lord Snatchal is to be punctual, only a few short minutes remain before his arrival. Up the stairs they run, and Francis is ordered to stow the religious icons away at once, while Matthew concerns himself with hiding the rudimentary work he is undertaking on his re-creation of the Cornhill wig - a project which at present looks nothing more than just what it is: a bunch of old beards. All this is accomplished just in the nick of time, because as the clock in Cheapside strikes the hour, a glance through the windows to the yard below confirms that a single private chair, maroon in colour, lacquered and emblazoned with a spectacular gilt motif of grapes and cornucopia, and carried by men in the distinctive liveries of a prestigious household, has already been set down, and that Lord Snatchal has stepped from it. Flourishing an elaborate silk handkerchief, the corners of his mouth turned down in distaste at the sights of inevitable squalor that surround him, he is clearly in no mood to dally - and after brushing down his laced sleeves with the back of his hands several times, as if the very corrupting dust of the East End must be removed from his person as quickly as possible, he locates Matthew's sign and the door to his stairs and hastens towards its sanctuary. Matthew goes out to greet him on the gallery, and within moments, the noble lord is inside, removing his coat and hat and chatting away as urbanely and with as much familiarity as if he and Matthew were the best of chums.

'I must apologise for my untidy appearance, m'Lord,' Matthew explains, drawing up a stool for his visitor and bidding him take a seat. 'I have only just this minute managed to negotiate the crowds and arrive home. Did you encounter any difficulty?'

But Lord Snatchal looks unconcerned. 'No, no. Just come from the heart of the City, as a matter of fact. Banking matters, you understand. Though I noticed the queues were forming as I left. They say they'll only be paying out in pennies now, so it's chaos, and oddly enough no one after me seemed to be able to withdraw a thing. Anyway, got another little job for you, Wildish, if you are of a mind to oblige me. I'd like to keep this one a bit quiet, though, if you don't mind?' he adds in a voice which is unusually furtive all of a sudden.

'Of course, Sir, a pleasure,' Matthew responds, wondering what it could be.

'Good. You see, it's like this - the Countess is out shopping in Cornhill at the present time, which is not only an interminable process but a damn expensive one as well. So the least I thought I could do was to treat myself to a new wig - a necessary item soon, anyway, in the event of being called upon by His Majesty to command a division of the army. You never know. There's always an outside chance of it, even at my time of life - and I'll obviously need a new wig for that. Can't go into battle wearing an old one. What would the fellows think!'

'Well, yes indeed,' Matthew concurs, 'I can see how that would be a problem, yes.'

'Maybe one of those bob wigs - a shorty - you know, what do they call it these days, a campaign wig, eh?'

'Ah, you mean one of these, Sir?' Matthew suggests, indicating a short-length, powdered specimen on a block nearby, the very latest innovation with its triple row of neat side curls at the temples and which, upon inspection, appears to command Lord Snatchal's obvious approval.

'Um, I say! Very nice,' he remarks, ever the epicure, and sampling the perfectly fashioned curls between finger and thumb. 'Most handsome - and ideal for a man at my time of life, of course - as the actress said to the bishop, what!'

'Yes, well that can certainly be arranged for you, m'Lord,' Matthew responds with alacrity reaching for his order book. 'I will just need to take a few measurements first, if you would care to remove your present piece?'

To which Lord Snatchal peels of his periwig, to reveal the recently shaved pate beneath, with just the slightest dusting of silver-grey hair remaining at the temples, and upon which Matthew sets to work with the tape measure, working swiftly and with expert eye, ascertaining the distance from the front to the rear hairline, from ear to ear and across the horizontal plain from temple to temple, all the while making careful observations of any anomalies in the shape of his client's cranium, and recording these in the latest page of his order book.

'Heavens, can't say I've ever been in this part of town for a while,' Snatchal remarks indignantly as he takes his perfumed handkerchief once more and flaps it about several times in front of his nose - and looking particularly old all of a sudden without his resplendent wig to frame his pasty old face and badly painted lips. 'Beggars, loiterers, cutpurses in every doorway, and the very air reeks of gin.'

'Gin Sir?' Matthew echoes, endeavouring still to concentrate on his work, and bemused by such a diverse outpouring of scorn, for he has never heard the old boy so vehement.

'Yes - gin, Sir! *Mother Geneva!* Brewed up in every scullery or kitchen by unscrupulous women, and with catastrophic consequences. A penny to get tipsy; tuppence for a drunken stupor. Such an inordinate carnality of manners brought about by the addiction of the common people, Wildish, that some may even choose it over food - and which, I might add, seriously damages their capacity for work. That's what I'm concerned about. I mean, where are the future generations of labourers, soldiers and farmers to come from when we are raising such weak and distempered stock - conceived and nurtured at the breast by mothers addicted to this vile concoction? Surely we have laws, don't we - Parliamentary legislation against all this sort of thing. But nobody around here seems to be paying the least bit of attention to any of it! I can see now that all those stories one hears about these parts are true, moreover - that whenever a gentleman goes unattended in a liveried chair or carriage, his vehicle is liable to be pelted with mud and turds. Disgraceful! What on earth possesses you to work and live in such a benighted part of the metropolis, Wildish? This kind of outrage would never be tolerated West of Temple Bar. If you want my advice, you should be considering moving your shop forthwith to somewhere more civilised like Pall Mall.'

'I do apologise, Sir,' Matthew says, endeavouring to continue with his measurements - while also noticing down in the yard that a couple of stableboys with bucket and sponge have already been enlisted by the Earl's men to wash down the chair of its various unpleasant encrustation's. It is a fine looking chair, with walnut inlays and a most elegant frame sculptured into a fancy 'S' shape at the rear. Very impressive. 'In fact, I choose to live and work here amid all the comings and goings in order to glean intelligence,' Matthew continues to explain, 'the better to further my services to His Majesty's government, as you might recall. And I usually go out to my more distinguished clients, anyway. I visit them in their homes - all part of the service.'

'Oh, yes, of course. I do understand,' Lord Snatchal remarks, beginning to calm himself by this time. 'Oh, I don't know - I just can't comprehend why they detest us so much, the common herd,' he continues. 'Do they not grasp the fact that we are just the same as them - that we have our sorrows, our frailties and our pains just

like anybody else. Why despise us for our differences when we
have so much in common?'

'Perhaps they are envious,' Matthew suggests.

'Envious?'

'Yes. That a minority among us have so much, while so many
among them have so very little.'

'Nonsense! They should think themselves jolly lucky,' the
noble lord argues, indefatigable. 'Why, when I go among them they
have all the pleasure of admiring the magnificent gilded
craftsmanship of my chair; my smartly turned out staff and me
inside, immaculately dressed and coiffured. A darn sight more
edifying than when I have to look out at them. Then all I see is a
load of filthy people walking about in rags. Who gets the better of
that bargain, I ask you?'

Matthew, meanwhile, and much to the other man's curiosity,
has taken up some scissors and has begun to cut a profile from
black paper - creating in minutes a remarkable likeness of
Snatchal's features as seen from the side and over which he
attaches a paper cut-out of the intended wig, thereby producing an
almost instant representation of how the finished article might look.
'I shall put your order to the top of my list, Sir,' Matthew assures
him, pasting everything into position onto a square of blue card that
also bears his business address. 'I expect it to be ready within a
couple of weeks - at which you might like to arrange a final fitting.
The best of all bob wigs, it shall be - suitable for the field - though I
cannot guarantee it will protect you from a cannon ball should one
come your way.'

'Not to worry, young man - I became an expert in avoiding such
inconveniences long ago - the last time the Jacobites planted their
standard: the 1715 campaign. A bit before your time, of course,
what!'

'Just a little,' Matthew laughs, while fetching some glasses and
a good claret, already opened as luck would have it, and to which
the noble Lord expresses his favour straight away. In fact, Matthew
is pleasantly surprised at how well he is getting on with the old
fellow who, although as cantankerous as ever, has gradually
become a good deal more amenable in the temporary absence of his
grand peruke. 'May I enquire, do you have children, Sir?' he adds,
his curiosity piqued by recollections of the numerous portraits he
had observed upon the walls at Snatchalcombe House during his

recent visit - and knowing, too, how imperative the principles of continuity and lineage are to families such as this.

'Oh, yes, the Countess and I were blessed with a fine son quite early in our marriage,' Snatchal replies, taking up his glass. 'Big lad now, of course. In the Americas, making his fortune in commodities of various sorts.'

'Commodities?' Matthew echoes with interest.

'Well, yes, slavery, to be precise. Not altogether sure I approve - considering what all those liberal philosophers are always telling us. They do say, don't they, that no man should assume the right to exercise absolute power over any other, not without just cause? Naturally, those of us in government must always give the impression of considering these matters. But the young men ... well they just see a chance to get rich quick. That's what my boy's doing. And I suppose if I were in his position I'd be doing the same, and somebody would be grumbling at *me*. The trouble is, by the time a man discovers his father was right, he usually has a son who thinks he's wrong - and so it goes on, each generation plagued with the same vices as the last. What do you think, Wildish? Do you concur with this business of shipping humans across the oceans to work on the plantations?'

'I suppose every civilisation has only ever prospered on the back of exploitation of one kind or another,' Matthew replies carefully, 'even when those who are enslaved are unaware of it at the time. I do not think, though, that it becomes us to engage in cruelty, whether in peace or in war, as we are now contemplating yet again. Men should not suffer.'

'Um ...' the old boy mumbles, glancing at Matthew rather icily while replacing his own wig and then, with the aid of a looking-glass on Matthew's bench, adjusting his curls with a small comb taken from his waistcoat pocket, thereby becoming his old, imperious self once again - and all this within a remarkably short space of time.

Just at that moment, the clatter of dainty feet can be heard: someone coming from the upper doorway of the inn and hastening along the gallery outside - arriving, moreover, at Matthew's entrance within seconds, accompanied by the familiar melodious salutation of 'Oooh hoo!' and at which both men turn to behold the lovely aspect of the laundry girl Sarah May who, with Matthew's splendid periwig from the other evening in her hands, strolls in as if she owned the place. Matthew, who has clean forgotten she was due, gets to his feet to greet her - a greeting which must, for obvious reasons, be subdued on this occasion - for had they been alone, they would have rushed to each other's embrace. What a nuisance they can't just be themselves. He would have so enjoyed learning about all the scandalous details of her encounter with Lady Snatchal on the night of the masquerade.

'Ah, yes, Miss May, thank you!' Matthew declares loudly, taking the wig from her and carefully placing it on one of the mannequin heads, trying to ignore the surprised face of Lord Snatchal. 'My linen you'll be wanting, yes. It's in the usual place, young lady, if you care to step this way,' he instructs her, guiding her needlessly towards his bed chamber at the far end of the long room before returning to his guest - whose narrow eyes, meanwhile seem transfixed on the periwig she has brought in - his face gradually altering from one of puzzlement to downright suspicion, as if straining to recall just where he might formerly have seen it - such a magnificent piece - for he *has* seen it, of course, and she who wore it - though in the disguise of a young gallant on that occasion. Would Snatchal have recognised Sarah in her present garb? Would he be aware of what, by all reports, had taken place between her and his wife at their house in St James's Square while he was still attending the masquerade that night? It all makes Matthew feel terribly nervous.

'Is everything all right, Sir?' he inquires of his distinguished guest, his voice cheerful - as if a laundry girl walking in unannounced with an almost priceless periwig tucked under her arm were all perfectly normal procedure.

'Oh, yes - er - thank you, Wildish,' he responds, his eyes following Sarah with fascination whenever she appears going about her chores, for she does indeed look most lovely today, Matthew thinks, her lustrous brunette hair all loose and tumbling about her shoulders, her slender figure with its narrow waist clad in a tight peacock-blue waistcoat - so different to her normally tawdry and common-place attire - surely a hand-me-down or a present from someone, as the item is clearly of an expensive material that would normally be beyond her means. It shows her shapely figure to good advantage as she sways and turns this way and that - so graceful, almost like a dancer - and with a waist and loins of a length so extraordinarily generous: enough for even the most indulgent of exploring hands. It thrills him, knowing that he has enjoyed her already, and even - in a novel sort of way - that the wife of the man seated beside him has almost certainly done likewise. And he wonders, also, how she would be feeling, considering the changes that have swept through her young life in the past several weeks. There is a self-confidence and worldliness about her this afternoon and which now, given her exposure among people of rank, will doubtless continue to commend her to others of a like kind and steer her destiny in a far more advantageous direction. He is happy for her. Having completed her tasks, she throws all the linen together, and then, with obvious disappointment that she has not found Matthew alone, makes for the exit without further ado, the sheet with all its laundry tied up in a bundle slung over her shoulder as she goes.

'Bye, bye, Mr Wildish,' she says, plaintively and with a sorrowful glance his way as she passes. 'Until next time,' she adds, before dipping into a modest curtsy to the noble Lord - and then the men are alone once more. It is, Matthew thinks, as if a light in the room has suddenly been extinguished. He watches out the windows as she walks away across the yard below, followed by the admiring eyes of the stable boys and chairmen. She has come to him often of late, his luscious dark beauty - and each time it is a joy to him. In a simple, unaffected way she is quite adorable, and he feels just a little bereft on each occasion whenever she must depart - and today far more so than ever, of course, it being all so incomplete.

'Um ... jolly nice!' Snatchal declares, craning his scrawny neck to look down into the yard also. 'She could come and iron out the wrinkles in my britches, any day, what! I do like to see a nice tight waistcoat on a woman, don't you? Lady Snatchal has one just like that. Oh, and - er - by the way, Wildish, that reminds me: may I just enquire of your progress with that other - er - rather special commission we honoured you with some weeks ago?' he adds, almost as an afterthought - though all the while, Matthew realises, his eyes have been casting about among all the mannequin heads for the familiar and much venerated Cornhill wig. He appears to be disappointed and even slightly alarmed in not being able to detect what he is looking for among all the other specimens on display.

'Oh, *that!* Yes, the work's coming along splendidly, my Lord,' Matthew replies, as if the business of resurrecting ancient wigs compiled of pubic hair was all in a typical days work and perfectly normal. 'It's in the oven at the moment.'

'The oven?'

'Oh, yes - the postiche oven, that is. I have had to reconstruct the foundation of the piece, you see, and have applied a little finishing sculpture to the hair itself after the process of *ventilating*, as we call it - that is, sewing all of the fibres into place once more. This usually requires moistening of the hair afterwards and then drying in a special oven to set the style.'

'Ah, yes, I see,' Lord Snatchal responds with a grudging acquiescence. 'It's just that, what with the deteriorating political situation, you understand, I don't think we can risk waiting until Christmas to take delivery. It would be in danger - should the rebels reach London, for example, and sack the place - which is looking increasingly probable, I regret to say. To be frank, had it been finished today, I would have taken it back with me this weekend to Snatchalcombe.'

'My apologies, Sir,' Matthew remarks and then, trying to change the subject as swiftly as possible. 'It does all seem to be coming to a head, doesn't it. I was caught up in the muster myself this morning, over at the Haymarket. Quite hysterical, of course.'

But Lord Snatchal seems surprised at such a flippant observation. 'I hope you are not underestimating the gravity of the situation, Wildish,' he asserts, a little irritable once again, Matthew detects, perhaps due to not getting what he has really come for. 'We are going to need all the troops we can get hold of, y'know. Charles Stuart and his generals are exceptionally well organised and swelling in numbers all the while, and there's not much we can throw at them that can prevent them proceeding right to the capital - especially if the French launch a simultaneous invasion onto the south coast. They could, if they are of a mind to, put a ring of fire around the capital, leaving those caught inside to choke to death and the rest of us to be overrun in a matter of days: a new kingdom, new government, new religion, everything. Oh, we've tried, naturally, to set false intelligence in the way of the rebels - with letters, rumours, employing double agents, and so on, anything to convince the Pretender that our forces are more powerful than they really are. But Lord Murray, the Prince's general, is a wily fox, and seems to know instinctively whenever we attempt to trick him. Listen, what I am about to tell you, Wildish, must go no further, but I am reliably informed that His Majesty is about to abandon the

kingdom and to remove the royal family out of harm's way. His
secretary is already at work determining which art treasures and
valuables to take - all to go off by barge along the Thames and
thence away to the Netherlands or ...'

But then Lord Snatchal's voice trails off unexpectedly.

'Is everything all right, my Lord?' Matthew inquires at the
sudden lapse into silence, having been aware for some moments of
his client straining his eyes and squinting in a certain direction
across the room, a look of some suspicion and distaste upon his
face.

'Yes ... but do tell me, Wildish, what precisely is *that?* Over
there?'

And as Matthew, his order book still in hand, turns to discover
what is being referred to, he sees, to his horror, a tall, brightly
painted figurine of Saint Patrick, still set proudly upon the
chimneypiece - one among the several placed about the room by
his valet this morning, and this one not having been spotted in time
to have been removed from view.

'Oh, *him,* yes,' Matthew declares with a rueful shaking of the
head, walking over and picking up the object.

'Yes Sir - *him!* Surely not yours?' Snatchal demands, hardly
able to believe his eyes or contain his indignation.

'Wax!' Matthew says, endeavouring to explain. 'We're always
on the look out for anything made of wax. My man Francis fetches
them from the markets for melting down, you see. Makes excellent
candles.'

'Candles - really?'

'Oh yes,' Matthew asserts. And then, snapping poor Saint
Patrick in half and placing him into a crucible normally reserved
for the warming of glue, he applies a taper to the oil burner beneath
and lights a flame. The unfortunate patron saint of the Emerald
Isles, the very same as once adorned a special niche of finest
walnut shelving in the morning room of his family home in Dublin,
quickly melts away, and within seconds has dissolved into a
swirling puddle of various muddy-looking hues.

'Well, I am relieved to learn that's all there is to it,' Snatchal
states, observing the process with a certain approval, though still
shocked.

'I'm afraid that wretched candle tax is no inconsiderable burden
to a man in my line of work,' Matthew continues, especially in the

winter months when it is so dark.'

'Really,' Snatchal remarks with surprise. 'Can't say I've anything against taxes on candles, Wildish. One should make a point of always having the best wax lights - and plenty of them. It demonstrates affluence. Same with windows. As soon as that window tax became law, all the top families started putting more of them in, not taking the ruddy things out! Anyway, enough of all that. Can't hang around all day putting the world to rights,' he adds with abrupt decision, glancing at his pocket watch and getting to his feet. 'Got some - er - pressing business to attend to on the way home this afternoon at an address in Cockspur Street.'

At which, rising also, Matthew assists the noble Lord on with his topcoat.

'Oh, incidentally, Wildish,' he says by way of parting words, 'I would appreciate it if you could keep my order for the campaign wig quiet. I wouldn't want to appear vain or to have *jumped the gun*, so to speak, in the event of not being called upon to serve this time around. You do understand? Not even a word to Lady Snatchal, if you don't mind.'

'Of course, my Lord,' Matthew replies and bows his compliance. 'I can assure you, always, of the utmost discretion, Sir.'

And with that, a parting nod and a look upon his face of genuine gratitude which surprises Matthew, the noble lord is gone. Matthew, glances down to the yard as the Earl becomes reunited with his chair - the door held open for him, then closed softly behind. In perfect unison, the men lift the box and, with nimble feet and all the care and dexterity of those who are fresh and solicitous in their work, carry their master away at top speed, leaving Matthew to contemplate not a good few days and nights of hard graft ahead, whether by candle light or lamp, working on both wigs now in order to discharge his obligations as swiftly as possible. Only then will he feel safe - for, as none other than Lady Snatchal herself had intimated at the masquerade the other evening, his life is already forfeited, at least for the time being, and the arrival of the marauding Jacobite armies would be as nothing compared to the repercussions for him personally should his misdemeanours ever be laid bare.

And so Matthew takes another glass of wine for his solace and, as so often when faced with an unpalatable problem or task ahead, turns his thoughts instead towards his poetry and, by definition, his love life also. What a shame he had no opportunity to partake of Sarah's refreshing company this afternoon. He must send out a card to her - ask Francis to deliver it. That will please her; and he has a very special present for her, too, a little something which he located in a jewellers in Cornhill the other day in the shape of a pendant necklace with a beautiful oval-cut sapphire. Perfect for her.

Before any of that, however, he knows he really must attend to his more personal needs. Delightful as the experience undoubtedly was this morning at Mrs Armstrong's establishment, he must have something more substantial than a champagne breakfast to satisfy his hungry stomach. So he calls for Francis, and sends him to fetch a hot meal and a loaf from the inn. And then, reclining on his couch, he takes the opportunity to sift through his trayful of papers, including those items of correspondence that have arrived today - and among which he discovers, to his surprise, sealed with a big daub of red, shiny wax, a letter from a former sweetheart of his, a certain Miss Harriet Swift. How wonderful. He recollects that she had left London some time ago to work as a governess at a home in Hertfordshire, but now, by the looks of it, seems intent on returning.

*Croxly House, St Albans, Herts*

Dearest Matthew,
I trust you are well and have not forgotten your loving friend, and that you would not object to renewing our acquaintance shortly when I return, as I must, to London. You might recall from my last letter to you in April of this year, that I have enjoyed a most stimulating period in the service of Mr and Mrs Davis. My work as governess to their three children has proved most pleasant and rewarding, but alas this must now be concluded due to the perceived dangers of the advancing Jacobite army. My employers are of a persuasion that to remain here, adjacent to what would be the very highway along which the rebels would be advancing, places us all in the most grave and imminent danger, and they have resolved to pack bags and flee for safety as far south as possible (I believe with family, somewhere in Sussex). All this means that my services must be terminated - at least for the time being. Thus, I shall be

departing at the end of this week for London - though I regret that I shall have to do so unescorted, and at such a hazardous time. If you should be so disposed, therefore, I would be indebted to you if you could find it in your generous heart to come and bring me back. If you are able to arrive ahead of Friday, moreover, we could spend a day together here in the countryside, or I could introduce you to all the fascinating sites and history of the Cathedral. I shall, in any event, look forward to seeing you upon my return to the capital. I expect to be staying with my Sister in Bow until I can secure new employment.

Yours in hope, your ever faithful friend,
Harriet

How wonderful! All at once the memories of their time together come flooding back to him - memories of trips to the theatre, of discussing poetry and music deep into the night, and of the most delicious and adventurous love-making that often accompanied it all. And suddenly, picturing her in his mind's eye, her remarkably dark brown eyes, her slim lithesome body, her most unusual crinkly brown hair that was, he remembers, always styled so unusually short, he realises that an opportunity to unite himself with the very body and soul of Mercury might well have just presented itself. A brief dip into the pages of his book of astrological lore confirms it beyond all doubt - for the slightly androgynous, busy and intellectually driven Harriet is described perfectly therein. Even had it not been so, he could hardly refuse her. Only now, of course, inspired by his own personal mission, it becomes doubly imperative that he rise to the occasion and go to her aid - and this, he immediately resolves to do.

'Ah, Francis, my man,' he says, as at just that moment the valet returns with his meal, brought in on a tray straight across from the tavern and stored piping hot as ever in an array of metal dishes and tureens. 'I wonder if you could prepare an overnight bag for me. I have a lengthy coach journey ahead of me tomorrow, so a little brandy in a flask would also not go amiss.'

To which Francis nods his understanding, and Matthew, setting out the dishes upon his bench, commences his meal full of anticipation for his reunion with the lovely Harriet. How very heroic it will be, he reflects with a blend of pride and keen anticipation - going forth to rescue a damsel in distress. Excellent. And as for all that tiresome work on Lord Snatchal's wigs ... well, once again, that will just have to wait.

# ~ 16 ~
## OBSERVATIONS OF THE
## HEAVENLY BODIES - MERCURY

*Of the planet Mercury, its general and particular significations: She who bringeth intellect and reason. Comely, neat and clever. Of body, not tall, but lean and fine-boned. Inclining to androgynous appearance when young. A straight chin and high forehead and somewhat narrow face. Sparkling eyes, quick and alert. The authoress of subtlety, tricks and devices of learning and argument. In apparel preferring of checks and variegated patterns. Sardonyx for her gemstone.*

The outward journey to St Albans had not been easy - it being bitterly cold, and the thick leather curtains of the stagecoach had to be pulled across the windows the entire time - rendering the interior of the carriage dark and dreary in the extreme. Nor was the general talk among the passengers particularly edifying, the main topic being the scarcity of able bodied men these days - so many of the local justices, bailiffs, watchmen and so on, having already been enlisted into regiments fighting the rebels to the North - men who might otherwise have been employed protecting the citizens at home or upon the highway. The outcome was a state of lawlessness in which footpads and highwaymen roamed free. Rumours were even abroad to the effect that the villains themselves, no longer merely content with the business of holding up the coaches and relieving travellers of their valuables, were beginning to flirt outrageously with whoever took their fancy. During Matthew's long twelve-hour journey, this became the topic of conversation that gradually began to take over from all else, and in the confined and monotonous atmosphere of the coach, as the brandy flasks were handed round, one tale inevitably led to another, each one becoming more improbable than the last, until soon some of the more eloquent of the gentlemen passengers were describing tales of highwaymen actually demanding amorous favours of the ladies at pistol point, which might take the form of kiss or - far worse - a request to oblige the highwayman with more intimate services behind the nearest bush, before allowing the coach to proceed. The lady passengers, as might have been expected, were particularly horrified by these revelations. All this was as nothing, however, in comparison to the rumour of there actually being a highway-*woman* at large, who would single out some of the more handsome of the male passengers to oblige in a similar fashion - and to which Matthew in particular tut-tutted and shook his head in studied indignation, inquiring upon which route such outrageous behaviour might have taken place ... so he might avoid it in future. There were even stories concerning the infamous 'Lisping Highwayman of Buckinghamshire,' who had a most dainty, foppish way about him and seemed to enjoy a wide range of favours among both sexes - so much so, that he usually didn't bother to rob anyone at all!

Despite all these dire predictions of imminent doom, the coach and everyone on board did manage to reach its destination safely - the distinguished cathedral and market town of St Albans and, within its walls, the White Hart Inn, a particularly busy and bustling place from where, after tips had been handed out to the driver and likewise to the porters of the inn; after some measure of feeling had been restored to frozen feet and numb backsides, and a hot meal had been taken in the tavern to replenish body and soul, Matthew could at last send out a messenger to the location where he knew his friend Harriet was staying - a manor house a few miles distant from the town itself - to inform her of his arrival and that he would, as requested, be honoured to come to her aid early tomorrow and help convey her and her luggage safely back to London.

And so it transpires that he finds himself here this morning, outdoors and walking through a pleasant meadow by a stream, hand in hand with that very young lady herself, his former sweetheart, dearest Harriet. Though cold, it is a fine day, with the sun putting in an appearance to celebrate their reunion - that all-too-rare radiance at this time of the year shining on their faces and casting long shadows over the barren fields behind them as they go, arm in arm, so full of laughter and fun - there being so much to talk about since they had last seen each other: all the latest books they have read, the music they have heard; and, throughout it all, the sense of anticipation, too, that soon they might be returned to London, to Matthew's home and there, with leisure and privacy, to enjoy each other's warmest embrace once more.

'I am most grateful to you, dearest Matthew,' she says.

'Not at all - it is my pleasure,' he replies, continuing to play the part of *knight-errant*.

She is as he remembers her, a most comely young woman, in her mid-twenties now, with unusually short reddish brown hair and a quick and alert intelligence animating the most lovely of features, her high cheekbones, her chin so finely cut, and yet a mouth that widens so temptingly whenever she smiles. He is as intrigued as ever by her prim appearance, her slightly upturned nose that can imply a certain censorious attitude at times - yet which belies the presence of one who, when the moment is ripe, will surrender herself freely to the most intricate exploration of her senses. Clothed today in a military-style jacket with rows of brass buttons and a plumed tricorn, her gingham skirts cut in a simple, practical flare, there is a delightful jauntiness about her, too, as she walks, a most pleasant companion.

Suddenly, an indignant robin, excited no doubt by Matthew's red waistcoat, and standing out very scarlet himself amid the bare branches, pipes up loudly at their approach, his ear-piercing song causing them to stop in wonder.

'Hark at that little fellow up there!' Matthew exclaims. 'What do you think - is that not how a man should be! Our feathered friend here has but a short time on this Earth, oppressed by dangers and hardships on every side, and yet he puffs out his chest and shows off and sings his heart out until he dies. A fine philosophy.'

But Harriet, is not impressed, and instead turns up her nose and smiles with superior knowledge. 'The unseasonable warmth tricks him into thinking that winter might have been postponed, that's all, and that spring is coming. The soppy bird.'

'And I am the same when I am with you,' Matthew states. 'I always feel happy and full of hope.'

'Matthew - stop it!' she exclaims, admonishing him, though there is a flash and twinkle of merriment in her eye also as they set off walking again. Harriet, he should have remembered, can never be seduced by smooth-talk. A most perceptive and forthright young woman, she has, in the past, always managed to brush aside any of his attempts at conquest via flattery. Any poem he might have for her today will need to be free of too much romance. 'I will concede,' she continues, 'that your happiness in my company is a genuine sentiment, and I shall content myself with that for the time being. As for your hopes ...well, we shall have to see about those at a later date, when we are back in London.'

'Well, perhaps not so very long to wait, then,' he suggests, indefatigable. 'We could take the noon coach and be back at my apartments at the Pig and Whistle by late tonight?' he adds, pulling her closer in a playful hug.

'You *are* speaking in jest, I take it!' she reprimands him again, though pleased with his cuddle, because she nestles in close to relish the warmth of it. 'I agree, today would be nice, but you must understand my darling Matthew that there are so many people here of a similar purpose, wanting to leave and take refuge to the South. Unless you have already booked our places, I cannot anticipate us getting away today. It's all one-way traffic.'

She is right. Even out here in the country where news arrives slowly and where it is also normally received with relative calm, there is a distinct atmosphere of agitation at present, of people wanting to be gone. He had sensed it yesterday among those working at the inn, the dread of having armies marching through, of having soldiers billeted on them - even the prospect of yet more English redcoats marching north to join the battle as had occurred, they said, just the other day. None of it could be regarded entirely with equanimity, and everyone seemed resigned to some level of disruption. Yes, he thinks, even the tranquillity of the countryside is changed; and he wonders, too, whether Harriet has been happy here, away from the city and all its amusements. Would she be sorry to leave, he asks her?

Not replying at first, she looks down, uncharacteristically silent for a while, and he senses that he has hit a sensitive spot with his question.

'I have enjoyed my stay - it has been most agreeable, yes,' she answers, giving the question her usual rigorous analysis, her head inclined from time to time upon his shoulder as they go, still nestling close. 'The children in my care, they have been a delight, and I trust they will have benefited from what modest education I have provided. It is a singular existence, though, I should tell you, that of governess - since one is neither a servant like the others, nor an equal of those who pay the wages. Women such as myself are stranded somewhere in-between, therefore, mistrusted by both sides. And so yes, I have yearned at times for just a little more sophistication. I have longed to go to the theatre - the proper theatre, that is, and not just some valiant provincial endeavour to *put on a show,* as they say in these parts. I have longed to hear some proper music, played and sung by those who *can* play and sing, not merely those who would if only they had more time, more training, and so on. I hope I am not sounding too haughty. They are all fine people, those I have described, and trying their best. But really, I have missed London society so very much.'

'And old friends, too?' he quizzes her, wanting her to say how much she will have missed him, as well. 'I expect you have missed those, eh? As we have missed you.'

'Oh, don't go giving me the old flannel, Matt,' she complains, 'telling me how you have been pining for my company. I shall not believe you. How often have you written to me in all that time? How often? Not a lot, my dear.'

Stopping once again, he draws her close, more tenderly this time and runs his fingers through her hair - that amazing hair! He adores the slightly coarse, chaotic texture of it, a texture quite special to her, as if the heat of her busy brain had somehow singed and scorched a myriad of tiny crinkles into it. 'Well, despite what you think, I *have* missed you,' he protests. 'And I don't mind owning up to it. Why I have even written a poem for you on the way here.'

'For me - really?'

'Oh yes.'

They proceed again, walking in silence for a moment, with still a jaunty step and a linking of her arm beneath his, nestling close - until she can bear in no longer.

'Well, come on, Matt - out with it! I shall not pretend I am not eager to hear it.'

And he smiles, congratulating himself on having found a chink in her armour at last. He does enjoy Harriet. It really is as if the very essence of Mercury, the winged messenger of the gods, has suddenly come to life from the pages of his astrological guidebook, strolling with him here at his side. He cannot help make the comparison - as though every woman he encounters now and henceforth must inevitably fall within the compass of one of the seven celestial bodies. She is all his desire. And thus, without further ado, speaking in time to their steps, he summons up his lines for her:

*Shall I proclaim the orator to thee?*
*Debate the law, or weigh the skies above?*
*No, not when I your fairest face I see.*
*I'd rather use my mouth and lips for love.*

*Should pleasures wait on speech and stories told?*
*Should tongues debate, should rivals fuel their spite?*
*No, no - for in the mouths of lovers bold,*
*What instruments of joy and sweet delight!*

*Thus, let us turn from this so dull obsession.*
*Of speech we shall no more lament.*
*But rather feed that darkest old transgression,*
*Where passions discourse 'til they all be spent.*

*Let wise men prate, divines proclaim their word!*
*In thy love-sighs is all my study heard.*

At which she turns away and clears her throat of any emotion before removing her arm from his. 'Ah, but Matthew, now you are trying to provoke me,' she grumbles, kicking through the debris of twigs and old leaves upon the path, 'knowing me to be the woman of words. I should not mind, though - for I have missed the sounds of a little fun and romance in my life. You were ever the master of both, Matt - and so yes, I suppose it must follow that I have missed you as well. I have missed you so very much. It's true.'

Pressing herself to his side once more, she conceals her face in the fabric of his coat lapels. And there he suspects she has shed a tear or two, for she applies a handkerchief to her eyes.

'Then I suggest, my dearest,' he murmurs, 'that we not waste another minute and that we turn now and retrace our steps. Let's see if we can, indeed, catch that midday coach - who knows, we might be lucky. Come home with me, Harriet, that we might talk more of fun and romance again.'

And thus with her agreement, and full perhaps of unreasonable optimism, they return quickly to the manor house where Harriet's modest items of luggage, consisting of no more than a small portmanteau and a hat box, are already placed in the lobby in readiness for her departure. A fast ride in a chaise brings them to the White Hart Inn and to the booking room in the yard where, as luck would have it there have been two cancellations for the afternoon stagecoach to the City - though it will entail some hours travel through darkness, they are told - an uncomfortable prospect in the inclement weather that is expected. Would they not rather wait until the early morning coach, the booking officer inquires?

'Oh, no, I think rather our needs must choose for us,' Matthew remarks with a discreet wink to his companion who responds with a vigorous nod of the head and a squeeze of his hand as, smiling fully for perhaps the first time today, she links her arm beneath his.

But just then, she turns and jumps at the sight in the doorway of a man in a greatcoat and riding boots, of middling height and conservative attire, not young and who, upon seeing her at the booking counter calls her name, *'Miss Swift!'* loudly and in some distress.

'Why Mr Bland!' she declares, releasing herself to stand alone quickly as the gentleman advances, a look of confusion upon his face and, Matthew notices, upon hers also.

'My dearest Harriet, are you going away?' he inquires, his eyes also darting to Matthew at her side, and not entirely with approval.

'Oh - er - this is my dear friend Mr Wildish, from London,' she says, doing the necessary introductions. 'Matthew - this is Mr Bland.'

'How do you do,' Matthew says, and offers his hand.

But the reaction, though polite, is not entirely one of concord, and a moment later Harriet reveals to him what would most likely be the reason: 'Mr Bland and I were engaged to be married some time ago.'

'Harriet - it was but a few weeks ago,' the gentleman argues. 'And you are aware, I trust, that I remain heartbroken?'

'I do not wish to discuss the matter,' Harriet responds, turning from him and linking her arm beneath Matthew's once more as they walk away, but only to be pursued by Mr Bland.

He has a strong smell of the countryside about him, Matthew thinks - a residue upon his boots, no doubt - and of stale tobacco, also.

'Harriet, is there no hope at all?' he inquires, coming around to her side with what seems to Matthew a shallow protestation of fondness. 'I had entertained hopes that your decision was but temporary, that we had a certain understanding.'

Harriet appears most displeased, especially by being pursued physically in this way. 'Mr Bland,' she begins, disengaging her arm from Matthew's once more and turning to face him, 'tell me: what was the most recent book you read in a single day?'

'In a day - why, I cannot recall,' he answers, looking puzzled over such a singular departure in conversation. 'It is surely forgotten to me by its triviality.'

'Exactly Sir. Thus, be advised: I am a volume that requires more than a passing acquaintance. My pages have a complexity and a meaning far beyond the triviality of a day's study, or even that of a few weeks or months before one should assume any understanding. Therefore, you are mistaken, I regret to say, if you ever felt, in your haste, that you understood anything at all of my purpose. And so I must bid you a *final* farewell, Sir.'

Upon this devastating rebuttal, a dejected Mr Bland falls back at last, and allows her to walk from him, and Matthew, after a brief exchange of sympathetic glances with the unfortunate gentleman, (for he could have told him he would never win an argument with Harriet) follows in her wake. Outside in the fresh air, he finds her standing alone, her head held high - and at which, suddenly, and with all the good fortune that bravery and spontaneous decisions often evoke, the stagecoach from Coventry, pulled by a team of four, comes thundering into the yard outside, and within minutes the horses are changed, a new team installed, and he and Harriet are inside and making acquaintance with their fellow passengers. Their luggage is stowed in the cage at the rear of the vehicle under the watch of two young gentlemen who have elected to pay the cheapest fare and to ride on the roof, and whose groans and curses and shuffling of feet above as they endeavour to cling on for dear life, can be detected by those inside, beneath them, as soon as the carriage itself gets under way.

Conditions inside the coach, though, are scarcely any less salubrious. A row of three passengers huddled together must face three more in very close proximity, so close in fact that their knees must all dovetail together - the company opposite consisting of a pair of elderly ladies, possibly widows, seated alongside a well-met and chubby clergyman, leaving Harriet to occupy the place on the seat to Matthew's right, nestled close, while to his left is located a further individual of indeterminate age - indeterminate since his face is not visible and who, by the expedient of long hours of travel through the cold winter landscape, has availed himself of so many blankets as to be virtually indistinguishable from the contents of an upturned laundry basket. The only clue that might inform of the gender of this person is the presence of a man's tricorn hat placed on top of the pile and which shudders and trembles from time to time in unison with the occupant's snores and grunts. Given this unpromising collection of individuals, conversation is limited - at least at first. But eventually, with a few jests and timely observations, Matthew dispels the formality and in no time the ladies in particular have warmed to him. They are clearly of the opinion that if he and his sweetheart were married they would make the most excellent of couples, and if not married ... why, would surely be most suited to be so. Fortunately, his and Harriet's gloved hands manage to cover up any evidence one way or the other as to which of these suppositions is the more likely, allowing Matthew to feel perfectly at liberty to snuggle up as closely and as lovingly to Harriet as he pleases, which helps in no small measure with the business of trying to keep warm - for the draughts cutting in through the curtains and ill-fitting windows are so sharp as to be almost beyond endurance at moments. Eventually, Matthew's brandy flask emerges from his coat pocket, therefore, and the ladies, accepting of his offer, imbibe gladly from the cap which he fills for them each time and passes across. The clergyman declines to share in the liquor to begin with, as befits a man of the cloth - at least for the first circuit of the flask. By the time it next comes around, however, even he surrenders to temptation.

'Harriet,' he whispers into her ear at one stage, 'I swear I am so frozen to the marrow that you will have to thaw me out tonight before I can even begin to rise to the occasion.' To which she whispers back words to the effect of having the warmest lips that might melt a mountain of snow if need be - which intrigues him greatly, and provides him with the impetuous to continue similar closely whispered messages of utter sauciness, thereby helping at least to relieve some of the monotony of the journey.

The hours pass, horses are changed, and a peep through the curtains indicates that a red, broadly glowing sunset is already reaching its conclusion and that night is about to fall, that awful bleak and friendless rural night that travellers dread. The windows are sealed with the application of padding from every available handkerchief, and the scent of lavender from the ladies clothing that most evocative and cloying of fragrances, becomes so strong in the confined space that they might just as well have been rolling in a field of the stuff: a distant remembrance of warm summer meadows.

Outside, the road steepens, and their vehicle begins to struggle in the mud - and thus, as so often happens at least once or twice upon any coach journey in winter, it is necessary to halt and for the gentlemen to step out and walk alongside in order to lighten the load. And this they must do, including those hitherto on the roof, all five men walking alongside as the poor creatures in harness continue to struggle and to haul the coach up the hill. At least it provides an escape from the smell of lavender and an opportunity, also, to make the acquaintance of the man in the blankets, who is, he tells everyone once he has roused himself sufficiently from his slumbers, a solicitor in the process of journeying southwards to flee the rebel advance, his home having been directly on the road south of Manchester.

At least the walking helps restore a degree of feeling to the limbs, and everyone tries to make the best of it. It is a bleak landscape, with tall trees either side of the road and no buildings in sight. Frost is already forming in the still air and upon the various clumps of scrub or grass at the side of the road; and puddles that were once muddy water, now crunch beneath the feet.

'Halt!' comes a loud, *very* loud voice, and as they lift their heads they see, from the side across an unfenced field, a man on horseback, dressed all in black, masked and, even worse, pointing a cocked pistol towards them as he advances.

'Your valuables, if you please, gentlemen,' the highwayman demands - as the coach must, at his behest, be halted and the breaks applied. 'I require at least something from each of you and will brook no refusal,' he adds with chilling determination.

Matthew, being the only one armed, already has his hand upon his sword, but quickly thinks better of drawing when the pistol is aimed directly towards him in response. Any weapon of steel is useless in the face of a bullet, of course, so he raises his arms above his head instead - joining the others who, in deference to the inevitability of the situation, have all instinctively adopted the same pose. 'Watches, jewellery, cash of any description,' the man urges them, 'and quickly, if you please, for I do not wish to detain you any longer than is necessary.'

Everyone rummages through their clothing and a quantity of watches, rings, cravat pins and sundry valuables are duly handed over, along with any coins that might be available, and placed as instructed into the robber's hat which he lowers gracefully to the side of his steed expressly for that purpose.

'And now perchance you could ask the ladies to step outside also,' the man demands next - and it is all Matthew can do to prevent himself leaping at the rascal's throat. But he suspects he will have little or no assistance from the others, who are all clearly petrified - their hands above their heads once again. The last thing he desires is to cause any additional distress through yet more violence.

So out they come, poor Harriet shaking visibly, whether from the cold or fear he cannot rightly tell, and the two ladies clearly none too pleased either, sounding like a couple of broody old hens, mumbling and grumbling among themselves as they are assisted down onto the muddy road by the clergyman. They must remove their rings and necklaces, brooches and combs - anything containing precious stones or metals. All are placed into the very same hat - with Harriet tending to hurl hers in rather than surrender them lightly. What with the darkness and silence all around, it is, Matthew feels, like some terrible dream.

But just then an owl screeches nearby, the team of horses become startled and the coachman seizing the moment of confusion in the darkness removes the break and cracks his whip. The coach moves off, driver included, leaving everybody stranded, all eyes staring in disbelief - everyone watching open-mouthed, including the robber himself, equally bemused at the man's cowardice and stupidity, they know not which is the greater, as the vehicle trundles away. For one terrible moment the robber aims his pistol, steadying it upon his forearm, and is clearly considering firing off a shot - but thinks better of it, for it would leave him vulnerable.

'Idiot - come back!' Matthew calls after the driver, but to no avail. He keeps going, the coach gaining momentum, and all the easier now for having no passengers onboard, until eventually it vanishes over the brow of a hill and is gone.

'I am sorry you appear to be inconvenienced,' the highwayman states, emptying the contents of his tricorn into an open saddlebag in one sweeping, well-practised movement before replacing it upon his head. 'In any event, your generosity is already quite sufficient - and I shall likewise take my leave of you now.'

'Oh,' one of the elderly dames interrupts, 'aren't you interested in anything else?'

'No Madam, I am content. I have no wish to tarry any longer than is conducive to my safety, or yours. You will find the nearest habitation but a mile farther along the highway. And so good evening to you all.'

And with another flourish of his hat in theatrical fashion, his horse is turned and the man gallops away at speed, back across the same field from whence he came, and vanishing into the darkness as swiftly as he had appeared.

With nothing for it but to walk, they set off in the tracks of the stagecoach - though at a necessarily slow pace that might accommodate the elderly among them, all the while hoping that the vehicle might be waiting in readiness just a little farther down the road. But they are to be disappointed - and in fact, they do not encounter the coach until much later, parked outside a tavern in a small hamlet at least one mile from where they had been abandoned. By the time they locate the coachman himself, clearly repentant and drowning his sorrows in ale, everyone is too tired to remonstrate with him, and it is with much relief, therefore, and following some much-needed nourishment provided by the tavern keeper, that they take their places once again and the coach proceeds on its way, but with the knowledge that it will be much, much later than scheduled before they have any hope of reaching their destination.

The remainder of their coach journey from St Albans to London passes in a sleepy, frozen passage of hours, punctuated by the occasional collection of lights or noises of the roadside as they roll through the northern outskirts and finally the densely built-up city itself. The roadways here, even at this late hour, are more congested than Matthew had expected, packed with people either arriving from the North as refugees, or else residents leaving in fear. It is well past midnight, moreover, when they do eventually trundle into the yard of the inn - not unfortunately the Pig and

Whistle but a much larger establishment, the Boar's Head in Cheapside itself, only to discover a few moments later that not a single room is available for anyone to bed down.

'Oh heavens! What are we to do?' one of the elderly ladies cries, wringing her hands as they all gather disconsolately outside on the pavements.

'They don't expect us to sleep in the streets, do they!' one of the young men who had been on the coach roof adds, his voice one of exhaustion and trembling with the cold that has, by this time penetrated to the very bones of all concerned.

Matthew squeezes Harriet closer to his side to comfort her. He longs to take her home without delay - for the Pig and Whistle is only a short walk away - but how can he possibly abandon all these poor people.

'Our needs are simple, we wish only for shelter,' the clergyman asserts, appealing to no one in particular.

'Ladies and gentlemen,' Matthew intervenes, feeling an unavoidable sense of responsibility - perhaps because this is his home ground, after all: the familiar streets and taverns of London. 'I recommend you go inside and remonstrate with the staff once again. If they still refuse you, try across the road at the Tuns Tavern where they will invariably have a dormitory bed for those in extreme need. Hardly luxurious accommodation, but adequate. And if in the unlikely event that even *they* are full ... well, look, here is my card. I have my own apartments and workshop not a few minutes walk from here at the Pig and Whistle Inn - in Broad Lane, just off of Cheapside. Enter the coach yard and look for the covered stairs on your right - the one with the sign of the wig above the door. If all else fails, therefore, and though I cannot vouch for too great a supply of provision for your breakfast, I can at least promise you a roof over your head this night.'

Gratified, they resolve to follow his advice. And so with Harriet at his side Matthew leaves them at last, setting off at a brisk pace along Cheapside - so that they are at his home within minutes.

'Ah, how wonderful!' he thinks, as he opens the door to his apartments and invites her in. Peace and quiet, and alone with the gorgeous Harriet! It is warm and snug, too - his chimney being a shared one with much of the rest of the building, so always giving off a welcoming heat.

'Don't worry, dearest, our fellow passengers will have no need to pursue us here,' he declares as he kindles a fire in the hearth, as well. 'The Tuns Tavern always has beds of some description.'

Able to remove her heavy topcoat and hat at last, Harriet makes herself comfortable on the couch, and soon he has joined her, accompanied by a hastily produced jug of warm mead to share. What a pleasure it is to see her here, the absence of her coat revealing a most delicate *pet-en-l'air* of silk brocade - the first time he has seen her thus - and the ties of the bodice between its lapels she loosens a little now, as well, so she breathes more easily as a consequence.

'Well, my sweetheart,' he says, after a grateful sip of the honeyed drink, the log that he has set upon the hearth crackling and glowing merrily already. 'Here we are - and at liberty to speak freely at last. There is so much I have been longing to ask you.'

'And I you, Matthew. How wonderful, being back in London. I do like your new home - I have not seen it before. What, then would you ask me?'

'About your love-life, of course,' he continues with brazen enthusiasm. 'Your time away from the capital might well have been a touch parochial, as you say, but clearly not entirely without the affections of the gentlemen of St Albans. Were you really engaged to be married to that fellow, what was his name, Mr Bland?'

She seems reluctant to answer right away - as if it were really none of his business, which indeed, he has to admit, it probably isn't.

'Well, yes,' she responds at last, kicking off her shoes, as well, and drawing up her feet upon the couch: quite at home already, he is thrilled to see. 'In answer to your rather impertinent question, Matthew, yes of course. You don't think he would have made such a scene in the booking hall otherwise, do you! A local gentleman, a widower with land and property.'

'I see ...'

'Oh, Matt, it is not like you think,' she protests. 'I wonder if you can appreciate how difficult it is being a woman and single - the wiles and snares that are set against us. And when endowed with some intelligence, it is even more so. I am sure I do not need to remind you, for you endeavoured often enough to have it otherwise, that I was still a maid when last you saw me. You may smile - and I was not exactly *virgo intacta,* I'll own that much - but you know what I mean: I had never actually embraced the ultimate deed. Anyway, Mr Bland and I met socially, being introduced to each other at an assembly in town. We became friends, and I suppose I must have perceived some qualities in him at the time, because eventually we became engaged to be married. It furnished me with some security, some social standing at last. Everything seemed fine until one evening when ... well, we had been drinking, and I without a chaperone, we found ourselves suddenly alone at his family home. There was a big fluffy woollen rug by the fire, and one thing led to another ...'

'Harriet!' he exclaims in mock indignation. 'Don't tell me you have surrendered, at last?'

'I have, Matthew. I surrendered - and immediately wished I had not. Thank mercy there were no repercussions. And it was an experience that, as I made clear to Mr Bland, I did not intend to repeat, not until he made good his promise of matrimony. All seemed well for a time, but then I started to consider and analyse my situation more rationally. The experience was so disappointing, you see - not at all as I had anticipated. You and I had rehearsed it and practised towards it on so many occasions, providing us both with so many hours of enchantment along the way, that gradually I was forced to conclude that Mr Bland was not likely to come anywhere near to pleasing me in such a fashion, not even with the ultimate act itself at his disposal - that very act, moreover, which, paradoxically, I had always denied to you. And although I am not entirely certain I should compliment you further - for you are already in little need of having your own excellence confirmed in such matters - he was certainly no *Matthew*. And I longed so much for a *Matthew* at that moment, yearned for even a fraction of your delicacy and kindness. Even as I lay there at the conclusion of it, I felt so empty - and more than a bit frustrated. It was not painful - not for me. I did not feel degraded or anything like that, as maids often lament. No ... it was simply disappointing, that's all I can say. And if that's what married life was to be like, I reasoned, I want none of it, at least not with the present prospect. Oh Matthew, who of us can tell what the future holds, how long any of us have on this earth, and it is surely only logical that one should strive for a quantity of pleasure in that interval, would you not say so? And thus, only quite recently it was, that I returned his ring - and, with regret, as I told him, ended our relationship. Was it a mistake? I don't know. I'm not getting any younger, Matthew, am I? I even wonder sometimes lately if I am being left on the shelf. Are my looks fading? You would tell me, wouldn't you?'

He draws her closer, and cradling her face in his hands kisses her softly upon her forehead and then gently on her lips. 'Your looks are not fading in the least,' he whispers. 'Why, I should say, Harriet, my little love-engine, that you are even more beautiful than ever, and even more desirable than ever, if such were possible. And anyway, I must say I do quite like - er - *experienced* women.'

'Oh, now you are making merry at my expense!' she cries, and throws a mock punch - that lands on his shoulder and actually does hurt. 'Experienced I might well be - but only from one evening of tedium. What I mean is, I cannot just allow the passage of time to turn me into some shrivelled-up old prune. I wish to try again, Matthew. I wish to do it properly, all the way through. To put it in concise terms - and you will think me a slut, but I don't care - I am most curious to discover exactly what you can make of me if I allow you the full liberty of my person - for I suspect there might be a considerable variety of experiences that I have yet to be exposed to in this respect. Does that meet with your approval?'

'Entirely, my lovely,' he answers - most eager, even at this late hour, to commence upon that very adventure.

'Oh, how fine is this!' she sighs as he, running his fingers through the ever fascinating crimpiness of her auburn hair, kisses her most self indulgently, her eyelids, her nose, her ears and neck - with ardent lips all afire for her.

'I had thought that weariness would be my traitor tonight,' he murmurs, 'and weaken my desire for you, but if anything the waiting has given such spice to the dish.'

'Am I your dish?' she asks, looking up into his eyes.

'Yes, you are ... my tasty dish.'

'Then eat me up, my darling Matthew,' she sighs. 'For I am seasoned and ripe and all aglow with readiness.'

And as the flames rise in the hearth, so too do their passions, and soon he is exploring beneath her clothing, and she, aiding him is removing it herself with increasing impatience to get to the purpose, so that he is just about to guide her towards his bed chamber, when the sound of a number of people, walking through and into the yard below, all speaking loudly, can be heard - unusual for this late hour - and when, turning he looks down through the windows he sees, to his dismay, even by the scant light available, the entire troupe of his fellow travellers arriving. Clearly, they have - every one of them apart from the coachman - failed to secure any place to bed down, and are therefore about to take him up on his offer of shelter. Seconds later, having quickly located his porch, they have all scaled the stairs and assembled on the gallery outside and where, finding the bell out of order, begin immediately hammering on his door.

'Oh, my darling Harriet, I am so sorry,' Matthew groans as, with a gentle squeeze of Harriet's hands he leaves her and goes to open the outer door - at which, without even attempting to offer a greeting or to explain themselves, they all pile into his lobby, all talking avidly amongst themselves and almost crushing him and his manly pride, still prominent in his tight breeches, as they go bumbling past him in the dark and narrow passageway.

Oh dear! he thinks, with regret. It is one thing to be making a gesture of generosity to those in need. Quite another when they actually take you up on it! And at which he is forced to conclude, that it is not just a new bell-pull that needs installing outside but preferably a broad moat, a drawbridge and portcullis as well for any peace of mind.

'We are indebted to you, Sir,' one of the young men declares at last, discarding his hat upon Matthew's bench. Everyone is looking very cold and hungry, and yet surprisingly chipper and loquacious, as well - as if taking part in the adventure of a lifetime.

'Oh, what a lovely little boy, that was!' One of the ladies suddenly declares rather cryptically, removing her shawl and bonnet and placing these on one of Matthew's mannequin heads.

'Such a dear!' the other agrees, doing likewise and making herself at home right away on the nearest stool.

'*Boy* - what boy?' Matthew demands, already most irritated by the disruption taking place in his workshop. 'Who are you talking about?'

'Why, the little link-boy outside!' one of the widows replies, as if it were obvious to all. 'He showed us the way with his light. Why, we would surely never have found the place otherwise.'

'A most fortunate happenstance!' the clergyman declares, nodding in vigorous agreement. 'Most provident, indeed. Good lad!'

'Indeed!' says Matthew, busy tidying away his most expensive wigs and working tools from the temptation of curious eyes or mischievous fingers as, glancing down to the yard he sees him now, the link-boy, his mop of curly hair gleaming golden in the light of his torch. Catching Matthew's eye, he even has the audacity to wave before turning on his heels and departing under the arch - and just in time, therefore, to prevent an ungracious Matthew from brandishing his fist back at him in response - for as he watches the tiny glow of flame playing on the walls for a final time and then fading, Matthew realises that all his manly ardour has likewise vanished, extinguished as irrevocably as if a bucket of iced water had been poured upon it.

In desperation, he hastens out onto the gallery and rouses Francis the valet from his rooms at the far end, enlisting his help in locating for everyone concerned either a blanket or an extra layer of bedding. By the time Matthew has returned inside, however, his arms laden down with piles of the stuff, it is only to discover that the elderly ladies have already commandeered his bed in the other room and are ensconced beneath the covers and fast asleep. The clergyman, meanwhile, has seized upon the next-most-comfortable spot, the magic-couch in the alcove by the windows, while the three remaining gentlemen have bedded down nearby as best they can upon the floor amid all the various wig-stands and benches - and from which it is clear that there is not much more Matthew can do other than to drop the blankets upon them and then to make sure Harriet is comfortable in the armchair she has appropriated for herself. This accomplished, and with a farewell kiss on her forehead, all that remains is to undertake the dubious pleasure of joining Francis in his quarters once more where he must spend what is left of the night next to him on his bed: not exactly as he had expected things to turn out. For one brief moment he curses his luck, wondering how fine it would have been to have had the lovely Harriet by his side, her slim waist and narrow maiden's hips, her pert little breasts and crinkly auburn hair to enjoy, but then sleep descends - the deep and dreamless sleep of utter exhaustion.

The next morning, Matthew returns from Francis's room along the gallery to his quarters where he finds everyone already up and about. Having brought in some food and extra stools from the inn and putting his workbench to good use as a tabletop upon which they are all busy tucking into pies and toast, the conversation, as might be expected, is all about their misadventures of the previous night - though also inspired in no small measure by the latest headlines from an open newspaper on the bench, confirming the worst: 'Jacobites take Manchester. Gaining support, they march now on Derby.'

*Derby!* Only just over a hundred miles from the outskirts of London itself. Why they could be here within a few days, Matthew tells himself as he sits down next to a bemused Harriet and greets her silently with a kiss. With this astonishing piece of news, even he is beginning to feel anxious. Because if anything will persuade the Royal family to take flight, this will. The kingdom really is about to fall - just as Snatchal had said: a catastrophe is unfolding before their very eyes.

Assuring himself that his guests have consumed sufficient sustenance to see them on their way, he leaves them and escorts Harriet to her sister's home in Bow, only a short walk - trusting, as he does so, that by the time he returns all of his guests will have gone. But this is not to be. Upon his return, they seem, if anything even more entrenched. As ill-luck would have it, it transpires that no one among them seems to have any home to go to or employment waiting anywhere at all. They are, they tell him, all desperate people, with no immediate plans of any kind other than survival - over which they do, at least, appear most resourceful. Matthew's special oven that he uses for drying of hair, for example, has already been set to work for the re-heating of edibles from the chop house, and his crucible commandeered for cooking soup! The men, meanwhile, having made themselves quite comfortable, and having already washed their socks in his sink and hung them out to dry on a line above the chimneypiece normally reserved for switches of expensive hair, seem perfectly content to spend their time sitting up at the bench playing cards - trying to keep their language as decent as possible in earshot of the clergyman in the armchair, who is, however, far more interested in the newspaper and its contents as to be paying too much attention. Smoking at their clay pipes, the men deal hand after hand, playing for pennies while all the time making bold assertions about the need to enlist in the City Bands - the various regiments of volunteers expected to defend the City. The authorities are taking all comers, apparently, in order to protect the business quarters around the Royal Exchange and also the Palaces at Whitehall and St. James's. The men agree it is a worthy objective, and that they really ought to be considering something of that nature shortly, though perhaps not today - it being rather damp and chilly outside.

'I think it's all well and good, being a hero,' one says, 'but it's dangerous work, being in the heroic line of things. I think I'd prefer something more in keeping with my natural talents, anyway.'

'Oh, and what might they be, then?' his companion asks, dealing out a fresh hand.

'Taxidermy - that's what I am by trade, you see. Only there isn't really a lot of demand for stuffed animals in wartime. So I am at a bit of a loose end, so to speak.'

The ladies, meanwhile, have made another cup of tea - they seem constantly to be making tea - their discourse returning to the unsettling prospect of an occupying army roaming the streets.

'How will it all end, I don't know, Martha, my dear,' one declares, shaking her head dismally. 'You know what soldiers are like!'

'That's right, Dolly - and you know what they say, too … it's anything in petticoats. And I don't suppose these ones will be any different. Or any more ... well, fussy.'

'No, indeed not, my dear. Of course, one isn't suggesting that some of them, the Clansmen and the Highlanders, might not be anything other than quite handsome and dashing, especially the officers.'

'Oh, yes, I am sure some of them are most presentable,' Martha agrees, 'and that they would know exactly how to treat a lady, as well. But, there again …'

'Exactly, my dear. We will need to be vigilant.'

Matthew, meanwhile, taking advantage of a vacant chair, one of those requisitioned from the inn, sits himself down and weighs up his options. Clearly, no one is going to offer to leave. And, sooner or later, he is going to have to say something to encourage them to do so. But then, as he catches sight of the headline in the clergyman's paper once again, that special word - *Derby* - leaps out at him. There is, he is certain, a memory, a definite association with that town? And then abruptly it comes to him - of course! Derby - that was the hometown of his Jacobite sympathiser Mr McNiel, the very one who had commissioned a wig from him last summer and who had spoken so vehemently, even then, about the imminence and necessity of rebellion. Matthew had pledged his assistance at the time so as to gain his trust and to garner intelligence, and he cannot help wonder what might come of all those idle promises now - and whether he might even be held to them. In addition to that, there is another train of thought insistently playing upon his mind as he listens to the talk of his guests - about *being in the heroic line of things*, one of the young men had said. Yes. And then there was the link-boy, Ralph, the other evening. What was it he had spoken of as he walked along: 'That a man should be doing at least one heroic deed, if the honour comes his way.' Yes, that was it. *One heroic deed*. And gradually Matthew begins to comprehend that a quite momentous idea is beginning to formulate itself in his mind. Suddenly he knows what he must do.

'Francis,' he says, noticing the valet coming in, all long-faced and gloomy over the prospect of having to tidy up piles of dirty food dishes yet again, and beckoning him to a corner of the room where he can speak discreetly. 'Francis, who's on duty downstairs, in the stables? Do you know?'

'I believe it is John, today, Sir.'

'Good. Go down and ask John to reserve for me the best horse available - tell him it is for me personally, mind you. Bring up saddlebags. Then, if you please, you should lay out the following items: riding boots and the warmest clothes suitable for a lengthy journey, hat, woollen scarf and cloak - oh yes, and woollen stockings and spatterdashes, too. I also require my lightest sword - that would be the copper-bound handle - and my pistol with powder and shot. Tinder box also, if you please, and some dry biscuits. I will also need a brandy flask again, and some small beer in bottles. I will check through the items before I leave. During my absence, my man, you must do your utmost to encourage these good people to depart, also, and this as soon as possible.'

'And when might I expect your return, Sir?'

'Francis, I wish I could answer that question, but I cannot. There is something I must attend to which is important - a rather unfamiliar task, and I am not at all sure how much time will be required to accomplish it.'

And with that, Francis, shaking his head in further mystification and not inconsiderable dismay at the uncertainty of everything, goes down to the stables and begins the preparations as instructed.

# ~ 17 ~
## LETTERS CROSSING

*The Pig and Whistle, Cheapside, London*

Dear Sam,
      I trust this finds you well. At the present time of writing, my valet Francis is endeavouring to empty my apartments at the Pig and Whistle of some guests who are beginning to outstay their welcome. If you could assist him at any time in my absence, I would be most grateful. They are all decent people, and every one of them shared in my fate recently when, on a journey from St Albans in the company of a young lady of my acquaintance, we were robbed at gun point. Unlike my friend and I, they found themselves, much later that same night and upon their arrival in London, without accommodation. Their plight seemed so pitiful that I offered them shelter. At the moment, however, I must say they seem reluctant to move on. If you can persuade them of the necessity to do so and to render what practical assistance is necessary to ensure their safety, I shall be beholden to you and shall take this opportunity to thank you in advance with all my heart.

      The reason for my inconveniencing you in this way is that I have resolved to go forth for a few days once more, though this time with the intention of actually doing something useful with my life. I hope this sudden lapse into nobility of sentiment does not strike you as too out of character, and even if it does, you are not to be alarmed. If I am successful in my endeavours, I shall look forward to explaining to you upon my return the precise nature of the enterprise. If, on the other hand, I fail, then I will probably not be returning at all, at least not in one piece. Do not, however, I repeat, be anxious on my behalf. I remain as desirous of my own self-preservation and continued life of idle pleasure as any man, and can assure you I will not be placing myself in any unnecessary danger. At least that is the plan as it stands at present.

Trusting in your safety and continued good health in these difficult times, and please commend me to your dear lady wife,

Sincerely, your friend,
Matthew

Woolveston Cottage, Greenwich, Kent

S alutations, my Wonder,

It has been so long since we last had the pleasure of conversing, and I trust that you will excuse the liberty I have taken in writing these few lines - hoping as I do so that this will find you in the very best of spirits.

I am anxious to discover what you are making of your 'Heavenly Bodies' and to have the pleasure of reading your sonnets in full. It does, I must own, seem an exceptionally long wait. I know I am impatient, but it is a project over which you have been engaged for so many weeks, if not months. Naturally, I am curious. Write to me, please, and share with me your progress, or better still visit us once again, Sam and I. We shall dine together and make music once more - even though, alas, this cannot be conducted at our home here in Greenwich, at least not for a while, because Sam has resolved that, being so close to any possible field of conflict, we must leave the capital and make plans for an extended stay in Tunbridge Wells with his mother - the better to be removed from the dangers. It is not such a lengthy journey from where you reside, however, and you would be most welcome, I am sure, to stay over.

How tiresome it is, all this talk of war. A most frightening time for everyone - though there are other matters which concern me even more than this, and which pertain to your preservation most of all. Allow me the liberty of being plain with you, my Wonder, since I cannot conceive of any other way of forewarning you of the danger that you are under at present unless I tell you the truth as it has come to me. It concerns a certain lady of nobility of our acquaintance who, I am sure you cannot have helped but notice, has very obvious designs upon your person. I have spoken with her on occasion recently and she has quite brazenly boasted to me (to me of all people who care and cherish your welfare almost as much as my own) of her intention to bed you. How disgraceful! She seems, moreover, of the persuasion that her ambitions must inevitably be crowned with success - and this within a very short period of time. What furnishes her with such confidence I cannot say, but whatever it is, it seems a most powerful conviction on her part and one with which she seems to rejoice in taunting me, and this in the most cruel and unbecoming fashion. I really do think I am beginning to dislike her. I entreat you, therefore, to be on your guard, my Wonder, since to succumb to her advances would expose you to a danger of terrible magnitude, and one through which even you, cat of nine lives, may not be able to traverse unscathed. Resist, resist, and turn instead to your art, your poetry and keep in your heart a regard for those who care for you and who look each day for a letter or message to confirm your safety. I do so look forward to discussing your noble project with you again soon. Until then, know that you remain in my thoughts, and that even when your feet must run so far to seek your friend, your mind need not.

Affectionately yours,
Johanna Woolveston

# ~ 18 ~
## THE SILK MILL

There has been ample time to consider his decision, that the journey he has undertaken is foolhardy in the extreme, of a most improbable likelihood of success and not without considerable danger. But he will not turn back.

The first fifty miles or so were familiar enough - retracing on horse-back the very route by which Harriet and he had travelled from St Albans to London just a couple of days previous. The overnight accommodation at the White Hart was as adequate to his needs as on his previous visit, and the next day, refreshed and full of hope, he rode out at a cantor, north and westward along the old Roman highway of Watling Street - the tall cathedral tower upon the horizon receding rapidly into the distance with every periodic glance back over the shoulder, his progress impressive. But that was some time ago, and for all Matthew's enthusiasm at the outset, he is already beginning to suspect that the weather is not likely to co-operate for very much longer. It is becoming bitterly cold, with tiny flurries of sleet and then snow driving into his face as the skies become more and more overcast - that typical early gloom of a December afternoon. A north wind is never an encouraging sign at any time of the year, but in the depth of Winter it is positively treacherous - and very soon, with the approach of evening he discovers that he is not only riding into darkness but also into an increasingly desolate landscape. There are villages and hamlets along the way, yes - but silent places, for the most part. And whether they are genuinely deserted or their inhabitants simply resolved to keep safe behind closed doors and shuttered windows, the overall presentation is the same - one of cold and friendless indifference to any traveller upon the open road.

Inevitably, too, he has had to concede that the various inns where he must now change horse or bed down for the night will be of a far more modest standard when compared to the comforts of the White Hart or those of his own home in London. There is not much by way of conversation to be had with the staff at these places, either, while any fellow travellers are likewise most reticent to speak, preferring to keep themselves very much to themselves in these dangerous times. The only news he can gather is to confirm that the Jacobite army has left Manchester and, with their ranks swelling all the while, are continuing upon their relentless march south towards Derby with their sights set on London in just a few days time. Meanwhile, His Majesty's own forces under his son the Duke of Cumberland have made the journey north to meet them and are already at Lichfield, seeking to outflank the enemy or to cut off their supply lines. A major confrontation is only days away, possibly already taking place at this very minute, and the uncertainty leaves everyone feeling most restless and dejected.

The next morning comes with an even worse deterioration in the weather, and with his saddlebags stocked for another lengthy day's riding, Matthew notices almost immediately the tell-tale signs of a marching army having gone before - Cumberland's redcoats for sure, having passed this way perhaps as recently as just a day or two ago. Wagons and gun carriages have rutted the road, and everywhere the surface has been churned into a slippery morass - made worse by the harsh overnight frosts that has transformed it into a fine powder and thus, with the onset of yet more sleet and snow today, into a slurry of fine mud - heavy going now for any stagecoach. And sure enough, it is not long before he encounters one such ill-fated vehicle abandoned by the side of the road, and then an hour later another, almost at a standstill on a hill with its passengers walking in front.

Apart from this, there is very little by way of traffic going north - most of the commerce, predictably enough, being in the opposite direction: with everywhere people, especially the well-to-do, taking to the road in carriages or on horseback, their servants and their belongings alongside in covered wagons with heavy loads straining the axles, their horses breathing out great clouds of mist as they go. Even those of a more humble station can be seen out on the highway, seeking to remove themselves from harm's way: labourers, farmers and their families, even in some instances accompanied by their livestock - trotting alongside or else secured upon litters or carts, improvised vehicles of all shapes and sizes pulled by mules or even by men and boys, all fleeing the area of conflict - everyone, young or old, rich or poor alike on the move. Extraordinary.

Relieved that he will not be encountering Cumberland's forces at this juncture, for his route takes him off the Lichfield road now, he continues up through all the various turnpikes towards the town of Leicester - this being reached just prior to sunset. After so long upon the highway and among so many relatively primitive and insanitary settlements, the appearance of such a substantial, well-populated town comes as a relief for Matthew. A community set in the centre of the woollen and tanning industries, Leicester is a thriving market town, and he has fond memories of it from a former visit many years ago. At present, however, there is an eerie, nervous feeling even here, the streets empty and many of the shops boarded up. The market, meanwhile, and which would normally be so vibrant, appears today to have consisted of just a handful of stalls, their owners already folding their awnings, packing up early, fleeing what is considered to be the inevitable occupation of the town by the rebels in just a couple of days time - for once Derby, such a strategically placed town on the river Derwent just a few miles to the North is taken, anything is possible. Even among those at the inn in which he stays that night, with its roaring fire and plenty of good food and wine, an almost apocalyptic sense of impending doom can be felt - though also, perversely at the same time, a mood that is celebratory in tone - everyone resigned with a kind of gallows humour to the approaching cataclysm that would signal if not exactly the end of the world, then at least a dramatic change in affairs that would leave no one upon its surface entirely unaffected. 'Drink and be merry!' seems the order of the day - one to which he gladly unites his sentiments, with much bragging, jesting and colourful language enjoyed by all.

The next day, the final leg of his journey, Matthew comes to the long causeway and stone bridge at Swarkestone over the river Trent, unguarded, he is relieved to discover, and then finally to the southern outskirts of Derby itself, his intended destination and the home of Mr McNiel and his family - residing, Matthew discovers, in a fine building with an impressive classical facade, just inside the town walls. Dismounting in the gathering darkness of the winter's afternoon, he is met in the grounds by a groom who asks him his business before leading his horse away to be stabled, while another, a butler in smart livery and wig, takes his calling card and conducts him into the lobby of the house itself. Here, he remains, standing, his saddlebags at his feet admiring the panelled interior and the many fine paintings upon the walls - until the tall and elegant figure of Mrs McNiel, her hair covered in a neat linen cap, appears. He has already made her acquaintance, of course, albeit briefly during the summer when she and her husband had first come to his workshops in London, and she seems to recognise him, too.

'Why, Mr Wildish - if I am correct?' she says.

'You are, Ma'am,' he replies with a bow.

'Well, you are, of course, most welcome - yes, most welcome,' she adds, and Matthew can sense the strained cordiality in her voice, though her manner still most gracious for all that. 'I know not what the purpose of your visit might be, Mr Wildish, but my husband is at present in the town centre with the army. By that, I mean, those soldiers of Prince Charles - for the vanguard entered yesterday evening via Eastgate and our town will soon be occupied entirely as additional troops arrive.'

Her candour and trust in conveying all this vital information to him is quite touching, for she is evidently of the opinion that he is a sympathiser, a supporter of the Jacobite cause, the very impression he wishes to convey, of course.

'The Prince has already requisitioned Exeter House, close to the river,' she continues. And for a moment her hand strays to her forehead, as if to steady her thoughts. 'He has made it his Headquarters. I am in dread that soldiers will be billeted upon us at any moment. Forgive me, then, if I seem disturbed - for on being informed of the arrival of a stranger just now, I feared the worst. I thought ... Anyway, I presume that it is, indeed, my husband that you are seeking, Sir?'

'Yes, Ma'am. And I can assure you I would not trouble you at all if it were not a matter of considerable magnitude. If you could indicate to me where precisely I might locate him? You mentioned Exeter House? Where might that ...'

'You will surely take a little refreshment first, Mr Wildish?' she remonstrates with continued kindness 'And I will then supply you with someone who will guide you safely to where my husband is to be found.'

Feeling suddenly weary almost beyond endurance, he accepts the good lady's hospitality, allowing her to usher him through into the drawing room where a welcome fire is already burning in the hearth and where, appearing calmer now, she offers Matthew a seat close by. After ringing for service, she also takes her place across from him.

It is a most excellently appointed room, he reflects, with an abundance of silks everywhere, these incorporated in the upholstery and in all of the drapes and hangings, as well, resulting in a delicate, shimmering air of the utmost refinement - the equal of any town house in London. A perfect setting for one such as Mrs McNiel, in fact, who is attired in a variety of similarly outstanding fabrics. All this, Mrs McNiel explains, is the result of the family business in the weaving of silks, one of the mainstays of local industry in these parts. And thus, by the conversation, spoken with exceptional civility and composure over tea, and with the addition of some welcome food hastily brought up from the kitchens by the same nimble-footed butler of earlier, Matthew is able to learn yet more about the current state of the town and of the opposing armies and their intentions - for Mrs McNiel, he discovers, is no mere passive spectator in these developments but is in fact a well-informed observer with considerable practical knowledge. Seeing her like this in her own home, moreover, as she continues to relate the details of the campaign, she appears a far more significant and commanding figure than when he had encountered her on the arm of her husband last summer. Referring to the various divisions of loyalties current in the locality, she explains that whereas some families have always prevaricated concerning the Jacobites, others have from the very start welcomed the prospect of their coming, including her husband who is about to throw in his lot entirely behind them. The possible repercussions for him and his family as this enthusiasm becomes public knowledge are immense, of course, and it is evident that Mrs McNiel herself is fully aware of them and most apprehensive.

Just then, there is the sound of dainty feet running, and two young children, females, their hair all dancing ringlets and plaits, enter the room - excited and wanting to see for themselves the visitor. 'Are the soldiers coming, Mummy?' the eldest inquires, clearly anxious, looking Matthew up and down, as if he were one of the very ogres sent in advance, while the younger of the two, coming closer and clutching a little dolly to her breast, cowers behind her mother's broad skirts.

'No dearest, no. This is Mr Wildish, an associate of your father's. Mr Wildish, may I introduce my daughters Judith and Emily.'

Matthew rises from his chair and, making a leg, bows most elaborately, which pleases them greatly, all giggly now.

'I am delighted to make your acquaintance, ladies!' he announces.

Both the girls are immaculately dressed - with, as might be expected, an abundance of fine silks on display.

'There, you see!' Mrs McNiel asserts with a smile, a hand on each child's shoulder. 'Mr Wildish is a gentleman, and you have nothing to fear. Hurry away now, both of you, and see if you can complete your embroidery lessons. And, all being well, I will see you before bedtime.'

And with that, and just one final examination of Matthew's countenance with bold, probing eyes, the girls depart the room, exiting with far greater composure than upon their entrance.

'I can see you have many blessings,' Matthew observes.

'Indeed, I have, Mr Wildish. Thank you.'

'Tell me, did the Jacobites not encounter any resistance here at all?' he asks, resuming his quest to learn as much as possible, and even now hardly able to believe the ease of their continued advance.

'Prince Charles employed a successful diversionary movement,' she replies. 'He dispatched a small number of his troops Westward, thereby giving the false impression that the entire army would be marching to Wales where they would have additional support to swell their numbers. Consequently, the bulk of Cumberland's redcoats moved westward also from Lichfield to intercept it, leaving the road into Derby and most of the countryside to the North and West free of obstruction. In the meantime, our own local garrison failed to stand their ground. In fact, I am ashamed to report that no sooner did the Prince and his men come marching in at one end of the town, when they with much haste rode out by the other, and we have not seen or heard anything from them since. It is not known how soon the Duke of Cumberland will realise his error, but even the diversionary troops that were sent to steer him away have rejoined the main body of Highlanders now, and are about to continue farther south, I understand, to secure the bridge at Swarkestone. Meanwhile, the Prince has demanded billets for nine thousand men in and about the town - which is a most disproportionate amount for such a small place as Derby. They will then be ready to begin their final march to London, maybe as early as tomorrow.'

'Then it is perhaps all the more urgent that I speak with your husband,' Matthew states, reluctantly setting aside his tea and climbing to his feet. 'For I have some significant details to impart to him.'

'I understand,' Mrs McNiel responds, rising also. 'If you would care to wait here for just a moment, Mr Wildish, I will fetch someone to show you the way.'

Upon her exit, and in the absence of conversation and the need to appear alert - for he is indeed feeling quite exhausted all of a sudden - Matthew takes his seat once more and allows himself to close his eyes. It feels good. And gradually he realises that he is dozing off. He fights against it for a while, but it is so very homely here, so comfortable with the gentle crackling of coals on the fire and the ticking pendulum of a casement clock in the room, that he persuades himself there would really be no dishonour even to be found thus, upon Mrs McNiel's return, resting his eyes. And so he surrenders.

He has no way of knowing how long he has been asleep, but at one moment he is aware of children running in again, the two girls and a small boy, as well, this time. He half opens one eye only to see them running off, and discovers that a blanket has been draped across his legs, which he instinctively pulls up over his chest - all so blissfully comforting that he slips away into slumber again and this time most deeply.

'Mr Wildish! Mr Wildish,' a voice calls, and as he opens his eyes it is to behold Mrs McNiel once more who has returned this time with a footman. 'I have a gentleman here who will take you to my husband forthwith, if you are so disposed.'

'I am much obliged, Ma'am,' Matthew says as he draws himself slowly to his feet, aware of his own reluctance to leave. 'You have been most kind. And my gratitude also to your three children for their kind gesture,' he adds, folding the blanket slowly and placing it onto the chair back.

'My *three* children?' Mrs McNiel echoes, mystified. 'Oh, I am afraid you must be mistaken, Mr Wildish. We have only the two girls in this house.'

'My apologies, Ma'am. I must have dreamt there were three,' he replies, feeling still drowsy - though, once outside, the cold evening air revives him straight away as he accompanies the footman the short distance across the market place and into the road where Exeter House is located - a stylish three-story mansion, set within a rectangular park and courtyard - the most substantial building in the area, in fact, other than the church with its tall, almost cathedral-like tower nearby. The snow must have been falling heavily, he notices, for it has settled with ease upon the roofs and cornices of the buildings, and it is very noisy everywhere, with the entire town most evidently full of soldiers, including many Highlanders - unmistakable in their distinctive plaid dress, some busy clearing away undergrowth to make space, pitching their field tents in gardens, others chopping firewood, cooking at campfires or else, with whet-stones in their hands, sharpening and maintaining their weapons, their swords and axes - the sparks flying sometimes in the darkness as they work. It is the first time Matthew has seen anything like it - all these battle-hardened soldiers, many of whom would have been on the march from one skirmish to the next for almost half a year. A good few of them have long, unshorn hair, and beards to match. They seem so strong; so powerful; so full of purpose and intent. The momentum is with them, these blood-hardened fighting men, anticipating each new confrontation, no doubt, with all the ease and practised skill that familiarity of warfare brings. Some stare across at him in his fine clothes as he and his escort proceed along the long, straight driveway up to the house, his blatant and provocative *Englishness* clear for all to see.

Passing through the broad door of the entrance with its illuminated fanlight above, Matthew encounters McNiel by chance straight away in the hallway, so that after the initial surprise on his part, a handshake is all that is needed by way of introduction.

'Mr Wildish, what brings you here?' he inquires.

'Good Evening, Mr McNiel,' Matthew begins. 'I have come directly from London. I have information that I feel would be to your advantage.'

'Really! Well, you'd better step this way then, Mr Wildish,' he responds, though not, Matthew senses, without a certain unwillingness on his part as he tears himself away from the conversation in which he has been engaged: important business, it would seem, among a number of neatly attired men in long wigs, each with the white cockade in their hats and therefore, Matthew surmises, most likely to be commanding officers of the Jacobite army.

McNiel ushers Matthew through to the back of the building, to a window seat in the library where they place themselves close to each other in order to converse with some measure of privacy. The window is undraped and through the glass Matthew can see the fields and rear gardens of the houses sloping down to the river, and upon these yet more soldiers are assembled, the smoke and embers of campfires rising vertically into the still air and around which most of the men are already bedding down upon straw. It cannot be easy - trying to sleep under such freezing conditions, he thinks. But, there again, these *are* Highlanders.

'What I am about to say might already be known to you,' Matthew begins without delay, looking the other man steadily in the eye, 'and if this is the case, forgive me for troubling you - but the forces at the command of the Duke of Cumberland and the English army are almost certainly far more numerous than you would be aware of at present. In addition to the troops of General Wade to the East, only one day's march away, and those of Cumberland not so very far to the West, there is a massive third wave advancing as we speak from the South.'

McNiel slumps back into the comfort of the upholstered seat, and he emits a long sigh before answering: 'I thank you Mr Wildish. However, the Prince and his General, Lord Murray, are fully aware of the enemy dispositions,' he states, unimpressed. 'Even if Cumberland and Wade were to come together in any coherent way, which so far, of course, they have singularly failed to do, the Bonny Prince's forces are equal to them - and more than a match, also, to any rag-tag band of volunteers that might be defending the London road.'

'No, no, this is precisely my point,' Matthew argues, more strongly while endeavouring still to keep his voice low. 'The third wave I speak of is not merely defensive, but is comprised of several thousand enlisted men, divisions from Flanders, infantry, cavalry, all equipped with heavy artillery and ready to take the fight directly to the Prince.'

'I see. So exactly what is it that you are suggesting?' McNiel asks, irritable now. 'That we should halt our advance - or even retreat? I must inform you, Mr Wildish, that such an inference would hardly be met with universal approval by those in command here. Many of us suspect reports of this kind to be exaggerated, or simply a case of misinformation being fed to us from - if you will forgive me - dubious sources.'

'Then, I take it, a retreat of some kind has already been mooted?' Matthew inquires, boldly.

McNiel looks away, and appears to clench his jaws, his countenance if anything even more distressed. 'Correct,' he answers. 'Most of the generals, and Murray, too, are of the view there has been an insufficient response from those we had considered our allies; and that this has been most damaging to our prospects.'

'Really. How unfortunate.'

'I understand, that in certain quarters the opinion is that His Highness may have misled us - regarding, for instance, the strength of the French determination to join. I, too, am most disappointed, I must own, with the response here in the Midlands. Even though the Prince has made it clear he has no intention of abolishing the Union with Scotland, or meddling in matters of worship, still, without an indication from the French as to the timing of an invasion, there have been few here willing to rouse themselves to any public commitment to the cause.'

'Not even here, not even in Derby?' Matthew asks.

'Especially not here in Derby, not now,' he replies and suddenly his voice has become much calmer and more measured, almost with an element of resignation to it. 'As you can see, the town is in disarray at present, Mr Wildish, and many here are much troubled to see it thus. The army, furthermore, has not exactly commended itself to the populace. Far from it. Oh, the officers on the whole have conducted themselves commendably, and the Prince and Lord Murray are honourable men. But the soldiers, the common soldiers - well, by all accounts, a marked deterioration in discipline has occurred since Manchester, and here in Derby they have plundered everything they can lay their hands on - food, bedding, clothes, candles - anything they can carry off. They say a young serving girl has been slain at the Dolphin Inn, not one hundred yards from where we speak - the soldiers having been drinking there all day. It has not taken them long to line their pockets, either - and no sooner had they entered the town, when they established an office in the

Market Place to collect excise duties that would otherwise have gone to London. It is, of course, nothing less than extortion, with local tradesmen facing the prospect of having to pay duties twice over as a consequence. Anyone who refuses to comply is threatened with the firing squad.'

And suddenly Matthew begins to comprehend the unease he saw in the face of this gentleman's wife earlier, the sheer anxiety of it all. For a while, McNiel looks inward, ruminating over not only the validity or otherwise of Matthew's earlier assertions, but also perhaps his own plight, of what might become of him were he to continue to declare publicly for the rebel cause. To proceed with the advance, in the light of this new information, would mean certain failure; yet a retreat would mean worse - shame and ignominy for the families of any English sympathisers left behind, including the possibility of prosecutions, the forfeiture of their estates and even a death warrant for treason being issued. It really would be, Matthew thinks as he examines the face of the other man for any signs of emotion, the worst possible news that he is now having to digest.

From the gardens, Matthew can detect the playing of bagpipes - a most unfamiliar sound to him, and also to the citizens of Derby, no doubt. There is some raucous singing in places, too. And as Matthew glances through the window once again, down towards the swift-flowing waters of the Derwent, he notices, illuminated by a sudden shaft of moonlight, the presence of a massive mill situated at a bend in the river, a silk mill most likely - a broad weir of foaming water, all white and silver, tumbling and dancing in the darkness. Really quite beautiful.

'You had better come along with me, Mr Wildish,' the other man mutters, raising his head at last. 'I would like you to repeat what you have just told me to General Murray.'

Together they take the broad staircase with its carved balustrade, overhung with portraits of the noble past, up to the first floor and where, following a word with a soldier, a message is sent in to the drawing room on their behalf. They have only a few minutes to wait on the landing until the guard returns. The tall, double doors are opened and together they enter into a finely panelled and wainscoted room where, amid a profusion of candles on every available surface, from chandeliers and candelabrum, a substantial number of well-groomed military men and sundry

gentlemen sit in orderly fashion along the length of a long
mahogany table strewn with maps and papers. Many of those
present are clustered in groups or pairs, in animated conversation,
and yet it all seems to Matthew, given the circumstances, a
surprisingly orderly and civil gathering. Even though it is late in the
day and wine has been served, no one appears to be anything other
than entirely sober, looking up to meet the eyes of the newcomers
with a blend of battle-weary wisdom and inquisitive interest - the
look of resignation and uneasy calm that would come from months
of harsh campaigning and fatigue.

After a moment, McNiel, evidently a familiar face to them,
takes the opportunity to introduce Matthew to the commander,
Lord Murray, a man of around fifty years in a very neat campaign
wig, white-powdered and which contrasts, oddly in this instance,
with his black, perfectly arched eyebrows which are raised in
curiosity as he bids Matthew and McNiel to be seated opposite him
at the table where, with the utmost courtesy, places are hastily
cleared for them - though not before offering McNiel an apology -
because a number of soldiers, he is informed, have been billeted on
him already, and that he will find them at his home when he
returns. McNiel, his spine stiffening visibly in response, seems
none too pleased at this news, and Matthew finds himself sharing in
the other man's discomfiture. Even several others at the table
appear to be sympathetic, regarding him with a look of uncommon
kindness - no doubt realising all too well the unpleasant
consequences for the local man.

Murray is a softly spoken Scot, with just the slightest indication
of strain, a certain tightness at the temples as he talks, as if
struggling to maintain composure, and after a few more moments
of conversing with gentlemen on either side, he turns his attentions
to Matthew, providing him at last with an opportunity to repeat his
story. And yet, when Matthew is allowed to speak, conveying his
information exactly as told to McNiel, much of it is received with
surprising indifference.

'Mr Wildish, we are indebted to you,' Lord Murray responds at
length, just catching the eye of one or two colleagues as he does so,
though all remain silent. 'I must tell you, however, that the details
you have furnished us with regarding the strength of the opposing
forces is nothing we have not already heard several times today.
We have people - men, you understand, who are spies within the

ranks of the Redcoats themselves, but who have turned double agent and foolishly believe they can relay false information back to us as a consequence. We know who they are, and we tend to ignore what they say, particularly regarding any flagrantly implausible figures concerning those forces ranged against us. In other words, we have heard it all many times before. Why, therefore, would you expect us to give any special credence to *your* information in this instance?'

'Because it's the truth,' Matthew replies, perhaps rather naively, for it is an assertion that causes a ripple of merriment around the table.

'*The truth,* Mr Wildish, may I remind you, is always the first casualty of war,' Murray replies without passion. 'And I regret to say there have been quite a number of such casualties of late.'

A further cackle of polite laughter circulates around the table - with more than a few wise old heads nodding in agreement. He must, Matthew tells himself remain calm, to bluff his way through this moment with all the steely nerve of the greatest of gamesters - for it is, of course, the most flagrantly inaccurate information concerning the strength of the English forces that he is trying to impress upon them. In the event, he need not have worried, for it is McNiel who comes to his aid and who, alone among them in his unwillingness to share in any gaiety, ventures to speak next.

'May I, with your permission gentleman, contribute to this discussion,' he says, addressing Lord Murray in particular: 'Mr Wildish here is a gentleman I have known for some months. I have dealt with him in a business capacity, and long ago he even volunteered his assistance if and when our forces were to enter the capital. He is not, as should be obvious by his apparel, a member of the armed forces, nor is he anyone sent by you to spy, and who might subsequently have turned double agent. Rather, he has journeyed here of his own volition from London where he is a wig-maker.'

A chorus of embarrassed coughing and even the odd smirk or overt chuckle ensues now as everyone gives in to the absurdity of it all. It is the laughter of weariness.

'*A wig maker!*' a large, red-faced man at the far end to Murray declares with dreadful irony, his chair well back from the table so that he almost seems to be reclining. 'Well, well, that is something different, I must say: the destiny of the nation brought to perfection by the word of a man who makes wigs!'

Murray smiles at this, the first time he has done so, indulging the speaking-out of his colleague with the countenance of one who has a certain familiarity with the tone of it, and also as one long-past caring whether or not it is perceived as pertinent or helpful, or either. 'My Lord Drummond, Duke of Perth,' he announces by way of introducing Matthew to his detractor, his hand, with its white-laced sleeve held forth and extended in the man's direction, 'a noble colleague of ours who, like His Highness, Prince Charles, would gladly have us all marching at the double upon the London Road at first light - but who, mercifully, remains in a minority at this table. Though, it has to be said, the observation is a fair one, for yours does seem, if you will excuse my plain speaking, Mr Wildish, a curious qualification for one who professes to be privy to sophisticated military intelligence. What knowledge, pray, should a wig-maker, have of the dispositions of the Hanoverian troops?'

'It is inaccurate to describe me as a wig-maker, Sir,' Matthew responds straight away. 'I am a *master* wig maker. I am also a poet and ...'

'*A poet!*' Drummond exclaims and this time almost falls off his chair laughing, his bare knees protruding from his plaid doing a little jig of uncontrolled merriment.

'A poet, and a socialite,' Matthew continues patiently, allowing himself a glance of contempt towards his distinguished heckler. 'I have, numbered among my clients, men of the highest station, both in the Privy Council and among the Admiralty. The information I am exposed to in the course of my work, even when I try my hardest not to listen to it, is usually accurate, therefore, because it is given me during moments of unguarded conversation. As my name and possibly accent might already indicate, gentlemen, I am of Irish descent and, like you, I detest the Hanoverian usurpers who sit on the English throne. And because I am anxious that the overall mission of Charles Stuart to restore the rightful succession should not founder though ill-conceived optimism, I have taken it upon myself to journey here, alone and at some hazard to my personal safety, that I might explain the facts as I understand them. I am no military tactician, gentlemen, but through the information that has come to me, I have arrived at the conclusion that the only hope for the preservation of your enterprise is if the Prince now returns to

Scotland, perhaps for the duration of the worst of the winter months, in order to regroup, to replenish his forces and await the arrival of the French. I can assure you, again through intelligence that is known to those in Whitehall, that the imminence of French troops on English soil is what George fears the most. But again, my understanding is that any invasion will not be forthcoming - I repeat, *not* be forthcoming at all, until early next year. To proceed towards London at present would be to invite disaster. Your are already outflanked and your forces are hopelessly outnumbered.'

An eerie silence descends, and it remains that way for some moments, punctuated merely by a return to yet more embarrassed coughing. One of the men opens his snuffbox and takes a pinch.

'Well, Mr Wildish,' Murray responds at length, after making a show of studying his papers for a second or two, 'we thank you.' And then turning to the others: 'So, what say you, gentlemen? Interesting? In any event, we must arrive at a decision soon and convey our views to His Highness when he returns from dinner. I take it, Mr Wildish you will be remaining here in Derby this night?'

Matthew nods his compliance.

'Mr Wildish is welcome to lodge at my house,' McNiel interjects, glancing in Matthew's direction by way of invitation, 'if there is room, that is, after your troops have done with us.'

'It will be but a few days inconvenience at the most,' Murray responds with a vaguely humorous smile. 'They are mostly officers of the Highland regiments, and are instructed to be on their best behaviour.'

At which, and amid a certain degree of frivolity from those present, clearly well apprised of what Highlander officers might be like even when on their 'best behaviour,' McNiel and Matthew rise from the table and, with a mixture of relief but also much anxiety for what the local man might find at home, eagerly take their leave.

Emerging outside into the cold air once more, McNiel leads his guest speedily across the market place and back towards his house. It is much quieter now, so that the turbulent rush of the river can be detected upon the air, the snow falling once more as they trudge along the street and into the courtyard of McNiel's home, and even as they approach the building it is obvious that the whole place is much changed since Matthew had left it only a couple of short hours ago. Horses and mules are tethered everywhere in the garden, tied to anything that might remotely be used to secure them; bales of straw are scattered elsewhere, being made ready for bedding or feed for the animals, while from the façade of the house itself every window appears to be either lit or occupied by moving shadows or figures within. A good fifty-or-so Highlanders have been placed here, according to the testimony of the butler as they encounter him on the doorstep, wringing his hands and trembling with fright - for whereas just a short time ago everything about the place had exuded an air of order and homely comfort, now there is an almost palpable feeling of aggression. Inside, it is worse. Amid a hubbub of noisy bombast, they encounter men everywhere, some already bedding down on any available floor space they can find - in the hall, in the drawing room, the library - some drinking, some eating, others playing at cards, everywhere the sound of harsh voices, the smell of damp clothes and bodies unwashed. The wonderful, gorgeous interior of shimmering silks and brocades, of finest velvets and chintz now all covered over by the dull russets of tartan and coarse plaid, besmirched by muddy boots and the touch of a hundred grimy hands.

McNiel hurries to seek out his wife and there is the sound of sobbing somewhere far back in the house where he has gone - though he does return shortly in order to show Matthew to a place where he might sleep the night. All the bedrooms are already occupied, he states, so it must needs be the attic. Matthew is unconcerned, however, since with the addition of a pillow and blanket supplied by his host, it appears comfortable enough up beneath the eves, and after preparing his bed, and not wishing to retire too early, he elects to return alone downstairs - to the drawing room once more and where, nodding a greeting to a couple of tartan-clad officers lolling feet-up on a sofa, he locates a chair and makes himself comfortable. Elsewhere, several other soldiers have settled themselves in the room, and for the most part they ignore his arrival. Bare-legged with only short woollen socks, their heavy plaid thrown over their shoulders, their bonnets and hats still upon their heads, the men have ranged their weapons, broad swords, daggers and, in one instance, even a poleaxe of some kind, upon the floor around them, their knapsacks and palliasses nearby also - these items much the worse for wear and covered in mud and excrement. The smell, particularly in the proximity of the fire, is appalling, as they continue to converse loudly with one another in their Gaelic language, of which Matthew has no understanding. But then, when another soldier, dressed differently in more conventional English garb and who has evidently already discovered the location of the wine cellar, enters with several bottles under his arms, they revert in large part to English - though this still with a heavy accent that is nearly every bit as impenetrable.

'Hey, I could get used to this, eh!' one of the men says to his colleague after managing to remove the corks from a couple of the bottles with the aid of a dagger, so that soon they are passing them around and drinking heartily, spitting out any pieces of cork that have inevitably fallen into the bottles. Matthew declines at first to join them, not relishing present company sufficient to participate, which seems to annoy them - his comparatively dainty civilian clothes and gentlemanly manners already being sufficient cause for some suspicion on their part. So eventually he does relent - though still insisting on locating a glass, so he might imbibe in a civil manner.

'Your health, my friend!' one of the Highlanders states, raising the bottle, almost as a kind of admonishment rather than a salutation, and to which at first Matthew merely remains silent. But by the second and then third repetition of the toast, he knows he is obliged to utter at least something by way of response.

'It would be a pity to have come all this way for nothing,' Matthew jests, addressing the men with a cheeky smile - and immediately realises he should have kept his mouth shut.

'There is no way we are coming here for nothing, friend!' one of the men on the sofa argues very loudly, almost like a battle cry itself and pointing a long grimy finger in Matthew's direction. 'We are a-going all the way my friend, all the way to London - where we are a-going to have King George's balls for dinner!'

'Aye!' one of his companions shouts in response, his voice almost like a song. 'Watch out Georgie Boy. We are a coming for you, no mistaking!'

'Are you not concerned about the redcoats, then?' Matthew inquires, swirling the liquid in his glass and enjoying the aroma of what is in fact a fine vintage claret. Poor McNiel - all his best wine vanishing down the throats of these oafs.

'Listen, friend,' the biggest and loudest of the three replies, 'do you see that there sword over yonder on the carpet? Bit frightening, isn't it! Oh - you don't think so! Well, I'll tell you something, friend - seeing as you seem to be such a fine judge and connoisseur of drinks, with your fancy ways - I can tell you that I am a connoisseur, as well, but of killing. Aye. And when I am charging at a soldier, and all he's got is a wee musket with a bayonet on the end, there is nothing he can do - *nothing,* but turn and run. There's many a redcoat has already showed me his backside in the heat of battle, and those that didn't are to be found in pieces on the road back yonder.'

But suddenly the rebels' attentions are drawn elsewhere, and Matthew's also, because at the doors to the room can be seen the most incongruous site of the two young daughters of the McNiel's, standing in their night-gowns and staring in curiosity at the outlandish men who have brought such disruption to their home, for they would probably never have seen such specimens before, such grubby bare legs, such beards!

'Why hello, pretty Lassies!' one of them says. 'Won't you come in - we shall not bite, you know!'

Both frightened and clutching at each other's arms, the younger of the two becomes tearful, the older one more stoic. But the worst of it is when Matthew catches the look in the eyes of the soldiers as they stare back - and he is appalled at what he suspects would be going through their minds. They seem about to get to their feet to fetch the girls, and Matthew prepares to step up also to prevent them - but then suddenly the tall figure of Mrs McNiel appears at the doorway behind, all agitated and flustered, gathering the girls up in her arms and crying aloud in anguish as she hurries them away.

How she would be feeling at a time such as this - the utter horror of being under the same roof as so many of these dangerous and lawless men, he can only guess, but it cannot be easy. Matthew sincerely hopes the conversation is not about to turn base, but suddenly, he catches sight through the window, and so do they, of a courier coming up the pathway. Hurried footsteps are heard on the marble floor as he enters followed by a cold blast of air from outside rushing through the hallway and into the room.

'Mr Wildish, if you please?' a voice calls out as the man quickly locates the drawing room and coming to the door calls Matthew's name once more. Getting to his feet, Matthew goes to meet him, only to learn to his shock that he is requested to attend General Murray once again at his earliest convenience. And the reason for it causes his heart to skip a beat and then to pound wildly in response. For it is none other than His Highness, Charles Edward Stuart who wishes to see him.

Upon receipt of the surprise summons to attend the Prince, Matthew finds himself once again outside, cloaked and hatted, retracing his steps in the company of the messenger the short distance through the snow-covered streets to Exeter House where he is met by General Murray himself in the front hall.

'In your absence this evening, Mr Wildish, we have had a further vigorous exchange of views with the Prince,' he announces in a hushed, discreet voice, though without any preliminary greeting. 'It has not been easy, but he is nearly full-persuaded now of the need to halt our advance and this will almost surely be followed by the decision to retreat. Your testimony contributed to the debate, you'll be pleased to learn, and because of this, His Highness wishes to see you briefly - though you should be advised that when he says "see you" that might well be precisely all that he means: just that. Understand, that you do not address His Highness yourself, not unless invited to do so.'

'I am familiar with the etiquette,' Matthew replies curtly, a rebuke of sorts which Murray takes in good heart, nodding a little apology to him as they go - until, within just a short time, he has escorted him upstairs once again towards the drawing room and where, with a gentle knock at the door, they are shown in by a steward.

Much darker than when he last saw it, the interior of the room is lit by a solitary candelabrum now, and in comparison to all the noise and commotion taking place elsewhere in the building it is also uncannily quiet, the table occupied by just one person, in fact - for here, seated behind the centre of the large, uncluttered expanse of polished mahogany, his eyes cast down, occupied in writing and not looking up at all at their entrance, is a fine-looking young gentlemen in a white powdered bob wig, slight of build, with pale, slender hands framed by lavish and voluminous lace cuffs and with a complexion as fair and as unblemished as a child's. No one speaks as the moments pass. The blue sash or the Order of the Garter is across his left shoulder, Matthew notices, just showing beneath a fine brocaded coat of scarlet and gold. And then, calmly, his work at a point at which he might pause from it, the young man avails himself of a blotter and rolls it over the page. He then looks up and his eyes gaze into those of his visitors. This is, of course, the Bonny Prince himself, Charles Edward Stuart, the Young Pretender. Even had Matthew not been introduced, there could be no doubt in his mind as to whose company he is in. And no, he does not speak, but rather, with just the faintest gesture, he summons Lord Murray to his side - this accomplished with little more than the raising of an eyebrow - and to which the General, marching quickly round towards him, leans over so that the Prince might whisper into his ear, his lips almost without movement, his face expressionless. Murray replies in measured tones, softly also, as if explaining something, solicitous as ever.

Then, abruptly, the prince raises his eyes, his vision settling with a special look of observation upon Matthew. He seems to be examining every detail of Matthew's countenance, his clothing, his hair, his complexion, his very origin perhaps - peering not only into his past, but also into his very soul, the quality and totality of the man standing before him.

So, this is what it is all about, Matthew thinks as he gazes back, engaging the other man's eyes for what seems like an eternity. This is the reason so many men have died and will die; why so many families will suffer, why towns and even whole cities might fall into ruin and desolation: for this one extraordinarily refined and very quiet young man seated at the table, and who considers himself to be the rightful heir to the English throne.

Resuming again their whispered conversation, the Prince and Murray exchange further observations, almost of a trite and casual nature now, it seems - with the Prince appearing somewhat remorseful before he takes up his pen again, and thereby allowing Murray to return to Matthew's side.

'We may go now,' Murray whispers, a gentle hand on Matthew's arm. And then, with hardly having had a moment to assimilate all that has taken place, Matthew finds himself outside in the hall once more without quite knowing how he has gotten there. The door behind him is closed, and his moment of destiny, for good or ill, is over - and all so very quickly. He feels shocked, almost bereft. He wants to go back; he wants to look into the extraordinary pale eyes of the Bonny Prince once more, but he cannot. He may not. He is instead guided by Murray down the stairs and towards the front door; told that he must keep any suggestion of the retreat, which is almost a certainty now, he states, an absolute secret at all costs; and then as they emerge from the portico of the building, the Scotsman bids him a good night - though not before providing Matthew with an armed escort of two men who have, it seems, been waiting for him. Surely not necessary for the short walk back to McNiel's? But Matthew accepts, and the men, volunteers or mercenaries from overseas by the look of them in their well-tailored breeches and braided tunics, greet him with a wry smile as they all go forth together.

'Oh, Mr Wildish?' the softly spoken Murray calls out after him from the doorway as they make their way along the path where the snow has settled thickly once more. 'You have no objections, I take it, if we invite you to accompany us tomorrow upon our journey. I have taken the liberty of placing these gentlemen at your service.'

Matthew understands. Yes, of course - why had he not anticipated as much! And he bows his concordance towards Murray before turning away once more. The men - their breath smelling strongly of alcohol - walk close to him, one each side. And the reason for their solicitude is obvious now. He has been placed under arrest. He has become a prisoner.

# ~ 19 ~
## A WINTER JOURNEY

His two guards, Frenchmen who go by the names of Claude and Jacque, both from a division of Drummond's infantry, remain with him at McNiel's throughout the night, sleeping in turns, stationed outside his loft entrance. But it is a short night. The billeted troops downstairs in the rest of the building, eager to eat, must by necessity rise far in advance of the slow dawn of an overcast December day - while outside, at the campfires upon garden lawns or in the market place, huge, steaming cauldrons of broth or of porridge are already on the boil, providing sustenance to queues of hungry men gathering in the darkness. McNiel is up too, still in his night-cap and dressing gown, hurrying to-and-fro and, with the inextinguishable courtesy of a born gentleman, ensuring that everyone in the house has at least a hot drink of some kind before they leave for the march ahead - soup and bread mostly - a bowl of which Matthew, once dressed and downstairs, gladly consumes under the eagle eyes of his guards. Elsewhere in the house, men standing unceremoniously in all manner of places are devouring freshly baked loaves smeared with butter or honey, or else picking through various items of food filched from neighbouring houses and gardens, bartering with one another all those small but vital necessities that hunger and the impulse of survival bring to a man faced with the prospect of a day's hard marching and possibly fighting.

But where is everybody going? The men, he hears, are being supplied with a fresh issue of powder and shot - just as they would at the approach of a battle - so everyone assumes the direction will be southward to engage the forces of the Duke of Cumberland at last. Matthew, however, suspects something quite different is taking place, and that orders would already have been circulated among the officers to organise the retreat. Unless plans have altered drastically overnight, the majority of the soldiers are simply being deceived.

Amid the chaos, Matthew manages to secure a word with McNiel in the hallway, the poor man doing his best to make sure his valuables and silver plate are not vanishing into the knapsacks and sporrans of the soldiers as they file past on their way out.

'Are you well, Sir?' Matthew inquires.

'Yes, but I am frightened half to death by all of this,' McNiel answers discreetly. 'My dear wife and babes I have locked in our bedchamber. I only hope this will be over shortly.'

'Do not be in any doubt - there will be a retreat,' Matthew whispers. And they will not be coming back.'

'Really?' McNiel inquires under his breath. 'I thought they were off to take Swarkestone bridge, to fight?'

But Matthew shakes his head. 'There would be a mutiny if they knew where they were really going. I will not presume to instruct you on what you should do now, Sir, but I can only hope you will not declare in favour of what is already a doomed enterprise. For the sake of your dear family, I beg you to refrain from action. A better opportunity might present itself one day, but for now, believe me, the settlement we have hoped for is all but lost.'

'I shall exercise caution,' McNiel responds, just as a soldier, his musket slung over his shoulder, shuffles past towards the exit, barefoot but otherwise fully clad in his Highland plaid and drawing McNiel's attention especially in this instance since he still appears to have his breakfast, a bread roll and mutton pie, attached to the silver platter on which it was served. 'Have you forgotten in your haste to leave my plate behind, Sir?' he inquires, taking the valuable object and clasping it tightly.

The soldier looks cross, but because he is being hurried along by the others, and the drums of the muster are already sounding in the market place outside, he grudgingly relinquishes his grasp upon the object, and with a quick mumbled curse, leaves the building.

It is then when McNiel, still clutching a whole quantity of assorted valuables to his breast, notices the two soldiers nearby - clearly not leaving but rather attending upon Matthew himself. 'What's happening? Surely you are not detained by these men?' he asks.

'I am. They tell me it is a precautionary measure. General Murray does not wish me to be captured and interrogated by Cumberland's redcoats and thereby to divulge the retreat. He is reckoning on a quick getaway, and not being pursued for at least a day.'

'I see. You have no choice I take it?'

'No. I have been told I must march with the infantry - my horse, boots and riding accoutrements having already been requisitioned - as alas, have most of the items from your stables, as you know. At least they have left me in possession of my sword. My detention will be but for a short time only, I hope. A gentlemen's agreement.'

'Beware of your hopes, Sir,' McNiel says, a hand on Matthew's shoulder. 'Your detention might be the lesser of two evils at present - for your liberty would, as you say, only leave you at the mercy of the redcoats - or much worse if the locals apprehend you and conclude that you are a rebel deserter or a spy. You will be hanged without ceremony, or else interrogated within an inch of your life.'

And realising the terrible truth in McNiel's statement, Matthew bids him farewell, uniting his fortunes with his French companions - they being the last to vacate the house - and leaving the poor man, he sincerely hopes, to better days and the blessings of peace. But as Matthew reaches the end of the path, a woman, tall, cloaked and hooded, comes running after him. It is Mrs McNiel, he realises, once he is able to discern more of her face - which, even in the half-darkness, and though her eyes are swollen and red from much crying, is one full of kindness and concern.

'You have no cover for your possessions, Mr Wildish,' she cries above the din of the soldiers assembling all around. 'Here, please take this. You will find it well stocked for the road.'

At which, she hands him a knapsack containing, it appears on a cursory inspection, a quantity of food, and some items of warm dry clothing. It has to be inspected by the others, of course, in case it might contain weapons, but nothing is taken from him, and it is with great pleasure and gratitude that he slips the knapsack over his shoulders and tightens the straps.

'Thank you. Thank you so very much, Ma'am,' he says with a bow, though there is no further opportunity for gallantry as his unchosen companions are anxious to be gone; and with firm hands they guide him away.

Having set off prior to any semblance of proper daylight, and marching ostensibly southward to engage the enemy, the mood of the men is one of reasonable good cheer at first, with very few among them who appear to know in what direction they are really going. Gradually, however, and as the more astute begin to comprehend, with the advancing light it becomes clear that they are in fact retracing their steps, marching northwards again, along familiar ground and past landmarks on the road that they would have observed only a couple of days ago - and at which the mood begins to alter - until finally, shortly after dawn and with the direction of the sun, albeit masked by cloud, most obviously to their rear, everyone begins to understand that they can only be retreating. A sense of disgust and betrayal sweeps through the ranks - and after which nothing can be heard from any of the men but grumbling and exclamations of rage. Highlanders do not turn, they say. Highlanders do not retreat. To have come thus far, to have been but a four-day march from London, and yet to abandon the venture like this is an abomination to them.

Nor does the weather appear to be offering very much cheer. It remains heavily overcast with flurries of snow once more - and bitterly cold. The army itself, meanwhile, and together now in almost its entirety, is truly vast, Matthew realises, because from time to time, whenever a vantage point or high ground presents itself, he is able to look down at the road ahead, down towards the vast serpentine ribbon of marching men - the reds and ochre colours of their plaid the predominant hue, an unending rivulet of dull scarlet, reminding him of blood haemorrhaging from a vessel - and with all the lugubrious pack horses, mules and wagons among them, ranging as far as the eye can see along the same line - their combined heat rising as mist into the air, taking all that creature-vitality and dispersing it far and wide beneath the grey sky.

Over the course of the day, Matthew, overhearing or occasionally also contributing to episodes of conversation, must by necessity be subject to a somewhat enforced lesson regarding the conduct and method of marching men, the bravado and counterfeit show of strength that is *de rigueur* among them. It is a mask that must never slip, he learns - for no weakness must ever be shown. He also learns much about the structure of the Highland army itself, of all the different clans comprising it, their histories, their chieftains and all their differing loyalties - the MacLean's, the Cameron's, the Frazer's and so on. After a while, his head begins to spin with such an overload of information. At least it is mildly entertaining - and for this he is grateful, since there is not much else to punctuate the monotony of the march, at least not until later that same afternoon when, as they approach the village of Ashbourne, there comes the sound of galloping horses, the vibration of their iron hooves within the hard frozen ground audible at a distance as several guards and officers, perhaps with Lord Murray and even the Bonnie Prince among them, advance along the road behind - for Matthew has heard that Charles is no longer marching at the head of his army, something that once endeared him so much to his men. His retreat must now be swift. Clean, resplendent, cloaked and hatted, tall in the saddle, they thunder past - so close to all the poor wretches on foot, unheeding as they go of any hazard, indifferent to all the mud thrown up into faces, or of the proximity of stirrup and jagged spur so close to those negotiating the narrow highway. Such arrogance! Matthew is almost certain that he recognises one of them - General Drummond it is, the one member of the council of war who had wanted to take the campaign to London.

Yes, it is him for sure, Matthew concludes a moment later as, unexpectedly, the man reins in his horse. Coming to a position just behind and where Matthew's two French minders are tarrying, he leans down from the saddle to speak with them, and then as Matthew glances back over his shoulder once more, he notices how their eyes turn to him briefly as they talk; their faces devious, as if discussing his fate. It might be something benign, Matthew thinks, but most likely not - since the look that Drummond throws in his direction as he passes without word or salutation before galloping away in pursuit of the others is none too kindly. It verges on contempt, Matthew thinks, for Drummond would be well aware how the decision to retreat was, at least in part, a result of his, Matthew's, interference. And from that moment on, his two companions become far less amicable, electing to speak with each other exclusively in their own language - not realising that Matthew, being a fluent French speaker after his years in Paris, is able to understand what they say. Most of it is typical of their kind, for they are mercenaries, of no loyalty but to themselves, and their speech reveals a woeful lack of education and manners - their imminent return to the town of Carlisle apparently being what interests them the most, a place where they won a significant victory during the previous days of the campaign and where they hope to be doing 'a good bit of whoring again,' as they put it. How very unpleasant, Matthew concludes, and so he endeavours instead to turn his attention to the sights and sounds of the extraordinary landscape in which he finds himself, because it really is quite spectacular, he has to admit.

Strange - that he has never been this far north in his own country, a peculiar omission considering how widely he has travelled throughout most of Europe, doing the *Grand Tour* through France and Italy, and touching upon the Low Countries and Flanders en route. Yet here in England - his own England - the landscape and customs of parts such as this are as alien to him as the most remote and exotic of continents: a wild, rugged England, it is, with mountains and peaks - and these already appearing, even at a distance, to be taller, more exposed and unforgiving than he could ever have imagined, towering so high and steep that at first when he had seen them this morning he had mistaken them for clouds upon the horizon.

These are the Pennines, of course, the 'Backbone of England' as they are called - a term which, even as a child, had always struck Matthew as peculiar because it was always evident, looking at the maps in the geography books at school in Dublin, that the 'backbone' never really got started until half way up the page, towards Scotland. But here they are now, laid out for his edification: the vast, stark mountains of the North, drawing him ever closer, becoming ever more magnificent in their snow-capped isolation. All rather beautiful, in a haunting, frightening kind of way, he thinks. And so the day passes.

That first night's accommodation, billeted indoors and spent on the floor of an inn at Ashbourne, proves tolerable enough. But the march the next day is harder than the previous one and must, they are told be done at a faster pace, moreover - the redcoats being aware of their retreat now and, it is rumoured, coming closer all the while - with reports, not usually verified, that sightings of Cumberland's light horse have been detected on the eminences of the hills behind, while somewhere the other side of the mountains, far to the East and unseen, the substantial redcoat army of General Wade would, they say, be marching, too, flanking them and, unlike their own ragged stream of demoralised and hungry soldiers, would be a well-nourished, well-supplied body of professional fighting men. For the time being they remain a distant threat - but for how much longer?

To Matthew, now, the road ahead really seems at times to be without end, with nothing but walking to be done - walking through bleak heathland or bog, through barren winter pasture, always the peaks of the mountains to their right, and with always a target, of some kind, their sights set on one place or another, on some village or farm settlement ahead and which, once reached, is celebrated merely with a moment's pause, some ghastly broth or piece of grisly bone to gnaw on, and then immediately superseded by a new target, a new destination, and then marching, marching once again - until, with the approach of afternoon and with still no let-up to the pace, his feet finally begin to ache and then, a mile later, to become painful. He knows that he needs some proper walking boots instead of the ridiculously impractical soft-leather shoes and spatterdashes that he has been left with after the commandeering of his horse and riding accoutrements. A mile or two farther on, and he discovers that his shoes are actually falling apart, cracking at the sole, so that his feet are becoming damaged and blistered. A request to a sergeant for some decent boots is merely met with derision. 'Impossible.' The concern, therefore, for Matthew is the exposure of any open wounds to the filth and the mud of the road - walking as he must in the wake of hundreds of men spitting, vomiting and relieving themselves without shame anywhere and everywhere they choose. For a while, it worries him, but then he becomes numb to the pain and to the danger also, and even ceases to notice the squalor and the filth beneath his feet. He is lifted above it by some unfamiliar necessity, carried into a space of utter indifference. There is only the march now, only the eternal presence of men ahead, behind, at his side, and many of them bare-foot themselves, he notices - so why should he worry! Why should he be so precious, he thinks, as he casts off his broken footwear and hurls the pieces across the road and into the distance. He becomes a cipher, an undistinguished smudge upon the trail of the great march northward. And should he by any misfortune fall by the wayside and perish in the mud it would hardly make an impression, scarcely a ripple in the relentless torrent of indifference and cruelty by which a retreating army such as this is sustained. And so he keeps walking … walking, walking, hoping not to stumble or fall, for in so doing he fears he might never be able to rise again.

And then just as he thought it could not possibly get any worse, they are informed that this evening, at the outskirts of Macclesfield, they must sleep in an open barn, with merely some filthy straw for bedding. He has never felt so cold - a cold that seeps into his very bones, and which never once allows him to sleep for more than a minute at a time. And as he lies upon the ground in the darkness, shivering and with every item of clothing he possesses upon him and all to no avail, his thoughts wander into the most unfamiliar and depressing territory, the kind of bleak delirium that might be the very precursor of death, he feels. For death surely cannot be far away in such an extremity of discomfort.

Being compelled to listen to the assorted snores and grunts of his fellow travellers freezing likewise, his sense of hearing becomes uncommonly acute, and he becomes aware of every scrap of conversation nearby, and that of two men in particular - whispering mostly - furtive, gruff and disputatious, for they cannot sleep either. Their language for the most part is French; so these must surely be his companions, Claude and Jacque, lying nearby. Inevitably, unavoidably, Matthew translates their words as they mumble and hiss and curse their way through their broken fragments of speech.

'I tell you she had it coming to her,' one says - Matthew is not sure which of the pair is speaking.

'You shouldn't have tried it on,' the other admonishes him. 'You could see she was a maid - not just some tart to be doing the likes of us a turn.'

A pause ensues, and then the other one grunts and curses: 'She was a stuck-up little bitch!' he says, his voice resentful and derisive. 'All I did was give her a slap. I didn't know she was going to fall over, did I! She shouldn't have led us on like that.'

Matthew, with a terrible sense of revelation dawning upon him, is appalled - because he knows now that they can only be referring to the tragedy of that poor servant girl at the inn in Derby - the one McNiel had told him had been slain. He had heard, later, that she was no more than seventeen years; a decent girl, they said, of a good family and hoping soon to be married.

'If Murray finds out, you will be court-martialled and shot, you know that, my friend?' one of them continues, most likely Claude, whose voice is slightly deeper than the other.

'Who's about to tell on me, then? I'll do for anyone who as much as breathes a word of it!'

'Not I, Jacque, not I,' comes the frantic whisper. 'My God I swear I am going mad. I'm the same as you - I haven't had a woman in weeks. What we all need is a good battle, to take a town

- take it good and proper with a bit of plunder. This campaign has been a joke under Murray. Too many scruples.'

'Yea - the bastard English and Scots, they're all the same,' Jacque curses. 'What the hell are we doing here. I'm going back to France for soldiering when all this is over. Give myself a treat.'

'Yea, me too, my friend. Me too.'

And with that, they fall silent.

So, Matthew thinks, feeling most distressed, one of these scoundrels, has done the deed. One of these shabby little men he is travelling with is a murderer - Jacque by the sounds of it, and the other not much better. How very dreadful it all seems.

Eventually, closing his eyes yet again and which he realises are full of tears this time, he does manage to fall asleep: a few minutes of fitful slumber, only for his peace to be shattered a moment later by the sound of drums from the road. Those hideous drums. And although dawn is hours away, it is nevertheless time for everyone to rouse themselves and prepare. His own rations and all the generous additions supplied by Mrs McNiel upon his departure, have all been consumed by now, and nothing much is forthcoming, therefore, but cold bread to nourish him and some kind of dried biscuit that is inedible in the absence of any liquid. And thus as the day begins, with hunger in his belly and with limbs as stiff and frozen as a cadaver, he knows that he must march again.

'Here!' Claude calls to him as he struggles with his knapsack ready for the off, speaking to him as if addressing an animal as he throws down a pair of old boots to the ground at his feet. 'The owner of these won't be needing them any longer,' he adds with irony as Matthew seizes them, a pair of old woollen socks still inside - for these boots, he is informed, are those of one who has frozen to death in the night and buried with haste in a ditch already.

Matthew feels no remorse as he pulls them on. The boots are so comfortable. Becoming once again the favourite of fortune, he feels happier than he has in days - and foolishly he thanks both of his companions with the words: *Merci mon ami.'*

But the two Frenchmen look at him not with good-natured approval as he, in his unguarded state, had half-expected they might, but instead with the utmost unease and then suspicion; and he only requires a brief moment of sobriety to comprehend why. 'What a fool you are, Wildish!' he mumbles to himself. For would they not thereby conclude, or at the very least strongly suspect, that he would have been privy to their conversations - including those concerning their crimes at Derby? Of course. They know now that he knows: and they appear none too comfortable with the idea.

He has no time to dwell on his indiscretion, however. For even before proper daylight lends its assistance, they are off again, marching - destination Macclesfield this time, or is it Manchester? He forgets. And it really doesn't matter. He just obeys the orders. For now and always it seems there will only ever be the march, the endless tramping and squelching of thousands of feet through mud, interrupted only by the sounds of the occasional explosion from far back as bridges are blown up to prevent the redcoat's pursuit - or at least that is what they are told. In fact, everyone knows it is just a matter of time now until the rearguard will be forced to engage the enemy, catching up all the while. It sets Matthew to thinking: there is no rationale any longer for his continued detention. He would far prefer to take his chances alone now, anyway, even if it meant being captured by Cumberland's men - who could surely be no worse than present company.

'Gentlemen,' Matthew begins at one stage, attempting to strike up some useful dialogue as his captors happen to draw alongside, 'all of the redcoat armies are surely aware of our retreat by now. You could release me, therefore, could you not?'

'We have no orders to let you go, friend,' Claude replies, not bothering to look at him as he speaks, simply marching onwards, his head down, almost buried in his chest to avoid the driving sleet.

'Surely your original orders would not have been to detain me indefinitely?' Matthew argues.

'What do you mean? I don't understand,' Claude replies, his voice waspish and irritable above the wind. So Matthew puts it in French - though their response is still far from encouraging. They cannot release him without orders, they tell him, and even when pressed to explain the exact wording of their original commission, they refuse to do so, or cannot do so. And the very officers, Murray or Drummond, or whoever it was who gave those orders could, they tell him, be a hundred miles away by now. Matthew can only feel disappointed, bitterly so, that his first attempt at a rational appeal to his captors has been dismissed out of hand. It seems a hopeless situation - so that he is forced to contemplate the dreadful and dangerous alternative that at sometime in the near future he is simply going to have to make a run for it. But how? Even though the pistol that Jacque carries in his belt is not primed and he probably has no dry powder for it anyway, both men are armed with sabres - awful weapons of slashing and cutting which they would know well how to use. And although his own sword is a fine enough weapon against its own kind, with its sharp thrusting point and a modest edge to the blade to prevent grappling, it is no match for the long, razor-sharp sabres that could slice the top of a man's skull away at a stroke. Together, the Frenchmen would be impossible to overcome, and of course everywhere, at almost every moment of the day, they are surrounded by whole troops of men with muskets at the ready to shoot any deserters. It is a depressing, intractable situation - and he fears he will finish up in Edinburgh before too long at this rate, and even begins to wonder if he will ever see his home again? Meanwhile, his captors are already turning their talk to the noble recreation of whoring once more, and of getting drunk.

With no desire to converse anymore with the Frenchmen, Matthew weary now and feeling often faint with hunger, turns his attention instead to whatever snippets of information he can glean from those marching with him, strong Highland men who, like himself, are all fully occupied with the task of personal survival. He wonders if there is anything he can learn that might help him devise an escape; or even to locate a bit of extra food, since many now appear to be foraging for themselves. But it is all rumour, nothing substantial, and in his half-delirious state all their stories simply mingle and become lost among all the various fleeting images, sights and sounds, half-heard, half-imagined that surround him; of oaths and curses; of arguments and disputes; of reports of altercations with farmers over the taking of their livestock or grain; of Highlanders incurring the wrath of locals by sharpening their swords on the gravestones of churchyards; of a Vicar's wife driving soldiers from her doorstep and who, they say, died of fright a short time after; of the inn keeper beaten to death for refusing to open his tavern, or of another, a gentleman farmer, his face cut with a sabre for refusing to relinquish his daughter's horse. There are stories of people in a village who took refuge in their church, locking themselves inside, only to have the solders open fire through the door, leaving it peppered with musket shot and inflicting heaven-knows what injuries to those inside; stories of villagers, emboldened by the ragged state of the infantry men passing through their streets, to throw rocks or even to fire shotguns from hidden places. There is even a story of a mortar cannon left behind somewhere by careless soldiers and the furore this engenders as its bearers, exhausted and demoralised, abandon it and desert from the army altogether. And as if all this were not enough, there are tales, perhaps even more dishonourable, of some among the deserters turning in desperation to crime - of robbing travellers in the way of common highwaymen and even, it is rumoured, of rape.

And so, Matthew Wildish, what price your refined tastes and pretty manners in such company as this? he asks himself as they scramble across yet another slush-covered ditch. What price all your soft feather beds and clean linen now? What price your braided waistcoats, your white stockings and kid gloves; your own valet brushing the tiniest stray hair from your shoulder as you prepare for the fragrant delights of the theatre or masquerade? What price your dancing and your flirtation with the ladies, your gallant smile and practised flourish of the tricorn as you bow to a pretty face or fluttering fan? What price the gentle lips and welcome embrace, the lilting sigh, the tender kiss in a moonlit bower? Where is Matthew Wildish now, that devotee of fine wines, of poetry and all the glorious music of the orchestra and the human voice? The answer is that he is left far behind, that dear man - somewhere in London, in the sparkling capital that is no more than a fabled memory to him now and at a distance that might just as well be a million miles. Matthew Wildish, in other words, is no more. He is dead - as dead as the man in whose boots he is marching, and almost as empty and frozen of all feeling as if he were lying beside the poor wretch back there in his grave.

Evening approaches, and some of the ever increasing number of stragglers, among whom Matthew and his two guards are numbered, deliberately fall back to take advantage of a small cluster of deserted farm buildings off the main highway. Here, the three of them, having caught themselves a rabbit, locate a yard that provides excellent shelter and where, backs against an angle between two walls, they are able to build a small fire over which Claude is busy brewing a stew while Matthew prepares bread for toasting, cutting it into pieces with his knife. They have chosen well. Plenty of dry bedding is available in the barn, and they have a roof of sorts under which to shelter later on. Alternatively, they could, Matthew suggests, ever hopeful, always emulate the many hundreds of men who have already slipped away and vanished from the disorderly ranks. But this proposal is met with universal indifference from both men, and despite Matthew's misgivings that the smoke from their fire might draw unwelcome attention, neither seems in the least perturbed by any possibility of danger - until, that is, the sound of a distant explosion is heard, and then another much closer; and it makes everyone feel jittery.

'Some fool playing with that captured mortar,' Jacque remarks and then spits and curses for good measure.

'You don't think Cumberland would be marching through the night, do you?' Matthew speculates, turning to gauge the reaction of each of his companions in turn, but who remain as surly and as blasé as ever.

'No chance! They need to rest and stuff their bellies same as us,' Claude remarks and stokes up the embers, eager perhaps to have the cooking over and done with and for the fire to be out, after all, Matthew thinks, for even the Frenchmen now appear to be apprehensive over the presence of the smoke. Would the owner of the farm be seeing it? Without the proximity of the main body of Highlanders, they are vulnerable.

With time, and with the common purpose of consuming their food, Matthew begins to entertain hopes that now is perhaps the time to broach again the subject of his captivity; that if only he can humour his companions a little more they might be persuaded to turn a blind eye and allow him to escape especially with the expedient of a modest bribe, for he still has some money on him.

'Forgive me for raising this issue again, gentlemen,' he begins with studied courtesy. 'But even if you wish to remain with the army, as you insist, you could let *me* off, could you not?' he adds, probing for some reaction. 'I would be pleased to show my gratitude with a little beer money. I do not have much, but what I have I would gladly exchange for your indulgence, to smooth over any misunderstandings concerning your orders.'

But Jacque, getting to his feet and walking away, seems displeased at the offer. It is getting dark now and difficult for Matthew to see his face. Claude, meanwhile, his thickset features just visible by the dying embers of the fire, looks similarly troubled, fidgeting restlessly from his resting place between two piers of brickwork where he has set his own substantial bale of straw for comfort. And then, to Matthew's horror, as he glances back to Jacque, he sees that he has drawn his sabre.

'You should know, my fine English friend, there has never been any misunderstandings in our orders,' he states, his back turned away still, his shoulders tense about his ears. 'Our orders regarding you were made clear to us soon after we began the retreat. Our task has never been to detain you indefinitely, as you seem to think, but rather to kill you.'

And as Claude also gets to his feet, and likewise draws forth his sabre, Matthew realises that it is a terrible trap that has been set for him, wanting merely for an occasion such as this to spring it. He is ensnared, caught just as surely as the poor rabbit whose entrails they had removed earlier.

'Anyone not of the army and suspected of being a spy is to be slain,' Jacque declares as he turns, his voice cold and without emotion, his thick, heavy eyebrows knitted together in concentration. 'That is what we were told.'

'Surely such extreme measures are not necessary,' Matthew says, sensing the inevitability of what is about to happen and compelled with urgency to his feet also. 'This is surely some misguided desire for revenge - from your general Drummond. Come now, gentlemen, I think this is the case, is it not?'

But there is no response, at least not from Jacque.

'We could have been in London by now,' Claude shouts, his throat hoarse with emotion and pointing an accusing finger. 'We could have been walking down the streets with a wench on each arm and food in our bellies, the victory there for the taking.'

Matthew knows that his only hope, and it is a slim one, is to maintain a triangular formation to the men, and this he does. Drawing his own weapon and flexing the blade with his free hand gripping low towards the tip, he strides in a circular fashion, provocative in his movements, taking advantage of the expanse of the yard itself - his heart beginning to pound in his chest.

'Yeah. And what have we got instead!' Jacque cries in agreement, his voice also gaining in vehemence. 'What have we but dishonour and hunger, our men dying by the roadside or deserting in droves - and you and your turncoat friends to thank for it!'

'No, Sir,' Matthew argues, still in motion, keeping the formation, keeping them at arm's length. 'It is not my fault. There were many sources of intelligence at play during the discussions at Derby. Reason and logic were also applied.'

'Your reason and logic be damned!' Jacque cries closing in on him with determination - and with Claude stepping up at the same time, one each side.

Matthew knows it is his life or theirs.

'Well and good, gentleman!' he announces, hand on hip, chin raised. 'Do your damndest - but I shall mark you both well before you conclude your business, for you will find me somewhat more intractable, I trust, than a poor maid in a tavern.'

At this, they seem mad with rage, seething with pent up frustration - rushing towards him, everything happening so fast. But again Matthew leaps to form a triangle, while at the same time pinking with his sword point into Claude's face as the man advances, which makes him flinch, allowing Matthew to stoop - exceptionally low, as he throws his rear foot back - just in time to avoid the anticipated swipe of Jacque's sabre from the other side. It has been aimed at Matthew's head and, failing to meet with its target, the momentum of its swing takes the aggressor stumbling off-balance and thus exposing his side - at which Matthew is able to rise and thrust upwards, straight under the ribs, severing the aorta of his opponent or piecing the heart - he knows not which - but upon withdrawal the blood pours forth, audible in its intensity and accompanied by a terrible gurgling scream as the man collapses onto his back - and where, with the addition of a crack of an unprotected skull on the flagstones he has come to a place from which, Matthew knows, he will not rise again.

With stunned silence, a look of utter bewilderment on Claude's face at the rapidity of it all, for the entire engagement had lasted no more than a few seconds, there comes an inevitable pause in proceedings, and Matthew allows the man to go tend to his colleague, cradling his head in his hands, the blood pumping forth from his abdomen into the muddy ground, though more moderately now and with an ever slowing rhythm until it becomes all but a trickle.

'You bastard! Claude cries leaping to his feet, the knuckles white around the hilt of his sabre, clutched so tightly, almost blind with rage. Matthew knowing it will be relatively easy to deal with him in this state, is unconcerned, and simply positions himself *en garde,* ready to do the terrible deed once more.

But just then there is a peculiar whistling sound in the air, not like wind but more shrill, and a split second later a loud thud like a gigantic rock landing - accompanied by a bright flame and an explosion so powerful that it throws both men, whether from force of the blast or else by instinctive response, immediately off their feet and onto the ground. A mortar shot has landed near to them, and shrapnel has peppered the walls of the yard, some pieces appearing to have hit Claude in the legs, who cries out with it and, unlike Matthew who is up immediately, seems incapable of rising.

'There, you ruddy fool!' Matthew shouts, advancing on him, angry even though the man's proximity has acted as a shield and saved him from injury. '*There* you have the enemy - the real one. We should all of us have been more vigilant. But all you could think of was your pathetic revenge.'

'Spare me!' Claude cries, struggling once more to get to his feet, but still he cannot rise.

'Do not fear, Sir. I shall not allow you to seduce me into another act of despicable violence, for that man's demise over there pains me more than even the thought of my own. And you have been the cause of it.'

'Are they coming, the redcoats?' Claude asks, unheeding of Matthew's reprimand. 'I cannot move.'

He really is badly wounded, Matthew perceives now - the pain etched into his face; a certain incoherence in his speech, also, as the initial shock of the explosion wears off.

'Who gave you orders to kill me - Drummond, was it?' Matthew demands, though sheathing his sword now.

'No. We lied to you. We had no orders, none but that we should detain you for a couple of days. But we thought you would tell - about the girl. You heard us speaking. You knew what we did. It wasn't my idea,' he whimpers, his head rolling in a curious fashion, maybe already beginning to lose consciousness.

'Then God help you,' Matthew says, his knapsack on his back once more and already preparing to make good his escape, for they can hear the sound of drums in the distance and the intermittent crackle of musket fire. 'You must look to your own preservation now, my friend, and think no more of curtailing mine.'

And with that, taking to his heels as quickly as possible, Matthew leaves his would-be executioner to his fate.

# ~ 20 ~
## ELEMENTS OF CHOICE
## AND TEMPTATION

The voice is a delight: the sound of her singing, accompanied by harpsichord. And it is this, more than anything, the gentle, lilting rhythm of the music that brings everything back to him, the rhythm exactly as he had heard it again and again, a measure of his own footsteps, walking, striding relentlessly on: the presence of her sweet voice and the aria he knew so well and whose words could not have been more incongruous amid the bleak, snow-bound landscape in which he had heard them:

*Where'er you walk, cool gales shall fan the glade;*
*Trees, where you sit, shall crowd into a shade:*
*Where'er you tread, the blushing flow'rs shall rise;*
*And all things flourish where'er you turn your eyes.*

How bizarre it had seemed - this evocation of warmth and pleasure - for the snow had been deep and treacherous beneath his feet then, the mountainous slopes unforgiving. Never had he been so close to losing his life. The awful fight with the Frenchmen had been bad enough, but afterwards it was worse, the dangers more pervasive - knowing, too, that Johanna and Sam would be worried half to death over his absence, and thus conjuring up the notion, even in his utter desolation and loneliness on the mountain trail, of a kind of togetherness, as if her voice were real, sent to him across the skies by the power of thought to become the very stuff that had sustained him through his hunger and pain as he stumbled his way southwards, always southwards, thinking of her, Johanna, time and time again, surely just as she would have been thinking of him.

At first it was by night that he would walk, the overcast and starless sky above, and with merely a light of some distant farmhouse or village nearby to cheer him - the existence of humankind, even if unapproachable through fear he would be thought of as a spy or deserter, and other lights, too, which often seemed to elude him, to be extinguished and vanish before he could ever quite identify their source or location - while by day he would hide, in barns or in shepherds' huts, beneath bushes or under stony outcrops, and sleep as best he could. And then, as soon as the threat from the armies of Wade and Cumberland, proceeding north in the other direction, had abated, he would at last take courage to walk by day instead, more confident by then, guided by a more substantial light, the sun, or what was visible of it behind the mists and swirling clouds, signifying the direction in which he must go, making use of a combination of well worn pathways or pack horse trails and, eventually, the roadway itself leading down into Derby. This ever present beacon of light in one form or another, combined with the sound of her voice had blended into a most persuasive alchemy, a determination and a faith that he would survive, and survive he did.

Even now, seated in the drawing room of his dear friend's home in Greenwich, even in the company of familiar and kindly faces, all full of Christmas cheer and celebration, the recollection of it, and the triumph of it, too, remains constant and, at times, almost too much to bear. For yes, it *was* a triumph - or at least it had felt that way to him - the triumph of having battled the elements, to have found his way back to the very place where he had been captured, and then to McNiel's home - a place where he experienced perhaps the most surprising revelation of all, for whereas at the very start of his journey when he had first set off from London, his estimation of McNiel had been little more than that of a foe, one who must be overcome and deceived, now upon Matthew's return from the hills that day, in his very hour of need, the man had revealed himself to be the kindest and most solicitous of people. How they had welcomed him, he and his good wife, and with such generosity. And how he had slept! - slept for a whole day and night - and then, upon waking, eaten as he had never eaten before.

Thus, restored to something like his old self, and wanting so much to reflect a little kindness back, he had gone with McNiel to the Dolphin Inn to inquire of the whereabouts of the family of she who was slain there, so they should no longer suffer in ignorance over the terrible event that had taken their daughter from them. They were humble people, good people, and took great solace,

Matthew felt, by his testimony - that the culprit had been uncovered and that retribution had been visited upon him.

And thus, his duties discharged, thankful to be alive, and even at one time having joined the McNiels for a service in their secret chapel, he was able to continue his journey home - though this time by stagecoach to London, finding, upon his arrival, that his own apartments were mercifully empty of unwelcome visitors and, thanks to Sam and the good offices of Francis his valet, secure and undamaged. What a relief.

It was, moreover, as he soon discovered, a very different sort of London to that which he had left just a couple of weeks previous - with the gentle snow here falling upon a calm and unusually hushed capital that could, it seemed to him, scarce persuade itself that everything was well - a London preparing for Christmas, with a fair in full swing upon the frozen Thames, and an almost palpable sense of relief that the invaders had been repulsed, at least for the time being. Peace, in fact, had never felt quite so peaceful. And this evening, on the very eve of Christmas itself, and as Johanna's charming song reaches its conclusion, everyone present applauds with joyous gratitude for their deliverance, and Matthew among them applauding with perhaps the greatest enthusiasm of all.

'Anyway, my dear, you can definitely count me in,' Lady Snatchal declares speaking to Johanna from her place on the settee where most of the long seat is taken up by her vast gown, spread out to display the stunning opulence of embroidery upon all the various black silks and purple brocades that comprise her skirts and elaborately laced bodice.

Johanna, far more elegant and simply attired in cream satin, has been mooting the possibility of taking the waters at Bath this coming season, and Lady Snatchal, no doubt thinking as much of the pleasant society of the town itself and of all the assemblies and masquerades that take place during the spring and summer months, is perhaps rather predictably all for it - 'once the ruddy weather warms up a bit, naturally,' she adds, accompanied by a shiver of the shoulders by way of emphasis - and to which Sam, ever the attentive host, immediately responds by stirring himself from his place at the harpsichord in order to throw another log upon the fire - though the great Yule log of Christmas that the men had dragged back earlier today, this being of a size that must burn for the next twelve days, of course, remains untouched upon the floor by the grate, no one having ventured yet to manoeuvre it into the fireplace, let alone try to light it! Working with the poker to stoke up the embers, his face remains downcast, betraying more than a little indifference to the proposal. A journey of miles all the way to the famous spa town, and then, as he observes, 'to sit around all day consuming gallons of foul water or else watching people float up and down like stranded whales in the pools,' is not at all to his liking.

Everyone smiles, aware that Johanna is always trying to turn him into something more adventurous: a futile exercise against one who is, by his own admission, so very fond of his home comforts.

'Doctors of medicine testify that immersion in the hot springs is most beneficial,' Johanna protests, though with good cheer, as she returns to her seat - this being a luxurious pile of cushions near to the fire and occupied at present by her two bonny children, John and Samantha who, in the company of their Nanny, are doing their best to be inconspicuous so as not to have to retire too early for bed. There is also the ubiquitous Boris, the terrible pug as Matthew still unavoidably thinks of him, chasing around after any quarry that happens to take his fancy, real or imagined, or else chewing at any shoe he can find not attached to its owner's foot - for everyone is very relaxed and merry, warming their toes at the fireside or resting their stockinged feet on stools or cushions. 'Moreover, the waters once taken internally do engender, they say, a most noble purging of the system,' Johanna continues in a voice of suitable gravity, 'these being both emetic and laxative in nature.'

'Huh!' Sam responds in a gruff voice, returning to the keyboard and making a show of leafing through his sheet music for the next recital. 'Why, I could drink of any ditch water hereabouts and achieve the same results. The difference is only in the reputation of one and the anonymity of the other.'

Noises of accord can be detected from Lord Snatchal, who would in any case be expected to rejoice more in the prospect of the annual festivals of racing at Epsom Downs or Newmarket than in any excursion to Bath this coming spring and who, seated close to the fire and taking a pinch of snuff between finger and thumb, sniffs loudly and nods his head with additional male scepticism regarding, 'the dubious attractions of any of the popular spa towns,' a statement which prompts a by-now decidedly morose Lady

Snatchal to declare very much for Johanna once more, and the pledge that they will therefore go together, alone, without the encumbrance of the men, who can stick with their tobacco and snuff in some filthy old tavern for all she cares.

Despite all this banter and friendly baiting of one another, it is, Matthew reflects, most pleasant to see the Woolveston's family home at this season of the year, the drawing room hung with loops of cane entwined with holly, ivy and fragrant rosemary, and with little figurines of the nativity, Mary, Joseph and the baby Jesus placed inside, framed and secured with coloured ribbons. Red apples and even-redder berries have also been included - and some tiny candles that Johanna occasionally attends to and replaces as they burn down, much to the delight of the children. There is a sideboard upon which fine wines and tasty items of jugged food and fruits are displayed - and the air is full of the most enchanting aromas of spices and mulled wine.

'Anyway, Matthew, do remind us once again, won't you,' Sam pipes up, appearing exceptionally inquisitive once more as he takes up a ladle and helps himself to a glass of punch, 'just how exactly did you manage to overcome so many of your captors? A most fascinating tale,' he adds filling Matthew's glass for him also.

Although Sam has heard the account of Matthew's intrepid escapade to the North on at least two occasions earlier this evening, a journey that has already taken on legendary proportions in the estimation of some of Matthew's listeners, he seems especially keen on having it retold yet again - most odd - as though he were trying to catch him out all the while.

'Oh well, I didn't exactly need to overcome the entire Jacobite army, you know!' Matthew responds with a look of kindly admonishment towards his friend. 'There was really only a modest contingency of men keeping their eye on me,' he adds, faintly aware that, having perhaps consumed a little too much punch already, he is succumbing to a certain tendency to exaggerate his achievements.

'A modest contingency? Really!' Sam retorts, more than a little expressive of suspicion, Matthew thinks, his face waxing scarlet by the light the hearth fire. 'I thought you said earlier there were just a couple of them looking after you?'

'Oh, did I? Oh, yes … well, two or three,' Matthew says, continuing to feed off the silent adulation of the lovely Johanna and

Lady Snatchal, their chins resting on interlaced hands, continuing to gaze admiringly in his direction. He has never been so feted. 'The numbers varied. But I fought them off, you know; hand-to-hand combat until I eventually got away. We were engaged in a ferocious rearguard action at the time, you see. So I had to dive down the hillside into a hollow to let the enemy pass, and then I escaped by moonlight along a narrow ravine in which a frozen stream lay hidden in the undergrowth.'

'Oh, how exciting!' Lady Snatchal exclaims and fans herself vigorously.

'Yes - yes, that's right. It was!' Matthew echoes with escalating enthusiasm. 'That night I had to sleep in a barn with the cattle, otherwise I would surely have perished. A milkmaid discovered me in the morning, took pity on me and brought me some provisions. And then ... well, I just had to carry on, naturally, clambering over mountains, fighting my way through blizzards and hurricanes and all the enormous, terrible wild animals they have up north, you know, until eventually - and armed with little more than a pen-knife by that stage - I managed to claw my way back into Derby. Safe at last, but only just by the skin of my teeth.'

'My hero!' Johanna exclaims with unguarded admiration, almost reclining now, her yellow kid slippers kicked off, and abandoning her lace tucker, as well, which she casts aside from her breast as if the heat generated by all the excitement was simply too much to endure.

'*Our* hero, you mean!' Lady Snatchal corrects her, clearly not wishing to allow Johanna to have him all to herself. 'And you say you actually met the Prince - Bonny Prince Charlie?' she adds, almost beside herself by this time.

'Oh, yes, that's right, I did,' Matthew replies proudly. 'The Young Pretender himself.'

'And is he really as right-handsome as they say?' the Countess continues to delve, almost squealing with curiosity, her knees visibly knocking with excitement beneath the great folds of her petticoats.

'Yes - a fine looking gentleman,' Matthew responds. 'Such remarkable blue eyes. So fair, and of course still so very young.'

'Oh, how marvellous!' Lady Snatchal declares as if about to swoon.

'Astonishing, Wildish - astonishing!' Lord Snatchal exclaims,

equally in awe as the revelations keep coming. 'Prince Charles
Stuart himself. I mean, what the devil did the two of you talk
about?'

'What did we talk about? Oh ... this and that. A very - er -
erudite man. Very bright; very bright indeed. Good old Charlie!'

'And you really persuaded him to turn back, to retreat?'
Johanna inquires, her eyes so large, her lovely crescent-shaped
eyebrows as wondrously animated as he has ever seen them.

'Well, I suppose I might have contributed in some small part to
the decision,' Matthew admits. 'Though of course I would prefer it
if we could refrain from making too much of a fuss over all this. I
am not at all for gloating, you see, or wishing to appear boastful in
any sense. Just a matter between the few of us here this evening, if
you please.'

'Of course, dear fellow. Of course!' Lord Snatchal asserts, his
face full of concern and deference still, and snapping his chin back
into position with a little tap of the fingers underneath.

'Anyway, enough of me!' Matthew states with studied modesty,
not very convincingly perhaps. 'Wouldn't it be fun, after hearing
my story again, if everyone else were to tell one, too.'

'What a good idea!' Sam agrees loudly. 'A bit of variety
certainly wouldn't go amiss. Yes, let everyone tell a story. It
doesn't always have to be about *oneself* all the time. Anything at all
to feed the imagination. Let the subject be *Choice* - the choices we
make in life and their implications. How about that?'

'Well, you begin then, darling,' Johanna says, trying to hide her
disappointment at having to leave the wild North and Bonny Prince
Charlie behind at least for the immediate future.

The children and their Nanny, meanwhile, after numerous
diversionary tactics, are finally persuaded with great reluctance to
take their leave - accompanied by kisses all round as Sam, himself
more than willing to take over the entertainment, bustles about in
his chair, adjusting the cushions, and in the manner of an actor
preparing for an announcement at a theatre, draws himself up and
commences his story: 'Ladies and gentlemen, I give you the
notorious incident of The South Sea Bubble.'

A frisson of modest anticipation spreads around the room.

'Yes, the saga of that infamous trading company that almost
plunged the nation into ruin. It was really not that long ago, after
all, when an enterprising gentlemen in the vicinity of Exchange

Alley - an area of the city not unfamiliar to me, as many of you already know - decided he could assist the government with their debt by allowing the public to purchase shares in a special company formed for trading in the Americas - the South Sea Company, as it was called. The monies from selling shares in this would then go to financing the government who would pay back interest to the shareholders based on the projected taxes they would raise from the trade itself. In other words, everyone was going to be a winner - it being such a splendid idea, in fact, that many people, from every level of society, went ahead and purchased shares in the company. The value of the shares rose over the subsequent months, soaring with each fresh issue - as more and more people, even those who would normally never dabble in the stock market, became anxious to participate. Huh! The fear of missing out, you see - it became irresistible. Some chose to invest all of their savings. They sold their property, their jewels, their valuables, even their homes, just to buy South Sea stock - which eventually shot up from a little over £100 a share when first issued to almost £1000 at one stage - even though not a single ship had yet sailed and not a single transaction or trade of any worth had yet been undertaken by the company itself. Extraordinary!

'In fact, the whole thing was a delusion, without any potential for new trade in the region, anyway, because the Spanish already had everything sewn up. Eventually news seeped out that the owners of the company had lost their nerve and dumped all their shares. Well, you can imagine what happened next. People panicked - everyone rushing for the exit at once, as it were, and the price of South Sea shares plummeted overnight. No one could find a buyer - not anywhere. The bubble had burst, and all about the country the most pitiful stories were to be heard; of honest, well-meaning individuals having lost everything; of whole families becoming destitute and cast out of their homes, and of men, suddenly facing ruin or plagued by enormous debts, taking their own lives in despair. And so, ladies and gentlemen, there I must conclude my sorry tale: not a happy ending, alas, but instead a valuable lesson in the importance of the choices we make in life, and also of course, of the dangers inherent in fabricating things or of exaggerating, which I would hazard to suggest is one of the greatest imperfections in any man - would you not agree, Matthew?'

'Oh, yes, indeed, Sam,' Matthew responds, ignoring his friend's intimidating stare. 'A most edifying story, to be sure.'

'Excellent!' Snatchal declares. 'I remember it well, the whole business. I sold my stock near the peak, as a matter of fact. Got a tip-off from the owner - good friend of mine, you know. As for the stock market ... well, it's for the experts not just for any old Tom Dick or Harry. And I should think it'll be a while before any of the common herd go sticking their noses in those parts again - as the actress said to the bishop, what! Anyway, who's next for telling a story? Dorothea, how about you, my dear?'

Lady Snatchal nods her acquiescence - though she seems unusually taciturn and lost for words for a second. 'Well, I don't know really - let me think. All I can say is I am right glad I don't have a story about all them rebels entering London. I can't even imagine how one would cope with the Jacobite army coming to stay, can you! For a start, there simply wouldn't be enough chairs and teacups to go round. It would be right embarrassing. Unless they came to Snatchalcombe House, that is. I suppose we could accommodate the whole lot of them there!'

'Yes, quite, my dear, quite right,' Lord Snatchal confirms. 'But what about a story, Dorothea - come on, my pet, you must have one!'

'Oh, all right. I know what, I'll tell one of them there biblical stories, one that goes right back to Adam and Eve.'

'*Adam and Eve?*' Lord Snatchal echoes, amazed and clearly a little anxious.

'Yes, why not! You see, as we all know, at the time of the Creation, God made Adam and Eve more or less equal, didn't he. Well, what's not so well known, is that after he'd finished, he had a few bits and pieces left over that he didn't know what to do with. So he decided to let Adam and Eve choose if there were any that they would like to take away with them. "Look, Adam, me boy? What do you think of this bit here?" God said. "It's called a penis? It enables you to stand up and pee." Well, Adam tried it out. He found he could do all kinds of other things with it, as well. He could point with it, shake it about, play with it, sign his name in the sand with it. All very impressive. "I like it!" Adam said. "I reckon that'll suit me just fine." Well, God agreed he could have the penis. And then he turned to Eve, who was waiting patiently for her turn to choose, and said, "Now, young lady, what about this other bit here? Do you think this might be something that would interest you? It's called a brain." *"I'll take it!"* she said.'

To which Johanna bursts into the most raucous laughter - so very loud! In fact Matthew cannot ever recollect having heard or seen her quite so undignified, rolling back into her cushioned nest, her dainty feet in the air as she chortles in utter abandonment. Sam, meanwhile, smiling ironically, glances in Matthew's direction.

'Well, there, you have it, Matt,' he observes waiting until some decorum is restored before rising to make sure everyone is well accounted for by way of wine or punch. 'Another salutary lesson for us men folk, wouldn't you say - led not only by the nose most of the time, but also by the organ of procreation through every venture, mishap and foolish vanity of the world.'

To which Matthew makes no reply other than defiantly holding forth his glass so it might be topped up.

'Well, I must admit, that really was rather good, my dear,' Lord Snatchal declares, 'even if just a trifle lacking in taste.'

'What?' the Countess responds straight away with bemused indignation. 'I hardly think you should lecture me on matters of taste, Cornelius - not with some of them there stories you come home with when you return from the club late at night.'

'Men simply have a better way of putting it, my dear - more subtle.'

'What do you mean?'

'Well ... it is difficult to quantify, the precise distinction,' the Earl mumbles, realising he is getting himself into deeper and deeper water. 'But everyone understands. We just have better taste, that's all.'

'You are perfectly right, of course, my darling,' Lady Snatchal responds straight away with an aloof smile. 'As I recall you once asked me to marry you precisely because you had such good taste, and I, as a woman, accepted because I had so very little.'

At which Johanna really does lose any remaining vestige of self-control, dissolving into a frenzy of giggling. 'Oh Goodness! I am sorry,' she says, spluttering now and, from a near-horizontal position by this time, her big hazel-green eyes clouded with tears of laughter as she peeps over her fan towards Lord Snatchal - who does, however, take it all in good heart.

'Yes, well, your little parable, Dorothea, is obviously going to be rather difficult to follow,' Lord Snatchal asserts, feigning indifference, 'so in the meantime, while I try to come up with something sufficiently vulgar, perhaps our lovely hostess could take up the challenge next? Once she has finished laughing, that is.'

Johanna nods her compliance. 'Well, yes, fair enough,' she agrees, hoisting herself back into a sitting position, 'I do have a little story for you all. I know not whether it is in good taste or not, but it is about flying and birds. Could we have a little music please, husband, while I prepare my contribution and attempt to regain my composure?'

To which Sam retakes his place at the harpsichord and toys with a little rendition of seasonal tunes from the Messiah by way of an interlude until his wife is ready to begin.

Once satisfied that the mood in the room is sufficiently calmed, she smoothes off her dress, sits up in her nest of cushions and takes a deep breath. 'Well, once upon a time,' she begins in a voice which is calm and soothing, 'there was a jackdaw who was troubled and went to his friend, the wise old owl, and asked him why it should be that birds live such short lives compared to so many other creatures. The owl replied that it is because birds can fly, and such immeasurable joy has only been given to birds in exchange for a relatively brief mortality. Well, the jackdaw went away and thought about that. He reasoned that although it was good fun flying, he would rather prefer to live longer, and the best way to achieve this would be to embark upon a regime of abstinence and careful living, choosing to take special care of his diet and not to go tiring himself or over-extending himself in the flying department. At first, he felt very satisfied with his progress, but after a while he began to notice that his little wings had begun to atrophy and that he could not really fly very much at all any longer. Then one day, watching all the young birds flying about and, in the spring, mating and having young, all without a care, he suddenly became aware of what he was missing. He felt sad. He did not live an especially healthy life either, and not long after, when he realised he was dying, he returned to the wise owl and asked him what happened to the deal? "Goodness! No one said there was any deal," the owl replied. "That was merely your false reasoning. You cannot trade with God, foolish jackdaw. You have wasted your life, and not spread your wings and flown as you should." And that was the end of the Jackdaw, and it is the end of this story. And the moral of it all is … well, enjoy the magic that is given to you, since it is magical indeed, our time we have on this earth, and it lasts only for a short while in which we must seize a-hold of it according to our nature and make it our own.'

Lady Snatchal sniffs loudly and dabs a tear from her eye. 'Gawd, that's very lovely, dear,' she says and reaches over with her closed fan to tap shut Lord Snatchal's mouth with the handle - for he is also looking uncommonly moved, his thin little chin trembling with emotion.

'Lovely, my dear,' says Sam and, taking his wife's hand in his, he gives it an appreciative and gallant kiss on his way back to his chair.

It is quite possible, Matthew thinks, that we have already had far too much to drink than is at all good for us - himself included. And yes - of course – *flying*. Matthew had almost forgotten the mission she has set for him, the poetic quest. It is a project that has become lost in a morass of sensuality of late; in more than a little folly and time-consuming heroism, as well. But this coming New Year will be different. He pledges it to himself. He will spread his wings and fly as intended. He *will* - or else perish in the enterprise. He knows that now. And he knows, too, as his eyes meet those of Johanna, that he has never felt more in love with her than at present.

'Well m'Lord,' Sam says, turning to the Earl. 'Perhaps you would care to honour us presently, with your contribution, Sir?'

'I shall … I shall, indeed,' he replies as Johanna makes a little round of her guests to make sure everyone is well stocked with items to eat - a house-maid having just been called upon to replenish a fascinating array of tasty nibbles, including various little caprices in sugar and chocolate, edible architecture conjured up by Johanna herself in her own kitchens. A hobby of hers.

Lord Snatchal, meanwhile, has elected to take a seat upon a tall-backed chair, the better to be seen, and with head raised looks every inch the orator as he settles into his story - though sadly his feet do not quite touch the ground, and so a stool is brought over quickly on which he might place them.

'Are you sure you don't need to go outside first, Cornelius?' Lady Snatchal inquires, quietly and with uncommon tact, aware as always of her husbands unfortunate weakness.

'No, no, not at all,' he answers a little tetchy over the inference and keen to get started. 'Now listen, everyone, this is really interesting. Many people have asked me over the years just what exactly has shaped my enlightened philosophy and my politics. The answer you might be surprised to learn lies in my formative years and in a visit I once made to the eternal city of Rome - on the Grand Tour, y'know - the one which all of our young men of distinction - *present company excepted Sam, sorry* - must make at some stage. It was at Easter, no less, on the day of Good Friday, when I observed the custom, as it was at the time, in the Sistine Chapel for penitents to flagellate themselves - just precisely the kind of sordid pastime favoured by the Papists, of course, when not persecuting our brother Masons in Italy. Anyway, I digress. It was in deference to this unwholesome public demonstration some years later when I resolved at one of our illustrious gatherings of the Cornhill Club to bring forth a riding crop among those assembled and to thrash each one of our fellow debauchees soundly on the buttocks - where available, that is - because quite a few of them, there were, who fled from me in terror. Nevertheless, it is a tradition which, as some of you know, still continues to this day among the Knights.

'Anyway, it was in the early hours after one such meeting when I returned by coach late to Snatchalcombe House and, unwilling to cause a disturbance or awake the household, retired instead to the seclusion of one of my pavilions in the park. And there, somewhat worse for drink, I must admit, I fell into a stupor and slept like a log. I was awoken shortly before dawn, however, by the sounds of a frightful inhuman shrieking and was aghast to observe in the darkness there before me a most terrible sight. This was nothing less than a beast from the most damned reaches of hell - an apparition with four glowing green eyes peering in through the window at me. Well, convinced that I was being visited by demons, I fled at once and repented my sacrilegious ways with fervent prayers, resolving to embrace the faith of Rome forthwith instead of mocking it. And this I did. Truly. Lady Snatchal will testify to it. I was a changed man. I would attend Mass regularly and was never to be seen without a crucifix and a rosary about my person. Society shunned me, doors once opened to me became closed and I just had to abandon completely any hope of public office, of course. This unnatural behaviour continued until some months after the event, when my gardener, who was also wont to spend the odd night in the pavilion, for reasons best known to himself, confided in me that he, too, had experienced the apparition but informed me that what I had taken that night to be a dreadful four-eyed fiend with its inhumane shrieks and cries of retribution was in fact nothing more than a pair of feral cats copulating on the window sill outside the building and which he had witnessed himself on several occasions. This in turn, as you can probably imagine, led me to an equally swift de-conversion, relinquishing my newly acquired Papist proclivities forthwith. Thus, ever since, I have rejoiced only in the powers of reason or, occasionally for my recreation, also in a celebration of the sacrilegious and the profane. And that, my friends, brings me to the conclusion of my story, the story of how I came to be the very man of prudence and sobriety you see before you today.'

'Most interesting, Sir! Most interesting,' Sam declares, endeavouring to ignore the struggle Johanna is clearly experiencing in keeping a straight face, her usually fair complexion reddened at the cheeks - while Lady Snatchal merely glances up to heaven, her comparatively swarthy features by contrast lacking in emotion of any kind, most likely because she had heard the story before, and heard it many times.

'It certainly must have been a challenging time for you, Sir. A horrifying experience,' Sam concludes.

'It was. It was indeed!' the noble Lord confirms with a look of immense seriousness, not quite willing to relinquish being the centre of attention. 'Even now, after so many years I can still re-live the terror of it. To be perfectly frank with you, Sam, I just wet myself.'

An almost tangible ripple of embarrassment spreads around the room at this rather indelicate confession.

'Well, yes, that would be forgivable, I should think,' Sam eventually responds, filling the awkward silence, 'in the face of such a spectre ...'

'No, no!' Lord Snatchal interrupts. 'I mean just now, just this minute. I just wet myself.'

'*Cornelius!*' Lady Snatchal snaps angrily, with a glance up to the heavens.

'I'm terribly sorry,' the Earl continues. 'I do hope you will excuse me, therefore, if I leave the room for a moment. Oh, and I don't suppose you could supply me with a fresh pair of britches, Sam, could you, old boy?'

To which Sam, with the utmost alacrity, rises and assists the

noble lord, somewhat unsteady on his feet, from the room - and a
short time afterwards, both can be heard upstairs in the bed
chamber, in avid discussion presumably over the merits or
otherwise of Sam's breeches - none of which, Matthew reflects,
would be a particularly good fit - one man being at least twice the
girth of the other.

'My Goodness, what an evening of fun we are all having!' Johanna
exclaims, endeavouring to dispel any embarrassment as she takes a
seat beside Lady Snatchal on the sofa. But she need not have
worried. The Countess remains as indifferent to her husband
occasional *faux pas* as ever, and Matthew, for his part, rising to
stretch his legs, continues to find it all wonderfully amusing. After
the trials of the past few weeks, nothing that comes his way amid
such fine and amiable company could possibly be unwelcome. It is
simply a delight.

'Perhaps some more music to end the evening?' Johanna
proposes.

'Oh no, no! I want to hear more about our hero and his
exploits!' Lady Snatchal squeals, and even stamps her foot several
times in protest until Johanna and Matthew both agree to it.
'Matthew, come and sit by us - look between us here. See, I have
made a place for you,' she says, patting with her hand the small
available surface of the settee just visible between the women.

And thus, a moment later, Matthew finds himself squeezed in-
between his two excitable and inebriated admirers, both of whom,
he suspects, are about to make a terrible fuss of him all over again -
each one, moreover, with an ample expanse of bare throat and chest
exposed by this late hour, displaying that much celebrated 'rising
moons' configuration that tightly laced stomachers and stays
inevitably engender. He is caught, therefore, flanked by his evil
temptress on one side and his faithful muse on the other, and
realising that it is really impossible to ignore the allure of either one
at the expense of the other.

'Tell me Matthew - is it true you woke up with a milk maid in
your barn that morning?' Lady Snatchal inquires. 'Gawd, I bet she
thought her luck had changed, don't you! Something a bit more
interesting to get her fingers around that day, eh!'

Johanna laughs, too. 'Yes, I should think so!' she giggles, her
voice sounding tipsy. 'Anyway, Dottie, don't you think our

Matthew is greatly changed by his adventures? I do believe there is a certain appealing ruggedness about him since his return, wouldn't you say?'

'Oh yes. All sort of roughed-up, like, and ... well rather dangerous-looking,' Lady Snatchal agrees.

'Ladies, please!' Matthew protests, staring fixedly ahead, aware of their eyes upon him, possibly examining his stubble - since it is a good many hours since he last shaved.

'Oh dear! I do rather suspect we are embarrassing our hero,' Johanna exclaims, peering around him to her friend on the other side with a smile of complicity, her shoulders trembling in mirth.

'Yes, poor Matthew!' Lady Snatchal coos, pursing her lips extravagantly and raising her open fan, which she flutters above him to cool his brow. 'But Matthew, you must tell us: were you required to wear a uniform when you went off with all them soldiers?'

'Oh, yes, do tell!' Johanna echoes. 'I must own that I do rather admire a man in uniform. I think it would suit you ever so well, Matthew.'

'Oh, definitely, yes - because of his height and broad shoulders,' Lady Snatchal concurs. 'I reckon a man always shows his true qualities to best advantage in the manner of his equipage. All that braiding, and them there epaulettes on the shoulders. So very engaging and ...well, *so assertive.*'

'Well, most of the men in my company wore tartan, as a matter of fact,' Matthew states, managing at last to get a word in. 'And thick woollen socks. I can't imagine you would be getting too excited by any of that!'

'No - probably not,' Johanna admits.

'No, not unless it's true what they say,' Lady Snatchal chuckles and winks, 'you, know, about them there Scots and what they don't go wearing underneath their kilts!'

'Oh Goodness, yes!' Johanna exclaims and claps her hands in glee, followed by another bout of giggling. 'Poor Matthew,' she finally coos once a degree of calm is restored. 'We are rather overwhelming him, aren't we.'

'Not at all!' Lady Snatchal argues, raising her glass to her lips once more. 'I bet our Mr Wildish here, like any soldier, can handle himself right-well when pinned down in tight situations.'

'Indeed, one would assume so,' Johanna agrees. 'And after all, we are as nothing compared to the Jacobite army - being but two tender, helpless females.'

And suddenly Matthew realises that they each have a hand upon his knee - their dainty fingers all a-tremble and creating thereby a very constricted situation indeed - and upon which after only a few seconds, he has to reach for the modesty of a cushion to place over his lap - though this expedient, accompanied by a guilty smile on his part, only results in further uproar. Lady Snatchal, putting down her wine, opens her fan once more and applies it to his brow again - and then Johanna does likewise, and with such contrived felicitations, that all three find themselves completely dissolved in merriment for a good while, especially when the Countess attempts to pluck his cushion away and, upon his struggling without success to retain it, declares that she has never in all her days seen a recruit so better equipped and fitted out for action!

But just then there is an abrupt change - a different presence in the room as all three turn their heads simultaneously to behold, standing in the doorway having just descended the stairs, a most indignant Sam, hands on hips, and Lord Snatchal, looking most puzzled and clothed in what appears to be the largest pair of breeches ever devised by humankind.

'Look. What do you think?' he inquires with immense seriousness. And, coming around to the front of the sofa so all might have a view of his diminutive form in his enormous new breeches asks: 'Do I look all right in these?'

And there is very little sense or sanity can be got from anyone for quite some time thereafter.

## OBSERVATIONS OF THE
## HEAVENLY BODIES - THE MOON

*Of the Moon, her general and particular significations:*
*She who bringeth sustenance and fertility. The face pale, the eyes*
*rounded and expressive of feeling. Much hair and of a lustrous*
*kind. Short limbs, roundly proportioned and inclining to fleshy or*
*plump. Merry and most good the company. Kindly and sympathetic*
*in nature, tender in thought and given to dreams and imagination.*
*In apparel preferring of shimmering pale shades. The pearl for her*
*gemstone and all things of silver.*

'So, a little more clarity in this matter, Sir, if you please,' Sam begins, allowing his body, draped in little more than a towel around his waist, to recline against the hot, tiled wall - and thus resembling, with his ample rolls of blubber moistened by the steam, nothing so much as a large white sack of lard that might have been placed upright in that position. 'You say you have already four of your seven ladies on standby ready and willing?'

'That's right,' Matthew answers, hoping this is not destined to be another meddling mission on Sam's part to dissuade him from his enterprise. Removing his own woollen gown and, draped in little more than a loin cloth cleverly tied to gain the maximum exposure to the steam to his skin, he joins his friend on the bench, his own body, he is pleased to observe, appearing relatively slim and athletic alongside that of his companion. They are in the bagnio of Mrs Armstrong, a place designed specifically for the cultivation of a polite taste in pleasurable vice and to which Matthew has become a frequent visitor of late. Sam, meanwhile, and encouraged by favourable reports of the excellent facilities, and perhaps out of a certain lascivious interest, too, has joined him this afternoon in this oasis of self-indulgence. It is early still, and they have the place to themselves.

'Yes, *four down three to go,*' Matthew continues in wistful fashion, a little subdued by the heat. 'Already I have my extravagant and very special Caroline, the lady I encountered in Ranelagh Gardens who is fulfilling the role of Jupiter. There is my enchanting young Sarah - the former laundry girl and the very embodiment of Venus but who upon the recommendation of our very own Lady Snatchal, is now employed by a baroness in Mayfair, as a *special* chamber maid, they say.'

'Another devotee of the game of flats?' Sam enquires, accompanied by a salacious pursing of the lips.

'Most likely, yes. They have me to thank for that, of course, having brought her to the masquerade that evening. Who would have thought it!'

'Um, Y*errz...*' Sam responds, his voice also uncharacteristically languid in the heat. 'They say, though, that Snatchal is content to surrender to the inevitable regarding the inclinations of his wife in this respect. I even heard he has a little peep-hole installed for his delectation - by mutual consent between the walls of his own and the Countess's chamber.'

'Disgraceful!' Matthew declares with hollow disapproval, for it is really more a case of anxiety that he is feeling, that he could lose his lovely Sarah to all the temptations of her new life among the *Beau Monde*.

'Anyway, who else?' Sam inquires further. 'That's only two you've mentioned.'

'Oh, sorry. Yes, not forgetting dear Harriet, my lithesome Mercurial governess whom I escorted back from St Albans that day. And of course there is still my old flame, Rose Tidey, the lovely brewer's daughter - you met her that evening in the tavern garden, remember, when you nearly lost your wig in that brawl. It is she, I trust, who will fulfil her part as the Moon, even though I must confess that we have yet to consummate our newly discovered fondness for each other in any practical sense.'

'Huh! You're slow!' Sam grumbles with irony.

'Ah, but I am anticipating putting that particular omission to rights very soon, my friend, do not fear - for I am to visit her later this very afternoon in her new home, not far from here, and where I shall present to her my very latest sonnet to the mysteries of fair

Luna. An evening of mutual gratification awaits. She is keen - and by heaven so am I.'

Matthew, meanwhile, is aware of Sam studying his back, intent on looking at it with curiosity whenever Matthew bends forward for any reason.

'I say, that's rather a nasty collection of scratches you've got there,' he remarks with puzzlement. 'How on earth ...'

'Oh, those!' Matthew responds with nonchalance 'Old battle scars.'

'Battle scars - *you?*'

'Well no, not really. Wounds from sharp nails, actually,' Matthew elucidates. 'Before one knows what's happening it's usually too late.'

'I see. Um, a bit over-zealous, some of your ladies, aren't they?' Sam observes, his voice a mixture of curiosity and disapproval.

'One can never be over-zealous in the pursuit of pleasure,' Matthew answers patiently, hoping he will not need to elaborate.

'*Yerrz,*' Sam responds, already languishing, his voice fading once more.

But at just that moment, the doors swing open and the commanding figure of Mrs Armstrong herself appears, unheeding of any abundance of flesh on display as she undertakes her customary function of hostess, checking on her visitor's comfort. Fortunately, they have been conversing in hushed tones, so she will not have been privy to Matthew's itemised account of his amorous intentions - just as well, Matthew reflects, because Lucy would hardly be the kind of woman to accept being part of a set.

'I trust everything is to your satisfaction, gents?' she inquires, standing tall and glorious above them, resplendent in a panniered gown of candy stripes, all powder blue and lemon colours, and eyeing them both in unabashed and appreciative fashion, her dimpled cheeks manifest as she smiles most generously with that innate combination of approval and benevolence unique to her. 'Will either of you lascivious monsters be requiring a private room this afternoon?' she asks with still the most brazen forwardness, as Sam reaches for his robe the better to cover a little more of his torso.

'No thank you, Mrs Armstrong,' Matthew replies. 'We must both shortly depart your excellent establishment, alas.'

'Well, I am gratified to have made the acquaintance of your

guest,' she states, turning to Sam. 'I trust you shall not neglect to return to us at some future juncture, Sir, to sample the broad range of services we provide and which, if I may remind you, consists of overnight accommodation; a hearty breakfast; bathing and steam baths; an expert Turkish massage; flagellation with birch, horsewhip or riding crop to your predilections, with or without a second lady to attend upon you during the process; and a nice drop of fine wine to boot if you intend to indulge in the sordid vices of Bacchus.'

Sam clears his throat and splutters his gratitude, while also declining Mrs Armstrong's kind offer to show him her specialist furnishings consisting of various frames and chairs upon which one might be bound. And with that, she smiles her most abundantly dimpled and radiant smile before leaving the room, a departure which leaves Matthew quite bereft and with the distinct sensation of the sun just having gone in behind the clouds.

'Isn't she magnificent!' Matthew declares admiringly.

'Um. Even if a trifle formidable,' Sam agrees, letting his covering fall away once more. 'So you have, I take it, already - er - sampled the goods, so to speak?' he continues, unusually timid - the look of puzzlement on Matthew's face, meanwhile, only serving to encourage him to still greater heights of euphemism. 'I mean to say, I assume you have enraptured the practice, applied the finishing stroke, so to speak - drank from the well of ...'

'We have enjoyed a good shag together, Sam, yes, if that's what you're trying to say. Heavens, man, will you speak plainly! You never used to be like this in your bachelor days. You don't think you are in danger of becoming a bit of a prude lately, do you?'

'A prude! Not I, Sir. A person of respectability and propriety, yes - but that is a process that naturally comes with maturity and the onset of age.'

'For heaven's sake, Sam, you're only twenty-eight!'

'Yes, but I am a married man, Matthew. And you will discover for yourself one day, should you ever attain that exalted state of felicity, that lurking within every carefree, rampant bachelor, there is a gentleman desirous of becoming a person of substance, a man of property and family - and of reaching that time of life, therefore, when certain unfortunate customs and manners of speech are naturally cast aside. *A good shag,* as you so indelicately put it, being one of them.'

But Matthew merely shakes his head, unimpressed by his friend's excuses. Sam has been in a foul mood all morning, anyway, ever since discovering that his wretched barometer had broken yet again and must be taken back for repairs. An interminable process.

'I needed warming up, Sam - especially after the freezing snow of the North. And a visit here for a hot bath with Mrs Armstrong was just the remedy I needed to restore the vigour to my limbs.'

'What! And to have your bum spanked?' Sam demands, incredulous.

'Not at all,' Matthew replies with dignified calm. 'Like any woman, Mrs Armstrong is not averse to the pleasures of a normal congress, as you would perhaps prefer me to describe it. We have a mutual regard for each other's requirements. I must say, also, that is quite heavenly, being embraced by Mrs Armstrong. Why, it's just like when you bare your chest and forehead to the sun on a summer's day and bask in all that warmth and radiance. And so, Sam, by way of revisiting our earlier discussion, it is really more a case of *five down, two to go*. For I am confident that the redoubtable Mrs Armstrong will fit nicely into the little play I shall perform - and soon - where she will occupy the fourth rung upon that magical ladder to the stars, there in the role of the bountiful and resplendent Sun made flesh.'

Sam shakes his head - a bewildered kind of admiration.

'Well, Sir, all I can say is that I shall have to revise my earlier scepticism concerning your abilities. How do you do it?'

'What do you mean? How do I gain the trust of the ladies?'

'No, I mean how do you manage to seduce them so readily and keep them coming back for more?'

'Well, that's just it - precisely what I was saying. *Trust.*'

'Really? *Trust?* Is that all there is to it?'

'It is the beginning and end of the entire process, Sam - the trust that comes from being attentive, caring, wanting to understand the needs of another. For every woman has needs, do not doubt it - and the desire is always present for these to be answered one way or another. Oh, it's nothing to do with good looks, with bravado or contrived demonstrations of passion or romance or anything like that. They can see right through all that nonsense straight away. No, it is the agreeable and supremely seductive and irresistible sensation of trust that is the key, a trust that says you will not inconvenience or harm your lady in any way, that you will not be indiscreet or embarrass her, and that you will, with all your heart, endeavour to become solely the vehicle of her joy. Is that not what we all of us, deep down, long for in a lover, anyway? We are born to trust, immediately when we suckle at the breast. It is a quality, therefore, appreciated most of all through the medium of touch.'

'What, you mean you give them a good squeeze and cuddle to get them going?'

'No, Sam. A good squeeze, as you put it, must only be considered much later, if at all. Rather, one must first wait, and to wait patiently, for that moment of surrender, that precious moment of calm and tenderness. You see it in her eyes, feel it in her heartbeat, hear it in her breathing and in her sighs. It can arrive with the lightest of touches, when she turns her senses entirely towards her pleasure and then you know she is yours. Though to be sure, we should always bear in mind that no woman likes her man to be bashful. No, no. that would never do. And it is always better to seek forgiveness afterwards than to ask permission at the start.'

'Um, *yerrz*,' Sam mutters by this time clearly more than a little befuddled, folding his arms obstinately about his chest. 'All sounds a bit complicated, if you ask me. And rather a lot of waiting around for things, as well. Still, I think I've about got the gist of it, thank you. I'll try it on Johanna, sometime. See if it works.'

'Johanna?' Matthew echoes, mystified. Sam would surely be in no quandary in that respect, not after so many years of marriage. Whatever it is he is referring to, Matthew thinks it would be best to change the subject or at least divert it onto safer ground. 'It was a beautiful rendition, the aria your good lady sang the other evening,' he continues. '*Where're you Walk*. Delightful.'

'Well, I should think so, too! She was rehearsing it for the most part of every evening during your absence. Even singing it in her sleep.'

'Really?'

But Sam does not respond. He seems to be untypically pensive all of a sudden, and his next words leave Matthew in no doubt that something is troubling him. 'You are - er - rather fond of Johanna, aren't you?' he inquires after a lengthy pause and, for once, Matthew senses, deadly serious.

'Of course. You are both among the very dearest people in the world to me.' Matthew replies. 'And the obvious happiness of your marriage commands my eternal respect.'

'*Obvious happiness,*' Sam echoes. 'Huh! You don't know the half, my friend,' he adds, his lips pressed in contemplation, and for just that instant his face, all flushed and red with the heat and without the splendour of his wig to frame it, appears old and full of care. 'Oh, I know what people say,' he continues. 'They say it was never a proper love-match. They say I only married Johanna because of her family's endowment of three thousand per annum. That, my friend, is utter nonsense. By heaven I would have taken her to the altar for half that sum!'

'Most magnanimous!' Matthew remarks with an irony that is, he suspects, wasted on his friend at just this moment, and which still does not seem sufficient to lift him out of his despondency.

'What I am trying to say,' Sam begins again, and still unusually dismal, his eyes cast down, 'is that sometimes one may derive a false impression when looking in from the outside, a marriage being no exception. And yes: I have, occasionally erred - but not, mind you, from any want of regard for my wife. I do love her. And I would not have chosen such a path were it not, since the birth of our second child, for Johanna's reluctance to indulge me. She does not, I believe, wish to endure further pregnancies. As a result, particular days of the month are out of bounds - as are other times prior to her courses when she is most irritable and prone to headaches. To be frank it is more than I can keep up with sometimes, having my desires circumscribed by so many dates upon a calendar.'

'I see,' Matthew murmurs, saddened by his friend's confession, and as perplexed as ever by the impenetrable mysteries of marriage, an institution whose curtailing of adventure and spontaneity must surely outweigh any advantages it might bring in comfort and security.

'Well, there are ways to avoid such inconveniences, anyway,' Matthew says. 'I mean the matter of unwanted pregnancies.'

'What, you mean cundums? Huh! The sport is much pleasanter without them. Like trying to bite your nails with your gloves on!'

'No, no. On the contrary, Sam, there are some excellent products these days. Those old, coarse linen ones that you are probably referring to have been entirely superseded lately by those made from sheep's gut. Mrs Constantia's emporium just around the corner from here has, they say, an excellent line in some that have, moreover, been especially rendered and softened by a chemical treatment - most comfortable, and of course totally reusable.'

'How often can they be re-used, then?'

'Well, I suppose that would be depending on the extent to which they are deployed each time,' Matthew answers with an unavoidable chuckle. 'A man who avails himself merely of five minutes on occasion will be able to use one many times more than a man who makes his dalliance with it for an hour - a matter of wear and tear.'

'I see, yerrz,' Sam responds, his brows furrowed with a multitude of additional questions, but which he restrains himself from asking immediately. They lie back instead and allow once more the wondrous steam and heat to penetrate their bones and sinews. Eventually, though, Sam's curiosity does get the better of him.

'I say, Matt, how - er - long do you normally go on for, then? You know, when you do the business.'

'How long - why, as occasion demands, I suppose. But it should not be rushed. I mean, why should the pursuit of carnal love not be favoured with the same expenditure of time and energy as our other appetites? Why should a man devote so many hours at his dining table each day, for instance, and yet spend so little time in the joys of the boudoir? It is, to be sure, a peculiar omission, Sam - would you not say - a strange contrariety when we do not feast for every bit as long on those delights. And this is the very essence of my project, of course. I have for several weeks now been endeavouring to establish the self-control necessary to reach an accommodation with those wayward urges that would otherwise terminate the practice too soon. And to my surprise my efforts have not once met with disapproval, in fact often the very opposite - they have been welcomed - the prolonging of the pleasure celebrated with sighs of the most joyous approbation.'

But Sam does not respond. Staring ahead, he seems thoughtful. 'I suppose, now you come to mention it, and looking back on my bachelor days, it does all rather make sense,' he says at length and, to Matthew's astonishment, seeming to agree with him for once! 'And how often has my mind revolved around that very thought - I mean, the recollection of how much more exciting it used to seem during those times of courtship - of taking pleasure with one's beloved through the most whimsical of activities, while by necessity always avoiding the main event, the deed itself, through fear of making babies. And then marriage came along, and straight away the need for caution was lifted. And what a falling off of ingenuity and invention there was then, eh! Married life became a predictable repetition of manners, rushing always straight to the main point, the finale of the performance each time, never the prelude - not even the first act very much at all - nor all those other parts that we once rehearsed with such artful curiosity, because in that was surely the greater part of the thrill and excitement. You are right, Matt. I can see that now. Maybe I should at least discuss this with Johanna, and visit your Mrs Constantia's emporium, after all.'

Matthew can only regard his friend with sympathy. He has rarely, if ever, heard him talk in such an overt manner, and with such seriousness.

'Anyway, Matt,' he concludes, getting to his feet, 'I am rather of the opinion that I am cooked. Look at me - my skin! We both of us look like ruddy lobsters. Time to take the plunge, eh?'

Oh dear! Matthew thinks. The dreaded plunge! That cruel, obligatory conclusion to the luxury of the caldarium that must be paid for by the horrors of a plunge into icy water. He would never live it down were he to demur, and everyone knows it is unhealthy to leave a bagnio thus, with the pores of the skin open. So they waddle into the adjacent room, stare abjectly into the cold-water pool ahead and prepare. A moment's hesitation ensues until the vast semi-naked figure of the masseur Mr Mustafa appears at the doorway behind - a man who is known to have a most firm hand by way of encouraging guests to take the plunge.

'Get in there, gents,' he says in his deep resonate voice which echoes off the tiled walls and floor. 'Or I'll have to fetch me prodder on you!'

And thus, without any further ado, their eyes full of glazed images of Neptune with his trident ranged upon the very walls about them, they emit a loud collective scream, and jump.

The directions provided to Rose's house prove more than adequate, and the chair brings him to the very door, thus ensuring that his fine shoes and stockings are without blemish. The house she has bought for herself is located in a terrace in one of the smart and still-fashionable courtyards off Ludgate Street, close enough to the exclusive shops and arcades of the Strand and Covent Garden while

being also not too far distanced from the breweries and pubs of the
East End and Clerkenwell that are her stock in trade. Only a brief
wait after ringing the bell is needed until the door is opened by a
bonny young maid who shows him through and takes his hat and
sword. Rose herself, meanwhile, appears at the foot of the stairs
and without formality invites him through into the parlour.

'Happy New Year, my Sweet Rose!' he declares greeting her
with a gentle embrace, making sure their cheeks brush tenderly
together.

'And the same to you, my dearest Matt,' she echoes with good
cheer as she pours wine and they snuggle up on her sofa. 'Yes, a
Happy New Year, and a Peaceful 1746, that is what we want -
though in this I suppose we still cannot be certain, for I read in the
papers that with the holiday over, the Duke of Cumberland is back
in the saddle and eager to engage the enemy once more. Is that
right?'

'They're already on their way to Scotland,' Matthew replies,
taking his first sips of the wine, a spicy and succulent Alsace and
which, as one might expect from Rose, is most excellent. 'The
enemy, they say, must be taught a lesson this time, and one that
they will never forget. God help them! And I'll wager there are one
or two of our boys on the cold road north to Edinburgh at this
minute, who would swap their places for ours, eh!'

'Quite right,' she agrees, allowing herself a moment of gloomy
introspection, trying to put herself in the position of the poor men,
while Matthew needs little stretch of the imagination to do so.
What a fine and rare young woman she is, he thinks - so fair, so
very rounded and feminine; so deep in thought at one moment, then
full of laughter and fun the next; a spirit brim-full of different
emotions - and these forever changing like the face of the Moon
itself, tugging at the tides of every sentient being who comes within
her range. She is, he thinks, especially yielding today, moreover -
with no silly barriers or formalities between them for once. Perhaps
it is the confidence of being in her own home, but here he suspects
she is not going to tease him, or fend him off with studied modesty
or reticence. They both know what is on the menu for this evening,
since they have arranged the feast in advance, and she has, she tells
him, made sure they will have ample time and provision for the full
relish of it.

'Well, at least for my family it shall be a happy year!' she continues, a smile back on her face already and her large, expressive eyes full of merriment. 'Our little Margaret will be wed to her porter Harold before the month is out, and if our boys in scarlet can keep the Scots at bay, then London will remain a place of peace and prosperity and you and I, dear Matthew, shall be the happiest of people.'

'Amen to that!' he declares.

'Anyway, you haven't told me yet - what do you think of my little home?' she asks, just as her maid enters bearing a dish of hot mutton pies - delicious. 'Not bad for a humble girl from Whitechapel, eh?'

And for the first time he takes the opportunity to properly cast his eyes around the parlour - almost a drawing room in size and appearance - everything immaculately appointed in the very latest Rococo style and with touches of unbridled French finery in the luxurious curtains, swags and decorative screens. Little items of Delftware placed here and there on shelf or chimneypiece, and a mahogany table set with cups and saucers, all lend touches of finesse, even if all a little rushed in composition, as though she has gone out and bought it all at once - which, he reflects, she probably has. Fresh flowers are placed in vases to add a homely and distinctively feminine touch - not yet vitiated by the presence of any overbearing male influence, he is pleased to note. And long may it continue! He would be saddened, he must admit, should Rose take up with anyone else, at least in the near future.

'I must say, you have furnished it all quite perfectly,' he says, and makes a show of being justly appreciative of what she has done.

'And every bit of it I have earned by my own wit and ingenuity,' she reminds him. 'The business is flourishing as never before, Matt, and almost every month or so I add a new establishment, a tavern or an ale house, or else we take on a new brewer or drayman. My accountant even says that I should consider - what do they call it - *a listing* on the Stock Exchange. What do you think of that? You will be able to buy shares in me! I hope you are impressed, Matt. For I always did think you were the kind of man who might enjoy the company of a women of substance.'

'Clever, clever, Rose,' he says, and kisses her now upon her lovely mouth. 'And yet you are so fair and desirable that I would strive to enjoy your company even were you clothed in humble rags and had not a penny to your name. That you should be mine, if only for an hour, is all of my desire.'

'Oh, only an hour?' she chuckles.

'For as long as our pleasure lasts,' he corrects himself, much to her obvious approval. And here at last he is able to reveal the little gift he has brought for her, a single pearl set in silver which he fixes for her now upon her gown, noticing as he does so all those other little echoes of sparkle with which she has already adorned herself, all the seeds and sequins that dance like stars upon her bodice - that place of endless fascination for him, criss-crossed by lacing and where the most exquisite embroidery in silver thread has also been woven, almost as if embossed upon the taut brocade, all caught in the candlelight - the pearls of the sea, the silver of the moon. She is, indeed, the very essence of all he, the ardent student of the mysteries, could ever come to associate with the lunar emanation, and she seems, moreover perfectly at ease with his silent observations, and pleased with his appreciation, too, for she would have taken great pains to have made herself so very beautiful, he knows.

'Thank you, Matt. You really are such a darling,' she says, softly now as she continues to rest her head so fondly upon his shoulder, her distinctive scent so delicious to him, their hands clasped as one. 'I have everything I could desire now, do I not? That's why I say to people, what need for someone like me to marry? None at all.'

'Then you are a brave Rose as well as a clever one,' he tells her, and not entirely in jest.

'Oh - quite right!' she agrees. 'And I shan't be falling for any brute who lives in a hovel down by Dung Wharf, that's for sure - like Margaret has done with her Harold. I shall remain single and take my fun - as and when. What do you think of my philosophy, Matthew? I am sure there must be some ancient Goddess or such like that you can name for me who might be my exemplar?'

'Oh, yes - there is the indomitable and chaste Diana.'

'Chased - chased by what?' Rose demands, sitting up again, alarmed and clearly feeling that Diana might not suit her aspirations after all.

'No, no, my sweet: *chaste*, as in chastity.'

'Oh, I see. Chastity. Why, that was never your preference in women, Matt, as I recollect,' she adds merrily. 'Chase Titty! Yes -

that would be more like it.'

And they laugh together at their silliness.

'Anyway, don't talk to me about chastity!' she continues, pouring a little more wine for them both again. 'I have met many a woman in my line of work, Matt, single and married alike, for whom chastity is little more than a convenience - a shield behind which they might then indulge in every other kind of vice. And so they go drinking themselves silly, gambling and wasting money, neglecting their children, cheating their customers and ruining their husbands with debt - yet all the while being the picture of virtue to the world because they are *chaste*. Well, my upbringing has at least taught me never be so false, so full of hypocrisy.'

'It might be more accurate to say that Diana's chastity was more in the interests of self-preservation,' Matthew argues patiently, 'of not being ruled by any man. In fact the myth goes that once, when an unfortunate hunter named Actaeon happened to spy upon her bathing one day, she was so enraged that, by her magical powers, she instantly transformed him into a stag, after which he was pursued by his own hounds and torn to pieces.'

'Oh, that's better. I like the sound of that!' Rose declares, lifting her chin very slightly as if bestowing the very same judgement on the entire male sex. 'Diana, hear me! I shall henceforth be your devotee. I must go seek out a bit of sculpturing of you for the mantelpiece, or even commission something from one of those painters. The celebrated Mister Hudson, will do well enough, I should think, for no other reason than that I have the money for the best. Fear not, though, Matthew. I shall always make the occasional exception for a man who can please me. And I don't think you would look very becoming with a stag's head.'

'Then I am honoured, indeed,' he declares, allowing his eyes full reign once more to explore the delights and prospects set before him.

'Matt, read me your poem - the one you said you wrote just for me, remember? Do you have it on you?'

'I do not have it, Rose.'

'You don't!'

'No. Nor do I need to - because I know every line by heart, and I have thought of you so often of late, that every time without fail the words have spoken themselves and implanted themselves in my memory so deep and tenderly that I can never forget them.'

'Oooh! Then let us fill our glasses again, my dear poet,' she says, reaching for the wine once more. 'For I am your most willing audience.'

And, thus, he recites his sonnet to the Moon - the very one he really should have had ready and prepared for her in his apartments all that time ago when she had visited, and when to their dismay his client McNiel had called and interrupted them at the cusp of their pleasure. How very far away it seems now, that warm summer's afternoon! And he wonders why it has taken him so very long to put the matter to rights.

*Should my full heart reject its humble station,*
*On seven oceans might I seek my fame,*
*Where sirens call and sing such sweet temptation,*
*And all our ships by tempest wracked in vain.*

*For then by chance I might yet swim to thee,*
*Thy silver'd bow commanding all the oceans deep,*
*And opening thy chest, thy gentle treasures free,*
*That ardent lips thy aching pearls shall seek.*

*My ebb shall be your flow, and never cease,*
*My foaming crest shall burst upon your side,*
*Where spending all would yet my love's increase,*
*Unto thy port shall all my craft abide.*

*No more will I the roving sailor be,*
*When we as waves shall rise and fall eternally.*

His lines please her, he knows, for upon their conclusion she lets forth a little sigh of delectation; and then, resolving to go at once to a place of comfort and privacy, they hurry upstairs - he with the wine and glasses in hand, she racing on ahead along the landing where, proudly, with a sweep of her arm, the door is opened to reveal a most sumptuous boudoir, an interior already illuminated by a wax light and a warm fire and one therefore shimmering with sparkling brocades, of curtains of satin, and of chairs and a bed draped in the most gorgeous and luxurious of quilted fabrics. And it is upon this most substantial and inviting item of furniture that they immediately position themselves, tumbling into it: as soft and inviting a place as any nest of love could ever be.

'I won't flatter you and tell you that I got myself this house solely for entertaining you, Matt,' she giggles. 'The mighty Diana would never approve if I said such a thing. But you are welcome to christen my new four poster with me if it meets with your approval.'

Rubbing noses in play, and with giggles of ardent mischief, and with their glasses filled once more that they might toast again their togetherness, he sips a little wine and then, pressing his lips against hers, propels the liquid into her waiting mouth, which excites her greatly. And they kiss again most passionately, mingling the sweet wine with their own moisture, celebrating their tryst with shameless indignities of mouth and tongue in wild-mingled pleasure. And here, with hardly time to draw breath, they are upon the task of renewing their long-neglected fondness with eager touch, tugging at buttons or fastenings, bit by bit releasing each their willing flesh to the purpose.

'Oh, Matt, let us not restrain our raptures a moment longer,' she sighs, her nimble fingers on the buttons of his breeches already.

And how good she feels, how warm and yielding to his touch as, abandoning all subtlety she grips his backside as an eagle setting its talons into its prey - both so engrossed in the joy that he is only vaguely aware of the door bell ringing away in the distance somewhere downstairs - though this does cause a momentary hiatus in proceedings, as Rose, catching the sound for a second time, lifts her head of tangled curls from the pillow in a bid to detect who might have had the temerity to have called unannounced at this hour.

'Do not be concerned, Matthew, my love,' she sighs, throwing her arms about his neck and bringing him down upon her once again. 'I have instructed my maid that under no circumstances should we be disturbed and that no matter who should call, unless it is a matter of life or death, none shall be admitted. Come, where is our wine? Let me drink from you again my wicked Bacchus - until I overflow with all your juices!'

And gladly he obliges. Relieved, they snuggle up once more, resuming their longed-for lovemaking again, with hot, fervent kisses and hands exploring every quarter, and with all the more spice to the deed knowing that visitors have been turned away. He has never felt more up for it, and wonders how he has ever managed to live all these months without his wondrous and voluptuous Rose to warm his heart and satisfy his desires.

'Oh Matt! Do it now!' she cries as the talons go in once again. 'I want that bottom of yours up and down like a fiddlers elbow - and never cease the jig until I expire in your arms!'

He can hardly believe it - but elsewhere in the house the voices of other women can be detected, shouting, arguing now, and then footsteps are heard, galloping up the stairs, and then along the hall towards them - so that before they can either of them regain their composure, the bedroom door is flung open.

As one, they both rise, lifted upwards instantly by a combination of fright and fury, to discover there at the foot of the bed none other than Rose's pretty younger sister Margaret in a long coat, all damp and bedraggled from the rain outside, the poor distraught house-maid behind her, wringing her hands, a look of tearful distraction upon both their faces.

'For God's sake, what is it?' Rose snaps at the intruder. 'It had better be something bloody important, that's all I can say!'

Margaret meanwhile, still puffing from the exertion of running up the stairs, and hardly concerned by the state of half-naked dishevelment upon the bed in front of her, waits only a second to restore her breath before gasping out her words: 'Oh Rose. Sister! Help me. My poor dear Harold - he's dying, I swear!'

'Harold? Your Harold? How can Harold be dying! Why a young man as strong as an Ox cannot be dying. What's wrong?'

'He fell into a dreadful fever yesterday, took to his bed and since this afternoon has been tossing and turning, and sweating so bad. He is all swollen up and in such pain and, I fear, becoming most confused in his speech. There is not a physician will risk coming out to our humble area in the darkness. I fear I shall lose him, my dear Harold. And we are to be wed in just a few weeks time. Oh what shall I do?'

Matthew, meanwhile, having raised himself upon the bed, takes up his shirt and begins to pull it on, feeling it might be prudent to make a discreet exit forthwith and leave the ladies to resolve the issue - for clearly Rose will not be wanting to do anything much now other than to aid her sister. He has not seen Margaret in the intervening months since that evening outside the Tavern in Southwark, and she has altered somewhat - looking prettier than ever, in fact, and also a little taller. But of course the man she would be referring to, her Harold, would be the porter who had flown into such a jealous rage that evening and set off the fight. A bit of a brute.

'Matt!' Rose cries in a voice which is harsh now and has the note of reprimand about it, the voice of one who in her own inimitable style is already taking command of the situation. 'You are a physician, are you not - or have been trained as such? You have often told me of your abilities when apprenticed to a Barber-Surgeon.'

'Er - yes. Though that was a long time ago and ...'

'Good!' she interrupts, brushing the hair from her face and composing herself, as if having reached a verdict as to what must be done. 'Margaret, my pet, listen: Matthew and I will help you. We will come to your aid at once. Now, while I put on my clothes, go down to my maid again and tell her to set out my greatcoat and hat in the hall, for it is chilly outside. And you, Matt, for heaven's sake hurry up! Get dressed and cover up that ... that *affair* of yours!'

Reluctantly, for the call to duty seems inescapable, and with the pride of his manhood having begun at last to subside sufficiently, he pulls on his breeches. His boots come next, while downstairs his sword and coat are already waiting for him in the hands of the capable maid so that within minutes, and with Rose also quickly clothed and booted, off they go - out into the street and if not exactly running than at least making suitable haste, led by Margaret along Ludgate Hill, then down various narrow lanes and alleyways until, after some fifteen minutes they are among the gloomy and dilapidated buildings of the Blackfriars quarter down by the river. Numerous unpleasant and unsanitary hovels are to be found in these parts and it is into one of these that Margaret guides them - up a flight of rickety outdoor stairs that seem as if they would scarce withstand the weight of all three of them together, into a garret, a dark, stinking place lit merely by a solitary lantern and where they behold, in the corner of a room that clearly serves as both living and sleeping quarters, a large bed and upon it the equally large figure of a man, fidgeting restlessly and with much of his bedclothes and blankets discarded despite the coolness in the air.

'Oh, just look at him!' Margaret whimpers plaintively. 'Have you ever seen a sight more pitiful!'

And, bringing the lantern a little closer, she illuminates the scene all the more vividly, while Rose clutches her hands to her breast in consternation - for it is, to be sure, a most disturbing site: this great giant of a man, laid completely low by illness.

'You'd hardly recognise him!' Rose declares. 'What's all that swelling on his face? He's got a head on him twice the size it ought to be.'

'Oh, that's not the only place he's all swelled up,' Margaret asserts, as, with hardly a semblance of protest from the poor half-delirious Harold writhing on the bed, she peels away the sheet to reveal the largest pair of testicles Matthew has ever seen upon man or beast - swollen indeed to many times what they should normally be. And even after Matthew's many years of absence from the field of medicine, the merest cursory glance at the poor fellow's countenance, the parotid inflammation of the jaw and neck, the obvious fever and clutching of the head as if in pain, are all sufficient indications to arrive at a diagnosis - though by way of confirmation, he does take the man's hand anyway and checks the pulse of his wrist, this being very rapid and feverish indeed, confirming the worst - that without doubt Harold is in the throws of a most severe case of parotitis with an additional complication of orchitis: in other words *mumps!*

'Doctor! Doctor!' Harold begins to murmur, catching sight of Matthew leaning over him in the gloom, his voice all hoarse and constricted by the swelling of his airways. 'What ails me? Tell me straight. Am I dying?'

'I trust not, Sir,' Matthew replies. 'It is serious, the condition what you have, but rarely does it prove fatal.'

'But me bollocks - they're all swollen. What have I got?'

'You have *orchitis*, my friend,' Matthew replies with authority.

'Orchitis? What does that mean?'

'It's Latin for … well, for bollocks that are all swollen.'

'Oh … I see,' Harold mutters with a sigh of relief and then, lifting himself with difficulty from the pillow, seeks out the face of his sweetheart in the gloom. 'See, I told you, Maggie - I told you it would be all right once we had a doctor. I've got orchitis.'

'Oh, thank you doctor!' Margaret says, turning to him, her hand trembling with gratitude upon his sleeve.

'Well, all right, Matt,' Rose interrupts with a reproachful slap on Matthew's other arm, 'but what the hell are you going to do about it?' she demands, not terribly impressed with his Latin.

'Well, I suppose there is really only one thing we can do,' Matthew replies. 'We must reduce the fever and the swelling as swiftly as possible to prevent any possible after-effects.'

'*After-effects!*' Harold exclaims, raising himself from the pillow again in panic. 'I ain't gonna lose anything, am I?'

'No, no, dear fellow. There will be no need for amputation or anything of that kind. It's what's called mumps, that's all.'

'*Mumps!* Oh, be careful, Matt!' Rose cries - that's contagious, is it not?'

'No, no, do not worry on my account - I had it already as a child,' he replies.

'And my sister and I, too, thank the Lord,' she declares, though crosses herself, anyway, for good measure.

'Anyway, we just need ice for now,' Matthew continues, as if thinking aloud, 'Yes, that's it: ice, and lots of it.'

'Well, that we *can* arrange,' says Rose - and with that, she is up and away out the door, her footsteps clattering down the stairs - most confident, it seems, in her ability to obtain what is required.

While they wait, Matthew takes a moment to glance around the interior of the place, the better now his eyes are more adapted to the gloom. How peculiar, he thinks, the variance at which people live according to their rank and station. And whereas only few days ago he had been luxuriating in the Palladian edifice of Snatchalcombe House, the country home of two privileged souls who owned more rooms than anyone had ever been able to count, this evening he has been called to the most humble of abodes, a hovel with a crumbling ceiling and where the lives of two people are confined in the utmost squalor in a living space that for some would be considered little greater than a broom cupboard. How very odd it all seems.

Along one of the adjacent alleyways outside, they can hear the distinctive, emotional voice of Rose, calling out to someone: orders being given - and then, within just a few minutes, the sound of her returning with haste, up the stairs in the company of what is probably a local tavern keeper with a substantial block of ice upon his shoulder, which he casts into the sink and begins to break into pieces with the aid of a hammer and chisel.

'Some clean rags in which to wrap the ice, if you please, Margaret,' Matthew instructs the little lady nearby, and within minutes two large ice packs have been applied and secured with bandages to the sides of Harold's face, and another, accompanied by groans of severe discomfort, to his testicular region, again secured by a kind of truss that keeps everything secure and in place against the hideously swollen area between his legs.

'Jesus! Are you trying to kill me?' Harold cries. 'It's bloody freezing!'

'Keep calm my friend. All is well. All is well,' Matthew asserts and even finds he has placed a hand of sympathy upon the man's brow. It is all clammy and wet, for he has clearly been perspiring heavily, and the smell of the dank bedclothes is abominable. But somehow this reluctant doctor keeps his hand in place, still cool from the ice, keeps it there upon the burning brow of the poor fellow, while he reaches out also to feel the pulse in his wrist once again. The rate is still very rapid, though possibly not quite as agitated as previously. But still Matthew knows that if any risk of damage to the poor fellow's brain and reproductive organs is to be averted, the ice will need to be kept in position and renewed regularly for some hours to come, and these requirements he puts into simple language and conveys to the women.

'Wait a minute,' Harold mutters in a moment of clarity, raising his great swollen head again, 'you're that bloke, aren't you, the one I had the fight with that evening?' he adds, pointing an accusing finger in Matthew's directions before falling back from the exertion. For a moment, Matthew feels apprehensive. But he need not worry, for when Harold gazes up at him again, it is not with any sort of grievance but with a remote, wondrous look emanating from his big brown eyes, his brows knitted in concentration. 'You're a fine fella!' he cries - struggling to sit up once again and reaching out a hand, much to the alarm of all present who together also thrust out their arms towards him, imploring him to lie down again. 'You're a fine fella! A *lovely* fella!' he adds in a voice even louder.

'Just try to rest and keep still, Sir,' Matthew asserts. But the unfortunate Harold seems anxious to say more, motioning with his hand that Matthew should come closer to him, perhaps because of the difficulty and pain of speaking.

'Let me embrace you, Sir,' he groans, more passive now. 'You're a fine fella and I want to show my gratitude. Let me just give you a kiss.'

'Really, my friend … that won't be necessary,' Matthew protests realising the poor man is surely delirious by this stage. 'I am content to have been of service.'

But this untypical modesty on Matthew's part is met with a loud plaintive bellow like that of a wounded animal and a further demand, this time brooking no refusal, that Matthew should allow himself to be kissed. Trying not to grimace too greatly, for the whole thing is really most unpleasant, he acquiesces, shutting his eyes tight as a big muscular, hairy arm embraces him and pulls him downwards.

Oh dear! Matthew thinks to himself, this is not at all how I had anticipated things turning out this evening. It should have been the lovely Rose whose lips were there. But it is no use protesting. Before he can do much about it, Harold has pursed his big slobbering lips and placed his token of gratitude upon Matthew's cheek. It is done. Harold sighs and with the final words, 'You're a fine fella,' repeated once more under his breath, falls asleep at last, a deep stupor of a sleep, punctuated only by a series of loud, gigantic snores that seem to reverberate all around the wooden walls of the room.

The ladies, meanwhile, a mixture of relief and admiration on their faces, turn from the patient and stare up at Matthew, already on his feet and hoping to slip away now.

'Don't forget to apply the ice again as soon as it has melted,' he reminds them, reaching for his coat and hat. 'A salt gargle every once in a while, perhaps with a little honey will help his voice once he regains consciousness. At the very least try to keep him out of any drafts.'

'Oh, Matthew, how can we ever thank you!' Rose exclaims at last, hardly heeding his instructions, so emotional has she become all of a sudden.

'I'll ... I'll try to think of something,' he answers. And with a squeeze of the hand in farewell to her and to Margaret, a little less agitated now, he is pleased to see, he ambles out into the cold night air.

Feeling weary almost beyond endurance, but glad to have escaped the filthy place, he wanders down the lane towards the river and towards a narrow gap between the buildings in which the busy, criss-cross network of traffic can be seen out on the water, their lanterns all bobbing up and down. The rain and sleet have ceased now, and the stars are out, those wonderfully bright winter constellations - the air clear and frosty. And it is suddenly all so very fascinating for Matthew: the sensations of being healthy and at liberty. How fragile and how full of variance is the human condition - how broad its spectrum! He can see that now. Ever since pledging himself to the mystery of the seven heavens, his life has changed almost beyond recognition, so that if he were to write his life's story now, it would no longer be the trivial booklet of his youth but rather an encyclopaedia in several volumes that would fill his shelves. If only, he thinks, he were more worthy of it all - for although he feels a certain satisfaction, knowing that he has done good by the poor, unfortunate Harold, he is also acutely aware of his own overly-refined sensibilities that inform him that he has never felt so unclean or so greatly in need of a hot bath than at this moment.

Someone, a small boy, is seated upon the end of the wharf. He rises as Matthew approaches. The by-now familiar face of Ralph the link-boy looks up at him, his mop of curly blond hair caught in the moonlight.

'Will it be Cockspur Street you'll be needing to go to next, Sir?' he inquires already striking at his flint to light the flame.

'What an inspired idea!' Matthew exclaims. 'Yes, lead the way, Ralph!'

Thus, with the bright wand glowing merrily ahead of him, Matthew follows the boy up and along into Ludgate Hill, then westward, destination Charing Cross and Cockspur Street and where for the second time in twenty-four hours he hopes to avail himself of the rejuvenating facilities and warm and loving hospitality of the redoubtable Lucy Armstrong. And he is not to be disappointed.

# ~ 22 ~
## UNSEEMLY AND PECULIAR
## FANTASIES

It was a shock, quite terrible - and an even greater shock that he did not let him know. Not once had Sam even written to him or mentioned his plans during any of their regular get-togethers. In fact, Matthew had learned of it only this morning, through a chance encounter at The Rainbow, heard that Sam had volunteered for the Duke of Cumberland's army as a surgeon and that he was soon to be on his way north to join the campaign against the rebels in Scotland. What ever could have motivated him to undertake such a folly? It is a gesture so at odds with the man's self-avowed fondness for domesticity and indolence as to be almost beyond belief. In addition to this, the papers this morning are full of news of a serious setback for the English forces in Scotland under general Hawley who has suffered an ignominious defeat at a major battle near Falkirk. The Jacobites are claiming a huge moral victory as a consequence, and are also reported to be receiving reinforcements of French troops and supplies because of it. Success is breeding yet more success for the rebels, ensconced now in their stronghold of the Highlands, and bringing every possibility this coming summer of a repeat performance and an invasion south of the border into England - unless, that is, the Duke of Cumberland can strike a decisive blow in the next few weeks. Hell-bent on revenge upon all those who have dared to question the legitimacy of his father's reign, the Duke is, they say, already in Aberdeen with thousands of well-equipped professional soldiers, while the forces of Charles Stuart, the Bonny Prince, remain centred on Inverness. Apparently, the weather north of the border is so appalling at present that no one can make a move either way, but once the thaw comes, there could be a dreadful slaughter. And Sam ... Sam, the fool, wants to join the fray!

But it is not all bad news this morning; and if the rumour in the coffee house has been a source of sadness for Matthew, the letter he has discovered waiting for him upon his return home is one of contrasting jubilation - this being news from Rose, stating that her sister's fiancé has made a full recovery from his illness, and that everyone wishes to send their deepest gratitude to Matthew for his timely intervention the other evening. It seems the soon-to-be-wed couple are ready to attribute a minor miracle to him in his absence - an absence which, despite their overtures of hospitality, he is determined to maintain. He is happy for Margaret, of course, to have her man restored to full working order once again, but even happier that he has done well by Rose, and that she will aspire more than ever now to become his willing partner in pleasure - if and when they do ever get around to it, that is!

In the meantime, he is resolved to see Sarah again, his beautiful dark Venus - for no one is better suited to banishing his cares than she. Only, he must send out his invitation for Sarah these days. Circumstances have altered; her station in life continuing to rise, as is only right and proper for one of such unique and delightful society. By all accounts, it is not an arduous job, her new position as serving maid to a friend of Lady Snatchal's, since it is Sarah's remarkable beauty and charm that her employer is most interested in, and which therefore leaves her plenty of hours in which she might come and go as she pleases. And he is resolved that within the next day or two it will please her to come to him - to enjoy a little music together perhaps and then to return here for an evening of blissful passion. Yes, he knows that she is young; knows that she is no great intellect, and that for him there is probably no lasting romance in the making either; and yet her company is an inspiration to him - her exuberance and youthful impetuosity a joy. He knows he must make the most of it while he can - and so he puts pen to paper, full of anticipation for an opportunity to enjoy her once again.

Yes, life is good. And as he sits at his bench and sips at his customary mid-day glass of wine, he knows he should try to put the shock of Sam's decision behind him. Today, especially, should be one of celebration, anyway, because it marks the completion of one particularly onerous task, the removal of a heavy cloud that has blotted his horizon for far too long but which now is about to be dispelled permanently from his sight - for yes, at last it is done, displayed there proudly upon his bench for all to see in all its falsified and dubious glory: the finished restoration of the Cornhill Wig!

And what an excellent job he has made of it. With Lord Snatchal consenting, albeit reluctantly, to allow him a little more time into the new year to complete the commission, Matthew has found himself applying more and more enthusiasm to the task, until during the last couple of days he has even wanted to put in extra hours to perfect it - operating with all the furtive enthusiasm and self-satisfaction that anyone who is a forger must feel in making visible the deception fashioned by his own hand. It really has become a magnificent piece, he thinks: the hair woven finely onto the new foundation, and so beautifully blended, all the textures and colours so perfectly balanced. The Knights and Companions of the Wig will be impressed, he is certain. Never for one moment will they or anyone have so much as an inkling that the object they will be parading and venerating upon the dates of all their major ceremonies, from this day forth until the end of time, will be nothing more than a clever fake composed of the beards of dozens of miserable vagrants from the rookeries of Seven Dials. No one will know - no one, that is, accept for two people: Sam, and, a little more worryingly, Lady Snatchal.

And then, as if the very thought of the ogress had summoned her up via some magic incantation, he notices that a chair has been carried into the yard below and placed down, the distinctive motifs of cornucopia and grapes emblazoned on its side putting him in no doubt as to whom it might belong. Visiting without any prior announcement or warning whatsoever, out from it steps Lady Snatchal, waving up at him before he can withdraw and thus permitting him no opportunity for concealment or escape. Quickly, she dismisses the chairmen, and a footman, too, who has followed them in, and then, smoothing down her great, voluminous panniered skirts, she scurries across to Matthew's stairway door below.

'Francis! Francis!' Matthew calls in panic, summoning his valet from the other room - for as luck would have it he is attending to the contents of the wardrobe there. 'Francis, come in here at once and pay heed: I want you to remain in this room with me for the duration of my next visitor's entire stay. Do not, under any circumstances leave me alone with this lady - do you understand, *not under any circumstances?*'

Francis nods his compliance, even if a little too obviously mystified by the request, since under normal conditions it is just the opposite that is expected, that he should make himself scarce upon a visit from any lady and not to return at all until after her departure. But there is no opportunity to explain, for the footsteps of Lady Snatchal in her elegant heels can already be heard ascending the stairs and along the gallery outside, and Matthew hurries to meet her, her great wide petticoats hardly able to squeeze themselves along the narrow gallery let-alone through his doorway.

'Lady Snatchal - what a pleasant surprise!' he exclaims. 'Do come in. I must get that bell fixed, mustn't I.'

'Mister Wildish, good morning. I trust you have no objection to this unscheduled call, as it is by way of business, naturally,' she states, looking around the studio and more than a little disconcerted to discover the tall visage of Francis looming at one end, busy applying a clothes brush to one of Matthew's coats and acknowledging her arrival with a little bow of courtesy before turning his attentions back to his work.

'Ah yes, Francis, my man! Make sure that is done good and proper,' Matthew declares in a loud voice. 'Not a hair or fleck of scurf in sight, if you please - *no matter how long it takes.*' And then turning to Lady Snatchal herself, he explains, more sedately: 'My valet, Francis, you see. Good fellow. I trust you and Lord Snatchal are well, Madam? I was under the impression you were staying in the country?'

'Yes. Cornelius is with the hunt at Snatchalcombe. So, too, was I until yesterday. But it was so frightfully gruesome: all those houseguests bringing in endless carcasses of dead animals and doing unspeakable things with them on the kitchen tables. I thought I would rather come up instead and do a spot of shopping over the weekend. And there's some right thrilling executions going on at Tyburn, next week, they say.'

'Executions, Lady Snatchal? Do you really think those are an edifying spectacle - anymore than what might be taking place in your kitchens at home?'

'Why, yes, that's a different business altogether,' she answers with surprise. 'Everyone likes to see them there criminals dangling and kicking their heels, don't they! Really, Matthew, unless those who break the law are punished, those who abide by it can only ever feel cheated. And that would never do. Anyway, it's always such a festive occasion. I was even going to buy a new hat and gloves this very afternoon. But as misfortune would have it I went and had a serious accident.'

'An accident, Lady Snatchal - are you hurt?'

'No, it's my stays. Look - can you not see? One of them there bones in the bodice has gone and broken. It makes such an unsightly bulge, and will damage the lining of my mantua if it sticks through.'

To which, by way of demonstration, she draws aside the edge of her gown to reveal the offending object at the side of her bodice.

'Why Madam, perhaps you should rather make a call to your stays-maker?' Matthew suggests, endeavouring not to sound too alarmed at where all this might be leading.

'Mr Podger? Oh no, I'm afraid he is far too busy. I understand he's gone and lost his apprentice, anyhow, so he's quite rushed off his feet, poor chap. Anyway, I was in the vicinity, and knowing that you have all those working implements at your disposal here, I thought you might be able come up with a handy tool of some sort to help me out. The pieces need removing, that's all. A little operation with a sharp knife and some pincers should do the trick.'

'Nay, Madam,' Matthew responds with composure. 'I am woefully lacking in the requisite skills to perform such a delicate procedure, particularly as it would require the removal of your gown to gain access to the stays.'

But at this, Lady Snatchal, irrepressible as ever, appears to lose patience, leaning over closely to him and whispering with annoyance, 'Matthew stop being so bloody tedious! You know perfectly well it would take only a moment. Send that man of yours away that we might converse in private. What on earth are you doing employing people like that, anyway - he's far too tall.' And then, catching sight of the man himself staring at her, and no doubt eavesdropping, also, she presents him with her most engaging smile in a bid to disarm the situation. At that moment, however, she also notices the Cornhill Wig upon its mannequin head, and at which she becomes more serious, squeezing past Matthew and wandering along to it. 'Oh my word! Would you look at that!' she says. 'I see you've done the job, then?'

'Yes, just this very morning I put the finishing touches to it.'

'And very nice, too. You'll be able to bring it to Snatchalcombe House yourself, of course. Have you received your invitation?'

*'Invitation?'* Matthew echoes, puzzled.

'Yes - Sam's farewell bash. We are going to give him a good sending-off before he departs for the wars. Oh, silly me! You have perhaps not heard of his intentions?'

'Well, actually, yes I have heard, Madam. But from a source, I hasten to add, other than our good friend himself. I can't imagine what has persuaded him to undertake such a rash and impulsive course of action.'

'Oh, can't you! Well, *I can.* I can tell you perfectly well, Mr Wildish, what it is,' Lady Snatchal asserts with confidence and continuing to address Matthew formally in the proximity of the valet. But then, returning closer again so as not to be overheard, she whispers: 'And I can also tell you why, no doubt, he has neglected to discuss it with you my darling. It's because his dear Johanna has not been able to stop talking about that time when you went off to the North; about all your dashing heroism and what not. Naturally, he wishes to demonstrate that he can do likewise, only he intends to surpass you by journeying to the ends of the earth to join the entire campaign with Cumberland. Heaven only knows how long it'll take until he returns with all his medals! Anyway, Matthew, I really do think it is time you asked your valet to disappear, don't you? Then I can let out my stays a bit and you can get to work with that there tool of yours.'

'I really must apologise, Madam,' Matthew protests earnestly. 'But I'm afraid Francis has rather a lot of important things to attend to here this afternoon and ...'

But the Countess will clearly brook no dissent. Guiding Matthew by the arm, in fact almost hauling him along towards the other end of the room, her voice suddenly full of menace, she hisses into his ear: 'Listen, Matthew. I have been very patient so far with your failure to fulfil my wishes, but you really must concede that it would be more than a little embarrassing if my husband were to learn the truth behind his club's newly woven wig over there - if anyone were to tell?'

'Really, Madam, I cannot conceive that you would resort to such unpleasantness.'

'Oh, can't you! Well, Matthew, you might just be mistaken. And you might also be interested to learn that I have written a letter - yes, a letter, explaining precisely what happened to that there wig. The sealed document is lodged with our family lawyer. Should anything untoward happen to me, if I should die from the unrequited passion or of a broken heart, for example - which I might well do at my age, you know - he has instructions that the letter be opened and read. That would prove more than a little problematic for you, would you not say so, Matthew? If not downright dangerous. Therefore - your valet, if you please. Send him away.' And for special emphasis she loudly adds the word: '*Now!*' followed by an acerbic smile to Francis himself down the other end of the room as he, somewhat taken aback, raises he eyes in alarm at the sudden intonation.

Matthew bows his head in thought - and despondently, too, because it really is an impossible situation. He will simply have to comply and then try to think of something else to fend her off.

'Francis - thank you, that will be all for today,' he says.

'I beg your pardon, Sir?' Francis inquires, raising his eyebrows inquisitively and quite understandably confused as he continues his assiduous brushing of Matthew's coat - by this time almost threadbare at the collar.

'That will be all. You may go now.'

But Francis, perhaps recalling Matthew's precise instructions earlier, merely smiles and responds with a disdainful, 'Oh, no, Sir. I shall not leave. *Not under any circumstances.*'

But this is too much for Lady Snatchal who stamps her feet angrily. 'Good God, man!' she cries, advancing down the room towards him. 'Do you refuse to obey your employer?' she rebukes him. 'How dare you! Do as you are told, at once.'

Her commanding attitude, the self-assurance of one familiar with the process of giving orders and expecting them to be obeyed without question, is sufficient to persuade Francis this time to set down his brush and to depart - which he does, most reluctantly, and with a bewildered shrug of the shoulders in Matthew's direction as, with his customary bobbing up and down motion to avoid the low beams of the ceiling, he finally exits the apartments, returning along the gallery outside to his own room.

'There, that's better, isn't it!' Lady Snatchal declares wasting no time in unfastening and removing her cumbersome outer garments - and this with remarkable dexterity and speed, shedding her mantua and stomacher to reveal herself in merely her stays, with her shift beneath, and then, by this time, having also taken off her hat she positions herself on one of Matthew's high stools and presents her side to him and thus the offending whalebone for his inspection. True enough: it is indeed broken and protruding somewhat, ready and waiting for his ministrations. 'You see Matthew,' she continues, speaking all the while as if it were all perfectly normal and acceptable behaviour to be disrobed and thus attired in front of him, 'there are certain realities, certain reasons why some people are so eminently suitable for one another. A single man, like yourself, for instance, having to flit here and there for his satisfaction, naturally longs for a state of regularity - and so he's invariably attracted towards the wives of his friends. On the other hand, those women who've been married for a while, like me, usually find themselves yearning after the bachelor friends of their husbands, because they represent excitement and the world of the risqué. People like us should do well to recognise their illicit needs and to assist each other, would you not agree?'

'Now, now, Madam, just a minute - how can you be so sure that I am single, anyway?' Matthew demands, searching about for some tools that might be appropriate for the task. 'You really have so little knowledge about me. How can you be certain that I am not engaged, promised to another? Why, for all you know I might even be a widower or ...'

'Oh, Matthew, really!' she interrupts with a glance up to heaven. 'You do realise, surely, that you are not husband material. No woman would ever have you for a husband. You're the kind of man a women wants as a lover - that's all. And jolly nice too!'

He is not entirely certain whether he approves of this line of reasoning, but there is no time to offer up a counter-argument to this all too obvious provocation.

'I reckon, you'd better undo the laces a little, to set it all free a bit more,' she suggests, turning her back to him now, her tight ringlets of black curls tumbling about her shoulders.

Reluctantly, though with an irresistible curiosity nonetheless, he draws up a stool behind her, and cannot help but marvel at the fabulous quality of her attire, all those secret parts now revealed to him - the quality and opulence of all the varied textures and shades of the fabrics, the satin and silk brocade, the white stockings, the delicate embroidery of her shift, and all those little touches of ribbon or lace that contrast with the robust architecture of her stays. He feels quite fascinated and bewitched by it all as, leaning forward from his seated position, he unties the cords, allowing them to glide audibly through their eyelets, thus allowing the magnificently crafted garment to spread itself apart, almost of its own volition.

At first, the shape of her waist remains constricted but, as she breathes out, it appears to expand - though not greatly. She has a naturally slim waist, he is fascinated to discover. Rare in a woman of her years. The slackening is clearly a relief to her, however, because she emits a most delectable sigh upon experiencing the liberty of it.

'Did you say your regular stays-maker had lost his apprentice?' Matthew inquires, suddenly delivered of an appealing idea.

'Mr Podger - oh yes. Why? Are you considering a change of profession, Matthew?'

'Well, it would surely put me in contact with lots of ... er, interesting people,' he murmurs, as if thinking aloud.

'You mean lots of interesting women?' she corrects him, wriggling a little with pleasure and even giggling as he feels for the location of the whalebone strips.

'Oh, yes, I suppose so,' he admits. 'If you could just keep still a moment, Madam. I must diminish the force of tension a little more.'

'Oh, but now you are undressing me, Mister Wildish,' she jests and suddenly all a-tremble. 'Is there no end to the troubles you will heap upon yourself, reckless youth!'

Ignoring this nonsense as best he can, Matthew works away in silence, taking a sharp knife and cutting some of the stitching either side of the bone and thus being able to extract the offending fragment easily with the aid of a pair of pliers. This accomplished, he is just about to down tools and tie up the laces for her once again, when she emits a soft but lengthy groan of pleasure, and allows her head to loll back upon his shoulder, rotating it slightly to look up into his eyes. 'Oh, Mister Wildish, what is this! Will you take me at knifepoint now, you scoundrel! Why, I can do naught but surrender to you if you must ravish me thus.'

Matthew, alarmed, immediately throws down both knife and pliers onto the bench and gets to his feet.

'Madam, enough! I must make it clear that I cannot, nay *will not* dishonour your good husband by consenting to these, your unseemly and peculiar fantasies.'

'Don't be ridiculous! He dishonours me often enough, I should think,' she protests, also getting to her feet and, turning round, pursuing him now along the length of the studio.

'Ah, but two wrongs can never make a right,' Matthew asserts, backing up.

'Ha! *Two wrongs!* If only it were as simple an equation as that!' she argues, continuing her passionate tirade, her breasts wobbling in such agitation that they seem to be almost entirely free of her stays. 'The wrongs that I have endured from him over the years are of such a profusion that any rule of natural justice must allow at least one to be requited by me. Oh, Matthew, if only you knew the half of it - all those unkindnesses, of how often, even when we were first wed, that Cornelius would satisfy himself so crudely upon my person, and so selfishly! So many nights I would lie awake sobbing, listening to his snores. And then the treachery that followed - his roving eye; his drinking; his constant whoring over the years; and now, with the declining of his vitality, the surfacing of those most unnatural vices by which he now seeks his satisfaction - gross, monstrous enormities that I feign not tell you about (though I might if you're interested). In the end, our sordid infidelities have become the only thing remaining in our marriage that we have in common. So yes, I have suffered terribly, the humiliation of it all, and deserve at least the consolation of being able to share my sorrows with someone before I die.'

At which, seizing the knife from the bench, she clutches it to her breast, the handle nestled in her cleavage and, to his utter consternation, the blade pointing up towards her throat.

'Madam, please! You know full well that you have not suffered. You have led a life of great privilege,' Matthew argues. 'And there is, furthermore, that letter you told me about with your lawyer, isn't there? I really would prefer it, therefore, if you did not kill yourself.'

'Oh, Matthew!' she cries, the back of her free hand resting upon her brow in ever more theatrical fashion. 'Can you not understand, it is *you* who are killing me? You are killing me every day with unrequited desire.'

But at this, their attentions are suddenly diverted, because people can be seen in the yard below, staring up in a bid to ascertain the source of all the commotion. Noticing this, the Countess seems most perturbed, surprised by the realisation of being in such a semi-public space, Fortunately, there is no walkway running immediately outside of his windows, and it would only be her head and shoulders that would be visible from below. But there is, of course, always the gallery on the opposite side of the yard, and plenty of windows there, too.

'Oh, what a ridiculous place this is!' she grumbles, and hurls the knife down into the wooden bench where it embeds itself with a mighty thud and a twang. 'Perhaps if I were a pretty little blond, like a certain person we both know, with arched eyebrows and big startled eyes - or at least they're like that when you're around - it would be different. Yes, then you would soon change your tune!'

'Madam, I know not to whom you are referring, but ...'

'Don't give me that! You know full-well to whom I'm referring,' the Countess complains, wriggling and using her hands to bring her bosom more prudently back behind the upper margin of her stays. 'I've seen the way you look at her. You can't hide that kind of thing. And I am just as clever as she is, you know. Why, you could, if you are so keen on meddling with married women, converse with *me* about the moon and the stars. I know a right good thing or two about all that. And do not flatter yourself, foolish boy, that she cares for you. Ha! Do not be deceived, Matthew. She feels sorry for you, that's all. She told me so. Yes, that's right! She takes pity on you - and tries to encourage you, and help with your funding and all that. But it's miniscule, whatever she and Sam might be able to contribute. I, on the other hand, could assist you proper in obtaining some serious patronage - and from the highest sources. Never forget, I have the ear of His Majesty - the King himself - and, if I was to give him half a chance, a lot more besides just his ear! In other words, I can be all things to you, Matthew - and every rung on the ladder that you require to fame and fortune can be reached through me. Oh, you might think she can give you what you're seeking, but I can give you what you really need. You should choose what makes sense, therefore - and, by thunder, I am determined that you shall!'

Matthew, though realising he is probably safe in this part of the room from any further assault, cannot help but feel disconcerted over what she has told him - about Johanna - that she feels sorry for him. How humiliating if that were really the case. And what a fool he would have been, to have thought for one moment that she might really have cherished some regard for him - doubly foolish, in fact: to have thought it and then to have acted upon it, as well, allowing himself to be so influenced by her ideas.

Meanwhile, the Countess, conceding defeat, for the time being at any rate, has turned round to present her back once more, that he might tie her stays, and to which he gladly obliges.

'Are you worried about sin, Matthew? Is that it?' she inquires at length, and in a voice still edged with indignation.

'No Madam, not at all - though I would prefer to avoid it where possible,' he answers, trying to sound amused but aware that his voice is wavering, because he still finds himself thinking of what she said about Johanna. 'Our scruples are surely what sets our class apart, the only thing that can ennoble us or commend us to the poor.'

'Don't talk nonsense,' she snaps back. 'The rich are every bit as venal as the poor, Matthew. The distinction comes through our education, that's all: that we should not feel guilty for our sins, and that we usually manage to avoid being punished for them, as well.'

'I meant, Madam, that it is surely the mark of a gentleman to be in command of his own animal urges,' he argues, beginning, he suspects, to sound more and more pompous by the minute.

'Oh Matthew, for heaven's sake stop taking yourself so ruddy seriously! Sex was God's joke on us. Didn't you know that? But when nobody laughed he got so angry that he made it a sin instead. Don't fall for it, my dear. I don't.'

'Madam, there is a certain logic in what you say, I must admit,' he says, as he continues to make good the laces, 'though I must tell you that I cannot quite believe what you told me a moment ago about Mrs Woolveston.'

'Oh, you're such a fool, Matthew - such a simple fool!' she responds, turning to him again as soon as he has finished. 'I suppose that's why everyone loves you. But, I tell you this, my dear, loveable Mr Wildish, whatever you believe, or choose to pretend to me you believe, it matters not a jot - because you shall not spurn me for much longer. Oh no. We will give our good friend Sam a right merry sending off at Snatchalcombe next week - and you and I, especially, will be merry, because I have the key to the rooms that will be assigned to you, and there I shall visit you and you will give me full satisfaction. If not, I shall broadcast all of your misdemeanours concerning the wig the very next morning. That is my final word on the subject. Anyway, where is my gown?'

'Here Madam,' he answers at once, locating the fabulously opulent object, replete with its petticoats and all so well padded and hooped that it is still standing up by itself in the corner where she abandoned it. With petulance, she snatches the collective bundle from him and, to his relief, climbs nimbly into it with an almost equal speed to which she had removed it earlier - a double relief, in fact, because a glance down to the yard once more reveals not only the curious and amused faces of the stable boys still peering up but also the arrival of a local coach that has just trundled in, its passengers quickly alighting, and among them, dressed in a neat riding jacket and a beautiful felt hat trimmed with scarlet plumes, none other than Johanna. Within seconds, she is at the doorway below and upon the stairs, and before Matthew can squeeze past Lady Snatchal to intercept her is upon the gallery outside, rapping on the door with her knuckles and calling out his name as she enters.

'Johanna!' Lady Snatchal cries, fortunately almost fully clothed by this stage as she looks up at the visitor. 'What are you doing here?'

'Why, Dorothea!' Johanna declares, likewise indignant, hands on hips. 'Perhaps if I were someone of less temperance, I might venture to ask the very same question: what are *you* doing here?'

'I had a problem - with my boning,' Lady Snatchal replies lifting her chin in defiance. 'Mister Wildish here has obliged me by removing an unfortunate protuberance, that's all. He had it out in a jiffy.'

'Oh, did he! Well, I have something far less-frivolous and in fact very important to ask Matthew, if you do not mind,' Johanna states with astonishing audacity and then, taking a seat on Matthew's couch, glances up at him - a little provocatively, he thinks - and then downright tearfully as he comes to her aid. 'I have been shopping, trying so much to distract myself from some terrible news, and felt that I must speak to you, Matthew, since I do not know who else to turn to. Sam is going to join Cumberland's army as a surgeon. He is perfectly qualified to do this, of course, and they are appealing for people to come forward. But I am so anxious. Everyone says there will be terrible bloodshed. You could dissuade him, Matthew, could you not? You could make him see sense! I beseech you to at least try - if only for the sake of the children.'

Upon which she begins to weep in earnest, though silently, her handkerchief held to her face. Matthew comes to sit beside her, knowing that it is acceptable enough to do so in the proximity of the other woman - Lady Snatchal being busy still making the final adjustments to her clothing, much to Johanna's obvious perplexity and annoyance once she does raise her face again. And then she catches the pain in Matthew's eyes.

'Goodness, Matthew, why are you looking at me like that?' she asks, startled. 'Whatever is wrong?'

How can he express his despair - how could he possibly repeat what the other woman had just told him, about her pity for him, her contempt even!

'Madam, I do understand your predicament,' he says, brushing aside her concern with a gallant smile and telling himself not to be so self-absorbed. It would have been a dreadful shock to her and a worry almost beyond endurance, what Sam would have told her.

'Do you? Do you really understand why I am upset, Matthew?' she replies, with words directed to him alone. 'There might be more than one cause of it,' she adds with special emphasis.

'Madam, regarding your husband, I would willingly do all I can,' he continues, ignoring her inference - of her distress in finding another woman here upon her arrival (and not for the first time, of course). 'As a matter of fact, I was already aware of Sam's intentions, though I learned of them only this morning. Lady Snatchal has just confirmed the news - and that a farewell party is to be staged, too, at Snatchalcombe. Possibly then I might be able to bring some reason to bear.'

'Yes, there is a party, that's right,' Johanna acknowledges, still a little tearful and snuffly. 'We are indebted to you, Dorothea, for your generosity in organising it,' she adds, glancing back over her shoulder, a little more kindly by now. 'Yes. It is our only hope.'

'My dear!' the other woman declares, coming to her assistance with a fresh handkerchief. 'Chin up now! We will all be together, won't we, and we'll have a right jolly time of it, I know. And I am sure Matthew will be able to come up with a solution to our needs - I mean in respect of reasoning with your brave husband. Because it is of course preposterous, that Samuel should risk life and limb - a man of his responsibilities. It's not as if he has any military training or anything like that.'

'No, that's right. Thank you Dorothea, I am so appreciative of your empathy,' Johanna murmurs and dries her eyes again.

And then a few minutes later, following a large glass of Sherry offered by Matthew to stay everybody's nerves, not least of all his own, and a few more awkward pleasantries spoken among the three, it appears that Lady Snatchal in particular is suddenly anxious to depart.

'Well I really must be getting along now,' she states, 'and Johanna, my dear, perhaps you should consider accompanying me. We'll take a carriage. It would be just a little unseemly for you to remain here unattended with Mr Wildish - would you not agree? What would people think! Not that I would tell anyone, of course.'

'I do have my maid downstairs,' Johanna protests.

'And I my footman,' Lady Snatchal confirms with equal reassurance of her propriety.

And thus mutually satisfied that everything has been in the very best order, after all, Matthew's two surprise visitors do take their leave of him - with the intention of going for tea together, they say. And so within just a few short minutes, full of kind words and gratitude for Matthew's time and 'handy ministrations,' as Lady Snatchal puts it, Matthew finds himself alone at last, able to take a seat at his bench and to look down from his windows as his visitors depart, arm in arm, and with a maid and footman in tow - each laden down with numerous hat boxes and shopping bags as they disappear under the arch.

Allowing himself another glass of sherry, he emits a long sigh of relief. It has been a lucky escape for him. But he cannot help wondering, as he glances back over to the mannequin head nearby and to the resplendent but utterly fraudulent Cornhill Wig seated upon it, just how much longer will his luck last?

# ~ 23 ~
## NEMESIS

'Can't you go any faster?' Matthew cries, craning his head through the lowered window of the carriage, its wheels grating and grinding beneath him with a sound not unlike that of a discordant quartet of demented musicians as it bumps its way through the Surrey countryside until, at long last, it reaches the towering iron gates of Snatchalcombe House. The coachman, meanwhile, as they pass through, turns his head very slightly, but does not deign to respond very much in any other way to such an outburst of discourtesy. He is, after all, going quite as fast as possible for the road and the conditions, which are atrocious - the sleet driving into his face, and the two horses slipping and sliding in their harness as they go. Matthew is late, that is the trouble. He is late, and any luncheon that might have been put on will almost certainly have ended by now, and he will be in disgrace once more, branded yet again as the impolite miscreant, the one who spurns hospitality. It is almost as bad as getting lost in the woods that afternoon on his previous visit. Whatever will they think of him now!

Up the long, arrow-straight drive the carriage goes, flanked by frosty grass and the bare branches of ash trees, and culminating in the great spectre of the mansion itself in the distance, pale and stark, even more austere in its classical symmetry than when he had last seen it. Set now in a suitably bleak Winter's landscape, its myriad empty windows remind him of the eye sockets of a multitude of skulls, and in a way just as intimidating. During his last stay, it was at least tolerably warm. What it might feel like now inside this mighty stone and marble sarcophagus is anybody's guess. He is not even permitted the convenience of his own Valet, Francis, to accompany him - this having been discouraged by his hostess again. The man would have been an interference to her plans, no doubt. Oh, this dreadful predatory creature! Matthew thinks with dismay - Lady Snatchal, holding all the aces in this weird and twisted game she has initiated, one in which Matthew himself seems destined to be the loser this very night - and this in a most dishonourable fashion. Damned if he does, damned if he doesn't, whatever comes to pass, he will continue to be in the gravest danger. And as if all this were not enough, he is also suddenly reminded that somewhere at the end of that drive is Johanna - waiting for him, pinning her hopes on his somehow being able to persuade her husband not to proceed with his insane plan to enlist as surgeon in the Duke of Cumberland's army. Could it be done? What would Sam's resolution be like - or to be more accurate, his level of sheer obstinacy? - because he could be as stubborn as a mule when the mood takes him. It is, whatever way you look at it, Matthew concludes, a situation from which he himself would be unlikely to emerge entirely unscathed. If he had any sense, he would be urging the driver outside to turn around and hurry him back to London and thence to the earliest ship to the Americas - the only way to escape the madness of it all and to at least live to tell the tale. For a second or two, he really does contemplate it.

Just then, however, he is aware of a deep, rhythmic thudding outside - louder and louder until it becomes the unmistakable sound of a galloping horse. Seconds later, a great black steed with a cloaked rider thunders past, so close to the carriage that it almost touches it, and accompanied by a screech of excitement from the person astride the animal - all of which spooks the two horses of his carriage, for they neigh and protest loudly until they are coaxed back to their regular tempo. Ahead, meanwhile, the rider has reigned in her mare and waits for his carriage to approach - and as it draws alongside and as Matthew glances out the window and upwards, it is to the face of Dorothea, Lady Snatchal herself, revealed now from beneath the hood as, unfastening a button, she allows it to slide down upon her shoulders, her jet black hair hanging in sportive ringlets.

'Why, Mr Wildish, I had a feeling it might be you hiding in there,' she says as, urging the horse to keep pace, she sets off at a brisk canter alongside. 'Good day to you!'

'And good day to you, your Ladyship!' he declares, raising his tricorn and, with a little bow of the head, trying to avoid the great steaming nostrils of the beast and the cold sleet driving into his face at the same time. 'I trust you are well and in good spirits?'

'By Jove, I should say so! A good half-hour in the saddle perks one up no end,' she replies, speaking loudly against the wind.

'I must say Snatchalcombe House looks quite splendid this afternoon,' he ventures a compliment, though rather wishing he could close the window again as soon as possible and allow the accursed place to be swallowed into the ground.

'Oh, rather!' Lady Snatchal agrees loudly with her usual intensity, still riding at a canter, though possible becoming restless already with the slow pace. 'We always tell ourselves we should employ an artist one day to paint the north aspect with all them steps and pilasters and what not. A proper oil painting - you know, like in one of them there *Camelotos*.'

'Indeed, yes. A shame about the weather, though.'

'What?'

'A shame about the inclement weather today, Ma'am!' he shouts a little louder against the howling wind and creaking axles.

'Oh, doesn't bother me,' she replies cheerfully - and clothed, as he can see now, not in skirts but in baggy breeches, and fully astride the animal rather than side-saddle. 'I always enjoy a good ride, Mr Wildish, no matter what the conditions. My physician says it gets a lot of the aggression and heat out of the system - so I'm ready to return to the masquerade now and do a turn of duty among Sam's guests, who are all frightfully dull, I might add.'

'*Masquerade?* I had no idea,' he responds in horror, having come totally unprepared for such an eventuality.

'Oh, yes, did you not know? Last minute whim on Sam's part. Don't you go worrying, though. Just come as you are, Mr Wildish - so to speak. That'll do nicely.'

At which she lets forth another shriek of mischief, raises her hood, and with a kick of her heels and a flourish of her riding crop sets the animal off at a gallop once more - while for Matthew, watching her hurtling into the distance towards the house like some demonic phantom in the gloom, it is as if he is witnessing his very nemesis leading him on. His presence having been recorded now, there is no possibility of retreat.

As he alights from his carriage and settles the fare with the driver, and as he is met by a butler who assists him with his luggage and shows him into the vast, colonnaded atrium with its domed central ceiling, it is indeed evident that a masquerade is taking place - the house populated by many more guests than Matthew had bargained for, most in some variety of costume in addition to masks. It is, however, surprisingly welcoming in tone, with every room that he can see having a good fire set in the grate.

'Ah, Wildish!' a voice cries in salutation - this, coming from one attired as a Satyr, half-man, half goat, complete with a mask supporting a neat little pair of horns attached to his temples, and which can only be, as Matthew perceives straight away, Lord Snatchal. 'Welcome, m'boy! Do not be alarmed. Most of those you see here are guests for the afternoon only. It will be just the five of us at dinner this evening, during which we should, I trust, have an opportunity to put our case to Sam concerning his ill-advised plans.'

'Lord Snatchal, how good to see you again!' Matthew says by way of greeting. 'I have brought those items you require, by the way.'

'The wigs - oh, capital, my boy, capital!' Lord Snatchal declares, though looking around a little uneasily, Matthew thinks. 'Tell you what, come with me now, and we'll just pop up to the closet and take a look at them in private.'

And this they do, fetching Matthew's wig box from the foyer and then setting off on the lengthy route march that such an exercise inevitably entails, firstly up the great double staircase and then along the many anonymous passageways that Matthew recollects from his last visit. Why in heaven's name, he wonders, do people insist on building these enormous places, let alone trying to dwell in them for any length of time? Acres of empty state rooms and bed chambers - of a quantity quite beyond the wit of man to keep a tally of, as was remarked upon by none other than Lady Snatchal herself on Matthew's last visit, he recalls - and which inevitably compel those unfortunate humans who must occupy them to huddle together in a small parlour or closet somewhere where they can at least keep warm and where their voices are not echoed back at them constantly from cold marble walls.

'Everything, all right, Wildish?' Snatchal inquires, perhaps sensing that Matthew is already flagging somewhat with the awkward bulk of the wooden box under his arm.

'Yes, Sir,' he replies, his eyes full of the satyr's tail ahead, ascending yet another flight of stairs and swinging as he goes, 'it's just that one can perhaps become a little overwhelmed at times, by the dimensions of places such as this - magnificent as they undoubtedly are.'

'What do you mean? This is nothing compared to the foundations of the monastery on which it was built. Half the size!'

'Monastery?'

'Oh, yes, our family was awarded it with the Reformation, you know,' Snatchal continues with urbane nonchalance. 'Services rendered, and all that. Naturally, we knocked the ruddy thing down straight away - or rather my Great, Great, Grandfather did - and built the present edifice - of which the Palladian facade and interiors are the most recent additions. Anyway, what's your objection, exactly, Wildish? I don't understand! Surely it's preferable that a few of us enjoy a decent slice of the cake now and again, than to have the whole thing shared out and everyone living on a diet of crumbs?'

Matthew realises straight away that he should have kept quiet - but he is determined to hold his own. 'Indeed, Sir, yes - it's just that one wonders sometimes why we need to bake the cake on such a vast scale.'

'Good God, Wildish!' Snatchal groan with indignation. 'Because we can!' he adds with an odd kind of abandonment, almost hilarity, as if his explanation must be patently obvious to anyone with half a brain. *'Because we can,'* he repeats - and by which time, mercifully, the remote sanctuary of the noble Lord's private closet has been reached and Matthew can at last hand over the Cornhill wig, a duty he has never been more eager to discharge. Also in the same box is the finished campaign wig that Lord Snatchal had ordered way back in November. Both are taken out, still mounted over their wooden blocks, and placed with great care upon the table. And here, removing the lower segment of his mask, which does however leave his horns still intact, the Earl, draws up a stool and, bidding Matthew do likewise, appraises both items in turn with an obvious satisfaction - though as his eyes settle on the campaign wig, his little red-painted lips pucker up somewhat in sorrowful fashion and then seem to vanish almost entirely as he sucks them inwards before speaking.

'Pity. Doesn't look like I am going to be needing this one, after all,' he laments, his chin resting in his hands as he leans over it to examine its fine workmanship more closely. 'Do you know, I have not received a single request from Cumberland or Hawley for my services in the field. Most sad!'

'I am sorry, Sir,' Matthew says, commiserating.

'Yes, and I hope, therefore, that you have not gone and mentioned this embarrassing *faux pas* of mine to anyone, Wildish?'

'About the campaign wig, Sir? No,' Matthew answers, feeling disappointed that having given his assurances of confidentiality already some weeks ago that his discretion should be called into question again. 'I never discuss the details of my commissions, Sir, not with anyone,' he reminds the other man.

'Oh good. It's just that ... well, I would rather appreciate it if we could keep the whole thing hush-hush now,' the Earl continues, almost as a murmur as they both continue to gaze at the luxurious item which Matthew has already had powdered for him and which presents, therefore, a most resplendent, snowy-white appearance. 'The epitome of folly really, on my part, to have considered that anybody would want me at my time of life. I'm past it - and that's all there is to it.'

'Oh, surely not, my Lord!' Matthew exclaims with diplomacy. 'Life in the old dog yet, as they say.'

'No, no, Wildish,' the Earl overrules him, 'I really am past it. In fact, it's so long ago since I passed it, that I believe I've even forgotten what it was that I passed. Fine job, though, I must say. And better coming late than never, what! As the actress said to the bishop.'

'My apologies, Sir, that it took so long,' Matthew remarks, finding it hard to respond to the Earl's humour, which does seem more than a little hollow at present, he senses.

'Um, yes ... any particular reason for that, by the way?' Snatchal inquires, 'apart from your unanticipated adventures in the North, that is,' he adds, thereby tending to dismiss the question anyway.

But just then, as Matthew stares across into the face of the bizarre Satyr seated there before him, he is quite spontaneously delivered of a moment of inspiration - a perfectly unique idea. It might come to nothing, he thinks, or it might just be an opportunity to save his life. Either way, he knows he must seize the moment and speak:

'It was savaged,' he announces, managing to contrive a smile, 'by a dog.'

'What? The wig? Savaged ... *by a dog?*'

'Yes - the campaign wig, that is. I had it all finished, and a visitor came with a pug, and - what do you think! - the little rascal grabbed it and made off with it down the stairs. Well, to be sure, I gave chase, as you can imagine, but by the time I had apprehended the little scoundrel, the wig was shredded to pieces. I had to start from scratch and do the whole thing all over again.'

'My dear fellow - I had no idea,' Lord Snatchal declares with a note of sympathy. 'How very unfortunate. Naturally, I would be more than willing to compensate for any additional cost ...'

'Oh, that won't be necessary,' Matthew is swift to interject. 'Just one of those things, my Lord, and no harm done, after all.'

'Indeed no,' Snatchal agrees, as his eyes turn next to the other, far more keenly anticipated piece set upon his table. With a slow nod of approval and unusually hesitant hands, he sets aside its ceremonial box that Matthew has also returned today and reaches out to rotate the mannequin head on which the Cornhill Wig itself is set, viewing it from all angles to obtain a comprehensive observation of it in all its varied colours and pleasingly crinkly textures. 'Now, of course, if an accident of that kind had befallen this little beauty here ... well, that would have been a very different matter. Most regrettable, what!'

Matthew watches the face of the other man with amazement as, learning ever closer to the object of his admiration, his eyes widen and become illuminated with a extraordinary blend of excitement and awe - as, with index finger and thumb, he probes and toys and twiddles about within the curls for a further moment of unabashed joy. 'I must say it is quite remarkable, Wildish, quite a transformation - and so very spruce! All the different colours are so much more vivid now it's cleaned up. And I can even detect that little addition we requested, as well. Yes - here, it is. And dear Mrs Mountfast's as well. Ah, look, and little Molly just over here - that pretty blond. Such memories ... Anyway, what I really should be saying, Wildish, is *hooray and huzzah!* It's a masterpiece. You have done us proud.'

Upon which, the Earl rises and, still with the utmost care and veneration in his movements, replaces the Cornhill wig in its special box, which he then carries to his curio cabinet at the far end of the room, there to be deposited and locked securely away.

'What a relief to have it returned to us, safe and secure again,' he sighs as he draws out his watch and glances at the time. 'I say,

Wildish, we'd better go back and join the others, eh? And maybe we ought to lend you a mask - just to see you through the next hour or so, until that lot downstairs go home.'

Availing himself of a drawer below his desk, the noble Lord rummages around inside among various items. 'Oh dear! I've got some in here, but I'm afraid most of these seem to have horns of one description or another,' he says. 'Oh, wait a minute, here you are, here's one!'

'I don't mind horns, Sir,' Matthew asserts.

'No, no ... wouldn't suit you, Wildish,' he mutters, adjusting his own pair at just that moment.

It is an unfortunately skimpy piece that Matthew is presented with, and as he takes possession of it he knows full well that he will still be recognisable. But no matter: eager to conceal, if only a little, any guilt or apprehension that might be detected upon his face he dons it straight away.

'First-rate animal, you know, the goat,' Snatchal observes, still on his feet, looking at Matthew with a strange kind of interest, as though sizing him up.

'Really?' says Matthew, rising as well and feeling slightly disturbed for some reason, a chill running down his spine - a state not relieved at all as the old fellow's eyes meet his - the wrinkled face beneath its heavy powder and rouge surface looking surprisingly creature-like and menacing at just that moment before he slips his own mask back over his head and then with his thin little fingers wriggles himself into it, a process that does not improve the overall picture very much.

'Yes: amazing virility,' he continues with a purse of the lips, 'yet possessed also of so many additional qualities. I mean, have you ever observed, for example, the goat in its natural state, its perseverance; the way it climbs; the way it leaps in small increments, and always with the greatest of care from crag to crag, making its progress steadily up the mountain-side in search of its food, and always ready to butt any rival out of its way - calculating, relentless, *ruthless*. Altogether an ideal metaphor for the ambitious politician and leader of men, wouldn't you say?'

'Indeed, Sir, yes,' Matthew concurs, trying not to show his alarm, gazing back into the face of the terrible satyr standing next to him and hoping his feelings of distress are not obvious.

But he need not have worried. Abruptly, without any further

ado, Snatchal turns and leads the way out of the room, setting off at a brisk pace upon the return journey, which they undertake together, side by side, back downstairs to the ballroom and where a good number of guests are still to be found, raising their glasses and toasting in brandy, port and wine the imminence of Sam's departure - a departure which, Matthew is given to understand, could be as early as tomorrow morning, without even returning to his home in Greenwich.

Matthew, glad to be alone once again, mingles and tries his best to appear jovial. The music is provided by a modest ensemble of strings and bassoon from a gallery somewhere above - a fine sound, in fact, being just sufficiently classical in tone to meet the requirements of taste, but jaunty enough to urge many of those present to be up on their feet and dancing - at just this moment progressing through a modest formation of opposing rows, from which partners interchange and mingle in orderly fashion. Almost everyone is in costume, and again Matthew can only feel mildly irritated that he has not been forewarned. And then, with a chilling reminder of the incident at the most recent masquerade he had attended in London, a domino, heavily cloaked and hooded, approaches him from across the room. Detecting the fragrance of a heady perfume, this is, he suspects, his hostess, Lady Snatchal, an elaborate bejewelled mask of black velvet covering almost her entire face.

'Why, Mr Wildish, once again, is it not?' she says, her arm extended as if she would envelop him and spirit him away within the lavish folds of her sinister outfit. 'Perhaps we should show you to your rooms forthwith.'

'I am obliged to you, Ma'am,' he answers with a bow as she signals for a footman to take Matthew's overnight bag from the foyer and then, with Lady Snatchal herself clearly keen to accompany him, and each equipped with a candle fixed within a brass holder, they commence upon what appears destined to be Matthew's second expedition of the day through the dark, cavernous halls of Snatchalcombe House. Another servant, meanwhile, is enlisted to do the duties of laying the trail of sand as they go, a fine silver crystalline texture that shines and reflects in the candlelight and by which, he recalls from last time, one is able to retrace one's steps back to the centre of the house. This time, the journey seems to be using up an inordinate amount of the stuff, taking them to the farthest-flung outposts of the building, towards what, he is given to understand, is an area called the annex to the west wing, an interminable trek along endless passageways and up and down desolate staircases, stopping only occasionally to consult a small map which Lady Snatchal peruses each time by the light of her candle prior to proceeding.

'It's a bit out of the way this time,' she states, rather needlessly as, at just that moment, a resident bat which they seem to have disturbed flies along the entire length of the passageway and past their heads. 'Nice and peaceful for you, Mr Wildish - down the end here.'

It is, indeed, *down the end*, he reflects - in fact it could as well be half way back to London before they finally turn into a small, darkly panelled cul-de-sac of doorways - one of which, it is concluded by the expedient of an additional glance at the map and the trying of a key in lock, to be Matthew's very own bed chamber at last.

'That will be all for the moment,' she tells her men. 'Wait here outside and you may accompany me back to the ballroom shortly.'

At which, gratefully placing Matthew's case over the threshold, the men close the door behind them, leaving Matthew alone with his hostess.

'Well, what do you think of it?' she asks, approaching him more closely.

Holding forth his candle, he glances around to what, he has to admit, is a most pleasant interior, featuring a large four-poster bed - everything lavishly draped and carpeted. Nearby, set on a stand is a fine china washbowl with towels, and a more-than-adequate supply of wine and sherry positioned on a nearby sideboard. A log fire, having already been lit in the hearth, has settled into a mound of brightly glowing embers - making for a most pleasing ambiance.

'One way or another, I reckon you should be right comfy here tonight,' she announces. 'You have your set of keys on the washstand, Matthew, and I will look after these ones here myself. In the meantime, you should not be reticent in discussing your requirements with any of our staff.'

'Thank you, Ma'am.'

'Oh, for heaven sake, Matthew! Stop calling me *Ma'am!* I am Dorothea - Dottie, to my friends - remember?' And then, in a far quieter tone of voice, adding: 'You really must begin to call me something less formal, my darling - seeing as we are going to be on such intimate terms later on. And you do know that, don't you? You cannot prevent it, Matthew. You cannot resist the inevitable any longer.'

Matthew bows in curt fashion, as one would to an opponent at the onset of a boxing match - sufficient to bring a smile to her face, though an ominous one of anticipated victory in this instance. And then, stepping up, she places her hands upon his waist and runs them up and down his sides before standing on tiptoe in order to plant a surprisingly tender kiss upon his lips.

'Poor Matthew,' she says. 'The plight of the bachelor - I know well how it is for a young man - to have always such constant needs, that dreadful itch of desire that no matter how often it is scratched must always return, and then to sleep at night so often alone and not to be awoken by kisses.'

'You will be relieved to learn ... *Dottie,*' he replies, realising that his own hands have somehow instinctively found their way around her waist also, 'that the frustrations you describe are not ones that trouble me that often.'

'It will certainly not be the case tonight, I'll warrant,' she murmurs. 'Oh, Matthew, you will not be disappointed in my taking advantage of you, I promise - for I know right-well how to please. And anyway, you know what they say: *the older the millstone, the better the grind.*'

'I do not doubt it, Dottie,' he replies, acutely aware, and most disconcertingly so, of her hand examining him for one fleeting moment as a farmer might do a ram at a market.

'Your little Sarah the laundry girl has told us all about you, of course. You naughty boy,' she whispers. 'You should come and join us all sometime, Matthew. You are evidently well equipped for such a service.'

And as the margins of her cloak slip a little wider apart he cannot help casting his eyes over her - she being lightly and informally attired beneath. It is a rare moment, her being complicit and approving of his looking, and so he lingers in the study of it. Slim, with prominent bones at her throat and chest, she is blessed with a naturally vigorous countenance - no doubt sensitive to the attentions of gentle fingers or lips - while those sweet prominences, so bold even beneath the covering of her shift, have an erect aspect to them, and of a length that indicates one who, in her time, has perhaps taken much pleasure thereby. Intriguing. Under normal circumstances, she would present to any man a most attractive prospect - though he tells himself that this temporary fondness is only an aspect of his own baser instincts, and perhaps in no small part engendered by her teasing him with her ridiculous invitation to some unlikely and unspecified orgy. The rational part of him remains most disturbed, therefore - and it is greatly to his relief when all of a sudden she disengages herself and, with a swift glance at the clock on the chimneypiece, and speaking in an entirely different, more formal tone of voice, declares: 'Alas, Mr Wildish, I must leave you now, and embark upon the journey back to organise dinner, following which we must put our fondest expectations aside, at least for a while and try our best to prevail upon our dear Sam to change his mind. One would not wish poor Johanna to be lonely in London.'

'Indeed, yes,' Matthew agrees as he watches her securing her cloak once again. 'Until later, then ... *Dottie,*' he adds.

'Oh yes,' she whispers, 'until later - and even later still. That will be the best of it. Toodle Pip!'

At which, accompanied by a busy rustle of her cloak as it chafes the floor, she turns from him and departs. He listens as she strides away along the passageway in the company of her footmen, and suddenly he is alone - the deep, deep silence of the vast empty building becoming quite extraordinary in its intensity.

Taking a seat by the dresser to attend to his hair, he knows he should probably follow in her footsteps soon and return to the masquerade - an obligation of courtesy, like all the other obligations that have somehow ensnared him of late. He has not even the possibility any longer of taking the cowardly option, the one he has already considered on more than one occasion this afternoon of simply running away, for the anguish and embarrassment that Sam and Johanna would experience if he were to do so would be unthinkable. She is right, this terrible ogress - it is inevitable, his surrender. He is caught, like some poor fly enmeshed in a spider's web; reprieved for an hour perchance to roam a little and struggle on its gossamer thread, only to be drawn back later to await its fate. There is, he has to concede, really no answer to his predicament.

Having changed to more formal attire and returned by slow degrees along his trail of sand to the ballroom, Matthew takes a turn at dancing, participating with his fellow revellers in a lively minuet and joining in a modest formation with some of the remaining guests, admiring as he does so many an alluring pair of eyes beneath the masks - some of which he endeavours to put a name to from among Sam and Johanna's circle of friends and relatives, but this mostly without success because it is becoming even more difficult to see now in the advance of the early darkness that attends the winter's afternoon. The staff are simply not lighting the candles and chandeliers quickly enough to keep pace with it. Consequently, and although the music from the gallery continues, many of the guests begin to depart. It is only then when he finally encounters Johanna. She is attired as a shepherdess in a frock and *bergère* hat, her stomacher laced with pink ribbons, her ankles bare, her mask a full visor of leafy velvet with little touches of sparkling paste or glass beads that hang from delicate silver chains. Really most lovely.

'Pray, Sir, why are you not in costume?' she appeals to him, clearly exasperated again over yet another of his social blunders at the Snatchalcombe Estate.

'No one told me to bring one,' he replies curtly. 'Anyway, do I know you Madam?'

'Yes, of course! You know full well who I am, Matthew. Stop being so pretentious.'

Undaunted, he offers her his arm, which is always acceptable practice at a masquerade, of course - and she, taking it, allows him to steer her away from the others - just as well, this opportunity to converse alone, because he knows that he must confide in her. He simply cannot keep things to himself a moment longer.

'Johanna, please listen to me,' he begins with audacious intimacy as they locate a peaceful and discreet area behind one of the marble columns of the ballroom.

'I always listen to you, Sir,' she snaps, turning her face away, 'particularly regarding your assurances of punctuality, which is why, no doubt, I am often so very disappointed.'

'No, listen, I am serious,' he protests, ignoring her jibes. 'Johanna, I hope in advance that you will forgive me for getting myself into what you will shortly apprehend is a most dreadful mess, but I must tell you that I am in mortal danger.'

'Mortal danger - what again!' she observes, opening her fan and flicking it with a vigorous petulance beneath her chin, clearly still not prepared to moderate her annoyance with him. 'Why, Matthew, are your legendary exploits and daring-do not already celebrated sufficiently - so much so that my poor husband must now insist on emulating them? You must try to perceive the situation from someone else's perspective, my Wonder, just for once, and understand that my concerns over *your* danger are as nothing compared to those I must endure concerning the father of my children.'

'Yes, I understand that,' he concurs. 'I am sorry. But please, Johanna, do hear me out. I am in danger because I am compelled by forces beyond my control to commit adultery ...'

'Beyond your control, Matthew? Oh, how very convenient!' she declares, still waspish and, turning from him yet again, folds her arms indignantly about her chest.

'This very night,' he continues undaunted, 'and with the person of our hostess, moreover, Lady Snatchal, who has knowledge over a certain failing of mine and which, if made public would almost inevitably result in my demise. Oh, be assured, this will not be in the form of a duel, or entail any public demonstration of violence. The people I have offended have far more subtle ways of dealing with those who besmirch their honour - a lethal poison that cannot be detected, an unfortunate accident whilst travelling - whatever means they choose, it will be the most thorough retribution, believe me.'

'I don't understand. What on earth could you have done to render yourself so vulnerable?' she asks, appearing to be genuinely concerned for the first time - those little lines of concentration forming between her brows just above the margin of her mask.

'Can you remember that afternoon when you came to my workshop at the Pig and Whistle - no not last time: I mean the time prior to that, with your little pug, Boris, who ran off with that curious wig?'

'Goodness ... yes! And that terrible business with all those sailors. You were so very forgiving towards little Boris, I remember. I was quite touched by your tolerance.'

'Yes, well the rather shabby and humble hair piece that Boris took such a fancy to on that occasion did in fact belong to Lord Snatchal's elite society of companions and knights - the Cornhill

Wig Club.'

'Oh, yes, I know the Cornhill. Sam is a member. I never heard it called that before - *Wig Club*.'

'Yes. Those initiated into the ranks call it by that name only among themselves because - and this, I fear, might come as rather a shock to you, so forgive me - but the wig they venerate and incorporate in all their most important ceremonies and customs is compiled of the privy hair of their mistresses - or wives, as the case may be.'

'What!' Johanna cries, so loudly that he fears it might be drawing unwelcome attention, and he instinctively raises a finger to his lips to silence her.

'Over the decades it has been added to, bit by bit,' he continues, 'until it has become an indispensable icon of their fraternity. I was given the dubious honour of its restoration, and upon its loss that day, I had to find some means of reconstructing it - not from pubic hair, I hasten to add, but from other sources - and this I have managed to do. It even passed muster with Lord Snatchal when I delivered it into his hands this afternoon. The one problem in all this, is that Lady Snatchal knows. She put two and two together after you - and please do not blame yourself for this - after you had occasion to mention that very incident in conversation.'

Johanna lets forth a great sigh and drops her shoulders in exasperation. 'Oh, that awful old harridan!' she gasps with scorn. 'That snake in the grass! This would certainly explain why she has placed you in such a distant wing, miles from anywhere. I saw your trail of sand earlier, or some of it. It did seem inordinately long.'

'Precisely. And the door where it eventually terminates, is one to which the Countess herself has the key. Anyway, that is my predicament. I thought I had better inform you - though of course, I wouldn't want you to feel sorry for me.'

'Goodness, no - why should I feel sorry for you? What do you mean?'

'Isn't that what you said to the Countess the other day? That you only offered your help and patronage because you felt sorry for me.'

'Really? Is that what she told you? Goodness, are there no depths of deceit to which this awful Jezebel will not descend! Don't be such a fool, Matthew. Me, feel sorry for you - that'll be the day!'

Coming closer to each other in the silence that ensues, he senses a certain tenderness emanating from her. The frankness and temperature of their verbal exchanges has excited him, moreover, and he longs to take her hands in his, to prolong this all too rare moment of such intimate discourse. It would be a gesture, however, that would not pass unnoticed in the sparsely populated hall, he knows; and in any case, they cannot converse further because Sam has spotted them and is already advancing in their direction. Unmasked by this time, he is clothed in his Roman Emperor's costume once again, though with bare arms which do look somewhat blue and cold on this occasion.

'Matt - at last!' he exclaims in his usual blunt and forthright manner, coming up and looking disapprovingly on Johanna's proximity to him, while Johanna, for her part, can only regard her husband with a silent, simmering gaze of contempt, one that no mask could ever succeed in hiding - for it is almost palpable, the abhorrence she obviously feels concerning the true nature of the Cornhill Club. And without a word, she pushes past him and strides away.

'What's the matter with Johanna?' Sam demands, being equally as irritable, as if it were all somehow Matthew's fault.

'Sam, what on earth is all this going away nonsense about?' Matthew responds, not bothering to reply to his friend's question and unable to stem his own distress and curiosity over the whole affair a moment longer. 'Why did you not tell me your intentions?'

'Why? Because you would only try to dissuade me, Sir,' Sam replies, flicking his toga petulantly over his shoulder. 'And I am not for dissuading. No, Sir, not at all.'

Matthew stares in silence into the eyes of his friend which are uncommonly agitated and disturbed, he notices. So, yes, it really is true, he thinks to himself, and not without sadness. Poor Sam really is jealous. How ridiculous. Oh, if only they could all be friends again, he thinks, return to the simplicity of life as it was even just a few short weeks ago. But it cannot be - it seems it can never be so again - and then, before he can respond or even try to put the matter to rights, a footman approaches and, softly speaking, informs them that dinner will be served in precisely one hour, and that drinks will be available in the dining room in thirty minutes - all sufficient stimulus for Sam to hurry off, though not without a parting shot in Matthew's direction to the effect of his determination not to be diverted from his chosen destiny, and other high-minded sentiments which, emanating from Sam, sound so untypically lofty and exalted as to be almost comical.

And so, Matthew, locating his trail yet again begins the long march back to his room where, in the absence of his forbidden man-servant, he will be compelled to change for dinner unaided and from where, due to the distances and time involved, he will most likely be late again in returning to the dining room. The prospect of the evening ahead fills him with foreboding already. How will it all end? He dares not even contemplate it.

# THE REVEALING ART
# OF PERSUASION


'Would you care for some more oysters, Mr Wildish?'
Lady Snatchal inquires from her seat at the head of
the table, and for what must surely be the fifth time
this evening, even though Matthew has so far steadfastly declined
to partake in any of the renowned aphrodisiacal food himself. For
her own part, she appears intent on consuming as many as possible
and often intersperses proceedings by encouraging her guests to
share in her enthusiasm, raising the shell to her lips with a great
slurping sound each time as the item is slid, gannet-like, into her
mouth and straight down her throat.

Apart from this, the dinner at Snatchalcombe House is as civil
and as politely lavish as ever, the atmosphere one of cordiality and,
in fact, everything that one would expect from the renowned
hospitality of their hosts, topped with an array of succulent dessert
fruits, miraculous specimens preserved long-past their season by
the able ministrations of the estate gardeners. Upon the meal's
conclusion, however, everyone is aware that things must change,
that some serious and very plain speaking must be called for in
order to have any hope of dissuading Sam from his misguided
ambitions. To this end, and at Lord Snatchal's instigation, they
dispense with the usual after-dinner formality of the gentlemen
being left with their brandy, and elect instead to retire, all five
together, to a relatively warm and comfy drawing room - the very
same, Matthew notices, in which they had attended the
demonstration of the air pump upon his previous visit last year.
And so, once all the servants have been dismissed and guests have
been provided with wine and are comfortably cradled in armchairs
around the fireside or, in the case of Sam and Johanna, together on
a nearby sofa, Lord Snatchal, assuming the role as self-appointed
master of ceremonies calls everyone to order with a little jingle of a

spoon upon the rim of his glass and then, with one foot resting on his adjustable gouty stool, proceeds to address the assembled company thus:

'Ladies and gentlemen. I trust you have enjoyed a satisfying repast. It is now time for us to apply ourselves to the matter for which we are here met, and that is the imminent departure of our good friend for the campaign in Scotland. Sam, we have given you a good sending off with the masquerade earlier, and thus your family and friends are well aware of your noble and patriotic intentions - and from which it should be clear that there would be no disgrace if we were to persuade you now not to proceed. Your gesture will have been noted, your bravery acknowledged without you having to actually go through with it. To this end, I propose that each of us be permitted to speak uninterrupted for a few minutes, so that we might put our case to you as to why you should remain. The one condition I am going to impose upon each of us, however, is that we reinforce our reasoning with a confession of some kind, an intimate revelation on a topic not known to the rest of those present. The case that each of us presents will therefore be charged with all the more force and potency because of its element of self-sacrifice. Thus, I should just remind everyone present, that whatever is said will naturally remain within these four walls, and never be repeated elsewhere. Does that sound interesting, Sam? That we should all of us be moved to such a passion to keep you among us that we are prepared to compromise ourselves, even to our own detriment?'

'You are all welcome, of course, to try what you will,' Sam replies, looking down his nose in his most sententious fashion - and being clothed this evening in a waistcoat of scarlet, trimmed with braid, already seeming to have something of the military about him. 'I can assure you all that your efforts will be in vain, though,' he adds, 'nay, utterly futile. I am resolved.'

Ignoring Sam's bumptious protestations, Lord Snatchal takes a long sip of his claret, clears his throat and commences upon proceedings forthwith by presenting his plea: 'Samuel, the rational part of my argument is plain enough, and it is this. There is, as many of us know from experience, nothing glamorous about war. It's a rotten bloody business, and the work you will be undertaking will place you in the thick of it. To be perfectly frank, I do not believe you're cut out for such an ordeal. You would simply be too big a target, anyway, and wouldn't last five minutes under fire. Anyway, that said, let me go on now to provide additional weight to my contention (no pun intended, Sam, sorry) with a confession of sorts. Ladies and gentlemen, you will be aware that Sam and I have over a good few years enjoyed an excellent working relationship within the Admiralty. I refer not only to our shared interests in national security, but also to our close business ties. And in this context - and listen, because this is where it gets really interesting - Snatchalcombe House and its environs represent not only one of the most magnificent Palladian mansions to be found anywhere in the kingdom, but it's also a working farm; and Sam here, in his capacity as a procurement officer for the Navy, has bought heaps of our salt pork and potatoes over the years, always paying a handsome price for them, moreover. An impartial observer, I suppose, might even describe these prices as somewhat inflated; over and above the market value, you understand. You might also recall, Samuel, that we were hoping to sign a particularly lucrative deal later this year concerning our wool, in order to supply the Navy with blankets. Ladies and gentlemen, you may just recognise, I trust, the forces at work here - because money, as they say, makes the world go around, and a little extra over the odds never did anyone any harm. None of this is Sam's fault, I hasten to add - but merely the result of my own inveterate greediness and which I freely confess to you this evening.'

Everyone nods with a grim kind of comprehension. And Matthew, beginning to understand all too well the basis of Sam and Snatchal's working relationship, is not sure whether he wants to laugh or cry - though sensibly he restrains himself from doing either.

'Anyway, that's it,' Lord Snatchal concludes. 'I must say, those Papists have it all over us with this confessional lark, don't you think? Quite a cathartic experience. And so, Samuel my friend, you see how determined I am, that I have sacrificed my own integrity this evening among those present? And I have done so, because I do not wish you to be blown to smithereens on some ruddy godforsaken battlefield - not just yet, at any rate, not until the blankets are ready, and that won't be for months, by which time Cumberland will have kicked the Young Pretender's arse back into the Irish Sea, anyway, where it belongs. I rest my case, therefore, and trust that you will reconsider.'

Sam, simply hangs his head. He does not respond, while the look of disappointment and horror on Johanna's face, as the grubby reality of her husband's less-than-wholesome business dealings becomes apparent, is sufficient to indicate her displeasure. No small shock for her, it would appear.

'Well now, Dorothea - would you care to go next, my dear?' Lord Snatchal inquires, replacing his foot on his stool, and addressing his wife, who, seated alone, has been listening to all this with a singular indifference, her face appearing sallow and bloodless, almost skull-like in the eerie light of the candles which for once do not flatter her all that well. It is an aspect rendered all the more bleak by the usual preponderance of darkest colours that she favours, a gown bedecked in flounces of black lace, redeemed only in its centre by a stomacher of silver brocade to lend a little sparkle. Most dour. It is her child-wanting-to-stamp-its-feet appearance - her lips tightly compressed. But eventually she does rouse herself.

'What can I say, Sam?' she begins in an untypically drawling sort of voice - but gradually gaining vigour as she continues, 'I think it to be a right folly, and most unwise that any man should go leaving a young wife alone for months on end. I mean, don't you reckon, in them sort of circumstances, that a woman might feel tempted - how shall we say - to stray from the straight and narrow? Not that I am implying for one moment that my dearest friend Johanna would ever be prone to such inconstancy. But there again, you must admit you could be detained north of the border for some while. And like they say: When mending the bedroom door, one nail's as good as another.'

'I can assure you, Dorothea,' Johanna interrupts, 'that I would never compromise my marriage through any kind of sordid infidelity, if that is what you are alluding to - no matter what the circumstances.'

'Why naturally, my dear. I was merely trying to say that as a general observation on human nature, that women of a less sturdy resolution than ourselves might be led into temptation. Which brings me to my own disclosure and confession - and I trust you will pay heed, Sam, because it is intended to add force to my contention. I must own, that in my younger days whenever Cornelius was absent for extended periods, on business matters or court affairs, that even *I* was tempted to ere. *Tempted,* I say. Never to succumb, of course. This came especially to the fore after my unfortunate riding accident, the fall that I had, which sometimes inclined me in those darkest moments of loneliness and painful solitude to seek diversions and amusements elsewhere. And, even you my dear Johanna will surely agree, there are always enticements a-plenty in the capital, especially during the Season with so many amorous and handsome young men, *writers and poets* and what not on the loose.' At which, Lady Snatchal appears to falter, and her eyes dart, albeit very briefly, in Matthew's direction - just as Sam's eyes dart with similar rapidity towards his wife. 'To confess to you all yet further, I can tell you that I even took myself off once or twice in the evening to them Vauxhall Gardens - masked naturally - in order to discover just what sort of temptations a woman finding herself alone in the capital might be exposed to. Most enlightening, it was. Yes. An interesting experiment.'

'Really?' Lord Snatchal inquires, clearly surprised and agitated. 'And - er - how many times, exactly, did you engage in this - er - *experiment*, Dottie?'

'Oh ... not all that *offen*,' the Countess replies with untypical diffidence and beyond which she is clearly not willing to elaborate. 'And in any case, no matter what the temptations, at the last minute I would naturally always make my excuses and leave.'

'I see,' Lord Snatchal responds amid the sounds of various throats being cleared in the room, which otherwise does seem to have become exceptionally silent all of a sudden.

The Countess, meanwhile, has turned her gaze back to Johanna and by way of summing up continues with: 'Anyway, if my sordid revelations might go a ways towards persuading Sam here to reverse his decision and stay at your side, my dear, I reckon it would have been well worth it, don't you think, and a right good conclusion to have reached, *for all concerned*.'

'Most enlightening, Dorothea,' Lord Snatchal declares, still clearly a little disturbed. 'I am gratified by your assurances of fidelity, moreover, even under such extenuating circumstances, because it is true: all manner of naughty things do take place in Vauxhall Gardens, or so I hear - from what I have been told, you understand. All those shrubberies and lilac bushes at the far end of the gravel path to the South of the Chinese Pavilion. Um ... yes. Anyway, now Matthew, what about you, young man? What can you forfeit by way of secrets - something, I trust, of sufficient gravity that will persuade our friend here to refrain from leaving us?'

'Why, yes, of course,' Matthew responds, aware that all eyes are keenly upon him. 'I have, alas, had no opportunity yet to tell you, Sam, for you have neglected to discuss your intentions with me at any length, but I must say I dismayed by your decision. It is many years since either of us undertook our training as barber-surgeons and our skills with the implements and tools of the trade will have been all but lost. You will be obliged to learn everything all over again, and quickly. You will be called upon to entertain all manner of hardships and perform operations in the field that will be harrowing and gruesome. The experience will change you, and not for the better, I fear. Anyway, that is my argument based on reason. As to furnishing you all with some kind of titillating revelation by way of demonstrating the extent of my convictions, I am afraid I must disappoint. I really do not have anything unsavoury to be reporting to any of you. My only vice, if it be a vice at all, is that I am possibly a little too liberal with my person when it comes to affairs of the heart. Some might say that my behaviour verges on the libidinous. But I am a single man, after all.'

'Heavens, Wildish, that's hardly a damning disclosure!' The Earl protests, scoffing at Matthew's dismal efforts. 'There must be something else a bit more saucy to give us - as the actress said to the bishop, what?'

'Yes, come on Matthew!' Lady Snatchal joins in. 'You must have something just a tad scandalous?'

'No Madam. *Not as yet,* anyway.'

'Why, then, one might reckon you were quite keen on Sam going!' the Countess declares with a bold turn, opening her fan and letting it droop provocatively.

'To be sure, yes,' Matthew replies straight away, maintaining his confidence while glancing all the while with kindness towards Sam, 'and thereby I might perhaps do him the greatest service in preventing him from going at all, for he will then wonder why I am so cool.'

'Ah, yes,' Lord Snatchal chortles with approval. 'Clever! What say you, Sam? Perhaps you had better just stay after all. Keep an eye on the young rascal.'

But Johanna fails to see the funny side of any of this and is increasingly losing patience. 'I can assure you, again, *all of you,*' she states most firmly, leaning forward from her seat as if she would get up and charge, 'that my husband has no need to keep an eye on anything or anybody in respect of the vows I took upon my wedding day. I resent this entire line of reasoning. I shall prove steadfast - as faithful as Penelope during his absence. I shall wait a hundred years if need be for his return.'

To which Sam looks with appreciation once more concerning his wife's vigorous demonstration of loyalty, surveying one by one the faces of the others with a look of unguarded pride and satisfaction.

'Well then,' Lord Snatchal observes, turning again to Johanna, 'perhaps it is time then for you to present us with *your* plea, young lady? In the face of all our manifest failures, our hopes now rest with you. And unlike the virtuous Mr Wildish here, perhaps you might just reveal to us one little secret in order to strengthen your case, something about your good self that we don't already know and admire?'

'Thank you, Sir,' Johanna responds crisply and still with dignity, smoothing down her fine silken petticoats with her hands as if to steady herself. She looks most lovely this evening, Matthew thinks, delicately bedecked in pastel shades, a minimum of lace upon her wrists: a natural humility and poise. 'I shall, indeed, satisfy you presently in that sense, if you will give me leave,' she continues. 'But first, I will appeal to you, husband, as I have already appealed to you so many times in private these past few days, to remain with us for the sake of our children. Consider: how poorly they will fare, should anything unfortunate befall you and you fail to return to the bosom of your family. What sorrows must our babes endure without the moral authority of their father; without the guidance of manly experience; the rough and tumble of play. Goodness - how will *I* manage, having to face the remainder of my days without the support and joyous society of the man I love?'

Sam, clearly taken aback my such a passionate appeal, looks to be unusually blubbery and tearful all of a sudden. Putting down his wine glass and patting her on the knee with one hand as he blows his nose upon his elaborate lace handkerchief, he mumbles a tremulous, 'thank you my dear, thank you so very much.'

'Yes, but what about the confession?' Lady Snatchal demands,

surveying the loving couple seated together on her sofa with a look
of mild exasperation, not quite stamping her feet, but almost. 'What
we want to know is one of your naughty secrets, Johanna - if you
have any, that is.'

'It is true, Dorothea, I probably do not have that many to draw
upon,' Johanna responds straight away, her eyes narrowing with
venom, 'and none I suspect that you yourself would find
exceptional. I am not, for instance, one of those shameful women
of society with too much time on their hands who might wantonly
amuse themselves by lusting after younger men, or - to imagine
another instance - one who might indulge in the vile practice of
blackmail in order that others might succumb to her wishes, as I
suppose does go on *in some parts of the world.*'

A certain unease can be detected, a certain flapping about and
fidgeting among those present, troubled no doubt by Johanna's
untypical vehemence.

'No, quite, quite!' Lord Snatchal interrupts, a little puzzled over
why so many unwholesome topics might be surfacing all at once.

'Oh, how boring, then!' Lady Snatchal declares, sulking now
and pretending not to be concerned, though fanning herself with a
certain peevishness, for all that. 'Why, if I did not know you for the
delightful and engaging young woman that you are, Johanna, I
might be inclined sometimes to think you terribly dull.'

'And if I did not know you for the temperate and magnanimous
woman that you are, Dorothea, I might well mistake some of your
suggestions this evening as shot through with rudeness and
hypocrisy!'

'Now, now, that's enough of all that, you pair of lovelies!' Lord
Snatchal interrupts, a finger raised in reproof and who, having cast
aside his gouty stool, is at just that moment on his feet and, not
altogether steadily, hopping about making sure everyone's glass is
re-filled and to which Matthew, rising, lends a helping hand.
'Whatever Johanna has to say, we must be patient and hear the
young lady out,' he insists, evidently still keen on getting to the
confessional, and which seems to embolden Johanna, because she
draws herself upright on the sofa next, hands on knees as if
preparing to make an important announcement.

'Thank you, Sir,' she says as the men take their seats again.
'And, indeed, with your permission, I intend to reveal the
emotional side of my argument forthwith - since I have ... I have a

secret vice.'

'Really!' exclaims Lord Snatchal. 'Do enlighten us, my dear,' he says, a little thrilled already, it appears, judging by his colour.

'I shall, though I should in advance also apologise to my husband. Sam, my darling, I shall have to tell them. It is that I enjoy having my feet caressed. Yes. In fact, I enjoy it so much that I rarely achieve any satisfaction unless such a kindness is bestowed upon me. My long suffering husband will testify to the sincerity of this statement.'

All eyes, of course, immediately fly to Sam, who is looking most uncomfortable, raising his glass to obscure the trembling of his lips and spluttering somewhat as he attempts to imbibe.

'Why ... yes, that is true, my love,' he mumbles. 'You do enjoy having your little feet caressed ... occasionally.'

'No, husband. That is not entirely accurate to say *occasionally*. I have perhaps not informed you in the past of the full extent of my preferences in this sense, since I would much prefer to have it done *always*. When it is not done, in fact, I find myself feeling frustrated and incomplete. And when you are not present I often take a little almond oil from the cook and in the privacy of the bed-chamber apply some to my feet, gently rubbing and stroking all over the soles, my ankles and in-between my toes - all of which provides me with the greatest of pleasure.'

'Good God!' Sam declares. '*Almond oil!* So that's what I can smell in the bedroom when I return home late in the evening. And I had always assumed you were indulging yourself in confectionery!'

'I'm sorry,' she says, and lowers her gaze somewhat. 'But you see how fervent my wishes are that you should stay with us - that I should reveal to such a degree my most private eccentricities?'

Lord Snatchal, meanwhile, quite agog, appears far more interested in this revelation than should be at all proper under the circumstances - not exactly licking his lips, but almost.

'Cornelius!' Lady Snatchal barks loudly. 'Stop it at once!'

'Stop what, my dear?'

'Why, whatever it is you're thinking about there.'

'How do you know what I'm thinking, Dottie?'

'Huh!' she exclaims, raising her eyebrows in a rather salacious way herself and with an involuntary glance down towards Johanna's feet and her neat little brocaded shoes in sky blue.

'Huh!' echoes Sam in similar fashion, almost recoiling from his wife and appearing embarrassed as a result of this demonstration of his own ignorance.

'Um,' Matthew murmurs quietly and with, he sincerely hopes, a not-to-obvious smile, but at which Johanna raises her face to regard him with a most delicious and helpless look of surrender. Who would have thought it! What fun a man could have with one such as this, he thinks. And if he did not already desire her almost beyond endurance, then he knows, now more than ever, that he will never cease to be completely fascinated by her.

Unfortunately, despite all these sacrifices of honour and pride by which Sam has been assailed this evening, he still appears unmoved as to his resolution to leave for the wars - though he does at least agree to 'sleep on it,' as he tells them, and to announce his final decision in the morning - by which provision it eventually, becomes clear that it is time to retire. Everybody knows it has come, observing once again, as one must, all those signals that portend it: the signal, for instance, of Johanna's discreet yawning from behind her fan a little too often; the signal of Lord Snatchal beginning to snore and of the servants with the field stretcher having to be called to carry him off to his chamber - or of Sam not faring much better this evening, either, and beginning to slump into his seat at quite an early stage. There is also the signal when Lady Snatchal, a little uncharacteristically for her this evening, takes herself off early to her rooms with the parting statement that 'it's probably time to get a good night,' though exactly what she might mean by a 'good night' being perhaps open to interpretation in this instance. For Matthew it does not bode well, he thinks as, being the last to leave and, after taking a breath of fresh air from one of the windows, he wanders out through the atrium and up the vast curving double staircase to the first floor, eventually to locate his own silver trail of sand and, by the illumination of a solitary candle and a little ambient moonlight filtering in through the many undraped windows, to make his way back towards his distant chamber in the far-flung western annex of the gigantic edifice that is Snatchalcombe House, his heart full of cares for what the night may bring.

Although the renewed fire in the hearth has now faded once again to little more than a few dying embers, it remains warm and cosy in his room, the perfect love nest, in fact, if only a more edifying prospect were in store than a visitation from the Countess. To lock the door at this stage would be a provocative and futile act of defiance, of course. So he merely closes it softly behind him, takes a seat by the dresser and, with his face illuminated by a solitary candle, stares with abject observation at his own weary reflection in the glass.

So, Matthew Wildish, it has come to this, he thinks - all those years of poetic conquest and sweet dalliance - all leading to this moment of ignominy. Behold: the face of the soon-to-be adulterer! How very dishonourable.

He tells himself not to be so stupid, not to be so damn finicky about it all. The Countess, after all, and though hardly in the first blush of youth, is still a fine looking woman. Should he not instead just make the best of it - enjoy the experience? She would be highly experienced, adroit and passionate as a lover - and under any other circumstance, he would have not the slightest hesitation in obliging her. But he knows it is wrong, and with all the social ramifications attending the deed itself ... why it was little short of a disaster in the making.

'Ah - women, women!' He mutters to himself a little ruefully as he unfastens his cravat and sets the jewelled pin carefully aside. These wonderful creatures of charm and endless fascination. They have been his passion, his inspiration, his salvation and, more often than he would care to admit, his downfall, too, over the years - years in which it seemed at times as if his entire life had been set to the purpose of their society, of unravelling their mysteries. He had been vaguely aware of this destiny even at an early age, when the growth of a beard on his chin was still enough of a novelty for him to marvel at. He suspected, even then as a boy, that women would be important to him, immensely so - though he was also aware that he lacked the necessary experience to confirm the notion in any practical sense. All he knew was that his view of love-making was at variance to those of his contemporaries, the other young men around him at boarding school, who spoke about it in such disparaging terms in the dormitories, or at play upon the sports fields - those boisterous knaves whose sole aim in life, according to every report he received from them, was to emulate the beasts in the field and to simply satisfy themselves as swiftly and as frequently as nature would permit their urges to become renewed each time. He had, he recollects, even then, considered alternatives, wondered if a more protracted, generous engagement with the person of one's lover might be possible, a congress in which the passage of time could be used to explore sensations and feelings that he only half-suspected might exist but which, of course, once a little practical experience came along, he quickly learned *did* exist and could be located in such abundance in so many varied parts if only a little patience and imagination could be applied.

Never was he naive enough to assume that every woman he met would suit his ways, of course, nor was he ever vain enough to assume that he might suit every woman. How preposterous that would be in a world of such infinite variety! Instead, he discovered very early on that every woman was so wonderfully varied and different. Each one was motivated by different needs and desires. And once this principle was discovered, and once the approval of those lovers who *did* suit became apparent through its practise, he could no more cease his exploration of these territories of human endeavour than a seeker of treasure might abandon his search for *El Dorado*. And thus, so often in his amorous encounters, he would find himself asking, voicing the question silently to himself: where does she wish to be touched, where kissed? What words does she wish to hear, this dearest creature of desire? And the answer always came, as if the voice of some wise and discarnate being were prompting him and inviting him on to greater and greater delectation. And then, as wild youth blossomed to accomplished manhood, his reputation would go before him, with favours and opportunities becoming more and more his constant companions, urging him to indulge his curiosity still further. He became what is termed in polite society a man of pleasure, or what in some quarters might better be termed a rake or libertine. Yet throughout it all, even during his years overseas, he tried to be always the gentleman, endeavoured to avoid the blandishments of married women and to maintain some measure of honour ... until now, that is. Now, how very futile everything seemed, the realisation that all of it, everything, had been leading to *this* - this disgrace: to betray the hospitality of a friend, to lie with another man's wife - and this beneath his very roof, moreover. Would her kisses taste of oysters, he wonders? It is, he knows, the least of his concerns.

With nothing for it now but to wait, he undresses, dons his nightshirt and takes to his bed - and where, to his surprise, it being so soft and comfortable beneath the covers, he does eventually find himself drifting towards slumber. What prevents him from dropping off entirely, however, is the variety of unidentifiable noises that come in the otherwise deep silence of the building, noises which against such an ambience of isolation become amplified to alarming levels: the whistle of wind outside, the creaks of floorboards settling in the room, the rattling frames of sash windows, or other barely perceptible sounds - of distant footsteps maybe, though whether these are human in origin or that of rodents it is impossible to determine - or perhaps none of these. Perhaps they are the ghostly echoes of monastic feet from some bygone age, searching desperately for the noble cloisters or towering halls of prayer that once were theirs. In truth, he is probably imagining it all, anyway, he concludes - until eventually he discovers that it is actually daylight and that he is walking through the meadows outside in the grounds of Snatchalcombe House, where the maze is located, and there ahead he sees upon the hillock in the centre, housed in her little crenellated turret, and perched upon a swing which gentle sways and tilts this way and that in the pleasant sunshine, none other than Lady Snatchal. With one hand, she beckons him silently towards her, and he knows he must obey. But the maze surrounding her and the hedges are so tall and so confusing! What should he do? He scurries in various directions, tempted into false turns, becoming stranded in every cul-de-sac, endeavouring all the while to penetrate any one of the concentric rings of tall dark hedging and bring himself closer towards the elusive centrum of delight where his lover awaits. But it is no good. Only occasionally does he catch glimpses of her, Lady Snatchal - her face pale, her dark tresses flowing as she sways back and forth upon her swing, this monstrous overgrown child, her petticoats lifting to reveal evermore tantalising glimpses of gartered thigh, the gates of pleasure parting all the while to tempt and tease and to draw him ever onward - so close, moreover, that he can even hear her singing now, siren like, as she beckons him yet again with her hand, urging him towards the mound at the centre. But all to no avail, for he is lost - lost because it is fast becoming dark. A wind begins to blow, whistling in from the West, ahead of the setting sun, and the whole world quickly dies in a blaze of scarlet - until there is only darkness, a darkness that flies towards him as if upon the wings of a gigantic raven that is called night.

Opening his eyes, he discovers the candle has burnt down and that there are definitely the sounds of footsteps outside in the passageway now. Unmistakable. But whether these belong to someone actually approaching his room, or to one simply shuffling about aimlessly he cannot tell. Most odd. The door remains inert; the big round handle of brass does not move; the heavy iron lock with its noble escutcheon does not stir or make a sound - and yet still the noises, those same peculiar scratching noises, persist. Unable to bear it any longer, he slides down from the bed and, negotiating his path merely by the moonlight, which is intermittent and at times almost entirely absent, makes his way quietly across the chamber. Locating the door, he manages to ease it open just a little, and there he sees, along the passageway the figure of a young woman in a night-dress, a delicate shawl wrapped about her shoulders and fastened with a brooch that glints a little in the moonlight as she turns and turns, this way and that - her sole occupation being that of sweeping. With a long broom of birch, she sweeps the silver trail of sand from the floorboards, brushing it into corners, dispersing it, concealing it in every variety of ways to render it no longer visible. Along the passageway the lovely Johanna, her eyes cast down, her hair all loose and tossed about her shoulders, like a luminous angel, continues her gradual progress in silken slippers, sweeping, sweeping, until she vanishes from sight, lost around some distant corner where the sounds of her work fade only slowly - because not for one moment does she cease in her labours, the dainty steps almost on tip toe and always the distinctive, rhythmic swish, swish of the broom, becoming more and more distant, fainter and fainter all the while.

Closing the door, Matthew returns to his bed and draws up the covers once more. How very strange - for although she has gone, it is as if he can still detect the sounds, still hear the swish of the broom, the sound that will continue forever through the vastness of the building, dispersing as it goes all his cares into the darkness. It is a most comforting sensation; and carried thus upon the gentle rhythm that seems to merge with that of his own quiet breathing, he closes his eyes and sleeps the sleep of perfection from which he does not stir or wake until dawn.

# ~ 25 ~
## ICE AND ROSES

'Ah, good morning gentlemen,' Lord Snatchal declares, glancing back over his shoulder from where he stands in abject fashion, hands on hips in front of a large display cabinet in the spacious morning room of Snatchalcombe House. Although still early, with the light of the new day creeping through the windows hardly sufficient to see very much at all, he appears intent on inspecting the contents of the cabinet - and to be none too pleased with his findings. 'Breakfast will be served presently, gentlemen,' he adds, 'though I mention this more in hope than expectation, since I seem to be having rather a difficult morning so far.'

'Really, Sir?' Sam inquires, trying to muster some interest in the minutia of his host's domestic life as he and Matthew wipe the slumber from their eyes and rouse themselves to what promises to be a particularly challenging day, a day of destiny, at least for Sam who, having the luxury of his own valet for the duration of his stay, is dressed immaculately, even at such an early hour, in his very best embroidered waistcoat and periwig, all in readiness presumably for whatever announcement he is about to make.

'Yes, all very frustrating,' Lord Snatchal continues shaking his head and setting in motion the long tassel on his night-cap as he leans forward and peers once more, with the aid of a candle this time, into the deep, cavernous reaches of the cabinet. 'Nothing seems to be going right. I was just about to inspect my little collection of weapons here and polish them up a bit, as I often do before breakfast - I have an old musket from the 15 campaign, y'know, and a shotgun for field sports - look, here they are! Numerous decorative pistols, too. Yet, for the life of me, I just can't seem to locate my old duelling swords anywhere. They were on display here - a pair of them mounted in a most attractive cross motif within their scabbards. Odd. And then everybody seems to have deserted me all of a sudden. The Countess, and Johanna, your good wife, Sam - they were both down here already a moment ago all fresh as daisies and joking with each another about witches' broomsticks or something, and now they've gone and vanished as well.'

Instantly, Matthew and Sam exchange glances of extreme alarm.

'Quickly!' Matthew cries, vaulting into action and making for the doors already.

'Indeed, with all haste, Sir!' Sam agrees, hurrying behind.

'Oh, I say, you don't think any of this could be connected, do you?' Lord Snatchal calls after them.

'Oh, come on, you silly old bugger!' Sam shouts back at him from the great echoing hallway outside, losing all decorum and bidding, with a frantic wave of the arm, his astonished host to follow.

Together, they fly from the building, searching firstly the paddock, running in their fine shoes and white stockings, a most curious jig, all in single file, prancing through the mud and straw. But no one is here. They race around the house, and into the kitchen gardens, then through a narrow archway to the rose parterre. But no one is here either apart from one solitary gardener, couchant and who stares up at them, open-mouthed in amazement at the sight.

'You have, I take it, not - er - seen Lady Snatchal this morning, have you, my man?' the Earl inquires hastily trying to maintain his composure. *'With a sword?'* he adds, still hopeful. But the bemused shake of the head from the poor rustic offers no guidance.

With nothing for it, the distinguished trio must therefore exit the formal gardens and hurry out to the park, to the wide vista of meadows and grazing sheep, the lakes, the woods of oak and elm, and where, at last, they behold far in the distance and much farther down towards the water, the two figures of the women. Standing facing each other some good few paces apart, both dressed simply in *pet-en-l'air* and without coats of any kind - these having been discarded nearby - they do, indeed, appear to be contemplating making use of Lord Snatchal's duelling swords - these being held and lowered in readiness. No one else is with them; no seconds enlisted to regulate the contest, no physician in attendance to provide succour to the injured or dying afterwards: just the extraordinary spectacle of two elegant women facing each other upon the crisp frosty grass, gloved and hatted, their dainty shoes and petticoats so colourful in the dull winter's landscape. Matthew can hear their voices, intermittently shrill and angry, hurling insults at one another as he and his companions run down towards them, endeavouring to keep their feet from sliding upon the slippery grass, and with Lord Snatchal lagging some way behind by this stage.

'This is all your fault!' Sam complains, breathless at his side. 'I knew we should have insisted on you bringing some female company with you this weekend.'

'Nonsense!' Matthew protests, just as the women are seen to raise their weapons and, somewhat haphazardly, take the first tentative step towards each other.

Suddenly, though, becoming aware of the men advancing down the hillside, they turn their swords in their direction instead.

'Johanna!' cries Sam, quite beside himself by this stage, bellowing in despair.

'Dorothea!' Lord Snatchal gasps, catching up at last and even venturing to continue his advance and to stagger towards his wife, arms outstretched in a desperate attempt to dissuade her from her actions - but it is futile, for the men, being unarmed, are helpless to intervene.

'Halt!' Lady Snatchal screams, a blood-curdling cry of utter passion. 'Do not tamper, gents - any of you - or I'll make a right big hole in whoever tries it on.'

Upon which, seeing the weapon pointing very much towards him, Lord Snatchal, without turning, promptly reverses his direction and takes several rapid steps back, which causes him to stumble and then to topple down onto his backside, where he remains, seated on the grassy slope, puffing, staring in helpless agitation at the spectacle taking place before him.

Satisfied that there will be no further meddling, both women return their attentions to each another - the distinct and yet unseasonable fragrance of roses from their perfume so peculiar in the icy winter landscape - their bosoms white, their faces illuminated by shafts of sunshine cutting between the trees, all sparkling-bright upon their brooches, and upon the razor-sharp tips of their swords.

'Now, my young Mistress Flibbertigibbet - seeing as you

believe me to be so wanton, I am ready to give you satisfaction forthwith!' Lady Snatchal cries, brandishing her weapon in earnest now.

'Then do your damndest, strumpet!' Johanna retorts stridently. 'And seeing as you think me such a fool, be forewarned that I am of sufficient knowledge of this weapon to know where an evil heart resides. *En garde!'*

'*En garde!'* Lady Snatchal shouts back, placing her best foot forward with its stylish heel. 'And for your impudence - you, you, d*razil-drozzle,* you! - be ready to be marked right proper. By the time I'm done with you, wench, you'll not be looked upon by any man with anything other than pity.'

'Oh, I do not think so, Madam!' Johanna responds with a violent swish of the blade that removes the plume from Lady Snatchal's bonnet in one stroke.

Furious, the older woman retaliates instantly. There is a clash of steel as she strikes the side of Johanna's sword with her own - the farcical encounter resembling nothing so much as a couple of ham actors upon the stage, with little realisation that the aim of fencing is not to hit the sword of one's opponent over and over but rather to thrust directly to the face or vital organs. Johanna, however, being clearly far better acquainted with the process, and making use of the youthful flexibility of her knees to extend her range, does eventually make a very genuine and convincing lunge at Lady Snatchal's throat - at which, visited by the prospect of the Countess being mortally wounded, and mindful of the letter, lodged with her lawyer which she had once told him would be read upon her demise, Matthew finds himself stepping forwards in utter panic.

'My Lady!' he hears himself cry, almost as if the words are not his at all. 'Turn yourself edgeways to your opponent. You must make the target as small as possible!'

At which, Sam, incensed, strides up to Matthew and slaps him on the side of his arm with such force that it nearly knocks him over. 'Good God, Sir! Whose side are you on?' he demands before taking a step forward and bellowing to Johanna, 'My dear, your free arm - place it behind your back, for pity's sake!'

At which Lord Snatchal, seeming to be equally displeased pulls himself to his feet and, dusting the frost and old leaves from his britches advances on his friend. 'I beg your pardon, Sir!' he cries. 'How dare you instruct your wife on how to kill mine more effectively!'

'I - er - do apologise, Sir,' Sam responds, 'I was merely advising my beloved on how to protect the delicate vessels of her wrist,' he explains, somewhat taken aback by the uncommon ferocity of the puny little man glaring up at him, his fists clenched in impotent rage.

Meanwhile, another terrible clash of steel compels all three men to turn their attentions back to the duel.

'Why, my dear, what a right thick stomacher you have to protect you!' Lady Snatchal declares, lunging forward again, and far more confidently this time, learning fast, and coming within an inch of Johanna's chest thereby - which is only parried away in the nick of time. 'I knew all along you were a sheepish little creature, but I did not expect you to fight in armour,' the Countess adds. 'How very handy!'

'Then I shall cast it off, Madam!' Johanna cries and, stepping back and thrusting her sword upright into the turf for a moment, swiftly unfastens and peels off her jacket on which the stomacher is attached. To everyone's astonishment, she also quickly removes her petticoat, as well, before hurling the heavy bundle of quilted fabric away into the undergrowth - and with such ferocity and vigour that Lady Snatchal emits a cry of astonishment at the sight. Retrieving her weapon and clothed now merely in her chemise and stays, the younger woman with the firmest of grips, next raises and circles the blade above her head most impressively before thrashing the air at her sides several times in spectacular and audible provocation. 'So, Madam, which of us has the armour now?' she demands, it being her turn now to point her weapon directly at her opponent and the thick stomacher, almost like a cuirass breast plate across her chest. 'A fine piece of upholstery we have here - to cover a piece of old baggage!'

At which Lady Snatchal, her eyes arrested at just that instant by the sight of a little pink ribbon impaled upon the tip of her opponent's sword, and clearly not intending to be upstaged, emulates the other woman by tearing away her own gown. And thus, standing likewise in her long-sleeved chemise and stays, appropriately black in contrast to Johanna's lighter shades, she shouts back defiantly, 'There, my jade! Look - I have nothing to hide now. Here is a proper target for you to aim at - a real bosom, the like of which you will not have seen in the looking glass lately.

*En garde!*' At which, taking up her own sword once again, she likewise swishes and thrashes about with it in the air to make a suitable display of violence. Unfortunately, her grip is not as firm as that evinced by her opponent earlier, and the weapon escapes her grasp - flying off into the sky in a great, arching trajectory which seems to last an eternity before finally embedding itself with a loud and resonate twang into the trunk of a nearby tree.

It is the moment for which the men have been waiting. Sam and Lord Snatchal, being closest to the Countess, are upon her in seconds, while Matthew makes a bee-line for Johanna, avoiding her feeble lunge of the sword and tripping her by hooking his foot around her standing leg. She falls and he manages to spread himself upon her and pin her down, gripping and securing her sword arm, squeezing the wrist until the weapon is released. Her chest heaving breathlessly she stares up into his eyes and he likewise finds himself transfixed, staring back into hers - her beautiful, startled eyes. It seems like time without end, aware of her breast rising and falling beneath his, surveying with wonder the beauty of her face - her magnificent tangle of blond hair, much of it all loose about her shoulders, her breathing becoming if anything even more pronounced, until she is positively heaving like a mighty ocean beneath him. 'Oh, my dear Matthew,' she sighs.

And suddenly he is aware of her other arm being around his waist, no longer trying to repel him but pressing him to her.

'Johanna. Such a passion!' he whispers, fully aware of what is happening. He is utterly lost in her eyes for that moment. Why, what need of a harem when a man could enjoy a feast such as *this,* he thinks in one brief moment of disconnected observation.

But Sam is hurrying towards them now - a big dark shadow looming over them as he approaches. 'By your leave, Sir!' comes the loud voice bursting forth, and most threatening in tone, Matthew thinks, as he turns his head to look up. 'Will you kindly remove yourself from on top of my wife, Sir!'

'Oh, sorry,' Matthew mutters. 'Needs-must, you know,' he adds as, with the utmost reluctance he extricates himself from Johanna's embrace and, by slow degrees, they both rise and brush themselves down - Johanna looking most flushed in the cheeks, her teeth bared, her lovely almost naked breasts continuing to heave from within the casing of her stays - a condition of obvious frustration and excitement combined which does not appear even under the present mitigating circumstances to entirely meet with Sam's approval, though Lord Snatchal, himself hastening alongside, his lips tremulously pursed, appears most interested in the spectacle.

'Trollop!' Lady Snatchal cries from her own seated position a little distance off, while Sam retrieves and returns to his wife the hat she has lost in the fray, and also chivalrously draping his own jacket across her shoulders - her own discarded coat being far too wet and cold to be of much use. 'You've had a lucky escape this time,' the Countess continues to shout, her body quivering with emotion and pointing an accusing finger in Johanna's direction, 'but that darling poet of yours: he's done for now. I'm telling Cornelius. Yes, I'm telling everyone. Listen to me everybody: he went and ruined that wig!'

'The wig?' Lord Snatchal echoes, shaking his head in puzzlement. 'What do you mean, Dorothea?'

'The wig, Cornelius - the ruddy wig he was doing for you. A dog had it! Her dog. The piece was totally destroyed. Matthew had to make it up again, using new stuff!'

'Oh, yes, I know that,' Lord Snatchal replies, looking slightly embarrassed all of a sudden.

*'You know?'* Lady Snatchal demands in exasperation, getting to her feet and striding up to her husband.

'Yes - Matthew told me. That's why it took so long. It doesn't matter, does it?'

'Doesn't matter! What do you mean! What do you think people will say, then?'

'Well ... nobody will know, will they?' Lord Snatchal argues with calm, 'not unless you make it public knowledge, my dear, which is hardly necessary, surely,' he adds as he begins to shepherd her away, up towards the house. Emulating Sam, he also places his own frock-coat across her shoulders as they go.

'But what about all them knights at the Cornhill Club? What about when they find out?' Lady Snatchal continues to protest with confusion, glancing back over her shoulder at Johanna and the others walking behind, each with bundles of discarded petticoats or swords held in their arms.

'The knights? Oh there's no reason any of them should know, either,' Lord Snatchal continues with a shrug of the shoulders. 'And even if they found out, they wouldn't really mind, I'm sure. Just an unfortunate error on my part, a miscalculation, that's all, and no harm done because, like I say, Matthew replaced it straight away.'

'I can't believe this!' Lady Snatchal cries, unremitting and evidently still very hot from her exertions as she drags off her husband's coat and petulantly hurls it back at him.

'*Dorothea!*' Lord Snatchal shouts, his patience coming to an end with this latest tantrum, his hand gripping his wife's wrist as he retrieves his coat from the ground. 'That really is quite enough now. I would prefer it if we could refrain from speaking about this embarrassing matter any further. Nor, if you please, will you go mentioning any such nonsense outside to other people. Not a word, do you understand? Or I shall have to call in the doctor and have you pronounced insane.'

'Insane!'

'Why, yes! *Insane,*' he repeats, releasing his grasp with a look of regret, though still angry. 'Do you not think you have already provided us with enough evidence of your instability this morning: trying to kill our guests? That is most discourteous, Dorothea. Enough, I say! Not another word about the wig, either. Otherwise you will be registered as mad and I shall have you put in the attic.'

And it is with this final and terrible threat ringing in her ears that Lady Snatchal at last seems to comprehend the logic of keeping quiet. Endeavouring to regain some composure, she accepts the coat from her husband this time and then continues her march back up towards the mansion without another word. In fact, no one utters another word. They all reach the building in silence and here, with cold limbs and hungry tummies, enter and take their seats in the morning room where they devour a grateful and substantial breakfast of eggs and sausages.

There is little by way of conversation during the meal, nor for that matter during the remainder of the strained and uncomfortable morning's activities. Without too much regard for anyone else, Lord Snatchal, with only a pot of coffee for company, sits alone in the morning room, where he cleans and polishes his precious duelling swords before re-uniting them with their scabbards and restoring them to their allotted places within the cabinet. Sam and Johanna elect to depart just as soon as they have partaken of a little bathing and have been tended to by the resident nurse for some minor bruising - Sam's final words being a demonstrative farewell rather than an *adieu*, and that he would not be able to say with any certainty when he would see any of them again, for he was now as determined as ever to journey to Aberdeen and to volunteer his services as field surgeon with the Duke of Cumberland: there to serve, as he said, 'in any capacity necessary to defend the kingdom from the Popish hoards.'

Lady Snatchal, meanwhile, having succumbed to a fit of the vapours retired very quickly to her chamber after breakfast and would not be available, her maid reported, to say farewell when Matthew himself departed by carriage shortly after noon. It was all over, the world in fragments, shattered by petty jealousies and intrigue, a situation of utter desolation that, Matthew could not help feeling, was surely beyond repair.

To be deprived of the society of Lord and Lady Snatchal into the foreseeable future is not, for Matthew, a sorrow beyond endurance, though any withdrawal of patronage will no doubt hurt his pocket, he reflects. Even if they do ever speak to him again, it is unlikely, moreover, that the Snatchal's *noblesse oblige* would ever extend to the private printing of his next book of verse, as they had once intimated it might. Never mind. At least he has his payment for the two wigs - and a most handsome one: seventy guineas - the equivalent of a year's salary for a common peruke maker in London, and which Matthew took receipt of during one final excursion up to the noble lord's closet just prior to his departure, presented rather icily by the Earl and enclosed in a neat little envelope bearing his coat of arms.

No - none of these considerations is of any importance this afternoon. Instead, as Matthew's carriage swerves and rumbles its way back along the rutted winter's roadway to London he can only wonder with a terrible anguish in his heart over the devastating impact the events of the past twenty-four hours might have on his friendship with Sam and Johanna. Whatever could have possessed the two women to have behaved in such a reckless fashion! Even though both insisted afterwards that it had only been a contest to 'first blood,' as they described it, anyone familiar with the science of the duel could have told them that the innocuous sounding 'first blood' could easily mean anything from permanent disfigurement to the loss of an eye - not to mention the possibility of a morbid descent into gangrenous infection from even the most minor of cuts or grazes. Madness. And what with him being the perceived cause of it all, it might well prove to be a step too far in their relationship. How sad - and he really cannot help wondering, therefore, if he will ever see either of his dear friends again or ever experience again such pleasant and innocent times in their company - the informal dinners with music and laughter; the enchanted evenings high up on the rooftops gazing at the stars. When, he wonders, if ever, will any of those precious moments ever return? And as he takes out his notepad and trusty carpenter's pencil - he never travels anywhere without one - with the intention of turning his thoughts instead to a little versifying, a tear of genuine remorse forms in his eye at the prospect of such a sad and unwelcome change in his life.

Perhaps it has all been a foolish distraction, anyway, he tells himself; this absurd preoccupation with the unattainable. And yet he cannot escape his feelings so easily. Even now, he has only to close his eyes, and he is reminded of her, of Johanna just a few short hours ago lying upon the ground beneath him, of her beautiful hazel-green eyes, her body heated and convulsed by a passion that was quite involuntary, it seemed. Where would it have stemmed from, that fire? How could it lie dormant for so long beneath such a normally placid exterior, captive in her heart until such a glorious moment? These and other idle meditations feed his attempts at composing verse for another hour, but it is no use. Having scratched out line after line of untidy black graphite, he finds himself simply spelling out her name instead - those seven little letters, writ large on the page, just as he has allowed them to be writ so excessively large in his dreams: J.o.h.a.n.n.a.

Is that all that is left to him now? he wonders. Should he pine away? Should he go carve the letters in a tree like some love-sick adolescent? No, it is all too ridiculous.

Glancing out of the coach window to the darkening sky, he notices how late the sunset is becoming - the days becoming longer - and reminding him that in just a few weeks time the new outdoor season and social calendar of London society will commence, all the gardens and spas opening their doors once again, all the glittering abundance of theatre, masquerades and assemblies - and everywhere a profusion of so many beautiful females with whom he might revel in it all. And with the prospect of being home safely in just a few hours time (something he could scarcely have hoped for when he set out with such foreboding yesterday morning), he resolves instead not to waste another minute of his life in self-torment but to devote himself instead in all the giddy lusting of his own personal obsession, his very own stairway to heaven in which he will enjoy the pleasures of not just one but *seven* beautiful women. Yes, he will take *their* names instead and carve them in oak - and more! A forest will not suffice! And to this end, he takes up paper and pencil once again - but this time setting his purpose to the marking out of a series of concentric circles, to create a diagram in the style of the venerable astrologers and alchemists of old, and by which he might clarify his progress thus far by labelling each space in-between with the name of one of the seven heavenly bodies and, alongside it, that of the fair lady and agent of desire who will guide him on his way.

To begin with, he already has in place his Moon in the shape of the voluptuous and clever Rose. That is the first sphere at the centre. The eloquent, crinkle-haired Harriet, meanwhile, the young governess he so gallantly escorted back from St Albans to London that fateful night, remains his Mercury and occupant of the second. Then, of course, there is dear Sarah May, his dark and lovely young Venus who remains as attentive to all the novelties and joys of the flesh as ever; and it is she, therefore, who shall occupy the third sphere. The magnificent Lucy Armstrong from Cockspur Street is forever his resplendent Sun with dominion over the fourth. He must skip a space next, this sphere being vacant still, before recalling to mind the very special charms of Caroline Bolter, she of the masked intrigues of Ranelagh Gardens and whom he hopes will long-remain his inspiration for all the extravagant emanations of Jupiter and to thus inhabit the sixth sphere of heaven in all her glory. All this leaves him wanting of only two more: a vigorous, fiery Mars to occupy that still-vacant fifth place, and finally a dark, mysterious Saturn for the seventh. Only a matter of time, he is confident, and all will be complete - while, even better, throughout it all he has still managed to adhere to the standards he had set for himself at the very outset: that none of his heavenly lovers will have been bought with money, and that none will have been taken dishonourably from within the bonds of marriage. Even Caroline, despite her occasional commitments to her distinguished paramour, remains a free agent; and even Lucy at the end of her working day of servicing with birch twigs or riding crop the nether regions of impotent reprobates, would give herself to him freely and without remuneration.

Yes, it is all so near now that he cannot help but wonder: will he undergo some singular life-changing experience upon its attainment? Will he discover gold at the end of his beauteous rainbow of the senses - some kind of fabled alchemy or transformation of the self as hinted at by all those philosophers and mystics? Will he be liberated from his body by the experience? Will he fly without wings? Will he die? There is only one way to find out. He will set his course for that star now, and will savour every flirtation; every sigh of pleasure, every lingering kiss and passionate conquest along the way - never turning back until his universe is complete.

## ~ 26 ~
## BOUND IN RIBBON
## AND LACE

Surely he will drop the lot in a minute! Matthew tells himself as, signalling through the window for the chairmen to halt and to set him down, he watches in admiration the scene outside in the street as the juggler throws yet another item into the mix - a small skittle that one might find stacked up in any tavern garden - hurling it high into the air to mingle with the others. Not only does he have four or five skittles on the go at any one time, but he also manages to run and dance up and down upon the boards, the small piece of stage set out here in the field at the edge of the thoroughfare - and all the while accompanied by a harlequin playing furiously on a hurdy-gurdy. It is, Matthew, reflects, the same little square of ground on which various entertainers, acrobats, wrestlers, rope dancers, knife throwers and fire-eaters will all be taking their turns later on, and all performing to very much the same accompaniment, the same intoxicating mixture of cheering and hurdy-gurdy, with occasional drum and fife. What fun!

During each act, a young woman, somewhat lean and hungry of aspect, circulates through the crowd to gather contributions in a hat, and Matthew willingly hands her some coins through the window. The juggler, meanwhile, concludes his performance with a spectacular flourish in which the skittles are hurled even higher in a seemingly chaotic pattern until returning to his arms as if by some means of magical suction, and all to loud acclaim from the small gathering of around twenty onlookers - not many yet because it is still early. But later in the day, Matthew knows, dozens, maybe hundreds of spectators might be out here, with everywhere gin, ale and cakes for sale, plus a fair number of mountebanks, pickpockets and harlots in attendance doing their worst amidst it all: a typical day of outdoor recreation in this quarter, and with the advent of some warm weather at last after the long winter months, and the threat of the rebel armies at least temporarily dispelled, it comes as a welcome diversion for the citizens of London.

Sadly, an inspection of his watch informs him that he must be going, because today Matthew has two important matters to deal with, each one filling him with a certain degree of trepidation. And so, with a signal to the men outside, his chair is hoisted and carried forth once more, rocking and tilting along the cobbled roadways and only occasionally enjoying the respite of a pavement to shuffle along as it goes. He always admires the street players, and having had the window of the chair open for these few moments has been a welcome relief, as he is reminded straight away as soon as he rolls it shut again, because the stench within this particular chair is appalling, as if the collective belching and farts of an entire generation of London theatre goers have been stored up in the fabric of the upholstery itself - if one could call it that, this threadbare slab of defunct horse hair and wool to sit upon, as lumpy and as uncomfortable as a pile of old flints. What can one do! He has simply been unlucky with this one and, it being far too late now to locate another, he places a perfumed handkerchief to his nose, instead, the very one given to him by Harriet this morning, his young mercurial governess, and which thereby allows him to direct his attentions to more pleasing meditations, in particular the wonderful night he has just spent with her.

Ah dearest most adventurous Harriet! Since her return to the capital, she had by her own express wish become his full and willing partner in pleasure - for he had never come to any proper extremity with her until this time. It had also not taken them long to rediscover all their previous fondness for each other's society. And yesterday, after a trip to the theatre where she had worn for the first time the brooch he had bought for her, a fine silver filigree inlaid with a most 'mercurial' sardonyx stone, they had hurried back to his home, and there, in each other's arms, had surrendered to all their sweetest desires once more. How very fine it had been, the presence of his lovely companion writhing in pleasure there beneath him - that, or else he would keel, and she facing him and seated in his lap, would engage with him in kisses perpetual, their mouths never parted and thus, in their coupling, an upright loop of love from top to bottom would be fashioned. It was as if all the world were still, with time in which every wish and question might find a resolution - for Harriet was ever the explorer in matters of the senses, and seldom reticent in the articulation of her requirements - a most attractive aspect of her character by which she would brazenly explore all the sensations available, and then voice her wishes, discuss them quite calmly: 'Darling, I do rather like to be touched here, and a little there, as well, if you please,' she would whisper, 'and if I could prevail upon you to do this once more, and not to stop, I would be yours and only yours for eternity,' and such-like romantic and delightful play. And he would answer in turn, that 'no my dearest treat, I shall not stop - not ever. I shall not cease to oblige you in whatever way you desire.'

And he did - oh, by heaven how he did! The delectable, ever intriguing Harriet! For equal to her attainments in (or upon) his bed, Harriet was also the most wonderful joy to be with, so that this morning's dawn, with all its attendant demands and obligations, found them cursing the passage of time and the cruel daylight that had insisted on intruding so soon upon their happiness.

The recollection of it now, for Matthew, is comforting indeed, matched only by his sense of anticipation for what awaits this coming night when he is due to stay once more with his very special Caroline Bolter in Hanover Square. They are due to meet again in the warmth of the Rotunda at the opening of the new season at Ranelagh Gardens; and there, masked once again, he is to pursue her as a stranger and she, in whatever guise she might present herself - he knows not what it might be - will deny him with ever more extravagant measures of resistance. He recalls it had been just the kind of intrigue that she had enjoyed enacting last year at the close of the old season; and he will not be an unwilling participant in it with the start of the next - so that later in the darkness of their homeward carriage, as they couple so deliciously and furtively, their limbs entwined, he will again touch and feast his senses not only upon her lovely flesh but upon every item of her apparel - feeling as would a blind man with his fingertips upon the face of his beloved every texture, every tracery of lace and ribbon. It is a delight, a fascination, and will surely result, he knows, in another bout of excessive and exultant love-making once they return to her home - for Caroline is not so much a partner in pleasure as a devourer of it - and one, furthermore, who continues to require her satisfaction in the most theatrical of ways - she, his ever more adventurous and ever more demanding Jupiter to be chased and tumbled from one room to the next, and with always the most voluble exclamations of passion at every turn - not only upon her bed but upon every rug and carpet, every chair and table top along the way. Not that he is complaining. Not at all. He is throwing himself into this life now. Immersing himself in the dizzy sensuality of it all. Is it immoral? No, not at all. Is it self-destructive? Quite possibly - though only for one of less vigour and resilience than himself. He has no qualms.

And thus fortified with this sense of self-congratulation, he has ample opportunity, as his carriers continue to trudge and squelch their path through the crowded streets, to reflect the life he is leading at present is perhaps not unlike that of a juggler, too. Five lovers on the go now - soon to be seven if he has anything to do with it - and always with such strong and determined women - women who, each in their own way, are expecting him to be their source of joy and satisfaction, so that with each additional one brought into his sphere it is becoming, he has to admit, more and more difficult to locate the next, if for no other reason than the scarcity of free time available for him to do so. Adding a third and fourth to the mix had not been difficult; even the fifth had been relatively trouble-free. But a sixth, and then a seventh? That would require something special in organisational skill, not to mention sheer stamina if his plans were ever to come to fruition. Even if he were to serve the needs of one of his special amours each day, a hiatus of seven days would still be experienced by each of them in-between his ministrations. Thus, he has to admit, the possibility will arise as time goes by that they themselves might seek their amusements elsewhere in the arms of other lovers, and perhaps already have.

It is this knowledge, that he might be exposing himself to an increased risk of contagion that has prompted him today to arrange a visit to the shop just off the Strand in Half-Moon Street of a certain Mrs Constantia, the very one he had spoken of and commended to his friend Sam not too long ago; for here among the many luxury articles such as wine and snuff, chocolate, tea and tobacco, are to be found all sorts of fine items that go by the name of cundums or 'implements of safety for gentlemen.' In other words, sheaths to protect from the pox. He has heard, moreover, that among the clientele are to be found a rising number of women - since the cundum itself is also being viewed more and more these days as a preventative measure against pregnancy. Not that this is the only attraction for the ladies at the premises of Mrs Constantia, since also for sale, they say, and this most discreetly, are those recreational items euphemistically termed 'widows' comforters' - carefully moulded and shaped in leather and ivory and celebrating all the varied manifestations of the cult of Priapus. All in all, a most interesting establishment, and Matthew finds himself wondering why he has rarely given it anything other than a cursory glance on his travels to and from all the other, perhaps more obvious attractions of the area.

He asks to be set down in the Strand, and from here a brief stroll is all that is necessary to bring Matthew to his destination with its neat double-fronted shop windows - and a place which looks to be especially popular today, with all the seats within the window recess already occupied, and with customers queuing up at the counter for service. Upon entry, therefore, Matthew has ample time, standing in line amid all the boxes, jars and cases of luxury merchandise, to peruse the various notices on the walls advertising those very items he has come here to investigate - these being fashioned from a wide and ingenious variety of materials, some of which, he reflects, would surely be of greater comfort and convenience than others. There is, for example, the 'Faithful Weave of Penelope,' a lubricated linen sheath covered in a special herbal preparation for, as it states, 'the consummate ease of the glide.' There is also the 'Slippery Glove of Neptune,' a cundum constructed from the intestine of the blowfish, but which is currently unavailable and crossed off the list - there presumably being a shortage of blowfish in the vicinity at present. Sealskin appears to have been a viable substitute for the blowfish at one stage, but this too is marked as unavailable. These shortcomings are more than made up for, however, by the accessibility of the 'Horn of Plenty' - a veritable 'cornucopia of pleasure,' as it is described - or, more accurately, an item made from the skin of a goat's bladder and of a 'snugness and comfort unsurpassed.' And as if all this were not sufficient, there is also the 'Ram of Darius' to be reckoned with - the ever popular sheep's-gut cundum, against which 'no siege can ever withstand.' This comes in two different grades, moreover - the more bespoke variety being 'of the thinnest gossamer comfort' and which, as the notice proudly proclaims, 'manifestly divideth the sheep from the goats.' All very entertaining, Matthew concludes, while the poet in him can only be heartened by the unique engraving, neatly framed in copper and gold above the chimneypiece:

*Happy the man in whose pocket found,*
*Whether with green or scarlet ribbon bound,*
*A well-made cundum.*
*By this machine's secure romance,*
*The willing maid may taste loves joys.*
*And wife of man unfettered toys,*
*With all his pleasant dalliance.*

Just as Matthew is reaching a decision on whether he should elect for the Horn of Plenty or the Ram of Darius, his attentions are arrested by an irate gentleman standing at the counter, engaged in an altercation with a stout lady in a gigantic mob-cap trimmed with lilac ribbons and who, if rank might be signified by size of bonnet alone, would surely be none other than the proprietress herself. She has apparently been called forth from the back of the shop by another lady assistant in order to deal with the awkward customer.

'Can *I* help you, Sir?' she inquires icily. 'My name is Mrs Constantia. I am the owner of this establishment.'

'Why, yes,' the gentleman answers, removing from his pocket a long flaccid sheath which he dangles aloft between finger and thumb. 'I wish to lodge a complaint. I purchased this article here last week, it being commended to me by your advertisement in the Gazette. It has proved most unmanageable, in fact so unpleasant an experience for both myself and my lady wife that I wish to exchange it for another. Or else to have my money back.'

*'Exchange!'* Mrs Constantia cries with the utmost indignation from behind the counter, hands on hips. 'We do not, Sir, exchange cundums, especially them that has been used. How dare you!'

'I have only used it once,' the man argues with what he clearly believes to be a persuasive and irrefutable logic.

But Mrs Constantia is having none of it. 'You disgusting little man. Get out of my shop immediately,' she cries, as all heads in the room turn her way.

'Shan't!' the man answers with a wide-eyed stare of disobedience, folding his arms about his chest and glancing defiantly around the shop as if seeking support from the other customers - though little seems to be forthcoming.

'Listen to me Sir,' Mrs Constantia responds, lifting the counter and striding out to confront the man at close quarters, her patience clearly at an end. 'I'll have you know that the item you are referring to has been manufactured to the very highest standards here in our own workshop, fashioned with much solicitude from the intestines of a sheep. This is not an easy substance to work with, Sir. It is a material that has to be carefully prepared, saturated and softened, turned inside out, macerated in an alkaline solution, scraped with great care of impurities, exposed to a brimstone vapour, washed again, gently inflated, dried, checked for imperfections and finally adorned with an attractive ribbon for your convenience. It is a complex, time consuming process, Sir, and one of immense artistry and skill, and if we were to exchange every one simply because its owner failed to make good and proper use of it, we should be out of business very quickly, I should think.'

'*Failed?* What are you insinuating, Madam?' the man demands.

'I am insinuating nothing, Sir, other than that you are not a welcome customer. Kindly leave!'

'Not until I am in receipt of a full refund,' the man declares and thrusts the tip of his cane against the stone floor for emphasis.

At which Mrs Constantia, far from daunted by this display of wilfulness, merely turns from the man and, directing her voice through a doorway to the rear of the shop, calls out: 'Mr Webster, would you care to step this way for a second?'

Upon which a giant of a man, ducking his head to avoid the low lintel of the doorway, steps forth into the shop, seeming to fill the entire room as he squeezes himself through the gap in the counter and then draws himself up to his full height as he advances.

*Webster?* Matthew ponders the name, and then remembers. Of course! This is none other than Bone Crusher Webster, he who is employed by the Cornhill club for dealing with various inconveniences. The very same man he had seen, albeit at a distance, skulking in the shadows outside his apartments last year. Clearly, he is one of that fraternity of pugnacious men employed in various establishments around Covent Garden for the purposes of protecting vulnerable business women - those of all professions. This is his day job!

'Are you experiencing problems using our merchandise, Sir?' Webster inquires, speaking in a deep rumble of a voice, not unlike thunder.

'Why, yes - in a way, yes,' the man answers, squirming a little.

'Are the dimensions of Mrs Constantia's items perchance proving to be a bit too much on the generous side for you? Or would you be having difficulties gaining sufficient vigour to fill the receptacle itself, Sir, is that the matter?' Webster inquires further.

'Certainly not, no!'

'Well, that's a bit of a puzzlement, then - because, you see, in my humble opinion, Mrs Constantia's products are of the highest calibre,' Webster states, in a voice even louder this time and which seems to shake the very walls and floorboards. 'That's what I think, anyway,' he adds, interlacing his fingers and cracking his knuckles loudly as if in readiness for a boxing match. 'Or do you wanna argue about it?'

The troublesome customer finally seems to understand. 'Oh ... no, not at all,' he states, all a-quiver, peering up into the vast face above him before turning quickly and vacating the premises forthwith - not quite running, but almost, and whereupon the terrifying beast that is Bone Crusher Webster returns by slow degrees beneath the lintel at the rear of the shop and back into his lair.

This unfortunate obstacle to the normal proceedings of business having now been overcome, and with an atmosphere of renewed concord having descended upon the shop, Matthew is at last able to be served, and it is Mrs Constantia herself who honours him.

'Oh, and how may I help *you* Sir?' she inquires with, he senses, a special emphasis on the '*you.*' Although not a particularly attractive woman, she has, Matthew thinks, the most remarkable eyes, extraordinarily deep and perceptive, with lashes that are of an inordinate length and which flutter at moments with all the alluring rapidity of a butterfly's wings.

'I would like to purchase a protective sheath, Madam. The sheep's-gut would do nicely, I should think. An essential precaution, you understand in these uncertain times.'

'Oh, yes, indeed, young Sir,' she responds in florid and obsequious tones, fluttering wildly. 'As the philosophers so rightly say: *a night with Venus - a lifetime with Mercury* - that baleful substance being still the only cure for the pox, and one, I regret to say, which in the application of its curative properties is scarcely kinder to the constitution than the disease it seeks to remedy.'

'Indeed, Madam, it is true,' Matthew responds as the ever more lyrical Mrs Constantia brings forth a beautifully inlaid tray of rosewood from beneath the counter in which are arranged a number of neatly presented samples, graded it would appear according to size and from which Matthew is invited to choose. Curiously, the ribbons used as ties are what fascinate him the most. Such a wide array of attractive colours.

'I must say it is nice to have a fine young gentleman to provide for, especially after the kind of disgraceful behaviour we have just witnessed,' Mrs Constantia declares fluttering her eyelashes once again - until, suddenly, Matthew realises they are false, as are her eyebrows, though very well constructed pieces, for all that. 'I take it by your apparel, Sir, that it is the bespoke service that you will be seeking here?' she adds, pursing her lips.

'Oh, yes - definitely,' Matthew replies, pleased with this little token of approbation. 'The bespoke service, certainly,' he echoes as he returns his attentions to the tray.

At just that moment, the other assistant, having recovered from her previous encounter, is seen returning to the shop. 'Mr Smith?' she calls in the direction of a number of other customers waiting patiently in a row upon the window seats, and to which quite a number of gentlemen raise their hands: a collection of 'Smiths' in fact, their nervous little movements reminding Matthew of a bunch of schoolboys answering an awkward question in class. The assistant smiles to herself, for she probably has many a name of Smith signed into the pages of her guest book. 'A Mr *John* Smith,' she clarifies, which seems to narrow it down to just the one.

'Ah, yes, that must be me!' the gentleman says.

'Mr Webster will see you for your fitting now if you would like to come through,' the lady informs him as he, getting to his feet, and, a little reluctantly, follows the young lady through and into the back of the shop.

*Fitting!* Suddenly Matthew feels less enthusiasm for the venture, particularly as the ministrations of Mr Webster appear to be included in the service.

'Er - excuse me, I wasn't aware that you took the trouble to do individual fittings?' Matthew inquires, and when informed by Mrs Constantia that this is the very essence of the *bespoke service* that he has just agreed to, he resolves at once to interrupt by stating that he would really be content, after all, just to have one 'off the peg, so to speak.'

At which Mrs Constantia's face appears to drop by at least an inch, evidently disappointed at such an abrupt change of heart.

'I hope, young Sir, you have not gotten a false impression by what just occurred in the shop,' she says. 'Mr Webster is really very gentle.'

But this is an assertion that, rather than putting Matthew at ease, has the opposite effect - and when he reiterates that 'off the peg' is indeed, his preference, Mrs Constantia merely sighs. Raising her moleskin eyebrows disdainfully she quickly replaces the trayful of brightly ribboned samples with another of far less attractive fare, all jumbled up.

'Off the peg it is, then,' she says, slamming the new tray down on the counter top. And in a loud and strident voice that seems to proclaim to all the world the accumulated vexations of her day, demands of Matthew: 'Will that be *small, medium or large?*'

Armed defiantly with the largest cundum available from Mrs Constantia's shop and realising with frustration, therefore, that it would be totally useless for his requirements, Matthew wanders for a while around the Piazza and checks on the latest performances to be posted upon the theatre billboards. It looks good - with still so much of the operatic season to look forward to. The weather is improving, too, and the whole city always looks so much more inviting whenever a little sunshine graces its walls and colonnades as it does today. Wonderful!

Feeling hungry, he elects to drop in for a pie and coffee at Tom's - one of the best coffee houses in the area and from the windows of which he often sits and watches with fascination the various games of flirtation and pick-up that men and women play hereabouts among the traffic of private chairs and carriages. For here above the rough and tumble associated with the market and the commerce of the humble hackney chairs carving out their progress along the crowded pavements, their bearers utterly regardless of the ribs and toes of those who do not make way for them, can be detected the more sedate and aloof traffic of slowly dawdling vehicles, those occupied by men or women often incognito, sometimes cloaked, hooded or even masked, looking out for sexual adventure. Matthew is a seasoned observer of all the subtleties of the process. A chair would often draw alongside another, and lengthy glances or idle chatter would be exchanged between its occupants, the gentlemen flourishing their hats, the women brandishing their fans, each sometimes signalling their interest by exchanging little gifts or tokens, all the while their respective chairmen or coachmen - for later in the evening the larger vehicles would often join in - maintaining a show of indifference to whatever might be taking place. Often people would alight from one coach and hop into another; sometimes they would both alight from their chairs and stroll off together; at other times a convenient collision would be contrived that might then result in an exchange of calling cards. The demirep and the rake have no need of the masquerade in such a place as this - for it is the masquerade of the real world, with similar rules of engagement, and with all the additional spice of anonymity among the crowds. At the very least it is, for the informed bystander a fascinating performance, on occasion every bit as entertaining as anything taking place in the theatres hereabouts. Matthew himself has never been tempted to indulge in any of it. But, he reflects, as he continues to sip at his dish of coffee and survey the players on this great stage of concupiscence outside, maybe it is time he did. Why not!

To be frank, he knows this endless pursuit of beautiful females and the life of dissipation it entails has become a necessary distraction of late. It takes his mind off things - because despite his earlier resolve to remain indifferent, he is still worried half to death for his friend Sam - he simply cannot help it - and distressed beyond measure for poor Johanna, too, and of how she might be faring in her husband's absence. It has been weeks now, and yet still not a single word, not a single letter from either of them, while the headlines in the papers and upon the billboards in Fleet Street regarding the war are far from encouraging. As feared, a long and arduous military campaign is underway north of the border amid the snow and freezing temperatures that still grip the Highlands at this time of the year. What dear Sam, a gentle soul who luxuriates in the warmth and cosy domesticity of married life, will be making of it all in the bleak and inhospitable foothills of the Scottish mountains is anybody's guess. Would Johanna have news from him? Perhaps. He knows he should write to her. He knows he should call. But he cannot bring himself to do either of these things. It is, for him, simply impossible. His heart could not withstand it. And as for the wars - well, he tells himself, they are far enough away not to be a concern. Apart from the ever present threat of a French invasion, London is safe for the time being, and there are, he reminds himself with a quick glance at his fob watch, far more interesting things to be doing.

And thus sufficiently fortified and nourished, Matthew leaves the coffee house and takes a stroll to his second scheduled appointment of the day: just up into Long Acre, where it is his intention to offer his services to the illustrious and celebrated stays maker, Mr Podger, the very gentleman referred to by Lady Snatchal some time ago and who, Matthew sincerely hopes, might still be casting about for that new apprentice that she mentioned. What an opportunity that would be! He feels most excited by the prospect.

The entrance to the workshops of Mr Podger is an impressive one Matthew thinks as he climbs the short flight of stone steps from the street and into the marble hallway of the ground-floor - a narrow room with a number of stylish chairs for clients to take their ease, but with wide doorways at both ends to accommodate ladies visiting in even the most extensive of panniered skirts - a fine and striking example of which just happens to be leaving the establishment as he is coming in: a beautiful woman, in fact - not young but with the most gorgeous curled tresses of red hair just visible from beneath her bonnet, its wide brim placed at a jaunty tilt to one side. Quite stunning in her self-confidence, her cuirass-style bodice an elaborate array of ties and ribbons, almost like a military tunic and thus the very fashion of the hour, she regards him with a glance of barely repressed flirtation as she saunters past - observing with approval the execution of one of his most perfectly executed salutations as he, with a flourish of his hat, makes a leg and bows low. The lessons he has taken from his dancing master has left him with a striking fluency in such displays, of course; and this afternoon he draws upon all of his youthful flexibility and acquired technique expressly for her benefit. Rising, he turns discreetly to watch her as she goes - being just in time to hasten to the doors and to hold one open a little wider for her as she passes through, there to descend the steps outside where she is met by a solicitous footman in smartest livery.

How very interesting! The place is very much to his liking already, he tells himself, as he returns inside and raps with enthusiasm upon Mr Podger's double doors - soon to be admitted by what is clearly the proprietor himself, a small, bespectacled elderly gentleman in a brown nankeen overall and tie-wig, a pair of well-used tailor's shears in hand and a carpenter's pencil behind one ear.

'Ah, yes, it's Mr Wildish, is it not,' he inquires, with an unusually weak handshake by way of welcome, ushering his visitor in as soon as Matthew has presented him with his card. 'You have come to see me about the possibility of becoming an apprentice, I understand. Won't you take a seat.'

'Your most obedient servant, Sir,' Matthew replies fulsomely, smiling down kindly at the old gentleman and responding to his offer by pulling up a stool to join him at his workbench.

It is obvious that this is a busy establishment, Matthew thinks. Like his own rooms at The Pig and Whistle, a similar compromise between comfort and practicality is in evidence - a place lavish enough to entertain clients in some measure of style, while also being workman-like and large enough for the practical business of manufacture and the storage of materials - all of which does indeed engender a most welcome and reassuring sense of familiarity, with everywhere the ordered chaos of mannequins in various states of undress, and clothes patterns pinned to walls. The subtle fragrance of fresh silk and cotton can be detected, along with the faintest opalescence of fabric dust that pervades the air wherever such materials are used on a continuous basis.

'I do hope my age, for I am already twenty-eight, will not prove a barrier in your considering me for such an honour?' Matthew adds, watching as Mr Podger attends to a few outstanding touches to his current piece of work, cutting from a pattern some pieces of bright scarlet silk.

'Oh, no, not at all,' he answers at length, finally putting down his shears. 'In fact, I would say you are still far too young as it is,' he adds, drawing up his stool closer to Matthew in order to examine his face for any obvious signs of advancing years and, after encountering little evidence for such a condition, shaking his head dismally in response.

'Forgive me, I'm afraid I don't quite understand,' Matthew responds, trying to hide his disappointment. 'I began my apprenticeship as Barber-Surgeon, for example, at sixteen, and as Master Wig Maker not much later. Apprentices are, by definition, of tender years, are they not?'

To which Mr Podger gazes upon Matthew with something not

unlike pity before shaking his head once again and then, getting to his feet, fetches a bottle of port. A frail old fellow, to be sure, he shudders a little as he goes, as if suffering from the cold, and Matthew catches himself wondering how he would have the energy sufficient for his labours, which would surely involve no inconsiderable degree of dexterity and strength. How would he even thread a needle with such tremulous hands? Never, in fact, has Matthew encountered anyone more in need of an assistant, if only to undertake some of the more arduous demands of the profession. Resuming his seat once again with a deep protracted sigh, he pours a generous glass of dark ruby-coloured port for his guest and another for himself.

'Well, Mr Wildish: here's to your health, and to your youth!' he states raising his glass. 'I suppose, at the very least, I owe you a more substantial explanation for my reticence. You see, the fact of the matter is that the making of stays, or corsets as they are coming to be called on the continent, is not really for the likes of an upright young gentleman such as yourself. Can you imagine, for instance, the temptations that might be in store if you were to expose yourself to such an exercise on a daily basis - especially, as one presumes, you are already possessed of a natural inclination to find such an occupation agreeable?'

Matthew can only respond with a bemused shake of the head as Mr Podger drains his glass. He encourages Matthew to do likewise before filling it for him once again.

'Think about it, Mr Wildish,' he continues. 'Clearly, we do not go naked like the animals, and the art of fashioning undergarments has developed over the centuries of civilised conduct not only to bestow a goodly shape where nature has not deigned to provide one, but also to display to perfection all those most beguiling and enticing attributes of the female form - quite breathtakingly beautiful at times, the body thus so perfectly sculptured, so artfully bound in ribbon and lace. You observed, I take it, the distinguished red-headed lady who left this establishment some ten minutes ago just as you were entering?'

'Why yes, as a matter of fact I did,' Matthew replies, his voice eager. 'Rather a splendid ...'

'Baroness Martina von Klapperstein,' Mr Podger interrupts by way of elucidation. 'A most comely Hanoverian widow: wealthy, accomplished and entirely devoted to a life of shopping. She calls here to my studio for a new corset every few weeks, to be fitted for any of the latest designs that may have become the fleeting and ever changing toy of fashion. I have through the years of familiarity come to know her body, to be acquainted with each and every changing measurement of her curvaceous torso as intimately, if not more intimately than her late husband - may he rest in peace. Her image haunts me, because even when I work upon her garments in her absence, I am compelled to picture her in my mind, and not merely the measurements of her waist, but also the wayward locks of red hair falling upon the freckled whiteness of her shoulders, the outstanding line of her breast lifted into prominence by the very artfulness of my own contrivance and design. I am hardly ever free of her, therefore, or of any number of equally beautiful apparitions.

'Ah, I know what you are going to say, young man. You will tell me that the familiarity of such an experience must surely lead to a certain equanimity over time, an acquired indifference to the temptations laid before us. But sadly this is not the case - because, believe me, every day those temptations will not only be renewed, but they will also be magnified - and with the passage of time increased rather than diminished. Can you imagine, for instance, sitting here at your bench faced constantly with the sight of so many beautiful women coming towards you through those very dressing-room doors over there, clad merely in their chemise and stays? Can you imagine having to spend hours each day encasing the female torso in the items that you have fashioned, of having to fit and measure and make adjustments each time until the garment fits snugly and becomes entirely to the satisfaction of your customer? And then, if that were not enough, to have to face over and over again the business of drawing tight the laces, of surveying the glorious female figure in all its varieties of shape and size - the slender waist, the rising breasts, the curvaceous allure of hips and nether regions taking shape before you, moulded by the ministrations of your very own hands - only to have to slacken and release such delights from their constrictions, over and over again, and to harken endlessly as you must do to the sighs and gasps of relief from your ladies - sounds, moreover, which you will inevitably associate with the sighs of passion? For yes, believe me, Sir, you will make such a correlation. It is inescapable. Yet all the while, you must reign in your natural instincts, you must conduct yourself in an impeccable and professional manner. Even should you be able to command your eyes not to persist in gazing, you will still be compelled to labour within a universe of sounds and fragrances, and these every bit as distracting. Every creak of whale bone, every swish of cordage within a pair of straining stays, every nuance of breath, every fragrance of perfume, nicety of manners or custom of feminine charm must, each and every moment of the working day bewitch and inflame you to the point of utter exhaustion. And every day - every day I tell you, it will be the same. How could you, as a young man, ever begin to negotiate the perils of such an occupation!'

'I could always try,' Matthew answers.

But Mr Podger merely shakes his head in despair. 'No, no, Sir. Believe me, you could never succeed. You are far too young. I was young once. Now look at me. Look at what being a maker of stays has done to me at the age of thirty-nine.'

'*Thirty-nine!*' Matthew exclaims, and immediately wishes he had not gasped or demonstrated his surprise in such an overt manner, for the poor man looks most disturbed and trembling more than ever with the exertions of his speech.

'Exactly,' he mutters as if reading Matthew's thoughts, a certain look of exaltation upon his face, engendered perhaps by the novelty of confession. 'Exactly - and you would do well to be shocked and alarmed, Sir. Indeed you should.'

Matthew lets forth a sigh every bit as heavy as that of his companion. It is, to be sure, a sorry tale - and, moved almost to tears, he really does feel himself sharing in the other man's grief.

'Well ... I must say I am indebted to you, Sir, for your sincerity,' Matthew responds at length, laying a sympathetic hand upon the arm of the other man as he gets to his feet - for the plight of Mr Podger is not too dissimilar to that of any other red-blooded male tormented by the temptations of the flesh. And who could fail to forgive a man for that!

Realising that it is probably vital for the preservation of his sanity that he make his escape as soon as possible from the sorrowful atmosphere of Mr Podger's workshop, he drains his glass once more and, with additional noises of gratitude and courtesy, prepares to take his leave - though not until being called to one side momentarily by Mr Podger himself who, seeing the distress he has occasioned in his visitor gives him a wink and a surprisingly hearty smack on the shoulder as he accompanies him to the door.

'I trust, Mr Wildish, you will not take the case I have made for declining your offer too much to heart,' he says, a hint of laughter at the back of his voice. 'I am a great story-teller, you know. The fact is, if I were to have anyone as fair as yourself working here as apprentice, I would never get a look in with the ladies. And that would never do. And so good day to you, Sir.'

'Good day,' Matthew responds, comprehending the real cause of his rejection with a mixture of relief and amusement. 'You're not really thirty-nine, are you?' he asks, retracing his steps for a moment to look a little more closely into the face of his host.

'No ... no,' Mr Podger replies with a smile of complicity. 'Forty last September.'

'Oh ... good,' Matthew says, and bows once more.

Outside, in the fading light of the late afternoon, Matthew returns to the Piazza where already many of the shop windows and dwellings show the glow of candle and lamp-light within. It is disappointing, not being able to take up with Mr Podger. But Matthew is not dejected. Far from it. He is elated, fired with a renewed enthusiasm for his plans - because all the while he finds himself wondering about *her*, she who has ignited the flame once again and made it burn even brighter - and searching, therefore, as he goes - glancing into every shop window, every dress maker or milliners, speculating with a passion just where or how he might contrive to encounter again she whose name is engraved indelibly in his memory, that very exemplar of fiery Mars, the red-headed widow 'addicted to shopping' - the magnificent Martina von Klapperstein.

# ~ 27 ~
## FURTHER LETTERS OF
## A PRIVATE NATURE

*Aberdeen this 7ᵗʰ day of April 1746*

Matthew, my good friend,
I hope fervently that this letter will reach you,
because I have reason to believe that very few of my letters
are reaching anybody at all at the present juncture. Nor
should you endeavour to write back to me after today,
because no one even seems to know where we shall be
tomorrow, let alone in a week's time. Damn this business of
letters! The army is a hopeless postmaster. We have been
stuck here for weeks, trapped by the appalling climate,
driving snow and ice underfoot. At this time of year,
everywhere is shrouded in perpetual darkness, as well, even
by day. I have never experienced anything like it. My
understanding is that as soon as there is a break in the
weather, we will march out to engage the enemy. Everyone
is chomping at the bit for some proper action, in the absence
of which, I have been gainfully employed among His
Majesty's troops in the lancing of boils or providing enemas
to the generals whose diet remains, even in this remote
outreach of the kingdom, as rich and inhibiting to the proper
functioning of the bowels as ever.

The fact is, the Duke is enjoying the good life here in
Scotland just as completely as if he were in London, and has
even had his own cook sent up to satisfy the prodigious royal
appetite - a man so steeped in grease and fat that if one were
to throw the scoundrel at a wall he would stick to it - all of
which has given rise to many an idle jest among the troops
that we should adopt a stratagem of allowing our cooks to
fall into enemy hands - the view being that if we could
introduce the lean and hungry fighting Highlanders into

some of our luxury ways, we should soon find it a much easier task to overcome them.

On a more serious note, the rebels have taken Inverness, regrouped to the North, and with supplies and reinforcements from their friends overseas have again become a significant fighting force. Naturally, I am not permitted to convey details of our numbers nor of the Duke of Cumberland's intentions in this letter, otherwise it will be censored with big black marks. Suffice to say I am keenly anticipating seeing Charles Stuart and his tartan army within the sites of a musket - and soon!

I will not be permitted to fight, you will be relieved to learn, except in an emergency, as my skills are expected to be in demand in attending to casualties. How I will cope with this I am not yet sure. There have been some minor skirmishes, and I have seen bodies. War is a bastard occupation in which regular laws are often set aside, and Cumberland and Hawley amuse themselves here in Edinburgh by building gibbets in order to hang without trial anyone they can lay their hands on from the enemy camp. The rebel Highlanders are not proper soldiers, you understand, and should not be granted the courtesies normally reserved for prisoners of war, or so they tell us. I agree, of course. I have to agree, as must we all.

Anyway, my friend, I have received a letter from my dearest Johanna, which is a minor miracle, that it should have reached me. She and the children are well, and I am also reliably informed that she and Lady S. have patched up their grievances. That is good news. However, she also tells me that you have not once called upon our home in Greenwich since the unfortunate incident of my going-away party at Snatchalcombe. Why, Matthew? This is most out of character. You should not feel you are unwelcome simply because the master of the house is not in residence. I have no qualms about your visiting Johanna, in fact I would strongly encourage you to do so, since I know you both to be honourable people. Do not, Sir, underestimate my sincerity in this matter. It would provide my dear wife with much needed support at such a difficult time, and I wish her to be under no misapprehension as to the extent of my love for

her. And if, through this constant failure of dispatches, I am
unable to convey my sentiments, I would be obliged if you
might do so on my behalf. I would also wish you to be on
hand, should anything untoward happen to me of a more
irreversible nature. Do not feel diffident about it, Matthew.
Just go. Take my dear one's hand in yours and bless my little
children for me when they say goodnight. These are my
wishes. Never doubt them, or me.

    Your good friend,
    Sam

*St. James's Square, 8th April*

My Dear Mr Wildish,
    You will have been puzzled, I should think, over
my tardiness of late in writing to you, or in matters of my
avowed commitment to your welfare and all that jolly fine
versifying that you do. I trust you have not taken this as an
indication of any cooling off on my part. Despite any
unfortunate misunderstandings that might have arisen that
weekend at Snatchalcombe, both my husband and I remain
as devoted to your preservation and advancement as ever -
particular in regard to how best to sponsor those sonnets of
yours. I have been in frequent communication by letter and
in person with your friend Mrs Woolveston - our dearest
Johanna - and thus stimulated by a deeper understanding of
their literary significance, I am as enthusiastic as ever about
seeing these, your better parts, displayed for a wider
consumption.

On the subject of Johanna, the poor young woman is
quite hopelessly besotted with you, of course, as I am sure
you understand. We had a right good chin wag about it the
other day when we agreed to make up any quarrels between
us - a frank exchange of views - as them politicians might
say - and we agreed that it would be best if she did not have
too much to do with your work in future - or with you, in
fact. So, do not be surprised if she does not write to you,
since that is what we agreed upon.

Regarding your ongoing project, perhaps we could
bundle your sonnets with some of your earlier bits and
pieces to make up a nice thick volume - and naturally with a

good few pages of dedication to the Earl and me at the beginning. We should then consider a worthy presentation, a binding with lots of gold leaf and the Snatchalcombe crest prominent, so I can give plenty of copies to friends. The King would also receive a copy, naturally. I must see you in person, however, to discuss this proper. I am now to be found here at our town house, giving the mattresses and what not a right good airing in advance of the coming season, and would consider it a pleasure if you could gratify me by popping in at your earliest convenience.

Until then, I remain, your devoted admirer in all matters poetic and artistical,

Dorothea, Lady Snatchal

*Snatchalcombe House, Surrey, 10th April*

Wildish,
Some news that might just be to your advantage. I understand from sources close to His Majesty that there is to be a massive battle near Aberdeen within the next day or so. The intention is to ensure there will be no repeat performance of the Jacobite rebellions at any future date. In other words, Cumberland is ready to give old Jock up there a bloody nose. And because the victory will be widely celebrated here once news reaches the capital, it would be to your credit to get your foot in the door in advance of this with a poem in dedication to his Highness the Duke of Cumberland. Everyone in the know is already preparing for his triumphal return, and Handel, I understand, will do something specific. If you could run up a worthy dedication to the King at the same time, you would score a bulls-eye by extolling the praises of both father and son. I urge you to think about this in a serious fashion. Naturally, I can ensure you that whatever you do has the full ear of His Majesty. An excellent opportunity, that you should seize with both hands - as the actress said to the bishop, what!

I received a letter from Sam, by the way. It looks like the censor has been at it, because it has lots of thick black splotches all over the paper and I cannot say I ever recall him writing that way in the past. Anyway, from what I can make of it, he confirms exactly what I just stated - that once the weather starts to improve they will all be lining up for 'the big one.' Trouble with those Highlanders, as I know from experience, is that they are just too damn obstinate to know when they are beaten, and what with our boys having so much heavy ordnance at their disposal, there will be a bloodbath for sure and plenty to keep our Sam busy in the medical department. Let us hope he keeps out of the firing line and that we have him back with us soon, and safely. I would hate to see that pretty little wife of his becoming a widow and draped all in black for months on end (though I'm sure we would all be round there damn sharpish with the almond oil to offer consolation, what!)

Anyway, Lady Snatchal is off getting the town house ready for the summer season and I am here all on my own with the painters and decorators. Boring, boring, boring! And I am poisoned half to death by the fumes. So, I intend to ride to the market this afternoon with some of my top porkers - to do a spot of trade and pursue some of those handsome village girls. (Don't tell Lady S.)

With Kind Regards,
Snatchal

*Woolveston Cottage, Greenwich, Kent, 10th April*
Salutations, my Wonder,
    Forgive me, my dear friend, for troubling you, as I am sure you are much occupied with all your noble thoughts and creative endeavours at the present time, and I interrupt your concentration hereby only with the greatest reluctance, trusting that you will not think me too much of a nuisance. I am faring well under the circumstances, and remain as resolute as ever to remain brave and steadfast in Sam's absence, so that every day I reassure the children that his return to the heart of the family will be accomplished within a very short time. I only hope I will be proved accurate in these predictions, or the little ones will never forgive me as they grow older - that I have given them such false hopes each evening as they kneel at their prayers.

Lady S, being back once more in London for the season,

has called here at Greenwich and I am able to inform you in all good faith that we are once again the very best of companions. She has confessed to me a certain infatuation with you, which led her to mistake our friendship, yours and mine, as something different to what it has been and to have supposed, quite preposterously of course, that you cherished some romantic sentiments towards me. Hence, her peculiar and jealous behaviour - something more than obvious, I should have thought, to everyone in recent times. I assured her that any such suspicions on her part were unfounded, and consequently, we had a lively exchange of views regarding her plight and also of how she might overcome it. We determined that this should best be achieved by her keeping her distance from you - for at least a good while to come. So, you need not be too concerned or puzzled if she does not write or seek your society at the present time, as this is what we agreed upon.

I must tell you, my Wonder, that I am so desperately lonely and unhappy, and so anxious for the welfare of my Sam, that for two pins, and if it were at all possible, I think I should acquire for myself a soldier's uniform, disguise myself as a redcoat and journey north to join him. If it is true, as the philosophers insist, that all men are born free, why must the plight of women be to abide always in their homes and to languish away? It seems so unfair, and sometimes I think I will never enjoy a peaceful night's sleep ever again, lying awake with apprehension and such uncertainty as to the future. I fear Sam is simply not prepared for the rigours of warfare - though, there again, as Lady S stated the other day, 'men often rise to the occasion in the most unexpected ways when in a crisis.' I am not entirely sure what she meant by that, but she seemed sincere. After all, her own husband fought with valour all those years ago during the previous uprising. She said all the violence made a man of him. I am not entirely sure, however, if it is the sort of man I would wish to have return to me at the end of it all. We shall just have to wait and see.

I cannot help but ask myself why you have not written to me at all. I trust and pray you have not taken it into your head to go north once again to join the fighting. I do not

think I could bear it to know that you were placing yourself
in such danger as well. Tell me you have not left us, my
Wonder. If you could write a few lines or even call upon us
here at some time in the near future, I would be most
gratified. The children, John and Samantha, often ask of you
- their 'uncle Matthew' as they say - while Sam has urged
me to notify you of his faith in your integrity and that you
should not feel inhibited in respect of visiting. Believing, as I
do, that inhibition has never been an obvious weakness on
your part, I trust that it will not be a hindrance to your
coming, if only for an hour. And thus I remain in hope of
hearing from you soon.

 Affectionately, your dear and ever faithful friend,
 Johanna Woolveston

  Matthew reads through each of the four letters once again
before consigning them all to a bottom drawer in his desk. He will,
of course, probably not have time to write to Sam, especially as, by
his own admission, the letter would be unlikely to reach him. He
will not go to visit Lady Snatchal at her St James's house, either,
nor will he compose some grovelling poem to commemorate any of
the dubious achievements of the Duke of Cumberland in order to
satisfy Lord Snatchal. Most reprehensible of all, however, and he is
fully cognizant of it himself, is that he will not visit Johanna at her
home. How could he even contemplate anything so foolish! The
fact is, some things in life are risky and would be ill-advised.
Walking on a tightrope, as he has seen done at Vauxhall Gardens;
or riding full pelt in a carriage down Shooter's Hill - those are risky
- as is walking alone unarmed through the Rookeries of Seven
Dials at night. All these things are dangerous - but they are as
nothing compared to his venturing forth to visit Johanna in
Greenwich. For it is inevitable what would happen.

  For a moment, he opens the drawer again, as if he would read
again her letter, but then slams it shut once more, most firmly, and
gets to his feet. Damn it! He does not wish to be in love. It is far
too inconvenient. He wishes only to forget - to forget them all.

# 28

# OBSERVATIONS OF THE
# HEAVENLY BODIES - MARS

*Of the planet Mars, its general and particular significations:*
*She who bringeth strength and vigour. A bold countenance,*
*impulsive, courageous and fiery of nature. Of middle stature and*
*lean. The complexion of a high or ruddy colour. The hair red or*
*sandy flaxen and many times curling. Sharp eyes, ever observant.*
*Outspoken, sometimes being the authoress of quarrels and*
*contention. Accomplished with implements and weapons. In*
*apparel preferring of scarlet. The garnet and ruby for her*
*gemstones.*

If this happens just once more, Matthew thinks, I shall surely finish up punching someone on the nose.

'Magnificent - the news, Sir! Have you heard?'

With dismay, Matthew looks back with an impassive apprehension into the face of the latest passer by who has just waylaid him, hoping at the very least that it might be someone he has a passing acquaintance with, someone from The Rainbow or some other coffee house. But no. This, again, is a total stranger.

'Yes, thank you, I have heard the news - already some days ago,' Matthew replies hardly bothering to stop, shielding his eyes from the sun as he seeks out the face of the other.

'Not so bonny now, is he - Prince Charlie,' the man adds with continued jubilation as he hurries on.

It is futile, Matthew tells himself, trying to quarrel with anyone or to moderate their enthusiasm. London, basking in the glow of triumph and victory, is scarcely any more reasonable a place than it was when exposed to the chill of apprehension and conflict. Both bring out the worst in people, and both are equally ill-informed and unpleasant to experience at close quarters, because even now, even after nearly one whole week having elapsed since the news broke, still the bells of the churches continue to ring out, and at night the most extravagant and expensive of illuminations continue to be applied to the walls of prominent buildings, especially around Whitehall and Mayfair – gigantic pictures in light of the King or the Duke of Cumberland.

The reason for all this unbridled celebration is that the Jacobites have been routed at a place called Culloden Moor in the Highlands, not far from the former rebel stronghold of Inverness. From what Matthew can make out, thousands of rebel fighters have either been killed or taken prisoner, with very few serious casualties on the government side at all. A well drilled, well-nourished army of professional English redcoats set against a hopelessly outnumbered collection of hungry, tired and disparate Highland clans, the outcome was never really in any doubt. Just as Lord Snatchal had predicted in his letter the other day, it has been a massive victory.

The battle took place on the 16th April, but it took a good few days for the news to reach London. But when it did, it was received rapturously and with what can only be described as a state of over-bearing and drunken euphoria. Thousands of Scots have been slaughtered; the Young Pretender, Bonnie Prince Charlie nowhere to be found and, if he is alive at all, clearly isolated and on the run. And for the good citizens of London, four hundred and fifty miles from the carnage, strolling beneath the chestnut blossom and scented lilac of their parks and pleasure gardens in the sunshine of a warm afternoon at the start of May, it is a joy of inestimable proportions. Everywhere, people are smiling at one another. Complete strangers stop and exchange greetings, all the normally sober and dignified men and women of the city mixing with one another in a perpetual state of gloating - and this often most raucously - the victory secured by others far away having bestowed fresh virility, pride and arrogance upon so many here at home - while when night falls and the common street whores emerge from their dark recesses and hovels, the euphemistic offers describing their services are expressed with appropriate topicality: 'A Highland Fling' for sixpence, 'Tossing the Caber' for a shilling or 'A Grope up the Kilt' (nothing on underneath) for little more than a cup of gin. Never has Matthew known anything quite like it. And it makes him feel just a little nauseous.

By way of diversion from all this grotesque nonsense - the Cull of Culloden, as he has heard it described by one particularly tasteless wit - he has, for the most part, continued to throw himself into what has become his own increasingly obsessional world of self-indulgence and rampant sensuality. He has just returned from a long and passionate night with Rose, his dreamy and voluptuous lady Moon, and upon that sea of dreams, enfolded by such succulent curves of devotion, he had set his purpose with a dalliance that was most constant - never once breaking his embrace with her; they resting in each other's arms in gentle bliss the night through until the slumber of contentment finally washed over them - and then, with the morning, their parting was of such tenderness. Dearest Rose! How good it had been.

But that was hours ago. Now he is on the loose again and searching, as he has searched most every day recently, for any sign of the resplendent flame-haired widow whom he had encountered at the workshops of Mr Podger, the stays maker - searching, still for the ideal candidate that he has determined for the role of Mars: the delectable Martina von Klapperstein.

Assuming by her name that her departed husband would have been associated with one of the numerous Hanoverian families who followed the first King George into England some decades ago, Matthew has been investigating all the arcades and shops that retail German delicacies, food or clothing - home-from-home items and furnishings from Hanover or Cologne, from Hamburg or Berlin. Yet not a trace of the elusive Lady von Klapperstein has he detected anywhere - until today when, quite by chance, walking past the shop window of a well-known gunsmith in The Strand, he finally discovers her. Yes, that magnificent tangle of red curls falling from beneath a vast wide-brimmed hat with a long purple plume, her gown a resplendent maroon colour of brocade silk - simply stunning! She is inside the shop inspecting various weapons - and despite the incongruity of such an elegant woman in her fine apparel standing there amid so much cruel steel and ordnance and all the paraphernalia of hunting and trapping, she is clearly there with a view to buying.

Entering the shop and manoeuvring himself close, and while pretending to be inspecting some pieces from the firearms section, he listens, hoping to ascertain her business. The place is crowded - it being suddenly very fashionable to be absorbed in things of a martial nature. Swept along upon the tide of victory, everyone wants to be their own hero in their own little kingdom; everyone wants to demonstrate what a *jolly good shot* they might be, just like all those brave redcoats who have vanquished the foe north of the border. And what better way to satisfy such patriotic inclinations than to go shopping for a good gun!

'Oh, most certainly, Madam, yes, a muff pistol is an essential accessory for any lady these days,' an obsequious sales assistant remarks, hovering nearby, his fingers interlaced in a clumsy sort of way, his body bent forward in deference to the fabulous vision of opulence and style standing there before him in the panniered skirts and conspicuous diamonds of Lady von Klapperstein.

'Exactly so, Sir!' she replies, handling the miniature, beautifully crafted flintlock pistol, no bigger than the size of a small hairbrush, with an already accomplished ease, as if she has surely held weapons of this kind before and is no novice to the mechanics of them, either. Matthew can hear her conversing with the man concerning such technical details as 'the calibre' and 'the bore,' and so on - her accent only very slightly Germanic. 'And you say it is effective even beyond close range?' she enquires further, her prominent chin with its elegant curving jaw directed towards the man.

'Over ten feet, Madam, a reasonable accuracy. But at close quarters, deadly.'

'Especially if I am getting him through the neck, eh!' Lady Klapperstein urges him, her voice firm and rasping in tone all of a sudden. *'Bang!'* she exclaims wielding the weapon in one incisive movement upwards to the shopkeeper's throat, aiming with confidence and panache with the unloaded weapon at a place just beneath the chin through which a bullet might enter upwards and into the brain - and at which the poor man, shocked and stunned by the swiftness of the move, takes an involuntary lurch backwards, as if mortally wounded - though he endeavours to laugh it off straight away; a nervous laugh, pretending to be entertained.

It is then, smiling to herself over her display of martial prowess, that she catches sight of Matthew standing nearby. She seems, moreover to recognise him, though whether she is able to place him precisely in the context of their encounter in the atrium of Mr Podger's workshop, he cannot tell. But she regards him with a blend of puzzlement and amusement for a good while before turning back to the shopkeeper and announcing in the same firm and slightly strident voice: 'I will take it. Do not wrap it. Load it for me. I wish to carry it home in my handbag.'

The shopkeeper appears taken aback by this unusual request.

'Are you sure, Madam? It would be most irregular and quite dangerous to ...'

'Load it for me, I say! The weapon has a safety catch, not so? Are you, then, without confidence in the safety mechanism of your product?'

'Why no, Madam, we are perfectly confident ...'

'Then you may follow my instructions without further disputation. The customer is always correct, I believe.'

The man nods in meek and subservient fashion before hastening away, the weapon in his hands, to do her bidding as required with powder and shot.

Matthew, meanwhile, seizing the opportunity to engage the lady while she waits, embarks upon the execution of one of his most accomplished bows, or as best he can manage in the confines of the shop, making a leg and sinking almost entirely to one knee as he removes his tricorn by way of salutation before flourishing it magnificently in the air as he rises.

'At your service my Lady,' he says. 'Matthew Wildish is my name, if I might be so bold.'

'Yes, of course. Who is not bold in London at this time!' she observes in a similarly assertive manner, and then turning from him as if distracted by some items of interest in the shop, adds: 'I trust, though, that you are a worthy gentleman in addition to being merely a bold one. That is of equal importance, would you not agree?'

The shopkeeper, meanwhile, has returned with the loaded pistol and Lady Klapperstein sequesters it into a small satin and finely embroidered handbag. She does not pay or even offer to pay, presumably having a line in credit. And then, it being obvious that she is preparing to leave, Matthew, anxious not to lose her, accompanies her out of the shop.

'Do you intend taking a chair, Ma'am? If not, perhaps we might share a carriage?' he suggests, allowing her thereby the opportunity of refusing his approach. But she does not refuse, at least not entirely.

'It might be convenient,' she replies, though a little reproachful, he feels, walking at a brisk pace towards the Piazza. 'What direction are you taking, Sir?'

'Why the same direction as yourself, Madam.'

'How do you know which direction is mine, Sir?'

'You have, Madam, stepped already into the sphere of my curiosity and, if I might say so, my admiration, as well. Naturally, one would wish to protract such an agreeable experience for as long as possible. I shall not pretend otherwise.'

'You are a fine talker, Sir.' she says, though without mirth, as though chiding him as she walks at his side.

Undaunted, he takes the opportunity to introduce himself more fully and to explain that he is a poet. To his surprise, it is something that appears to be acceptable, even to this most singular devotee of weaponry and violence - so that within minutes they are ensconced together inside a hackney carriage, seated opposite each another and here, having provided the coachman with her card, they are driven at a gentle pace towards Leicester Square: her home, he surmises, though he does not pry.

'I must say it is a rare individual who would occupy himself with verse at a time such as this,' she declares, drawing the curtains across against the intermittent glare of the setting sun, which is very bright at just this moment and sparkles on various little diamond points upon her throat and ears as she turns. 'Are you not more interested in killing, Sir? Most of the men I have encountered today seem convinced they have personally dispatched a dozen Highlanders on the field of Culloden, even though none was ever farther north than Finchley.'

Matthew responds without merriment, but rather acknowledges her appraisal of the current state of London's manhood with a magnanimous bow of the head. 'No Madam, I have no interest in such things,' he replies. 'I find the conquest of ideas through the medium of words far more gratifying.'

'Indeed,' she agrees. 'And how might one experience an example of your *conquests,* Mr Wildish?'

'Why, here Madam, for I can, if you would give me leave, sit by you, and recite some verse gently to your ear.'

'Gently? Can you not speak up from where you are?' she asks, her voice abrasive.

'A poet does not shout, Madam.'

'Oh! What does a poet do, then?' she asks, while sliding almost imperceptibly to one side, making a little space for him next to her.

While taking care not to embrace this welcome opportunity with an all too-obvious demonstration of haste, as is very much his natural inclination, he chooses instead to rise from his seat only gradually, rotating himself into the place alongside her - she folding her voluminous skirt over her lap to accommodate his proximity before allowing it to spring back and thus to enfold him - all the while feigning disapproval.

'How dare you!' she says, her voice rasping once more despite her acquiescence in the deed.

It is rather like having a welcoming rug placed over one's thighs, he thinks, as he leans over, ever closer in order to respond to her challenge: 'Why, Madam, do you not think that a poet should be daring if he is to penetrate such a spirit of resolution? And when he has the ear of a beautiful woman, he must sigh and breathe his words with due tenderness - the better, then, to season the object of his admiration in flavours of sweet herbs and spice, and to lament his longing in all the warmth of chocolate and brandy.'

'Um - your poetry is sounding quite delicious already,' she murmurs in return.

And in the pleasant shade of the carriage, still faintly scarlet in the light of the setting sun and where her hair is consequently even more aglow with its radiant colour, their eyes meet properly at last, indulgently for what he realises is perhaps the first time in any lengthy engagement. He feels quite captivated by those eyes, which seem to invite him and yet which are steely and defiant at the same time, as if their contradictions might go on forever; and he also notices that her hat is trimmed not only with plumes but with a naked stem of rose. There are ruby-red rosehips preserved and entwined therein, and with the sharpest of thorns still intact. An unusual statement under normal circumstances - though not perhaps for she who is, after all, the very exemplar of Mars. And how red is her hair - and even her eyebrows have the faintest hint of russet gold within them. It is all he can do to extricate himself from the fascination, or to resist the temptation to kiss her there and then. But instead, he stills his beating heart, breaths deeply and prepares to recite his verse - and never before has he been more certain which of his sonnets it must be:

*As empires brandish arms and fall from grace,*
*As they with Mars and forceful strife contend,*

*Then would I make my peace in thine embrace,*
*That all our ardent yearnings might we mend.*

*Within thy rose and fragrant scarlet bower,*
*I am therefore a probing humble bee,*
*Who separates the petals of thy flower,*
*And there will make my greedy sport with thee.*

*Oppose me not. Surrender to me, love.*
*Lay all thy thorns aside as vanquished bloom,*
*And let my hand of friendship fit thy glove,*
*Or be henceforth full-punished in thy doom.*

*My wishes all are only this to bring,*
*That thou should'st feel the venom of my sting.*

'Leicester Square!' comes an abrupt and coarse cry from the driver outside and, much to Matthew's annoyance, shattering the magic spell of silence that had met the conclusion of his poem.

'Driver - go round once more,' she calls, lowering the window a little so she need not shout. 'And continue thus until I give you instructions to stop.' This accomplished, she then sinks back to her place, if anything even more intimately adjacent to him, their bodies touching. 'You see, Mr Wildish, this is where I live, though I am in no hurry to return home. Where, may I inquire, do *you* live, Sir?'

'Why do you ask, Madam?'

'Why? Because I wish, if you should be so inclined, that I might go home with you instead,' at which astounding statement she removes the rose stem from her hat and places the thorns upon the back of his hand. 'Ah, I can see you are shocked, that I should be so impulsive and have so little regard for my safety,' she continues softly, her eyes engaging his all the while. 'But look - I am armed, and with the sharpest of thorns.'

'Madam, I shall not presume to judge you, but can only assure you of my most tender care for your person. I shall inform our man outside of a change in destination, if you will give me leave.'

At which she rests her hand firmly upon his sleeve, almost clasping it, with the rose crushed between her hand and his. He can feel the sharpness of it, piercing. 'Yes, do so, please,' she murmurs, raising her eyes. 'And let it not be too great a distance. For I have a fire in my breast that will consume me if it is not extinguished by those very deeds your words portend.'

Matthew, lowering the window on his side this time, conveys the newest instructions to the driver who, with the carriage being stationary, is busy lighting his lamps in any case, and accepting it all with little more than a nod of tactful comprehension - being well inured, as any driver of carriages in these parts, to the perpetual round of manoeuvres, assignations and flirtations to which his vehicle and many others coming from the Piazza are so regularly enlisted. And then, settling once more by her side, Matthew takes the gloved hand of his lovely companion and contrives that their lips shall meet softly. It is delectable, and intoxicating - this lightest of touches - and so they repeat the gesture again and again, lingering a little longer each time yet not once allowing their kiss to become complete. Her fragrance is exquisite, and mingled with those creature scents that are so unmistakable and urgent in their intensity. And when she inquires of the distance and time they must wait until they reach their destination, and when with regret he informs her it will be all of thirty minutes, she seems hardly able to contain her frustration.

'What shall become of me!' she complains. 'The fuse you have ignited is not of sufficient length to sustain my needs that long.'

'Then we would do better to distract ourselves, Madam. Let us rather converse a little more - for you will find me an ardent listener if you will only tell me your story.'

'My story?'

'Yes,' he replies, taking her hand again, and above the silken margin of her glove, planting a delicate kiss upon the flesh of her wrist. 'And thus, by my tender ministrations I will make sure your fuse, though smouldering more slowly, shall not be totally extinguished.'

'But what do you wish to know?' she asks, as if stunned - though, he senses, also with surprising intensity.

'Anything, Madam. Or *everything* - as you feel disposed. We have time.'

At first with reticence, but eventually gaining interest in the idea, she does begin to speak more earnestly. 'Well now, there is no great mystery, Sir. You see me as I am - and, as you have already deduced, a widow. I united my fortunes when young to a nobleman, already some years my senior and who, like our King George and his father before him, never lost his fondness for the customs of his native Germany. We were both Hanoverian, and consequently, we would find ourselves travelling back for the summer months each year, following the progresses of the English court. My dear husband was a man who enjoyed life to the full, you see, and I was but a part of that enjoyment, for I was very beautiful when young.'

'Madam, it is a quality that has not deserted you, as any impartial observer would surely avow,' he states, and to which she smiles, though in a grim kind of fashion, with the look of one who has heard such blandishments many times yet who for all that is pleased to hear them spoken again. 'You are most kind, Sir,' she responds. 'Do not for one moment ever assume that we women do not value flattery, no matter how irritated we pretend to be upon hearing it.'

'Was it as agreeable an existence as one might imagine, following the court?' he asks next, keen still for her to speak as the carriage begins to settle into a more steady pace - while he, fulfilling his earlier promise, continues to bestow the occasional tender kiss upon her cheek or hand.

'Oh, yes, it was an agreeable distraction,' she replies in wistful fashion. 'I might even say a lavish one, spending much of our Summer dining, attending dances and masquerades, and also staying on through the hunting season - since I am a very good markswoman. And there is nothing better than to feast on a haunch of young venison that one has dispatched oneself but a few days previous and butchered in the autumn woods. Yes, agreeable times - but also somewhat artificial, our happiness, because alas no children came our way, and as any married couple will inform you, with the passage of the years and the onset of ever more predictable routines and customs, a certain languor and slothfulness arises. This, we both slipped into, until our life together became one of contentment and familiarity rather than anything of passion or adventure. It remained thus up until the end, when all of a sudden I lost him. It was most pleasant, though, our final day together - not that we knew it was to be our final day, of course - but it was a joy. We were at home in our house in Leicester Square, the very place where I almost allowed you to abandon me a moment ago. We had tea served to us, and he said to me, "My dear, let us be utterly indulgent. Why should we not have as many buttered crumpets as we like today?" And so, I buttered his crumpets and served them to him. We drank our tea, with a little brandy therein, and then I called for some more crumpets and buttered them with my customary generosity once again. Oh, he was so happy, I will always remember the look on his dear face - following which he went off for his usual afternoon nap ... and did not wake up. I became, thus, a widow before even reaching my fortieth year, and discovered at the same time that my husband had but poorly organised his estate, and many debts were outstanding. Altogether a brutal shock. I shall not disclose to you how many years ago that was, but since that fateful day, the time has passed without joy or very much contentment. I live off my good name, preferring to associate with those who are not aware of the impecunious condition into which I was thrown upon my husband's passing. Instead, I have come to mitigate the pain of my sorrow each day by shopping, and at nights by attending the theatre. Thus, it will be obvious from what I have told you, Sir, that although my style of living in the absence of my husband has remained visibly extravagant, it has not, alas, been matched by any significant income to support it. It is an illusion. And as a consequence, I have run up debts in every milliners of worth on the Piazza, every mantua maker in Bond Street and many honest craftsmen in sundry places about the city such as the premises of Mr Podger, where I avail myself of a new set of stays most every other week according to my whim and fancy - anything that might pass the time or assist me in ignoring the evidence of my decline. You see, it is not at all easy loosing one's good looks, Mr Wildish. You will discover that one day, also, I trust. For the skin upon your face which is so soft and tender now in the bloom of youth will one day come to resemble nothing so much as a faded composition of cracked old leather.

'And so it was, with a disproportionate amount of these cares and sorrows weighing upon me like so many great stones about my neck, that you, Mr Wildish, encountered me today at the gunsmiths where I purchased this very item here. Look, let me take it from my bag and let us, if you will forego your caresses for a moment, examine it once again. Is it not a fine machine! There is, would you not agree, every bit as much comfort and peace here as there is malice and severity. And so I can inform you now, Sir, without any fear of retribution, for I trust you will not judge me harshly, that with this elegant and finely crafted item at my disposal, it has been my intention this evening to journey to the park before St James's, to locate the most fragrant and pleasant place of seclusion by Rosamond's Pond - and there, amid the song of the nightingales and the melodies of music and laughter from the gardens, to place this dear instrument of release to the side of my head, thus, and to blow my ruddy brains out.'

She watches him with eyes that suddenly seem to burn with a strange ecstasy as she raises the tiny pistol to that very place, almost lost beneath the brim of her bonnet, nestled within the curls and locks of her resplendent red hair.

Slowly, he extends his hand to take the weapon from her, relieved to see that the safety catch is still in place. 'Madam, it is as well the story has a happier conclusion in prospect,' he murmurs, his voice firm.

'Yes ... yes, it is, my poet. Thank heaven! And I promise you within the hour that I shall expend upon you a passion every bit the equal to that which would have inspired me to pull this trigger. For you have saved me from myself, and I will therefore give myself to you as I would unto death.'

As mercy would have it, for he is burning with desire for her now, they arrive at the inn far sooner than anticipated. Quickly, paying off the driver with ample coin, they are at Matthew's entrance and, within a few swift bounds, are up the wooden stairs laughing together now with shared excitement and little fleeting words of endearment and sauciness as they hasten along the gallery.

'Ah, so it's here that we shall kiss - really?' she inquires.

'Oh yes, indeed, my mistress dearly,' he answers in rhyming couplets.

'And bite the night?' she asks, taking his hand.

'And knead, indeed, that's right,' says he.

'And squeeze and tease,' says she.

And stroke and please,' says he - and so much other silliness, all the while hurrying towards his door - which, to his surprise, is ajar and where, he is even more surprised to discover, a lamp-light is already showing from inside. What - has Francis anticipated his return so perfectly?

But no. The reason for the welcoming light is there to behold -

for here inside, hatted and gloved, sat upright upon his couch, gazing up at him in the company of her maid, is the beautiful face and searching, tearful eyes of Johanna.

Matthew is speechless, while Lady Klapperstein bringing up the rear as they charge in, still holding hands, can only stare with a mixture of shock and bewilderment at the presence of the other women.

'Yes, Matthew, it is me,' Johanna says, the tears streaming down her face now. 'Forgive this intrusion. Your valet let us in.'

'My dear Mrs Woolveston!' he exclaims, 'Johanna, what is this?'

At which her shoulders tremble and shake as if any icy blast had engulfed her.

'Matthew - it's Sam,' she cries, getting to her feet and most distraught. 'He is returned.'

'Sam! Returned? But where?' Matthew demands, looking around the long expanse of the darkened workshop for any sign of his friend.

'No, not here!' she cries, sobbing and wringing her hands. 'He is imprisoned - in Newgate. They have arrested him for treason and brought him back by ship yesterday. They will not allow me see him.'

And a second later she has thrown herself into his arms, shedding further tears, hot burning tears of utter desolation. He has never seen her so moved, so utterly wretched, and it makes the tears well up in him also as inevitably he must share in her grief. Her hands claw and tug at his arms, and then squeeze his shoulders so tightly he feels he cannot breathe - and how he needs to breathe, and to let forth his astonishment in groans and sighs also. The very idea of Sam being arrested and languishing in gaol is so utterly appalling. Whatever could he have done to have incurred such a degrading punishment?

At length, disengaging himself with reluctance, for a good part of him wants to hold her close and to continue to comfort her, Matthew clears his throat and, once assured of some measure of calm, turns from her in order to introduce his guest, Lady von Klapperstein - for it seems only right and proper that he do so. But the two women are far from willing to acknowledge each other with anything other than the most superficial of courtesies, and with good reason, no doubt. Johanna appears irate and disappointed at the sight of his sordid conquest being dragged in on his arm - while Lady Von Klapperstein, for her part, remains similarly unimpressed over being introduced to someone untitled, a social inferior and consequently one who should rather have been introduced to *her*. Being exposed also to one who by her own admission is the wife of a traitor is also clearly far from meeting the approval of the noble Hanoverian lady. And so it is, that Matthew feels it prudent to arrange a carriage for his handsome widow. And because the hour is late, he also realises he will need to order up some accommodation in the inn for Johanna and her maid, as well. So much to do, and he must try to see Sam this evening, of course.

Within a mercifully short space of time, therefore, and with the assistance of Francis his valet, all these things are arranged. Mrs Klapperstein, escorted by Francis himself, is dispatched to Leicester Square with promises of a more thorough explanation in the morning; Johanna is housed at rooms here at the inn where, after providing the proprietress, Mrs Block, with special instructions to ensure that she and her maid, Mary, are honoured with every comfort and service possible for their overnight stay, Matthew dons a warm coat and begins his walk, the not too great a distance through the streets to Newgate prison where, according to the scant information Johanna has been able impart, his friend is being detained in the Gatehouse itself - that baleful building, evoking for Matthew such an image of grief and oppression, that the very thought of it leaves him hardly able to draw breath.

Although Cheapside is still busy at this early hour of the evening, the usual frantic pace of street life is moderated by the presence of a thick, swirling fog, wafting up from the river and which envelops everything, smothering it into an uncommon silence. The lamps in the shop windows barely make any impression on it, becoming little more than two ranks of nebulous haze either side of the wide thoroughfare, so that everything in the darkness becomes more difficult to see than ever. Ahead, however, he notices a sharp little flame, distinct and gaining in brightness as it approaches. It is the flaming torch of the link-boy - and not just any link-boy, naturally, but rather the familiar face of Ralph, the one Matthew has by this time almost expected to find available in a crisis.

'Towards Newgate Street is it, Sir?' he inquires merrily as his face comes into view and, having already anticipated Matthew's destination in his usual perceptive way, his first words are as pertinent as if he and Matthew had finished their last conversation only yesterday.

'Yes, in fact to the gaol itself, I regret to say, if you would be so good, Ralph,' Matthew replies without breaking stride.

'My pleasure, Sir - even though the smells attending the place are most rank at present.'

'Surely no worse than usual?' Matthew argues, aware of the notorious pestilent odour of filth and disease that has for centuries permeated the very ground on which the prison stands and which occasionally wafts eastwards along Cheapside to the disgust of all who work and live here.

'Oh, much worse of late, Sir, the boy replies, marching on ahead his little chest puffed out in his usual cocky manner, looking back over his shoulder as he speaks. 'They have some prisoners of war, and other traitors from Scotland. And there is, they say, nothing so rank as the stink of treachery. A difficult death to face for the accused - the bowels being drawn out before death.'

'Yes, all right, thank you. I am aware of the procedure,' Matthew snaps back, wondering why he needs the boy at all for such a short distance. But it is foggy; his company is a distraction of sorts - and surely such a fate would not be applied to Sam. Not hanging drawing and quartering. Not dear Sam!

Soon they are beneath the tall, crenellated walls of Newgate with its imposing archway and portcullis, one of the gates through the city walls that Matthew has usually avoided. There is always something irredeemably vile about those double towers of blackened bricks and those grotesque life-size statues over the lintel depicting Justice, Fortitude and Plenty - so absurdly inappropriate when inside there has always been such malice, cruelty and inhumane neglect. And yet, if this is the location where Sam is being held, it would at least provide the poor fellow with some degree of isolation from the morass of common felons that would be resident in the other, more substantial prison block alongside.

Availing himself of the blackened brass knocker on the gaoler's door, Matthew is eventually admitted - and even before he steps inside, is compelled to acknowledge the execrable stench of the place, so bad that he wonders if he will be able to prevent himself from retching. He feels compelled to hold his handkerchief to his face, until realising that such a foppish gesture would create the wrong impression, not at all helpful if he is to be firm with whoever is in charge. There is only one other person in the reception room at the end of the hallway, a short, stocky warder in a felt hat, mittens on his hands, his exposed nails black with filth and who from the confines of his tall-backed chair behind a counter-top, and without ceremony of speech or formality of any kind demands straight away what Matthew's business might be - the visitor's fine apparel and manners being already sufficient to arouse the fellow's suspicions, no doubt.

'I understand you have a Mr Samuel Woolveston incarcerated here?' Matthew inquires after introducing himself and presenting his card.

'Woolveston ... let me see,' the Warder mumbles, leafing through some sort of ledger. 'Oh yes, we've got him. He's not permitted to see anyone, in case you were wondering.'

'Not permitted! On what grounds?'

'Well ... on grounds that I say, so, I suppose.'

'Would this persuade you that a little leniency on your part might be to the advantage of all concerned?' Matthew inquires, sliding a silver half-crown across the counter top. The man seems astonished - it being more than an acceptable sum for a petty bribe. But Matthew feels he has no time to waste on bargaining and longs to have the whole sordid business over with - and quickly.

'Oh, indeed, Sir. Very right, very right,' the Warder states picking out some keys from a secret place beneath his bench. 'If I might just relieve you of your sword first, Sir, then you may accompany a colleague of mine thence.'

With reluctance, Matthew relinquishes his sword. This safely stowed by the gaoler, and with an encouraging thrust of his stubbly chin in the direction of a doorway behind, Matthew is given over to the company of another man, a turnkey who - availing himself of an oil lamp and a huge set of iron keys, conducts Matthew up two flights of stairs, through a barred door and into the bleak, darkest reaches of this most dreadful of buildings. Certain, Matthew is, that there are rats scurrying from them as they go, while, to either side, stand various chambers, likewise with iron bars upon their doors and through which in the half-darkness he can sometimes detect the vague, reclining shapes of prisoners huddled in corners. It is not a long walk in distance, but it seems like an eternity before they reach their destination, a chamber high up at the far corner of the building and where, with the turn of a key the door is swung open to reveal a surprisingly large room in which a wretched man, alone, in ragged scarlet military tunic is seated on a bed, head in hands, slumped over a small stool upon which rests a book which the man endeavours to read by the scant light of a single piece of tallow burning from a nearby shelf. Matthew can hardly believe it, but this very man, his shoes filthy, his clothes tattered, his wig bedraggled, is none other than his dear friend Sam. And when he raises his black-circled eyes languidly from his reading, clearly expecting to behold nothing other than the face of his turnkey or gaoler, and yet seeing Matthew standing there before him, he lets forth a little cry of astonishment and pain and struggles to his feet.

'Sam,' Matthew murmurs, and then, as he approaches, endeavouring to put a brave face on it, admonishes him in jest, his voice more loud: 'Why, this is a fine bloody mess you've got yourself into!'

Sam, rather unsteady on his feet, hurries to embrace him, tears in his eyes at first, but these he quickly disperses and wipes away with his filthy sleeve, responding in kind with, 'Refrain from your disparagement, Sir! It is but a minor inconvenience. They will cut off my head in the next few days, they tell me, and consequently I shall be well out of it.'

At least a couple of stone less in weight than when Matthew had last seen him, his features are strained and gaunt and framed by a substantial margin of stubble.

'Don't talk nonsense, Sam!' Matthew declares, trying still to maintain the banter, though not very convincingly. 'I can't believe this - I really can't.'

Removing the book - it is a bible - from the stool, Matthew sits himself down as his friend retakes his previous place on the edge of the bed, the frame of which, Matthew notices, is attached to the wall by chains and is hardly wide enough for anyone to lie down on. The turnkey is dismissed - though he must, he tells them, lock them both in for the length of Matthew's stay. They are not worried, for at least they are alone and able to talk without being overheard.

'Is Johanna safe? Have you seen her, my friend?' Sam asks with an eager look, grasping Matthew's hands in his - suddenly more desperate in his ways. 'And the children?'

Matthew explains that he has indeed seen Johanna; that it was she who told him of his misfortune, and that she is safely housed at the Pig and Whistle where she will remain with her maid overnight.

'And the children?' Sam inquires again, his eyes searching Matthew's face as if he would devour every nuance of emotion present there.

'They too are safe, my friend, do not fear,' Matthew answers softly, endeavouring thereby to calm the other man's continued agitation. 'They are at your home in Greenwich with all the staff to look after them. But Sam, for heaven's sake, tell me - in all earnestness, for I know not how much longer we might be granted to converse like this - whatever has occurred to bring you to this condition? I have been told that the charge against you is treason? When will you be tried?'

'Tried? Oh that's done already,' Sam replies with bitterness. 'Next-door, at the courts yesterday, almost as soon as I arrived. I was fifth or sixth on the list that morning, I believe, along with various vagrants, debtors, petty thieves, forgers and harlots all standing trial for their misdemeanours. The jury were averaging about ten minutes per case - being sent off each time into a cold basement with no fire for their deliberations which, as you can imagine under the circumstances encouraged them to return to the warmth of the courtroom with their verdicts sooner rather than later. My trial, I am proud to say, did last a good while longer, though - fifteen whole minutes before they returned with their verdict. And because their adjournment for lunch was in abeyance there was not much longer, to wait for the judge to pass the mandatory death sentence. After that, and with everyone satisfied with their morning's accomplishments, they all went off to eat - excepting me, of course. I was dragged here, manacled. I bribed my way out of that particular encumbrance, using what little money I had on me, but it did not come cheap. I do not know when the date of execution is to be, but it will not be far off. My only hope is that I might have an opportunity to appeal and to have myself beheaded rather than hung drawn and quartered, as many in a similar position have already been subject to at Carlisle.'

At which Sam appears to lose consciousness for a second, and it is only by Matthew's timely intervention, thrusting out his hands, that the poor fellow is prevented from toppling forward from the bed - an expedient which succeeds in rousing him once more.

'Are you well, Sir?' Matthew inquires once the other man has opened his eyes, the expression on his face being one of bemusement at first.

'I am, Matt,' he answers slowly, 'But I must tell you that I have not eaten for a while. What little coinage I had on me at the time of my arrest has already vanished in that bribe and in payment of Garnish, as it's called - that is, food and drink allowed me upon my arrival and which has long gone. I would be indebted to you, Sir, if you could with some urgency, therefore, procure some sustenance for me - for otherwise, I feel I will be unable to impart any details of my history at all.'

Looking into his friend's haggard face, Matthew needs little persuasion of the necessity of this request, and once assured of his safety, allowing him to lie back onto the bed, he calls out for the turnkey. Accompanying the man back down into the shabby little office at the front of the building, Matthew inquires of the warder what might be got by way of provisions for the prisoner.

'What here? At this time of the evening? None at all, I should think!' the warder answers, appearing astonished that anyone should consider asking such a thing.

'I take it you will have no objections, then, if I fetch some food for the prisoner?' Matthew inquires, to be met merely with a shrug of the shoulders. And thus assured that he might be allowed back in if he were to leave, Matthew exits the building and hurries around the corner to fetch some food from the nearest chop shop. Anything cooked will do, anything that might be packaged to retain its heat and taken away - mutton pies and baked potatoes are what he finishes up with. He also adds a bottle of brandy and one of fortified wine for the poor fellow, all of which does not take more than fifteen minutes to accomplish. Then, as soon as everything has been inspected by the warder, the whole lot is brought to the cell and Sam's vigour is somewhat restored, while Matthew, for his part, and retaking his place on the stool once again, imbibes a little brandy with him and waits patiently, in silence to hear anything that might go some way to satisfying his burning curiosity.

'I made a mistake,' Sam says, finally responding to the unvoiced question - and hitting the brandy bottle at the same time as if his life depended on it.

'What kind of mistake?' Matthew asks without being insistent in any way.

But the provision of any explanation in the matter is still not likely to be forthcoming, Matthew perceives, because suddenly the comfort of the hot food and brandy is too much for Sam who, reclining now upon the bed has no sooner started to speak when he appears to be losing consciousness once more. He is clearly utterly exhausted. Catching Matthew's inquisitive and anxious gaze through one half-opened eye, he laughs weakly and with hardly sufficient vigour to speak, murmurs: 'Matthew, my friend, would it be at all possible for you to return to me tomorrow, when I promise I will be in far better condition to satisfy your inquisitiveness.'

Matthew agrees, of course.

'And do not, please, I beg you, bring my dear wife with you when you come. Not yet. I have such things to tell you, Sir, that I would not wish her to be exposed to. I would also like to be a little more presentable in order to receive her. If you might, therefore, bring me some fresh clothing and clean towels I would, likewise, be indebted to you.'

'I will do that, Sam. And I'll bring some shaving gear, and some money, too - some small change?' Matthew suggests.

'Yes, that would be much appreciated,' Sam replies, though rather incoherently by this time, Matthew thinks, as the poor fellow stretches out upon his bed. 'Forgive me, Sir,' he continues, 'but for now I am almost too weary to offer you my gratitude which, believe me, is most sincerely ... most sincerely felt.'

Matthew, knowing now that it is time to go, removes his own coat in order to cover his friend, for he has little more than a filthy moth-eaten blanket to protect him from the gnawing cold of the cell, even more acute now as the night comes on apace. And although the process of leaving, cannot be accomplished in silence, - since the turnkey has to be called from the other end of the building once more, and keys must be applied again to all the various ancient and intractable locks along the way - even then, as Matthew glances back over his shoulder and through the bars, he sees that his friend, his coat snuggled up beneath his chin, is already fast asleep, his breathing deep and heavy as would befit a great fallen giant, his eyes closed and with something not unlike a smile upon his lips - the first time Matthew has seen such a phenomenon upon his poor face all evening.

Outside, where many of the lights and regular lamps are already extinguished at this late hour, and where the fog has become if anything even thicker, Matthew is relieved to discover the link-boy once again - his flame already lit, almost as if he were anticipating Matthew's coming.

'Shall it be back to the Pig and Whistle, then, Sir?' he inquires, already marching on ahead.

'Why, yes, if you would be so kind, Ralph, thank you,' Matthew answers, quickening his pace and endeavouring to shrug off the terrible despondency he feels.

'No coat Sir? Chilly night to be abroad without one.'

'I lent it to a friend back yonder,' Matthew answers, turning up the folds of his cravat to cover as much of his neck as possible.

'Nasty business - being behind bars,' the boy continues. 'I've had some of that myself. It isn't difficult, y'know - getting yourself on the wrong side of the law when you work the streets like I do.'

'Really? Well, that should never be - that they would place one of your tender years in gaol for no other reason than being homeless.'

'Oh, I do have a home, Sir. With my father - I dwell with him.'

'Oh, I see - I'm sorry. I just assumed ...'

'Keep up, Sir! You will be warmer if you walk faster. Not far to go now, Sir.'

'Thank you,' Matthew responds, duly chastised and quickening his step as they march along the now almost deserted Cheapside.

'Do you have hopes, Sir ... for your friend?' the boy asks.

It makes Matthew aware all of a sudden just how very despondent he feels and of how very little hope one might reasonably have. 'Well, I don't know,' he replies, realising that the boy is trying to cheer him up. 'He's sentenced for treason, you see. It would be a miracle for him to be spared.'

'Miracles do sometimes happen, Sir.'

'Not in Newgate,' Matthew argues with grim realism.

'*Miracles, manacles, madrigals,*' the boy declares in his usual sing-song voice, making up silly rhymes as he marches ahead. 'God's grace is not always among incense and prayers, Sir. There is always hope, no matter where.'

The time flies, and soon they are at the archway into the Pig and Whistle.

'That makes two occasions this evening upon which you have assisted me, young Master Ralph,' Matthew states, and I don't suppose, if your past reticence is anything to go by, that you will be any more inclined to accept payment from me than on the last?'

But no answer is forthcoming. What with the darkness and the fog, which is now so thick that he cannot even see his hand in front of his face, Matthew knows that the boy is already gone, the precious light extinguished, and just the faintest clatter of tiny feet on the cobbled lane as the sounds of his steps fade around the corner. Matthew is left alone to climb his stairs, therefore, and along the gallery once more to his apartments. A dismal homecoming and an outcome to the day he had definitely not anticipated at the time of his dramatic coach journey here this afternoon in the company of the delectable Lady von Klapperstein. Now, in place of all those anticipated joys, there can only be a thousand new cares to occupy his mind. What would become of poor Sam? What would become of Johanna and her children? These questions are ones he can scarce bring himself to ask at present, let alone find answers to, because the penalties for treason are, indeed, as Sam had intimated, grim and harrowing in the extreme – hanging, disembowelling, beheading, quartering of limbs and, for those of the family left behind, confiscation of all lands and property, which would throw Johanna herself into penury of course. And thus for Matthew, his thoughts full of such horrors, the common pleasure of sleep remains a stranger to him for most of the night, punctuated only by fitful half-dreams and visions - of glimpses into dark chambers, of hangmen's nooses and axe heads and all the savage barbarities of retribution that his dearest, dearest friend would now be subject to.

# 29

# TALES FROM THE DARKNESS

Morning in Newgate prison, Matthew reflects, is not much of an improvement on evening, and with no further light to be had either way - what little there is, struggling at present to enter through a small unglazed window with bars, high up in the wall above their heads. By this scant illumination, he endeavours to inspect the edge of the razor that only by an additional inducement of silver coin has the gaoler permitted him to bring in this morning for the purpose of administering to the ten-day growth of stubble upon poor Sam's weather-beaten face - applying soap to his chin with his shaving brush and then, in the absence of any clean water, rinsing him off each time with a quantity of small beer from a bottle, much to his amusement.

'I was among the very core of Cumberland's forces when we left Aberdeen,' Sam announces proudly - and laughing, too, as he makes a mighty show of licking his lips, for a shave has never tasted as good. 'What a relief we all felt, being on the move after so many weeks of inaction,' he continues. 'Even the weather seemed benign, or at least it did at first. After some good amount of manoeuvring and minor skirmishes, we were finally within ten miles of the Jacobite's encampment. Everyone was ready.'

'Were you excited?' Matthew asks, as he applies a little lather again and commences upon some finishing strokes, endeavouring to concentrate on the task in hand and not to nip his friend's lips, these being in constant motion as he describes the location and condition of the two armies, English and Scots, with such relish. For whereas yesterday it had been a challenge to keep Sam awake, this morning he was as alert and loquacious as ever and clearly looking forward to what, later today, would be the first visit from his wife.

'Yes, we were all excited,' he replies. 'In fact, I would say the term *excited* is not adequate to describe how we felt, and when we lit our fires that evening we were full of longing for the morrow and the fight that would come. It was then, I understand, that over in the enemy encampment, the Bonnie Prince's quartermaster, of all people, had persuaded everyone that it would be a good idea to send the greater part of their men out through the darkness, to march eastwards in freezing temperatures across the most inhospitable terrain with the intention, once they reached our camp, to pounce upon us in our sleep and to slit as many throats of our soldiers as they could. Ridiculous, of course, because by then, even we knew that the poor devils were so weakened and hungry that they would be incapable of such an arduous exercise. Yet march they did - it must have taken them hours - all the while failing to predict that we would be up late that night anyway, celebrating the birthday of the Duke of Cumberland, and there was much carousing, with cheese and brandy all round. Can you imagine, Matt - thousands of men toasting the health of their leader into the early hours! The poor Highlanders must have heard us from a distance of miles away, and then of course they would have realised the futility of surprising us at all and so they simply turned round and retraced their steps, exhausted, I shouldn't wonder - while our boys when they did retire to their tents and warm blankets, slept like babes.'

'What a mad thing to have attempted!' Matthew observes with a rueful shaking of the head, concentrating still as he makes a final pass with the razor to any growth remaining between nose and mouth and which really does, this time, require that Sam remains silent for at least a few moments.

'It *was* madness, you're right,' he acknowledges at length, after Matthew releases his friend's lips from a determined pinch to keep them closed. 'I heard later that many of the rebels were in disarray even at an early stage of their progress and became lost in the fog and darkness, anyway. The combined hike would have been around twenty mile, and not a bite to eat for any of them even upon their return, they say. The idiot in charge of bringing up provisions from Inverness had made a mess of the whole thing. Dreadful organisation. As for us ... well, the morning came with a feeling of jubilation because everyone knew that the battle would be waged within hours. The drummers struck up as we marched westwards, knowing that the rebels would be catching the first sounds of it almost instantly - the Bonnie Prince's army being under Lord

Murray, or so we believed, as we taunted him and chanted his name.'

'Murray?' Matthew echoes, thoughtful.

'Yes - didn't you encounter him in Derby that time - in December?'

'Yes, that's right,' Matthew replies, taking a seat on the by-now familiar and rickety stool - while Sam, getting to his feet and applying the clean towel to his skin with obvious enthusiasm, begins to pace up and down as he speaks:

'Well, it was your friend Murray who seeing his men limping back and collapsing with hunger and fatigue that morning, who was the first to voice misgivings. He knew the men were in no fit state to fight and said as much to Prince Charles. He must have suspected that they were outnumbered, too, and that the moor where he had been urged to set up his lines, just north of the river Nairn, was a hopeless place for Highlanders to do battle, anyway, being boggy and difficult for them to charge their enemy - which, as you know, has always been the forte of the clansmen. He related all these misgivings to the Prince, and the Prince was not pleased - this not being the first time he and Murray had failed to see eye to eye, of course. They say that Charles had never forgiven him since the retreat from Derby, feeling always that he had been over-cautious - holding him back from his glorious destiny. The truth of it is, on that morning, and after months of frustration, the Bonnie Prince just could not bring himself to decline a battle any longer, not even for a single day. And so, allowing his impatience and vanity to get the better of his judgement, he overruled Murray for the very first time and took command of the troops himself, giving out his dispositions according to his own less than perfect understanding of the arts of warfare - not to mention his woefully unrealistic expectations of what five thousand hungry, ill-shod and exhausted Highlanders could do against almost double that number of well-fed, well-drilled government forces - advancing in formation towards them with fife and drum. He would have heard us coming for the best part of an hour, I should think. Oh, they all roared their defiance when they finally caught sight of our standard - but they would have been concerned, as well, we knew that - a vast wall of red advancing towards them out of the mist, and all our dragoons, too, with their sabres and lance and their fine horses that skipped and ran onto the high ground to take their positions. What a sight we must have been to them, so terrible, so eager in our cruelty - because believe me, Matt, we were ready to be cruel. Our scouts had informed everyone by then of the night raid that they intended to inflict upon us; so we hated the Jacobites then; we hated them as never before that morning, and every one of us wanted to get at them.

'Our infantry, we lined up in two main waves facing West,' Sam continues, taking up various little objects, coins, shaving implements and playing cards and placing these on the table top to represent the positions of the armies on some imaginary field of battle. 'The first was here, look, set up to take the initial advance of the rebels when they charged and it was expected to crumble somewhat. But the second, which they would not have been able to see all that well, was carefully laid out - three-deep behind to provide a barrage of continuous fire-power when needed. I have never seen anything like it - so many men in uniform. What with the snowflakes falling on all those lines of scarlet coats and black tricorns, all ranged in such symmetry: a sight to behold, Sir, I can tell you. The Highland clans, on the other hand, to the West, were in comparative disarray, the wind in their faces, their front line uneven and with a difference of at least two hundred yards between their left and right flanks in relation to ours. They'd also somehow managed to hem themselves in, with dykes and stone walls in various places either side. They seemed to think these offered protection. In fact it merely inhibited them.'

'Were your ranks composed only of English soldiers, or were there others?' Matthew asks, taking the opportunity to speak while Sam pauses to pour some of the wine that Matthew had fetched in yesterday. Ever the attentive host, he carries a generous cupful over to Matthew, as well.

'Actually, you might be surprised to learn that we had plenty of Scots on our side, too,' he replies. 'You see, what we sometimes fail to understand is that many of the lowland Scots despise the Highlanders. Rightly or wrongly, they dismiss their culture as a relic of the past, almost something barbaric. There were plenty of old scores to settle between rival clans, as well, and we even had a couple of those fighting on our side. Nor is it fair to assume this was just some religious quarrel, a Catholic versus Protestant grievance. Having been at the very heart of it, Sir, I can assure you it was far more complex than that. There were numerous Catholics on our side fighting against the Highlanders - and many a Highlander who had no religious affiliation either way. At bottom, it was a choice between the old ways versus the new, the past or the future, and so all the merchants, all the academics and the money-people from Edinburgh, they were always set against the uprising from the very start.

'Anyway, there they were that morning, the enemy - so many of those old warriors, ranged beneath their blue and white standards, each of the clans led by its own chief, with the different plaids of their tribes wrapped about them and all the special hierarchies and customs of their societies informing the placement of every man according to rank and status - in their own way most impressive. They brandished the swords of their ancestors above their heads; they roared their obscenities at us; and they played their wretched bagpipes as best they could - because the snow was turning to sharp, freezing sleet by then and was driving in their faces, which were all red and swollen. And how odd - I thought that I could see all those faces in perfect detail, or imagined I could, every one of them. I suppose our senses become heightened when ready to fight like that. At that moment, the armies were little more than four hundred yards apart, Matt. And then finally it began, the madness.

'The first salvoes of cannon came from the rebel artillery, such as it was - just a few pieces of outdated or captured cannon, each manned by a motley crew, inadequate in their training and quite ineffective. They seemed more intent on hitting Cumberland himself than on fulfilling any tactical plan. But the king's son had been astute. He was a large enough target, that's for sure, all that scarlet and braid up there upon his unfortunate sagging horse, but he'd stationed himself well out of range, on higher ground to the North. Our guns fired in reply then, playing upon the Bonnie Prince, in turn, who *was* in range - not far behind his own right flank. I had a good view of him, at least at first. Astride a fine grey horse, he was, wearing a tartan jacket and a buff waistcoat and, most conspicuous with that famous blue sash around his shoulder, the Order of the Thistle on his chest, and the white cockade in his bonnet. And for just that one moment, Matt, I could understand why they all followed him, even into the jaws of death like this, because he was indeed a bonnie man: tall, handsome and possessed of all the graces. Ah, but then his fine apparel was tarnished a second later, spattered with gore as his groom, who had been standing alongside, had his head taken clean away by a cannon ball. The position the Prince adopted thereafter was a little more discreet, therefore, and well back. Trouble was, he was then on lower ground, which afforded him only an incomplete view of proceedings: a trifle unfortunate, given that he had earlier taken over command of the entire battle himself.

'Our guns had turned their attention on the front line of the Jacobites by then. Cannon and grapeshot - these being just crude canisters mostly of stones and jagged metal fragments packed together, but lethal enough. Believe me, Sir, these men had courage. Without any orders either way, to charge or to retreat, they just stood their ground while dozens, maybe hundreds of them were mown down. Even though you are, as a soldier, prepared for the spectacle, you can scarce believe what is happening even as you see it - the cannon shot and shrapnel like a hail of iron, cutting through the flesh and bone of the poor wretches, like a gigantic scythe through a hay meadow. I saw limbs flying, heads rolling, and all the driving rain and sleet behind them stained red with showers of blood. And all the while the noise and the thick black smoke; the terrible explosions of the ordnance that made your whole body shudder from your boots upwards - the stench of the gunpowder and the smell of blood, too, and all the cries of the victims. It was a horror almost beyond endurance, Matt, and yet one from which I could not turn away. No one could. And still they held their places - all those brave, half-starved, half-mad Highland men and boys - and yes, there were boys among them, as well, even these maintaining their discipline with a will of iron, waiting for their officers to sound the advance - waiting, waiting for an order which just never came.'

'Whereabouts were you positioned during all this?' Matthew asks, as Sam, no longer pacing up and down, draws to a halt, transfixed in silence, as if occupied with some awful, vivid recollection playing there before his mind's eye.

'Myself? Oh ... well back,' he answers at length, startled for a moment like someone waking from a dream. 'I was placed with Cumberland - yes, that's it - along with all the other surgeons, playing it safe, though we all knew well-enough by then we would have plenty to do before the morning was out. Someone had a spyglass and they passed it round, so we could all arrive at very close inspection of what was taking place. Too close, perhaps.

There wasn't much that we missed - the terrible carnage. The bombardment itself must have gone on for at least ten minutes. Can you imagine! I heard later that Murray, who was positioned to the North and who could see everything, rode down to the Prince and begged him to allow the men to advance, and this was agreed. But the messenger sent with the command was slain in the saddle before he got through. By the time Charles was aware of what had happened and had sent forth another, yet further precious moments had been lost and many more of his Highlanders had been slaughtered. Eventually, even they could stand it no longer, especially on their right flank, to the south of the field, which was taking the worst of the bombardment. And so it was, with a furious war-cry, hundreds of them broke ranks and commenced their charge. Like the swarming of a hornet's nest, they descended the slopes, their shields across their breasts as they ran, their broadswords brandished. There was an extraordinary kind of poetry in it, Matt - I can't explain - this doomed bravery of theirs - and all their plaids of different colours, all their bright weapons raised, like a vast, shining silver cloud as they came on, and with a terrible kind of roar, too, like a thunder that made every one of us, even at a distance of a quarter-mile, quake in very fear.

'The ground between the opposing forces was just too boggy for them, though. That was the problem - and they were obliged to swerve to their right as they came on, being funnelled into a wedge rather than keeping a proper line, so that many of them just finished up running into one another. Our front line, in the meantime, waited until the rebels were within very close range before opening up with their muskets - and a lot of them fell then, bodies on top of others in some places. Murray was correct. That famous highland charge of theirs, the very tactic that had proved so devastating in the past was useless in these conditions. The narrow shape of their line also meant they became an easy target for any additional musket fire. There were some stone walls below and on these our fellows rested their weapons, calm as you like - using the rebels nearest them for little more than target practice. Assailed on all sides and caught in the crush, it also became difficult for them to wield their broadswords. Everything conspired against them on that morning. What's more, Cumberland had trained his men to withstand any close engagement. You see in the past, once our troops had fired off their muskets, and with no time to reload, it would usually come to hand-to-hand fighting - our boys with fixed bayonets and the Highlanders with shield and sword. The Highlander would deflect the thrust of the bayonet with his shield and then follow through and upwards with the sword - devastating. And for our fellows, seeing their comrades being dispatched like that, with a lot of bloody hacking about as well, it was not uncommon in the past that they would turn tail and run for their lives. But Cumberland had spent weeks drilling the men this time - urging them not to thrust with their bayonets to the advancing Highlander in front, but instead to the one immediately to the right - each soldier covering the one next to him in strict order. The thrust to the sides of the rebels took them totally unawares to begin with, and they could not use their shields in the usual way. Hundreds were skewed in the sides - liver and kidneys, and terrible pain, of course. It worked for a little while, anyway, until the chaos of battle did eventually take over, but by then it was too late for the rebels, anyway, because another line of musketry had advanced. Within seconds they fired off a great salvo - then as they knelt to reload, a further salvo came from the ranks behind them, wiping out even more - continuous, synchronised fire. Eventually, even those who were left standing had no choice but to retreat, and this in a most disorderly fashion, cut to pieces by yet more artillery fire as they went.

'Meanwhile, the left flank of the Highlanders, farther to the North, and which had held its shape through most of this, had at last received their orders to advance - by which time, despite all the black smoke, they should have seen that the day was ours. But still the came on. And, even then, you have to say that Murray himself was magnificent. Not a young man, as you know, but by God, Sir, he could fight! At one time he had lost his horse from under him, lost his sword, his bonnet and even his wig - his coat shredded with bayonet slashes - and yet somehow he got hold of another sword and stormed back into the melee, urging on as many men as he could muster, even those who were terribly wounded, to return into the teeth of the battle. And then, when even this began to fail, he got back on a horse and covered the retreat, leading some of his own meagre cavalry into position - just a few dozen mounted men against hundreds of our dragoons, but somehow their presence sufficient to hold them at bay for a while, enough to prevent a much worse outcome - at least for those who were endeavouring to escape in reasonable order.

'The Bonnie Prince, meanwhile, was mad with despair seeing all this - and ready to spur his horse forward and charge headlong across the field alone. But they held him back, grabbing the bridle. He shouted again and again to his men as they made off, urged them to rally and return, but either they could not or would not understand. No one was of a mind to hurl themselves towards certain death anymore across a field strewn with the limbs of their comrades - except one or two brave chieftains, that is - madcaps with the smell of blood in their nostrils and who continued to run at us with little more than a pistol or a dagger in some instances, and who were shot down within seconds - though I did see one who was well-armed and who managed to hit home with his claymore - on one of our officers who had his head cleft from crown to collar-bone with a single blow. But it was all futile, of course. I tell you at that point there was not a fixed bayonet among those of our men who had taken part that was not either bent or else stained with blood up to the muzzle and who, with half-mad cries and beating of drum, traversed the field from east to west, then, bayoneting or cutting down with sabres any stragglers or wounded upon the ground. They slew them all, Matt - not heeding a single cry for mercy - splashing through the blood that by then lay in puddles all over the moor and even scooping it up in their hands and hurling it at one another in jubilation until they resembled nothing so much as an army of filthy butchers rather than any company of decent soldiers. Even then, they were not satisfied. They pressed forward, casting ever further afield for their sport, to hedgerows, ditches, anywhere they could locate a wounded Highlander, or even to those who had collapsed from starvation from the previous night's march, dispatching them with bayonet or dagger, cutting their throats where they lay. Elsewhere, others were being pursued by our cavalry who descended upon the rebels most cruelly, thrusting down with their lances and sabres as they endeavoured to retreat along the road towards Inverness, many hardly able to walk, let alone defend themselves. No quarter given.'

Listening to all this, Matthew can only feel utterly appalled by what he hears. 'What in God's name did Cumberland say to all this?' he demands, almost speechless with outrage, learning that English soldiers could behave so dishonourably, against all the normal customs of warfare and common decency.

'Cumberland! Why his conduct was every bit as reprehensible,' Sam rages and forces himself to break off for a moment, taking a substantial sip of wine to steady himself before continuing. 'Later, towards dusk when he was riding over the field to inspect the carnage, and attended by some of his officers, he came upon a young Highlander even then still alive and endeavouring to rise from the ground and to flee but unable to do so, being badly mauled in the legs. The Duke asked the man to whom he belonged, and he replied, "to the Bonnie Prince." Cumberland called instantly for one of his officers to shoot the boy, the *insolent scoundrel* as he called him - to shoot him like a dog. I was there, Matt. I heard the order. The officer in question, and to his credit, a certain Major Wolfe, declined, saying that although his commission was at the disposal of His Royal Highness, his honour was not. And quite right, too! The Duke, infuriated, ordered several other officers, one after the other, to pistol the man, but with the same response each time. Finally, locating a common soldier, he demanded of him if he had a charge in his musket and when answered in the affirmative, commanded him to do the deed. The boy was slain, therefore - a single shot to the head at point blank range.'

Sam ceases then. He takes a seat on the edge of his bed as if suddenly exhausted by the horror of it all - having perhaps recounted the details, Matthew reflects, for the very first time to any willing listener. And when he speaks again it is with head bowed, his face in his palms. 'We could have helped him, Matt - we could have dressed the poor boy's wounds, saved him, I swear. But it was impossible. We were not permitted to touch a single one. Oh, these are tales from the darkness, Sir, the deepest darkness, and you who have not been exposed to such horrors would be forgiven for doubting their veracity. Yet I can assure you they are true. One of my fellow surgeons even had his instruments and vials taken from him when they suspected he was about to aid someone from the enemy ranks. And then the worst of it began. Because if you think my story until now has been dreadful to hear, I must tell you, Sir, that it is merely a prelude to the most disgraceful and abominable, the most barbarous and inhuman acts ever perpetrated by an army at war. Listen to me, Sir! Do not turn away - for you are a man, as I am a man, and you must know what men have committed in our name. We did what we were there to do, those of us who were surgeons or stretcher bearers, we dealt first with our own casualties that afternoon and much of the evening, dressing wounds, performing the occasional amputation, which never became any easier for me - especially the sawing of the bone - receiving all those proud young men who but a few hours earlier were brandishing musket and sabre at the enemy, but who now in their agonies could only cry out for their sweetheart's kiss or mother's embrace. Terrible. And then the next morning, just as I and my colleagues were preparing to go forth again, with the intention this time, upon our own volition, of seeking out any of the wounded from the other side that yet had been spared, the orders were given to the redcoats to go ahead of us to make certain of their previous day's work and to search this time the outlying settlements for any wounded who had sought refuge. A number of the injured Highlanders had gone to what they would have thought was the safety of barns or abandoned cottages. Some had been rescued by local people who had taken pity on them, and these were receiving basic medical aid; while others, outside in the bitter cold, were being tended by their own women folk, camp followers, wives or mothers. They must have been out there cradling the dying men in their arms through the whole night. We were prevented from giving aid to any of them - only perhaps to the occasional officer who had been captured. The rest were all taken, torn from the arms of their women or friends, all their cries for mercy ignored. They were laid out in rows upon sloping ground and executed, shot dead with musket fire or, even more shamefully, by crude canister-shot ranged upon them. Why, I even heard that some of those very same women were slain by our redcoats - those who tried to plead for some clemency for their men, cut down with sabre. There was a barn, little more than a hut really, used for sheltering of sheep during the inclement weather, and into this some of the Highlanders had taken refuge - many of them too badly wounded to move. Upon discovery, it was locked shut and just set ablaze. Everyone inside, between thirty and forty persons and the animals, too, all perishing in the flames. Nowhere was safe, after that, Matt. Nowhere. I even heard that the troops were dispatched into Inverness, as well, to go from house to house, cutting the throats of any wounded as they lay in their beds.'

At which, Sam, as if profoundly agitated once again, gets to his feet and begins to pace around the cell once more, his fists clenched at his sides as he goes.

'I could tolerate it no longer, Matt,' he continues. 'Blinded with rage and the shame of it all, I just had to take myself away from it for a while. And then, when riding out on my own a little later that day, I chanced upon a remote habitation of some dozen or so houses, a good few miles from the field of battle by this time - and it was here I was approached by a lady who by her dress and manner I could see was no common country woman, but rather a person of some standing and who, seeing me equipped merely with a surgeons bag and no weapons to speak of, and probably not yet aware of the atrocities being committed by His Majesty's troops elsewhere, urged me to accompany her to her home, a finely appointed stone building over two floors and where I was taken to attend upon several injured men - all Jacobites. These, I learned, were unknown to the lady herself, a widow, but all had sought refuge at her door in the hours immediately following the battle. I ordered water to be boiled, and asked for any ale or spirits that were available to be bought to me; and I then set about, with the assistance of one of the servants who seemed reasonably able in such matters, to the business of removing shrapnel, and the cauterising and dressing of wounds. I knew I had to work fast, because it was surely only a matter of time before Cumberland's cut-throats would discover the place. I then took an injured man with me upon my horse and rode with him to where he told me he could locate a crossing of the loch to his family and a place of safety in the North. Returning to the house some hours later, I then undertook a similar service for another, a poor fellow who had lost an arm at the elbow.

'None of this was easy, Matt, because after the battle, all the passes up to the Highlands were beginning to be guarded by our militia. But these men were not without local knowledge, of course. They knew all the smaller, winding tracks, or safe houses where they might be hidden by friends - and so by slow degrees I got another couple of them away. By then it was dark and impossible to return to camp, and so I slept that night at the house, lying in the hall with the remainder of the poor men, one of whom, taken with gut-shot, I rightly expected would not last the night. I listened to all their pitiful groans and to many of their tales of courage during the campaign. They had always fought, they said, with decency, adhering to the conventions of war, of burying the dead where possible and honouring any prisoners taken - so that as I listened with admiration, all the while comparing it to what I had witnessed of our own despicable and cowardly behaviour, I felt then that I had become a Jacobite, that in my heart I was one of them. Believe me, Matt, if I could have saved every last one of those fellows I would - because these were not barbarous savages as we have been led to believe, nor were there among them any of those ruffians you encountered at Derby that time. No, these were educated, noble men. They conversed upon the humanities, and upon literature and science. One was an architect; another that I attended had studied mathematics and music - and all so courteous and stoic, these men, even in the extremity of their suffering. I felt I had been lied to, lied to and duped by everyone I had associated with these past several weeks. I never wanted to return to the English camp, and resolved to continue aiding the fugitives the next day. But my rash and untypical conversion to heroism was not to last. Upon riding out with another early that morning, I was intercepted by a patrol and, my crimes being obvious, they arrested me on the spot.

'As for those I left behind, why I heard that, in a gross parody and mocking of my own efforts, that the redcoats went in and finding still a number of rebels present, told them to make ready for another surgeon who was outside and who would minister once more to their ills. But as they staggered out or were carried out by their fellows it was only to be shepherded to a ditch and shot. As for the good widow, who had sheltered them, I fear her fate was not a kind one either - because in the days that followed the battle, Cumberland's men embarked upon a campaign of the most savage retribution against the people, ransacking every house, burning every hut, every barn, breaking farming equipment. Every habitation for miles around met with the same fate, and all the cattle and provisions carried off.'

'So they will starve,' Matthew observes with bitterness.

'Yes ... they will starve. And by then the rumour had began to spread, anyway, or was deliberately fostered among the troops, I know not which, that a written order had been found upon the person of a Highlander after the battle, signed by Lord Murray, no less, and stating that no quarter was to be given to any of our men if taken. We think it referred to the rebel's attempted raid on the eve of the battle. No one I knew ever managed to see this document, by the way, and if it did exist it was probably a fabrication. But the lie served its purpose - and after so many months of ignominious defeat the redcoats were out for revenge, so that Cumberland rather than ordering them to be merciful in their victory, allowed them to be commanded by their basest instincts. Over the next several days, consequently, every kind of outrage was not only permitted but actively encouraged, and any woman encountered was violated and turned out with their children on the heath. And as you say, even those who did survive such violence will surely all perish now anyway, without shelter or food, without their men-folk and with no means to restore themselves. By all accounts, this despicable behaviour continues. It is probably taking place even as we speak, all over the Highlands. Every tradition or trace of native life shall be erased - that is what I heard - even their way of dress will be forbidden, they say. Even their wretched pipes will be outlawed. The Highland race is done for, Sir, and will never come again. That perhaps has always been the intention. And, by God, our brave boys have gone about their business with a purpose and a brutality the like of which I should not wish myself or anyone else to witness ever again.

'And so, Matthew, my friend, there you have it,' Sam concludes as he takes a seat once again on the edge of his bed. 'That is how I fell foul of His Majesty's government. Cumberland, when he heard, had me clapped in irons, and, shortly after, I found myself upon a ship bound for London. I was later informed that one of those I had helped escape was a high-ranking officer in the Jacobite cause, and thus the charge of treason was brought against me. The rest, I have already related to you yesterday - a swift trial, sentence passed. And now, for the mercy that I showed towards those in most dire need that day, I am to forfeit my life.'

Matthew looks into his friend's eyes for a long while - clearly so terribly distressed. What can he possibly say? What could any man say? 'I'm so very sorry, Sam,' he finally ventures - finding it difficult to maintain his own composure.

'You would have done the same, Matt,' Sam responds kindly. 'Any man of principle would have done likewise. I know now that we are not creatures of warfare or of hatred - none of us really in our heart of hearts. We are beings of love and mercy. That is our natural state. All else is a construction put upon us by our masters for their own ends, their greed, their pride and bloody hunger for victory or revenge - and so we must all become butchers for their feast.'

Again, Matthew does not respond, not for a while, allowing Sam to settle himself - and, taking the clean shirt that Matthew has brought in for him, stripping off and changing into it with great relish, smelling the clean linen with a lingering, self-indulgent delight that seems to illuminate his entire face.

'Sam, you are a good man,' Matthew states. 'And a damn brave one, too. No one among your family or friends will ever blame you for what you did. Your dear lady wife, I am sure, will take pride in your story.'

But Sam, rather than agreeing, appears to be smiling now - buttoning up the shirt and with a strange, exultant look, almost reminding Matthew for one peculiar moment of Sam the musician, making music, his bright blue eyes full of merriment.

'Leaves the field clear for you now Matt,' he says.

'What do you mean?' Matthew demands, knowing full well, however, what he does mean. And he is shocked.

'It would not displease me, Matt - you know that, my friend. Do not pretend you do not care for her.'

'Don't be silly!' Matthew states, and this time it is his turn to get to his feet, feigning a false indignation. But then realising that he must not, really *must not* be cross with the poor man, he returns to his stool, leaning forward that he might look closely into his face once more. 'Listen to me, Sam: this is a serious business, this is your life we are talking about here, and the bond of friendship between us is such that there is no happiness in the world that I would not sacrifice in order to preserve it. And if we share an admiration for a fair and beautiful woman, why that can only strengthen that bond. And anyway, we will surely be getting you out of all this mess. There must be something that can be done - an appeal for clemency. And if so, rest assured, I will find it, and I will make it happen.'

And thus, by slow degrees, eventually, Matthew manages to calm and to reassure his friend, reminding him that if Johanna is to be brought to him later today, as they have agreed, then he must look his best for her, and to be calm and put on a good show. His wig, expertly brushed and curled by Matthew, is now restored to him, therefore, and he allows himself to be preened and managed a little more, having his nails pared and - availing himself of Matthew's almost forgotten skills in such procedures - even consenting to have a rotten tooth pulled. All seems well, but then, just as Matthew is preparing to leave and packing up his barber's pieces into his bag, he realises that the razor he had used earlier is not to be found.

'Sam. My razor, if you please,' Matthew requests, holding out his hand and knowing full well that his friend, in his desperation, has somehow sequestered it.

'I beg your pardon, Sir!' Sam responds obstinately folding his arms about his chest and looking away. 'What is a mere razor to you, Sir, an object that can be replaced for a few shillings - while for me it will allow me to administer a little medicinal bloodletting on myself here from time to time.'

'Bloodletting? How much bloodletting had you in mind, exactly?'

'Oh, around eight pints,' Sam replies, re-visiting their shared knowledge of just how much blood exactly the average human body contains.

'Sam! The warder is aware that I have brought the razor in. He will ask to see it upon my departure.'

'Are you sure? Why not try - test him and see?' he says with a mischievous glint to his eye.

'No, Sam!'

'They will drag me to Tyburn, Matt,' Sam pleads, deadly serious now, though speaking under his breath. 'They will pelt me with stones, insult my good name; they will hang me till I nearly choke; lay me on a block; cut my belly and pull out my guts before I die. And you would deny me the alternative of being able to simply open my veins here in the quietness of my cell?'

'Sam! For heaven's sake! If I were to sanction this, they would have me following you to the gallows for aiding and abetting your suicide.'

Sam appears pensive for a moment, looking down. 'Ah ... yes, I see,' he admits, a bit crestfallen all of a sudden. 'I hadn't thought of that.'

'No, I rather thought you hadn't,' Matthew admonishes him with good humour. 'Anyway, listen, my friend. I promise you this - and most faithfully - that whenever we hear that a warrant has been issued or a date appointed for your execution, I will smuggle in a serviceable device of this kind for you once again. Thus, you will only be tempted to have recourse to such an expedient on the eve of your passing - by which time I will have made plans to make myself scarce, even if I must go overseas to escape the authorities. Therefore, be of good heart, my friend. And return to me my razor now, if you please.'

With the utmost reluctance, Sam reaches down behind the buckle of his breeches at the knee and retrieves the object from its place of concealment, handing it over with a rueful shaking of the head. 'Promise?' he urges Matthew. 'Promise me, Sir, that you will honour me with this favour when necessary?'

Matthew gives him his word. He swears he will do it, and then he calls for the turnkey, allows his bag to be searched in the office outside, as anticipated, and hurries back towards the inn to prepare Johanna for her visit, for she must be told her husband's story in advance, and also advised on the condition in which she will find him.

As he goes, rejoicing in the bright sunshine outside, all the more remarkable by way of contrast to the dark squalor in which he has been confined for the past couple of hours, he notices the newspaper bill boards along Cheapside, which continue to be full of news concerning the hunt north of the border for Bonnie Prince Charlie who, without troops or protection of any kind, is still thought to be in hiding somewhere in the Western Isles, hoping for escape by sea. But the coasts are being patrolled, and the French ships that have been sent for him are prevented from coming near. Whatever the outcome for the Young Pretender, the rebellion is clearly over, and has no hope of ever being resurrected. As for poor Sam's predicament, meanwhile, there is only one course of action that Matthew can possible take now: he must appeal for clemency from the highest source - in other words the King himself. And for that there is only one avenue of access. All pride must now be swallowed, therefore; all reticence laid aside. He must make an appointment now - and do it fast - to speak with Lord and Lady Snatchal.

# ~ 30 ~
## PLEASURES OF THE
## PHYSIC GARDEN

'**D**ottie!' the King exclaims, a voice mildly admonishing in tone, as one might use to a child.

'Porgie!' Lady Snatchal responds in kind, taking the proffered hand and sinking into a curtsey upon the lawn outside St James's Palace so low that one might think that a gigantic hole in the ground had opened up and swallowed her - a most extravagant and untypical demonstration of humility on her part, and one accompanied by much creaking of whale bone and panniers as she descends. 'Georgie Porgie!' she adds, puckering her lips as she glances up at him from amid a mountain of billowing satin and silk that threatens to engulf her entirely.

Matthew is terrified - because, for all the familiarity and playfulness, she is, after all, still addressing the King of England. It is a risky stratagem, and he cannot help wondering whether they might both finish up alongside Sam in Newgate this evening as a consequence.

'Dottie, Dottie, Dottie!' King George repeats in a tuneful way this time, bidding her rise with a regal hand and, speaking in his renowned and immovable Germanic accent. 'How vonderful to see you! Where is your lucky husband today - surely not letting you out on your own looking so ravishing and damn fine!'

'Cornelius is incapacitated, your Majesty. He is at home with the gout.'

'Oh, damn shame!' the King replies disingenuously, since he is no doubt more than a little pleased with the situation - until, that is, he catches sight of Matthew some paces behind, on lower ground and consequently peering at him from behind the slopes of the vast, voluminous court mantua and petticoats of Lady Snatchal. Surprised and becoming disgruntled over the discovery, he nods curtly in Matthew's direction and inquires: 'And you, Sir, are ...?'

'This is Mr Wildish, your Majesty,' Lady Snatchal intervenes, turning and ushering Matthew upwards and into closer range with a wave of her fan. 'He is a distant cousin of mine and a right good gentleman and friend of that person we were hoping to speak to you about this afternoon.'

'Good day, your Majesty,' Matthew responds, bowing his most elaborate of bows, flourishing his tricorn hat in the bright sunshine and which thereby casts a series of swift, fleeting shadows upon the grass at the King's feet.

King George, clothed here for outdoor diversions in satin breeches and a braided, knee-length waistcoat of unparalleled magnificence, is not especially tall but is of prodigious girth - as wide as he is tall, in fact - and with big china-blue eyes that seem to bulge out of their sockets at whoever he looks upon. His wig, being of the highest quality, is most likely French, Matthew surmises - perfectly combed and tied with a bejewelled blue velvet ribbon at the nape.

'Oh, well, yes - and good day to you, Sir!' he responds with a further curt nod in Matthew's direction before returning his attentions to the beaming face of Lady Snatchal at his side, and allowing her to take his arm as they, all three, shadowed by an solicitous and vigilant equerry at some distance behind, begin their walk through the lovely private garden - the Physic Garden, as it is called - featuring beds of medicinal herbs and fruits - all flanked by glasshouses and interlaced with meticulously trimmed hedges of yew and box no higher than the height of one's knee. Beyond its boundaries can be seen the park of St James's, the public space with its formal avenues of lime and ash trees stretching away as far as the eye can see in the sunshine and haze of a glorious spring afternoon.

'Remind Us again, who is it you wish to speak to Us about?' the King asks, while signalling with an imperious wave of the hand to the various footmen and lackeys that dance attendance on him to make themselves scarce for once - for they continue to follow him around the garden, pandering to his every whim and fancy ever since his appearance a little over twenty minutes ago when he emerged from the Palace and strolled at a very leisurely pace to the point where he had arranged to rendezvous with the Countess.

'Samuel - Samuel Woolveston, your Grace,' she reminds him. 'His wife, Johanna, is the daughter of Lord Bridges, a baronet. Sam is a rising star in the Admiralty and destined for high office, my husband assures me - and I simply cannot comprehend how he could have got himself into such a pickle with your son, the Duke.'

'Oh, I see! Well, sorry, Dottie - all I can say, is if my boy Villie doesn't like him, then he must be a trouble maker,' King George asserts with a regretful shaking of the head. 'And if he's for the chop, as the law says, then that's all there is to it. He'll just have to go. Sorry, my pet.'

'But he attends the Cornhill Club - and he's a Knight of the Wig,' Lady Snatchal protests confident still.

'Really! Oh, I suppose that's different. All right - I am listening. Vot has he done, then?'

'Well perhaps at this point I might call upon my cousin, Mr Wildish, who will be able to explain far better than I. You have a lot in common, by the way, Sire. Mr Wildish is a great admirer of Handel.'

'*Hendel!*' the King exclaims, gaining a little interest. 'Oh ... he's all right. Some good tunes now and then - at least my father always used to say so. But he will insist on using bloody fiddles all the time. I told him - I said to him, Mr Hendel, I said, if you could only stick to proper martial music with plenty of drums and trumpets you will make me a happy man. But no ... no, he keeps on putting those screechy fiddles in all the time, or else those infernal castrato creatures spoiling everything with their silly songs. Anyway, speak up, Sir! Vot has this friend of yours done to upset my Villie?'

'If it please Your Grace,' Matthew begins running around to his other side - the one not yet occupied by Lady Snatchal's blandishments and thus the better to have more intimate access to the royal ear, 'Mr Woolveston and I both trained as barber-surgeons when young, and although Sam in particular has not practised his skills in this respect for many years, he resolved to lay aside his Admiralty position for a certain time in order to volunteer as a surgeon alongside the Duke's army. He was apprehended doing little more than tending to the sick and wounded on the enemy side following the battle at Culloden.'

'Really - oh, that won't do!' the King remarks, taking a pinch of snuff from a silver box as they wander out through the garden and into the wide Mall, there to join with the many well-heeled and aristocratic visitors parading up and down. 'That must be the reason he has offended my Villie,' he continues. 'My son was not up there to attend to the health of the Scots, y'know! He was up there to teach them a bloody lesson.'

'Mr Woolveston was not aware at the time, we believe, that it was against orders to perform the duties natural to his profession,' Matthew counters, though taking care to maintain an appropriate tone of obsequiousness - or at least he sincerely hopes so, 'it being customary in the treatment of soldiers taken prisoner to attend to their wounds, of course.'

'We are fully conversant with the customs of warfare, Sir!' the King bellows, suddenly outraged, and colouring brightly as he turns to face Matthew, as though all his previous calm and conviviality had been a contrivance on his part. 'We have led men into battle, Ourselves, Sir - against proper soldiers. But these ... these were not proper soldiers. These were Jacobite rebels: a bunch of treacherous, heathens - with beards!'

'Now, now, Porgie!' Lady Snatchal chides the King. 'We all know how upset you are, what with that nasty little Charlie boy wanting to take your throne from you. But Mr Woolveston is a very nice man, a decent chap. And yet, y'know, he works awfully hard, as well. Why, he and Mr Wildish here have been faithful servants of the crown in the spying way of things, for ages! He's the right sort, in other words. One of us. And it really would be jolly nice, therefore, if you could alter his sentence to something a little less harsh than having his head chopped off.'

'Um ...' the King mumbles, doing his best to listen, but also compelled all the while to be turning this way and that to acknowledge the salutations of spectators, all bowing and curtsying, the hats of every fashionable promenader sweeping the ground as he passes. He clearly enjoys being recognised in public.

'Your Grace,' Matthew begins again, realising he must not let the moment slip by. 'As one of extensive and worldly experience, your Grace will understand how it is that some men may come to grief in the course of their lives. Some, for example, might squander their fortunes in gambling; others may ruin themselves over a woman; others through debt or even some in the pursuit of an ideal or dream that is ill-advised. Our good friend, Mr Woolveston, however, has done none of these, and has brought his misfortunes upon himself through no other fault than that of human compassion. Thus I can only appeal to your Grace's wisdom and magnanimity in this instance, and ask whether you might agree with us that his sentence has been disproportionately harsh for what is at bottom a tragic misunderstanding.'

'Um, well, We are not without magnanimity, Mr Wildish,' the King responds at length as they continue walking towards the long, decorative canal that runs through the centre of the park. 'Anyone will tell you that. Why, even when at the side of my dear wife, the Queen, as she lay upon her deathbed some years ago, and when she urged me to marry again - I answered her "no!" I shall never marry again, I told her. I shall only ever continue to have mistresses.'

'That must have been a great comfort to her, Sir,' Matthew suggests.

'Yes, yes, that's right. It *was* a comfort. Everyone said so at the time. And so, Mr Wildish, We give you Our assurances now, that We shall consider your request with the utmost care. You have, I presume, a letter or document of some description detailing your plea?'

To which Matthew produces a written summary of the situation as they perceive it, couched in his most florid prose and written this morning with many a flourish of his finest crows-feather quill. It is signed by Lady Snatchal, Johanna and himself, and includes details of all they have told His Majesty this morning regarding Sam's character and their plea for clemency on his behalf. Taking it, His Majesty gives it a cursory glance before tucking it away into his coat pocket - after which Matthew concludes there is little more that can be done to save poor Sam but to put their trust in God and King George.

'Jolly good!' the King declares in a curt business-like fashion. 'Anyway, Mr Wildish, why don't you take yourself off now on a little stroll, eh? Enjoy my nice park here - or take a walk along the canal or something. And Dottie, you and I can go off on our own for a bit, eh?'

'*A bit,* Porgie? A bit of what, exactly did you have in mind?' the Countess inquires.

'I mean, allow me to take you back into the privy garden, my dear,' Matthew hears the King explain - though from a distance now, as already they have begun to walk away together. 'I have a certain succulent specimen I would like to show you in my glasshouse and we can - er - discuss further the business of your friend there, eh?'

Lady Snatchal, nodding her acquiescence and supposed pleasure at the proposal, glances back over her shoulder in Matthew's direction for a second, as if to say - *see, I told you it would work!* And then off they go, entering by a wicket gate into the mysteries of the privy garden once again and where they vanish from sight amid a congregation of parterres, intimate rose arbours, and exotic glasshouses.

It is becoming very warm in the park as Matthew, realising he had best not stray too far while he waits for Lady Snatchal's return, takes a leisurely stroll along Birdcage Walk - a shady avenue where every other tree is hung with a cage in which a songbird sings - before returning, back in the direction of the Mall in search of a bench from which he might survey at leisure the area's most extraordinary variety of people and visitors - the Mall, one thousand paces long, they say, and the finest and most frequented walk in London. And it is here, promenading up and down the long avenue or along the margins of the canal with its swans and pelicans, that one may find the lovely young ladies up for the season, ready to be introduced at court, wanting to *see and be seen*, their solicitous and ever attentive beaus alongside, and all accompanied by chaperones and maids who follow discreetly several paces behind. There are young pages in cheap white wigs - the shimmering light of the water dancing upon their faces. There are elderly divines from the Abbey, taking the air - gaunt, puritan figures in black robes. And there are tall guardsmen in their scarlet coats and white breeches, off duty for a precious hour, maybe - the distinguished Grenadiers among them, too, in their tall mitre bonnets - all seizing the opportunity for some fresh air or to feel the sun upon their skin. Lots of different people, from all walks of life. Yet for all that, it remains uncommonly hushed and dignified - an occasional raised voice of conviviality among the gentlemen, perhaps, or a little chuckle to accompany the many varied signals and configurations of the fan among the ladies; but not a harsh word to be detected anywhere. It is an oddly pastoral scene, as well. Cattle and deer are grazing in the fenced areas between the avenues; and at stalls and trestles set up nearby, fresh milk is being served for a penny a cup - the customers wiping the creamy deposits from their mouths upon the backs of their hands - that or else with picnic basket upon the grass, they sit in groups, pouring wine or cherry brandy, so that even the most innocent and chaste of lips are sometimes stained just a little red.

How Matthew comes to be here at all and having moreover just a few moments ago spoken to the King of England in person, is a minor miracle - it having been only a matter of a couple of days since Sam's return, and just a few short hours since, at a most unseemly time of the morning, he had called on the Snatchal's London address and left his card, expecting to speak with the noble occupants only much later. But to his surprise, he was intercepted by the butler on his way out to his chair, the man hurrying after him with a message urging the visitor to return at once. Lord and Lady Snatchal were at breakfast in the morning room and, being at that stage still unaware of Sam's incarceration, they were so disturbed to learn of the whole affair that they immediately sent out cards to St James's, not expecting a reply for days, if ever - only to have a message back within the hour from the King's secretary stating that His Majesty would have a few moments this afternoon during a walk he intended to take within his private physic garden, and if Lord and Lady Snatchal would care to attend upon him there, he would be glad of their society. Astonishing!

And so it was, with the gout-ridden Earl genuinely laid low by his afflictions and unable to make the journey, that they determined that Matthew should pose as a distant relation and thus become eligible material to escort Lady Snatchal to St James's instead. With such a prestigious destination, however, the matter soon began to take on an additional life of its own, so that rather than take chairs, or even to just walk to the garden - since it was only just around the corner - Lady Snatchal, keen to make as much social capital from the occasion as possible, elected to take her own finely appointed carriage instead. And thus, with great aplomb, dressed for the occasion in a sumptuous ensemble of black and purple taffeta, scalloped, tiered and tasselled, bowed, ruched and gathered to every possible extravagance, and looking more like a Duchess going to a coronation than a simple garden assignation, she allowed Matthew to hand her into her gilded coach-and-four, its horses short docked, with plumes upon their foreheads and accompanied by a pair of liveried footmen striding out alongside, to be subsequently conveyed the short distance towards the mighty brick edifice at the end of St James's Street and where they rode as if in state between the formidable gateway of Tudor turrets built so long ago by Henry VIII and into the shaded, colonnaded courtyard of the palace itself - all busy with marching guardsmen and sedan chairs coming and going. At that moment, had some invisible celestial orchestra suddenly struck up Handel's coronation anthem from beyond the clouds, nobody would have been in the least bit surprised. Otherwise known as the 'Whalebone Court' due to the curious presence of one half of a gigantic whale skeleton clamped to one wall (the rest of which, Matthew could not help thinking in one unkind moment, might well have been requisitioned for the construction of Lady Snatchal's gown), here they were met by a surprised and bewildered chamberlain who guided them most solicitously through the palace itself, up a grand staircase and along a passageway to a reception room among the royal apartments - only to guide them instantly and with equal alacrity, once their business became known, down another staircase and out to the gardens the other side.

Though brief, it was a memorable experience, Matthew had to admit, because he had never been inside St James's before - the interior of which transpired to be every bit as formal and squarely regimental in tone as the exterior: all the walls of the hallways and staterooms, or those that Matthew could discern, at any rate, decorated with various geometrical arrangements of swords, pikes and muskets, punctuated by vast, gilt-framed paintings depicting members of the Hanoverian nobility or famous battles from European history - all very martial in tone and replete with images of smoking cannon, charging cavalry and fallen soldiers at every turn. Perhaps, Matthew reflected, one should not be surprised at such a predominantly masculine taste being in evidence - dictated by one who had been without a wife for almost ten years. Understandable, yes. Fascinating, certainly. But Matthew felt much relieved when they were set free, to be outside again and beneath the pleasant sun.

Here they had walked together for a while and waited for the King's appearance - the Countess determined to take Matthew's arm, but this being far from easy due to the enormous lateral dimensions of her hat and gown.

'Now, now, Mr Wildish, you need only step a little before or behind me, rather than at my side,' she had instructed him, raising the hem with her hand all the while, 'and I shall be able to take your arm and we can become proper cousins - just like you and Johanna were *proper cousins* once when you two walked arm in

arm over the bridge that time. Oh yes, I know all about it,
Matthew,' she added as they waited for the King to approach.
'Women do talk about that sort of thing, you know. Once the blue
porcelain and the silver spoons come out over tea, everything is
aired, all our little triumphs and indiscretions.'

He had laughed then, and so had she, helping him to calm
himself ahead of the ordeal. And now, bringing it to his
remembrance once again, seated thus alone upon his bench,
shielding his eyes against the sun as he seeks still for any sign of
Lady Snatchal's return, he cannot help wondering just what else
women might talk about on such occasions, and just how much of
himself might be featured in the conversation. But no matter. Any
minor discomfiture he might be forced to acknowledge today
would, he tells himself, be as nothing compared to what poor Sam
would be going through languishing in his cell.

And so he waits: increasingly anxious at the passing of the time
- because he has promised to accompany Johanna to Newgate later
today so that she might spend a few hours with her husband once
more. Having kept her room at the Pig and Whistle, she has already
been to visit Sam - twice yesterday and once on the evening prior
to that. On all these occasions Matthew guided her into the horrid
building where, in the presence of a turnkey or warder, they would
pick their way upstairs and along the bleak and dingy passageway
to the room where Sam was kept. And each time, with a wink of an
eye or a discreet wave of bravado to his friend behind his bars,
Matthew would leave him and Johanna to converse alone - hardly a
convivial environment amid all the filth and squalor, and with still
the terrible uncertainty of the prisoner's fate in the balance, but
surely better than nothing at all - and meanwhile providing
Matthew with time in which to haggle and negotiate all the various
petty bribes and inducements necessary to make Sam's detention
tolerable, including how much time his visitors might be permitted
to spend with him. It was, Matthew felt, the least he could do.

And yet if these precious hours of company were an obvious
comfort to Sam, they were also, Matthew was beginning to suspect,
becoming increasingly arduous for Johanna. The strain visible on
her face this morning, when he had joined her for an early breakfast
over at the inn, was already beginning to alert him to the
probability - with the poor woman's normally calm, tranquil
exterior having become agitated and strained, her skin tight around

the temples where little lines of discomfiture had formed, her complexion becoming paler than ever and showing the dark circles of sleeplessness beneath her eyes - those once so-sparkling eyes. He felt almost ashamed over having to conduct her to such a dreadful place once more. And she would not, she said - simply *could not* - ever go there alone.

Dining together, as they have been compelled to do of late, they have, Matthew realises, probably been granted the pleasure of each other's company far more in this short period than in the whole of their several years of previous friendship. And whereas before it had always been under the formality of some social engagement or the other - at Greenwich with Sam, or else conducted out and about in the company of so many noisy, intrusive people - here it was just the two of them, brought together by the simple necessity of taking food and refreshment - that, or else walking together along Cheapside towards the prison, dressed modestly as befitted their destination, he in a simple velvet coat, she in a country style jacket and skirts, all dark and sombre in colour: anything that would not be tainted too obviously by the filth of the place. Thinking of it now, he has to smile, despite himself - for the streets of East London or the tavern of the Pig and Whistle were hardly ever the most sophisticated or romantic of places in which one might pass the time with someone so fair. Yet, whenever they had met to share a meal together, he had hardly noticed his surroundings. She had never once appeared unduly concerned, either - the noise, the vulgarity, the rowdy chaos of a typical coaching inn providing if anything a kind of protective boundary of commotion around them in which everything was conducted at a different tempo. They were as two people upon an island, therefore, seated opposite one another at a rough, uncovered table amid an ocean of unobservant, indifferent humanity. Here they spoke of their lives, of Sam's life, of Johanna's children's lives and even, in lighter moments reminiscing over the mischievous pug, Boris, and his antics - and all the while with such an uncommon luxury of time and leisure at their disposal, with horizons of conversation that seemed to stretch away to an inexhaustible infinity of possibilities. And then he would sometimes read her one of his poems, or discuss with her those sonnets, the allusive seven that seemed such a long time in coming to perfection and which even now were not quite ready for her.

'I do not know, Matthew, whether I can face attending again tomorrow,' she confessed at one stage, with a serious turn but in every other respect relaxed, ungloved, leaning back a little in her seat after they had eaten and taken more than a little wine together. 'I wonder if you can understand my feelings?'

'Yes, I can understand,' he said, still deeply troubled for Sam's sake - for it seemed that everything mentioned between them excited his sensibilities of late. 'The worst of it is to see him in such a vile place among so many base individuals, all the common thieves and villains. For my part, I know only that I must go tomorrow for his sake. If you do come, though, you would, I take it, still wish to spend time with Sam alone?'

'I don't know,' she replied, and then her lips compressed themselves as if to fight back some tears. 'I am not sure about that either. The last occasion became so impossibly harrowing and dreadful. We talked of such awful things - that he should die, and die so miserably; that I should be cast out of our home with our children, and all our capital and means of support taken from us. It is all the worse for him, that he is so powerless to remedy it. And to me, naturally, he reveals the full measure of these afflictions. It is an aspect of his character that even the closest of friends would not have been privy to: only perhaps a wife or mother. He weeps, and then I weep, and we just go round in circles thinking about the agonies of what might befall us. If you were to be present, as well, next time, my Wonder, keeping things on a more even keel, so to speak, it might help. It might be ... well, less intense?'

With little more than a nod of the head, he let it be known once more his understanding. How different she seemed, he thought - everything about her. This was no longer Sam's wife seated there before him. No longer the formidable and almost unattainable Mrs Woolveston. It was Johanna herself - a person if not exactly new to him, then at the least one who was revealing a facet of herself that *was* new. The intriguing quality of pensiveness that he had once admired and which on occasion had seemed merely a passing shadow across her lovely face was now, more and more with the events of the past several days, becoming a permanent cloud that had settled there. And yet if it was a cloud, it was never an oppression to behold, not for him - never dull but rather one of gentle lamentation and tenderness - and one, therefore, from which he simply could not withdraw his eyes. He realised then that one of two things was surely taking place: that either she was miraculously becoming even more beautiful than ever or - the more likely explanation - he was falling more deeply in love with her by the hour - a love which he almost dreaded to contemplate because he knew it really could not be concealed for much longer.

'It just occurred to me,' he said, almost as if thinking aloud, 'that maybe even Sam would appreciate my being there. After all, it cannot be easy for him either, having you all to himself - I mean, to be exposed to the object of his devotion in such a vile place, to be so near to that which is so lovely and yet to which he cannot respond, not in the way that is natural to him, by embracing you and enjoying your society. It cannot be easy.'

'Do you think I am lovely, Matthew?' she asked, though not frivolously as he might have reasonably expected, but rather seizing on that one remark, that one word, and ignoring all else. An earnestness was in her voice, then, and when he raised his eyes to meet hers, he saw an urgent questioning there, as well. What he had said could never be unsaid, of course. They both knew that.

'Yes,' he replied simply. 'I think you are the loveliest creature on earth.'

She clasped her hands together then and raised them to her lips, as if she was about to stifle a cry, and tears were forming in her eyes - eyes that suddenly looked so large - larger than he could ever remember seeing them, making it all the more remarkable, the way she looked.

'Your eyes,' he murmured, smiling despite all the gloom and miseries of the day that had just passed, 'they are so big!'

'And yours. I was just thinking the same,' she said. 'Your enormous eyes. Why, Matthew, whatever are you thinking about!'

'I'm sorry,' he said, furious with himself - for surely the last thing this unfortunate, dear woman would have wanted at present was his ridiculous and inappropriate overtures. It was as if he could not spend more than a few minutes with any woman these days and not automatically endeavour to seduce her. But then she surprised him.

'Goodness, Matthew, we should not jest, should we? We should not even think like it. Yet we do. You spoke a moment ago about being with us - but don't you see, you have always been there, somehow always there between us? And if thoughts are as bad as deeds, as they say, then what sinners we must all be deep inside,

that we should betray all our better instincts of what is right and
dutiful. What treachery there is in love!'

'*Love,*' he whispered and inadvertently he reached out - and
why he reached out he could not say because, again, it was a
gesture once made that could never be undone - but their hands
touched then and suddenly they were clasped, one hand in the
other, and then all four hands somehow all locked together across
the table. And all of his body from the top of his head to the tips of
his toes felt alive as he had never felt before. She had spoken the
word: love. And he understood then - yes, *love* - genuine,
irrepressible love that overpowered everything in little more than
the duration of a breath. And all those cares, all those duties and
sacred vows that people so foolishly place as an obstacle to stand in
its way were simply swept aside, annihilated in a moment with that
one word shared and acknowledged between them.

At length, they disengaged their hands, unravelled slowly every
finger, lingering on each one with a little squeeze or stroke,
knowing all the while that they must let go, yet doing so only with
the greatest reluctance. And then, having composed himself once
again as best he could, and she having done likewise, and replaced
her gloves, they each, like responsible people ought to do, resolved
to behave themselves and to bid each other good night in the most
civil of ways. She went to her rooms, and he went out and through
the yard to his door and up to his rooms, too, feeling utterly bereft,
as though he had left his very heart and soul behind, and that he
ought, instead, to surrender to every compulsion in every limb that
was urging him to turn around at once and go seek her again - and
yet all the while knowing that he must not, that he simply must be
sensible about it all and go to bed. Yes - go to bed, damn it! And so
he did go to bed; but sleep would not come. Sleep was impossible.
And later, sitting up at his bench, he found himself wide awake,
drinking coffee and examining from the darkness every window
across the yard, trying to fathom, as he had tried to fathom on the
previous evening, just where in the vast sprawling building of
forty-odd guest-rooms the one belonging to her might be situated.
Would there be a light? Would he, if he waited long enough catch a
glimpse of her - a glimpse of the one person he revered and
cherished more than anything in the entire world? He was, he
concluded, utterly and hopelessly love-struck. And the answer was,
of course: no, he could not see her. Her room was not even on the

gallery; it was the other side of the building, hidden from sight.
And he was a bloody fool.

And so, now, this afternoon, back in the park, with these
exhilarating recollections burning in his memory, and looking
forward to the hour when he might return home and be able to
escort her once more to Sam and then perhaps to dine with her
afterwards, he casts his eyes about the busy meadows and verdant
avenues once again, and then back up to the Palace, hoping still to
detect some sign of a returning Lady Snatchal. But no. It is, he is
forced to conclude, obviously going to take a little more time,
whatever it is the King has in mind.

The sun has become hazy now, and gradually clouds have
begun to gather - bringing with them an oppressive and even
stormy feel to the afternoon. Everything is hushed, governed by
that uneasy and troubled mood that comes with the approach of
thunder. Down towards the river at Westminster where a breeze is
beginning to ruffle the tops of the trees, the view of Hawksmoor's
towering additions to the Abbey catches his attention - newly
constructed, their stones pale and unblemished against the
darkening sky behind them. How magnificent they look. Yes, it
will rain shortly, that is for sure - and people are glancing upwards
at the change, expectant. And then, all of a sudden, it occurs to
Matthew that there might be something decidedly suspicious about
their assignation with the King today - the ease and speed with
which everything had fallen into place. Maybe His Majesty already
knew about Sam's predicament and that the poor fellow was a
friend of the Snatchals? Perhaps it was all some elaborate charade,
a handy opportunity for the man to have his way at last with his
much coveted Dottie? But more significant for Matthew this
afternoon, and with leisure now for the first time to reflect upon it
more fully, is the recollection of reading again through their
petition for clemency during the coach journey here today, the
same that was presented to the King, only to discover that Lord
Snatchal's signature had not been upon it. When asked about the
omission of her husband's hand, however, Lady Snatchal had
merely shrugged her shoulders and brushed the matter aside,
adding words to the effect that for all the love he bore for his friend
and colleague, Cornelius was forever the true patriot. Believing that
the signature of the Countess would be sufficient, he had simply
elected not to sign, therefore. Odd - *most* odd. Let us hope,

Matthew reflects, it does indeed prove to be sufficient, else how would he ever be able to forgive the old reprobate for his negligence. Patriotism be damned!

And thus, Matthew, with even more reason to be anxious, must continue to bide his time here in the park, amid the increasingly threatening approach of a storm, waiting for whatever might come to pass regarding the fate and destiny of the two dearest people in all the world to him - with Sam's life or death and the future welfare of Johanna being determined by little more than the outcome of a sordid flirtation somewhere in a privy garden. Would they be deceived? Would the King simply refuse to budge or to countermand the wishes of his son, his precious *Villie?* - already beginning to attract to himself the dubious nickname of 'Butcher Cumberland' as a result of his atrocities north of the border, and from where, to the continued detriment of the poor Scots, he is yet to return.

He tries to stop thinking about it, and instead turns his attention to the scene around him once more - for rarely does one have the opportunity to observe so many of the great and the good of London society outdoors at such an early hour. And suddenly, for him, it is no longer such an edifying spectacle. No flattery of candle light is present here to soften the complexion; no twilight or seductive moonbeams to deceive the eye. And when a gap appears in the clouds and a wedge of sunshine sweeps across the scene like a spotlight upon the stage of a theatre, it leaves everyone just a little exposed to the harsh reality of it all. And although every kind of opulence, every silk, every sumptuous brocade and variety of wig is on display, there are also more than a few glimpses of faded glories, the presence of canker or withered bloom in the hat-bands and décolletage, the dull powdered complexion of the rake or libertine, the badly painted lips or chipped cochineal of the bawd or dowager. Here suddenly, all the myriad sparkles of gold or silver, all the diamond-studded brooches, snuff boxes, hair pins, buckles, canes and every other accessory of genteel ornament or beauish decoration, appear to Matthew as little more than tinsel against the magnificence of the sun. Everything loses its lustre and fades into paltriness, leaving instead - and the more he looks the more he sees it - merely a profusion of moles, wrinkles, pencilled eyebrows, stubble chins, false hair, smiles of manufactured teeth, and everywhere the white faces and powdered wigs that seem like so much straw and dust compared to the splendour of the verdant leaves and blossom in the trees above. And he cannot prevent himself reaching the inevitable conclusion that because of this, in deference to this distasteful parody of civilisation taking place before him, young men have had to go away to fight, to sacrifice themselves and to die in war, and by the command of those above them to commit the most heinous acts of barbarity against their fellow men and women. Even in the fair light of a glorious day in May, he hears the words of Sam from his prison cell, recounting the horrors of Culloden. They thunder in his ears, as everything and everyone ranged in front of him now appears as little more than some grotesque circus, a freak-show of overdressed and unpleasant smelling creatures of various assorted shapes and sizes - while all their speaking and laughter, every word they utter sounds to him like so much bestial jabbering.

And then, without warning, Lady Snatchal in her distinctive purple and black is all at once to be seen hurrying back across the Mall, the breezes ruffling her gigantic dress – several stray tresses escaping from beneath her hat as she waves to him and makes her way down across the park. And as he rises, to greet her, his heart pounding almost audibly in his chest, he examines her face for any sign of resolution, searching for the faintest hint of accomplishment and, dare he hope, even triumph concerning the fate of his friend. And then, to his surprise, and in one peculiar and detached moment of observation, he realises that her face looks different. It does not look old to him, as it often does, but is instead full of the most remarkable vitality and intensity.

'Sentence commuted to transportation!' she announces as soon as she is within earshot, a hand raised to steady her hat in the wind. 'They will send him overseas, probably to America.'

'Thank God!' he cries, jubilant as they stand for a moment gazing into each other's eyes.

She, too, is overjoyed, even though they both know it is still far from a totally agreeable outcome. 'Naturally, it will all need to be cleared with the Judge who dealt with the case, and Sam's estate will be confiscated just the same,' she continues by way of clarification as, taking his arm and gripping it tightly, they walk with brisk steps back to the rear entrance of the Palace. 'But it will all go through, he reckons - within a matter of days.'

Matthew knows he should be jubilant, and yet he cannot help

recalling Johanna's words to him some while ago, confessing her dread of Sam ever having to go to sea for any length of time, the very sea that had claimed the life of her own brother. How very strange. Could the poor fellow withstand such a journey? And would Johanna go with him? Oh, whatever is to become of us all now, he wonders? These and so many other questions come tumbling towards him so fast: so very upsetting.

'I suppose it is as much as we could have hoped for,' he observes, after breathing a protracted sigh of relief, still walking and speaking in a voice of reason that bears little relation to the turmoil inside. 'It definitely could have been worse. Was it difficult?'

'No - not difficult at all,' she answers, just as the first drops of rain begin to fall, and still a little breathless with the excitement as they enter the shelter of a narrow alley-way leading through into the courtyard, the roofs above them lit suddenly by a flash of silent lightening. 'We had a pleasant stroll in the garden. Jolly educational it was, too, amid all them-there herbs and rare shrubs and things. Oh, and I - er - did him a bit of a favour, that's all.'

Looking at her face, it seems to him then, along with that unusual intensity that he had observed a moment ago, that a certain melancholic dignity pervades her countenance now, something he has never observed in her before. But then, he reflects, perhaps he has never bothered to look for it before, either. Whatever has taken place in the seclusion of the garden is clearly not entirely to her liking, so he refrains from pursuing the matter, and Lady Snatchal herself says not another word on the subject either, merely clearing her throat from time to time and, rather unladylike, spitting occasionally into her handkerchief as they return together to their carriage.

# OBSERVATIONS OF THE
# HEAVENLY BODIES - SATURN

*Of the planet Saturn, its general and particular significations:*
*She who bringeth age and wisdom. A broad forehead, the eyes*
*inclined to black and looking downward. The complexion pale or*
*swarthy. The hair dark and rugged of texture. The body lean and*
*the waist slender. Of a serious, melancholic nature. Sometimes*
*given to irony or to be occupied with morbid fantasies. In dress,*
*elegant - often preferring of black. Diamonds and black agate for*
*her gemstones.*

The uncertainty of it, the combination of guilt, love, desire and sorrow is tearing him apart. How on earth, he asks himself, will he ever manage to retain his sanity over the next few days?

The first thing they decided was not to inform Sam straight away of his sentence being commuted. The matter of formal judicial proceedings was yet to take effect. It could take weeks, and if anything were to go wrong, it would be dreadful to have to tell him his hopes had been dashed. So, when Matthew had taken Johanna to see him that evening, they contrived together to conceal their expectations. They also endeavoured to hide the more personal feelings that attended them - since those in love can rarely ever disguise the fact when in each other's company. Without needing to talk about it, therefore, they reached the conclusion that it really would be best to visit Sam separately, and so Matthew went in only much later, after Johanna had taken a carriage back to Greenwich, there to be re-acquainted with her children after so many days of absence. He was able to sit with Sam for an hour then, and managed to drop a hint or two, as she had surely done, to provide him with at least a modicum of hope - words to the effect that they were already doing their best to seek clemency on his behalf, that he should not be too downcast, and so on. But, it was a difficult hour; and the next day, in Johanna's absence (for Sam had insisted that she not return to expose herself anymore to the indignities of Newgate), it became even more fraught, with the poor man wanting to recount again and again all the horrors of Culloden or to contemplate the gory procedure of his own execution, should it come to pass - so disturbing, in fact, that Matthew could only secretly long for the time when he could return with a proper signed and sealed confirmation of the man's reprieve. Perhaps, he thought, Sam himself would be informed of it anyway within the next day or so. He could only hope, with all his heart, that it would happen. The burning question was would Johanna elect to follow her husband - or even to accompany him to the New World? As yet, she had revealed nothing of her intentions.

'Huh!' Sam had exclaimed at one stage after asking about the weather outside, 'I wonder what my old barometer would say?'

'Yes, I wonder,' Matthew echoed, unsettled by such a peculiar observation. It would have seemed the least of Sam's worries now, the weather.

'You're right, Matt,' he said with a bitter smile, as if reading his thoughts. 'Maybe I never needed to know what the weather was going to do, eh? I should rather have applied myself to forecasting my own doom, my own rash stupidity - the better to have avoided the consequences. No, I never got that barometer of mine working properly. And you never got your doorbell fixed, either. Life somehow always got in the way, didn't it. Oh, what fun we have had, Matt, you and I. What fun it all was!'

What could Matthew possibly say to this? The whole experience, of seeing this most excellent of men brought to such a pass, to such a ponderous confusion of mind, was more than depressing. It was heart-breaking. And so it was that he had left his friend yesterday and gone forth to visit the impetuous flame-haired widow, Martina von Klapperstein for a night of unbridled passion and forgetfulness in the bedchamber of her residence in Leicester Square. And how he had needed to forget - to erase from his mind not only the vision of Sam languishing in his filthy prison, but of the love he now felt for Johanna. He just could not face another night alone without something to distract him. So he had gone to her, bearing with him the gift of a handsome ruby pendant, the very gemstone of Mars, replete with a purple ribbon that he had fastened around her naked throat before covering her with kisses - enjoying her fully at last, that fiery redhead who with such shameless impetuosity would roll upon him, sit astride and whinny like a mare as she took the lead again and again. He had pleased her well with that gentle violence that she craved, holding her fast, gripping her flesh, and she, rejoicing in the struggle, calling out in her native German any number of harsh obscenities while twisting her long red hair into a braid that she gave him to tug upon, for it seemed she desired to be commanded thereby. Ah! What indelicate and sordid delight was there - his fiery, passionate lady Mars! And he rather suspected he would be returning to her in the not too distant future for a further bout of loving combat.

This afternoon, feeling sated and with a certain clarity of mind restored to him once more after his night with Martina, he has elected to venture out to Ranelagh Gardens, to re-acquaint himself with the fragrant walks, ponds, pagodas and pavilions and to perchance locate that final note upon his magical octave and rainbow to heaven, the woman who might represent the emanations of Saturn. He has completed his sonnet to the seventh sphere, only just this morning. So would the magic work again?

The day is warm, slightly oppressive and threatening rain - though inside the Rotunda all is cool and fragrant, and here he discovers to his delight that an orchestral rehearsal is imminent, to include selections from Handel's Water Music. Irresistible! And already the vast space is becoming populated with excited visitors.

'Why, Mr Wildish, fancy seeing you here!' comes the voice from behind, and even before he turns he knows full well to whom it belongs.

'Lady Snatchal!' he declares. 'What a pleasant surprise!'

Dressed as always in the most extravagant of outfits, panniered skirts and embroidered jacket, all in a striking variety of dark and dramatic colours, she holds forth her gloved hand, a cascade of lace ruffles from elbow to wrist as she advances towards him. Her maid and a footman, some distance behind, have clearly been instructed not to attend too closely through fear of spoiling the effect - for the presentation of such splendour requires, above all, plenty of space around it by which its bearer can be properly seen and appreciated. With the additional obstacle of a similarly elaborate wide-brimmed hat, tilted upon one side of her head, it is all Matthew can do to reach over and get close enough as he attempts to take her hand and raise it to his lips in greeting.

'Would you care to join us upstairs in our supper room, Mr Wildish?' she inquires, indicating one of the private boxes ranged around the circumference. 'We are just up there, overlooking the bandstand. There is champagne and nibbles - oh, and a certain document from St James's Palace which might be of interest.'

Catching the twinkle in her eye, he understands at once.

'Why, Dottie, Dottie, Dottie!' he exclaims, mimicking somewhat the King's endearments of the other day - those he had been privy to, at any rate. 'If this is what I think it is, I do declare you are a genius every bit my equal.'

'How very perceptive of you, my dear,' she responds, just as playful, as they continue towards the stairway, a broad ascent that takes them to the circular passageway above and where she, walking ahead, continues to speak to him over her shoulder. 'By the way, my real name is not Dottie, you know - or even Dorothea.'

'Really?'

'No. Dorothea is just my middle name. My proper one comes from my Italian mother, Malaena. I cannot bear it because it means something like *black serpents*, apparently.'

'Ah - the head of the Medusa!' he chuckles, recalling the evening of the masquerade and thinking, too, that the name really does suit her - though she does not seem amused by the inference.

'I assume you have not been home yet today,' she continues, 'because I have already sent out letters - to yourself and to Johanna at Greenwich - recommending that we all gather at your apartments at The Pig and Whistle this evening, and from there go to Newgate to convey the good tidings to Sam - since the authorities won't be telling him for ages. I take it Johanna is at Greenwich?'

'Yes, that's right - though I have furnished her with a set of keys to my rooms this time, should she need to return quickly.'

'Her own keys - really!' the Countess echoes with obvious amusement. 'How very convenient - I mean, that you and I can enjoy the music here this afternoon and come at our leisure, so to speak.'

Turning sideways to negotiate the relatively narrow door, she allows him to open it and show her through. He follows. But inside the supper box, a wainscoted room of small dimensions though furnished with every convenience along with several chairs and a fine table arrayed with ice bucket and champagne, there is no sign of Lord Snatchal.

'Oh dear! Cornelius must have just popped out for a moment,' she says, closing the door behind her and sequestering the key somewhere within the voluminous folds of her petticoats before descending by slow degrees onto a broad chair between Matthew and the door. 'Do take a seat, Matthew - and yes, I know what you are thinking: I have fibbed to you just a little about Cornelius. In fact, he's gone off today to Snatchalcombe House - or will do, anyway, once he has concluded a little business somewhere in Cockspur Street, he says - and he'll take the coach out from there. We are quite alone.'

'I see,' Matthew responds, realising that he is trapped but, oddly, not caring one bit for his predicament. And as the music, with all its familiar and seductive charms, strikes up from below, he feels inclined, especially in the light of all she has done for Sam of late, to acquiesce and to bear his obligations to her - and this with a sense of resignation verging on enthusiasm now, even above the interests of his own self-preservation which had impeded him so often in the past.

'The truth of the matter,' she begins again, leaning forward to draw the curtains of the box a little further over, 'is that my dear Cornelius has been rather a naughty boy. He admitted it to me this morning.'

Matthew raises his eyebrows - a gesture of inquiry, though he feels he should not pry by asking directly for an explanation. Instead, making himself comfortable in his armchair, he releases his sword belt and sets it aside, waiting for her to continue. Which she does, though in a voice of some displeasure.

'My ever resourceful Cornelius knew at the start of the year that Sam would be in no small peril going off to enlist with Cumberland. So he went down to Garraways and took out one of them insurance policies. On Sam's life, it was, for the period of one year - to pay out handsome upon his death, whether by misfortune, legal judgement or failing health.'

'Really!' Matthew exclaims, shocked. 'I didn't know that kind of thing was possible?'

'Oh yes. You can take out a policy on just about anything, these days. Anyway, I only discovered it this morning when, upon sharing with him the good news about Sam, he appeared somewhat peevish. It was then that I wrung it out of him, what he had gone and done. I was, to be candid with you, Matthew, most displeased, and we quarrelled.'

'But I thought Sam and your husband were supposed to be friends,' a stunned Matthew protests, reaching for the champagne and unfastening the cork, 'or at the very least colleagues?'

'Oh, you don't know my Cornelius,' she says, proffering her glass, her eyes downcast - and for once he feels it is not a counterfeited sorrow that she is presenting to him. 'Where money is concerned there are no friends, no colleagues, no honour really much at all. Now, of course, we know why he neglected to put his signature to that there petition. Moreover, you do apprehend, I take it, the nature of the business he's engaged in when he makes those little excursions of his to Cockspur Street?'

'Oh ... no, not really, Dottie,' Matthew replies with tact as he fills their glasses, suspecting that he does know, and yet dreading that he might be correct. 'What exactly do you mean?'

'That tart, of course - that most consummate, dissembling harlot and bawd: Lucy Armstrong,' she replies reproachfully, a sour expression on her lips at the very mention of the name of she who has no doubt claimed many a man, and his money, from among the society in which the Countess moves. As if considering just how much she should reveal, she stares ahead, sipping at her drink. 'I suppose I can tell you, now, can't I, Matthew my darling,' she murmurs, 'seeing as you and I are arriving at a certain understanding, I can let you into some of the more intimate details of my marriage - and of how, over the years, my husband has become a devotee not only of the steam baths and massages of the bagnio, which is forgivable, I suppose, but also of the many dubious and varied pleasures of flagellation - which is perhaps not so easy to countenance. You see, even in the early days of our marriage it became obvious that nature had, alas, not furnished Cornelius with the natural strength and vigour adequate to his desires. Having strained and over-taxed his constitution through all manner of perverse follies and fancies, he began to suffer quite early on from a certain corporeal debility - so that with the passing years, more and more extreme measures were called for in order to *raise the flag*, so to speak - measures which I was no longer able or willing to provide. As a consequence, I occasionally sought my own diversions elsewhere, which is why, of course, I have endeavoured for so long to win your affections. Oh Matthew, my darling, all this reminds me so much of being young again, being here with you. Do you know that? Of being carefree. I had almost forgotten what it was like.'

'Now, now, Dottie. I don't believe that for one moment,' he says.

'You have never been trapped in a broken marriage, Matthew,' she argues, untypically serious all of a sudden. 'You have not experienced neglect and indifference from those who once loved you - all the more unpalatable when one has still the recollection, as I do, of happier days - times when I was properly admired, so adored that now I sometimes wonder if it was true - was it really me?'

And, raising her eyes again to meet his, she takes her fan and applies it with vigorous movements to her face, though also keeping it open afterwards as she thereby invites him further into her confidence, all the while watching him closely, waiting for his reaction, aware perhaps that for some time now she has been taking command not only of the conversation but of his feelings, too.

'Tell me ... tell me more, my mysterious Malaena,' he murmurs as raising her gloved hand to his lips he places a delicate kiss upon her fingers.

'Yes ... was it really me?' she continues, not minding his intimacy or his use of her unliked name, 'or was it just some recollection of another life, a story that has been told to me and which, with all the nostalgia and fondness one has for things past, one remembers only imperfectly? That's what I wonder sometimes. Can you imagine, my darling, that once upon a time I was considered to be one of the most beautiful women at court, and my Cornelius was a dashing young guardsman - so handsome, so tall and upright in his scarlet uniform! And so devoted, too. He would worship at my feet then - quite literally so - and would go about all the shops in town with one of my shoes in his pocket as a pattern in his search for pretty footwear - it being the perfect pleasure for him, he used to say, just to wash and paint my pretty toes in readiness for the ball. And then, when I heard music such as this and took to the floor, my heart used to jump for joy because when I danced it was as if my feet had wings and that I was soaring through the very sky itself and taken off to heaven. Everything had

a freshness about it then, you see - a zest! There was not one cloud
in my sky, Matthew, just as there was not one blemish upon my
beautiful skin. So strong, so confident, my thoughts were alive with
anticipation in that morning of my life - with nothing that could
ever persuade me that my future could be anything other than one
of complete happiness. And, you know, the funniest thing about it
all is that one only understands this later, much later when one is
old. And that's me now, you see. And my dear Cornelius, my
dashing hero, has shrunken and shrivelled up and become so very
old and foolish, too, hasn't he! So very *outré*. He is little more than
a convenient embarrassment now; a torment to my spirit. That is
what I felt this morning. I felt so ashamed of his disdain towards
our dear Sam. It brought it all home to me, the awful truth of what
Cornelius and I have become. I hope my candour does not
displease you, Matthew, or my keeping you here in this place?'

'Why, no, not at all,' he replies. 'In fact. I would not wish to be
anywhere else in all the world at this moment but here.'

She seems surprised at his sudden conversion. But she need not
be - for he is resolved now to pleasure himself on the delights set
before him, to avenge Sam for the greed of that old reprobate of a
husband of hers, as well - though whether he can really believe any
of what she has told him today concerning her companionate
marriage, he cannot say. She is a mystery, this saturnine sorceress,
a painted enigma in so many variations of black taffeta and purple
silk.

'Malaena,' he says, looking into her eyes with curiosity, 'tell me
something: I have always wondered at your preference for black. I
must say, it is a shade that becomes you, and yet ...'

'Age naturally inhibits the use of colour, Matthew,' she
interrupts with confidence. 'And then, of course, black is infinitely
preferable to white. At least with black one appears to possess a
certain finesse. With white, one merely becomes a grotesque
testimony to all the excesses of red wine and chocolate. Which
reminds me - I almost forgot. Look - on a far happier note - here is
that special document I mentioned!'

To which, with a little purr of satisfaction, reaching forward into
her portmanteau, she draws forth a rolled parchment, with its
already broken circle of red wax that has taken the seal of St
James's Palace upon it. With a smile of triumph, she hands it across
to him for his perusal. 'Delivered by special courier this morning,'

she adds with pride, 'signed by all the necessary parties. It's a duplicate - the original will be sent to Newgate once a ship has been determined for the prisoner.'

It is a lengthy legal scrawl written in a copperplate hand, the bulk of which is beyond Matthew's comprehension - and anyway, he still feels so disturbed over what he has just heard about Snatchal's skulduggery that he can hardly bring himself to concentrate. He has time to note the signatures, however, from both the King and what would presumable be the judge responsible for the original sentence - the words 'Transportation to the American Colonies' clearly emblazoned near the top, indicating that within days his friend will be taken on board ship. Whoever would have thought it! Life in the colonies as a felon would not be easy - but at least it will be *a life;* and, knowing Sam, he will surely strive to make the best of it.

'And so, my dear Matthew, what a fortunate happenstance that we find ourselves here alone together with time on our hands,' she says, taking the document into her custody once more and returning it to her portmanteau. 'How well we both did the other day, don't you think. I certainly did my bit. And now ... what will you do for me, my darling?'

'What shall I do? Why, I should like to recite a very special poem for you, if I may,' he answers, knowing he has every word of it memorised. Not only that, but looking into the face of Lady Snatchal, or *Malaena* as he really should be thinking of her, he suddenly perceives that behind all the elaborate display of studied irony and self-parody, there really is a woman of the most engaging complexity and depth of character - and that he has, all the while without really knowing it, been writing his sonnet to Saturn for someone very much like her.

*Now from the tower, the bat-wing glides from roost,*
*And night's dark portal opens up in dread,*
*I come to thee in cloaked disguise, all loosed,*
*To drape black silk o'er all your cherry red.*

*Do not fear me, love, I am tender mild.*
*Do not withdraw your open lips from mine.*
*Let us, instead, cling tight as tendrils wild,*
*With nightshade, thorn and white-flower'd columbine.*

*Then, as day and all its empty joys must wait,*
*Shall Saturn's leaded black hood fall,*
*And we no more shall care for that pale state,*
*But rather seek bewitchment in our thrall.*

*Thou cans't not hide thy loving heart from he*
*Who would be all thy sweet pain and ecstasy.*

'Oh, Matthew, I would happily die listening to your words,' she sighs.

'Why, that would surely be a terrible waste!' he says taking her hand once more, 'to relinquish life at just that moment when I would rather assist you in exploring so many of its pleasures.'

'Can you do that? Oh I would to heaven that you could,' she sighs as he busies himself with the buttons of her glove and then very slowly removing it, relishing the audacity of undressing her, even if only slightly in this way as he strokes her hand gently and then lifts it once more to his lips. 'I would so like it if you would enjoy me, Matthew,' she adds, her voice soft. 'Just take me.'

The music below is well-heard now; and so, not wishing to raise his voice any longer above that of a coaxing whisper, he brings his chair much closer, placing it in front of her, the better to continue the delightful prelude of wicked pleasure that they are engaged in, and also a position from which the dimensions of her mighty gown and petticoats will not inhibit his purpose as they commence upon a kind of languid, almost involuntary exploration of every part, as if suddenly wanting to touch every inch of each other.

And then, observing with approval the rising and falling of her shoulders as she breathes more deeply and eases herself back into her chair more comfortably, he, with hands that by slow and tender increments become all the more bolder, makes free with the seemingly impenetrable mystery of her attire, exploring the places of ingress through which he might reach beneath as he seeks all those secret parts by which to command - and she, aware of her own weakening self-restraint, sighs long and loudly to release her feelings. 'Oh ... how good!'

'Now, tell me, Madam,' he whispers boldly, 'that riding accident you once had ...'

'Yes, most unfortunate, Matthew. I do suffer from it terribly, you know,' she murmurs, speaking in words of strained decorum that bear little relevance to what they are now both engaged in, and even assisting him by raising herself from her seat for a moment to accommodate his hand still further.

'Indeed, Madam,' he concurs. 'But to which parts, precisely, are you the most afflicted? Is it here, perhaps? Or here? Tell me at once, Madam - for I am determined to apply my own tender physic and release you from your misfortunes forthwith.'

'Oh, yes, my gallant, do .... maybe just a little farther around - yes there. Yes, most certainly thereabouts.'

She receives his kisses then - her chin raised, displaying her long and elegant neck as if she would follow the lilting stream of the music with all its soothing delights - only now her lips are parted and her teeth are barred as she allows his free hand to caress her face, his fingers tracing a path through the tangle of ringlets and curls about her ear. And then, as he looks deep into her eyes, and as he teases her for just one further moment by withholding his favours, she, quite roughly, tears away the lace from her throat and chest to reveal almost the entire expanse of her bosom - seizing his hand and guiding it slowly along the length of her neck - not once, but again and again, returning it each time it to the length of her throat, emitting a long sigh each time and the words: 'You're taking me, darling, aren't you - taking me at last!'

Strange, he thinks, that she should be so repetitive in her statements of approbation - and slightly alarming, too - as guiding this time both his hands to her mouth and covering them in kisses, she wraps his fingers tightly round her neck again and cries more loudly this time, 'Oh, I shall be ravished! You're killing me, Matthew!'

'Sssh!' he whispers frantically, wondering if people would be able to hear - for even though the music is becoming conveniently loud at this stage, a vigorous hornpipe, there are, he knows, similar boxes on either-side of theirs. He can only hope these are not occupied at present. Meanwhile, she appears to be losing all composure - away in a kind of wanton intoxication of her own, clasping his hands once more and pressing them to her lips and then again to her throat, 'give me your hands! Give me your hands, Matthew,' and with always the same fervent declaration: 'Oh, I shall be ravished! I shall die! You're killing me!'

Well, whatever is happening, or whatever this is leading to, there is an intriguing intensity about her now that very few would have ever been privy to. It is, for him, as he continues to indulge her, most fascinating to perceive the transformation and surrender taking place - *if only she would keep her voice down!* But just then, while rising to cradle her face in his hands and kiss her fully, if for no other purpose than to moderate her cries, he notices quite by chance through the tiny gap in the curtains, a man below in the hall - and why Matthew's attention should be drawn to this individual over all others he does not know. Conspicuous by being tall and of powerful build, but also uncommonly scruffy for a visitor to Ranelagh, he must, Matthew concludes, be a servant or messenger of some kind rather than a footman or page - yes, because he is holding a scrap of paper in his hand as he directs his gaze up and along the rows of boxes. And then Matthew knows - it hits him like a thunderbolt. Quickly, he throws himself to the floor, sinking to his knees. For this is none other than Bone Crusher Webster!

'Matthew, whatever is the matter?' the Countess demands clutching abruptly at the folds of her petticoat as if sharing in his alarm.

'Look! That man down below, the one with the great cutlass of a sword harnessed to his side - hardly decorative! Do you know him?'

She leans forward and descends also - or as best anyone can descend in such a structure as she is clad in, thus rather collapsing into a vast supportive nest of taffeta as she parts the curtains a little more and looks down over the ledge, her face still all flushed and swollen with desire. 'Oh, bloody hell! It's Webster, isn't it? The gorilla who does all the dirty work for the Wig Club.'

'Precisely,' Matthew agrees, already seeking out his sword as Lady Snatchal fumbles for the hidden door key, unsuccessfully, amid the folds of her skirts. No escape.

'Oh my God!' the Countess cries, her voice muffled by her own hand 'He wants us. He's coming round here - look! He's coming up.'

Indeed, she is correct, because already the sound of mighty feet can be heard thundering up the stairs and along the passageway outside, then a moment later a loud rapping on the door and the call of, 'My Lady Snatchal?'

'I shan't let him in,' she whispers frantically, scrambling back onto her stool. '*I shan't, shan't, shan't!*'

But Webster is not to be dissuaded merely by a lack of response from within: 'My Lady, please answer,' comes the deep resonant voice again. 'I have come from St James's Square, and your maid downstairs has informed me of your whereabouts. I have news, grave news that I must impart to you.'

'Oh God! Quick, Matthew: get under here,' Dottie whispers frantically, pulling him down by the shoulders. And within seconds, he has manoeuvred the entirety of himself beneath the vast canopy of her petticoats, his knees drawn up beneath his chin. Seated in the humid darkness between her legs, he senses her leaning forward and then hears her unlock the door and then open it slightly.

'Oh, Mr Webster! Well, good afternoon to you!' she says, with utmost calm, though her thighs gripping the sides of Matthew's head indicate that a certain tension might be felt elsewhere. 'Can I help you at all?'

'Ma'am, it is news concerning your husband, Lord Snatchal.'

Silence ensues, a silence that seems to last an eternity - until Matthew hears the sounds of the door creaking on its hinges as the man steps over the threshold.

'Well - out with it, Mr Webster!' she demands, somehow managing to summon up her familiar imperious voice. 'What is your news?'

'That the Earl, your husband has been taken poorly Ma'am. At a certain establishment in Cockspur Street.'

'Poorly - what do you mean? How poorly?'

'Well ... poorly to the extent of being dead, Ma'am,'

'Oh my God!'

'The owner of the premises, a Mrs Armstrong, with whom I do business of a - er - delicate nature such as this, has suggested I inform you, m'Lady, in case you wish to recover the body and bring it to a location more salubrious for the discovery, as it were - it being otherwise normal in these circumstances to transfer any unclaimed cadaver to the anatomists for a prompt and discreet disposal.'

'Indeed! Yes, I do understand,' Dorothea concurs, though by now sounding tearful and panicky, her knees knocking against Matthew's cheeks with the emotion of it all. 'Anyway, perhaps you would be good enough to leave me for a moment, Mr Webster. I must compose myself. And I shall be with you anon.'

Webster is heard to grunt something to the affirmative as he leaves - and upon which, Matthew, hearing the door close softly, and with the raising of the skirts, is able to emerge, reborn, into the light of day once again.

'Oh Matthew, what a turn up is this!' she murmurs under her breath a little frantically at first but then tearfully, as Webster's heavy footfalls are heard retreating down the passageway. 'My poor Cornelius - expired in the arms of a whore; lying all cold in that horrid place while I have been here listening to a hornpipe with a man under my skirts. I am so ashamed! How are we to get him home and avoid a scandal?'

'I am so very sorry,' Matthew says, taking her trembling hands again, though with a mission of comfort this time rather than one of seduction. 'Webster will surely know how to proceed, and if you wish I will accompany you. I should tell you, too, that Mrs Armstrong is an acquaintance of mine, and together I am sure we can sort everything in a discreet and timely fashion.'

Though still distressed, she seems pacified by his optimism, and so with little more than a brief smoothing down of clothing, replacing of gloves and tidying of hair, they both emerge from the box - to the amazement of Mr Webster who unfortunately remains stationed a little farther down the passageway and can be left in little doubt, therefore, that they have both come forth from the same doorway. Looking puzzled at first and then down right perplexed, he raises a finger as if intending to ask a question, but quickly thinks better of it - before turning and marching off, leading the way down the staircase. Lady Snatchal's maid and footman, both still waiting outside, are dismissed with some money to find their way home, and within minutes she and Matthew, in the company of Bone Crusher Webster, have hailed a carriage from the ranks and are on their way: destination Cockspur Street.

The lengthy journey up to Westminster and into Whitehall is conducted in silence, with merely the sound of raindrops, increasingly heavy upon the carriage roof. Matthew is aware of Webster, seated at his side in the coach, surveying his face from time to time with the same look of bewilderment that he had worn upon seeing him emerging from the supper box earlier, though this eventually altering to one of calculating and sly comprehension. The fellow's silence is going to cost someone a pretty penny,

Matthew reflects. But Lady Snatchal it is, seated opposite, who strikes the bargain.

'Mr Webster, I take it one can rely on your discretion?'

'Of course, m'Lady,' he answers in his deep, resonant voice.

'And that we will naturally recompense you for your trouble - and that, most generously. Shall we say twenty guineas?'

Mr Webster, clearly satisfied, bows his head in concordance, for it is a substantial sum. Eventually they arrive at Cockspur Street and, alighting, hurry up the alleyway to the doors of the bagnio itself that Matthew knows so well. Inside, to their surprise, all is busy and festive - a group availing themselves of the steam baths, by the sounds of it. Business must go on, of course, Matthew reflects, as he introduces his guests to the maid - this being sufficient for Mrs Armstrong to be summoned.

Lucy is dressed as lavishly as ever and in bright pastel colours which might, under the circumstances, seem a little inappropriate, so that as the two women's eyes meet in a mutual, top-to-toe appraisal of each other's apparel, it is an exchange not entirely based on concord. In suitably hushed tones, however, the proprietress does express her 'profound regret,' before guiding them to a room away from the noise and to where inside they find him - poor Cornelius, laid out on a couch, shrouded in a blanket up to his chin, his wig and various items of clothing hanging from pegs above him and a gentle smile, almost one of contentment, upon his otherwise cold and impassive features.

'He had a seizure of a kind,' Lucy states, a little tearful now, and genuinely emotional, Matthew thinks. 'And even though he recovered, he said he was still feeling unwell, so I laid him down here and gave him a little cuddle. And then ... well, he just *went.*'

'*Went?*' Lady Snatchal repeats with mystified indignation, as though an occurrence of such magnitude should at least require a more substantial explanation.

'Well, yes ... you know: *expired,*' Lucy elaborates, her voice gentle and full of warmth as she gives forth a loud sniff. 'Doesn't he look peaceful, though,' she adds, turning her face towards him once again, almost with admiration.

But this is too much for Lady Snatchal, who flies at her - hurling insults to the effect that a worse harlot or base whore had surely never set foot upon the earth, and other most unkind comments that Lucy herself, and though she could probably knock the other woman down with little more than a flick of her wrist if she wanted to, resolves nonetheless to bear in stoic silence. But then suddenly a huge collective scream from both Lady Snatchal and Webster rocks the room to its very foundations, and Matthew leaps almost off his chair at the sight of Lord Snatchal's jaw dropping wide open of its own accord, as if in mute protest at the unseemly fracas - Terrifying! - but upon which Lucy, without a sound, reaches forward and with the utmost calm closes the old fellows jaw for what will surely be the final time.

Endeavouring to set aside his own jitteriness, Matthew manages to reconcile the two women once again with some words of kindness - until everyone agrees that it really would be best to shift the body into a carriage as soon as possible and transport it home to St James's Square where it could be duly 'discovered' in the morning. The doctor could then be called, and a scandal averted.

'Yes, but how could a carriage be brought up here - surely too narrow?' Lady Snatchal ponders, now calm again.

She is right, of course. The entrance to the alleyway outside is far too small to accommodate a vehicle, and the transfer of the body could not be done on the main road at this hour of the evening, not in full public gaze.

'Best to put him in a sedan chair,' Webster says. 'I know some lads that can be relied on. They'll bring it up outside once it gets dark, and then we could get his Lordship away unseen.'

Everyone exchanges glances. Though unsavoury, it does seem the only feasible course of action; and they must act quickly, of course.

'Fetch two chairs, if you will?' Matthew asks of Webster as he is about to don his hat and leave. 'One of us will have to follow closely without being conspicuous. In the meantime, Lady Snatchal, may I suggest, could go on ahead by carriage to prepare for our arrival.'

It is agreed. And no more than fifteen minutes have elapsed, though it seems much longer, before Webster returns from his nefarious mission - entering wet and bedraggled from the rain to report that all is in place, the two chairs awaiting outside. Meanwhile, Lord Snatchal's body has been clothed again, albeit not very tidily, since rigamortis has already begun to set in and it is difficult to get his arms into his shirt and coat - but eventually they manage. His wig and tricorn are placed on his head next; and then, with Webster taking one arm, and Matthew the other, they raise him into a vertical position and frog-march him out to the passageway.

'Ha - had a bit too much to drink!' Matthew observes, just as a gentleman coming from the steam room catches sight of them making for the exit.

'Time to take him home!' Webster adds by way of additional explanation, replacing Lord Snatchal hat as it tumbles off into his arms. The man from the steam room, however, encased in white towels and looking as languid and unconcerned with his surroundings as a boiled lobster, hardly responds. An over-inebriated customer being taken home would be a common enough site in places such as this, of course. And seconds later they have Lord Snatchal outside, down the steps and his body bundled into the waiting chair.

'There you are, gentlemen,' Webster murmurs to the chairmen, all sheltering from the rain under some eaves as he pays out their fees in advance, well over the odds by the looks of it, while Matthew, leaning into the cabin, busies himself propping up the body with cushions so it will not tumble. The men, for their part, appear surprisingly sanguine about it all - and it occurs to him that this might not be the first time they have been called to certain establishments in this area for a similar purpose. Webster does, indeed, seem to know some of them by name, so presumably they can be trusted. But at just that instant, Lady Snatchal emerges from the interior, surveying the scene from the topmost step of the portico with a haughty and imperious gaze, a presence of such aristocratic incongruity that it appears to spook the chairmen because, hoisting the chair instantly, they hurry off with it - not down the alleyway into Cockspur Street as Matthew had anticipated, but upwards, leading through to St Martin's Lane.

'What a peculiar route to be taking,' Matthew observes - and it is then when he notices the look of alarm on Webster's face.

'The fools!' the big man cries, his hands animated in panic. 'I had no time to give out the address. They must just reckon it's for the anatomists - the resurrection men up yonder in Seven Dials - to be disposed of.'

'The resurrection men!' Lady Snatchal echoes and begins to swoon - to be caught only just in time in the arms of Lucy who has just stepped out of the doorway behind. 'The body snatchers,' she continues faintly as if speaking from some terrible dream, her hand across her forehead. 'They're taking my Cornelius to the body snatchers.'

'Quick - come on!' Matthew cries, realising they are already losing precious time as he hurries towards the second chair waiting just a little down the alley.

'We'd be quicker running,' Webster suggests.

'Oh really! And do you happen to know where we should be running to?' Matthew demands, and when Webster admits with a dismal shaking of the head that he does not, it becomes clear that the only course of action is to enlist the other chairmen.

'Do you know of any anatomists up yonder?' Matthew asks with urgency, wondering if they might run with him there. When the men reply that they do, located in the Rookeries off Seven Dials, but that they cannot abandon their chair, Matthew has no alternative but to climb in and urge them to take him there at once - or if possible to overtake the chair of their colleagues that has just sped off in that direction - if they can find it, that is. Thus, once assured of Lady Snatchal's safety in the capable hands of Lucy, Matthew is lifted up and off they go - with Webster running alongside.

'With all haste, gentlemen, if you please!' Webster, already panting, urges them as they labour up the hill - soon to emerge from behind the sprawling complex of the Royal Mews into St Martins Lane and towards the Piazza. A whole host of chairs are to be found here, of course, all going in different directions among the crowds, so no one can be sure which of those ahead might be containing Lord Snatchal's body. Matthew's chairmen, however, seem to know where they must go, anyway, and manage to maintain a brisk pace - something that alas cannot be said for Webster, whose large, bulky body, looking as if it is running on the spot outside, can be detected less and less frequently through the glass as more often than not he falls behind. Matthew, rolling down the window, calls back to him to keep up. But he is clearly having difficulty, and it is only with a supreme effort that he manages to run alongside for one final time to offer an apology.

'It's my asthma, Sir!' he splutters, puffing and wheezing terribly. 'A distemper of the bronchial tubes. I fear I shall not be able to assist you further.'

And indeed, a moment later as Matthew glances back from the

window he sees that Webster has drawn to a complete halt, stooped, hands on knees and gasping for breath. But no matter - for suddenly a cry of jubilation is heard from the two chairmen as they catch sight of the other chair ahead. 'There it is, Sir!' the one in front cries, breathless, the steam rising from him in the rain which is falling even heavier now.

'Are you sure?' Matthew calls out through the window. And when the answer comes back in the affirmative, he orders the men to stop and let him out, that he might pursue it on foot. Throwing in some coins, he slams the door shut - though inadvertently crushing the scabbard tip of his sword in the hinges as he does so. Try as he might, he cannot extricate it, and so he simply pulls forth his sword instead and makes off with it in his hand, abandoning the scabbard to its fate. Unfortunately, this does rather create the wrong impression on the men ahead carrying Lord Snatchal's chair and who, upon seeing Matthew running behind, shouting to them while also brandishing a drawn sword, immediately respond by increasing their speed. Faster and faster they go - in fact, never have two pairs of stockinged legs run at such a rate of knots, like some demented four-legged creature pursued by the Furies - so fast that they become little more than a blur before the eyes of astonished theatre-goers and passers by as they race across the Piazza at a blistering pace and up towards the warren of lanes leading into the notorious district of Seven Dials. The rain is pouring down now as Matthew, splashing and tramping through the filthy mud, is forced to acknowledge that even with the combined weight of their chair and its occupant, the men ahead are making far better progress than he will ever be able to manage and that he is in very real danger already of losing them. Clearly, it has been a mistake to have abandoned his own chair so soon.

From time to time, turning a corner, he catches a glimpse of them, still going at an extraordinary pace, though more and more erratically all the while, wobbling with fatigue - until, with the torrential rain and slippery surface, the inevitable happens - the chairmen slip; they both fall down on their backsides, and the chair itself escapes their grasp. As ill-luck would have it, this occurs on the brow of a hill at the head of a long alley, and consequently the chair itself continues on its way sliding unaided, skimming along in the mud and the water that has by now formed something of a modest stream in the central conduit of the alley itself - all dark and totally unlit.

The chairmen, by this time, have made their escape down a side lane, leaving Matthew, still with sword in hand, to pursue the wayward sedan chair alone, which eventually comes to a halt with a crash, hard against the stonework of an overflowing water trough. What with this, and the rainwater pouring in torrents from the eaves above, Matthew feels as if he is swimming rather than walking as he approaches his goal. Drenched to the skin, but full of relief, he slides the last couple of yards towards the chair and where he is finally able to peer inside through the window only to discover, to his horror and cry of astonishment, the face of one very irate and shocked looking gentleman in a long periwig staring furiously back at him - not Lord Snatchal at all - but one very much alive and clearly in no mind to be getting out just yet. Matthew has been chasing the wrong chair.

Waving a hesitant and startled apology to the gentleman inside, at just that moment Matthew notices a glow forming around the corner of the alleyway, and seconds later Ralph the link-boy turns the corner, his torch spluttering and almost extinguished by the rain - though not looking particularly wet or bedraggled himself as he marches up to Matthew and surveys his wretched dripping countenance with a blend of amusement and pity.

'Bit of a rough old night to be out, Sir!' he observes. 'Will it be the other chair with the red top you're looking for - the one with the unfortunate gentleman inside with the stiff neck?'

'Yes, how did you know which ... or never mind. Where is it?'

'This way, Sir!' he says, his little chest puffed up, as he strides past and guides Matthew back in the direction from which he has just come. 'Quick-march, Sir!' he adds. 'No time to waste.'

The rain has turned to a mere drizzle by now, which is a small mercy as Matthew follows the light - down into the Piazza and where, sure enough, sheltering in the colonnade they locate the very chair he is seeking, its bearers standing alongside - and with Webster, too, restored to health and by all appearances having taken shelter somewhere during the worst of the downpour, most likely a tavern with the men. With everyone full of apologies, proper instructions are given this time to convey the gentleman inside to the nearest hackney carriage, which is no sooner said than done, just around the corner in Long Acre. Thus Matthew and Webster are able to place the body into a more substantial and private horse-drawn vehicle without needing to call upon the services of anyone else, and within minutes they are on board and travelling towards St James's Square - the link-boy by this time - and it hardly comes as a surprise to Matthew anymore - having vanished, of course, gone upon his usual enigmatic way.

The Countess is already home by the time they arrive, and by bringing the coach around to the unobserved rear of the building, they are able to carry her husband's corpse in through the back door and then, unseen by any of the servants, who are by this time retired to their chambers, to place him on his bed where they cut away his clothes, drag a night-shirt over him and tuck him up. The doctor will be called in the morning, they agree, when Lady Snatchal will pretend to have discovered the Earl's demise.

Breathing a gigantic sigh of relief, Matthew realises, therefore, that his mission is accomplished. He has succeeded in taking the old reprobate home to be buried as a Christian rather than have his bones bleached in the Rookeries to provide the surgeon's college with another handy skeleton to pore over. Webster, meanwhile, replete with a pink envelope containing a substantial amount of money, surely already a greatly inflated sum than the twenty guineas promised earlier, takes his leave, and Matthew, after cleaning up and drying his hair and receiving a tearful embrace from Lady Snatchal herself, does likewise - with little ambition now other than to bring himself home and to collapse onto the nearest item of soft furnishing or, preferably if he can stagger through that far, upon his welcoming bed. But it is then that he remembers, and the thought comes like an arrow-shot to his heart, that poor Johanna will be there. Of course she will! She will have received Lady Snatchal's jubilant letter earlier today; she will have responded by travelling into London and would have come to the Pig and Whistle as instructed, where they were all due to meet and to visit Sam. She would have been waiting for hours - all night, in fact. Whatever would have become of her?

Thirty minutes later, reaching the inn, he leaps from his carriage and hurries up the steps to his apartments, noticing as he reaches the gallery that the first light of dawn is beginning to brighten the sky and a blackbird is just beginning to pipe up his first notes of greeting to the day. The door, he quickly unlocks, hurries inside and here, wrapped in blankets upon his couch, the lamplight nearby having long-since extinguished itself, is the little bundle of braided blond hair - about all he can make out in the half-darkness - that signifies the presence of Johanna. He makes a light with the embers of the hearth fire and then a fresh candle - at which she opens her eyes and swiftly casts aside her blankets, getting to her feet and staring at him in a most peculiar way.

'Oh, Matthew, how I hate you!' she murmurs in a terrible voice - most deep and menacing, he thinks, as she stands before him, her clothes all dishevelled by her efforts to sleep.

'Johanna, I can explain ...!'

'They've taken him,' she interrupts, not interested in anything he might wish to say. 'They've taken Sam already!' she shouts now, her voice so shrill, hurling the set of keys she still has clutched in her hand onto the floor, before flying at him and punching his chest over and over until he seizes her in his arms. And as their eyes meet, those beautiful startled eyes of hers so given to pain, he sees her terrible anger blended with absolute disgust - that he should have abandoned her.

'Let me go!' she screams and extricates herself with force. 'Wherever have you been?' she demands. 'With *her,* I suppose? That awful woman! I can smell her all over you, her perfume - and worse.'

'Johanna, stop it! What do you mean they've taken him - where?' he demands, ignoring her accusations, able to think of nothing but poor Sam.

'Chatham - to ship - and without us having been with him on his departure. He will think we have abandoned him. Oh, how I hate you, Matthew! He is taken to ship, and we will never see him again - never, never, never!'

# ~ 32 ~
## EVENING STAR

Johanna seated opposite him in the carriage, her little daughter, Samantha, cuddled up at her side, raises her eyes again, as she has surely raised and lowered them, opened and closed them countless times so far this morning as he, meanwhile, endeavours to catch up on an absent night's sleep - for no sooner had she told him of Sam being taken from his cell in Newgate to a ship at Chatham, than they had hastened by chaise to her home and there, still with the march of dawn having hardly given way to day, had roused their coachman and groom to their posts, packed some hurried items of clothing into a wicker laundry basket, and with the two little ones, John and Samantha, carried from their sleep into the Woolveston's own coach-and-four, had continued immediately on their way, travelling farther out eastwards along the very same road.

She remains upset with him, of course, and they are both very tired. And yet even now, those extraordinary hazel-green eyes, so full of intelligence and beauty manage to enchant him. Dressed still in the same elegant, riding jacket with its deep collar and brass buttons, a flurry of lace upon the sleeves but in every other sense unencumbered by ornament, she remains the very picture of elegance. Were he to die in his sleep, and awake in heaven, things would look much like they do now, he suspects. And, thus still half-immersed in his dreams, he wonders for a moment whether it might actually have taken place. But no, a harsh bump in the road restores his senses, particularly those centred in his backside, to the land of the living - for a coach journey at speed, no matter how fine the vehicle, is never a smooth ride.

The naval dockyard at Chatham, near the confluence of the rivers Medway and Thames is over twenty miles from her home in Greenwich, but the straight Roman route leading out from the capital is a good one, and a safe one, too, at this time of the day -

and without the added encumbrance of footmen or servants on board, they are making good time, so good in fact that they have hopes of arriving no latter than mid-afternoon. Yet even then, they cannot be certain whether all their haste and urgency will have served them well. They do not know what ship Sam is likely to be taken to, whether it will be a navel vessel or a crude convict ship for the transportation of felons. They do not know when it would be due to sail, or even if it might call at another port prior to setting off on its Atlantic crossing. In brief, they know nothing - only that they are exhausted, confused and, in the absence of any further information, inclined to silence as the constant rhythm of the coach wheels rattle and churn upon the roadway beneath them, sending the familiar pitching, upward and downward motion through their bodies to which all seasoned travellers quickly lean to yield. His thoughts are a tempest of doubts and indecision - and yet throughout it all, a constant presence to his senses, there is always Johanna - looking back at him from beneath the wide brim and feathered plumes of her hat - at one time disapproving, pale and stern-faced, observing him with silent contempt, at others, pensive, full of a trembling anxiety, as if fearing that any word of tenderness might suddenly escape her lips. Even now, there has been nothing he has been able to say to excuse himself or to mitigate against his negligence. Presenting her with the information, as he had done almost straight away this morning, of the demise of Lord Snatchal and of the unfortunate debacle surrounding the recovery of his body, had hardly registered with her at all - his every explanation dismissed out of hand as just another fanciful excuse for his misbehaviour and inconstancy. It was as if she had chosen to suspend all belief in anything he might have to say, at least until the tribulations of this day might be over. And who could blame her for that.

'Mama?' Samantha inquires at one stage, as the first proper sunshine of the morning flickers through the layers of gauze and velvet curtains and proclaims to everyone that it is probably time to stir themselves and to put sleep aside. 'Mama, where are we going?'

Johanna runs her fingers through the child's hair, which due to the haste with which they set off early this morning remains still an uncombed nest of tiny golden curls. 'We are going to see Papa,' she answers with tenderness and patience. 'He is back from

Scotland, but is going away again. Perhaps we will be able to wave to him - to wave him goodbye.'

But why doesn't Papa come home and say goodbye to us first?' Samantha demands with undeniable logic.

'Because the King wants him to go to America straight away on important business - so very important that His Majesty won't even allow your Papa time to visit us before he goes.'

'What is America?' asks young John, who has himself been reclining against Matthew's side, the two of them being opposite the ladies. On hearing his sister's voice, he has roused himself from slumber and now, sitting up straight for about the first time since they had taken him from his bed and laid him in the coach a little over an hour ago, adds to the questioning by inquiring further: 'What does America do?'

'It is a colony, John, a part of the Empire,' Matthew explains, serious in tone, as if addressing an adult. 'It is yonder over the sea - a big, big country, and very exciting, with ferocious bears and wild men with spears who fight with bows and arrows. A place only for the bravest of men to venture forth, like your father.'

John appears impressed by the description. But there is of course always going to be the inevitable question: 'Will we never see him again?' Samantha asks a little tearful now, and obviously none too comforted by Matthew's lurid description of the natives.

'Hush now, of course we will,' Johanna replies, though with her eyes fixed on Matthew, as if addressing him as much as anyone else. 'We will follow him, my pet. We will go after him wherever he goes - since without Papa there is nothing here for us.'

And Matthew nods his understanding, for she has spoken now. In her own inimitable way, she has told him her decision. How foolish of him to have ever thought otherwise. And he knows now, should he have ever been in any doubt, that everything is coming to an end. Without Sam, what legitimate reason would they have for meeting? Sam's presence had always been their bridge, a way of linking them and bringing them together. His absence would now become an obstacle, a river and an ocean dividing them forever. Yes, it is the end, and they both know it.

Between the trees to their left, they sometimes catch glimpses of the bright ribbon of water that is the Thames - the road they are on being never too distant from its shores. The river becomes wider and wider as it runs its course towards the sea; and always so busy -

the barges of commerce and trade with their distinctive brick-red sails bright in the sunshine; or else the long, black colliers laden with coal for the capital. And always a profusion of magnificent tall-masted ships - these more often out in the centre of the water: robust, ocean going vessels, some sailing up-river into the docks of Deptford or Woolwich; others bound in the other direction and out to sea - out far and wide to the breezy Hansa ports of the Baltic or else upon voyages that might take their sailors or merchant seamen around the entire circumference of the globe before ever returning to their native shores. It is a river not only of London's pageant and theatre, therefore, but also one of trade and commerce, of conquest and adventure - magnificent - and yet for them this morning, travelling alongside it in their coach and four, it is all reduced to one very simple function: it is the river that carries Sam away, holding in the balance the fate of just one humble family, a wife and two small children bidding farewell to their father. And now, as they cross the historic bridge over the Medway and as their coach turns north towards the dockyards he can only hope and pray that they will not be too late.

Upon arrival at the vast sprawling brick and stone edifice of the dockyards, Matthew alights and makes inquiries at the gate house, and is informed that Sam's ship, the most likely candidate anyway for taking prisoners, a square-rigged navel vessel which can just be seen anchored far out in the haze and bedazzlement of the bright river, is due to sail on the tide at noon tomorrow. Most of the convicts down for transportation have already been embarked at Gravesend and Tilbury, the clerk tells him - but then, upon further enquiry and a renewed examination of the pages of a ledger, he discovers just one late addition, a certain Samuel Woolveston who arrived last night by water and who is detained still in the customs barracks, awaiting transfer. They are in luck. So, Matthew requests that the prisoner's family be allowed to visit and to speak with him; and with this being granted, and just as the bell above in the clock tower in the yard strikes two, he hurries back to the coach to inform Johanna.

Quickly, excitedly, the children's hair is combed; dresses and waistcoats are straightened and hats adjusted - and then, along the seemingly endless expanse of quayside they walk, past hemp house and sail lofts, sheds and warehouses, buildings of every possible use pertaining to the maintenance of ships and the men of His Majesty's navy; past all the smart and stylish terraces of admiralty houses, the walled citadel here having a most refined and civilised air to it, with officers in uniform out for an afternoon stroll admiring the well-tended front gardens and accompanied by their wives in their straw hats and summer dresses. Consequently, their own somewhat bedraggled looks - Johanna still in her crumpled petticoats from a night's sleeping on a couch in the Pig and Whistle, Matthew, his hair a tangle of unruly curls, and the two bonny children with hardly enough on top to cover their nightclothes - all conspire to make them feel more than a little misplaced. Johanna does not speak, except to encourage the children along - though she does take Matthew's arm at one stage, more for modesty's sake he suspects, rather than affection, for it seems any regard she might have had for him has all but fled now or else is buried beneath her cares. Perhaps, he reflects, she is simply unable to absorb any more feelings, any more agony or sorrow than what she has already had to endure - surely more than enough for one person to contend with. And yet, he suspects as he opens the door to the little fortress-like annex close to the quay, and as he hands her in to the rank, tobacco-and-rum-smelling interior of the building with its long wooden benches and bare floor boards that serves as barracks to the customs men, that the next several minutes might prove even more challenging for her than anything that has gone before. And he is right.

Without a word, and after perusing the note Matthew was given at the gatehouse, the official inside, a grizzle-bearded clerk in a dull blue uniform, indicates that they may approach the prisoner - the only other person present, in fact, a man seated with his back to them on a bench at the far, darkened end of the room, gazing out through the windows to the river. Still clad in his ragged scarlet coat, learning forward, his elbows on knees, he appears deep in thought. His legs are in irons, a long chain linking both ankles - a sorry sight - and yet, by the distinctive rotund shape of the body and the noble head with its excellent wig and tricorn, they know it is he.

'Oh, my dears!' Sam cries, looking over his shoulder at last and removing his hat in salutation. 'How wonderful ...'

But he cannot finish because the children have rushed towards him, covering his face with their kisses. Sam laughs, quite beside himself with joy. A moment later, however, both the children notice the irons, almost stumbling over them at his feet.

'Papa! What are these?' Samantha demands, more puzzled than alarmed.

But Sam is not to be embarrassed by his shackles, and with a faint echo of his old bumptious, irrepressible self he puffs out his chest and chuckles heartily. 'Why, young lady, these treasures of bronze and iron, I'll have you know, were put on by King George himself. And he alone has the key to them - for otherwise, he knows, I would surely fly to Greenwich to visit you and kiss you goodbye. And that, he told me, would take up too much valuable time. But look - now you are here anyway! So all is well, my little ones. All is well.'

Johanna meanwhile, standing apart, still some distance away, watches everything in silence - her body upright, her spine as taut as a bow string, her lips tightly compressed and her jaw set like granite in its pale visage of a face that seems now entirely void of blood as well as emotion. Only a heart of stone could fail to grieve for Sam's predicament and the prospects of what awaits him. And so eventually she, too, comes to him, and leaning over embraces him in mute stillness as best she can, resting her head upon his shoulder as he manages to make way for her on the bench, the clinking of his irons and rattling of his chains as he shuffles along, continuing to voice their own ignominious testimony as to his fate. How very wrong it is to have placed the poor fellow in such a shameful condition, Matthew thinks - because Sam, such a proud man, would have been a visitor to the dockyard here on countless occasions in connection to his work for the Admiralty, and yet now here he sits, a captive, an object of pity and, even to some of those who might recognise him from brighter times, of mockery as well. And as Matthew himself approaches, being the last to do so, as is only right and proper, he notices, most untypically for Sam, a grubby old scarf of wool around his neck. No silken cravat and diamond pin now - just an old rag instead, a precursor of all that is to come, no doubt. Already his cuffs are frayed, his breeches stained with all the grime and filth of his prison cell. He is becoming a convict in appearance now as well as in law: an untidy ragamuffin. And it pains Matthew more than anything to see such a splendid and once well-groomed man so terribly diminished.

'Matt - so good to see you again,' Sam declares, rising a little and holding forth his hand, which Matthew foolishly seizes over-zealously with both of his. 'I wish you had been at Newgate yesterday,' he adds, sinking back onto the bench again, 'because when they came for me, I thought at first ... well, I thought my time was up. I was frightened. But then they told me, that I would be spared - to serve on the plantations or else in His Majesty's army. Not so bad a prospect, eh! Though it was a cold journey last night. They left me out on the open deck for hours before they brought me in, the dogs! Someone gave me a scarf. A good fellow, he was ...'

'Sam, I am so sorry. We were all going to come to you. We had everything arranged for telling you the news ourselves. But ... something's happened. It was Snatchal. He died.'

'What - Cornelius, *dead?*'

'Yes. Just yesterday. It was a total surprise.'

'Oh, my word! I am sorry to hear that, Matt. How ..?'

'Most likely his heart - a palsy, or a seizure of some kind. He went peacefully.'

'So sad. So very sad,' Sam mutters, as if distracted. 'My dear friend Cornelius,' he adds, and for a time appears lost in his thoughts, as if the name of the Earl reminded him of a far different life, a life of prestige and comfort in which he, too, once shared but which is now almost forgotten, so remote as to be a puzzlement to him. But then, a second later, the sound of his children sobbing jolts him back to the present. 'Now, now, what's all this, you two, why are you crying?' he demands, reaching out once more and trying to be his old familiar self to them and taking charge. 'This is not what I expect of you. You must be brave little boys and girls now, and help your Mama!'

Prescient words, Matthew reflects - because the chances of their father arriving safely are far from good. He would be confined to the hold of the ship for the duration of the voyage, maybe even shackled for a good part of the time. He would be sharing that dark and pestilent space below decks with the worst kinds of vagabonds and villains - or even perhaps, later on, those poor unfortunate Negroes they take as slaves from Africa, half of whom will die before reaching their destination. And even then, even if he withstands the perilous and unsanitary conditions on board with its regular outbreaks of disease, his duties upon arrival amid the fierce climate of heaven-knows what region of that vast continent he will be sent to for military service or heavy labour, or else simply wander into by misadventure, will be harsh, indeed, often violent. The odds really are stacked against him. And for Matthew, the thought of these dear children and their mother following and sharing in that fate becomes almost too much to bear. For one moment, he contemplates the possibility of some mad, heroic deed - to draw sword, to overpower the guard, to somehow hurry Sam into their coach and gallop off with him, to hide him, smuggle him to safety. But it is impossible of course. They are in the midst of a fortified dockyard with a barred gatehouse, surrounded by high walls and populated by dozens of soldiers with sabre and musket. What a stupid idea! He admonishes himself for even thinking it.

Instead, with renewed calm and realism, Matthew wanders back, to talk quietly with the officer on duty and to inquire how much longer the family might yet have with the prisoner, to be told only a few more minutes. Apparently, Matthew is reliably informed, the silting of the river hereabouts of late means that the ship with its deep draught would not venture in close to the quayside, and they are therefore waiting to row the prisoner out the next time provisions are taken on board - which is imminent, and in fact if Matthew cares to glance through the window and across the water, he will see the rowboat approaching already, and soon the crew will be ashore and coming up the steps. It is sufficient information to urge Matthew to keep his distance now, watching the little family group on the bench from afar and realising that everything is going to happen so very fast for them now. It is, in any case, all so very remote, he suddenly feels, the scene he is witnessing: the little family group conversing, sometimes holding hands, sometimes busy attending to little needs - of tidying a lock of hair, or the wiping of a smudge from a cheek or nose with a handkerchief - sometimes laughing, sometimes cuddling - a world, *their world,* so very distant from his own narrow sphere of experience and into whose presence he can only ever be an intruder, an interloper and an irrelevance. Yes, of course she will follow. It might be weeks; it might be months - but she will follow. Sam is everything to her. She has even managed to bring him a clean shirt, which she takes from her little portmanteau and passes to him and which, with great care, he stows away in a sack they have evidently allowed him for his personal belongings. Yes, for her children's sake, for their father, her husband, for everything she holds dear, Johanna will follow Sam to the very ends of the earth. It was the most persuasive and powerful of forces - marriage and the family. And he himself could no more hope to stand in its way than hold back the ocean tide.

Footsteps of several men in heavy boots are heard outside, and suddenly the door is flung open and into the office stomp a group of loud and rowdy seamen roaring with assorted curses and bursts of coarse laughter. It is like an explosion of vulgarity, against which the family can only cower in horror upon their bench. One of the men calls out to the official that they are here to take on-board the late-comer, and when Sam is pointed out, a couple of them in their haste and total lack of sensitivity, simply stride over and haul him to his feet, almost colliding with Johanna, who has already leapt up in panic and staring in terror at their arrival. The children, meanwhile, have run to Matthew's side.

'Woolveston?' one bellows, that Sam might confirm his name. 'Right - off we go, then, Sir. Said all your goodbye's have yer?'

But this is too much for Matthew, who hastens to his friend's side to protest at the treatment. 'Take a care, Sir, please, and show a little courtesy in the presence of his family to a man who has been a loyal servant of His Majesty!'

But the sailors are unimpressed, and one already has his hand on Sam's arm, urging him away.

'Forbear, Matt,' Sam murmurs, just managing for a second to reach out and clasp his friend's sleeve. 'Do not trouble yourself anymore for my honour, because what remains of that will soon be extinguished in the holds of that vessel out there.' And then coming even closer and whispering more intimately, with words for him alone, 'I am a dead man, Matt. Forget me now. And may God preserve you and all those we hold dear.'

And before Matthew can reply or even decipher the meaning of these final words, poor Sam is hauled away, supported on each side because the chain makes it difficult for him to walk. The children, not understanding, endeavour to grab a hold of his coat tails for a second, but Johanna intervenes and releases him before the men do it for her, roughly as they surely would. And in a second, they have taken him to the door.

'Papa!' Samantha screams, a piercing cry. And Sam, his shoulders flinching, almost jumps at the sound. But he does not turn. He cannot turn to see such a sight any longer, for the pain would surely burst his heart. And then so very quickly, he and his uncouth company are gone - already outside, striding away with the characteristic rolling gait of sailors, the tall figure of Sam in their midst shuffling along in his irons as all together they disappear, descending some steps over the harbour wall. It is, indeed, all happening so fast. And by the time Matthew and Johanna have gathered themselves and have followed outside with the children and hastened to the edge of the quayside it is only to see the rowboat, stacked full of provisions and with its half-dozen crew and Sam already on board, casting off below. Within seconds the mooring rope is pulled in and oars are lowered, their blades cutting into the sparkling water, and off they go. Only now, does Sam turn, shielding his eyes against the sun and casting his vision back to where they are standing, but he does not call to them or even wave; and neither do they. No one wants to commit to that terrible act of finality: to wave goodbye. In silence, therefore, they stand together, watching the tiny vessel make its way out towards the ship, to that immense piece of wooden architecture, rigging and sail, anchored almost in the middle of the wide river - watch as it becomes lost in the haze of sunshine and water, like a boat being rowed out to heaven, so white and light and beautiful is it. And yet for poor Sam, they know, it is little more than the start of a journey to hell - one from which, even should he arrive safely, he will never, on pain of death, be permitted to return.

Evening finds them not far from the dockyard, in the nearby town of Rochester where they stable their carriage and horses and take rooms at one of the coaching inns close to the busy High Street. Here they also find accommodation for Johanna's coachman, while she and Matthew linger downstairs and eat together with the children at a big round table in a corner of the dining room. And here, amid all the old brown leather furniture and darkly panelled walls of the vast cavernous room where the staff must light the lamps and candles even at such an early hour, they all try as best they can to put a brave face on things. The food here is basic but wholesome, and everyone has had an opportunity to clean up and to change into the few hurried items of spare clothing that they had managed to take with them this morning - so that little Samantha and John appear to have forgotten quite quickly the drama and anguish of the afternoon and instead now begin to indulge their curiosity in all the excitement and adventure of their present surroundings - an utterly quaint and unfamiliar place where instead of being at the very centre of attention, as at home, they must now become a small part of the vast universe of adult life, spectators to all the busy comings and goings of customers, guests and staff, all forever in transit somewhere or other about the building, dragging bed linen and luggage through the hallways, or carrying aloft great trayfuls of food and drink from one room to the next, and who all appear, to the children's obvious astonishment, perfectly content to ignore them both completely. All rather humbling. And so here, a little later, Matthew orders up a gigantic pot of hot chocolate, while they nibble at fine wafer biscuits and talk again and again of the dear man who is no longer among them - an occasion to compare notes, too, because Johanna, having had time to question her husband during those final few stolen minutes of conversation, is able, at last, to impart her understanding of the situation and of Sam's immediate future.

The ship, a navy man-o-war bound for Boston is due to set sail tomorrow, around mid-morning, she says. The crossing could take anything up to ten weeks, and upon its arrival Sam was likely to be placed as a soldier in the British army - to be sent south, either for combat or else to be employed as surgeon in any one of the innumerable skirmishes and petty wars that are being waged constantly against either the French or the Spanish. It is hard to envisage a more precarious existence in prospect. What the future might hold for a wife following her husband from one battle to the next through the swamps and jungles of the Deep South is, moreover, anybody's guess. But probably not particularly glamorous or edifying, Johanna concludes with a glance to both children to see if they have understood what it all means to them.

'Will he have to fight Red Indians?' John enquires in-between mouthfuls of biscuits and chocolate.

'I sincerely hope not!' Johanna replies with a smile, though Matthew can perceive well enough that she speaks in earnest. 'Though I am sure they are a noble race, nonetheless.'

'Will we have to learn to speak American?' asks Samantha, a cloud of misgivings fleeting across her otherwise fair and animated complexion, her bright blue eyes, so like her father's, continuing to flit from person to person.

'No, no, my darling,' Johanna replies. 'They speak English

quite well, by all accounts. We might need to learn French, though, or even Spanish if we are captured.'

'Captured!' Samantha exclaims. 'I don't think I wish to be captured. Can't we just stay here instead, at home? Until Papa returns?'

'No,' Johanna answers patiently, 'because, my dears, I must tell you that we will be asked to move out of our home soon, anyway - since King George wants it for himself. We will go to live at Grandmama's instead, until Papa writes to us and lets us know when we might go to America to be with him again. That will be nice, won't it! It will be something we can look forward to. Something we can ...'

But suddenly it is all too much, too overwhelming for Johanna. Thinking surely of the imminent confiscation of their own estate, which is already marked for the Crown, she begins to weep, silently at first, but then, leaning over, she embraces each of the children in turn; and with a big long hug and an enforced giggle of reassurance, quickly dries her eyes. John exchanges glances with Matthew, man to man for a while until he, too, appears at last to understand the magnitude of the situation - so well, in fact, that following a few brief moments of brave defiance, his little chin begins to wobble and he starts to sob as well. There is only one thing for it, Matthew concludes in a moment of rapid decision, for he even feels a bit tearful himself. It is time to call for more chocolate.

After Johanna and the children have retired, he takes himself off for a stroll along the High Street, past the tall walls of the cathedral and up to the embankment of the river, as if the roadway were rising to meet it, and from where he can survey in the twilight the broad meandering curves of the water and the old battered castle ruins close to the shore, the square tower and buttresses of the cathedral to its side, and the bright 'evening star' just visible in the western sky - the planet Venus peeping out from between the occasional wedge of thin cloud. From inside one of the fine town houses nearby somebody is practising the violin - music lessons perhaps - improvisations around a tune Matthew recognises well: *'Let me Lament my Cruel Fate,'* and which does indeed seem most appropriate, he reflects, as he lingers and listens for a while.

Rochester is a fine little town, a city in fact, with an air of the academic about it. Even at this late hour, the whole place is so full of noise and vitality. Being on such a busy coaching route, moreover, always there is a vehicle, a carriage or a wagon of some kind clattering over the bridge or along the cobbled street. Even upon returning to the yard of the inn to check on the welfare of their own carriage, he is amused to discover the Woolveston's coachman still tending to it, standing in animated conversation, ale in hand, enjoying the warm evening and the company of several porters and ostler from the inn, all busy discussing the dazzling accoutrements of Sam's carriage with all its luxuries and advanced features of designs and suspension - for this is, they must surely appreciate, one of the newest, a Landau with elliptical springs, of German design - fast and light. And Matthew, as he passes by and returns into the dining room of the inn, smiles to himself - for how Sam would have relished all that if he were here now among them! He would have tarried with the men out there; he would have puffed out his chest and boasted and looked down his nose as he spoke, seizing upon any opportunity to converse on all the latest developments in the smart, competitive world of road vehicles and engineering. What price now, all that nonsense, Matthew thinks. Poor Sam this evening in his chains would surely not care. In exchange for his liberty, he would give the whole world now for a dung cart on an open road. And Matthew vows that he will not, henceforth, waste another moment on anything other than the most beautiful or the most worthy of pursuits. Never again will he allow anything to enter his world that does not in some way contribute to his well-being and happiness. Every beautiful woman, every work of art, every poem and every pleasured entry in the ledger of his life he would celebrate. And these wonders alone would occupy him entirely from here until the end of his days.

'For you Sam!' he whispers to himself, seated alone and toasting his absent friend in a glass of Riesling from the slopes of some noble, towering vineyard in Germany or France. 'May God watch over you, my friend. This and all the wonders of the world I hereby dedicate to you.'

The next day, following an investigation of the shops along the High Street and after making preparations for their return journey to Greenwich, they take themselves off in an open-topped chaise for an hour or so - a hired carriage with a blue satin lining, and a single strong horse that trots and canters upwards to the fine sweeping roadways and the hills above the river, and from which vantage point, they hope to be able to watch Sam's ship departing. It is a bright, sunny morning as Matthew sits at the reigns and guides the frisky creature on its way, drawing them on at what seems the most exhilarating pace - the breeze on their faces and the sun on their backs as they, all four, look down in admiration at the vista of hillsides and fields below, bordered in places with picket fences or wooded hedgerows, as grand a sight as any parkland by William Kent.

What a fine little group we all make, he thinks to himself with an unexpected sensation of pride - the lovely Johanna at his side in her light summer clothes, a wide brimmed straw hat with a feather and a garland of wild flowers upon her shoulder, as pretty as he has ever seen her, and the children squeezed in safely where the luggage would usually be to the rear and enjoying every minute of the adventure. Were it not for their mission today and the distress that attends it, he feels he might easily allow himself to become the happiest man alive.

A few moments later, and they reach a vantage point from which all of a sudden the entire river and hillside above the dockyard opens out, all sloping down to the water, the wide river Medway curving towards them, almost doubling up on itself before proceeding north once more on its meandering course to join with the estuary of the Thames, and thus revealing all the ships below - the one in which Sam is confined easily recognisable by its size, and already raising anchor and hoisting sail, setting itself gradually in motion as it allows the wind and the tide of the river to ease it on its way.

Finding a convenient spot, Matthew alights from the carriage and hands Johanna down also, and they take a few steps upon the grass towards the edge of the hill. The children join them, hurrying to their sides.

How odd it all seems, the beautiful countryside in such celebratory mood, so alive with the sound of birdsong, so vivid with wild flowers, of apple and hawthorne blossom - and already, everywhere across the fields, amid the cowslips and bluebells, the joyous swarms of wildly copulating butterflies in their dances of courtship - all this contrasting with the sorrow of Sam's departure. How very difficult it is to grieve at such a glorious moment!

'Shall we wave?' Johanna suggests to the children as the ship begins to gather knots - already quite some distance from them.

And they do, lifting their arms and setting them in motion as extravagantly as they can in the hope that, should their father, by some miraculous stroke of kindness on behalf of the captain, be allowed up on deck, or should he have access to some open gun port below, he might just have leisure and opportunity to glance out and up to the distant hillside and notice them.

'Maybe someone will lend him a spyglass - what do you think?' Matthew suggests. It is an appealing thought, a pretence that gives them some notion of being connected to him.

'Perhaps ... perhaps,' Johanna murmurs, allowing herself to be optimistic also as she waves again - a wide, generous sweep of both her arms this time, as they all continue to look down towards the distant vessel, shielding their eyes against the glare and gazing out towards the ever diminishing, ever more hazy vision of noble rigging and sail as it glides away - so lovely, so very graceful, until it vanishes round the brow of a hillside, heading out already into the vast estuary and thence to the unknown sea beyond.

A little despondently now, they return to their chaise but then, calculating that they might be able to see the estuary from a position farther along the road, they renew their enthusiasm for the task and, climbing back on board, take off at a pace again - it requiring only a short time for their powerful horse, prancing and tugging them onwards around the wide, sweeping curves of the highway, to bring them to a fresh vantage point and from where, sure enough, they can see not only the Thames estuary out in the far distance but also the very sea itself - so very blue in the sunshine; so sparkling and vast. Here they stop once again and gaze outwards, straining their eyes. But here at the busy confluence of the two rivers, there are so many vessels upon the water that it is almost impossible to distinguish with any certainty which of these might be Sam's. Remaining seated upon the chaise this time, they debate for a further idle fifteen minutes all the various possibilities of which ship it might be. It would surely be *that one*, someone speculates with excitement as they endeavour to point it out. Or would it instead be this one? Or rather the one behind? And so on, until even they must concede that the game is up. Sam is gone, and even were he to be furnished with the greatest spyglass known to humankind, even if he had the mighty telescope from the Royal Observatory at Greenwich itself on board, he would not be able to see them even if he tried.

It is time to go home.

Availing themselves of their own carriage once again, their return journey to Greenwich is a surprisingly pleasant one considering the gravity of the situation that had drawn them forth the previous day. Inside, they play games with the children, and talk again of Red Indians and grizzly bears, of huge mountains and canyons that they say are everywhere in America. And between it all, just occasionally their eyes would meet - Johanna's remarkable hazel-green eyes surveying him from that same inscrutable distance; her thoughts as guarded as ever and yet with a grudging tenderness he suspects that had not existed yesterday.

Eventually, towards sunset, they are brought to the road leading down to the pleasant houses and gardens of Greenwich and also, just showing through some of the trees, the observatory on the hill - all so familiar and reassuring. Johanna and the children are full of anticipation to be coming home. But then as they catch sight of their house, and as their carriage approaches the street outside and the path leading up to the portico, they are aware of a change; that all is not quite as it should be; that strangers can be seen outside of what is an open doorway. Even worse - and they can hardly believe it - there is furniture outside on the front lawns, as well, and other smaller items placed within the porch itself. Drawing up outside and alighting with all haste they run through the gate and up the short pathway to the door, there to be met by an agitated Mary, their young maid, and moments later their butler, Robert, looking very grave indeed.

'Oh, Ma'am!' Mary cries, wringing her hands, her pretty face all flushed and agitated. 'The king's bailiffs have come. They're taking everything, and say we must vacate the premises because the house is to be seized from you!'

'Robert, is this true?' Johanna inquires of her butler, holding in his arms, of all things at just that moment, Sam's barometer.

'Madam, it is. They have all the necessary documents with instructions to enforce their possession according to the laws of forfeiture. Everything must be removed, they say, though I have taken the liberty of setting aside those items that I know to be of personal value to Mr Woolveston and yourself. I am so sorry. I had no idea, Ma'am ...'

'No, no ... do not apologise, Robert, please. I regret we neglected to forewarn you of the possibility,' Johanna responds, one hand raised to the side of her head, as if to steady the turbulence within. 'And Mr Woolveston will not be returning anyway ... so the place must go, of course. I only thought it would not happen quite so soon.'

At which she fights back her tears, straightens her spine and marches in to speak with the bailiffs. Matthew follows and does what he can to reason with the men and to gain more time - successfully so, and they agree to return tomorrow to complete their task - though this, considering the late hour, they would probably have done anyway. Meanwhile, Johanna has hurried to fetch writing paper from the desk, at present positioned outside on the lawn beneath one of the lime trees, and in the fading light quickly pens an urgent message to her parents in Aylesford. Matthew, in turn, makes sure this is sent immediately by the fastest means, dispatching Sam's groom with instructions to take the swiftest horse. A letter is also dispatched to Sam's sister in London, though this more in hope than expectation, since she has not visited him once in prison or offered any support, and seems to have disassociated herself entirely from him since his ignominious return.

Thereafter, time passes very rapidly, with so much to do yet so little opportunity in which to do it. Retiring late, everyone sleeps as best they can in the half-empty house, availing themselves of any chairs and sofas still remaining, or of any blanket or mattress that can be found; and, with the dawn, a much-anticipated breakfast is brought in from a nearby inn.

All the staff are then asked to leave, dismissed each with this or that little memento given to them by their mistress, along with promises of assistance in finding placements elsewhere, or as much as can be provided at such short notice. How sad and stunned everyone seems - all the maids, cooks, footmen, grooms and coachmen, all those good people so intimately entwined in the running of the prestigious household, now to be dispersed far and wide - such devastating changes for them all within the space of little more than a couple of short days. As for the local populace, meanwhile, they remain conspicuous by their absence. Not one neighbour comes to their aid. For in such times as these, with the Bonnie Prince himself still somewhere at large in the Highlands of

Scotland and continuing to evade capture, and with still the possibility, no matter how remote, of a French invasion, who would wish to be seen aiding anyone associated with treason. The business of self-preservation reigns supreme - here in the tranquil, leafy avenues of Greenwich as much as anywhere else. And thus the Woolveston household, or what remains of it, has been left very much to fend for itself.

A little after ten o'clock, the bailiffs return - by which time, all those personal items, jewellery, musical instruments, family portraits, letters and documents that have been successfully set aside have been loaded by Matthew into a separate cart, Johanna's own covered wagon stationed in the paddock alongside, awaiting departure. The only thing he has kept back is Sam's barometer which, with Johanna's permission, Matthew elects to take home as a memento. The infernal thing seems to have been so very much a part of Sam's life, that Matthew simply cannot bear to see it go. A little label attached to the back reveals a recent repair, one of many, at the clock-makers in Deptford.

It is hot, backbreaking work, placing everything where it should be ready for moving, while with remarkable courage and efficiency, with hardly time in which to be sad or annoyed, the mistress of the house, Johanna, organises and marshals the bailiffs to make the process as painless as possible. Later that afternoon, her parents arrive in a coach and four, the coronet emblem of a baronet emblazoned on its sides, to collect their daughter and their grandchildren - a visible relief for her as she rushes to embrace them. And then, only shortly after their arrival in fact, the front door with its elegant fan light above is closed on Sam's once-so-happy home for the final time and His Majesty's locks and chains placed crudely upon it by the bailiffs, uncaring and unrelenting as ever in their ways - for they, too, are keen to depart - their own collection of wagons already piled high with furniture and all the expensive contents of the stables and coach-house. Sam's magnificent liveried carriage, the very one they had returned in from Rochester yesterday, is among their booty, of course - the leader of the team of bailiffs riding inside, and finding it all terribly amusing, waving in regal fashion from the window and jesting with the others as he goes. And then, almost simultaneously, amid the desolation of it all, Matthew realises that Johanna herself is also about to be whisked away, taken in her parent's coach and with hardly a moment's opportunity to say farewell as, all of a sudden, the vehicle is brought round to the front gate once more. The children, already inside, wave at their 'uncle' Matthew from the lowered window, and he waves back and smiles as best he can, while Johanna herself, who it seems cannot even bear to glance his way any longer, and standing for a moment by the coach door, merely concludes their time together with a brief, formal shake of the hand. Even then, the sensation of longing, of being so alive to each other's touch, is astonishing to him. For just the duration of this one exhilarating instant as they exchange glances, it is as if they would read and absorb every last secret from each other's faces - but at which she, disapproving, through moist eyes and with an almost imperceptibly shaking of her head as if to say: 'Don't, please, make it any more difficult for me, Matthew,' she draws her hand away, and in words designed to be heard by her ever vigilant and possibly slightly suspicious parents as much as anyone else, merely says: 'Our gratitude, Mr Wildish, for your assistance in all these matters. I trust your poetry will continue to flourish. I regret only that we will no longer be able to aid you as we have in the past. Instead, I must commend you to our good friend Lady Snatchal for your advancement. And I shall of course write to you, providing I have any further news.'

'And I shall write to you anyway, if I may,' he says, wondering at her sudden disdain and aloofness.

'I might not be able to reply if I am overseas,' she responds. 'Farewell, Sir.'

And, with that, it is done. Amid all the cares and frantic chaos of the day, the ending of it has come upon them so quickly. And now in the light of the low sun and fading bloom of the afternoon as it drifts towards evening, he alone remains, watching as the carriage containing Johanna and her family trundles away, pulled by its pair of horses up towards the Kent Road, accompanied by the covered cart within which the few remaining goods of the Woolvestons are now contained - all gone, leaving only her cruel parting words to torment him.

Apart from a little birdsong, the whole garden now has a most dismal air about it, Matthew thinks. He has surely carried a thousand items from the house, and his arms are aching. But thank heaven he had been here - for how ever would she have managed otherwise! All that remains now is for Matthew to shoulder his little travel-bag of personal effects, including the bulbous end of Sam's barometer protruding out of the top, and to walk the short distance to the local inn, there to hire a post horse by which he might ride home, returning to the city in the gathering darkness, wondering all the while whether he will ever see Johanna again - and rather cursing his fate, shaped in part by his own negligence, no doubt, by which he has allowed so much that is dear to him to slip so very quickly from his grasp.

# ~ 33 ~
## INVITATIONS TO
## A MASQUERADE

'Will there be anything else that needs fixing, Mr Wildish?' the man from the ironmongers inquires, packing up is tools and wiping the grease from his hands with an old blackened rag that he evidently keeps for just such a purpose.

Matthew walks into the hallway leading out to the gallery and, giving the barometer there in pride of place upon the wall a little tap with his finger as he passes, replies that, no, as long as the bell pull is functioning at last, and that the front door to the yard below can now be closed properly for the first time in living memory, he is more than satisfied. Just one of several improvements to his quarters he has made of late. His new business sign above the entrance that he commissioned from a local sign writer is also very much to his liking - more prominent - depicting an image of a splendid full-length periwig and the wording of *Matthew Wildish Esquire, Master Wig Maker,* emblazoned in a graceful, curving motif underneath: far more professional-looking than the last one. The most important enhancement, however, is undoubtedly the security aspect. At last, he has a door bell that works, and proper privacy in the form of new locks on both his stairway door below and his front door leading from the gallery into his apartments - particularly important features, these, considering the forthcoming endeavours he has in mind, because the last thing he wants is for any embarrassing mishaps or any unexpected visitors to be walking in on proceedings, as has so often been the case in the past, of course. And as the tradesman departs this morning at the conclusion of his labours, Matthew tests the bell and the locks on both doors several times with his new set of keys, and smiles to himself with unbridled satisfaction.

It is a glorious warm summer's day, and by the testimony of

Sam's barometer as Matthew stands before it once again admiring its polished mahogany casing and finest silvered calibration, the weather is 'set fair' for the future. Perfect. For it is not the only thing that is set fair according to his plans. He simply cannot wait!

'The new instrument holding up well, Sir?' Francis the valet enquires, calling out as he busies himself about the room, folding clothes, tidying here and there.

'It is, Francis,' Matthew replies with enthusiasm, returning inside. 'Extraordinary. It was always going wrong in its previous location, but here in its new home it seems to be behaving itself quite well. I must say, though, I do miss the gentleman who once owned it.'

'Any news of what has become of Mr Woolveston, Sir?'

'Oh, yes, I received a letter from him just the other day, as a matter of fact. They did their best to starve him to death during the voyage to Boston, apparently, but he survived and upon his arrival wasted no time in putting pen to paper, describing the miracle of his preservation. He said they are going to send him south to fight the French, as we rather feared they might.'

'And may I also enquire over Mrs Woolveston?' Francis asks - for he did, of course, come to know Johanna quite well during the days when she resided next door at the inn during Sam's imprisonment.

'You may, Francis,' Matthew replies, though feeling that his heart is sinking into his boots at being reminded of that dreadful evening when he had watched her carriage roll away from her home in Greenwich, the very last time he ever saw her.

'I believe she and her children have joined her husband already,' Matthew answers, not wishing to elaborate on his reasoning. 'I wonder what kind of life they will make for themselves? A new country, new opportunities - maybe it's all for the best. What a perilous journey to undertake with the little ones, though!'

'A fair helping of danger even upon arrival,' Francis observes dryly as he continues to go about his work.

Matthew nods his agreement. True enough. The dangers are well documented, and just about everyone has an anecdote or a story to tell on the subject - on the fate of a friend, a colleague or family member, brave souls who have attempted to settle in America and have come off the worse for the experience - or even, in extreme cases, having lost their lives. Matthew definitely has no intention of ever making the journey, while Sam will never be permitted back into England, of course. It is most unlikely, Matthew knows, that he will ever see him or Johanna again - and so, as he returns to his workbench and takes up his tools once again he endeavours to dismiss the pain from his mind, just as he has so often dismissed it of late. Each time it becomes a little easier - and this is important, for these are busy days for him, with an order book full of commissions, and he simply cannot afford too many distractions.

Electing a little later to take a pause for an afternoon glass of wine, he wanders over to the chimneypiece and leafs through his card box, the current tally of calling and acceptance cards received - so excited as he casts his eager eyes over them again - for none of these is associated with his business endeavours, but rather each is in response to a number of recent invitations he has sent out to 'a very special masquerade,' as he had termed it: seven eager acceptances from seven enchanting and, above all, passionate women who will open the fabled heavenly spheres to him during the course of one whole glorious day and night of love-making. Yes, it really is about to happen - at last: an adventure of the senses of such magnitude and intensity that its outcome, its destination and resolution is, he suspects, beyond his comprehension at present. Where will it take him?

In a peculiar way, though, it is almost incidental, this long planned-for apotheosis, since the past year of preparation has already proved to have been of inestimable value in its own right, an experience of unprecedented novelty and creativity - for with every new success in his amorous endeavours, yet more success seems to follow - as if a new kind of aura of self-confidence has come to attend upon his every deed and wish. Appreciative glances, opportunities to converse, to befriend and, should he be so inclined, to seduce, now present themselves with a greater frequency than he could have ever thought possible just a few short months ago. And with the constant preoccupation with his seven individual lovers and the unique pleasures he has already enjoyed with each of them, the most remarkable changes have already begun to occur. At first it was simply a comfortable physical sensation he felt, a pleasant, intriguing kind of warmth emanating from the lower abdomen, and this eventually reaching up to his heart, and then the most wonderful state of mind in which he felt joyous and full of the most exhilarating vitality. At first, it had occurred only rarely, for an hour at a time, but of late it has blossomed into an almost permanent state of transformation that prevails upon his entire being. It is a feeling of felicity that he wishes to share with the whole world - for there is hardly a man or woman he would meet these days to whom he does not feel in some sense well disposed. It is, he has begun to comprehend, a kind of love, but a different kind of love, a universal love. Extraordinary. And yet for all these remarkable changes, still he cannot help wonder whether there might, *just might,* be something even more exceptional awaiting him when his project is finally put into practice tomorrow, something mystical and other-worldly to be had from it, or from any repetitions that might ensue over subsequent weeks. There is, of course, only one way to find out.

To his surprise, the whole thing had proved remarkably easy to organise. It was just a few days ago, when he enlisted Francis to go forth and deliver the hand-written invitations to the addresses of each of his seven heavenly bodies. And the wording was simple:

*Matthew Wildish Esq. requests the pleasure of your attendance at an exclusive and very special masquerade for two at his workshop at the sign of The Pig and Whistle on Friday next to celebrate the very first reading to you of his seven sonnets to the planetary spheres. The entire experience to be enhanced by a special vintage of the rarest Claret smuggled in from France; accompanied by a profusion of exotic fruits and chocolate; and by the most tender and ardent ministrations of kindness and affection to be lavished upon you, and only you, by he who would be your loving host.*
*RSVP*

A different time for the 'masquerade' was inserted into each invitation to ensure a pause of two hours between guests - the intention being that at the conclusion of each tryst, he would send his lady happily on her way with the explanation of a pressing business appointment that would be due. Thus, Rose (the Moon) was due at eleven in the morning; Harriet (Mercury) at one o'clock; Sarah (Venus) at three; and Lucy Armstrong (the Sun) at five. This means that Lady von Klapperstein (Mars) would then be due at seven that evening, to be followed by Caroline Bolter (Jupiter) at nine, and finally the late-night visit at eleven o'clock from Lady Snatchal (Saturn) and who, because of the mourning for her late husband, he had scarcely seen since that fateful afternoon some months ago. But the Countess is, as her reply clearly demonstrates, more than willing now to relinquish her sorrows. In fact, the most intriguing aspect of the exercise so far has undoubtedly been the replies he has received, every one of his ladies having responded with some lines of her own - the messages themselves each so deliciously saucy and provocative. And surrendering to an additional moment of unashamed self-indulgence from the comfort of his armchair, he allows himself to read with pleasure each one yet again.

From Rose Tidey: *'Matthew, my love, my amour and finest buck. It is a little early in the day, you rascal, but do not doubt my devotion - I shall be there. I am feeling so emotional about it already. Like the restless sea, I am foaming and so very wild for you. Take me in my ebb and tide and let us sail away together upon every ocean of sweet desire.'*

From Harriet Swift: *'I shall come, of course. So much to tell you. I have discovered the most interesting sensation that can be elicited through a certain procedure. What will it be, you ask? Oh, Matthew my darling, wait and see! You will be shocked and surprised at my unnatural vices and chastise me, no doubt. At least I sincerely hope so.'*

From Sarah May: *'Look - I have got myself educated. I have learnt to read and write. And I do so want it, want it, want it. Your poetry, I mean, silly! What did you think I meant? Will there be music at your masquerade, or will you blow upon my reed and make me sing for you, instead? Tra La La, Tra, La, La. Can you hear me rehearsing already? (Better than a game of flats any day!)'*

From Lucy Armstrong: *'Can you feel my heart beating my lovely Icarus? I am smouldering with desire, my every part as glowing and brazen as the brightest of flowers that turn their faces always to the sun. Let me warm you, excite you and cherish you through all the glorious hours of pleasure that await us.'*

From Lady von Klapperstein: *'Your preposterous declarations of hostilities are accepted, Mr Wildish. Let the battle be joined! Strike the drums and prime your weapon. You will need to be on your very best metal, Sir, for my aim is to destroy you entirely (or else perish in defeat and surrender the spoils of cruel victory to your masterly hand).'*

From Caroline Bolter: *'Whatever you have in mind, Sir, do not, through any fear of my condemnation, moderate your demands upon my person. Be fulsome and extravagant, and as always you will meet with a most willing and enthusiastic participant in even the most outrageous or excessive of your endeavours.'*

And finally from Malaena, Lady Snatchal: *'Matthew, I shall come of course. I am right fed-up with all these long weeks of mourning. Being a widow, one is not expected to enjoy oneself at all - the very thought makes one feel guilty. I have not even pleasured myself proper since that terrible day. I am like one of them there volcanoes ready to explode, and I swear I shall flay alive anyone who dares stand in my way!'*

Well, it really is a most intriguing prospect, he tells himself. Wave after wave of such reckless enthusiasm and passion coming his way. How very splendid. Aware of Francis nearby, eyeing him with more than a little curiosity, however, he wipes the smile off his face and, feigning nonchalance as he replaces the cards in his neat little rosewood box and turns the key, declares: 'Francis, you are to be congratulated - look, all those invitations you delivered the other day: I have just checked through them, and every one has been responded to, and all most positively. Good man!'

'Thank you Sir,' Francis says with the faintest of smiles and a bow of the head, which he has to do anyway, of course, several times, as he advances along the length of the room, avoiding the wooden beams of the ceiling as he goes. 'Though I must confess the exercise of delivering them was not entirely without its difficulties due to ...'

'Oh well, never mind, Francis,' Matthew interrupts, all his emotions still churning with anticipation and excitement and in no mood for trifles. 'The main thing is you've done it. I am very pleased - and as a reward, you may take the entire day off tomorrow.'

'Really, Sir! But won't you be requiring assistance for such a gathering?'

'No, no, not at all, Francis. Not at any point during the proceedings. A number of visitors will be coming and going, that's all. It is a masquerade of a kind, you understand, but really also rather a refined matter of a private nature in which I shall be discussing the merits of literature and poetry with a number of ladies of taste and discernment. I alone shall answer any calls and you will not need to trouble yourself or come from your apartment, at all. In fact, I insist that you ignore me completely tomorrow. Do I make myself clear, Francis?'

'You do Sir. And I shall, indeed, accept your kind offer. I could visit my sister in Peckham, and upon my return that evening will go straight to my own room through the inn.'

'Excellent. Thank you Francis. Oh, and by the way, when you do return and as you avail yourself of the gallery outside, you should not be unduly troubled if you hear - er - various unusual noises, shouts or squeals or anything like that emanating from the rooms here. It is, after all, a masquerade, a festive occasion.'

'I understand, Sir.'

And with that, and still filled with an almost intolerable sense of anticipation for the morrow, Matthew dons a fresh shirt and takes himself off to The Rainbow, hoping to divert his thoughts from the heavenly prospects awaiting him and to regain at least some measure of calm.

The capital has almost returned to its old self, he reflects as he saunters along the south pavement of Fleet Street in the cool shadows of the afternoon. And although still the occasional vague rumour surfaces in the papers that the French will throw their weight behind a rescue mission to locate the Bonnie Prince, wherever he might be secreted in the Highlands and Islands of Scotland, most people believe it will not happen. And the salutary reminder of what might befall anyone misguided enough to try again to dispose the monarchy of King George is ever present in the shape of the various new traitors' heads, parboiled and impaled on the pikes atop the roof of Temple Bar - difficult to ignore - while from the shade of the arches below, enterprising young men are already letting out spy-glasses to passers-by at a halfpenny a time to get a closer look, and there is even a handy diagram as well for the more literate, a kind of 'who's who' of prominent Jacobite rebels for an extra halfpenny, so each head might be identified by name and title.

Somewhat more edifying indications of a return to normality can be detected, meanwhile, in the more regular trades and businesses of the city that have settled once more into their familiar routines: the shop windows full, the streets a cacophony of criers and hawkers again and the reassuring noise of the wagons and rumbling traffic of normal commerce. Visitors from the shires have returned to enjoy the summer season of parks and gardens and the operatic performances therein, and all is well with the world. And yet, a little later, as Matthew sits in his favourite window seat in The Rainbow, sipping at his coffee and gazing absently to the busy street outside, still he cannot help but think of his absent friends, of Sam and Johanna. And although Sam's head was not, after all, destined to be one of those swaying on its pike in the warm autumnal winds above Temple Bar or the Tower of London, his alternative fate has not been kind. The explanation Matthew had given his valet Francis earlier did not convey the entire story because he simply could not trust himself in front of his servant not to break down in the telling of it. The sad, tragic truth is that the plight of his friends of happier times is almost certainly now one of utmost desperation. Whether they are alive or dead, he simply does not know - nor will he ever know, it seems. The letter from Sam that he had referred to in his conversation with Francis was in truth no more than a brief, scribbled note, one of three received. And now, in the bustle and noisy detachment of the coffee house, he can take those very messages from his pocket and read through them again, endeavouring to shield himself from their impact by pretending that they are mere bulletins from the newspapers, just some impersonal scraps of news as he would have pondered over a thousand times in places such as this. Then it doesn't seem so bad.

Amid the dreadful privations of the voyage, Sam was confined below decks most of the time where he was seasick and had contracted some kind of febrile disease which, he stated, had weakened his constitution. It had, he believed, also affected his intellect and clouded his mind, possibly irrevocably, so that he could not think clearly and often suffered from headaches and dizzy spells. It made for uncomfortable reading, and his subsequent notes, only two more until they ceased altogether, were even bleaker, full of the greatest lamentations for his plight, detailing all the privations and hardships he must endure in the army and the dreadful prospect awaiting his family when they arrived. He was full of despair for what they would find, though without compunction, it seemed, of inviting them to share in it - the wreckage of his life - the little that remained of his dignity already long since crushed beneath the daily grind of fending off starvation and keeping body and soul together as a conscript in His Majesty's forces where discipline was harsh and punishment brutal. A glimmer of hope remained, he said. Perhaps, they could all escape once Johanna and the little ones were arrived - change their names, take a wagon joining the settlers going out West. Maybe he could try to get hold of some land, make a life. It was a despairing message - concluding with the statement that he had no permanent forwarding address and that he would only ever write again if he had any good news to report - something that he obviously did not contemplate being the case.

As for Johanna, it was even worse. Resolving not to respond to any of Matthew's own letters, and consequently to keep him in ignorance of her intentions, she had not even allowed him the opportunity of bidding her farewell, or of aiding her in any of the difficult practicalities of her departure. Her silence, when it was broken, came merely in the form of a brief letter sent from her family home, and this some weeks after her departure. He reads this next:

D ear Matthew,
    I trust this finds you well. I have left instructions that this be sent to you once I am at sea and already well underway towards my new life in America. Sam has assured me via a letter from Boston that he has organised everything for our convenience and comfort when we arrive. We will make the best of it. A new life for us all.
    You will wonder at my resolve in not permitting us to see each other prior to my departure. But I could not allow my heart to rule my head. There are many different kinds of love that people feel and act upon, but yours, alas, has not coincided with mine and can, therefore, only prevent me

from following my destiny, a destiny that lies elsewhere.

You will smile, I suspect, reading this, and be amused at my use of such an emotive word. Destiny. Please don't. We have spoken often about fate and whether we are free and at liberty to choose what we do. You are aware, I am sure, that many of the wisest of the philosophers believe that human nature is not ruled by the stars and that mankind has free will. It is true perhaps. But in this freedom a certain arrogance has bred itself. Now, intoxicated with our powers, we hurl all the insults of rationality towards the heavens, hoping they will be cowered into submission by our cleverness. We are like the dogs and the wolves who have howled at the moon for generations. But the moon has never run away because of that. And the heavens do not bend to our will even now. Nor can we destroy the mystery of our lives on this earth with cries of reason.

Do we have free will? I have concluded that it is true - we do - but only in the small and insignificant things: in matters of whether we put salt on our dinner or wear blue today, but not in the meaningful things, not in the important people we meet and those singular events and rites of passage that shape our lives. There is a fate, and we are subject to it. I am certain of that now. And although I am frightened half-to-death by what awaits me, I am ready to accept it - to embrace my future, whatever the outcome might be.

I shall not write to you again, Matthew, because I need to forget my former life. I intend to relinquish it entirely - or else the pain of recalling all those times of happiness will prove too much to bear in addition to all that I must now endure. The Johanna you once knew is a part of history, gone forever. And I must let you go also. I wish you every happiness my dear Matthew, and that you will find success with all that you wish for in this life.

Johanna


With a tear that he hopes will not be obvious should anyone glance his way in the busy coffee house, Matthew reads and folds the letter once again, just as he has already read and folded it a dozen times, and then replaces it slowly and with care into his waistcoat pocket - its words of misplaced courage and optimism all the more poignant in the light of the awful truth that will be revealed to her and the children upon their arrival: the hopeless future with the broken man who has called them forth. Whatever will become of them, he wonders, those brave souls? And the wondering, for Matthew, is a pain almost too much to withstand. So after a while he tells himself he must stop wondering. She is right. It is over - gone forever.

Friday morning dawns with the most joyous sunshine and a festive chorus of birdsong - the dew and moisture of the night rising in gentle vapours from all the red-tiled rooftops and walls of the yard, as if the very breath of God were upon the world. Never has a day dawned more beautifully or with more promise. Never has a man leapt from his bed with greater excitement for all that is to come. No eager bridegroom, no graduate awaiting honours, no noble prince upon the eve of a coronation would ever have felt so glad and full of anticipation as does he this morning - so ready, so full of desire!

Yes, he tells himself, as he stands in front of his dressing table and looking-glass for his customary sponge bath and then, unattended by Francis this morning, of course, shaves himself with special care before arranging his long, lustrous locks of hair with a little purple ribbon at the nape - today is the stuff of which legends are made. Let the Gods look down and wonder at the aspirations of man - that he, Matthew Wildish, should dare to emulate their excesses and seek a pathway to their very door. The first of his seven lovelies, Rose, is due in just a couple of hours time, at eleven o'clock. All is settled and will run its inevitable course. The only question that remains is how will he occupy himself until then? A young man awaiting the arrival of his lover must experience every minute as one would normally an hour; but when seven lovers are due in succession, it becomes an eternity. How ever can he take his mind off it? Does he even wish to take his mind off it!

So, after a leisurely breakfast, he goes to his bedchamber once more, dons his finest silken banyan and most elaborate of neck stocks, all ruffles and flounces, and here, in the seductive semi-darkness, busies himself for the tenth time already this morning, making sure everything is clean and in order, carefully arranging upon the bed's generous expanse of surface this or that silken pillow or braided cushion. It is a large bed, surrounded by various bolsters and woolsacks and thereby extending its dimensions from wall to wall - fit for play as much as for slumber. Wherever he has lived in recent times, he has taken it with him - this very special, almost magically imbued item of furniture which, through all the years of steady usage, has played host to so many amorous encounters that by now it is almost as if it has taken on a life of its own. Steeped in passion, sweetened by desire, impregnated with the nectar and juices of a thousand amorous embraces, and perfumed by layer upon layer of passion that lingers in the very air about it, no one can behold it without becoming enchanted, without sensing the invitation, the whispered irresistible siren call to plunge and loll between its posts and swags of curtains gathered, down into the soft, glorious embrace of it. Yes, it has served him well, and with loyalty over the years - and now it is ready, awaiting its master's finest hour. 'Oh, sound the trumpets,' he murmurs to himself, impatient for all that is to come. 'Hurry on eleven o'clock!'

Returning to his workshop, he takes a little coffee and decants the first of his bottles of claret in readiness. Then, perching himself upon a high stool by the windows from which he can survey the yard below, he patiently awaits the first arrival, waits for she who will place him upon the first rung of the magical stairway: his dearest, most-voluptuous Rose Tidey. Will she be wearing the lovely silver mask he has made for her with its sweeps of seed pearls and shell? What fun that would be!

He hears the clock in Cheapside strike eleven and his heart begins to pound as the appointed hour comes ... and passes. There is no sign of her. He waits a further thirty minutes, seated still upon his stool, full of anguish, observing with eager expectation every detail of the busy comings and goings in the yard below. Several undistinguished sedan chairs arrive and depart. A group of young stable-boys congregate for a minute or two in raucous idleness - being particularly fascinated and amused, it would seem, by his new, far more extravagant business sign. A coach and four from Essex trundles in and its visitors step down and waddle inside via the corner door of the yard. Horses are unharnessed, changed for fresh ones - slowly, lugubriously, for the day is already becoming warm - and then the coach departs. Life goes on, the dreary routine traffic of commerce and travel - until, before he knows it, a full hour has passed; it is already noon, and still no sign of Rose.

Whatever could have happened to her? With his nether regions beginning to turn numb with being seated on the hard stool for so long, he simply abandons his post, therefore, and sits himself down on his couch instead, head in hands, full of disappointment. Here, closing his tired eyes, he allows the time to pass a little more, the time that will at least eventually take him towards one o'clock when Harriet would be due. Something to relish - but he feels disappointed, that his elaborate scheme should apparently founder so soon, at the very start.

Wandering out onto the sunny gallery to take the air a little later, he tends to one of his hanging baskets of flowers, pouring water from a can, only to attract the attentions of the stable-boys below who, still entertained by his new sign above the door, and his particularly decadent appearance today in his resplendent banyan, resolve to detain him with a collective rendition of some ridiculous street song they have picked up:

*Barber, barber, shave a pig.*
*How many hairs will make a wig?*
*Four and twenty, that's enough,*
*Give the barber a pinch of snuff!*

'Bloody cheek!' he shouts down - his pent up frustrations getting the better of him for a second as, pointing a menacing finger, he singles out the ringleader among them. 'I've told you before: I am not a barber. And you behave yourself. I know where your mother lives!'

'I bet you do!' another one of them cries, only to receive a cuff round the ear from the first.

Just then the tall figure of Francis steps out onto the gallery, closing his door softly behind him - and upon which, the boys below make themselves scarce. He is preparing to leave for his day-off, of course, as instructed, looking very dapper in his straw hat and a sky-blue waistcoat - and Matthew hurries along to intercept him before he can make his exit via the inn door.

'Francis - a word with you, if I may,' he says, shielding his eyes from the sun, for the light is very strong out here.

'Oh, that's all right, Sir,' Francis asserts walking away. 'As per instructions, I shan't disturb you.'

'No, come here, Francis, I want to speak with you.'

'Oh no Sir, *I'm ignoring you!*' he adds in a little sing-song voice. 'I'm off to Peckham to visit my ...'

'Francis! Come here at once *or I'll kill you!* Listen - tell me, when you delivered that invitation to Miss Rose Tidey, the brewer's daughter - can you remember, was there any indication of a problem? I mean, did anybody there tell you that the time for the appointment could not be met?'

'No, Sir. I did not encounter any of the recipients of the letters at any stage, and spoke with no one as I put them through the doors.'

Matthew stares at his valet, still perplexed by what could possible have gone amiss - since every invitation had been replied to and must, therefore, have been understood. But just then, with the clock in Cheapside striking its single melancholic chime of one o'clock, a chair comes racing into the yard below, the men clattering in their shoes across the cobblestones, setting it down and opening the door straight away - to reveal not Harriet emerging from it, as expected, but the radiant and gloriously attired Lucy Armstrong, masked and outstanding in various bright pastel shades - she who was not expected until much later this afternoon.

'Listen, Francis - something must have gone terribly wrong,' Matthew appeals to him again in confusion, grasping the poor fellow by the lapels while trying, not altogether successfully, to conceal himself behind one of the wooden posts.

'Well, Sir, the only thing is, and as I endeavoured to explain to you the other day, I did have the most unfortunate accident on my way to deliver the first invitation.'

'An accident - what do you mean?' Matthew demands, as at just that moment another chair with its own coat of arms races into the yard below, its chairmen in such haste that it almost collides with the first - and out from it, by slow degrees, unfolding and rearranging her vast panniered skirts, emerges none other than Lady Snatchal.

'There was a torrential thunderstorm,' Francis continues patiently and still seemingly unaware of the terrible magnitude of the situation unfolding below.

'*A thunderstorm?* What the hell has that got to do with it?' Matthew demands, breathless, letting go of Francis's lapels at last as he continues to look down in horror, responding only vaguely with a wave of the hand to the smile of the Countess - for she has spotted him straight away. Any moment now, he thinks, and she will notice Lucy, as well.

'All the invitations, bar one, got ruined,' Francis answers. 'The ink had run, rendering them illegible. Fortunately, though, I still had the list of names and addresses, so I came back here and took the liberty of writing them out again, based on the one that remained. Naturally, I resealed them all and then ...'

'What - the same time? You put *the same time* down on all of them?'

'Why, yes, of course, Sir. One o'clock is what it said - the invitation,' Francis replies, still in bewildered fashion, while at just that moment a terrible shriek comes up from below as Lady Snatchal spies Lucy at last, hardly inconspicuous in all her best attire - and the very sight of which is sufficient to send her into a paroxysm of rage. Advancing on her, she demands to know what she is doing here.

'None of your damn business, you old baggage!' Lucy replies, her voice, unusually strident, echoing off the walls of the yard. 'And if you are intending to call upon Mr Wildish, you should be advised that I already have an appointment.'

'So do I! At one o'clock.' the Countess retaliates in a voice equally as loud. 'And you would do better, therefore, Madam, to take yourself back to your whorehouse!'

'I beg your pardon! Are you referring to my exclusive bagnio?' Lucy demands, incandescent by this time. 'How dare you, Madam!'

All very unpleasant - and the women are only prevented from coming to blows by the arrival of a chaise drawn by a fine grey that canters into the yard and straight between them, and which appears to have on board none other than the esteemed personage of Lady Martina von Klapperstein. Climbing down in her voluminous mantua with the assistance of her driver, she pays the man and upon his departure, looks around most contemptuously at the sight of the two ladies staring at her and whose appearance, being every bit as lavish as her own, suggests that they are also hoping to attend the exclusive 'masquerade for two.' With a continued look of disdain, she chooses to ignore them, however, and instead simply advances on Matthew's stairway door, where she pulls the bell several times most vigorously.

'Is anything wrong Sir?' the mystified Francis inquires, as the

other end of the bell itself clangs and rattles on its chain behind
him, his eyes full of admiration for the outstanding and beautiful
women arriving below. 'I must say you seem to have quite a good
showing down there already.'

But just then a missile of some sort, probably a flower pot,
comes crashing into the post by Matthew's head, shattering into
pieces, followed by something else more substantial - an old
horseshoe, by the looks of it - also hurled from below. Meanwhile,
Lady von Klapperstein, losing patience has begun to pound with
her fists upon the stairway door. All hell is breaking loose, with the
most unseemly curses and profanities - *Strumpet! Slut! Trollop!
Whore!* being cried - together with a few more lengthy descriptions
containing phrases such as *'Soiled Goods'* or *'Mutton dressed as
lamb'* echoing from the walls - and by which time, all around the
gallery, a substantial number of onlookers, guests and staff have
already assembled to watch the performance. The stableboys are
loving it.

'Out of my way. I am due to visit Mr Wildish at one o'clock!'
Lucy is heard to declare loudly, advancing on the doorway herself
now - and, worse, upon the woman baring her entrance. 'I do not
believe anyone else has been invited.'

'Not so! I have also an appointment, and a card to prove it.'
Lady von Klapperstein insists, shouting back over her shoulder
whilst continuing to hammer upon the door. 'And also, may I
remind you, that a menial such as yourself should address me as
my Lady. *Du Schlampe!'* she adds, reverting to her native German
in order to insult the other women more comprehensively.

'Don't tell lies!' Lady Snatchal shouts as she, too, advances on
the redhead, attempting to haul her away. 'You're not a proper
Noble, anyway - everyone in London knows that. You're just a
common, sausage-eating drab that came over with the Germans!'

This is getting worse and worse, and several blows have already
been struck when abruptly all heads turn to the entrance of the yard
as the lovely young Harriet Swift strolls in, dressed soberly in
gingham, a plain straw hat perched squarely on her head. With a
rapid glance around the yard, she appears to size up the complexity
of the situation instantly as would any governess in the presence of
unruly children, and is none too pleased as she claps her hands
thrice, loudly in an attempt to restore order - though this with only
temporary success. For at just that moment, the lovely Sarah May

also saunters in, twirling her mask around her fingers - cheerful and elegant in blue, unhatted, her luscious dark hair about her shoulders - and calling out a familiar salutation of 'Oooh hoo!' - only to be halted instantly, wide-eyed and incredulous at the sight she beholds. Seeing Lady Snatchal, pausing for only a short time from her by-now curiously silent grappling with several fistfuls of Lady von Klapperstein's red hair, Sarah seems at first surprised - but then, quickly begins to look most displeased and then breaks into tears, a terrible loud fit of sobbing - just as Rose Tidey arrives, in fact, strolling in on foot, all bosomy and brassy, but who is halted instantly by the astonishing sight that greets her - with no fewer than five sumptuously attired women, some in masks, some sobbing inconsolably, and the remainder arguing and shouting at one another - so very awful, that it is all she can do to prevent herself from turning on her heels and running straight out again. She is prevented from doing so, however, because at just that instant another sedan chair races in, containing the redoubtable Caroline Bolter, and who, alighting swiftly and seeing the pandemonium taking place all around seeks out Matthew's face straight away and cries out for an immediate explanation - *'Matthew - what is the meaning of this? Explain!'*

But there is no opportunity to do so - for within seconds, Matthew's stairway door below, still assailed by the fists and kicking heels of Ladies Klapperstein and Snatchal combined, finally gives way, and seconds later loud footfalls are heard thundering upon the stairs as they squeeze themselves through and upwards - all the others following in pursuit - an entire planetary system of furious women ascending to the gallery and baying for blood.

Matthew knows there is nothing left for it but to run. Thrusting a by-now somewhat alarmed Francis into their path with the words, 'Just deal with this, my man, will you,' he hastens along the gallery towards the upstairs doorway of the inn - and, once through, shuts it tightly behind him. Ignoring the cries of Francis outside, he lodges a chair beneath the handle to inhibit its opening - thereby providing himself with at least a few seconds advantage before he continues to hurtle through the building, much to the astonishment of all the customers and staff - several standing aside to avoid a collision and to let him pass unimpeded at top speed. Onwards he goes, along the passageway, down the staircase, straight through the dining room and the reception hall, tearing off his long banyan as he goes - finally to fly out through the front doors of the building, almost without his feet touching the front steps at all - down into the street, from where he races along to Cheapside, hails the nearest vacant chaise and leaps on board.

'Where to, Sir?' the driver next to him inquires.

'Anywhere you like!' Matthew replies. 'Only make it quick.'

# ~ 34 ~
## PRIMUM MOBILE

With a further sip of champagne, carrying his glass with him, he locates a vacant seat upon a couch at the back of the room. Not an ideal vantage point, he suspects, nor the most commodious or thrilling of places to take his ease - most of the seat being occupied by one very large elderly gentleman in a long, old-fashioned periwig and a cheap, over-sized black mask more like an executioner's hood than anything else. But it will just have to do. On this, his very last day on Earth, according to the astrological predictions made some while ago by the redoubtable Doctor Alcock, Matthew would ideally have liked to position himself a little closer to the musicians, or perchance to one or two of the more attractive female attendees - but that, it seems, is not to be, at least not for the moment.

With merely a perfunctory nod of greeting, therefore, in the direction of the gentleman with whom he must share his leisure, he collapses down in an undignified heap by his side, stretches out his legs in their white stockings and bejewelled knee buckles and, ignoring all else, closes his eyes and allows the music to entertain him.

Matthew has been invited to a soirée of the well-to-do of London society, a masquerade of sorts, set in the ballroom of a house by the Thames - and well attended, too. This is, in fact, the first stage for him today amid a defiantly hectic schedule of entertainments about the capital, to culminate this evening in the long awaited performance outdoors in Green Park of Handel's latest extravaganza: Music for Royal Fireworks, in celebration of an untypical outbreak of peace between England and France, and to be accompanied by a spectacular pyrotechnic display before the King who will be viewing it all from St James's.

The present modest rendition of orchestral selections is thus merely a curtain raiser for Matthew on what promises to be a most portentous final day, for he is determined to enjoy it - even though the elbow of his neighbour on the couch tends to poke him in the ribs from time to time as the man fidgets and beats time to the rhythm with his feet, compelling Matthew to turn and regard him angrily at one stage. Silly old fool! 'If he does that one more time,' Matthew thinks, 'I shall have to speak up and ask him to desist.'

Yes, all rather irritating. And as he casts his eyes around the lavishly appointed room and its crowded floor below he cannot help but feel mildly disappointed also in what he sees amid this sea of powdered wigs and extravagantly trimmed hats - those in attendance this afternoon being rather of the lower end of the self-styled *Beau Monde* of London Society, the kind of gathering in which the making of a leg by any gentleman would as like be better described as the *breaking* of one - a fiasco in which a fellow would likely get his sword caught between his ankles, topple, and then lose his hat in the process, twice probably, only to spend an additional ten minutes replacing it upon his head. The women are not much better - mostly of the trussed-up and over-painted variety - gross and indolent, celebrating endlessly their privileges of birth, but with little else by way of culture or intelligence to commend them to any man of taste or discernment such as himself.

As for the music ... well, the piece being played at present is not entirely to his liking, either - at least he has persuaded himself he does not care for it - for he is, by his own admission, a difficult man to please these days. It is an arrangement from Judas Maccabeus, including, naturally, the ever popular 'See, the Conquering Hero Comes!' - that musical trinket of thinly veiled Hanoverian propaganda celebrating in all but name the triumph of Butcher Cumberland over the poor starving Scots at Culloden some years ago. It has all the necessary martial affiliations, trumpets and drums enough to please the boorish tastes of the King - and yet it begins so sweetly, so very fine and delicately, a melody of such innocence and charm that it brings the tears to Matthew's eyes even now. And when the horns and trumpets join and the drums thunder and roll and draw the piece upwards to a crescendo, he feels quite carried away. But carried away upon what, exactly, he asks himself? Upon the barbarity and cruelty, the blood, grime and ignominy of war? Surely not! And he despises himself and his own stupid emotions that he should be so moved by any of it.

*See, the conqu'ring hero comes!*
*Sound the trumpets, beat the drums.*
*Sports prepare, the laurel bring,*
*Songs of triumph to him sing.*

Upon the wall to his side, among a number of paintings and gilded mirrors, all sparkling in a stray beam of April sunshine that has sneaked its way in-between the curtains, he becomes aware of what is surely his own unmasked reflection in the glass. And it is not an entirely pleasant experience. For one split second, he assumes it must be someone else, some other foppish young gentleman of fashion in his scarlet coat staring out of a window at him. But no - it is he, Matthew Wildish. And his powdered cheeks cannot conceal the fact that his face is altering - he is certain of it - and this in a most disconcerting way. It is a process that does not bode well for the future, he thinks, even should he live to see it - for it is as if all the excesses of his many amours were written there, the cynical, world-weary life he has thrown himself into - deeper than ever since his return to the capital after a lengthy exile (largely in the interests of his own self-preservation). No longer does he spare himself in the pursuit of seduction or conquest - as if he ever did! But now it has become a frantic, disorganised and decadent vocation - because these days he tends to be very clear in his mind regarding the extent of his personal requirements: these being chiefly music, wine and women. Those are his mainstay, and nothing much else excites his appetites or rouses his blood at all, not even poetry any longer.

In fact, Matthew Wildish has not written a single line of decent verse for quite some time, far longer than he wishes to contemplate. As one of the most sought-after and celebrated of master wig makers in the country, however, he knows he may safely classify himself as 'successful' - a man of substance, and with no shortage of funds, either, by which to finance his increasingly dissolute life style - all of which has begun to prove a slow poison to his health and to his looks, so that secreted now within every new line, every wrinkle or blemish, be it ever so slight and hardly anything one might notice at present, there is the seed of far deeper ravages that will surely increase with the passing of the years - for why should he be immune to the consequences of a life of dissipation any more than any other rake or libertine? Furnished by nature with all the gifts of honeyed speech, with intelligence and good looks, he has exploited it all, leading the life that many a man might envy. And now, as he gazes with amusement at his own reflection, the grim smile of resignation that comes back at him matches to perfection the conceited, arrogant and argumentative purveyor of wealth and taste that he has allowed himself to become. See the conquering hero? No, not exactly - and no happy ending either for his story. Instead, his epitaph, like so many other wretches like himself enslaved to their appetites, is destined to be a decidedly mediocre one. And perhaps it is only right, therefore, that he and everyone else should smile. Behold: the great jest and riddle of the world - Man - of which he has become little more than a rather undistinguished and second-rate example.

The orchestra breaks off for an interval now, and the silence that ensues once the little ripple of applause from the guests has died away invites some kind of conversation, and so almost inadvertently Matthew catches the eye of his masked neighbour on the couch and a further nod of acknowledgement is exchanged. And then it speaks.

'Ah, where have all the young beauties fled that you and I should find ourselves alone and sharing a seat today!' the old boy declares, sizing Matthew up no doubt by the foppishness of his attire. Ladies man.

Detecting just that faintest trace of an accent in the gravely old voice, this is, Matthew surmises, surely yet another one of those appalling old Hanoverians he is sat next to. Oh, how he is coming to loathe them, these half-German pretenders to the title of English Gentleman - for they permeate every level of society these days.

'It matters not to me,' Matthew answers with a shrug of the shoulders, not wanting his tastes and predilections to be identified so accurately, 'since this is, according to an astrologer of note I once visited, to be my very last day amid this vale of tears.'

'Then your astrologer is an ass, Sir,' the old fellow assets with confidence. 'No gentleman of that persuasion worth his salt would dare predict such a thing. The stars incline, Sir, they do not compel.'

'Let us hope you are correct, Sir,' Matthew responds, not deigning to turn his head to his unchosen companion any longer, 'and that your judgement of those I choose to associate with is superior to your manners in wishing to denigrate them. Either way. I have no regrets if it must end now. I must say it has all been quite delightful. And at such a time perhaps the charms and temptations of beautiful women should rightly be set aside, anyway - especially when one has the paradox of music such as this to occupy one's thoughts.'

'Paradox, Sir! What paradox?'

'That the exquisite piece we have just enjoyed should have been composed to celebrate the business of slaughter, to mark the Duke of Cumberland's return from Scotland after the '45. Even should I defy the predictions of my astrologer and live to be as ancient as you, Sir, I do not think I shall ever come to reconcile such an extraordinary contradiction of terms.'

'What!' the old boy exclaims and laughs. 'You don't seriously believe that music of that quality would have been inspired by such base sentiments? It is surely to the glory of God that it was dedicated, Sir - not to a purveyor of war - some overstuffed, parody of an ape that beats his chest and sits astride a cannon!'

'To the glory of God - inscribed where?' Matthew demands. 'If I were given to vain disputation, Sir, I would inquire of your qualifications for making such a remark - for I happen to be an expert in music of this kind, and I do not ever recall having seen that written down as such.'

'One does not ask a man who is masked for his credentials Sir. One dose not inquire of trifles. We are all children of God and the starry sky.'

'Well, I have no such scruples. I am Matthew Wildish. I am a poet.'

But the old fellow merely laughs - this rough, untidy haystack of a man, his belly heaving in merriment. How very unpleasant.

'Ah, a poet, eh! And are you a *good* poet, Sir?' he enquires. 'I cannot recollect having heard your name, not in that context anyway.'

'My following is a small and discerning one,' Matthew replies, feeling increasingly irritated. 'Were I to become excessively popular all of a sudden, and known to all and sundry, I should be anxious to re-examine the quality of my offerings and make the necessary improvements.'

'Um - literary genius and good looks!' the man continues

merrily. 'A rare combination. But no matter. It is possible, I suppose, that both might flourish within the same frame.'

'I am indebted to your perspicacity, Sir.'

'I have been known to be wrong, though,' he counters straight away and laughs again.

'I do not doubt it,' Matthew snaps back instantly. 'It is the misfortune of the elderly and their diminishing faculties to be so often in error when passing judgement on the young.'

'Indeed. But consider this: are you really so very young, Sir? My eyesight might well be diminishing with my infirmity, but do I not detect a certain profusion of silver or grey upon your temples? Are you not already reaching that age when the hair begins to wither and to thin, and that it is surely only a matter of time, would you not say, before you must consider shaving the lot off and availing yourself of a wig?'

'Never!' Matthew declares - unwisely, perhaps, for the old fellow might well be familiar with his name, after all - not as a poet, but rather in the context of his profession. 'You are, in any event, woefully mistaken in your understanding of fashion, Sir,' Matthew continues. 'It is true, some among us must wear a wig because their own hair is so loathsome; while there are others who cannot afford one anyway, and must therefore wear their hair to look as much as possible like a wig. There are, however, some, albeit a very few like myself, who have cared for and maintained their own hair so well over their lifetime that they have no need to pursue either course.'

'Then you are not entirely void of judgement, after all, Sir,' the old fellow concludes, getting to his feet unsteadily and availing himself of his cane for support, 'for most wigs are, in my opinion, overpriced. They are worn as a rule by fellows with more vanity than discernment - while those who peddle them usually have the most accomplished way of talking nonsense as any man in London. And upon that note of concord, Sir, I regret I must now take my leave of you, as I must shift my old carcass over to Green Park for the performance this evening.'

'Ah, you are going to the Royal Fireworks, too!' Matthew laughs. 'Perhaps I shall encounter your pointed elbows and tapping feet there, as well?'

'I doubt it,' the man replies. 'I shall be far too busy, and thus I regret we will not be able to continue our stimulating conversation even then.'

'Really! Will you be running around setting off the rockets, Sir?'

'No, not at all. And let us hope that the young fool who is charged with that honour does not succeed in burning the podium to the ground. No - it is my job to direct the orchestra. And so Good day to you, Sir!'

And with that, before Matthew can recover himself or rise or even call out after him, the old fellow has wandered into the crowd of guests on the floor below and has vanished from sight. There can, of course, be only one person conducting the orchestra this evening - and thus, Matthew realises with utter consternation, with feelings verging on despair, that seated next to him upon this very couch this afternoon, amid all his pompous banter and frivolous baiting of a poor old man, he has missed the opportunity of a lifetime to converse with none other than George Fredrick Handel.

With Ludgate Hill and Fleet Street congested due to just about everybody in London, it seems, making their way westwards towards Green Park and the stage of the Royal Fireworks, Matthew elects to walk down to the Bridge and river stairs in order to decide whether going by water might not be the better option. But not a single craft that might be hired is to be found anywhere - the entire river so full. Even if anything could be boarded at this hour, it would struggle to get through in time. It is getting late, too, the sun is low in the sky, the whole city alive with a buzz and hum of excitement as the terrible realisation comes upon him that even if he were to walk south of the river now and then cross again to Whitehall by wherry, he still might not be able to reach the performance in time. Nor is he the only one to have decided upon this alternative and somewhat dubious route. Carried along with the crowds now, he finds himself crossing the bridge whether he likes it or not, albeit very slowly with hardly room enough to spread his arms. Occasionally, a carriage or chair will encounter another, head-on in one of the narrow stretches between the buildings spanning the roadway, and everything then grinds to a halt. Fearing that his clothes will be ruined in the crush, or else a pickpocket will rob him of everything he has, Matthew takes the opportunity to make for the balustrade on one of the open sections; and here he finds some respite, seating himself upon the edge of the stonework.

A spectacular view of the water opens out from here, a vast armada of tiny craft interspersed with a number of more substantial private vessels - while away in the distance, towards the bend in the river below Whitehall, one of the royal barges can be seen, an enormous, serpentine vessel, its gilded hull catching the dipping beams from the sun. What a sight! The King, he has heard, is in St James's Palace, but the barge would surely be occupied by various favoured nobles, too, because even from Lambeth a reasonable view of the fireworks would be possible.

Lingering here now, the clamour of the crowd hurrying past, waiting for a pause or space that he might rejoin them and proceed on his way relatively unmolested, he is reminded that it was here, at this very spot where he and his old friend Sam had encountered the bird man that evening - so long ago now, so far removed from his present state: those happy, innocent times. And yet, for all his disappointment and self-criticism earlier today, since it sometimes seems to him that the entire story of his life has been one of missed opportunities, this evening he feels unaccountably buoyant - it having been the most astonishing couple of hours since leaving the recital and taking a meal at The Rainbow and then coming out onto the streets again - for during that time he has somehow managed to encounter just about everybody he has ever known in the capital. Perhaps it is understandable, with so many people out and about, and all in such celebratory mood, but this evening everywhere he turns he discovers people he has not seen for ages, faces almost forgotten until today and bringing back with them such a variety of memories.

A little while ago, for example, he noticed Rose Tidey's pretty sister, Margaret riding a wagon in the company of her burly husband, Harold. She had a babe in her arms, and there was another in his - twins! Full of good cheer, they waved from a distance as they passed. Then, at another moment, Matthew thought he saw those very same farmers who had lost the bull on that day at the inn, when the animal had got itself lodged in his stairway - though he could not be entirely certain, for they seemed to have prospered since he last saw them, and were well-dressed. Yet one of them called out and raised his hand in salutation. Amazing. Maybe it really was them! And then, shortly after this, Matthew even encountered the desperate gentleman from Lucy

Armstrong's rooms that evening, the very same fellow he had given his clothes to. Though a long time ago, Matthew felt certain it was him, and off to the performance himself no doubt, smiling from out of the window of his carriage in Fleet Street as he trundled by, with what looked to be his family inside - and surely just about the last vehicle to have got through unimpeded before the traffic jams had closed in. Lucky fellow.

Yes ... so many old faces from his past, that magical past that just this once, this evening, seems to have come back to haunt him in a most pleasant way. Perhaps this is what it is like on one's last day, he reflects - reliving so much of one's past all at once, like a collection of benign faces processing through the panorama of a weird and vivid dream before one finally slips away into oblivion. Why even now, even as he glances down to the water, Matthew becomes aware - and he really should not be surprised - of the tall figure of his former Valet, Francis, standing at the stern of a private boat. Having made a full recovery from the injuries sustained on that fateful day of the 'special masquerade' at the Pig and Whistle, he has clearly prospered - because there he is, going forth in the company of a fine gentleman, his new employer no doubt, and in his own private barge, heading West along the river to Whitehall. He will get a good view of the fireworks, too. Good man!

And so, inevitably, his meditations turn towards those seven very special women he had once been so fortunate to have encountered all within the space of a few short months, women he had enjoyed so well and yet betrayed so badly - or at least they would have perceived it as such at the time. Yet, even though they had no qualms over demonstrating their fury with him then, and even for a good few months thereafter, all is pardoned now. In the intervening period, the seasons have come and gone; time has healed the wounds and even those who are still here in the city are no longer baying for his blood. Life goes on, and with all the fair blessings of forgiveness, has a peculiar way of righting itself. The ever capable and beautiful Rose Tidey, for example, continues to prosper in the brewing business, and is even due to marry soon - a gentleman in the same trade, so that a regular brewing empire of sorts seems to be in the making. Clever Rose!

Meanwhile, the young and enchanting governess, Harriet Swift, now has a full time post with a prominent family somewhere in the West Country near Exeter, and is even about to open her own school, or so he has heard. She has done well for herself, and deservedly so.

The dark and delectable Sarah May, that youthful one-time laundress, turned maid, turned lover to a lady of wealth and fortune, is clearly also prospering, since Matthew just saw her go past him in a private chair - he swears it was her, blowing him a kiss from the window, and looking for all the world like the very Duchess she had once confessed to him she would like to become. How marvellous. How very splendid!

Elsewhere, the fiercely passionate Martina von Klapperstein has, he knows, found happiness, too: with a new husband some years her senior, again, and the heir to an estate overseas in the Prussian hinterland, and where she has enough money once more to go shopping every day. The ever resourceful Lucy Armstrong continues to expand her business, with a second bagnio, much larger and better appointed even than that located in Cockspur Street. And the redoubtable and demanding Caroline Bolter has moved to York with her noble paramour from the military and is, by all accounts, thriving at the head of her own fashion business.

As for Lady Snatchal, that arch temptress and would-be seducer, she no longer troubles him at all, not in any shape or form. Having suffered a second fall from her horse some time ago which resulted in a complete reversal of her immoderate appetites, she has now taken holy vows and gone overseas into a nunnery - her parting words to a friend one afternoon being that it is no great loss for a woman to give herself to God, providing she has at least had the pleasure of giving herself to the Devil for a certain period beforehand - an experience which, she avowed, she had surely already known in the fullest measure and was therefore content.

Yes, everything had righted itself. Why he even heard news the other day that Mr and Mrs McNiel of Derbyshire had been spared the wrath of the King's commissioners, being exonerated from any deliberate involvement in the Jacobite rebellion. It had taken an age to establish the man's innocence, but it had come eventually. Matthew was happy for him, for he was, he remembers, a decent fellow at the head of a perfectly charming family. Even Bonnie Prince Charlie managed to survive, having escaped back to the continent unscathed, largely thanks to being sheltered and aided by a brave woman from the Highlands, and is now feted in all the salons of Paris or Milan for his by-now legendary exploits among the Scots and where, it is said, he is prone to become over-inebriated more often than is at all good for him - an ignominious end for one upon whose shoulders the destiny of all of Europe once seemed to rest so handsomely.

And so it is, deep in these meditations, that he does not really register the salutation at first or the words, softly spoken - a voice vaguely recalled from some earlier, less troubled age and coming from somewhere just behind his shoulder:

'Hello my Wonder.'

He has heard the words, he is certain, not merely imagined them. Realising they are the herald of a miracle, he turns - turns quite involuntarily, as if rotated by the shoulders from some vast pair of celestial hands to behold the face of Johanna. For a second, he is struck dumb, simply gazing into her bright hazel-green eyes that he once knew so well. It is a slightly older, slightly changed Johanna, her face a little more altered to maturity - but it is her - it really is! And as she approaches, he finds he has taken her hands in his, that they are laughing like children, and that the tears are streaming down their faces.

'At this hour, so close to a performance of your beloved Mr Handel, I thought you would be out and about,' she says. 'I came here on a whim, knowing how much you love the bridge.'

'You have returned!' he exclaims, somewhat needlessly.

'I have, my Wonder. I have come back.'

But even as he looks into her eyes the question is shaping itself on his lips, and he knows he must ask: 'And Sam? Where ..?'

She shakes her head, and all is sadness for a moment.

'He died, Matthew. We lost him last year, in the winter. I cannot describe to you how harsh the conditions were. So many good people perished. He never really recovered from the journey to America, anyway. We did what we could but were unable to save him. I think it was camp fever, a kind of typhus that carried him off. We had no doctor to tell us for sure before we buried him.'

'I am so very sorry,' he says, her hands still held in his. He never wants to let them go.

'Thank Goodness it is over now, his suffering,' she adds. 'He often spoke fondly of you, Matthew. He never forgot all the good times you had, the pair of you. Oh, and he did miss his homeland so very much. As for America - what can I say! It is a land of amazement, so vast. And there are places of refinement there, too - Boston and Philadelphia - though we saw little of those. It was a very hard life, what we had to endure. My poor dear Sam.'

Without another word, for he feels so desperately sad and yet euphoric all at the same time, they begin walking, she taking his arm - just as she did all that time ago when they had met here by chance and strolled across the bridge together and she had spoken of her family and, oddly enough, the loss of her brother as well.

'Yes, you're right, I was intending to go to the performance,' Matthew states, aware that his own voice is full of emotion. 'But I'm not sure if it can be reached in time, now,' he adds, though suddenly none of it seems of very much consequence anymore.

'Don't say that!' she says, stopping and taking both his hands again, coming around in front of him as if she would haul him along. 'I'm sure we still have time. Come on my Wonder, don't give up.'

But although the crowds have dispersed somewhat, still he does not move. He wants only to linger and to look at her, to take in the presence of this miracle that has suddenly illuminated his life: Johanna in her neat little riding jacket, a jaunty tricorn trimmed with flowers upon her head. She is as delightful as ever - and yet there really is a difference to her face. It is a face upon which raw experience and wisdom have been etched, visible now in little lines where the passage of time has set itself and where once only the most temporary of furrows would have formed upon her brow. And it is then he notices the scar - that beneath her powder there is surely the faintest of lines from some wound, running from her left cheek down to just beneath her lip. And she, sensing his observation, disengages her hands from his and, quite inadvertently, places a finger upon it as she looks away with distraction for a moment before returning to look into his eyes.

'Oh, yes, *that!*' she says, and smiles a little uncomfortably. 'I wish I could tell you it was from some heroic episode, the outcome of some fierce battle with Red Indians in which arrows and tomahawks were flying, but the explanation is less glamorous, I'm afraid: merely a fall on board the ship on my outward journey. What modest looks I ever possessed have all fled me now, I regret to ...'

'Oh, my dearest, Johanna,' he says, raising her hands to his lips, 'if you had a thousand imperfections to your face it would still be the most welcome sight in all the world to me, or to any man with eyes not blinded by vanity and foolishness. You are beautiful, and always shall be.'

And she, looking modestly away, disengaging and taking his arm once again, gives him a further tug, almost as if annoyed with him, urging him on.

'When exactly does it begin, this performance of yours?' she asks.

'Eight-thirty, I think. But we would have well over an hour of walking ahead of us, unless we can locate a carriage. And even then we need to cross the water again to Whitehall.'

'We must try,' she says. 'Look, I am dressed modestly as befits a girl from the frontier. I will race you!'

He laughs. And this time they really do begin walking in earnest, and briskly - through the crowds and down from the foot of the bridge, weaving a path through the churchyard of St Saviours with all its jumble of old tombstones and monuments, and then along to Bankside, joining the throng, with everyone going in the same direction, hurrying westwards. How odd it all seems to be among so many well-to-do men and women, striding out along the rough roads and tracks of the south bank, here among all the timber yards, taverns and orchard gardens - the busy river to their side, and the stately buildings of the Strand opposite, where already some of the windows are lit with the approach of darkness and the water all ablaze with dancing lights. It is quite exhilarating, being part of this vast movement of people, everyone talking merrily, urging each other on, for some substantial groups there are to be found among them: whole families; dapper gentlemen in white stockings; elegant women with footmen holding up the hems of their skirts and looking as if they were about to stroll into an opera house rather than along a mile of rutted road. Inspired by all this, and by the infectious enthusiasm of Johanna at his side, he is determined now more than ever that somehow they will get across to Green Park in time.

To this purpose, he tries an alternative route, one closer to the river that most people appear to be ignoring, a sequence of narrow lanes with workmen's cottages and clumps of willow leaning out across the water. It is a gamble, but it pays off because just then, as luck would have it, and passing by a grim little wharf beside a timber yard, they discover at the bottom of a set of stairs - and they can hardly believe their eyes - a small black wherry tethered and bobbing up and down on the wash, its owner reclining on board and clearly taking a break from his labours and a much-needed bite to eat on what would surely be one of the busiest evenings of his life.

'Sir, if you would be so kind - across to Whitehall Stairs!' Matthew calls to him. 'I will recompense you generously for your trouble, I promise.'

'Oh, can you not see I am having my supper, Sir!' he complains.

But before he can protest further, overwhelmed with the vision of sheer exuberance and joy as the two of them, hand in hand, come hurtling down the steps towards him, he is forced to relent - a process all the more smoothly accomplished by Matthew placing a half-crown coin in his hand. The ferryman, gathers up his oars, therefore, and off they go, rowing at first most lugubriously, poor fellow, but eventually falling into the familiar rhythm of his work, as Matthew and Johanna snuggle up beneath an awning in the stern. Ahead, the sun has just set now, leaving a broad glow behind the distinctive towers and crenellations of the Westminster skyline. A young moon, a thin crescent, is visible low in the sky following it down, and already the first stars are beginning to appear as he and Johanna their hats removed the better to be close to one another, settle into their seat, her head upon his shoulder. Not exactly the most luxurious of places - squeezed together thus, and with a slice of cushion behind them thin enough to be almost transparent, so well worn is it. But they do not care. Nor are they unduly disturbed by the shock of the cool river air upon their faces still all-aglow from walking so briskly. There is no discomfort, no inconvenience in all the world that can possibly come between them and their happiness.

'Johanna, I think I am among the happiest of mortals,' he whispers closely, 'so much so that I am rather inclined to never let you go again. Do you mind?'

But she does not answer. She merely smiles again, looking into his eyes still. 'Do you remember that evening up on the leads at Greenwich?' she asks in a voice which is all tenderness and gentle recollection. 'That time when you visited us, when we had Sam's telescope, and all the stars?'

'Yes, I do,' he answers. We found ourselves alone, didn't we. Just the two of us, for so long a time, it seemed. Talking about the heavens and the planets? I felt very close to you then. That was when you gave me that idea, remember? - which became, I must admit, rather an obsession.'

'Your sonnets - an obsession?'

'Well, yes, there was quite a bit more to it than that. Not just poetry. A lot of odd things happened to me then - trouble with ladies and ...'

*'Trouble with ladies, Matthew!* Why, you do surprise me!' she laughs.

'I will tell you all about it one day, all about my seven heavenly bodies - though I think you encountered quite a few of them at various times, as I recall. I thought I might experience something exceptional, you see, something other-worldly through their beauty and passion. I thought I would succeed in flying that way. I know it sounds daft, but rather than drawing upon the intellect as you suggested, I chose a more profane and libidinous route to glory. And I failed, of course. I came crashing down to earth with a very harsh and unpleasant bump - no more able fly or to ascend the heavens than a man with cardboard wings jumping off of a bridge. Yes, it was an obsession - and I suppose I was lucky really, because it could all have turned out so much worse than it did.'

'I know,' she murmurs.

'You know?'

'Oh, yes - because I was worried about you even then. I thought to myself, I should not have sown those seeds in his mind, about all the planets and the magical stairway and so on. I became anxious. I prayed for you, then. I prayed that you would be kept safe through whatever hair-brained scheme it was you were trying to follow. And then one evening I heard a voice in those prayers, I know not whether from my own troubled mind or from some other place, but it told me that you had been sent an angel. Really! You won't believe me, Matthew, I know, and you will think that I have taken leave of my senses. But the voice said that you had been sent a guardian angel, and that it would appear to you and attend upon you in times of need. It said, that you would always have a light to guide you through the darkness; that all would be well and that I should never worry.'

'How strange!' he murmurs. 'A light through the darkness?'

'Yes.'

To which Matthew falls to reflection for some moments. 'Perhaps there *was* some kind of purpose to it all, then,' he murmurs, 'something good about it - though I don't suppose I could ever say with any certainty what it might have been. Perhaps we are not meant to know the purpose of what we do, not in this life. All I can say is that I never wrote a single line of verse again after you left for America. Those sonnets, I now believe, were really all for you. Does that make sense?'

'Now, now, Matthew, you are trying to flatter me!' she laughs. 'Goodness me, it won't do, you know. I am far too clever for you, especially these days - too cynical, after all I've been through.'

'All my poetry ... every line of it for you,' he repeats with determination, and presses his lips into her hair, drawing her close and resolved that she should accept the assertion, because it is true. 'The seven were always shadows - just that - just shadows to one radiant star. And that star was always you. I know that now.'

But she smiles again at his wild, romantic words, clearly reserving judgement. Yet, he knows that what he has told her is true. And not only that - but he is beginning to suspect that with the wonderful gift of this beautiful and gifted woman at his side, a substantial part of his old self might indeed have died this day. A part of him has perished, after all, and will not be missed.

'Oh, look: the new bridge!' she cries, raising herself from the seat and pointing with excitement as their boat reaches the bend in the river and the full extent of the new structure from the south bank across to Westminster is revealed, all the graceful arches and balustrades, its expanse so sleek and sinuous; so very unlike the old bridge of London, and totally unencumbered by any buildings at all upon its back. 'I remember seeing this at the start, as it was being built,' she continues, 'but never in its entirety - not until now. How very fine it is!'

'They wanted to open it ages ago,' he remarks, not without a certain note of amusement, 'but it had to be repaired after the central arch collapsed. You will be comforted, I'm sure, that we continue to build above our capabilities in this country - so much of what we do descending into farce, as always.'

'Goodness, Matthew, how peculiar you are!' she exclaims, though softly, her head still upon his shoulder. 'If this is a farce then I can assure you, my Wonder, it is infinitely preferable to the tragedy of struggling through the swamps of Louisiana or Virginia; a far better outlook than that of a wife of a convict in his Majesty's army. With all its faults, this is a paradise compared to where I have been, that place of such cruelty and conflict - a place where the English fight the French, and the French the Spanish, and every side enlists the alliances of different tribes of poor Indians to fight for them, or even against each other amid all the ruin and pillage of their culture. How very beautiful it is here - and the people - how very refined and gracious and polite they are. What a time and place we are living in, Matthew. I sometimes wonder if it is the beginning of something even greater, or is it perhaps the end? If only we knew, if only we could open up a window into the future and see, and tell people about ourselves. Do return to writing your poetry, my Wonder! Write again. Perhaps someone will be listening at that window one day if you do. Go tell the world what it was like to be alive at a time such as ours. For it is good, Matthew. Really, it is so very good.'

Amid all the profusion of lanterns out upon the water that often make it difficult to detect the other side of the river, the stairs at Whitehall are just coming into view at last, he notices - and their oarsman continues to make good time for them, as well.

'I'm a fool, aren't I,' he murmurs to her, sitting up now and replacing his hat in readiness for their arrival. 'It must have been hell - a journey to hell and back for you.'

'Yes.'

'And, so much I still want to ask! Why, I don't know the half of it yet. How are your children? Are the two little ones safe, Samantha and John?'

'*Three,* you mean!' she corrects him with a cheeky smile, sitting up now and weaving tight her hair upon the crown of her head.

'Three?

'Oh, yes. We were blessed with another - though Sam never lived to see his coming. But yes, three now. He is a bonny little boy and his name, of course, is Samuel. How could I have called him anything else! This evening he is all tucked up in bed with his brother and sister, at home in Aylesford, my parents home, as you may recall, and where I reside once again, my dear - when not chasing strange men about the streets of London, that is.'

'Three children!' Matthew sighs a little wistfully. 'Why you must be so proud?'

'Yes - just four more to go.'

'Four more? What do you mean?'

'Oh, Goodness, have I never told you - about when I was young?' she says laughing, replacing and repinning her hat. 'Once upon a time, long ago and even before I met Sam, I went to a wise woman - a fortune teller. She read my palm and she said I would have seven children, and that I would find a great purpose in the journey of seeing them grow, that each one would be a delight, and each so very different to the other, that one would become a miller, the other an actor, the other a lawyer, the other a wife of a scholar and a traveller, and so on. All different, she said. Well, we shall see. There is still time enough, I suppose, for it to happen ... even now. Really, did I never tell you that?'

'No,' he responds, slightly dazed. 'No, you didn't.'

'Well, like I say, it was a long time ago.'

'It certainly sounds like a lot of hard work,' he says, '*for all concerned.*'

'Perhaps that's the secret,' she answers.

With their boat arriving at the stairs, they alight and begin their walking again. They cross Whitehall and thread their way through some narrow lanes, converging with the crowds into the park, where everyone is hurrying along the tree-lined avenues towards St James's Palace where the tops of some outlandish stage architecture, turrets or pinnacles of some sort, can just be detected, all illuminated by lanterns, glowing and shimmering through the trees away in the distance - the stage, surely, on which the fireworks would be placed in readiness.

They are not late, not at all. He knows that nothing can prevent them from reaching their destination. And then suddenly from out of the gentle hubbub and murmuring of the crowd, there comes, so very loudly, the fabulous opening chords of trumpets and drums - surely, the very music they have come to hear, carried on the air from a distance not too far and accompanied by a great collective intake of breath as everybody gasps with the thrill of it, that most magnificent, unmistakable sound of the maestro, as they hurry now, all flocking together like hungry birds soaring through the sky in one direction. And then the fireworks commence - an explosion and a burst of flame and colour that mounts the sky - then another, until all the world is illuminated and bright as heaven itself. A space opens up, and they take it. Hand in hand, they quicken their pace. Two people amid all the wondrous multitude. And they run towards the light.

23552666R00320

Made in the USA
Charleston, SC
25 October 2013